John William Donaldson

The Theatre of the Greeks

John William Donaldson

The Theatre of the Greeks

ISBN/EAN: 9783337334994

Printed in Europe, USA, Canada, Australia, Japan

Cover: Foto ©Andreas Hilbeck / pixelio.de

More available books at **www.hansebooks.com**

THE

THEATRE OF THE GREEKS,

A TREATISE

ON THE HISTORY AND EXHIBITION
OF THE GREEK DRAMA,

WITH A SUPPLEMENTARY TREATISE ON THE LANGUAGE, METRES,
AND PROSODY OF THE GREEK DRAMATISTS.

BY

JOHN WILLIAM DONALDSON, D.D.,

FORMERLY FELLOW OF TRINITY COLLEGE, CAMBRIDGE.

EIGHTH EDITION.

WITH NUMEROUS ILLUSTRATIONS FROM THE BEST ANCIENT AUTHORITIES.

LONDON:
GEORGE BELL AND SONS, YORK STREET,
COVENT GARDEN.
1875.

PREFACE.

THE present edition is a reprint of the seventh edition (the last edited by Dr. Donaldson), with some slight modifications, which the publishers have thought desirable for the sake of issuing the book at a low price, so as to bring it within the reach of a large number of students.

Woodcut illustrations have been substituted for the two pages of coloured lithographs; and the translation of Aristotle's 'Poetic,' and the extracts from Vitruvius and Julius Pollux have been withdrawn, as they are mainly of use in substantiating references given in the body of the book, and are accessible in other shapes to those students who may desire to examine them critically.

Mr. Canon Tate's essay on the Metres, which is identified with the book, and records the honest research of that successful and experienced teacher, has been retained out of respect for his memory, no less than on account of its practical value.

LONDON, *January* 1875.

LARGER ILLUSTRATIONS.

A TREATISE ON THE HISTORY AND EXHIBITION

OF THE

GREEK DRAMA.

—◦◊◦—

BOOK I.

THE ORIGIN OF THE GREEK DRAMA.

CHAPTER I.

THE RELIGIOUS ORIGIN OF THE GREEK DRAMA.

οὐ γάρ τι νῦν γε κἀχθές, ἀλλ' ἀεί ποτε
ζῇ ταῦτα, κοὐδεὶς οἶδεν ἐξ ὅτου 'φάνη.

SOPHOCLES.

WE cannot assign any historical origin to the Drama. Resulting as it did from the constitutional tendencies of the inhabitants of those countries in which it sprang up, it necessarily existed, in some form or other, long before the age of history; consequently we cannot determine the time when it first made its appearance, and must therefore be content to ascertain in what principle of the human mind it originated. This we shall be able to do without much difficulty. In fact the solution of the problem is included in the answer to a question often proposed,—"How are we to account for the great prevalence of idol worship in ancient times?" For, strange as it may appear, it is nevertheless most true, that not only the drama, (the most perfect form of poetry,) but all poetry, sculpture, painting, architecture, and whatever else is beautiful in art, are the results of that very principle which degraded men, the gods of the earth, into grovelling worshippers of wood and stone, which made

B

them kneel and bow down before the works of their own hands. This principle is that which is generally called the love of imitation,—a definition, however, which is rather ambiguous, and has been productive of much misunderstanding.[1] We would rather state this principle to be that desire to express the abstract in the concrete, that "striving after objectivity," as it has been termed by a modern writer,[2] that wish to render the conceivable perceivable, which is the ordinary characteristic of an uneducated mind.

The inhabitants of southern Europe, in particular, have in all ages shown a singular impatience of pure thought, and have been continually endeavouring to represent under the human form, either allegorically or absolutely, the subjects of their contemplations.[3] Now the first abstract idea which presented itself to the minds of rude but imaginative men was the idea of God, conceived in some one or other of his attributes. Unable to entertain the abstract notion of divinity, they called in the aid of art to bring under the control of their senses the subject of their thoughts, and willingly rendered to the visible and perishable the homage which they felt to be due to the invisible and eternal. By an extension of the same associations, their anthropomorphized divinity was supposed to need a dwelling-place; hence the early improvements of architecture on the shores of the Mediterranean. His worshippers would then attempt some outward expression of their gratitude and veneration :—to meet this need, poetry arose among them.[4] The same

---

[1] The German reader would do well to consult on this subject Von Raumer's Essay on the Poetic of Aristotle (*Abhandl. der Hist. Philologischen Klasse der Kön. Akad. der Wissensch.* 1828). We do not think Dr. Copleston's view of this subject (*Prælectiones Academicæ,* pp. 28 sqq.) sufficiently comprehensive.

[2] Wachsmuth, *Hell. Alterth,* II. 2, 113

[3] See Wordsworth's *Excursion* (Works, v. pp. 160 foll.).

[4] Thus Strabo says, that "the whole art of poetry is the praise of the gods," ἡ ποιητικὴ πᾶσα ὑμνητική. x. p. 468. (The word οὖσα, which is found in all the editions at the end of this sentence, has evidently arisen from a repetition of the first two syllables of the following word ὡσαύτως, and must be struck out. For the sense of the word ὑμνητική, comp. Plato, *Legg.* p. 700 A.) And Plato, *Legg.* VII. 799 A, would have all music and dancing consecrated to religion. When Herder says (*Werke z. schön. Lit. und Kunst,* II. p. 82), "Poetry

feelings would suggest au imitation of the imagined sufferings or gladness of their deity; and to this we owe the
mimic dances of ancient Hellas, and the first beginnings of
the drama there.

But although art and religious realism have much in
common even in their latest applications, we are not to
suppose that all attempts to give an outward embodiment
to the religious idea are to be considered as real approxima-
tions to dramatic poetry. All art is not poetry, and all
poetry is not the drama.[1] Polytheistic worship and its

---

arose, not at the altars, but in wild merry dances; and as violence was
restrained by the severest laws, an attempt was in like manner made
to lay hold, by means of religion, on those drunken inclinations of men
which escaped the control of the laws," he does not seem to deny the
fact on which we have insisted, that religion and poetry are con-
temporaneous effects of the same cause; at all events, he allows that
poetry was at first merely the organ of religion. And although
V. Cousin endeavours to prove that religion and poetry were the
results of different necessities of the human mind, he also contends
that they were analogous in their origin. "Le triomphe de l'intuition
religieuse est dans la création du culte, comme le triomphe de l'idée du
beau est dans la création de l'art," &c. (*Cours de Philosophie*, p. 21, 2.)

[1] The view which we have taken in the text, of the origin of the
fine arts, is, we conceive, nearly the same as that of Aristotle; for it
appears to us pretty obvious that his treatise on Poetic was, like many
of his other writings, composed expressly to confute the opinions of
Plato, who taking the word μίμησις in its narrowest sense, to signify
the imperfect counterfeiting, the servile and pedantic copying of an
individual object, argued against μίμησις in general as useless for moral
purposes. Whereas Aristotle shows that if the word μίμησις be not
taken in this confined sense, but as equivalent to "representation." as
implying the outward realisation of something in the mind, it does then
include not only poetry, but, properly speaking, all the fine arts: and
μίμησις is therefore useful, in a moral relation, if art in general is of
any moral use. That he understood μίμησις in this general sense is
clear from his *Rhetoric*, III. 1, § 8: τὰ ὀνόματα μιμήματά ἐστιν· ὑπῆρξε
δὲ ἡ φωνὴ πάντων μιμητικώτατον τῶν μορίων ἡμῖν διὸ καὶ αἱ τέχναι
συνέστησαν, ἥ τε ῥαψῳδία καὶ ἡ ὑποκριτικὴ καὶ αἱ ἄλλαι. It was, however, as Schleiermacher justly observes (*Anmerkungen zu Platons Staat*,
p. 543), not of art absolutely that Plato was speaking, but only of its
moral effects; for doubtless Plato himself would have been most willing
to assent to a definition fart which made it an approximation to or copy
of the idea of the beautiful (comp. Plat. *Resp.* VI. p. 484 C); and this
is only Aristotle's opinion expressed in other words Von Raumer
truly remarks in the essay above quoted, p. 118. "The παράδειγμα

concomitant idolatry are the most favourable conditions for the development of art in all its forms and applications. And conversely, those nations and epochs which have been most remarkable for the cultivation of a pure and spiritual religion have been equally remarkable for a prevalent distaste and incompetency for the highest efforts of art. In ancient times, we have the case of the Israelites: for many years they strove with varying success to resist the temptations to idolatry which surrounded them on every side, and left to Greece and modern Europe the greatest aid to abstract thought, in the alphabet which we still employ. Yet we find that native art was, strictly speaking, non-existent among them. The few symbols which they employed in their early days were borrowed from Egypt or Chaldæa, and when, in the most flourishing epoch of their monarchy, their powerful and wealthy king wished to build a temple to the true God, he was obliged to call in the aid of his idolatrous neighbours the Tyrians.[1] Nay more, it would not be fanciful to connect the subsequent idolatry of Solomon with his patronage of the fine arts. It is remarkable, too, that the first trace of a dramatic tendency in the lyric poetry of the Israelites is visible in an idyll attributed to the same prince. And far as the book of Job is from any dramatic intention, the dialogues of which it mainly consists must be added to the

------

(*Poet.* xv. 11, xxvi. 28), which Aristotle often designates as the object to be aimed at, is nothing but that which is now-a-days called the 'ideal,' and by which is understood the most utter opposite of a pedantic imitation." Herder also was fully aware that although Plato contradicts Aristotle in regard to the Dithyramb, he was spe king in quite a different connexion, "in ganz anderer Verbindung" (*Werke z. schön. Lit. u. Kunst.* ii. p. 86). We may add, that our definition of μίμησις as a synonym for "art," which has also been given in direct terms by Müller (*Handb. der Archäol.* beginn.), "Die Kunst ist eine Darstellung (μίμησις) d. h. eine Thätigkeit durch welche ein Innerliches äusserlich wird," "Art is a representation (μίμησις), i. e. an energy by means of which a subject becomes an object" (comp. *Dorians,* iv. ch. 7, § 12), is the best way of explaining the pleasure which we derive from the efforts of the fancy and imagination, which, as has been very justly observed, is always much greater when "the allusion is from the material world to the intellectual, than when it is from the intellectual world to the material" (Stewart's *Elements of the Philosophy of the Mind,* i. p. 306).   [1] 1 Kings vii. 13.

many proofs which have been adduced of the comparatively modern date, and foreigu origin, of that didactic poem.[1] Even the incomplete metrical system of the Hebrews, as compared with the wonderful variety and perfection of Greek prosody, must be regarded as furnishing supplementary evidence of the inartificial character and antimimetic tendencies of the early inhabitants of Palestine.   So also in modern times, long after the drama had ceased to exhibit any traces of its original connexion with the rites of a heathen worship, and when it was looked upon merely as a branch of literature, or as an elegant pastime, in proportion as Christian nations adhered to or abhorred the sensual rites which the Church of Rome borrowed from heathendom, when it assembled its priest-ridden votaries within the newly-consecrated walls of a profane Basilica,—in the same proportion the drama throve or declined, and, in this country, either inflicted vengeance on the hapless author of a *Histriomastix*, or concealed its flaunting robes from the austere indignation of *Smectymnuus*.

To return, however, to the more immediate influences of polytheism and idolatry on the origination of the ancient drama, we observe that the dramatic art, wherever it has existed as a genuine product of the soil, has always been connected in its origin with the religious rites of an elementary worship ;[2] that is, with those enthusiastic orgies which spring from a personification of the powers of nature.   This was the case in India,[3] and in those parts of Italy where scenic

---

[1] Ewald, *poetisch. Bücher des alten Bundes*, III. p. 63.

[2] In connexion with the Phallic rites of Hindostan and Greece, we may mention that in the South Sea Islands, at the time of Cook's second voyage, a birth was represented on the stage.   See Süvern *über Aristoph. Wolken*, p. 63, note 6.

[3] " Like that of the Greeks, the Hindu drama was derived from, and formed part of, their religious ceremonies." (*Quarterly Rev.* No. 89, p. 39.)   The comparative autiquity of the Greek and Indian drama is regarded very differently by the most eminent orientalists.   For while Weber thinks it "not improbable that even the use of the Hindoo drama was influenced by the performance of the Greek dramas at the courts of Greek kings" (*Indische Skizzen*, p. 28). Lassen will not allow such an origin of the Indian drama, which he considers to be of native growth (*Indische Alterthumskunde*, II. p. 1157).   Even supposing however that the Indian drama was as old as the time of Asoka II. (*Asiat.*

entertainments existed before the introduction of the Greek drama. But in Greece this was so, not only in the beginning, but as long as the stage existed; and the circumstance, which gave to the Attic drama its chief strength and its highest charms, was its continued connexion with the state-worship of Bacchus, in which both Tragedy and Comedy took their rise.   We must not allow ourselves to be misled by our knowledge of the fact that the drama of modern Europe, though derived from that of ancient Greece, exhibits no trace of its religious origin.   The element which originally constituted its whole essence has been overwhelmed and superseded by the more powerful ingredients which have been introduced into it by the continually diverging tastes of succeeding generations, till it has at length become nothing but a walking novel or a speaking jest-book.   The plays of Shakspeare and Calderon (with the exception, of course, of the *Autos Sacramentales* of the latter) are dramatic reproductions of the prose romances of the day, with the omission of the religious element which they owed to the monks,[1] just as the Tragedies of Æschylus and Sophocles would have been mere epic dramas, had they broken the bonds which connected them with the elementary worship of Attica.   But this disruption never took place.   In ancient Greece the drama retained to the last the character which it originally possessed.   The theatrical representations at Athens, even in the days of Sophocles and Aristophanes, were constituent parts of a religious festival; the theatre in which they were performed was sacred to Bacchus, and the worship of the god was always as much regarded as the amusement of the sovran people.   This is a fact which cannot be too strongly impressed upon the student: if he

---

Res. xx. p. 50; Lassen II. p. 502, it is admitted (Lassen, I. 616, 625; I. 507) that Krishna, who stood in intimate connexion with the origin of the Hindoo theatre, was specially worshipped in the Saurasenic or eastern district (Arrian, *Ind.* VIII. 5), and there is every reason to believe that he was an imported deity; so that the Indian stage, even if aboriginal, may have derived its most characteristic features from the Greek.

[1] Malone's *Shakspeare*, Vol. III. pp. 8 sqq.; Lessing, *Geschichte der Engl. Schaubühne* (Werke, xv. 209).

does not keep this continually in view, he will be likely to confound the Athenian stage with that of his own time and country, and will misunderstand and wonder at many things which under this point of view are neither remarkable nor unintelligible. How apt we all are to look at the manners of ancient times through the false medium of our every-day associations! how difficult we find it to strip our thoughts of their modern garb, and to escape from the thick atmosphere of prejudice in which custom and habit have enveloped us! and yet, unless we take a comprehensive and extended view of the objects of archæological speculation, unless we can look upon ancient customs with the eyes of the ancients, unless we can transport ourselves in the spirit to other lands and other times, and sun ourselves in the clear light of bygone days, all our conceptions of what was done by the men who have long ceased to be, must be dim, uncertain, and unsatisfactory, and all our reproductions as soulless and uninstructive as the scattered fragments of a broken statue.[1] These remarks are particularly applicable to the Greek stage. For in proportion to the perfection of the extant specimens of ancient art in any department, are our misconceptions of the difference between their and our use of these excellent works. We feel the beauty of the remaining Greek dramas, and are unwilling to believe that productions as exquisite as the most elaborate compositions of our own playwrights should not have been, as ours were, exhibited for their own sake. But this was far from being the case. The susceptible Athenian,—whose land was the dwelling-place of gods and ancestral heroes,[2]—to whom the clear blue sky, the swift-winged breezes, the river fountains, the Ægean gay with its countless smiles, and the teeming earth[3] from which he believed his ancestors were immediately created, were alike instinct with an all-pervading spirit of divinity; —the Athenian, who loved the beautiful, but loved it because it was divine,—who looked upon all that genius

---

[1] See some good remarks on this subject in Niebuhr's *Kleine Schriften*, Vol. I. p. 92, and in his letter to Count Adam Moltke (*Lebensn.* Vol. II. p. 91).

[2] Hegesias ap. Strab. IX. p. 396.

[3] Æsch. *Prom. V.* 87—90.

could invent or art execute, as but the less unworthy
offering to his pantheism;[1] and considered all his festivals
and all his amusements as only a means of withdrawing the
soul from the world's business, and turning it to the love
and worship of God,[2] how could he keep back from the object
of his adoration the fairest and best of his works?

We shall make the permanent religious reference of the
Greek drama more clear, by showing with some minuteness
how it gradually evolved itself from religious rites universally prevalent, and by pointing out by what routes its
different elements converged, till they became united in one
harmonious whole of "stateliest and most regal argument."[3]

The dramatic element in the religion of ancient Greece
manifested itself most prominently in the connected worship
of Apollo, Demeter, and Dionysus. Thus at Delphi, the
main seat of the Dorian worship of Apollo, the combat with
the serpent, and the flight and expiation of the victorious
son of Latona, were made the subject of a representation
almost theatrical.[4]   And Clemens Alexandrinus tells us that
Eleusis represented by torch-light the rape of Proserpine,
and the wanderings and grief of her mother Demeter, in a
sort of mystic drama.[5]   Dionysus, who was worshipped both
at Eleusis and at Delphi,[6] was personated by the handsomest
young men who could be found, in a mimic ceremony at the
Athenian Anthesteria, which represented his betrothal to
the wife of the King Archon;[7] and there were other
occasions, quite unconnected with theatrical exhibitions, in

---

[1] Mr. Grote remarks (*Hist. of Greece*, VIII. p. 444), with special
reference to the Athenian drama, that "there was no manner of em-
ploying wealth, which seemed so appropriate to Grecian feeling, or
tended so much to procure influence and popularity to its possessors, as
that of contributing to enhance the magnificence of the national and
religious festivals."

[2] Strabo, x. p. 467 : ἥ τε γὰρ ἄνεσις τὸν νοῦν ἀπάγει ἀπὸ τῶν ἀνθρω-
πίνων ἀσχολημάτων, τὸν δὲ ὄντως νοῦν τρέπει πρὸς τὸ θεῖον.

[3] Milton's Prose Works, p. 101.

[4] Plutarch, *Quæst. Gr.* II. p. 202, Wyttenb.; *De Defect.* Orac. II.
pp. 710, 723, Wyttenb.

[5] *Cohort. ad Gentes*, p. 12, Potter.

[6] Plut. *de El Delphico*, p. 591, Wyttenb.: τὸν Διόνυσον, ᾧ τῶν Δελφῶν
οὐδὲν ἧττον ἢ τῷ Ἀπόλλωνι μέτεστιν.

[7] Demosth. *in Neær.* pp. 1369, 70; Plutarch, *Nic.* c. 3.

which the Bacchic mythology was made the subject of direct imitation.[1] But it was not in these forms of worship that the Attic drama immediately originated, however much it may have been connected with them in spirit. The almost antagonistic materials of Dorian and oriental mythology had to seek their common ground, and the lyric chorus of the Dorians had to combine itself with the epos of the Ionian rhapsode, before such a phenomenon as the full-grown Tragedy of Æschylus could become possible. We see these ingredients standing side by side, like oil and vinegar, and not perfectly fused,[2] in the first Attic tragedy which we open. It is the business of the following pages to point out how they came together.

In order to do this in a satisfactory manner, we must constantly bear in mind the important statement of Aristotle,[3] that " both Tragedy and Comedy originated in a rude and unpremeditated manner; the first from the leaders of the Dithyrambs, and the second from those who led off the Phallic songs." To reconcile all our scattered informa-tion on the subject with this distinct and categorical account of the beginning of the Greek drama, we must in the first place confine ourselves to Tragedy. We must see how the solemn choral poetry of the Dorians admitted of a union with the boisterous Dithyramb, which belonged to the orgiastic worship of au exotic divinity. And, we must inquire how the leaders of this lyrical and Dorized Dithy-ramb became the vehicles of the dramatic dialogues in which the Tragedy of Athens carried on the development of its epic plots. We shall then be able without much difficulty to consider the case of Comedy, which exhibited in its older form the unmitigated ingredients of the noisy Phallic Comus.

The following, therefore, will be the natural succession of the topics, to which we are invited by an inquiry into the origin of the Greek drama. As its first beginnings are to be sought in a form of religious worship, we must endeavour to

---

[1] Plutarch, *Quæst. Gr.* II. p. 228, Wyttenb.
[2] *Æschyl. Agam.* 322 :

"Οξος τ' ἄλειφά τ' ἐγχέας ταὐτῷ κύτει,
Διχοστατοῦντ' ἄν, οὐ φιλῶ, προσεννέποις.

[3] *Poet.* c. IV. ; below, Part II.

ascertain at starting what was the nature of the system which gave rise to a ceremonial capable of dramatic representation. It has been mentioned generally that the religion, which produced the drama, is essentially connected with the worship of the elements, and that the Greek drama in particular manifests itself in the cognate worship of Apollo, Demeter, and Dionysus. It will therefore be our first business to show that the Greek worship of these deities was implicitly capable of producing, and in fact did produce, both the solemn chorus of Tragedy, and the Phallic extravagances of the old Comedy of Athens. As however this comic drama, though expressing more plainly than Tragedy the original form and the genuine spirit of the religion of Bacchus, borrowed its theatrical attire from the completed Tragedy of Æschylus, we must trace the development both of the tragic chorus and of the tragic dialogue before we can speak of Athenian Comedy and its varieties; and we shall find that the latest form of ancient Comedy, while it approximates to the drama of modern Europe, in the machinery of its plot and incidents, derives its leading characteristics from the last of the great tragedians, and not only discards all allusions to the Phallic origin of the Comus, but even evades a direct reference to the religious festivals with which it was formerly connected. Accordingly, the order, in which we propose to treat the subject, will both exhaust the materials at our disposal, without incurring a risk of repetition, and will present the facts connected with the growth of the Greek drama in the legitimate order of cause and effect, and in accordance with the laws of their historical development.

CHAPTER II.

THE CONNECTED WORSHIP OF DIONYSUS, DEMETER AND APOLLO.

δεῦτ᾽ ἐν χορόν, Ὀλύμπιοι,
ἔπι τε κλυτὰν πέμπετε χάριν, θεοί.

PINDAR.

WHATEVER opinion may be entertained respecting the indigenous character of other Greek deities, there cannot be the slightest doubt that the worship of Dionysus or Bacchus was of oriental origin, and that it was introduced into Greece by the Phœnicians, who, together with the priceless gift of the Semitic alphabet, imparted to the Pelasgian inhabitants of the Mediterranean coasts a knowledge of those forms of elementary worship which were more or less common to the natives of Canaan and Egypt. The mythical founder of Thebes, the Phœnician Cadmus, is connected with both of these innovations. For while he directly teaches the use of letters,[1] it is his daughter Semele, who, according to the tradition, in B.C. 1544 gives birth to Dionysus, the Theban wine-god.[2] The genealogy of Cadmus connects him not only with Phœnicia, but also with Egypt, Libya, Cilicia, and Crete.[3] And the historical interpretation of the legend is simply this, that the Phœnician

[1] Herod. v. 58; Diod. III. 67, v. 57; Plin. *H. N.* VII. 56.
[2] Herod. II. 145. According to Herodotus, II. 49, Cadmus himself was a worshipper of Dionysus, and taught this religion to Melampus.
[3] The pedigree is as follows (Creuzer, *Symbol.* IV. p. 8):

Agenor, son of Neptune and Libya, in Phœnicia.————Telephassa.

Cadmus.————Harmonia. Phœnix.   Cilix. Europa.

Polydorus. Semele. Autonoe. Agave. Ino.

————— Jupiter.

Dionysus.

navigators, who visited every part of the Mediterranean, carrying their commerce and their language to the distant regions of Spain and Britain, succeeded, after some opposition, in establishing their own worship on the main land of Northern Greece about the middle of the sixteenth century before our æra.

In order that we may understand the true and original character of a religion, which the plastic fancy and eclectic liberalism of the Greeks modified by an intermixture of heterogeneous elements, it will be necessary to consider the forms of faith and worship, which were cultivated by the Phœnicians and other Semitic tribes in the country from which they set forth on their voyages for the purposes of commerce or colonisation.

Among the Semitic nations, as in all the most ancient communities of men, the Sun and Moon were the primary objects of adoration.[1] The Sun, on account of his greater power and brightness,[2] was worshipped as a male divinity under some one of the names *Bel* or *Baal*, and *Melek, Molech, Moloch, Milkom*, or *Malchan*, signifying "Lord" or "King" respectively.[3] The Moon, with her weaker light and the humidity which accompanied the period of her reign, was regarded as a female deity,[4] and worshipped as *Asherah*, the goddess of prosperity,[5] or *Astarte*, the bright star of heaven.[6] Each of these deities had its cheerful, as well as its gloomy

---

[1] The attributes and worship of these Semitic deities have been well discussed by F. W. Ghillany, *die Menschenopfer der alten Hebräer*, Nürnberg. 1842. pp. 118 sqq. See also F. Nork, *Biblische Mythologie*, Stuttgardt. 1842, Vol. i. pp. 12—137.

[2] Macrob. *Saturn.* 1. 21, 12: significantes hunc deum solem esse, regalique potestate sublimem cuncta despicere, quia solem Jovis oculum appellat antiquitas.

[3] See *New Cratylus*, § 479. That the sun-god was a king was an idea familiar to the Greeks also. Thus Æschylus, *Persæ*, 228 : τῆλε πρὸς δυσμαῖς ἄνακτος Ἡλίου φθιναςμάτων.

[4] Plutarch, *Is. et Os.* c. 53; Macrob. *Sat.* I. 17, 53.

[5] אֲשֵׁרָה from אָשַׁר "to be happy," = ἡ μακαρία. Fuerst, however (*Handwörterb.* I. p. 155), renders it *socia, conjux*, i. e. of *Baal*, as the Phœnician אָסַר (*Osir*) "the husband," is an epithet of the male god.

[6] Gesenius, *Thesaur.* p. 1083 : "nil fere dubito quin עַשְׁתֹּרֶת idem sit quod אֶסְתֵּר, *stella*, κατ' ἐξοχήν stella Veneris, ita ut Ἀστροάρχη,

aspect. The Sun, which ripens the fruit, also burns up vegetation. He is the god not only of generation but also of destruction. The Moon, which gives the fertilizing dew, is also the goddess of the dark hours of night from which she regularly withdraws from time to time her silver light. This division of attributes favoured the introduction of the other planets (for the Sun and Moon were classed with the planets) into the cycle of the deities to be worshipped. In his benignant aspect the Sun was occasionally represented by Jupiter;[1] as a malignant god he was generally superseded by Saturn,[2] though Mars assumed some of his functions as hostile to the human race.[3] On the other hand, Astarte was as often represented by the planet Venus as by the Moon.[4] If Mercury played any part at all it was as a subordinate and inferior manifestation of goodness.[5] In their supposed order of distance from the earth, the seven so-called planets were arranged as follows : Saturn, the most distant, Jupiter, Mars, the Sun, Venus, Mercury, the Moon. And assigning each of the 24 hours of the day and the night to a repeated series of the planets in this order, they found that if the first hour of a particular day was assigned to Saturn, the first hour of the following day

---

quomodo Astarte appellatur (Herodian. 5, 6, § 10), etymon bene referat." That Astarte was the Moon is distinctly stated by Lucian, de dea Syria, 4 : Ἀστάρτην δὲ ἐγὼ δοκέω Σεληναίην ἔμμεναι. And this is shown by her representation as a horned goddess: see the passages quoted by Gesenius, l. c.

[1] Phaethon was both Jupiter and the Sun. Cf. Cic. de Nat. Deor. II. 20; Athenæus, VII. p. 326 B: Horat. 2 Carm. XVII. 22: te Jovis impio tutela Saturno refulgens eripuit. Cf. Jul. Firmicus, p. 328. This opposition between Jove and Saturn is preserved in our adjectives "Jovial" and "Saturnine," derived from the Neo-Platonic school.

[2] Propert. IV. 1, 84; Lucan. I. 650; Tac. Hist. V. 4; Juv. VI. 569; Manetho, III. 245: Κρόνου βλαβεραύγεος ἀστήρ.

[3] Ovid, Am. I. 8, 29 : stella tibi oppositi nocuit contraria Martis.

[4] Cicero, de Natur. Deor. III. 23; Phil. Bybl. ap. Euseb. Præp. Evang. I. 10; Theodoret, III. Reg. Quæst. 50; Augustin, Qu. in Jud. VII.; Suidas, s. v. Ἀστάρτη.

[5] Mercury is regarded as the messenger of the supreme deity, because he is nearest to the Sun and of equal apparent velocity (Cicero, de Natur. Deor. II. 20 ad fin.; Tim. c. 9, p. 505; de Rep. VI. 17, § 17). He was often identified with Apollo (Macrob. I. 19, 16) or with the Sun (ibid. 8).

would belong to the Sun, of the next day to the Moon, and so on in the order preserved to our times by the names of the days of the week.[1]   According to the Semitic mode of viewing the supremacy of the distant and gloomy Saturn, the seventh and last day was consecrated to him,[2] and when it was discovered that the number six was a perfect number, it was inferred that no other period could be assigned to the creation of all things under his auspices.[3]   On the seventh day therefore the priests clothed in black made an offering to Saturn in his black six-sided temple.[4]   Similar offerings were made to the planets Mars and Jupiter on the third and fifth days of the week.   But although these specialities of planetary worship appeared in the religious systems of most of the Semitic tribes, these nations were always ready to fall back on the general worship of the Sun and the Moon, the latter being also regarded as the goddess of the Earth ; and while the former presided over all the modifications of the rites sacred to Baal or Moloch, the latter appears as his correlative in all that was either savage or lascivious in his peculiar worship.

As a malignant deity, or more specifically as Moloch, the sun-god is tauriform[5] and is appeased by the offering of human victims.[6]   In the same capacity his sister deity, whether representing the Moon or the Earth, has the head of a cow,[7] and is always connected in the oldest forms of her

[1] Dio Cassius, xxxvii. 19. p. 137, Bekker.   The passage is translated at length in the *Philol. Mus.* I. pp. 2, 3.

[2] Creuzer, *Symbol.* ii. p. 186.   We find the same number sacred to Apollo and Dionysus, who are other forms of the sun-god ; Creuzer, l. l. IV. p. 117.

[3] It seems clear that in the opinion of Plato, who echoed Pythagorean and Heracleitean theories more immediately derived from the last, the θεῖον γεννητόν, or the world (*de Anim. Procr. in Tim.* 1017 C, p. 142, Wyttenb.), was indicated by a period which was represented by the perfect number 6, the human creation, or the state, being represented by a series of arithmetical calculations based on this (Plat. *Resp.* p. 546 ; see our interpretation of the passage, *Trans. of Philol. Soc.* Vol. I. No. 8.

[4] Gesenius, *Commentar. über. d. Jesaia.* II. p. 344.

[5] Macrobius, *Saturnal.* I. 21, § 20.

[6] Kenrick, *Phœnicia*, pp. 315 sqq.

[7] See the figure in Gesenius, *Thesaurus*, p. 1083, and comp. *New Cratylus*, § 470.

worship, with the same horrid rites. It is very interesting to trace this Semitic development of the idea that the Divine Being is wroth with man and is best appeased with the blood of his noblest creature, as it spreads itself along the Mediterranean till it is checked every where by the purer humanity and juster sentiments of the Greeks.[1] Both in Palestine and at Carthage Moloch was represented by a metal figure either human with a bull's head or entirely bovine, in which the human victims, generally children, were burnt alive.[2] There can be no doubt that the brazen bull of Phalaris at Agrigentum was a remnant of Carthaginian or Phœnician worship established there,[3] and that the burning of human victims, inaugurated by Perillus, was due rather to the Semitic worship than to the arbitrary cruelty of a tyrant, whose name, though treated with living abhorrence by Pindar,[4] is perhaps as mythical as that of Busiris.[5] The fact that this bull was afterwards recognised at Carthage clearly proves its Semitic origin and religious use.[6] The rescue of Athens from the worshippers of Moloch in Crete is described mythically as the slaying by Theseus of an ox-headed Minotaur, to whom the Athenians were obliged to send every nine years a tribute of *seven* youths and *seven* maidens, the sacred number of the Semitic Saturn.[7]

[1] Creuzer, *Symbol.* II. 447.

[2] See the passage quoted from B. Jarchi, *ad Jer.* VII. 31, by Winer, *Realwörterb.* s. v. *Moloch*; the well-known description in Diodor. Sic. xx. 14; and the passage translated from *Jalkut* in Hyde, *Hist. Rel. Vet. Pers.* p. 132.

[3] See J. E. Ebert, Σικελ. I. 1, pp. 41—106, quoted by Creuzer, *Symbol.* II. p. 447; and Ghillany, *Menschenopf.* p. 226.

[4] *Pyth.* l. 95: τὸν δὲ ταύρῳ χαλκέῳ καμτῆρα νηλέα νόον ἐχθρὰ Φάλαριν κατέχει παντᾶ φάτις, where he is contrasted with the φιλόφρων ἀρετά of Crœsus.

[5] The tradition that Phalaris feasted on children (Aristot. *Eth. Nic.* VII. 5, § 2) clearly identifies him with Moloch. It is not improbable that even the name Φάλαρις may be connected with the Bacchic attributes Φαλῆς and Φάλλος (i. e. with the Semitic פֶּלַח and פָּלַח), and that he is merely himself a representative of the Διόνυσος Ταυροκέρως. If so, it will be a curious reflection that historical criticism arose in a controversy respecting the authenticity of some highly rhetorical epistles in Attic Greek attributed to this imaginary personage!

[6] See Cicero, *in Verrem*, IV. 33.

[7] That the Minotaur was an object of worship is clear from the re-

Hercules similarly liberates the Italians from their thraldom
to the semi-taurine[1] Cacus, who murdered men in a cave or
grotto corresponding to the Cretan labyrinth.[2] The man
of brass called Talos, who haunted both Crete and Sardinia,
and slew strangers in red-hot embraces, is another form of
the image of Moloch.[3]   Nor was the female goddess without
her share in these homicidal rites.   The Europa or broad-
faced moon, who is borne on the back of a bull to the
Minotaur's island Crete, is the same deity as the Ἄρτεμις
Ταυροπόλη of the coasts of the Euxine[4] to whom strangers
were sacrificed.   The interrupted sacrifice of Iphigenia
points to the prevalence of such a rite in her worship. And
the name Ὀρθωσία, or Ὀρθία, which was given to this
goddess in Lemnos and elsewhere, undoubtedly referred to
the loud wailings of her victims, for which the floggings of
the Spartan youth were a sort of compromise.[5]

Now it appears that Dionysus or Bacchus, the latter
name and its synonym Iacchus referring to the outcries
attending his worship, first appeared to the Greeks as a
tauriform sun-god appeased by human victims.[6] As late as
the classical days of the Greek drama it was customary to
address him as appearing in the shape of a bull, or at least
with the horns of that animal.[7] And many of his epithets

---

presentation on a vase, which exhibits the monster as about to sacrifice
the seven Athenian maidens on an altar (Böttiger, *Ideen zur Kunstmyth.*
Taf. v.).   The names of Pasiphae, the mother, and Ariadne-Aridela
(Ἀριδήλαν, τὴν Ἀριάδνην Κρῆτες, Hesych.), the sister of the Minotaur,
point to his true character as a form of the Sun-god.

[1] Virgil (*Æn.* VIII. 192) merely calls him *Semihomo*, but we may
supply the other half by a reference to Ovid's description of the
Minotaur as *Semibovemque virum semirirumque bovem* (2 *Ar. Am.* v. 23).

[2] When he is called the son of Vulcan, and is said to breathe forth
fire, the reference is no doubt to the brazen statue of Moloch.

[3] Apollod. I. 9, § 26.   [4] Kenrick, *On Herodotus*, II. 44.

[5] Creuzer, *Symbol.* II. 528.

[6] See the passages quoted by Ghillany, *Menschenopf.* p. 225.

[7] In the *Bacchæ* of Euripides (1008) the chorus says to the god:
φάνηθι ταῦρος, and we have in 1149: ταῦρον προηγητῆρα συμφορᾶς ἔχων.
In the festival of Dionysus of Elis, he was greeted as ἄξιε ταῦρε, and
invited to come Βοέῳ ποδί, i. e. with a blessing (Creuzer, *Symbolik*, II.
p. 204, IV. p. 56); and similarly he is bidden to approach καθαρσίῳ
ποδί in Sophocles, *Antig.* 1143.   The authority for the Elean usage is

pointed to the human blood which was shed at his altars. He was called Ὁμάδιος or Ὠμοφάγος, because he had human sacrifices at Chios, Lesbos, and Tenedos,[1] and his name Ζαγρεύς is best explained by a similar reference.[2] Persian prisoners were solemnly offered up to him on the day before the battle of Salamis.[3] The Delphic oracle sanctioned the yearly sacrifice at Potniæ in Boeotia of a beautiful boy to Dionysus, until, as in the story of Iphigenia, a kid was substituted for the victim.[4] At the feast called Σκιέρεια, a scourging of women took the place of the human sacrifice to Dionysus at Alea in Arcadia, in the same way as the boys were whipped rather than slain in honour of Artemis Orthosia.[5]

The Semitic sun-god and his Greek representative Dionysus were not only worshipped under the form of a wrathful and cruel Moloch, to whom the blood of human victims was an acceptable and even necessary offering. He appeared also as the god of generation and reproduction, as the cause both of human life, and of that annual growth of the fruits of the earth,[6] by which human life was sustained, above all, as the giver of the grape, which made glad the heart of man, and stimulated him to all that was pleasant and joyous. In

Plutarch, *Qu. Gr.* xxxvi., who gives the hymn addressed to Bacchus by the Elean women as follows: ἐλθεῖν ἥρω Διόνυσε ἅλιον ἐς ναὸν ἁγνὸν σὺν Χαρίτεσσιν ἐς ναὸν τῷ βοέῳ ποδὶ θύων· εἶτα δὶς ἐπᾴδουσιν· ἄξιε ταῦρε. He adds the question, πότερον ὅτι καὶ βουγενῆ προσαγορεύουσιν καὶ ταῦρον τὸν θεόν. Euripides defines Bacchus as ταυρόκερως θεός (*Bacch.* 100): and he was also called ταυρόμορφος, βούκερως, κερασφόρος, κερατοφυής, χρυσόκερως, and the like. See on this subject F. Streber's elaborate paper, *Ueber den Stier mit dem Menschengesichte auf dem Munzen von Unteritalien und Sicilien, Munich Transactions* for 1837, II. pp. 453 sqq.

[1] Porphyr. de *Abst.* II. 55.
[2] Creuzer, *Symbol.* IV. pp. 96 sqq.
[3] Plutarch, *Themist.* c. 13.
[4] Pausan. IX. 8.
[5] Id. VIII. 23.
[6] With reference to the functions of Dionysus as the god of all ripe fruits, Plato calls the γενναία ὀπώρα, or fruits which may be eaten from the trees, as distinguished from the ἀγροῖκος ὀπώρα, or fruits intended for ulterior applications, by the somewhat strange designation of παιδιά (not παιδεία) Διονυσιὰς ἀθησαύριστος (*Legg.* 844 D). Hence Bacchus is called δενδρίτης; Plut. *Qu. Sympos.* p. 675 F; Aθen III. 78 B.

C

this capacity, he was worshipped in his Semitic home as *Baal-Peor;*[1] in Byblus, and other Semitic cities, he bore the name of *Adonis ;*[2] and the Jews called him also *Thammuz,* from the name of the month July, in which his worship, as that of the glowing and triumphant Sun, was more especially celebrated.[3] In some parts of Asia Minor the Sun, as the fructifying principle, was worshipped as Priapus,[4] and though this deity was really another form of Dionysus, one of the mythological legends made him the son of Venus, and a doubtful father, either Dionysus or Adonis.[5] In Palestine, and wherever it appeared, the worship of Baal-Peor was accompanied by frightful immoralities,[6] and there is every reason to believe that the pure and divine religion of the Jews, which denounced the inhuman rites of Moloch, was based on a still more formal repudiation of the worship of a deity, for whose name the Israelites indignantly substituted the word *Bosheth,* signifying "shame."[7] The sun-god, as the giver of life, was represented under the more decent type of a serpent;[8] but the revolting emblem of the Phallus was openly displayed in every country to which this form of religion had penetrated;[9] it was a necessary accompaniment

---

[1] בַּעַל פְּעוֹר or פְּעוֹר only (*Numbers* xxv. 1 sqq., xxxi. 16; *Josh.* xxii. 17). The name is represented by the Fathers as βεελφαγώρ or *Belphegor* (*Etym. M.* ad v.; Hieron. *in Os.* c. 9).

[2] Creuzer, *Symb.* II. pp. 472 sqq. The name is the common Semitic expression for "my Lord," and is therefore nearly synonymous with Baal.

[3] *Ezek.* viii. 14.   [4] Lobeck, *Aglaophamus,* p. 499.

[5] *Schol. Apoll. Rh.* I. 932.   [6] Creuzer, *Symbol.* II. 411.

[7] e. g. *Hosea* ix. 10, "They went to Baal-Peor and separated themselves unto that shame, and their abominations were according as they loved."

[8] For the serpent as the Orphic first principle, see Creuzer, *Symbol.* II. 224; IV 83. 85; for its use as a symbol of Saturn or Moloch, see Creuzer, *ibid.* III 69; for its use in the worship of Bacchus and along with the Phallus, see Creuzer, *ibid.* IV. 137; Gerhard, *Anthesterien,* pp. 158, 160. It was, in fact, a type of the Agathodæmon (Creuzer, IV. p. 55), an Egyptian symbol (Lampridius, *Heliogabal.* 28), as such adopted by the Israelites (*Numb.* xxi. 8. Justin Martyr says rather too generally (*Apol.* I. 27, p. 71 A): παρὰ παντὶ τῶν νομιζομένων παρ' ὑμῖν θεῶν ὄφις σύμβολον μέγα καὶ μυστήριον ἀναγράφεται, but from the context he seems to have understood its meaning.

[9] See e. g. Herod. II. 48. That these figures existed in Palestine

of the rural feast of Bacchus in Attica;[1] till the last century it existed in all its most repulsive features in the heart of Christian Italy;[2] and the oldest traditions derive the indecency of this adoration of the reproductive powers of nature from the drunkenness of the vine-god and his festival.[3]

It was as a Phallic god and as the giver of wine that Dionysus retained his place in the worship of ancient Greece. And in this capacity his worship connects itself indissolubly with the mysteries of Demeter and her daughter, the goddesses of the earth and of the under-world.[4] Generally the productiveness of the earth is regarded as the result of a marriage between the god of the sky,—whether he appears as the genial Sun or as the refreshing rain,—and the goddess who represents the teeming earth, and weds her daughter to Plutus or Pluto, the owner of the treasure hidden below the surface of the ground, either actually, as metallic riches, or potentially, as the germs of vegetable growth.[5] To the last, this was the leading characteristic of the old Athenian worship of Dionysus, and his spring festival, the Anthesteria, was accompanied by mystic solemnities, pointing at once to this ideal of his religion, and to its Semitic origin.[6] At this

---

may be inferred from 1 *Kings* xiv. 23; 2 *Kings* xvii. 10, xxiii. 14; *Hos.* x. 1. For this worship in Italy, see Plin. *H. N.* xxxviii. 4, 7; August. *Civ. Dei,* vii. 21, 24, 2; Arnob. iv. 7.

[1] See *e. g.* Aristoph. *Acharn.* 243.

[2] At Isernia, one of the most ancient cities in the kingdom of Naples, situated in the Contado di Molise. It was destroyed by an earthquake in 1805, a judgment, as some might think, for this iniquity.

[3] Compare Tzetzes, *Chiliad.* viii. 211 :

Τοῦ οἰνουργίας εὑρετοῦ, φημί, τοῦ Αἰγυπτίου
Τοῦ Νῶε καὶ 'Οσίριδος·

with the tradition preserved by Berosus respecting the Phallic worship introduced by Ham : "hic est ille Belphegor" (says Cornelius Agrippa, *Opp.* ii. p. 63 , "idolum omnium antiquissimum, quod et Chamos dictum est, a Chamo filio Noe, qui, teste Beroso, idcirco *Esenna* cognominatus est, hoc est, impudicus sive ignominiosus propagator."

[4] This subject has been recently discussed by Gerhard, *über die Anthesterien und das Verhältniss der attischen Dionysos zum Koradienst,* Berlin, 1858.

[5] Petersen, *geh. Gottesd. b. d. Griech.,* 1848, p. 17.

[6] The principal passage for this ceremonial is in the speech against Neæra, attributed to Demosthenes, p. 1370.

festival the mysteries were entrusted to the wife of the king Archon, and to fourteen priestesses called γέραιραι, whose number is that of the victims sent to the Minotaur, and is obviously Semitic.[1]   As the representative of the State, and as symbolizing the virgin daughter of Demeter, who returned to earth in the spring, the king Archon's wife was solemnly espoused to Dionysus,[2] just as conversely the Venetian Doge annually married the sea, and she alone was admitted to gaze on the mysterious emblems of the god's worship, on which the welfare of the State was supposed to depend, namely, the sacred serpent and the Phallus.[3]   It is impossible not to recognize in this usage some connexion with the story of Theseus and his Cretan expedition.   For Ariadne, whom the Athenian hero carries away from Crete and leaves at Naxos, becomes the bride of Dionysus.   And the fourteen victims of the Minotaur reappear in the fourteen γέραιραι, and in the noble youths and maidens sacrificed to the sacred serpent of Bacchus.[4]   As Semele represents the earth,[5] Dionysus appears not only as her son, but also as her husband; for in his original form he is the main representative of the fructifying power of heaven.   These oscillations in the persons of the sacred allegory need not create any difficulty, for the free play of fancy has combined and recombined the elements of the picture, like the changing figures of a kaleidoscope.

The forms of elementary worship, in which the powers of the sky and earth were personified, and which we have thus traced from their Semitic origin, were established among the Pelasgian tribes of Greece long before the epoch called the return of the Heracleids, which marks the establishment of a Dorian, or purely Hellenic, race in the country which we

[1] Servius, *ad Æneid.* VI. 21, Müller, *Dor.* I. 2, 2, § 14, recognizes the worship of Apollo, i. e. of the sun-god, in the number 7, and the Ennaeteris in the period of the sacrifice.

[2] It was only on the day of these espousals, the 12th of Anthesterion, that the temple was opened (Dem. *in Near.* p. 1377).

[3] Gerhard, *Myth.* 450, 1.   [4] Id. *Anthester.* notes 43, 44.

[5] "Semele denotes the ground, not only according to Diodorus, III. 61, but also according to the certain derivation of the name, as θεμέλη, θεμέθλον (cf. ἠΰθεμέθλιος); Welcker, *Götterlehre,* I. p. 536." Gerhard, *Anthest.* note 96.

call by their generic name. According to the ethnographic
results which we adopt as most probable,[1] the Dorians or
Hellenes, properly so styled, were ultimately the same race
as the Persians. And they had from the earliest times a
sun-god of a very different character from that of the Semitic
tribes. The Ormuzd of the Persians was a god of light and
purity, an archer-god, the giver of victory and empire, the
charioteer of heaven, or the rider of the heavenly steed;[2]
and the Apollo of the Dorians possessed many of these attributes. But although, as an essentially warlike people, and
averse from agricultural employments, which they considered
the proper occupation of those whom they had conquered
with the spear,[3] the Dorians were not very likely to adopt
for its own sake a merely elementary worship, which is the
usual idolatry of the tillers of the soil, their national deity
Apollo would of course retain his traditionary position as a
sun-god ; and it was quite in accordance with the usual
procedure that he should supersede the corresponding
divinity, whom the northern tribes found established among
their Pelasgian or Achæan subjects. The Dorians, when
they conquered any country, generally introduced the worship of their own gods, but they endeavoured at the same
time to unite it with the religion which they found established in their settlements. Thus they adopted the
elementary gods of Laconia, the Tyndaridæ, taking care,
however, to give their worship a *military* and *political*
reference,[4] so as to make it coincide with the attributes of
Apollo, whose office of leader of the army was transferred
to them. Similarly Apollo was made the object of the
Hyacinthia, an ancient festival connected with the elementary religion of the Ægidæ.[5] Now the Dorians worshipped,
along with Apollo, a female form of that god, called by the

---

[1] *New Cratylus*, § 92.   Compare Gladstone, *Homeric Studies*, I.
pp. 545 sqq.
[2] *Varronianus*, p. 61, ed. 3.
[3] See the spirited drinking song by Hybrias, the Cretan, Athen.
p. 695 F, and cf. Isocr. *Panath.* p. 326, Bekker: Λακεδαιμόνιοι ἀμελήσ-
αντες γεωργιῶν καὶ τεχνῶν καὶ ἄλλων ἁπάντων.
[4] See Müller's *Dorians*, II. ch. 10, § 8, and compare our remarks in
the following chapter of this book.
[5] Müller's *Dor.* II. ch. 8, § 15.

same name (with of course a different termination), invested
with the same attributes, and looked upon as his sister.[1]
This need not surprise any one who has paid ordinary
attention to systematic mythology; for we constantly find
in all polytheisms sets of duplicate divinities, male and
female.[2] Now this is most particularly the case with those
divinities who were the ἀρχηγέται of the different nations.
Thus there was both a Romus and a Roma,[3] a Vitellius and
a Vitellia.[4] In some instances it may be accounted for from
the fact that the original division of the nation has been two-
fold:[5] and in this way we would explain the double form of
the national divinity of the Dorians; for it appears to us
that they were not always τριχάϊκες, but that they at first
consisted only of the two branches of the family of Ægimius,
the Dymanes and the Pamphylians, and that the Heracleids
were not till afterwards incorporated among them.[6] However this may be, the fact is certain; there were two leading
divinities in the Dorian religion. Now in the elementary
worship of the Pelasgians and Achæans there were also two
divinities similarly related.   These were the Sun and the
Moon, worshipped under the related names of Helios and
Selene, and by the Pelasgian old inhabitants of Italy, as well
under appellations connected with the Greek, as under the
names of Janus or Dianus, and Diana.[7]   In Greece, how-

---

[1] For instance, if Apollo was *Loxias*, Artemis was *Loxo*, if he was
Hecaergos, she was *Hecaergē*.   See Müller's *Dor.* II. ch. 9, § 2, notes
(*u*) and (*x*) especially.   Buttmann, *Mytholog.* I. p. 16.

[2] See Niebuhr, *Hist. Rom.* I. pp. 100, 101.   Aud sometimes deities of
doubtful sex: compare Thirlwall in the *Philol. Museum*, Vol. I. pp. 116,
117; and on the androgynous character of Bacchus, see Welcker *on
the Frogs of Aristophanes*, p. 224.

[3] Malden's *Rome*, p. 123.   [4] Niebuhr, *Hist. Rom.* I. p. 14.

[5] Niebuhr, I. p. 287; comp. 224.   [6] See Müller's *Dor.* I. ch. 1, § 8.

[7] Ἥλιος and Σελήνη are connected like ὕλη and silva (cf. the proper
name Sila, Paley, *ad Propert.* p. 52); Sol and (Se)luna are the same
words under another form.

On Janus, or Dianus, see Niebuhr, *Hist. Rom.* I. p. 83; Buttmann,
Mytholog. II. p. 73; Döderlein, *Lat. Synon. und Etym.* I. p. 6.   There
was also a Ἕκατος as well as a Ἑκάτη (see Alberti's note on *Hesych.* s.
v. Ἑκάτοιο).   Mr. Scott, of Brasenose College, Oxford, has given a
further development of these principles in a very ingenious and satisfactory essay on the mythology of Io, which appeared in the *Classical
Museum*, No. XII.

ever, the original denominations of these divinities fell into
disuse at an early period, and were rather employed to
designate the natural objects themselves than the celestial
powers whom they were supposed to typify; and Dionysus
or Bacchus was adopted as a new name for the sun-god, and
Deo or Demeter for the goddess of the Moon.[1] These
divinities, as we have seen above, were Phœnician importa-
tions; and, connected as they were in many of their
attributes with the old elementary worship of the Pelasgians,
they soon established themselves as constituent parts of
that worship, and were at length blended and confused with
the gods of the country. For Dionysus was the wine-god,
and Deo the fertile earth from which the vine sprang up.
How natural, then, was the transition from the god who
gave wine to mortals, to the Sun to whose influence its
growth was mainly owing! But if he ascended from earth
to heaven, it was necessary that his sister deity should go
with him; and as his bride Ariadne shone among the stars,
so might Demeter, Thyone, or Semele, his mother, sister, or
wife, be also translated to the Moon, and rule amid the
lights of night. Indeed, Bacchus himself is sometimes
represented as a night-god, and in Sophocles he is invoked
as the choragus, or choir-leader, of the fire-breathing stars,
as one celebrated by nocturnal invocations.[2] Thus Bacchus
and Demeter were the representatives of those two heavenly
bodies by which the husbandmen measured the returning
seasons, and as such, though not immediately connected with
agriculture,[3] are invoked by the learned Virgil at the
commencement of the Georgics.[4] They also represented
the earth and its productions; but there is still another
phase which they exhibit: they were, in the third place,
the presiding deities of the under-world.[5] This also admits
of an obvious interpretation. The Greeks, as a consequence

[1] That Bacchus was the sun-god clearly appears from the authorities
quoted by Welcker (*Nachtrag zur Trilogie*, p. 190).
[2] *Antig.* 1130.
[3] Welcker, *Nachtrag*, p. 191.
[4] I. 5—7:   —— Vos, O clarissima mundi
                    Lumina, labentem cœlo quæ ducitis annum,
                    Liber et alma Ceres.
[5] Herod. II. 123.

of their habit of imparting actual objective existence with will and choice to every physical cause, considered the cause of anything as also in some measure the cause of its contrary. Thus Apollo is not only the cause, but also the preventer of sudden death;[1] Mars causes the madness of Ajax,[2] he is therefore supposed to have cured the hero of his disease;[3] the violent wind which raised the billows also lulls them to rest;[4] night, which puts an end to day, also brings the day to light;[5] and Bacchus, the bright and merry god, is also the superintendent of the orphic or black rites; the god of life, he is also the god of death; the god of light, he is also the ruling power in the nether regions.[6]

The worship of Dionysus[7] consequently partook of the same variations as that of the sun-god whom he superseded; and while, on the one hand, his sufferings and mischances were bewailed, on the other hand, as the god of light, wine, and generation, as the giver of life and of all that renders life cheerful, his rites were celebrated with suitable liveliness and mirth. That mimicry should enter largely into such a worship, is only what we should expect.[8] A religion which recognizes a divinity in the great objects of nature,— which looks upon the Sun and Moon as visible representatives of the invisible potentates of the earth, and sky, and under-world,—is essentially imitative in all its rites. The reason why such a religion should exist at all, is, as we have already shown in a general way, also a reason why the ceremonies of it should be accompanied by mimicry. The men who could consider the Sun as the visible emblem

[1] Müller's *Dor.* II. ch. 6, § 2, 3.
[2] Soph. *Aj.* 179.   [3] Id. *ibid.* 706.   [4] Id. *ibid.* 674.
[5] Id. *Trachin.* 94. For this reason, says Eustath. ad *Iliad.* A. p. 22, Apollo is called the son of Latona, τουτέστι, νυκτός. Conversely Horat. *Carm. Sec.* 10:

> Alme sol. curru nitido diem qui
> Promis et celas.

[6] Herod. II. 123.
[7] It seems to us that Θυώνη or Διώνη is the feminine form of Διόνυσος, or more anciently Διώνυσος.
[8] Above, p. 8. The mirror which is given to Bacchus by Vulcan is an emblem of the mimetic character of his worship—οἵν Διονύσου ἐν κατόπτρῳ, Plotinus, IV. 3, 12 (see the passages quoted by Creuzer in his note on p. 707, I, 3, of his edition).

of an all-seeing power who from day to day performs his constant round, the cause of light and life ; the Moon, his sister goddess, who exercises the same functions by night ; the two though distant (ἕκατοι) yet always present powers (προστατήριοι); the men who could see in the circling orbs of night "the starry nymphs who dance around the pole ;" such men, we say, would not be long in finding out some means of representing these emblems on earth. If the Sun and the ever-revolving lights were fit emblems and suggestions of a deity, the circling dance round the blazing altar was an obvious copy of the original symbols, and an equally apt representation.[1]

The heavenly powers became gods of the earth, and it was reasonable that the co-ordinate natural causes of productiveness should also have their representatives, who would form the attendants of the personified primal causes of the same effects. The sun-god therefore, when he roamed the earth, was properly attended by the Sileni, the deities presiding over running streams ;[2] the goddess of the Moon by the Naiades, the corresponding female divinities; nay, sometimes the two bands united to form one merry train.[3] To the Sileni were added a mixture of man and goat called Satyrs, who were sometimes confounded with the former, though their origin appears to have been quite different ; for while the Sileni were real divinities of an

---

[1] See the author περὶ λυρικῶν, apud Boissonade, Anecd. Gr. IV. p. 458 ; Rhein. Mus. 1833, p. 169 ; cf. note on Soph. Ant. 1113, p. 224. Though all polytheisms are connected with the production of the mimetic arts, the modes of imitation differ with the nature of the religion. The *symbols* of an elementary religion are the objects of imitation ; but in a mental religion, art is called upon to produce from the ideal a visible symbol. The mimicry of *action* is the result of the former, the mimicry of *sculpture* of the latter. Hence the primitive gods, who were parts of an elementary worship, were not originally represented by statues (comp. Müller, *Eumen.* § 89, 90, 93). "Ye eldest gods," says Ion,

> "Who in no statues of exactest form
> Are palpable: who shun the azure heights
> Of beautiful Olympus, and the sound
> Of ever-young Apollo's minstrelsy."
>
> Talfourd's *Ion*, Act iii. Sc. 2.

[2] Welcker, *Nachtrag*, p. 214.   [3] Strabo, p. 468.

elementary religion, the Satyrs were only the deified
representatives of the original worshippers,[1] who probably
assumed as portions of their droll costume the skin of the
goat, which they had sacrificed as a welcome offering to
their wine-god.[2]

Such was the religion of Bacchus as it appeared in
Greece; and there is no doubt that it was speedily accepted
by the Pelasgian and Achæan tribes; that it presented
the duplicate form, which it had exhibited in its eastern
home; that the mixed religion became prevalent both
within and without the Peloponnese; and that the Dorians,
having a pair of deities corresponding in many respects to
those objects of elementary worship which they found
established in most of the countries they subdued, very
naturally adapted their own religion to the similar one
already subsisting; and that accordingly Dionysus took or
maintained his place by the side of Apollo even in the
Delphic worship.

In addition to the circumstances which adapted the
religions themselves to an amalgamation such as we find
in their ultimate form, there were features in the rites of
Dionysus, even in their most ancient halting-places in Crete
and elsewhere, which recommended them to the martial
tastes of the northern Hellenes. The dances of the Curetes
and Corybantes were decidedly military,[3] and the Bacchic
rites, at least as adopted by the Spartans, had a gymnastic
character, which accorded well with the rigorous training of
the female population in Laconia.[4]

---

[1] Strabo, p. 466: τούτους γάρ τινας δαίμονας ἢ προπόλους θεῶν, κ.τ.λ.
p. 471: καὶ ὅτι οὐ πρόπολοι θεῶν μόνον ἀλλὰ καὶ αὐτοὶ θεοὶ προσηγορεύ-
θησαν.

[2] Varro, de R. R. I. 2, 18, 19; Virgil, Georg. II. 376—383; Ovid,
Fast. 1. 349—360; Eurip. Bacch. 138.   [3] Strabo, p. 466.

[4] There were races at Sparta between young women in honour of
Bacchus. Hesych.: Διονυσιάδες. ἐν Σπάρτῃ παρθένοι αἱ ἐν τοῖς Διονυσίοις
δρόμον ἀγωνιζόμεναι. Pausan. III. 13. 7: τῷ δὲ ἥρωι τούτῳ (Διονύσου
ἡγεμόνι) πρὶν ἢ τῷ θεῷ θύουσιν αἱ Διονυσιάδες καὶ αἱ Λευκιππίδες [l.
Λευκόποδες]. τὰς δὲ ἄλλας ἕνδεκα ἃς καὶ αὐτὰς Διονυσιάδας ὀνουάζουσι,
ταύταις δρόμου προτιθέασιν ἀγῶνα· δρᾶν δὲ οὕτω σφίσιν ἦλθεν ἐκ Δελφῶν.
Something of the same kind appears to be alluded to in Eurip. Bacch.
853 sqq.: ἆρ' ἐν παννυχίοις χοροῖς θήσω ποτὲ λευκὸν πόδ' ἀναβακ-
χεύουσα.

From this brief sketch it will be seen that the connexion of the worship of Dionysus, Demeter, and Apollo, in which we recognize the earliest appearances of dramatic rites, was due to the common elements which they contained and to the readiness to adopt and appropriate the representative forms of human thought, which is universally characteristic of a plastic polytheism. We are now prepared to discuss the choral rites of the Doric Apollo, and to inquire into the circumstances under which the warlike dances of the northern Greeks came to be used in the celebration of religious solemnities consecrated to the Semitic wine-god.

CHAPTER III.

THE TRAGIC CHORUS.—ARION

Doch hurtig in dem Kreise ging's.
Sie tanzten rechts, sie tanzten links.
GÖTHE.

In the earliest times of Greece, it was customary for the whole population of a city to meet on stated occasions and offer up thanksgivings to the gods for any great blessings, by singing hymns, and performing corresponding dances in the public places.[1] This custom was first practised in the Doric states. The maintenance of military discipline was the principal object of the Dorian legislators; all their civil and religious organization was subservient to this; and war or the rehearsal of war was the sole business of their lives.[2] Under these circumstances, it was not long

---

[1] This is the reason why, according to Pausan. III. 11, 9, the ἀγορά at Sparta was called χορός. We are rather inclined to believe that the Chorus of Dancers got its name from the place; χορός is only another form of χῶρ-ος: and hence the epithet εὐρύχορος which is applied to Athens (Dem. *Mid.* p. 531) as well as to Sparta (Athen. p. 131 c, in some anapæsts of Anaxandrides). Welcker's derivation of χορός from χείρ (*Rhein. Mus.* for 1834, p. 485) is altogether inadmissible. See farther, *New Cratylus*, § 280; Antigone, *Introduction*, p. xxix.

[2] στρατοπέδου γὰρ (says an Athenian to a Cretan, Plato, *Legg.* II. p. 666) πολιτείαν ἔχετε· ἀλλ' οὐκ ἐν ἄστεσι κατῳκηκότων. All the Dorian governments were aristocracies, and therefore necessarily war-

before the importance of music and dancing, as parts of
public education, was properly appreciated: for what could
be better adapted than a musical accompaniment to enable
large bodies of men to keep time and act in concert? What
could be more suitable than the war-dance, to familiarize
the young citizen with the various postures of attack and
defence, and with the evolutions of an army? Music and
dancing, therefore, were cultivated at a very early period by
the Cretans, the Spartans, and the other Dorians, but only
for the sake of these public choruses :[1] the preservation of
military discipline and the establishment of a principle of
subordination, not merely the encouragement of a taste for
the fine arts, were the objects which these rude legislators
had in view; and though there is no doubt that religious
feelings entered largely into all their thoughts and actions,
yet the god whom they worshipped was a god of war,[2] of
music,[3] and of civil government,[4] in other words, a Dorian
political deity ; and with these attributes his worship and
the maintenance of their system were one and the same
thing. This intimate connexion of religion and war among
the Dorians is shown by a corresponding identity between
the chorus which sang the praises of the national deity, and
the army which marched to fight the national enemies.
These two bodies were composed, in the former case in-
clusively, of the same persons; they were drawn up in the
same order, and the different parts in each were dis-

---

like, as Vico has satisfactorily shown, whatever we may think of his
derivation of πόλεμος from πόλις (*Scienz. Nuov.* Vol. II. p. 160).

[1] "We and the Spartans," says Clinias, "οὐκ ἄλλην ἄν τινα δυναίμεθα
ᾠδὴν ἢ ἣν ἐν τοῖς χοροῖς ἐμάθομεν ξυνήθεις ἄδειν γενόμενοι." Plato,
Legg. p. 666.

[2] Ἀπόλλων—Ἀπέλλων, "the defender" (Müller's *Dor.* II. ch. 6, § 6),
who caused terror to the hostile army. Æsch. *Sept. c. Theb.* 147.

[3] He was particularly the inventor of the lyre—the original accompaniment of Choral Poetry. Pind. *Pyth.* v. 67 : (Ἀπόλλων) πόρεν τε
κίθαριν δίδωσί τε Μοῖσαν οἷς ἂν ἐθέλῃ, ἀπόλεμον ἀγαγὼν ἐς πραπίδας
εὐνομίαν.

[4] "The belief in a fixed system of laws, of which Apollo was the
executor, formed the foundation of all prophecy in his worship."
Müller, *Dor.* II. 8, § 10. The Delphian oracle was the regulator of all
the Dorian law-systems; hence its injunctions were called θέμιστες, or
"ordinances." See the authorities in Müller, II. 8, § 8.

tinguished by the same names. Good dancers and good fighters were alike termed πρυλέες, i. e. προ-ιλέες, or " men of the vanguard ;"[1] those whose station was in the rear of the battle array, or of the chorus, were in either case called ψιλεῖς, or " unequipped ;"[2] and the evolutions of the one body were known by the same name as the figures of the other.[3] It was likewise owing to this conviction of the importance of musical harmony, that the Dorians termed the constitution of a state—an order or regulative principle (κόσμος). Thus Herodotus[4] calls the constitution of Lycurgus, "the *order* now established among the Spartans" (τὸν νῦν κατεστεῶτα κόσμον τοῖς Σπαρτιήτῃσι); Clearchus[5] speaks of the Lacedæmonians who were prostrated in consequence of their having trodden under foot the most ancient *order* of their civil polity (οἱ τὸν παλαιότατον τῆς πολιτικῆς κόσμον συμπατήσαντες ἐξετραχηλίσθησαν); and Archidamus, in Thucydides,[6] tells his subjects that their good *order* (τὸ εὔκοσμον) is the reason why they are both warlike and wise; and concludes his harangue to the allied army, when about to invade Attica, with an enforcement of the same principle.[7]

This description of the Chorus may suffice to show, that,

---

[1] See *Varronianus*, p. 314; cf. Athen. xiv. p. 628 F: ὅθεν καὶ Σωκράτης ἐν τοῖς ποιήμασι τοὺς κάλλιστα χορεύοντας ἀρίστους φησὶν εἶναι τὰ πολέμια, λέγων οὕτως·

Οἱ δὲ χοροῖς κάλλιστα θεοὺς τιμῶσιν, ἄριστοι
Ἐν πολέμῳ·

σχεδὸν γὰρ ὥσπερ ἐξοπλισία τις ἦν ἡ χορεία, κ.τ.λ.

[2] Müller thinks (*Götting. Gel. Anz.* for 1821, p. 1051) that they were so called, because they were not so well dressed as the front-row dancers.

[3] See Müller's *Dorians*, B. iii. c. 12, § 10; B. iv. c. 6, § 4. And add to the passages cited by him, Eurip. *Troad.* 2, 3 :

———— ἔνθα Νηρῄδων χοροὶ
Κάλλιστον ἴχνος ἐξελίσσουσιν ποδός.

Herc. Fur. 967 : ὁ δ' ἐξελίσσων παῖδα κίονος κύκλῳ
τόρευμα (l. πόρευμα) δεινὸν ποδός.

[4] I. 65   [5] Ap. Athen. xv. p. 681 c.   [6] I. 84.

[7] II. 11 : κόσμον καὶ φυλακὴν περὶ παντὸς ποιούμενοι......ἐνὶ κόσμῳ χρωμένους φαίνεσθαι. This word κόσμος appears to be appropriated to dancing rather than to music : καὶ γὰρ ἐν ὀρχήσει καὶ πορείᾳ καλὸν μὲν εὐσχημοσύνη καὶ κόσμος, κ.τ.λ. Athen. xiv. p. 628 D.

being both regular and stationary, or moving only within
the limits of a particular space, it was distinguished, in the
latter respect, from the marching troop, which was a regular
body of men in a state of progress, and in both respects
from the Comus (κῶμος), which was a tumultuous procession
of revellers. We find the earliest description of the stationary Chorus in Homer's "Shield of Achilles,"[1] where, as we
shall see presently, the *Hyporcheme* is intended; and we have
the moving or processional Chorus by the side of the Comus
in Hesiod's "Shield of Hercules."[2] The regularity of the
Chorus always necessitated a leader (ἔξαρχος), who was
either the musician or some fugleman among the dancers,
who "set the example"[3] to the others. Thus in a dirge
the chief mourner was said "to lead off the lament;"[4] and

---

[1] Hom. *Il.* XVIII. 590—606.   [2] 272—285.
[3] Küster, *de Verb. Med.* I. 23, II. 5.
[4] The following passages will show the usage of ἐξάρχω:

Iliad XVIII. 50 :   αἱ δὲ (Νηρηΐδες) ἅμα πᾶσαι
     Στήθεα πεπλήγοντο· Θέτις δ' ἐξῆρχε γόοιο.

Ibid. 314 :   αὐτὰρ Ἀχαιοὶ
     Παννύχιοι Πάτροκλον ἀνεστενάχοντο γοῶντες.
     Τοῖσι δὲ Πηλεΐδης ἀδινοῦ ἐξῆρχε γόοιο.

Ibid. 604 :   δοίω δὲ κυβιστητῆρε κατ' αὐτοὺς
     Μολπῆς ἐξάρχοντες ἐδίνευον κατὰ μέσσους.

To which we may add,

Il. XXIV. 720 :   παρὰ δ' εἶσαν ἀοιδοὺς
     Θρήνων ἐξάρχους οἵτε στονόεσσαν ἀοιδὴν
     Οἱ μὲν ἄρ' ἐθρήνεον, ἐπὶ δὲ στενάχοντο γυναῖκες.

With which compare *Il.* I. 604; *Odyss.* XXIV. 60. The simple ἄρχειν
occurs in *Iliad* XIX. 12. Archilochus, fr. 38, Liebel. Athen. XIV.
p. 628 A :

     Ὡς Διωνύσοι' ἄνακτος καλὸν ἐξάρξαι μέλος
     Οἶδα διθύραμβον οἴνῳ συγκεραυνωθεὶς φρένας.

Archilochus, fr. 44, Liebel. Athen. iv. p. 180 E :

     Αὐτὸς ἐξάρχων πρὸς αὐλὸν Λέσβιον παιήονα·

which Müller, *Dor.* II. 8, § 14 (note *y*), mistranslates. He says : "there
was always a person named ἐξάρχων who accompanied the song on an
instrument. Thus Archilochus," &c. But ἐξάρχειν πρὸς αὐλὸν means
"to lead off the Pæan, either by words or as a dancer, *to the accompaniment* of the flute played by another person." See Eurip. *Alcest.* 346;
πρὸς Λίβυν λακεῖν αὐλόν: so that Toup has rightly introduced πρὸς

even the chief player in a game at ball is said ἄρχεσθαι μολπῆς;[1] whence it will be seen that the words μέλπεσθαι and μολπή, when used in speaking of the old Chorus, imply the regular, graceful movements of the dancers, and the *Eumolpids* were not singers of hymns, but dancers in the Chorus of Demeter and Dionysus.[2]

It would appear, then, that music and dancing were the basis of the religious, political, and military organization of the Dorian states; and this alone might induce us to believe that the introduction of choral poetry into Greece, and the first cultivation of instrumental music, is due to them. However, particular proofs are not wanting. The strongest of these may be derived from the fact, that the Doric dialect is preserved in the lyric poetry of the other Grecian tribes. We may notice this in the choral portions of any Attic tragedy. Now it has been sufficiently shown[3] that the lyric poetry of the Greeks was an offspring not of the epos, but of the chorus songs; and if the lyric poetry of the Æolians and Ionians was always (with the exception perhaps of Corinna's Bœotian choruses) written in the Doric dialect, the choral poetry, of which it was a modification, must have been Dorian also.[4] Nor can any argument against this supposition be derived from the fact that the most celebrated of the early lyric poets were not Dorians; for choral dances existed among the Cretans long before the time of the earliest of these poets; and it is no argument against the assumed origin of an art in one country, to say that it attained to a higher degree of perfection in

---

αὐλόν in Athenæus, p. 447 B (*Em. ad Suid.* I. p. 348).   Pausan. v. 18, 4 speaking of the chest of Cypselus, πεποίηνται δὲ καὶ ᾄδουσαι Μοῦσαι, κα 'Απόλλων ἐξάρχων τῆς ᾠδῆς καὶ σφίσιν ἐπίγραμμα γέγραπται,

  Λατοΐδας οὗτος τάχ' ἄναξ ἑκάεργος 'Απόλλων,
  Μοῦσαι δ' ἀμφ' αὐτόν, χαρίεις χορός, αἷσι κατάρχει.

Sophocl. Vit. p. 2; (Σοφοκλῆς) μετὰ λύρας γυμνὸς ἀληλιμμένος τοῖς παιανίζουσι τῶν ἐπινικίων ἐξῆρχε.

[1] *Odyss.* VI. 101; cf. Athen. I. p. 20.
[2] Müller, *Hist. Lit. Gr.* Vol. I. p. 25.
[3] By Müller, *Dor.* B. IV. c. 7, § 11.
[4] The weight of this argument will be readily appreciated by the readers of Niebuhr's *Hist. Rom.* I. p. 82, Engl. Transl.

another.[1] With regard to Athens in particular, it appears
to us, that we have in some sort positive evidence that
choruses were not instituted there until the Athenians had
recognized the Dorian oracle at Delphi; for some old
Delphian oracles have come down to us[2] particularly en-
joining these Doric rites, a command which could hardly
have been necessary, had they existed at Athens from the
first.

It must be obvious that so long as the choral music and
dancing of the Dorians were a religious exercise in which
the whole population took a part, the tunes and figures
must have been very simple and unartificial. A few plain
regulative notes on the tetrachord, and as much concinnity
of movement as the public drill-masters could effect, sufficed
for the recitation and performance of Pæans in Lacedæmon,
Crete, and Delos.   But, as a natural consequence of the
importance attached to music and dancing, in countries
where they formed the basis of religious, political, and
military organization, it was not long before art and genius
volunteered their services, and improvements in the theory
and practice of instrumental music were eagerly adopted
and imported, or cultivated by emulous harpers in the
Dorian states.   The Æolian colonists of Lesbos, from their
proximity to the coast of Asia Minor, were among the first
who sought to accommodate the more extensive and varied
harmonies of the Phrygians and Lydians to the uses and
requirements of the Dorian chorus.   Terpander of Lesbos,
who gained the prize at the Lacedæmonian Carneia in B.C.
676,[3] substituted the seven-stringed cithara for the old
tetrachord; and his contemporaries, the Græco-Phrygian
Olympus, and the Bœotian Clonas, exercised an influence
scarcely less important on the flute-music of the Greeks.
A little later, Thaletas, the Cretan, imported into the choral
worship of his own country and Sparta a more impassioned
style of music and dancing, which was intimately connected

---

[1] See Themistius, *Orat.* XXVII. p. 337 A, Harduin.: ἀλλ' οὐδὲν ἴσως
κωλύει τὰ παρ' ἑτέροις ἀρχὴν λαβόντα πλείονος σπουδῆς παρ' ἄλλοις
τυγχάνειν.

[2] Apud Demosth. *Mid.* p. 531, § 15, Buttm.

[3] Athenæus, XIV. p. 635 E.

with the rhythmical innovations of Terpander and Olympus;[1] and the Lydian Alcman, who was a great poet as well as a great musician, composed songs for the popular chorus, which may be considered as the true beginning of lyric poetry. As these improvements gradually developed themselves, they necessarily superseded the ruder efforts of the old crowd of worshippers; and the poet, as δημιουργός or " state-workman,"[2] with his band of trained singers and dancers, at length executed all the religious functions of the collective population.

The most ancient and genuine species of the Dorian choral song was the *Pæan*, which was not only practised in the rehearsals of the market-place, but carried to the actual field of battle. It was so thoroughly identified with the worship of Apollo, that we cannot doubt for a moment that its original accompaniment was the harp (φόρμιγξ), with which Apollo himself, in the Homeric Hymn, leads a chorus of Cretans; he dances with noble and lofty steps, and they follow him, singing the sweet strains of the Iepæan.[3] But as early as the days of Archilochus the flute had taken the place of the harp as an accompaniment to the Pæan at Lesbos.[4] That there was something grave and staid in the original Pæan may be concluded from the topics to which it was confined;[5] and as late as the time of Agesilaus it

[1] Müller, *Hist. Lit. Gr.* c. XII. § 10.
[2] *Od.* XVII. 385 :
  Τίς γὰρ δὴ ξεῖνον καλεῖ ἄλλοθεν αὐτὸς ἐπελθὼν
  Ἄλλον γ', εἰ μὴ τῶν οἳ δημιοεργοὶ ἔασιν,
  Μάντιν ἢ ἰητῆρα κακῶν ἢ τέκτονα δουρῶν,
  Ἢ καὶ θέσπιν ἀοιδόν, ὅ κεν τέρπῃσιν ἀείδων;
[3] Hom. *Hymn. Apoll.* 514 sqq.:
  Ἦρχε δ' ἄρα σφι, ἄναξ Διὸς υἱός, Ἀπόλλων
  Φόρμιγγ' ἐν χείρεσσιν ἔχων, ἀγατὸν κιθαρίζων,
  Καλὰ καὶ ὑψὶ βιβάς· οἱ δὲ ῥήσσοντες ἔποντο
  Κρῆτες πρὸς Πυθώ, καὶ ἰηπαιήον' ἄειδον
  Οἷοί τε Κρητῶν παιδόνες.
Cf. Pind. *N.* v. 22 sqq.
[4] Archiloch. apud Athen. v. p. 180 E. :
  Αὐτὸς ἐξάρχων πρὸς αὐλὸν Λέσβιον παιήονα,
above. p. 30, note 4.
[5] The ideal of a Pæan is very well given in the first Chorus of the

D

was performed at the mournful feast of the Hyacinthia.[1]
Whence Plato speaks with disapprobation of the later
practice of mixing up the Pæan with the Bacchic Dithyramb;[2] and in general we observe that the Pæan, as devoted
to the children of Leto, is kept separate and distinct from
the Dythyramb,[3] even in those countries where the worship
of Bacchus was cultivated along with that of Apollo, and
after the time when the characteristic Dionysian hymn was
raised to the dignity of lyric poetry.

From the Dorian *Pæan* three styles of choral dancing
developed themselves at a very early period, and most
probably received their chief improvements under Thaletas
in Crete. These were the *Gymnopædic*, the *Pyrrhic*, and
the *Hyporchematic* dances. The γυμνοπαιδία, or "festival
of naked youths," was held in great esteem at Sparta.[4]
The immediate object was the worship of Leto and her
children, and the music was that of the *Pæan*. But an
heroic and tragic character was given to the solemnity by
its formal reference to the victory at Thyrea. The praises
of the valiant Spartans, who fell on that occasion, were
always sung at the *Gymnopædia*, and the Exarchus wore the
Thyreatic crown.[5] The gesticulations and steps of the boys

Œdipus Tyrannus, 151 sqq. Plutarch (p. 389 B) calls the Pæan τεταγμένην καὶ σώφρονα μοῦσαν.

[1] Xen. *Ages.* II. 17: οἴκαδε ἀπελθὼν εἰς τὰ Ὑακίνθια, ὅπου ἐτάχθη ὑπο
τοῦ χοροποιοῦ τὸν παιᾶνα τῷ θεῷ συνετέλει.

[2] *Legg.* III. p. 700 D.

[3] See Pindar, *Thren. Fr.* 10, 103*, according to the emendations
which we have elsewhere proposed:

Ἔντι μὲν χρυσαλακάτου Λατοῦς τεκέων ἀοιδαὶ
Ἰηῖ[οι] παιάνιδες·
Ἔντι [δὲ σύγκω]μόν τισι κισσοῦ στέφανον
Ἐκ Διω[νύσου μεταμ]αιόμεναι.

[4] Ἑοστὴ δὲ εἴτις ἄλλη καὶ αἱ γυμνοπαιδίαι διὰ σπουδῆς Λακεδαιμονιοις-
εἰσίν. Pausan. III. 11, 9.

[5] Athen. XV. p. 678 B: Θυρεατικοί· οὕτω καλοῦνται στεφανοι τινες
παρὰ Λακεδαιμονίοις, ὥς φησι Σωσίβιος ἐν τῇ περὶ θυσιῶν, ψιλίνους αὐτοὺς
φάσκων νῦν ὀνομάζεσθαι, ὄντας ἐκ φοινίκων· φέρειν δ' αὐτούς, ὑπόμνημα
τῆς ἐν Θυρέᾳ γενομένης νίκης, τοὺς προστάτας τῶν ἀγομένων χορῶν ἐν τῇ
ἑορτῇ ταύτῃ, ὅτε καὶ τὰς Γυμνοπαιδίας ἐπιτελοῦσι. χοροὶ δ' εἰσὶ το-
μὲν εὐπροσώπων παίδων, τὸ δ' ἐξ ἀρίστων ἀνδρῶν, γυμνῶν ὀρχουμένων, καὶ

amounted to a rhythmical imitation of the wrestling match and pancration, which is partly implied by the absence of clothing.[1] The *Gymnopœdic* dance was considered as a sort of introduction to the *Pyrrhic*, just as the exercises of the *Palæstra* in general were a preparation for military discipline. To be able to move rapidly in armour was a leading accomplishment of the Greek hoplite, and we are expressly told that the *Pyrrhic*, which was danced by boys in armour, was a rapid dance.[2] Beyond this rapidity of motion, it had no characteristic steps ; the distinctive movements were those of the hands, whence it was called a "manual gesticulation" (χειρονομία), and might be performed by the horsemen as well as by the foot-soldier.[3] Connected with the rites of the Curetes in Crete, and of the Dioscuri in Lacedæmon, the *Pyrrhic* was danced in later times to the notes of the flute; and the same was the case with the Castoreum and the embateria. But we have positive evidence that the lyre was the original accompaniment in the Cretan and Spartan marches, and that the flute was substituted only because its notes were shriller and more piercing.[4] The *Hyporcheme* was, as its name implies,[5] a dance expressing by gesticulations the words of the accompanying poem. It had thus, in effect, two different kinds of leaders. Going back to the earliest description of this dance, we find that not only is the citharist, who sits in the middle of the

---

ᾀδόντων Θαλήτου καὶ 'Αλκμᾶνος ᾄσματα, καὶ τοὺς Διονυσοδότου τοῦ Λάκωνος παιᾶνας. See Visconti, *Mus. Pio-Clement.* Tom. III. p. 74, n. 4.

[1] Athen. XIV. p. 631 B.

[2] Athen. XIV. p. 630 D. The same is indicated by the *Pyrrhic* (‿‿) and *Proceleusmatic* (‿‿‿‿) feet, which are attributed to this dance. The latter, to which the ἐνόπλιος ρυθμός refers, is tantamount to the anapæst, which is the proper rhythm for *embateria*.

[3] This must be the meaning of what Pindar says of Bellerophon and Pegasus, *O.* XIII. 86 : ἀναβὰς δ' εὐθὺς ἐνόπλια χαλκωθεὶς ἔπαιζεν. Cf. Virg. *Georg.* III. 115 sqq.:
> Frena Pelethronii Lapithæ gyrosque dedere
> Impositi dorso, atque equitem docuere sub armis
> Insultare solo, et gressus glomerare superbos.

[4] Müller, *Dor.* Book IV. c. 6, § 6, 7. On the orgiastic nature of the flute-music see Aristot. *Pol.* VIII. 7, § 9.

[5] See Gesner, on Lucian *de Saltat.* (Tom. V. p. 461, Lehmann.)

chorus and sings to his lyre while the youths and maidens
dance around him, described as *leading off* (ἐξάρχων) their
μολπή, or rhythmical steps and gesticulations, but that
there are always two chief dancers, sometimes called
"tumblers" (κυβιστητῆρε), by whose active and violent
motions the words of the song are expressed, and the
main chorus regulated.[1]   These leaders of the chorus
seem to have been essential to the *Hyporcheme*, and
particularly to that species of it which was called the
"Crane" (γέρανος), where they led forward the two horns
of a semicircle until they met on the other side of the altar
of Apollo.[2]   The *Hyporcheme* originated in Crete, and was
thence imported into Delos, where it seems to have retained
its primitive characteristics even in the days of Lucian.[3]
Though connected originally with the religious rites of
Apollo,[4] it was subsequently introduced into the worship of
Bacchus by Pratinas,[5] and into that of Minerva of Iton by
Bacchylides.[6]

We have treated more at length of these three sorts of
choral dances, because each of them had its representative
in the dramatic poetry of a later age.   This appears from a
curious passage in Athenæus, probably derived from some
author of weight:[7] "There are," he tells us, "three dances
in scenic poetry, the *Tragic*, the *Comic*, and the *Satyric*; and
likewise three in lyric poetry, the *Pyrrhic*, the *Gymnopœdic*,
and the *Hyporchematic*; and the *Pyrrhic* indeed corresponds to
the *Satyric*, for they are both rapid" (he had given just before
a reason for the rapidity of the Satyric dance).   "Now the

---

[1] Compare *Il.* XVIII. 591—606 (*Od.* IV. 17—19) with *Hymn. Apoll.*
182—206.
[2] See the passages quoted by Müller, *Dor.* II. 8, § 14, note g.
[3] *De Saltat.* § 6: Ἐν Δήλῳ...παίδων χοροὶ συνελ᾿ όντες ἐπ᾿ αὐλῷ καὶ
κιθάρᾳ οἱ μὲν ἐχόρευον, ὑπωρχοῦντο δὲ οἱ ἄριστοι, προκριθέντες ἐξ αὐτῶν.
τὰ γοῦν τοῖς χοροῖς γραφόμενα τούτοις ᾄσματα, ὑπορχήματα ἐκαλεῖτο:
where οἱ ἄριστοι manifestly agree with the κυβιστητῆρες, which was
another name for particularly active dancers.
[4] See Menandr. *de Encom.* p. 27, Heeren : τοὺς μὲν γὰρ εἰς Ἀπόλλωνα
παιᾶνας καὶ ὑπορχήματα νομίζομεν.
[5] Athen. p. 617.   [6] *Fragm.* ed. Neue, p. 33.
[7] Athen. p. 630 D. He quotes Aristocles, Aristoxenus, and Seamo.
With regard to the Hyporcheme cf. Athen. 21 D: ἡ δὲ Βαθύλλειος
[ὄχησις] ἱλαρωτέρα· καὶ γὰο ὑπόσχημά τι τοῦτον διατίθεσθαι.

Pyrrhic is considered a military one, for the dancers are boys in armour; and swiftness is needed in war for pursuit and flight. But the *Gymnopœdic* dance is similar to the Tragic which is called *emmeleia*; both these dances are conspicuously staid and solemn. The *Hyporchematic* dance coincides in its peculiarities with the *Comic*, and they are both full of merriment."

The Bacchic hymn, which was raised to the rank of choral and lyric poetry among the Dorians, was the *Dithyramb*, which is regularly opposed to the *Pæan*.[1] Originally, no doubt, it was nothing more than a Comus, and one too of the wildest and most Corybantic character. A crowd of worshippers, under the influence of wine, danced up to and around the blazing altar of Jupiter. They were probably led by a flute-player, and accompanied by the Phrygian tambourines and cymbals, which were used in the Cretan worship of Bacchus.[2] The subject of the song was properly the birth of Bacchus,[3] but it is not improbable that his subsequent adventures and escapes may have been occasionally celebrated;[4] and it is a reasonable conjecture that the Coryphæus occasionally assumed the character of the god himself, while the rest of the Chorus or Comus represented his noisy band of thyrsus-bearing followers.[5] Whatever opinion we may agree to form respecting the etymology of the name, it is at least clear, from any justifiable analysis of the word Δι-θύραμβος, that it was addressed to the king of

---

[1] Plut. *De El Delphico*, p. 593: μιξοβόαν γάρ, Αἰσχύλος φησί, πρέπει διθύραμβον ὁμαρτεῖν σύγκοινον Διονύσῳ· τῷ δὲ ['Απόλλωνι] παιᾶνα τεταγμένην καὶ σώφρονα μοῦσαν. Ibid. p. 594: τὸν μὲν ἄλλον ἐνιαυτὸν παιᾶνι χρῶνται περὶ τὰς θυσίας, ἀρχομένου δὲ χειμῶνος ἐπεγείραντες διθύραμβον, τὸν δὲ παιᾶνα καταπαύσαντες τρεῖς μῆνας ἀντ' ἐκείνου τοῦτον κατακαλοῦνται τὸν θεόν. See also above, p. 34, note 3.

[2] Euripides, *Bacch.* 123—133, distinctly identifies the worship of Bacchus with the Corybantic adoration of Demeter.

[3] Plato, *Legg.* III. p. 700 B: παίωνες ἕτερον, καὶ ἄλλο Διονύσου γένεσις, οἶμαι, διθύραμβος λεγόμενος.

[4] This may be inferred from Herod. v. 67: καὶ δὴ πρός, τὰ πάθεα αὐτοῦ τραγικοῖσι χοροῖσι ἐγέραιρον· τὸν μὲν Διόνυσον οὐ τιμέωντες, τὸν δὲ ̓Αδρηστον.

[5] Bacchus is called ὁ ἔξαρχος by the Chorus of Bacchanalians in Euripides (*Bacch.* 141), and it seems obvious that the dithyramb must have endeavoured to represent the θίασος in all its parts.

the gods;[1] and Bacchus belonged, as we have already seen, to a branch of Greek religion which admitted an assumption of his character on the part of his votaries.

ARION, a celebrated cithara-player (κιθαρῳδός) of Methymna in Lesbos, who flourished in the days of Stesichorus and Periander, (i.e. about 600 B.C.) is generally admitted to have been the inventor of the *cyclic chorus* (κύκλιος χορός), in which the Dithyramb was danced around the blazing altar by a band of fifty men or boys,[2] to a lyric accompaniment. So intimately is Arion connected with this improvement, that he is called the son of *Cycleus*. We must be very careful not to confuse between this invention, or adaptation, of Arion's, and the improvements introduced into the older style of Dithyrambic poetry, some one hundred years later by Lasos of Hermione, the teacher of Pindar and the rival of Simonides.[3]   It is quite clear that the Dithyramb of Lasos gave rise to the style of poetry which existed under

---

[1] We have elsewhere discussed the etymology of this word at some length (*New Cratylus*, §§ 317 sqq.), and have endeavoured to show that it is the word θύραμβος = θρίαμβος appended to the dative of Ζεύς; that the termination is ἄμβος = ῖαμβος, a word denoting a dance of people in close order, or a hymn sung by such a body; and that the root θυρ = θρι is the same as that which is found in θύρ-σος. To this opinion we still adhere. The only doubtful point, as it appears to us, is the explanation of the root of θύρσος. Hartung (*Classical Museum*, VI. p. 372 sqq.) proposes to connect θύραμβος with θόρυβος. If the one were really a by-form of the other, it would be θόρυμβος, not θύραμβος. Cf. κόρυμβος, ἴθυμβος, &c. As however the dithyrambic dance was called τυρ-βασία (Jul. Poll. IV. 104: τυρβασία δὲ ἐκαλεῖτο τὸ ὄρχημα τὸ διθυραμβικόν), and as the root θυρ-, θορ-, θρο-, θρι-, might be connected with that of τύρβη, *turba*, from which this τυρβασία is formed, a question might arise whether the name of the θύρσος was derived from the tumultuous clamours (θρόος, θροέω, θρύλλος, &c.) of the θίασος of Bacchus; or whether it was expressive of the symbolical meaning of the Bacchic staff with its accompaniments.

[2] Schol. Pind. *Ol.* XIII. 26. Simon. *Epigr.* 76:

Ξεινοφίλου δέ τις υἱὸς Ἀριστείδης ἐχορήγει
Πεντήκοντ' ἀνδρῶν καλὰ μαθόντι χορῷ.

[3] Some of the older grammarians were unable to make this distinction. Thus the Scholiast on Aristophanes (*Aves*, 1403) says: Ἀντίπατρος δὲ καὶ Εὐφρόνιος ἐν τοῖς ὑπομνήμασί φασι τοὺς κυκλίους χοροὺς στῆσαι πρῶτον Λᾶσον τὸν Ἑρμιονέα, οἱ δὲ ἀρχαιότεροι Ἑλλάνικος καὶ Δικαίαρχος Ἀρίονα τὸν Μηθυμναῖον.

that name for many years, after the full development of
Tragedy and Comedy, and which is always distinguished
from the dramatic chorus. Instead of passing from the
flute of the Comus to the lyre of the Chorus, it multiplied
the appoggiaturas of the flute accompaniment.[1] Instead of
assuming more and more a dramatic form, it is expressly
described as having been distinguished from Tragedy and
Comedy by its expository style, and by the pre-eminence
given to the poet's own individuality.[2] Instead of approximating to the language of ordinary life, it became more and
more turgid, bombastic, affected, and unnatural. Even
Lasos himself indulged in an excess of artificial refinement.
He composed odes from which the sibilants were studiously
excluded; and his rhythms were conveyed in prolix metres,
which dragged their slow length along, in full keeping with
the pompous phraseology, which was to the last days of
Greek literature regarded as a leading characteristic of the
Dithyramb.[3] Pindar, the great pupil of Lasos, speaks with
disapprobation of this style of Dithyramb, which, however,
his own better example failed to correct: "Formerly," he
says, "the Dithyramb crawled along in lengthy rhythms,
and the *s* was falsified in its utterance."[4] Again, while the

---

[1] Plut. *Mus.* p. 666, Wyttenb.: Λᾶσος δὲ ὁ Ἑρμιονεὺς εἰς τὴν διθυραμ-
βικὴν ἀγωγὴν μεταστήσας τοὺς ῥυθμοὺς καὶ τῇ τῶν αὐλῶν πολυφωνίᾳ
κατακολουθήσας πλείοσί τε φθόγγοις καὶ διερριμμένοις χρησάμενος εἰς
μετάθεσιν τὴν προϋπάρχουσαν ἤγαγε μουσικήν.

[2] Plat. *de Republ.* III. p. 394C: ὅτι τῆς ποιήσεώς τε καὶ μυθολογίας ἡ
μὲν διὰ μιμήσεως ὅλη ἐστίν, ὥσπερ σὺ λέγεις τραγῳδία τε καὶ κωμῳδία, ἡ
δὲ δι' ἀπαγγελίας αὐτοῦ τοῦ ποιητοῦ, εὕροις δ' ἂν αὐτὴν μάλιστά που
ἐν διθυράμβοις.

[3] See Aristoph. *Pax*, 794—7; *Aves*, 1373 sqq. Hence διθυραμβώδης
signifies tumid and bombastic. Plato, *Cratyl.* p. 409 C. Cf. *Hipp.
Maj.* p. 292 C. Dionys. Hal. *de adm. vi dem.* p. 1043, 10. Philostrat.
p. 21, 6: λόγων ἰδέαν οὐ διθυραμβώδη, on which the Scholiast, published
by G. I. Bekker (Heidelbergæ, 1818), says: διθυραμβώδη συνθέτοις
ὀνόμασι σεμνυνομένην καὶ ἐκτοπωτάτοις πλάσμασι ποικιλλομένην· τοιοῦτοι
γὰρ οἱ διθύραμβοι ἅτε διονυσίων τελετῶν ἀφωρμημένοι.

[4] *Fragm.* 47: Πρὶν μὲν εἶρπε σχοινοτένειά τ' ἀοιδὰ διθυράμβων
Καὶ τὸ σὰν κίβδαλον ἀνθρώποισιν ἀπὸ στομάτων.

The adjective σχοινοτενής refers to rhythm, as appears from Hermo-
genes, *de Invent.* IV. 4 (Vol. III. p. 158, Walz), who, after defining the
κόμμα and the κῶλον says: τὸ δὲ ὑπὲρ τὸ ἡρωϊκὸν σχοινοτενὲς κέκληται

Dithyramb, as reformed by Arion, clung to the antistrophic and epodic forms introduced into the chorus by his contemporary Tisias, who derived his better-known surname *Stesichorus* from the stability which he thus gave to the movements of his well-taught body of dancers,[1] the Dithyramb of Lasos eventually became monostrophic, and returned in form to the primitive Comus, in the same proportion as it reverted to its original mimicry.[2] Above all, while the Dithyramb of Arion, influenced by the sedateness of the Doric muse, shook off by degrees all remembrances of the drunken frolics in which it took its rise, the other Dithyramb retained to the end many of its original characteristics. Epicharmus, who was a contemporary of Lasos, alludes to it in precisely the same manner as Archilochus, who flourished two hundred years earlier. That ancient poet says, that " he knows how to lead off the Dithyramb, the beautiful song of Dionysus, when his mind is dizzy with the thunder of wine."[3] Epicharmus tells us that " there is no Dithyramb, if you drink water."[4] And Simonides, the rival of Lasos, describes the Dithyramb as sung by noisy Bacchanalians crowned with fillets and chaplets of roses, and bearing the ivy-wreathed thyrsus.[5]

χρήσιμον προοιμίοις μάλιστα καὶ ταῖς τῶν προοιμίων περιβολαῖς. The second line alludes to the ᾠδαὶ ἄσιγμοι of Lasus: see Athen. VIII. p. 455 c.

[1] See the explanations given by the grammarians and lexicographers of the proverbial phrases πάντα ὀκτώ, τρία Στησιχόρου, and οὐδὲ τὰ τρία Στησιχόρου γιγνώσκεις. With regard to the significance of his name. as applicable to the Bacchic Chorus in particular, it is worthy of remark that when the Delphic oracle (apud Dem. *Mid.* p. 531) enjoins the establishment of the Dorian form of Dionysiac worship at Athens, it expressly uses the phrase ἱστάναι χορόν.

[2] Aristotle, *Probl.* XIX. 15, p. 918, Bekker: μᾶλλον γὰρ τῷ μέλει ἀνάγκη μιμεῖσθαι ἢ τοῖς ῥήμασιν· διὸ καὶ οἱ διθύραμβοι, ἐπειδὴ μιμητικοὶ ἐγένοντο, οὐκέτι ἔχουσιν ἀντιστρόφους, πρότερον δὲ εἶχον.

[3] Above, p. 30, note 1.

[4] Apud Athen. p. 628 B.

οὐκ ἔστι διθύραμβος, ὅκχ' ὕδωρ πίῃς.

[5] Simonides, *Frag.* 150, Bergk, *Anthol. Pal.* II. p. 542.

Πολλάκι δὴ φυλῆς Ἀκαμαντίδος ἐν χοροῖσιν Ὧραι
Ἀνωλόλυξαν κισσοφόροις ἐπὶ διθυράμβοις
Αἱ Διονυσιάδες, μίτραισι δὲ καὶ ῥόδων ἀώτοις

Although Arion was a Lesbian, it was in the great Dorian
city of Corinth that he introduced his great choral improvements. In enumerating the various inventions which were
traced to that city, Pindar asks: "Where else did the graces
of Bacchus first make their appearance with the ox-driving
Dithyramb?" alluding to the ox which was sacrificed as a
type of the god, who was also worshipped under this form.[1]
The account which is given of the specific improvements
imported into the Dithyramb by Arion, though brief, is very
distinct; and it is quite possible, from the notices which
have come down to us, to draw up an accurate description of
this Bacchic chorus as it was exhibited at Corinth in the
days of Periander.

Of our authorities, the two most explicit are the earliest
and the most recent, which stand related to one another as
text and commentary. Herodotus tells us that "Arion
was the most eminent cithara-player of his time, and that
he was the first, as far as Herodotus knew, who made
poems for the Dithyramb, who gave a name to these poems,
and regularly taught the Chorus; and that he did this at
Corinth."[2] The lexicographer Suidas gives the same information, but at greater length, and in such a manner as
to show that Herodotus was by no means his only authority.
He says: "Arion, the Methymnæan, a lyric poet, the son
of Cycleus, was born about the 38th Olympiad. Some

Σοφῶν ἀοιδῶν ἐσκίασαν λιπαρὰν ἔθειραν,
Οἳ τόνδε τρίποδα σφίσι μάρτυρα Βακχίων ἀέθλων
Θῆκαν· Κικυννεὺς δ' 'Αντιγένης ἐδίδασκεν ἄνδρας.

The student, however, must take care to remember that the Dithyramb
never actually became a *Comus* after it had once been raised to the
dignity of a Chorus. Even Pindar's processional songs, though
nominally performed by a *Comus*, were invested with the dignity of
choral poetry, and Comedy itself became at last choral. See note on
Pindar, *Fragm.* 45, p. 344.

[1] *Olymp.* XII. 18:

ταὶ Διωνύσου πόθεν ἐξέφανεν
Σὺν Βοηλάτᾳ χάριτες διθυράμβῳ;

See above, p. 16, note 7.

[2] Herod. I. 23: 'Αρίονα—ἐόντα κιθαρῳδὸν τῶν τότε ἐόντων οὐδενὸς
δεύτερον· καὶ διθύραμβον, πρῶτον ἀνθρώπων τῶν ἡμεῖς ἴδμεν, ποιήσαντά τε
καὶ ὀνομάσαντα καὶ διδάξαντα ἐν Κορίνθῳ.

have told us that he was a scholar of Alcman. He is said
to have been the inventor of the tragic style; and to have
been the first to introduce a standing-chorus, and to sing
the Dithyramb; and to give a name to what was sung by
the Chorus; and to introduce Satyrs speaking in verse."[1]
As these accounts are in strict agreement with one another,
and with all the scattered and fragmentary notices of Arion
which we meet with elsewhere,[2] we may conclude that we
have here a true tradition, and proceed to interpret it
accordingly. It appears, then, that the following were the
improvements which the Methymnæan citharœdus introduced into the Corinthian Dithyramb. 1. He composed
regular poems for this dance.[3] Previously, the leaders of
the wild irregular Comus, which danced the Dithyramb, bewailed the sorrows of Bacchus, or commemorated his wonderful birth, in spontaneous effusions accompanied by suitable
action, for which they trusted to the inspiration of the
wine-cup. This is the meaning of Aristotle's assertion that
this primitive Tragedy was "extempore" (αὐτοσχεδιαστική[4])
and some such view of the case is necessary to explain Archilochus' boast that he can play the part of leader
in the Dithyramb when the wine is in his head;[5] for this
presumes a sudden impulse rather than a premeditated
effort. Arion, however, by composing regular poems to be
sung to the lyre, at once raised the Dithyramb to a literary
position, and laid the foundations of the stately super-
structure which was afterwards erected. 2. He turned the
Comus, or moving crowd of worshippers, into a standing
Chorus[6] of the same kind as that which gave Stesichorus

---

[1] Suidas: Ἀρίων Μηθυμναῖος, λυρικός, Κυκλέως υἱός, γέγονε κατὰ τὴν
λη′ ὀλυμπιάδα· τινὲς δὲ καὶ μαθητὴν Ἀλκμᾶνος ἱστόρησαν αὐτόν. ἔγραψε
δὲ ᾄσματα, προοίμια εἰς ἔπη β′. λέγεται δὲ καὶ τραγικοῦ τρόπου εὑρετὴς
γενέσθαι, καὶ πρῶτος χορὸν στῆσαι καὶ διθύραμβον ᾆσαι καὶ ὀνομάσαι τὸ
ᾀδόμενον ὑπὸ τοῦ χοροῦ καὶ σατύρους εἰσενεγκεῖν ἔμμετρα λέγοντας.
[2] Dio, II. p. 101; Phot. *Cod.* 239, p. 985; Schol. Pind. *Ol.* XIII. 18;
Schol. Aristoph. *Aves*, 1403.
[3] This is the true force of the phrases ποιῆσαι, ᾆσαι τὸ διθύραμβον.
[4] Aristot. *Poet.* c. iv.
[5] See the lines of Archilochus quoted above, pp. 29, 30.
[6] Suidas: χορὸν στῆσαι. Schol. Pind.: ἔστησε δὲ αὐτὸν [τὸν κύκλιον
χορόν]. This standing chorus nevertheless might perform ἐξελιγμοί

his surname. In fact, the steps of the altar of Bacchus became a stage on which lyric poetry in his honour was solemnly recited, and accompanied by corresponding gesticulations. 3. He was the inventor of the *tragic style* (τραγικοῦ τρόπου εὑρετής). This means that he introduced a style of music or harmony adapted to and intended for a chorus of Satyrs.[1] For the word τράγος, "*he-goat*," was another name for σάτυρος, the goat-eared attendant of Bacchus ;[2] and we have just seen that Suidas specifies the appearance of satyrs "discoursing," or holding a sort of dialogue, in verse, as one of the peculiarities of Arion's new Dithyramb. 4. He gave a name to what was sung by the Chorus.[3] What name ? Not διθύραμβος, for that was the common designation in the time of Archilochus, some one hundred years before. As Arion substituted for the riotous Comus a stationary and well-trained Chorus, that which was sung— the ἀοιδή—could not be a κωμῳδία or *Comedy ;* but, as being the hymn of a Chorus of τράγοι or "satyrs," it was naturally termed a τραγῳδία.[4] This name could have nothing to do with the goat, which was the subsequent prize of the early Attic Tragedy; for we are expressly told, that in Arion's days the ox was the prize[5]. Nor could it imply that the goat was the object of the song, as if τραγῳδός signified a

---

and other evolutions on the ground to which it was limited. The Chorus, as a whole, was stationary, though the separate dancers were in motion.

[1] On the τρόποι, "styles" or "harmonies" of Greek music, the student may consult Müller, *Hist. Lit. Gr.* I. p. 152 [202].

[2] Hesych.: Τράγους· σατύρους—διὰ τὸ τράγων ὦτα ἔχειν. *Etym. M.* : τραγῳδία ὅτι τὰ πολλὰ οἱ χοροὶ ἐκ σατύρων συνίσταντο, οὓς ἐκάλουν τράγους.

[3] Herodotus says, ὀνομάσαντα τὸν διθύραμβον: but Suidas more definitely, ὀνομάσαι τὸ ᾀδόμενον ὑπὸ τοῦ χοροῦ.

[4] It is pretty clear that τραγῳδία was the name of a species of lyrical poetry antecedent to, and independent of the Attic drama. See Böckh in the Appendix to this Chapter. Welcker, *Nachtrag*, p. 244: "The lyrical Tragedy was a transition step between the Dithyramb and the regular drama. It resembled the Dithyramb in representing by a chorus Dionysian and other myths (hence the Pæans of Xenocritus were called myths, because they related heroic tales), and differed from it in being sung to the lyre, and not to the flute."

[5] Athen. p. 456 D; Schol. *ad Pind. Ol.* XIII. 18.

man ὃς τράγον ἀείδει.[1] For, as κιθαρῳδός means a man who sings to the cithara, so τραγῳδός and κωμῳδός denote the singer whose words are accompanied by the gesticulations or movements of a Chorus of Satyrs, or a Comus of revellers. That the form of Doric Chorus, which Arion first adapted to the Dithyramb, was the *Pyrrhic*, appears from what has been stated above.[2] It was probably not till the days of Thespis that the *Gymnopædic* dance appeared as the Tragic Emmeleia. In Arion's time the *tragic style* was still a form of the Dithyramb, strictly confined to the worship of Bacchus, to which the poet had been habituated in the early days of his Lesbian life,[3] formally satyric in the habiliments of its performers, and in every sense a new and important branch of the Dorian lyric poetry.

About the time when Arion made these changes in the Dithyramb at Corinth, we read that a practice began to obtain in the neighbouring city of Sicyon which could not be altogether unconnected with Arion's "tragic style." The hero Adrastus was there honoured with Tragic Choruses. And the tyrant Cleisthenes, for political reasons, restored these choruses to Bacchus.[4] The tendency, which was thus checked, shows that the Dithyrambic Chorus of Arion had proved itself well adapted for the representation of tragic incidents, and especially of those misfortunes which were traceable to an evil destiny; for Adrastus was a type of unavoidable suffering,[5] brought down by the unappeasable vengeance of heaven; and every reader of the later Greek Drama is aware that this was a main ingredient in the plots of the more finished Tragedies, in which the divine Nemesis was always at work. There may, therefore,

---

[1] This is Ritter's opinion; *ad Arist. Poet.* p. 113.

[2] It appears too from Aristophanes (*Ranæ*, 153) that Kinesias, who was a celebrated Dithyrambist, was also renowned for his Pyrrhics.

[3] Bähr, *ad Herod. l. c.*

[4] Οἱ δὲ Σικυώνιοι ἐώθεσαν μεγαλωστὶ κάρτα τιμᾶν τον Ἄδρηστον...τά τε δὴ ἄλλα οἱ Σικυώνιοι ἐτίμων τὸν Ἄδρηστον, καὶ δὴ πρός, τὰ πάθεα αὐτοῦ τραγικοῖσι χοροῖσι ἐγέραιρον· τὸν μὲν Διόνυσον οὐ τιμέωντες, τὸν δὲ Ἄδρηστον. Κλεισθένης δὲ χορούς μὲν τῷ Διονύσῳ ἀπέδωκε, τὴν δὲ ἄλλην θυσίην τῷ Μελανίππῳ· ταῦτα μὲν ἐς Ἄδρηστόν οἱ πεποίητο. Herod. v. 67.

[5] His name, as is well known, indicated as much. See Antimach. p. 71 (apud Strab. p. 588).

be some foundation for the claims set up by the Sicyonians.[1] By transferring the Bacchic Chorus to the celebration of other heroes, they made a step even beyond Arion towards the introduction of dramatic poetry properly so called; and it is very possible that Epigenes of Sicyon may have been the first of a series of sixteen lyrical dramatists ending with Thespis,[2] to whom, as we shall shortly see, we owe the actor,[3] the dramatic dialogue, the stage, and the epic elements of the Athenian Tragedy.

The only specimens of the Greek choral poetry which have come down to us complete are a certain number of the Epinician or triumphal Odes of Pindar, who was born three years after Æschylus, who was more than once an honoured guest at Athens after the establishment there of the tragic drama, and whose intercourse with Æschylus, in Attica and in Sicily, is attested by more than one indication of borrowed phraseology. We cannot therefore conclude the present chapter without endeavouring to ascertain how far the performance of one of Pindar's Epinician Odes partook of a dramatic or histrionic character.

We have already seen, on the authority of Plato, that the melic poem presumed a direct communication from the poet himself—it was δι' ἀπαγγελίας αὐτοῦ τοῦ ποιητοῦ, in other words, it represented the author of the poem as speaking in his own person, and was therefore distinguished from the imitative dialogue of dramatic poetry.[4] Now the ἐπινίκιον in particular belonged to the class of ἐγκώμια, which by the

---

[1] τραγῳδίας εὑρεταὶ μὲν Σικυώνιοι, τελεσιουργοὶ δέ 'Αττικοί. Themist. Orat. XXVII. 337 B.

See also Athen. xiv. p. 629 A: 'Αμφίων—ἄγεσθαὶ φησιν ἐν 'Ελικῶνι παίδων ὀρχήσεις μετὰ σπουδῆς παρατιθέμενος ἀρχαῖον ἐπίγραμμα τόδε·

'Αμφότερ', ὠρχεύμαν τε καὶ ἐν Μώσαις ἐδίδασκον
"Ανδρας, ὁ δ' αὐλήτας ἦν "Ανακος Φιαλεύς·
Εἰμὶ δὲ Βακχείδας Σικυώνιος. ἦ ρα θεοῖσι
Τοῖς Σικυῶνι καλὸν τοῦτ' ἀπεκεῖτο γέρας.

[2] Suidas in Θέσπις.

[3] Athen. xiv. p. 630 C: συνέστηκε δὲ καὶ Σατυρικὴ πᾶσα ποίησις τὸ παλαιὸν ἐκ χορῶν, ὡς καὶ ἡ τότε τραγῳδία· διόπερ οὐδὲ ὑποκριτὰς εἶχον.

[4] Plat. Resp. III. 394 C. Ast interprets ἀπαγγελία as "en exponendi ratio qua poeta lyricus utitur qui suis ipse verbis omnia refert, suæ ipso mentis sensa explicat."

nature of the case implied a festive meeting[1] and more than
any other form of melic poetry allowed the bard freely to
introduce his own personality. It does not, however,
follow from this that the poet was always present in person,
and took an immediate part in the public performance of
his ode. On the contrary, as the triumphal ode was generally celebrated in the victor's native city, and sometimes
repeated from time to time on the anniversary of his
success, the poet would more frequently than otherwise be
absent, and if the ode contained any direct ἀπαγγελία from
the author, he must have been represented by the leader of
the chorus, who thus became, to all intents and purposes,
an actor, or the exponent of an assumed personality. It is
probable in itself that there was a class of persons, who laid
themselves out for this species of impersonation, and the
fact that it was so is proved by the Orchomenian Inscription
(No. 1583), quoted in the Appendix to this Chapter. We
find there that a certain Theban named Nicostratus gained
the prize at the Charitesia as κωμῳδός in regard to the
ἐπινίκια, i.e. not the celebration of the victory, as Böckh
supposes, but the songs composed for that celebration.
For in order to sing the ἐπικωμίαν ἀνδρῶν κλυτὰν ὄπα, as
Pindar calls it,[2] it was necessary that there should be a
κωμῳδός, a leader of the band, that is, either the poet himself,
who is mentioned in the following inscription,[3] or some
professional leader, like this Nicostratus. There is sufficient evidence in Pindar's odes to prove that the ἀπαγγελία
of the poet himself was thus undertaken by a professional
representative, who was distinct from the teacher of the
Chorus.

There are two of Pindar's Epinicia, the sixth Olympian
and the second Isthmian ode, in which the poet directly
addresses the χοροδιδάσκαλος. In the fifth strophe of the
former he says;[4] "now urge your comrades, Æneas, first
to sing of Hera Parthenia, and then to make known whether
we truly escape from the old reproach—*Bœotian sow!* For
you are a true messenger, the despatch-staff of the fair-
haired Muses, a sweet-mixing cup of loudly uttered songs.

---

[1] Below, Chapter v.
[2] *Pyth.* x. 6.
[3] l. 47: τὰ ἐπινίκια κουφδιῶν ποιητής.
[4] vv. 87 sqq.

Then tell them to remember Syracuse and Ortygia." There is every reason to believe that this ode was sung at Stymphalus in Arcadia. Agesias had driven the mule-car himself at Olympia, otherwise the allusion to his danger[1] would have no meaning; but the chariot driven by his friend Phintis formed part of the triumphal procession which accompanied the performance of the ode, as appears from the address to the charioteer.[2] The "unenvying citizens,"[3] who are represented as taking part in the song of victory, are of course the Arcadians, tacitly opposed to the envious Syracusans, who slew Agesias three years after his victory, and who are implied in the statement that " envy impends from others envying him."[4] That Pindar could not have been present at the Arcadian festival is clear from his calling Æneas " a messenger " ($\ddot{a}\gamma\gamma\epsilon\lambda o\varsigma$) and "a despatch-staff" ($\sigma\kappa\upsilon\tau\dot{a}\lambda\eta$); and that Æneas was not the $\kappa\omega\mu\omega\delta\dot{o}\varsigma$, but merely the $\chi o\rho o\delta\iota\delta\dot{a}\sigma\kappa a\lambda o\varsigma$, is proved from this address to him. From the words immediately preceding: " Theba whose delightful water I will drink when I weave a varied strain for warriors,"[5] it appears that Pindar was at Thebes when he was meditating another hymn on the Olympic victory of Agesias, which was to be performed at Syracuse under the auspices of Hiero; for the $\ddot{a}\nu\delta\rho\epsilon\varsigma$ $a\dot{\imath}\chi\mu\eta\tau a\dot{\imath}$ undoubtedly refer to Agesias, who is described as distinguished by his military excellences no less than by his connexion with the prophetic clan of the Iamidæ.[6] In the other case, where the $\chi o\rho o\delta\iota\delta\dot{a}\sigma\kappa a\lambda o\varsigma$ is addressed, namely, at the end of the second Isthmian ode, although Thrasybulus, the son of the deceased victor Xenocrates, is accosted in the second person in the preceding stanzas,[7] the concluding epode is directed to the trainer of the choir, Nicasippus, and the

---

[1] vv. 9—11.   [2] vv. 22 sqq.

[3] v. 7: $\dot{\epsilon}\pi\iota\kappa\dot{\upsilon}\rho\sigma a\iota\varsigma$ $\dot{a}\phi\theta\dot{o}\nu\omega\nu$ $\dot{a}\sigma\tau\tilde{\omega}\nu$ $\dot{\epsilon}\nu$ $\dot{\imath}\mu\epsilon\rho\tau a\tilde{\imath}\varsigma$ $\dot{a}o\iota\delta a\tilde{\imath}\varsigma$.

[4] v. 74: $\mu\tilde{\omega}\mu o\varsigma$ $\dot{\epsilon}\kappa$ δ' $\ddot{a}\lambda\lambda\omega\nu$ $\kappa\rho\dot{\epsilon}\mu a\tau a\iota$ $\phi\theta o\nu\epsilon\dot{o}\nu\tau\omega\nu$.

[5] vv. 85—87: $\Theta\dot{\eta}\beta a\nu$, $\tau\tilde{a}\varsigma$ $\dot{\epsilon}\rho a\tau\epsilon\iota\nu\dot{o}\nu$ $\ddot{\upsilon}\delta\omega\rho$
           $\pi\dot{\imath}o\mu a\iota$, $\dot{a}\nu\delta\rho\dot{a}\sigma\iota\nu$ $a\dot{\imath}\chi\mu a\tau a\tilde{\imath}\sigma\iota$ $\pi\lambda\dot{\epsilon}\kappa\omega\nu$
           $\pi o\iota\kappa\dot{\imath}\lambda o\nu$ $\ddot{\upsilon}\mu\nu o\nu$.

We have maintained, in our note on this passage, that $\pi\dot{\imath}o\mu a\iota$ must be future here: and have compared *Isthm.* v. 74: $\pi\dot{\imath}\sigma\omega$ $\sigma\phi\epsilon$ $\Delta\dot{\imath}o\kappa a\varsigma$ $\dot{a}\gamma\nu\dot{o}\nu$ $\ddot{\upsilon}\delta\omega\rho$.

     [6] vv. 17, 18.   [7] vv. 1, 31.

poet speaks as though all that had gone before was a
message to be delivered to Thrasybulus, when Nicasippus
next saw him. He says :[1] "let him not be prevented by
the envious hopes of others from speaking his father's
praise and publishing these hymns" (the second Isthmian
and another composed for recitation at Agrigentum), "for I
have not made them to tarry in one place (like a statue, as
he says elsewhere)[2] but to pass to and fro among men.
Communicate (or impart)[3] these injunctions, O Nicasippus,
when you shall have come to my respected friend."

From these passages it appears that the κωμῳδός of the
Epinician Ode sometimes directly represented the person of
the poet.

---

[1] vv. 43—48.   [2] *Nem.* v. 1.

[3] ἀπόνειμον. The scholiast says it means ἀναγνῶθι, "read," as in
Soph. *Fragm.* 150: σὺ δ' ἐν θρόνοισι γραμμάτων πτύχας ἔχων ἀπόνειμον.

APPENDIX TO CHAPTER III.

ORCHOMENIAN INSCRIPTIONS.

1583.

Μνασίνω ἄρχοντος, ἀγωνο-
θετίοντος τῶν Χαριτεισίων
Εὐάριος τῶ Πάντωνος, τύδε
ἐνίκωσαν τὰ Χαριτείσια·
 σαλπίγκτας
Φιλῖνος Φιλίνω 'Αθανεῖος,
 κάρουξ
Εἰρώδας Σωκράτιος Θειβεῖος,
 ποείτας
Μήστωρ Μήστορος Φωκαιεύς,
 ῥαψάϝυδος
Κράτων Κλίωνος Θειβεῖος,
 αὐλειτὰς
Περιγένεις 'Ηρακλίδαο Κουζικηνός,
 αὐλάϝυδος
Δαμήνετος Γλαύκω 'Αργῖος,
 κιθαριστὰς
'Αγέλοχος 'Ασκλαπιογένιος Αἰολεὺς ἀπὸ Μουρινας,
 κιθαράϝυδος
Δαμάτριος 'Αμαλωῖω Αἰολεὺς ἀπὸ Μουρίνας,
 τραγάϝυδος
'Ασκλαπιδδωρος Πουθέαο Ταραντῖνος,
 κωμάϝυδος
Νικόστρατος Φιλοστράτω Θειβεῖος,
 τὰ ἐπινίκια κωμάϝυδος
Εὔαρχος Ε[ἰ]ροδότω Κορωνεύς.

1584.

Οἵδε ἐνίκων τὸν ἀγῶνα τῶν Χαριτησίων·
 σαλπιστὴς
Μῆνις 'Απολλωνίου 'Αντιοχεὺς ἀπὸ Μαιανδρου,
 κήρυξ
Ζώϊλος Ζωΐλου Πάφιος,
 ῥαψῳδὸς
Νουμήνιος Νουμηνίου 'Αθηναῖος,
 ποιητὴς ἐπῶν
'Αμινίας Δημοκλέους Θηβαῖος,
 αὐλητὴς
'Απολλόδοτος 'Απολλοδότου Κρησαῖος,
 αὐλῳδὸς

E

Ῥόδιππος Ῥοδίππου Ἀργεῖος,
    κιθαριστὴς
Φανίας Ἀπυλλοδώρου τοῦ Φανίου, Αἰολεὺς ἀπὸ Κύμης,
    κιθαρῳδὸς
Δημήτριος Παρμενίσκου Καλχηδόνιος,
    τραγῳδὸς
Ἱπποκράτης Ἀριστομένους Ῥόδιος,
    κωμῳδὸς
Καλλίστρατος Ἐξακέστου Θηβαῖος,
    ποιητὴς Σατύρων
Ἀμινίας Δημοκλέους Θηβαῖος,
    ὑποκριτὴς
Δωρόθεος Δωροθέου Ταραντῖνος,
    ποιητὴς τραγῳδιῶν
Σοφοκλῆς Σοφοκλέους Ἀθηναῖος,
    ὑποκριτὴς
Σαβίριχος Θεοδώρου Θηβαῖος,
    ποιητὴς κωμῳδιῶν
Ἀλέξανδρος Ἀοιστίωνος Ἀθηναῖος,
    ὑποκριτὴς
Ἄτταλος Ἀττάλου Ἀθηναῖος.
Οἵδε ἐνίκων τὸν νεμητὸν ἀγῶνα τῶν Ὁμολωΐων·
    παῖδας αὐλητὰς
Διοκλῆς Καλλιμήλου Θηβαῖος,
    παῖδας ἡγεμόνας
Στρατῖνος Εὐνίκου Θηβαῖος,
    ἄνδρας αὐλητὰς
Διοκλῆς Καλλιμήλου Θηβαῖος,
    ἄνδρας ἡγεμόνας
Ῥόδιππος Ῥοδίππου Ἀργεῖος,
    τραγῳδὸς
Ἱπποκράτης Ἀριστομένους Ῥόδιος,
    κωμῳδὸς
Καλλίστρατος·Ἐξακέστου Θηβαῖος,
    τὰ ἐπινίκια κωμῳδιῶν ποιητὴς
Ἀλέξανδρος Ἀριστίωνος Ἀθηναῖος.

These two Inscriptions were formerly in a chapel of the Virgin at Orchomenus in Bœotia. The stones are now removed. The first Inscription is written in Bœotic, and is supposed by Böckh to be of older date than Olymp. 145 (B.C. 220).

To the foregoing Inscriptions we will add a third; a Thespian Inscription, engraved in the later age of the Roman emperors, which relates to the same subject; and then give the inferences which Böckh has drawn from these three interesting agonistic monuments.

1585.

Ἀγαθῇ τύχῃ.
Ἐνείκων ἐπὶ Φλαουΐῳ Παυλείνῳ ἀγωνοθετοῦντι Μουσῶν, ἐ[π']
ἄρχοντι Μητροδώρῳ τῷ Ὀν[η]σιφόρου·
    ποιητὴς προσοδίου

Εὐμάρων 'Αλεξάνδρου Θεσπιεὺς
καὶ 'Αντιφῶν 'Αθηναῖος,
κήρυξ
Πομπήϊος Ζωσίμου Θεσπιεύς,
σαλπικτὰs
Ζώσιμος 'Επίκτου Θηβαῖος,
ἐγκωμιογράφος εἰs τὸν Αὐτοκράτορα
Πούπλιος 'Αντώνιος Μάξιμος Νε[ω]κορείτηs,
ἐγκώμιον εἰs Μούσας
Πούπλιος 'Αντώνιος Μάξιμος Νε[ω]κοοείτηs,
ποιητὴs εἰs τὸν Αὐτοκράτορα
Αἰμίλιος 'Επίκτητος Κορίνθιος,
ποίημα εἰs τὰs Μούσας
Δαμόνεικος Δάμωνος Θεσπιεὺς,
ῥαψῳδὸs
Εὐτυχιανὸs Κορίνθιος,
πυθαύλας
Φάβιος 'Αντιακὸs Κορίνθιος,
κ[ι]θαριστὰs
Θεόδωρος Θεοδότου Νεικομηδεύς
[κωμῳδὸs παλαιᾶs κωμῳδίαs]

. . . .

τραγῳδὸs παλαιᾶs τραγῳδίαs
'Απολλώνιος 'Απολλωνίου 'Ασπένδιος,
ποιητὴs καινῆs κωμῳδίαs
'Αντιφῶν 'Αθηναῖος,
ὑποκριτὴs καινῆs κωμῳδίαs
'Αντιφῶν 'Αθηναῖος,
ποιη[τὴ]s καινῆs τραγῳδίαs
'Αρτέμων 'Αρτέμωνος 'Αθηναῖος,
ὑποκριτὴs καινῆs τραγῳδίαs
'Αγαθήμερος Πυθοκλέους 'Αθηναῖος,
χοραύλης
"Οσιος Περγαμηνός,
νεαρῳδὸs
Κλώδιος 'Αχιλλεὺς Κορίνθιος,
σατυρογράφος
Μ. Αἰμίλιος Ὑήττιος,
*διὰ πάντων
Εὐμάρων 'Αλεξάνδρου Θεσπιεύς.

These Inscriptions were first printed by Böckh at the end of his treatise on the *Public Economy of Athens*. We subjoin some of the remarks which he there makes upon them (IIter Band, p. 361 fol.).

" Before I leave these two Inscriptions, I may be permitted to make

---

* "Haud dubie formulæ sententia est, *hunc inter omnes victores esse præstantissimum judicatum, victorem inter victores;* unde ultimo loco scriptus est."—Böckh in loc.

a few remarks on the games mentioned in them. We find in both, first of all, trumpeters and a herald who began the games: their art was doubtless an object of contest in most sacred games, and the heralds in particular contended with one another in the gymnic games (Cicero, *Fam.* v. 12); which may perhaps have been the principal reason why the ancients had trumpeters and heralds, whom no one of the present day could have matched in strength of voice. Comp. Pollux, IV. 86—92; Athen. x. p. 415 F. seqq.; Ælian, *V. H.* I. 26. These are followed by the Epic poet, together with the Rhapsodist who recited his poem: then we have the flute-player and harper with the persons who sang to these instruments respectively. Next come, in both Inscriptions, Tragedians and Comedians. At the new Charitesia, however, three additional dramatic games are mentioned: ποιητὴς Σατύρων and ὑποκριτης, ποιητὴς τραγῳδιῶν and ὑποκριτής, ποιητὴς κωμῳδιῶν and ὑποκριτής. At the Homoloïa in the second Inscription, Tragedians and Comedians occur, and for the celebration of the victory (τὰ ἐπινίκια) another Comedy, but without actors. It is sufficiently clear from this, that when merely Tragedians and Comedians are mentioned, without actors, as is so often the case in authors and Inscriptions, we are not to understand a play, but only a song: if, however, a Play is to be signified, this must first be determined by some particular addition. As soon as an actor (ὑποκριτής) is mentioned, we understand by Tragedy and Comedy a dramatic entertainment. For a long time Tragedians and Comedians alone appeared in the Charitesia at Orchomenus, and it is only in later times that we find there all the three kinds of dramatic representations, when the theatre of Athens had extended its influence on all sides: nevertheless, even then the tragic and comic poets are Athenians, and only the satyrical poet a Theban. But Tragedians and Comedians, as lyric bards, were to be found everywhere from the most ancient times. This has not been properly attended to, and many passages in ancient writers have consequently been considered as enigmatical or suspicious. In the list of Pindar's Works, given by Suidas, we have seventeen δράματα τραγικά. I have no doubt that Pindar wrote Tragedies, but they were lyric poems, and not Dramas. With this remark, we recognise at once what is true or false in this account. Simonides of Ceos is said by the Scholiast on Aristophanes, by Suidas and Eudocia, to have written Tragedies, which Van Goens (p. 51) doubts; but what objection can be raised to this statement, if we only understand in it lyrical and not dramatic Tragedies? Whether the Tragedies of the younger Empedocles (see Suidas in 'Εμπεδοκλῆς, comp. Sturz, *Empedocl.* p. 86, seqq., where, however, there are all sorts of errors) were just such Dorian lyric Tragedies, or real dramatic exhibitions, I leave undecided. Arion seems to have been considered as the inventor of this lyric goat-song, since the introduction of the tragic manner (τραγικὸς τρόπος) is ascribed to this Dithyrambic poet, although he is said to have added satyrs to the chorus as acting persons (comp. Fabric. *B. Gr.* Vol. II. p. 286, Harles' edition). It is admitted that the Drama grew out of a lyric entertainment, and was formed from the chorus; but it is not so generally known that among the Dorians and Æolians a lyric

Tragedy and Comedy existed before, and along with the dramatic, as a distinct species, but people usually referred merely to the rude lyrical beginnings in the Festal games. Thus tragedies before the time of Thespis remained a thorn in the eyes of critics, which it was needful to have taken out; and Bentley's services (*Opusc.* p. 276) in this respect have been very highly estimated. But let not us be deceived by it. The Peloponnesians justly claimed Tragedy as their property (Aristot. *Poet.* III.): its invention and completion as a lyrical entertainment belongs undoubtedly to the Sicyonians, whose Tragedies are mentioned by Herodotus (v. 67, comp. Themist. XIX. p. 487): on which account the invention of Comedy also is sometimes attributed to the Sicyonians (Orest. *Anthol.* Part II. p. 328, 326); and Thespis may very well have been the sixteenth from the lyric Tragedian, Epigenes (Suidas in Θέσπις and οὐδὲν πρὸς Διόνυσον). Aristocles, in his book about the choruses, said very well (Athen. XIV. 630 C): Συνεστήκει δὲ καὶ σατυρικὴ πᾶσα ποίησις τοπαλαιὸν ἐκ χορῶν. ὡς καὶ ἡ τότε τραγῳδία· διόπερ οὐδὲ ὑποκριτὰς εἶχον. Just so Diogenes (III. 56) relates, certainly not out of his own learning, that before Thespis the chorus alone played in Tragedy (διεδραμάτιζε). This Tragedy, consisting of chorus only, was brought to perfection in very early times, and before the people of Attica, to whom alone the dramatic Tragedy belongs, had appropriated the Drama to themselves: of course only romancers, like the author of the Minos, or dialogue of law, have placed the latter far above Thespis; a position against which I have expressed my opinion on a former occasion (*Gr. Trag. Princip.* p. 254). All that I have said is equally applicable to Comedy: in our Inscriptions we find a lyrical Comedy before the dramatical at Orchomenus; and lower down, the dramatical Comedy is introduced, as from Attica, along with which an actor is mentioned; the former was the old peculiarity of the Dorians and Æolians, among whom lyric poetry for the most part obtained its completion. Even if we pass over Epicharmus, and the traces of a lyric Comedy in the religious usages of Epidaurus and Ægina (Herod. v. 83), the Dorians, and especially the Megarians, might still have had well-founded claims to the invention of Comedy, which, according to Aristotle, they made good. Besides, the view which we have taken of the lyrical Comedy sufficiently proves that the name is derived, not from κώμη, but from the merry κῶμος : such a one took place at the celebration of the victory, and consequently we find in our Inscriptions τὰ ἐπινίκια κωμαϜυδός, and τὰ ἐπινίκια κωμῳδιῶν ποιητής, who is certainly in this place a dramatic Comedian, Alexander of Athens. We cannot, however, call Pindar's songs of victory old Comedies: and the greater is the distinction between the lyric and the dramatic Comedy, the less entitled are we to draw, from this view, any conclusions in favour of the opinion that the Pindaric poems were represented with corresponding mimicry."

Böckh has reprinted these Inscriptions in his *Corpus Inscriptionum*, Tom. I. pp. 763—7, with some additional remarks in defence of his view from the objections of Lobeck and Hermann.

CHAPTER IV

THE TRAGIC DIALOGUE.—THESPIS.

*C'est surtout dans la Tragédie antique, que l'Epopée ressort de partout.
Elle monte sur la scène grecque sans rien perdre en quelque sorte de
ses proportions gigantesques et démesurées. Ce que chantaient les
rhapsodes, les acteurs le déclament. Voilà tout.*

VICTOR HUGO.

IN addition to the choruses, which, together with the
accompanying lyrical poetry, we have referred to the
Dorians, another species of entertainment had existed in
Greece from the very earliest times, which we may consider
as peculiar to the Ionian race; for it was in the Ionian
colonies that it first sprang up. This was the recitation of
poems by wandering minstrels, called rhapsodes (ῥαψῳδοί);
a name probably derived from the *œsacus*,[1] a staff (ῥάβδος)
or branch (ἔρνος)[2] of laurel or myrtle, which was the symbol
of their office. Seated in some conspicuous situation, and
holding this staff in the right hand, the rhapsodes chanted
in slow *recitativo*, and either with or without a musical
accompaniment,[3] larger or smaller portions of the national
epic poetry, which, as is well known, took its rise in the

---

[1] Hesych.: αἴσακος. ὁ τῆς δάφνης κλάδος ὃν κατέχοντες ὕμνουν τοὺς
θεούς. Plutarch, *Sympos.* p. 615: Ἦιδον ᾠδὴν τοῦ Θεοῦ—ἑκάστῳ
μυρσίνης διδομένης ἣν Ἄσακον, οἶμαι διὰ τὸ ᾄδειν τὸν δεξάμενον, ἐκάλουν.
Welcker has established most clearly (*Ep. Cycl.* p. 364) that ῥαψῳδὸς is
another form of ῥαπισῳδὸς = ῥαβδῳδός. Comp. χρυσόρ-ῥαπ-ις, β-ραβ-εύς,
and ῥαπ-ίζεσθαι, as applied to Homer by Diog. Laert. (IX. 1).

[2] Hence they were also called ἀρνῳδοί, i.e. ἐρνῳδοί.

[3] It is difficult to determine the degree of musical accompaniment
which the rhapsodes admitted; the rhapsode, as such, could hardly
have accompanied himself, as one of his hands would be occupied by
his rod. We think Wachsmuth is hardly justified in calling (*Hellen.
Alterth.* II. 2, 389) Stesandrus, who sang the Homeric battles to the
cithara at Delphi, a rhapsode (Athen. XIV. p. 638 A). Terpander was
the first who set the Homeric Poems to regular tunes (see Müller's
Dor. IV. 7, § 11). On the recitation of the rhapsodists in general, the
reader would do well to consult Welcker, *Ep. Cycl.* pp. 338 fol.; Grote,
Hist. Gr. Vol. II. pp. 184 foll.

Ionian states; and, in days when readers were few and books fewer, were well-nigh the sole depositaries of the literature of their country.

Their recitations, however, were not long confined to the Epos. All poetry was equally intended for the ear, and nothing was written but in metre: hence the Muses were appropriately called the children of Memory. Now, the Epos was soon succeeded, but not displaced, by the gnomic and didactic poetry of Hesiod, which, as has been justly observed, was an ornamental appendage of the older form of poetry.[1] These poems therefore were recited in the same way as the Epos,[2] and Hesiod himself was a rhapsode.[3] If the *Margites*, in its original form, belonged to the epic period of Greek poetry, it cannot be doubted that this humorous poem was also communicated to the public by means of recitation. The Epos of Homer, with not a little borrowed from the sententious poetry of Hesiod, formed the basis of the tragic dialogue; and in the same way the *Margites* contained within itself the germs of Comedy. The change of metre, which alone rendered the transition to the other forms more simple and easy, is universally attributed to the prolific genius of ARCHILOCHUS, one of the greatest names in the history of ancient literature. This truly original poet formed the double rhythm of the trochee from the equal rhythm of the dactyl, and used this metre partly in combination with dactyls, and partly in dipodiæ of its own, which were considered as ultimately equivalent to the dactylic number.[4] He soon proved that his new verses were lighter and more varied than the old heroic hexameters, and employed them for nearly equivalent purposes. At the same time, he formed the inverse double rhythm of

[1] Wachsmuth, *Hellen. Alterthumsk.* II. 2, p. 391.

[2] Plato, *Legg.* II. p. 658.

[3] Pausan. IX. 30, 3: καθῆται δὲ καὶ Ἡσίοδος κιθάραν ἐπὶ τοῖς γόνασιν ἔχων, οὐδέν τι οἰκεῖον Ἡσιόδῳ φόρημα· δῆλα γὰρ δὴ καὶ ἐξ αὐτῶν τῶν ἐπῶν ὅτι ἐπὶ ῥάβδου δάφνης ᾖδεν. Hesiod could not play on the lyre, X. 7, 2: λέγεται δὲ καὶ Ἡσίοδον ἀπελαθῆναι τοῦ ἀγωνίσματος ἅτε οὐ κιθαρίζειν ὁμοῦ τῇ ᾠδῇ δεδιδαγμένον.

[4] It is expressly testified by Aristot. *Rhet.* III. 1, § 9, that the tragic poets passed from the trochaic to the iambic verse, the former having been the original metre in dramatic poetry.

the iambic from the anapæst, or inverted dactyl, which was the natural measure of the march, and was probably used from very early days in the songs of the processional comus.[1] Here again he had an admirable vehicle for the violent satire in which he indulged, and which found its best justification in the scurrilities and outrageous personalities that were bandied to and fro at the feasts of Demeter in his native island of Paros,[2] and paved the way for the coarse banter of the old Comedy at Athens. The iambic verse, however, was very soon transferred from personal to general satire, from the invectives of the *Margites*, and from the fierce lampoons of Archilochus, to the more sweeping censures and more sententious generalities of gnomic and didactic poetry. Simonides of Amorgus, who flourished but a little later than Archilochus,[3] used the iambic metre in the discussion of subjects little differing from those in which Hesiod delighted. For example, his general animadversions on the female sex are almost anticipated by the humorous indignation of the *Theogony*.[4] But in other passages he approaches to the sententious gravity of the later tragedians. Thus, his reflections on the uncertainty of human life might be taken for a speech from a lost tragedy, if the dialect were not inconsistent with such a

[1] See Donaldson's *Greek Grammar*, 647, 651, 656.

[2] Müller, *Hist. Litt. Gr.* c. XI. § 5, p. 132.

[3] Archilochus is first heard of in the year 708 B.C. (Clinton, *F. H.* I. p. 175), and Simonides the elder is placed by Suidas 490 years after the Trojan era (B.C. 693. See *Rhein. Mus.* for 1835, p. 356). It is interesting to observe how the poetry of the colonists in Asia Minor seems to have crept across, step by step, to Attica and other parts of old Greece. Homer represents the greatest bard and rhapsode of the Homeric confraternity in Chios; Hesiod was an Æolian of Cyme; Arion a Lesbian; and the isles of Paros, Amorgos, and Ceos produced Archilochus and the two Simonides'.

[4] Cf. Hesiod, *Theog.* 591 sqq. Simonides of Amorgos, *Fragm.* 6. Bergk. The 5th fragment of Simonides, quoted by Clemens Alex. *Strom.* VI. p. 744:

Γυναικὸς οὐδὲν χρῆμ' ἀνὴρ ληΐζεται
Ἐσθλῆς ἄμεινον οὐδὲ ῥίγιον κακῆς·

is merely a repetition in Iambics of what Hesiod had previously written in Hexameters (*Op. et D.* 700):

Οὐ μὲν γάρ τι γυναικὸς ἀνὴρ ληΐζετ' ἄμεινον
Τῆς ἀγαθῆς, τῆς δ' αὖτε κακῆς οὐ ῥίγιον ἄλλο.

supposition.[1] And the same remark is still more applicable to some of the trochaics and iambics of Solon, who lived to witness the first beginnings of Tragedy. Now all this iambic and trochaic poetry was written for rhapsodical recitation : for though we must allow (as even the advocates of the Wolfian hypothesis are willing to admit[2]) that the poems of Archilochus were committed to writing, it cannot be denied that the means of multiplying manuscripts in his time must have been exceedingly scanty ; and that, if his opportunities of becoming known had been limited to the number of his readers, he could hardly have acquired his great reputation as a poet. We must, therefore, conclude that his poems, and those of Simonides, were promulgated by recitation ; and as such of them as were written in iambics would not be sufficiently diversified in tone and rhythm to form a musical entertainment, we may presume that the recitation of their pieces, even if they were monologues, must have been a near approach to theatric declamation.

Fortunately we are not without some evidence for this view of the case. We learn from Clearchus[3] that " Simonides, the Zacynthian, recited (ἐρραψῴδει) some of the poems of Archilochus, sitting on an arm-chair in the theatres ;" and this is stated still more distinctly in a quotation from Lysanias which immediately follows : he tells us that " Mnasion, the rhapsode, in the public exhibitions acted some of the iambics of Simonides" (ἐν ταῖς δείξεσι τῶν Σιμωνίδου τινὰς ἰάμβων ὑποκρίνεσθαι[4]). Solon, too, who lived many years after these two poets, and was also a gnomic poet and a writer of iambics, on one occasion committed to memory some

---

[1] Simonid. *Fr.* 1.   [2] Wolf, *Proleg.* § 17.
[3] Athen. xiv. p. 620 c.
[4] This word is very often used of the rhapsode. For example, we have in Arist. *Rhet.* III. 1, § 3 : καὶ γὰρ εἰς τὴν τραγικὴν καὶ ῥαψῳδίαν ὀψὲ παρῆλθεν (ἡ ὑπόκρισις)· ὑπεκρίνοντο γὰρ αὐτοὶ τὰς τραγῳδίας οἱ ποιηταὶ τὸ πρῶτον. See Wolf, *Prolegom.* p. cxvi.; Heyne, *Excursus*, III. 2. It is also applied to the recitation of the Ionic prose of Herod tus, which may be considered as a still more modern form of the Epos. Athen. xiv. p. 629 D : Ἰάσων δ' ἐν τρίτῳ περὶ τῶν Ἀλεξάνδρου ἱερῶν ἐν Ἀλεξανδρείᾳ φησὶ ἐν τῷ μεγάλῳ θεάτρῳ ὑποκρίνασθαι Ἡγησίαν τὸν κωμῳδὸν τὰ Ἡροδότου.

of his own elegiacs, and recited them from the herald's bema.[1] It is exceedingly probable, though we have no evidence of the fact, that the gnomes of Theognis were also recited.

The rhapsodes having many opportunities of practising their art, and being on many occasions welcome and expected guests, their calling became a trade, and probably, like that of the Persian story-tellers, a very profitable one. Consequently their numbers increased, till on great occasions many of them were sure to be present, and different parts were assigned to them, which they recited alternately and with great emulation : by this means the audience were sometimes gratified by the recitation of a whole poem at a single feast.[2] In the case of an epic poem, like the Iliad, this was at once a near approach to the theatrical dialogue ; for if one rhapsode recited the speech of Achilles in the first book of that poem, and another that of Agamemnon, we may be sure they did their parts with all the action of stage-players.

With regard to the old iambic poems we may remark, that they are often addressed in the second person singular. We venture from this to conjecture, and it is only a conjecture, that these fragments were taken from speeches forming parts of moral dialogues, like the mimes of Sophron, from which Plato borrowed the form of his dialogues ;[3] for, except on the supposition that they were recited, we have no other way of accounting for the fact.

At all events, it is quite certain that these old iambic poems were the models which the Athenian tragedians proposed to themselves for their dialogues.[4] They were

---

[1] Plutarch, *Solon*, VIII. 82.

[2] Plato, *Hipparch.* p. 228: Ἱππάρχῳ, ὃς....τὰ Ὁμήρου ἔπη...ἠνάγκασ: τοὺς ῥαψῳδοὺς παναθηναίοις ἐξ ὑπολήψεως ἐφεξῆς αὐτὰ διϊέναι ὥσπερ νῦν ἔτι οὗτοι ποιοῦσιν. Compare Diog. Laert. I. 57, and Suidas v. ὑποβολή.

[3] Plato is said to have had Sophron under his pillow when he died. "Sophron—mimorum quidem scriptor, sed quem Plato adeo probavit ut suppositos capiti libros ejus cum moreretur habuisse tradatur." Quintil. I. 10, 17. See Spalding's note.

[4] This is expressly stated by Plutarch, *de Musicâ*, Tom. x. p. 680: ἔτι δὲ τῶν ἰαμβείων τὸ τὰ μὲν λέγεσθαι παρὰ τὴν κροῦσιν, τὰ δὲ ᾄδεσθαι Ἀρχίλυχόν φασι καταδεῖξαι, εἶθ' οὕτω χρήσασθαι τοὺς τραγικούς. Do not the first words apply to a rhythmical recitation by the exarchus, followed by a musical performance by the chorus?

written in the same metre, the same moral tone pervaded both, and, in many instances, the dramatists have borrowed not only the ideas but the very words of their predecessors.[1] The rhapsode was not only the forerunner of the actor, but he was himself an actor (ὑποκριτής[2]). If, therefore, the difference between the lyric Tragedy of the Dorians and the regular Tragedy of the Athenians consisted in this, that the one had actors (ὑποκριταί) and the other had none, we must look for the origin of the complete and perfect Attic drama in the union of the rhapsodes with the Bacchic chorus.

There can be little doubt that the worship of Bacchus was introduced into Attica at a very early period;[3] indeed it

---

[1] Whole pages might be filled with the plagiarisms of the Attic tragedians from even the small remains of the gnomic poets. The following are a few of the most striking.

Archiloch. p. 30, l. 1, Liebel:

χρημάτων ἄελπτον οὐδέν ἐστιν, οὐδ' ἀπώμοτον·

is repeated by Soph. Antig. 386:

ἄναξ, βροτοῖσιν οὐδέν ἐστ' ἀπώμοτον.

Æsch. Eumen. 603:

τὰ πλεῖστ' ἀμεινον' εὐφροσιν δεδεγμένη·

from Theognis, v. 762 (p. 52, Welcker):

ὧδ' εἶναι καὶ ἀμεινον' εὔφρονα θυμὸν ἔχοντας.

Æsch. Agam. 36:

τὰ δ' ἄλλα σιγῶ· βοῦς ἐπὶ γλώττης μέγας·

from Theognis, 651, Welcker:

βοῦς μοι ἐπὶ γλώσσης κρατερῷ ποδὶ λὰξ ἐπιβαίνων
ἴσχει κωτίλλειν καίπερ ἐπιστάμενον.

Soph. Antig. 666:

Τοῦδε [ἄρχοντος] χρὴ κλύειν
Καὶ σμικρὰ καὶ δίκαια καὶ τἀναντία·

(i. e. μεγάλα καὶ ἄδικα), from Solon's well-known line:

Ἀρχῶν ἄκουε καὶ δίκαια κἄδικα, as it ought to be read.

[2] When Aristotle says (Rhet. III. 1): εἰς τὴν τραγικὴν καὶ ῥαψῳδίαν ὀψὲ παρῆλθεν (ἡ ὑπόκρισις), ὑπεκρίνοντο γὰρ αὐτοὶ τὰς τραγῳδίας οἱ ποιηταὶ τὸ πρῶτον, he evidently means by the word ὑπόκρισις the assumption of the poet's person by another; which we conceive to have been the original, as it is the derived, meaning of the word. Compare ὑπόρχημα, &c. We think it more than probable that the names of the actors, πρωταγωνίστης, &c., were derived from the names of the rhapsodes who recited in succession (ἐξ ὑπολήψεως) in the ῥαψῳδῶν ἀγῶνες. See Pseudoplat. Hipparch. p. 228, and the other passages quoted by Welcker, Ep. Cycl. pp. 371 fol.

[3] On the early worship of Bacchus in Attica see Welcker's Nachtrag, pp. 194 fol., and Phil. Mus. II. pp. 299—307.

was probably the religion of the oldest inhabitants, who, on
the invasion of the country by the Ionians, were reduced,
like the native Laconians, to the inferior situation of
περίοικοι, and cultivated the soil for their conquerors. Like
all other Pelasgians, they were naturally inclined to a
country life, and this perhaps may account for the elementary nature of their religion, which with its votaries
was thrown aside and despised by the ruling caste. In the
quadripartite division of the people of Attica the old inhabitants formed the tribe of the Ægicores or goatherds, who
worshipped Dionysus with the sacrifice of goats. But
though they were at first kept in a state of inferiority and
subjection, they eventually rose to an equality with the
inhabitants of the country. There are very many Attic
legends which point to the original contempt for the
goatherd's religion, and its subsequent adoption by the
other tribes. This is indicated by the freedom of slaves at
the Dionysian festivals, by the reference of the origin of the
religion to the town Eleutheræ, by the marriage of the King
Archon's wife to Bacchus ;[1] and we may perhaps discover
traces of a difference of castes in the story of Orestes at the
Anthesteria. It was natural, therefore, that the Ægicores,
when they had obtained their freedom from political disabilities, should ascribe their deliverance to their tutelary
god, whom they therefore called Ἐλεύθερος : and in later
times, when all the inhabitants of Attica were on a footing
of equality, the god Bacchus was still looked upon as the
favourer of the commonalty, and as the patron of democracy.

As we have before remarked, it was not till the Athenians
had recognised the supremacy of the Delphian oracle that
the Dorian choral worship was introduced into Attica, and
it was then applied to the old Dionysian religion of the
country with the sanction of the Pythian priestess, as

---

[1] ——καὶ αὕτη ἡ γυνὴ ὑμῖν ἔθυε τὰ ἄρρητα ἱερὰ ὑπὲρ τῆς πόλεως, καὶ
εἶδεν ἃ οὐ προσῆκεν αὐτὴν ὁρᾶν ξένην οὖσαν, καὶ τοιαύτη οὖσα εἰσῆλθεν οἵ
οὐδεὶς ἄλλος Ἀθηναίων τοσούτων ὄντων εἰσέρχεται ἀλλ' ἡ τοῦ βασιλέως
γυνή, ἐξώρκωσέ τε τὰς γεραιρὰς τὰς ὑπηρετούσας τοῖς ἱεροῖς, ἐξεδόθη δὲ
τῷ Διονύσῳ γυνή, ἔπραξε δὲ ὑπὲρ τῆς πόλεως τὰ πάτρια τὰ πρὸς τοὺς
θεούς, πολλὰ καὶ ἅγια καὶ ἀπόρρητα. Pseud. Demosth. in Near. pp.
1369—70. Above, p. 20.

appears from the oracle which we have quoted above, and
from the legend in Pausanias, that the Delphian oracle
assisted Pegasus in transferring the worship of Bacchus
from Eleutheræ to Athens.[1] Consequently the cyclic chorus
would not be long in finding its way into a country so
predisposed for its reception as Attica certainly was; and
there is every reason to believe that the Dorian lyric
drama, perhaps with certain modifications, accompanied its
parent.[2]

The recitations by rhapsodes were a peculiarly Ionian
entertainment, and therefore, no doubt, were common in
Attica from the very earliest times. At Brauron, in particular, we are told that the Iliad was chanted by rhapsodes.[3] Now the Brauronia was a festival of Bacchus, and a
particularly boisterous one, if we may believe Aristophanes.[4]
To this festival we refer the passage of Clearchus, quoted
by Athenæus,[5] in which it is stated that the rhapsodes came
forward in succession, and recited in honour of Bacchus.
By a combination of these particulars we can at once
establish a connection between the worship of Bacchus and
the rhapsodic recitations. Before, however, we consider the
important inferences which may be derived from these facts,
we must enter a little into the state of affairs in Attica at
the time when the Thespian Tragedy arose.

The early political dissensions at Athens were, like those
between the *populus* and the *plebs* in the olden times of Roman

---

[1] I. 2, 5 : συνελάβετο δὲ οἱ καὶ τὸ ἐν Δελφοῖς μαντεῖον.

[2] It seems that the oscilla on the trees referred to the hanging of
Erigone, which probably formed the subject of a standing drama with
mimic dances like the Sicyonian Tragedies, with which the dramas
of Epigenes were connected. Welck. *Nachtrag*, p. 224.

[3] Hesych.· Βραυρωνίοις. τὴν Ἰλιάδα ᾖδον ῥαψῳδοὶ ἐν Βραυρῶνι τῆς
Ἀττικῆς. καὶ Βραυρωνία ἑορτὴ Ἀρτέμιδι Βραυρωνίᾳ ἄγεται καὶ θύεται
αἴξ. Does this mention of the sacrifice of a goat point to the rites of
the Ægicores?

[4] *Pax*, 874, and Schol.

[5] At the beginning of the Seventh Book, p. 275 B : Φαγήσια, οἱ δὲ
Φαγησιοπόσια προσαγορεύουσι τὴν ἑορτήν. ἐξέλιπε δὲ αὕτη, καθάπερ ἡ
τῶν ῥαψῳδῶν, ἣν ἦγον κατὰ τὴν τῶν Διονυσίων· ἐν ᾗ παριόντες ἕκαστοι
τῷ θεῷ οἷον τιμὴν ἀπετέλουν τὴν ῥαψῳδίαν. Welcker reads ἑκάστῳ τῶν
θεῶν, and takes quite a different view of this passage, except so far as
he agrees with us in referring it to the Brauronia (*Ep. Cycl.* p. 391).

history, the consequences of an attempt on the part of the inferior orders in an aristocracy of conquest[1] to shake off their civil disabilities, and to put themselves upon an equality with their more favoured fellow-citizens. Solon had in part effected this by taking from the Eupatrids some of their exclusive privileges, and establishing a democracy in the place of the aristocracy. At this time Athens was divided into three parties: the Πεδιαῖοι, or the landed aristocracy of the interior ; the Πάραλοι, the people dwelling on the coast on both sides of Cape Sunium; and the Διάκριοι or Ὑπεράκριοι, the highlanders who inhabited the north-eastern district of Attica.[2] The first party were for an oligarchy, the last for a democracy, and the second for a mixture of the two forms of government.[3] The head of the democratical faction was Pisistratus, the son of Hippocrates, of the family of the Codrids, and related to Solon : he was born at Philaïdæ, near Brauron, and therefore was by birth a Diacrian. Having obtained by an artifice the sovran power at Athens, he was expelled by a coalition of the other two factions. After a short time, however, Megacles, the leader of the Paralians, being harassed (περιελαυνόμενος[4]) by the aristocratic faction, recalled Pisistratus and gave him his daughter in marriage. The manner of his return is of the greatest importance in reference to our present object. "There was a woman," says Herodotus, "of the Pæanian deme, whose name was Phya : she was nearly four cubits in stature, and was in other respects comely to look upon. Having equipped this woman in a complete suit of armour, they placed her in a chariot, and having taught her beforehand how to act her part in the most dignified manner possible (καὶ προδέξαντες σχῆμα οἷόν τι ἔμελλε εὐπρεπέστατον

---

[1] See Arnold's *Thucydides*, Vol. I. p. 620. We think the fact that one of the classes in Attica was called the "Hopletes" points to a conquest of Attica in remote times by the Ionians.

[2] Herod. I. 59: στασιαζόντων τῶν παράλων καὶ τῶν ἐκ τοῦ πεδίου Ἀθηναίων. . . τῶν ὑπερακρίων προστάς.

[3] Plutarch, *Sol.* XIII. p. 85 : ἦν γὰρ τὸ μὲν τῶν Διακρίων γένος δημοκρατικώτερον, ὀλιγαρχικώτατον δὲ τὸ τῶν Πεδιέων, τρίτοι δὲ οἱ Πάραλοι μέσον τινὰ καὶ μεμιγμένον αἱρούμενοι πολιτείας τρόπον. Comp. Arnold's note on *Thucyd.* II. 59.

[4] Herod. I. 60.

φαίνεσθαι ἔχουσα[1]), they drove to the city." He adds, that they sent heralds before her, who, when they got to Athens, told the people to receive with good-will Pisistratus, whom Athene herself honoured above all men, and was bringing back from exile to her own Acropolis. Now we must recollect who were the parties to this proceeding. In the first place we have Megacles, an Alcmæonid, and therefore connected with the worship of Bacchus;[2] moreover, he was the father of the Alcmæon, whose son Megacles married Agariste, the daughter of Cleisthenes of Sicyon, and had by her Cleisthenes, the Athenian demagogue, who is said to have imitated his maternal grandfather in some of the reforms which he introduced into the Athenian constitution.[3] One of the points, which Herodotus mentions in immediate connection with Cleisthenes' imitation of his grandfather, is the abolition of the *Homeric* rhapsodes at Sicyon, and his restitution of the Tragic Choruses to Bacchus. May we not also conclude that Megacles the elder was not indifferent to the policy of a ruler who was so nearly connected with him by marriage? The other party was Pisistratus, who was, as we have said, born near Brauron, where rhapsodic recitations were connected with the worship of Bacchus; the stronghold of this party was the Tetrapolis, which contained the town of Œnoë,[4] to which, and not to the Bœotian town of the same name, we refer the traditions with regard to the introduction of the worship of Bacchus into Attica;[5] his party doubtless included the Ægicores (who have indeed been considered as

---

[1] See the passages quoted by Ruhnken on *Timæus*, sub v. σχηματι-ζόμενος (pp. 245—6), to which add Plat. *Resp.* p. 577 A: ἐκπλήττεται ὑπὸ τῆς τῶν τυραννικῶν προστάσεως ἣν πρὸς τοὺς ἔξω σχηματίζονται . . . ἐν οἷς μάλιστα γυμνὸς ἂν ὀφθείη τῆς τραγικῆς σκευῆς.

[2] See Welcker's *Nachtrag*, p. 250.

[3] Herod. v. 67: ταῦτα δέ, δοκέειν ἐμοί, ἐμιμέετο ὁ Κλ. οὗτος τὸν ἑωυτοῦ μητροπάτορα, Κλ. τὸν Σικυῶνος τύραννον. Κλεισθένης γὰρ . . ῥαψῳδοὺς ἔπαυσε ἐν Σικυῶνι ἀγωνίζεσθαι τῶν Ὁμηρείωνθεπέων εἵνεκα. Mr. Grote has shown good reasons for believing that the poems recited at Sicyon as Homeric productions were the Thebais and the Epigoni. *Hist. Gr.* Vol. II. p. 173, note.

[4] See the passages quoted by Elmsley on the *Heracl.* 81.

[5] The Deme of Semachus was also in that part of Attica.

identical with the Diacrians[1]), and these we have seen were
the original possessors of the worship of Bacchus; finally,
there was a masque of Bacchus at Athens, which was said to
be a portrait of Pisistratus;[2] so that upon the whole there
can be little doubt of the interest which he took in the
establishment of the rights of the Ægicores as a part of the
state religion. With regard to the actress, Phya, we need
only remark that she was a garland-seller,[3] and therefore,
as this trade was a very public one, could not easily have
passed herself off upon the Athenians for a goddess. The
first inference which we shall draw from a combination of
these particulars is, that the ceremony attending the return
of Pisistratus was to all intents and purposes a dramatic
representation[4] of the same kind with that part of the
Eumenides of Æschylus, in which the same goddess Athena
is introduced for the purpose of recommending to the
Athenians the maintenance of the Areopagus.[5]

Before we make any further use of the facts which we
have alluded to, it will be as well to give some account of
the celebrated contemporary of Pisistratus to whom the
invention of Greek Tragedy has been generally ascribed.
THESPIS was born at Icarius,[6] a Diacrian deme,[7] at the
beginning of the sixth century B.C.[8] His birth-place
derived its name, according to the tradition, from the father
of Erigone;[9] it had always been a seat of the religion of

---

[1] See Wachsmuth, I. I, p. 229; Arnold's *Thucydides*, pp. 659—60.

[2] ὅπου καὶ τὸ Ἀθήνῃσι τοῦ Διονύσου πρόσωπον ἐκείνου τινές φασιν εἰκόνα.
Athenæus, XII. p. 533 C.

[3] στεφανόπωλις δὲ ἦν.   Athen. XIII. p. 609 C.

[4] Solon (according to Plutarch, c. XXX.) applied the term ὑποκρίνεσθαι
to another of the artifices of Pisistratus. Diogen. Laërt. Solon, I. says:
Θέσπιν ἐκώλυσεν (ὁ Σόλων) τραγῳδίας ἄγειν τε καὶ διδάσκειν ὡς ἀνωφελῆ
τὴν ψευδολογίαν.   ὅτ᾽ οὖν Πεισίστρατος ἑαυτὸν κατέτρωσεν, ἐκεῖθεν μὲν
ἔφη ταῦτα φῦναι.

[5] This seems to be nearly the view taken of this pageant by Dr.
Thirlwall, *Hist. of Greece*, Vol. II. p. 60.   Mr. Keightley is inclined to
conjecture from the meaning of the woman's name (Phya—*size*) that the
whole is a myth.

[6] Suidas, Θέσπις, Ἰκαρίου πόλεως Ἀττικῆς.

[7] Leake *on the Demi of Attica*, p. 194.

[8] Bentley fixes the time of Thespis' first exhibition at 536 B.C.

[9] Steph. Byz. Ἰκαρία; Hygin. *Fab.* 130; Ov. *Met.* VI. 125.

Bacchus, and the origin of the Athenian Tragedy and
Comedy has been confidently referred to the drunken
festivals of the place :[1] indeed it is not improbable that the
name itself may point to the old mimetic exhibitions which
were common there. [2] Thespis is stated to have introduced
an actor for the sake of resting the Dionysian chorus. [3]
This actor was generally, perhaps always, himself. [4] He
invented a disguise for the face by means of a pigment,
prepared from the herb purslain, and afterwards constructed
a linen mask, in order, probably, that he might be able to
sustain more than one character. [5] He is also said to have
introduced some important alterations into the dances of
the chorus, and his figures were known in the days of
Aristophanes. [6] These are almost all the facts which we
know respecting this celebrated man. It remains for us to
examine them. It appears, then, that he was a contemporary of Pisistratus and Solon. He was a Diacrian, and
consequently a partizan of the former ; we are told too that
the latter was violently opposed to him. [7] He was an
Icarian, and therefore by his birth a worshipper of Bacchus.
He was an ὑποκριτής ; and from the subjects of his recitations
it would appear that he was also a rhapsode. [8] Here we
have again the union of Dionysian rites with rhapsodical
recitations which we have discovered in the Brauronian
festival. But he went a step farther: his rhapsode, or

[1] Athen. II. p. 40 : ἀπὸ μέθης καὶ ἡ τῆς κωμῳδίας καὶ τῆς τραγῳδίας
εὕρεσις ἐν 'Ικαρίῳ τῆς 'Αττικῆς εὑρέθη.

[2] See Welcker, *Nachtrag*, p. 222.

[3] "Ὕστερον δὲ Θέσπις ἕνα ὑποκριτὴν ἐξεῦρεν ὑπὲρ τοῦ διαναπαύεσθαι τὸν
χορόν. Diog. Laërt. *Plat.* LXVI.

[4] Plutarch, *Sol.* XXIX : ὁ Σόλων ἐθεάσατο τὸν Θέσπιν αὐτὸν ὑποκρινόμενον ὥσπερ ἔθος ἦν τοῖς παλαιοῖς. See also Arist. *Rhet.* III. 1, and
Liv. VII. 2.

[5] Welcker, *Nachtrag*, p. 271 ; Thirlwall's *History of Greece*, Vol. II.
p. 126.

[6] Aristoph. *Vesp.* 1479.

[7] Plutarch, *Sol.* XXIX. XXX. and p. 64, note 4.

[8] The names of some of his plays have come down to us : they are
the Πενθεύς, 'Αθλα Πελίου, ἢ Φορβάς, 'Ιερεῖς, 'Ηΐθεοι (Jul. Poll. VII. 45 ;
Suid. s. v. Θέσπις). Gruppe must have founded his supposition that
Ulysses was the subject of a play of Thespis (*Ariadne*, p. 129) on a
misunderstanding of Plut. *Sol.* XXX. in which he was preceded by
Schneider (*De Originibus Trag. Gr.* p. 56).

F

actor, whether himself or another person, did not confine
his speech to mere narration; he addressed it to the chorus,
which carried on with him, by means of its coryphæi, a sort
of dialogue. The chorus stood upon the steps of the
thymele, or altar of Bacchus; and in order that he might
address them from an equal elevation, he was placed upon a
table (ἐλεός),[1] which was the predecessor of the stage,
between which and the thymele in later times there was
always an intervening space. The waggon of Thespis, of
which Horace writes, must have arisen from some confusion
between this standing-place for the actor and the waggon of
Susarion.[2] Themistius tells us that Thespis invented a
prologue and a *rhesis*.[3] The former must have been the
procemium which he spoke as exarchus of the improved
Dithyramb; the latter the dialogue between himself and
the chorus, by means of which he developed a myth relating
to Bacchus or some other deity or hero.[4] Lastly, there
is every reason to believe that Thespis did not confine his
representation to his native deme, but exhibited at Athens.[5]

From a comparison of these particulars respecting Thespis

[1] See Welcker, *Nachtrag*, p. 248. We think that the joke of Dicæopolis (Arist. *Acharn.* 355 sqq.) is an allusion to this practice. Solon
mounted the herald's bema when he recited his verses to the people
(V. Plut. c. 8).

[2] See Welcker, *Nachtrag*, p. 247. Gruppe says quaintly, but, we
think, justly (*Ariadne*, p. 122), "It is clear enough that the waggon of
Thespis cannot well consist with the festal choir of the Dionysia; and,
in fact, this old coach, which has been fetched from Horace only, must
be shoved back again into the lumber-room." The words of Horace
are (*A. P.* 275—277):

Ignotum tragicæ genus invenisse Camœnæ
Dicitur et plaustris vexisse poëmata Thespis,
Quæ canerent agerentque peruncti fæcibus ora.

[3] p. 316, Hard. : Θέσπις δὲ πρόλογόν τε καὶ ῥῆσιν ἐξεῦρεν.

[4] This is the sense which the word ῥῆσις bears in Hom. *Odyss.* XXI.
290, 291:

—— αὐτὰρ ἀκούεις
ἡμετέρων μύθων καὶ ῥήσιος.

Æschyl. *Suppl.* 610: τοιάνδ' ἔπειθε ῥῆσιν ἀμφ' ἡμῶν λέγων.
See Welcker, *Nachtr.* p. 269. The invention of the ῥῆσις seems also to
be referred to by Aristotle, when he says (*Poet.* c. 4): λέξεως δὲ
γενομένης.

[5] *Nachtrag*, p. 254.

with the facts which we have stated in connection with the first return of Pisistratus to Athens, we shall now be able to deduce some further inferences. It appears, then, that a near approximation to the perfect form of the Greek Drama took place in the time of Pisistratus: all those who were concerned in bringing it about were Diacrians, or connected with the worship of Bacchus; the innovations were either the results or the concomitants of an assumption of political power by a caste of the inhabitants of Attica, whose tutelary god was Bacchus, and were in substance nothing but a union of the old choral worship of Bacchus, with an offshoot of the rhapsodical recitations of the Ionic epopœists.[1]

We can understand without any difficulty why Pisistratus should encourage the religion of his own people, the Diacrians or Ægicores; and why Solon, who thought he had given the lower orders power enough,[2] should oppose the adoption of their worship as a part of the religion of the state; for in those days the religion and privileges of a caste rose and fell together. It might, however, be asked why Pisistratus and his party, who evidently in their encroachments on the power of the aristocracy adopted in most cases the policy of the Sicyonian Cleisthenes, should in this particular have

---

[1] The conclusions of Gruppe are so nearly, in effect, the same as ours, and so well expressed, that we think it right to lay them before our readers (*Ariadne*, p. 127). "Thespis developed from these detached speeches of the Choreutæ, especially when they were longer than usual, a recitation by an actor in the form of a narrative; a recitation, and not a song. Thespis, however, was an inhabitant of Attica, an Athenian, and as such stood in the middle, between the proper Ionians and the Dorians. The formation of the epos was the peculiar property of the former, of lyric poetry that of the latter. So long as tragedy or the tragic chorus existed in the Peloponnese, they were of a lyrical nature. In this form, with the Doric dialect and a lyrical accompaniment, they were transplanted into Attica; and here it was that Thespis first joined to them the Ionic element of narration, which, if not quite Ionic, had and maintained a relationship with the Ionic, even in the language." We may here remark, that all the old iambic poets wrote strictly in the Ionic dialect. Welcker has clearly shown this by examples in the case of Simonides of Amorgus. (See *Rheinisch. Museum* for 1835, p. 369.)

[2] Solon, ed. Bach, p. 94: Δήμῳ μὲν γὰρ ἔδωκα τόσον κράτος ὅσον ἐπαρκεῖ. Is not Niebuhr's translation of this line wrong? (*Hist. Rom.* Vol. II. note 700.) Comp. Æsch. *Agamemn.* 370:

ἔστω ἀπήμαντον ὥστε κἀπαρκεῖν εὖ πραπίδων λαχόντα.

deviated from it so far as to encourage the rhapsodes, whom
Cleisthenes, on the contrary, sedulously put down on
account of the great predilection of the aristocracy for
the Epos.[1] This deserves and requires some additional
explanation. Pisistratus was not only a Diacrian or goat-
worshipper : he was also a Codrid, and therefore a Neleid ;
nay, he bore the name of one of the sons of his mythical
ancestor, Nestor : he might, therefore, be excused for feeling
some sort of aristocratical respect for the poems which described the wisdom and valour of his progenitors. Besides,
he was born in the deme Philaïdæ, which derived its name
from Philæus, one of the sons of Ajax, and he reckoned
Ajax also among his ancestors : this may have induced him
to desire a public commemoration of the glories of the
Æantidæ, just as the Athenians of the next century looked
with delight and interest at the Play of Sophocles :[2] and we
have little doubt but he heard in his youth parts of the
Iliad recited at the neighbouring deme of Brauron.[3] If
we add to this, that by introducing into a few passages of
the Homeric poems some striking encomiums on his countrymen, he was able to add considerably to his popularity, and
that it is always the policy of a tyrant to encourage literature,[4] we shall fully understand why he gave himself so
much trouble about these poems in the days of his power.[5]
Solon also greatly encouraged the rhapsodes, and shares

---

[1] Wachsmuth, *Hell. Alt.* II. 2, 389.

[2] See *Rheinisch. Mus.* for 1829, p. 62.

[3] See Nitzsch, *Indag. per Od. Interpol. præpar.* p. 37; *Hist. Hom.*
p. 165; Welcker, *Ep. Cycl.* p. 393.

[4] "Debbe un principe," says Machiavelli (*il Principe*, cap. XXI. fin.),
"ne' tempi convenienti dell' anno tenero occupati i popoli con feste e
spettacoli; e perchè ogni città è divisa o in arti o in tribù, debbe tener
conto di quelle università."

[5] " Quis doctior iisdem illis temporibus, aut cujus eloquentia litteris
instructior fuisse traditur, quam Pisistrati ? qui primus Homeri libros,
confusos antea, sic disposuisse dicitur ut nunc habemus." Cicero, *de
Orat.* III. 34.

Πεισίστρατος ἔπη τὰ 'Ομήρου διεσπασμένα τε καὶ ἀλλαχοῦ μνημονευ-
όμενα ἠθροίζετο. Pausan. VII. 26, p. 594.

Ὕστερον Πεισίστρατος συναγαγὼν ἀπέφηνε τὴν 'Ιλιάδα καὶ τὴν 'Οδύσ-
σειαν. Ælian, *V. H.* XIII. 14.

See also Joseph. c. *Apion.* I, 2 ; Liban. *Panegyr. in Julian.* T. I.
p. 170, Reiske; Suidas, v. "Ομηρος; and Eustath. p. 5.

with Pisistratus the honour of arranging the rhapsodies according to their natural and poetical sequence :[1] we must not forget, too, that Solon was one of those writers of gnomic poetry, whom we have considered as the successors of the Epopœists, and from whose writings the Attic tragedians modelled their dialogue. Now we know that Pisistratus endeavoured, as far as was consistent with his own designs, to adopt the constitution of Solon, and always treated his venerable kinsman with deference and respect. May not a wish to reconcile his own plans with the tastes and feelings of the superseded legislator have operated with him as an additional reason for attempting to unite the old epic element with the rites of the Dionysian religion, which his political connections compelled him to transfer from the country to the city? may not such a combination have been suggested by his early recollections of the Brauronia? did the genius of the Icarian plan the innovation, or was he merely instrumental towards carrying into effect? was the name Thespis originally borne by this agent of Pisistratus, or was it rather a surname, derived from the common epithet of the Homeric minstrel,[2] and implying nothing more in its connection with the history of the drama, than that it arose from a combination such as we have described?

But whatever reason we may assign for the union of the rhapsody with the Bacchic chorus, it seems pretty clear that this union was actually effected in the time of Pisistratus. And herein consists the claim of Thespis to be considered

---

[1] Comp. Diog. *Sol.* I. 57, with Ps. Plat. *Hipparch.* p. 228 B.

[2] Hom. *Od.* I. 328 :

　　τοῦ δ' ὑπερωΐόθεν φρεσὶ σύνθετο θέσπιν ἀοιδὴν
　　κούρη 'Ικαρίοιο.

—— VIII. 498 :

　　ὡς ἄρα τοι πρόφρων θεὸς ὥπασε θέσπιν ἀοιδήν.

—— XVII. 385 :

　　ἢ καὶ θέσπιν ἀοιδόν, ὅ κεν τέρπῃσιν ἀείδων.

See Buttmann's *Lexilogus*, I. p. 166. It was very common to invent names for persons from their actions, or for persons to change their own names according to their profession. Thus Helen is called the daughter of Nemesis, Arion the son of Cycleus, and Tisias changed his name into Stesichorus, by which alone he is known at the present day (above, p. 40, and see Clinton's *F. H.* Vol. I. p. 5); so that Thespis may even be an assumed name.

as the inventor of Attic Tragedy. Arion's satyrical chorus,
and even the lyric drama of Epigenes, may have been imitated at Athens soon after their introduction in the Pelo-
ponnesus. The cyclic chorus was performed as a separate
affair till the latest days of Athenian democracy,[1] and the
Pyrrhic dance, which was adopted by the satyrs, was also a
distinct exhibition.[2]   Nay, the Homeric rhapsody was
recited by itself on the proper occasion; that is to say,
generally at the great Panathenæa :[3] nor would the Homeric
hexameter have been so well suited to a dramatic dialogue
as the trochaic tetrameter and senarius, which the vigorous
and sententious poetry of Archilochus and the elder Simonides had made well known and popular in Attica and in the
Ægean.   Whether anticipated or not by Susarion, in the
employment of the iambic metre in dramatic speeches,
Thespis may claim the merit of having been the first to
combine with the Bacchic chorus, which he received from
Arion, a truly epic element, and he was clearly the first who
made the rhapsode appear as an actor sustaining different
characters, and addressing the audience from a fixed and
elevated stage.   At first he may have been contented, like
the exarchi of the improved Dithyramb, with personating
Bacchus, and surrounding himself with a chorus of Satyrs;
but there is every reason to believe that he soon extended
his sphere of myths, and that his plots were as various as
those of his successors.

Bentley was interested in the establishment of his propo-
sition that Thespis did not write his plays, and naturally
manifested the eagerness of a pleader rather than the im-
partiality of a judge.[4]   There is no antecedent improbability
in the statement of Donatus that Thespis wrote tragedies.
Solon, and, much earlier, Archilochus and Simonides committed their poems to writing; and in the days of Pisistratus
it is not likely that a favourite rhapsode would leave his
compositions unpublished.   The destruction of Athens, in

---

[1] Lys. ἀποδ. δωροδ. p. 698.
[2] Lys. u. s.; Schol. Aristoph. Nub. 988.
[3] Lycurg. c. Leocr. p. 161 ; Plat. Hipparch. p. 228 B; Ælian, V. H
VIII. 2.
[4] Dissertation on Phalaris, pp 237 sqq.

B.C. 480, made the older specimens of Attic literature very scarce, but there must have been some remains of his writings in the time of Sophocles, otherwise that poet would hardly have published strictures on him and Chœrilus,[1] which, as we may infer from his criticisms on Æschylus,[2] in all probability referred to the harshness of their style. Aristophanes speaks of him precisely in the same terms as he does of Phrynichus, predicating an antiquated stiffness of both these old Tragedians.[3] We may grant that the lines attributed to Thespis by Clemens Alexandrinus[4] contain internal evidence of their spuriousness, but there is no presumption against the authenticity of the quotations in Plutarch[5] and Julius Pollux,[6] beyond the ill-founded hypothesis, that Thespis composed only ludicrous dramas. This hypothesis, as we have seen above, rests on the old confusion between Thespis and Susarion. The forgeries of Heraclides Ponticus are themselves no slight proof of the originally serious character of the Thespian drama; for if his contemporaries had really believed that Thespis wrote nothing but ludicrous dramas, a scholar of Aristotle would hardly have attempted to impose upon the public with a set of plays altogether different in style and title from those of the author on whom he wished to pass them off. The fact is, that the choral plays from which the Thespian drama was formed were satyrical, for the Dithyramb in the improved form which it received from Arion was performed by a chorus of satyrs;[7] and there is little doubt that Thespis

---

[1] Suid. s. v. Σοφοκλῆς : περὶ τοῦ χοροῦ πρὸς Θέσπιν καὶ Χοίριλον ἀγωνιζόμενος.

[2] See Müller, *Hist. Lit. Gr.* Vol. i. p. 340, and our note on the translation.

[3] Comp. *Vesp.* 220: ἀρχαιο μελισιδωνοφρυνιχήρατα μέμη, "antiquated honey-sweet and popular ditties from the Phœnissæ of Phrynichus," with a passage in a subsequent part of the same play (1479):

ὀρχούμενος τῆς νυκτὸς οὐδὲν παύεται
τἀρχαῖ᾽ ἐκεῖν᾽ οἷς Θέσπις ἠγωνίζετο.

[4] Clem. Al. *Strom.* v. p. 675, Potter.

[5] Plut. *de Audiendis Poetis,* p. 134, Wyttenb.

[6] Jul. Poll. VII. 45. Another fragment has been lately published from a papyrus by Letronne. *Fragmens inédits d'anciens poètes Grecs.* Par. 1838, p. 7: οὐκ ἐξαθρήσας οἶδ᾽· ἰδὼν δέ σοι λέγω, where ἐξαθρέω is ἅπαξ λεγόμενον.   [7] Above, p. 43.

may have been a satyric poet before he was a tragedian, in the more modern sense of the word: but Chamæleon seems to have expressly mentioned the fact, that Thespis passed from Bacchic to Epic subjects.[1]   With regard to the titles of his plays preserved by Suidas and Julius Pollux, they are not really open to cavil.   For even supposing that they refer rather to the apocryphal compositions of Heraclides than to the lost tragedies of the old Icarian, there is no reason for concluding that the titles were not borrowed by the fabricator from obsolete but genuine dramas.   Unless we are prepared to maintain, against the prevalent tendency of all the authorities, that Thespis never wrote or acted a play of grave or pathetic character, we cannot assert that he was unlikely to have brought forward dramas, bearing the titles in question—namely, 'Pentheus;' 'the Funeral Games of Pelias,' or 'Phorbas;' 'the Priests;' 'the Youths;' indeed it would not be difficult to show that these subjects were very well adapted for the narrative speeches which must have abounded while the actor was limited to the personation of one character at a time.

With regard to the violent and ludicrous dances which were attributed to Thespis, and of which Aristophanes gives a somewhat ludicrous picture at the end of his 'Wasps,'[2] we have only to remark that all antiquated postures, attitudes, and movements appear ridiculous to those whose grandfathers practised them.   Apollo himself is described as leading the Pæan with high and springy steps;[3] and the gymnopædic dance, in which the Tragic Emmeleia took its rise, must have been originally distinguished by the agility which it prescribed.   In the early days of the drama a great deal of energetic and expressive gesticulation was expected from the chorus, and even in the time of Æschylus it is recorded that Telestes, the ballet-leader of that poet,

---

[1] This seems to be the proper interpretation of the passage in Photius, *Lex.* s. v. οὐδὲν πρὸς τὸν Διόνυσον—τὸ πρόσθεν εἰς τὸν Διόνυσον γράφοντες τούτοις ἠγωνίζοντο ἅπερ καὶ σατυρικὰ ἐλέγετο· ὕστερον δὲ μεταβάντες εἰς τραγῳδίας γράφειν κατὰ μικρὸν εἰς μύθους καὶ ἱστορίας ἐτράπησαν μηκέτι τοῦ Θεοῦ μνημονεύοντες, ὅθεν καὶ ἐπεφώνησαν, κ. τ. λ. καὶ Χαμαιλέων ἐν τῷ περὶ Θέσπιδος.   Below, p. [75], note 1.

[2] V. 1848 sqq.; Bentley, *Phalaris*, pp. 265 sqq.

[3] Above, p. 33, note 3.

invented many new forms of χειρονομία or manual gesticulations, and that in the 'Seven against Thebes' he represented the action of the piece by his mimic dancing.[1]

The statement of Suidas, that Phrynichus was the first
who introduced women on the stage (πρῶτος γυναικεῖον
πρόσωπον εἰσήγαγεν), which Bentley, perhaps purposely,
mistranslates, is no reason for concluding that Thespis
never wrote a Tragedy called 'Alcestis,' were there any
real evidence to show that this was the title of one of his
plays; for it would have been perfectly easy to handle that
subject in the Thespian manner, that is, with more narrative
than dialogue, without the introduction of Alcestis herself.[2]
Indeed we cannot conceive how she could be introduced as
talking to the chorus, whom she does not once address in
the play of Euripides, and there was no other actor for her
to talk with.

Of course, there could be no theatrical contests in the
days of Thespis:[3] but the dithyrambic contests seem to
have been important enough to induce Pisistratus to build
a temple in which the victorious choragi might offer up
their tripods,[4] a practice which the victors with the tragic
chorus subsequently adopted.

[1] Welcker, *Nachtrag*, pp. 266, 7; Athen. I. p. 21 F: καὶ Τέλεσις δὲ ἢ
Τελέστης, ὁ ὀρχηστοδιδάσκαλος, πολλὰ ἐξεύρηκε σχήματα ἄκρως ταῖς
χερσὶ τὰ λεγόμενα δεικνυούσαις. . . 'Αριστοκλῆς γοῦν φησὶν ὅτι Τελέστης
ὁ Αἰσχύλου ὀρχηστὴς οὕτως ἦν τεχνίτης ὥστε ἐν τῷ ὀρχεῖσθαι τοὺς 'Επτὰ
ἐπὶ Θήβας φανερὰ ποιῆσαι τὰ πράγματα δι' ὀρχήσεως. See Heindorf, *ad
Plat. Cratyl.* § 51.

[2] In the *Suppliants*, one of the most archaic of the extant plays of
Æschylus, no female character is introduced on the stage, although all
the interest centres in the daughters of Danaus, who form the chorus.

[3] Plutarch, *Sol.* XXIX.

[4] Πύθιον, ἱερὸν 'Απόλλωνος 'Αθήνησιν ὑπὸ Πεισιστράτου γεγονός· εἰς ὃ
τοὺς τρίποδας ἐτίθεσαν οἱ τῷ κυκλίῳ χορῷ νικήσαντες τὰ Θαργήλια
Photius. Comp. Thucyd. II. 15, VI. 54.

CHAPTER V.

*The best actors in the world, either for tragedy, comedy, history, pastoral,
pastoral-comical, historical-pastoral, tragical-historical, tragical-
comical-historical-pastoral, scene individible, or poem unlimited. For
the law of writ and the law of liberty these are the only men.*

SHAKSPEARE.

IT is generally stated that there were three kinds of Greek
Plays, and three only—Tragedy, Comedy, and the Satyrical
Drama. It will be our endeavour in the present chapter to
examine this classification, and to see whether some better
one cannot be proposed. With a view to this it will be
proper to inquire into the origin of the comical and satyrical
dramas, just as we have already investigated the origin of
Tragedy, and to consider how far the Satyrical Drama
differed from or agreed with either the Tragedy or Comedy
of the Greeks.

The word Tragedy—τραγῳδία—is derived of course from
the words τράγος and ῳδή. The former word, as we have
already seen, is a synonym for σάτυρος:[1] for the goat-eared
attendant of Dionysus was called by the name of the animal
which he resembled, just as the shepherd or goatherd was
called by the name of the animal which he tended, and
whose skin formed his clothing.[2] Τραγῳδία is therefore not
the song of a goat, because a goat was the prize of it; but a
song accompanied by a dance performed by persons in the
guise of satyrs, consequently a satyric dance; and we have
already shown how Tragedy in its more modern sense arose
from such performances. At first, then, Tragedy and the

---

[1] See above, p. 43, note 2.

[2] The word *Tityrus* signifies, according to Servius, the leading ram
of the flock: according to other authorities it means a goat; and some
have even supposed it to be another form of *Satyrus*. See the passages
quoted by Müller, *Dor.* IV. ch. 6, § 10, note (e).

Satyrical Drama were one and the same. When, however, the Tragedy of Thespis had firmly established itself, and Comedy was not yet introduced, the common people became discontented with the serious character of the new dramatic exhibitions, and missed the merriment of the country satyrs; at the same time they thought that their own tutelary deity was not sufficiently honoured in performances which were principally taken up with adventures of other personages: in the end they gave vent to their dissatisfaction, and on more than one occasion the audience vociferously complained that the play to which they were admitted had nothing to do with Bacchus.[1] The prevalence of this feeling at length induced Pratinas of Phlius, who was a contemporary of Æschylus, to restore the tragic chorus to the satyrs, and to write dramas which were indeed the same in form and materials with the Tragedy, but the choruses of which were composed of satyrs, and the dances pyrrhic instead of gym-nopædic.[2] This is the drama which has been considered by some as specifically different both from Tragedy and Comedy, but which was in fact only a subdivision of Tragedy,[3] written

---

[1] In his opening Symposiacal disquisition, Plutarch thus speaks: ῞Ωσπερ οὖν, Φρυνίχου καὶ Αἰσχύλου τὴν τραγῳδίαν εἰς μύθους καὶ πάθη προαγόντων, ἐλέχθη· τί ταῦτα πρὸς τὸν Διόνυσον;—οὕτως ἔμοιγε πολλάκις εἰπεῖν παρέστη πρὸς τοὺς ἕλκοντας εἰς τὰ συμπόσια τὸν κυριεύοντα—῏Ω ἄνθρωπε, τί ταῦτα πρὸς τὸν Διόνυσον ;—Sympos. I. I.

Zenobius gives this explanation of the phrase Οὐδὲν πρὸς τὸν Διόνυσον: —Τῶν χορῶν ἐξ ἀρχῆς εἰθισμένων διθύραμβον ᾄδειν εἰς τὸν Διόνυσον, οἱ ποιηταὶ ὕστερον ἐκβάντες τῆς συνηθείας ταύτης Αἴαντας καὶ Κενταύρους γράφειν ἐπεχείρουν. ῞Οθεν οἱ θεώμενοι σκώπτοντες ἔλεγον, Οὐδὲν πρὸς τὸν Διόνυσον. Διὰ γοῦν τοῦτο τοὺς Σατύρους ὕστερον ἔδοξεν αὐτοῖς προεισάγειν, ἵνα μὴ δοκῶσιν ἐπιλανθάνεσθαι τοῦ θεοῦ. p. 42.

Suidas, in his explanation of the same saying, after mentioning the opinion by which it was referred to the alterations of Epigenes the Sicyonian, adds: Βέλτιον δὲ οὕτω· Τὸ πρόσθεν εἰς τὸν Διόνυσον γράφοντες, τούτοις ἠγωνίζοντο, ἅπερ καὶ Σατυρικὰ ἐλέγετο· ὕστερον δὲ μεταβάντες εἰς τὸ τραγῳδίας γράφειν, κατὰ μικρὸν εἰς μύθους καὶ ἱστορίας ἐτράπησαν, μηκέτι τοῦ Διονύσου μνημονεύοντες·—ὅθεν τοῦτο καὶ ἐπεφώνησαν. Καὶ Χαμαιλέων ἐν τῷ περὶ Θέσπιδος τὰ παραπλήσια ἱστορεῖ. So also Photius, above, p. 72, note 1.

[2] Above, p. 36.

[3] Demetrius says (de Elocut. § 169, Vol. IX. p. 76, Walz): ὁ δὲ γέλως ἐχθρὰ τραγῳδίας· οὐδὲ γὰρ ἐπινοήσειεν ἄν τις τραγῳδίαν παίζουσαν, ἐπεὶ σάτυρον γράψει ἀντὶ τραγῳδίας.

always by Tragedians, and, we believe, seldom[1] acted but
along with Tragedies.[2]

We have already referred to the statement that the
Comedy of the Greeks arose from the Phallic processions,
just as their Tragedy did from the Dithyramb.[3]　Its progress, however, and its successive advances from rudeness
to perfection, are involved in so much obscurity, that even
Aristotle is unable to tell us anything about it; but he is
willing to concede that it was started in Sicily,[4] or primarily
in Megaris.[5]　And this appears very probable ; for not only
was Susarion, who is generally admitted to have been the
earliest comic poet,[6] a native of Tripodiscus in Megaris, but
continual allusions are made in ancient writers[7] to the
coarse humour of the Megarians and their strong turn for
the ludicrous, qualities which they seem to have imparted
to their Sicilian colonists.

But whatever may have been the birth-place of Greek
Comedy, it is quite certain that it originated in a country
festival: it was in fact the celebration of the vintage, when
the country people went round from village to village, some
in carts,[8] who uttered all the vile jests and abusive speeches

---

[1] If Pratinas wrote only eighteen tragedies to thirty-two satyrical
dramas, some of the latter must have been acted alone.　See Welcker,
Trilogie, pp. 497—8.

[2] It has been plausibly conjectured that the satyrical drama was
originally acted before the Tragedy.　Welck. *Nachtr.* p. 279.

[3] Above, p. 9.　Thus we read that Antheas the Lindian κωμῳδίας
ἐποίει καὶ ἄλλα πολλὰ ἐν τούτῳ τῷ τρόπῳ τῶν ποιημάτων, & ἐξῆρχε τοῖς
μετ' αὐτοῦ φαλλοφοροῦσι.　(Athen. p. 445 D.)

[4] Αἱ μὲν οὖν τῆς τραγῳδίας μεταβάσεις, καὶ δι' ὧν ἐγένυντο, οὐ λελήθασιν.
ἡ δὲ κωμῳδία, διὰ τὸ μὴ σπουδάζεσθαι ἐξ ἀρχῆς, ἔλαθε.　Καὶ γὰρ χορὸν
κωμῳδῶν ὀψέ ποτε ὁ ἄρχων ἔδωκεν, ἀλλ' ἐθελονταὶ ἦσαν· ἤδη δὲ σχήματά
τινα αὐτῆς ἐχούσης, οἱ λεγόμενοι αὐτῆς ποιηταὶ μνημονεύονται· τίς δὲ
πρόσωπα ἀπέδωκεν, ἢ λόγους, ἢ πλήθη ὑποκριτῶν, καὶ ὅσα τοιαῦτα,
ἠγνόηται.　Τοῦ δὲ μύθους ποιεῖν Ἐπίχαρμος καὶ Φόρμις ἦρξαν· τὸ μὲν
οὖν ἐξαρχῆς ἐκ Σικελίας ἦλθε.　Aristot. *Poet.* V.

[5] Τῆς μὲν κωμῳδίας οἱ Μεγαρεῖς, οἵ τε ἐνταῦθα, ὡς ἐπὶ τῆς παρ' αὐτοῖς
δημοκρατίας γενομένης, καὶ οἱ ἐκ Σικελίας.　*Poet.* III. 5.

[6] *Proleg. Aristoph.* Küst. p. xi : τὴν κωμῳδίαν ηὑρῆσθαί φασι ὑπὸ
Σουσαρίωνος.

[7] See Müller's *Dorians*, IV. 7, § I.

[8] Schol. Lucian. Ζεὺς τραγῳδός (VI. p. 388, Lehmann): ἐν τῇ ἑορτῇ
τῶν Διονυσίων παρὰ τοῖς Ἀθηναίοις ἐπὶ ἀμαξῶν καθήμενοι ἔσκωπτον

with which the Tragedy of Thespis has been most unjustly saddled; others on foot, who bore aloft the Phallic emblem, and invoked in songs Phales, the comrade of Bacchus.[1] This custom of going round from village to village suggested the derivation of Comedy from κώμη, and Aristotle has been misled by his own learning into an apparent approbation of this, on many accounts, absurd etymology.[2] One reason which has been advanced in defence of this etymology is extraordinarily ridiculous. We are told[3] that the word cannot be derived from κῶμος, because one of the meanings of that word is ἡ μετ᾽ οἴνου ᾠδή. This would scarcely be an argument if it were only the signification of the word κῶμος; but this is so far from being the case, that it is not even the primary or most usual meaning of the word. Κῶμος[4] signifies a revel continued after supper. It was a very ancient custom in Greece for young men, after rising from an evening banquet, to ramble about the streets to the sound of the flute or the lyre, and with torches in their hands; such a band of revellers was also called κῶμος. Thus Æschylus says,[5] very forcibly, that the Furies, although they had drunk their fill of human blood in the house of the Pelopidæ, and though it was now time that they should go out like a κῶμος, nevertheless obstinately stuck to the house, and would not depart from it. And as the band of revellers

---

ἀλλήλους καὶ ἐλοιδοροῦντο πολλά. See the passages in Creuzer's note on Lydus, *de Mens.* p. 127, ed. Röther.

[1] The reader will see these particulars in Aristoph. *Acharn.* 240 sqq.

[2] ποιούμενοι τὰ ὀνόματα σημεῖον, οὗτοι μὲν γὰρ (Πελοποννήσιοι) κώμας τὰς περιοικίδας καλεῖν φασίν, 'Αθηναῖοι δὲ δήμους. ὡς κωμῳδούς, οὐκ ἀπὸ τοῦ κωμάζειν λεχθέντας ἀλλὰ τῇ κατὰ κώμας πλάνῃ ἀτιμαζομένους ἐκ τοῦ ἄστεος. *Poet.* c. III.

[3] By Schneider (*de Orig. Comm.* p. 5).

[4] See Welcker in Jacobs' edition of *Philostratus*, p. 202. The remarks in the text are an abstract of what he says on the signification of this word. He supposes, however, that κωμῳδός is derived from the secondary sense of the word, in which he agrees with Kanngiesser (*Kom. Bühn.* p. 32).

[5] *Agamemnon*, 1161, Wellauer:

Καὶ μὴν πεπωκώς γ᾽ ὡς θρασύνεσθαι πλέον
Βροτεῖον αἷμα κῶμος ἐν δόμοις μένει
Δύσπεμπτος ἔξω συγγόνων 'Εριννύων.

"flown with insolence and wine," as Milton says,[1] not unfrequently made a riotous entrance into any house where an entertainment was going on,[2] the verb ἐπεισκωμάζω is used metaphorically by Plato to signify any interruption or intrusion, whether it be the invasion of a philosophical school by mere pretenders to science,[3] or the evasion of the proper subject of inquiry by the introduction of extraneous matter.[4] Hence the word κῶμος is used to denote any band or company. In a secondary sense, it signifies a song sung either by a convivial party or at the Bacchic feasts (not merely in honour of the god, but also to ridicule certain persons), or lastly, by a procession in honour of a victor at the public games. By a still further transition, κῶμος is used for a song in general; and a peculiar flute tune, together with its corresponding dance, was known by this name. It was in the second sense of the word that the Bacchic reveller was called a κωμῳδός, namely, a comus-singer, according to the analogy of τραγῳδός, ἱλαρῳδός, &c., in which the first part of the compound refers to the performer, the second to the song, and as τραγῳδία signifies a song of satyrs, so κωμῳδία means a song of comus. It is clear, from the manner in which the Athenian writers speak of the country Dionysian procession, that it was considered as a comus ;[5] and we think this view of the case is confirmed by the epithet ξύγκωμος, which Dicæopolis applies to Phales as the companion of Bacchus.[6]

The Phallic processions, from which the old Comedy arose, seem to have been allowed in very early times in all cities; Aristotle tells us that they still continued in many cities even in his time,[7] and the inscriptions quoted above[8]

---

[1] *Par. L.* I. 502.

[2] Like Alcibiades in Plato's *Sympos.* 212 c.

[3] *Resp.* p. 500 B: τοὺς ἔξωθεν οὐ προσῆκον ἐπεισκεκωμακότας.

[4] *Theætet.* p. 184 A: καὶ τὸ μέγιστον, οὗ ἕνεκα ὁ λόγος ὥρμηται, ἐπιστήμης πέρι, τί ποτ' ἐστίν, ἄσκεπτον γένηται ὑπὸ τῶν ἐπεισκωμαζόντων λόγων.

[5] Thus in an old law quoted by Demosthenes (*c. Mid.* p. 517) we have ὁ κῶμος καὶ οἱ κωμῳδοί.

[6] *Acharn.* 263: Φαλῆς, ἑταῖρε Βακχίου,
            Ξύγκωμε.

[7] τὰ φαλλικὰ ἃ ἔτι καὶ νῦν ἐν πολλαῖς τῶν πόλεων διαμένει νομιζόμενα. Aristot. *Poet.* c. IV.   [8] Above, pp. 49 sqq.

prove that a lyrical Comedy had developed itself from them. In the time of the orators, the ἰθύφαλλοι were still danced in the orchestra at Athens,[1] and we learn from the speech of Demosthenes against Conon, that the riotous and profligate young men, who infested the streets, delighted to call themselves by names[2] derived from these comic buffooneries. But probably they were always more common in the country, which was their natural abode; and if a modern scholar[3] is right in concluding from the words of the Scholiast on Aristophanes,[4] that there were two sorts of Phallic processions, the one public, the other private, we cannot believe that the private vintage ceremonies ever found their way into the great towns. Pasquinades of the coarsest kind seem to have formed the principal part of these rural exhibitions,[5] and this was probably the reason why Comedy was established at Athens in the time of Pericles; for the demagogues, wanting to invent some means of attacking their political opponents with safety, could think of no better way of effecting this than by introducing into the city the favourite country sports of the lower orders, and then it was, and not till then, that the performance of Comedies became, like that of Tragedies, a public concern.[6] When it was formally established as a distinct species of drama at Athens, the old Comedy was supplied, like Tragedy, with a chorus, which, though not so numerous or expensively attired as the tragic, was as carefully trained and as systematic in its songs and dances. In effect, it was the same modification of an original comus as that which

---

[1] Hyperides apud Harpocrat. v. Ἰθύφαλλοι.

[2] They termed themselves Ἰθύφαλλοι and Αὐτολήκυθοι. Demosth. *Conon*, 194 (1261). Cf. Athen. XIV. p. 622; Lucian, II. 336.

[3] Schneider, *de Orig. Com.* p. 14.

[4] *Acharn.* 243 (p. 775, l. 32, Dind.): πεισθέντες οὖν τοῖς ἠγγελμένοις οἱ Ἀθηναῖοι φάλλους ἰδίᾳ καὶ δημοσίᾳ κατεσκεύασαν καὶ τούτοις ἐγέραιρον τὸν θεόν.

[5] Platonius, περὶ διαφορᾶς κωμῳδιῶν: Ὑποθέσεις μὲν γὰρ τῆς παλαιᾶς κωμῳδίας ἦσαν αὗται· τὸ στρατηγοῖς ἐπιτιμᾶν, κ. τ. λ.

[6] χορὸν κωμῳδῶν ὀψέ ποτε ἔδωκεν ὁ ἄρχων. Aristotle, above, p. 76, note 4.

Gruppe labours under some extraordinary mistake in supposing (*Ariadne*, p. 123) that Comedy was not originally connected with religion.

performed the Epinicia of Pindar. It appears from several passages that the comic actors were originally unprovided with masks, but rubbed their faces over with wine-lees as a substitute for that disguise.[1]

The Tragedy and Comedy of the Greeks had, therefore, an entirely different origin. We must in the next place consider what were their distinctive peculiarities, how far they differed intrinsically, and whether any of the remaining Greek plays cannot be considered as belonging strictly either to Tragedy or Comedy. We shall do this more satisfactorily if we first set forth the definitions which have been given by Plato and Aristotle. Plato has rather alluded to, than expressed, the distinction between Tragedy and Comedy in their most perfect form, but his slight remarks nevertheless strike at the root of the matter. Comedy he considers[2] to be the generic name for all dramatic exhibitions which have a tendency to excite laughter; while Tragedy, in the truest sense of the word, is an imitation of the noblest life, that is, of the actions of gods and heroes. As a definition, however, this account of Tragedy, although excellent as far as it goes, is altogether incomplete. Aristotle's, on the other hand, is quite perfect. He makes the distinction, which Plato leaves to be inferred, between the objects of tragic and comic imitation, and adds to it the constituent characteristic of Tragedy, namely, that it effects

---

[1] Hence a comedian is called τρυγῳδός, "a lee singer." It does not appear that masks were always used even in the time of Aristophanes, who acted the part of Cleon in the Ἱππῆς without one. In later times, however, it was considered disreputable to go in any comus without a mask. Demosth. Fals. Leg. p. 433: τοῦ καταράτου Κυρηβίωνος ὃς ἐν ταῖς πομπαῖς ἄνευ τοῦ προσώπου κωμάζει.

[2] Legg. VII. p. 817: ὅσα μὲν οὖν περὶ γέλωτά ἐστι παίγνια, ἃ δὴ κωμῳδίαν πάντες λέγομεν . . .μίμησις τοῦ καλλίστου καὶ ἀρίστου βίου ὃ δή φαμεν πάντες γε ὄντως εἶναι τραγῳδίαν τὴν ἀληθεστάτην. The κάλλιστος καὶ ἄριστος βίος signifies the life of a man who is in the highest degree καλοκἀγαθός, and this term exactly expresses the persons who figured in the plays of Æschylus and Sophocles; for, as Dr. Thirlwall remarks, in his beautiful paper On the Irony of Sophocles, "None but gods or heroes could act any prominent part in the Attic tragedy" (Phil. Mus. II. p. 493). And this is perhaps the reason why Plato, in another passage (Gorgias, p. 502 A), talks of ἡ σεμνὴ καὶ θαυμαστὴ ἡ τῆς τραγῳδίας ποίησις.

by means of pity and terror the purgation of such passions.[1] Aristotle's definition of Tragedy is so full and comprehensive, that it has been adopted even by modern writers as a description of what modern Tragedy ought to be ;[2] there is one particular, however, which he has not expressly stated, and which is due rather to the origin of Greek Tragedy than to its essence, we mean the necessity for a previous acquaintance on the part of the audience with the plot of the Tragedy : this it is which most eminently distinguishes the Tragedies of Sophocles from those of Shakspeare, and to this is owing the poetical irony with which the poet and the spectators handled or looked upon the characters in the piece.[3] Aristotle is supposed by his commentator Eustratius to allude to this in a passage of the Ethics :[4] we are disposed to believe on the contrary, that he is referring to the different effects which events related in a Tragedy, as having taken place prior to the time of the events represented, and those events which are represented by action, produce on the minds of the spectators : for example, the calamities of Œdipus, when alluded to in the Œdipus at Colonus, do not strike us with so much horror as when they are represented in the Œdipus at Thebes.

If, however, all the prominent characters in the true Tragedy were gods or heroes, it follows that the Πέρσαι of Æschylus, and the Μιλήτου ἅλωσις and Φοίνισσαι of Phryni-

---

[1] ἡ δὲ κωμῳδία ἐστίν, ὥσπερ εἴπομεν, μίμησις φαυλοτέρων μέν, οὐ μέντοι κατὰ πᾶσαν κακίαν, ἀλλὰ τοῦ αἰσχροῦ ἐστι τὸ γελοῖον μόριον. Poet. c. v.—ἔστιν οὖν τραγῳδία μίμησις πράξεως σπουδαίας καὶ τελείας, μέγεθος ἐχούσης ——— δρώντων καὶ οὐ δι' ἀπαγγελίας, δι' ἐλέου καὶ φόβου περαίνουσα τὴν τῶν τοιούτων παθημάτων κάθαρσιν. Poet. c. vi.

[2] Hurd's definition (*On the Province of the Drama*, p. 164) is a mere copy of Aristotle. Schiller, who has a better right to declare *ex cathedrâ* what Tragedy aught to be than any writer of the last century, thus defines it : "That art which proposes to itself, as its especial object, the pleasure resulting from compassion, is called the tragic art in the most comprehensive sense of the word." *Werke*, in einem Bande, p. 1176.

[3] See Dr. Thirlwall's Essay *On the Irony of Sophocles.*

[4] I. 11, § 4 : διαφέρει δὲ τῶν παθῶν ἕκαστον περὶ ζῶντας ἢ τελευτήσαντας συμβαίνειν πολὺ μᾶλλον ἢ τὰ παράνομα καὶ δεινὰ προϋπάρχειν ταῖς τρα γῳδίαις ἢ πράττεσθαι.

G

chus, were not Tragedies in the truest sense,[1] and must be
referred to the class of Histories, which exist in all countries
where the drama is much cultivated, as a subordinate species
of Tragedy: the other Tragedies we may call myths or
fables[2] as distinguished from the true stories, to which they
bore the same relation in the subdivision of Ionian literature that the Epos bore to the history of Herodotus.

In the course of time another rib was taken from the
side of the primary Tragedy, and Tragi-comedy sprang up
under the fostering care of Euripides, which was probably
the forerunner of the ἱλαροτραγῳδίαι of Rhinthon, Sopatrus,
Sciras, and Blæsus.[3] One old specimen of this kind of play
remains to us in the Ἄλκηστις of Euripides, which was
performed as the satyrical drama of a Tragic Trilogy,
438 B.C., and we are inclined to consider the Orestes as
another of the same sort.[4] It resembled the regular
Tragedy in its outward form, but contained some comic
characters, and always had a happy termination.

Of the Satyrical Drama we have already spoken: we
cannot, however, quit the subject of Tragedy and its
subordinate forms without noticing a play called Εἵλωτες οἱ
ἐπὶ Ταινάρῳ, which was, according to Herodian,[5] a satyrical

---

[1] Niebuhr, *Hist. Rome*, Vol. I. note 1150: "The *Destruction of Miletus*
by Phrynichus, and *the Persians* of Æschylus, were plays that drew
forth all the manly feelings of bleeding or exulting hearts, and not
tragedies: for these the Greeks, before the Alexandrian age, took their
plots solely out of mythical story. It was essential that their contents
should be known beforehand; whereas the stories of Hamlet and
Macbeth were unknown to the spectators; at present, parts of them
might be moulded into tragedies like the Greek; that is if a Sophocles
were to rise up."

[2] The words of Suidas, quoted above, appear to allude to this distinction: κατὰ μικρὸν εἰς μύθους καὶ ἱστορίας ἐτράπησαν.

[3] Müller's *Dor.* IV. ch. 7, § 6.

[4] In an argument to the *Alcestis*, published from a Vatican MS.
(No. 909) by Dindorf, in 1834, we find the following words: Τὸ δρᾶμα
ἐποιήθη ιξ. ἐδιδάχθη ἐπὶ Γλαυκίνου ἄρχοντος τὸ λ. πρῶτος ἦν Σοφοκλῆς,
δεύτερος Εὐριπίδης Κρήσσαις, 'Αλκμαίωνι τῷ διὰ Ψωφῖδος, Τηλέφῳ,
'Αλκήστιδι. τὸ δὲ δρᾶμα κωμικωτέραν ἔχει τὴν κατασκευήν. The last
sentence is a repetition in effect of the statement in the Copenhagen
argument (Matthiæ, VII. p. 214). On the date see Welcker, *Rheinisch.
Mus.* for 1835, p. 508; Clinton, *F. H.* Vol. I. p. 424.

[5] See Eustathius on *Iliad* II. p. 297.

drama. This statement has occasioned some difficulties. It has been asked,[1] were the Helots, who doubtless composed the chorus, dressed like satyrs, or mixed up with satyrs? But if it was a satyrical drama, what mythological subject is reconcilable with a chorus of Helots? and, on the same supposition, how could the comedian Eupolis, to whom Athenæus[2] ascribes the play, have been its author? for a trespass by a comedian on the domains of the tragic muse, to whom the satyrical drama belonged, was, especially in those times, something quite unheard of. There is, it must be admitted, some difficulty in this, and principally in regard to the last question. The Helots, with their dresses of goatskin or sheepskin, and their indecent dances in honour of Bacchus, were very fit substitutes for the satyrs, and it is quite possible to conceive that a Dionysian myth might be represented in a play, the chorus of which consisted of Helots. From the statement, however, that Eupolis was the author, and from the purely comic and criticising tone of one of the fragments,[3] we are disposed to conclude that Herodian is mistaken in calling it a satyrical drama, and that he has been misled by the resemblance between the guise of the Helots and that of the satyrs; whereas the play was a regular Comedy with a political reference, perhaps not unlike the Λακεδαίμονες of the same author.

The Comedy of the Greeks first attained to a distinct literary and political importance in the country which witnessed its final development in a form corresponding to that of its modern representatives. Whatever may have been the value of the writings of Epicharmus, they have not reached our time except in fragments. For us Greek Comedy, both in itself and in its Roman transcriptions, is the Comedy of Athens. So far as we are acquainted with its literary history, it owes its first development and completion to the political and social condition of that great democratic metropolis; and it is so intimately connected with all that is characteristic of Attic life, that the greatest scholars of Alexandria, Lycophron and Eratosthenes, wrote

---

[1] By Müller in *Was für eine Art Drama waren "die Heloten"?* Niebuhr's *Rhein. Mus.* III. p. 488.

[2] IV. p. 138.   [3] In Athen. XIV. p. 638.

formal and elaborate treatises on the subject. Considered, then, as peculiarly Athenian, the Comedy of the Greeks admits of subdivision into three species, or rather three successive variations in form, which are generally distinguished as the Old, the Middle, and the New Comedy. These three subdivisions must be considered separately, and with a brief review of their distinctive characteristics.

The old Comedy was, as we have already seen, the result of a successful attempt to give to the waggon-jests of the country comus a particular and a political bias. Its outward form was burlesque in its most wanton extravagance. Its essence, or to use the words of Vico,[1] its *eterna propietà*, was personal villification. Not merely the satire of description, the abuse of words, but the satire of representation. The object of popular dislike was not merely called a coward, a villain, a rogue, or a fool, but he was exhibited on the stage doing everything contemptible, and suffering everything ludicrous. This systematic personality, the ἰαμβικὴ ἰδέα[2] of the old popular farce, would not have sufficed to obtain for Comedy an adequate share of attention from the refined and accomplished democracy which established itself at Athens during the administration of Pericles. It was necessary that the comic poet who would gain a hearing in the theatre at Athens should borrow from Tragedy many of its most striking peculiarities—its choral dances, its masked actors, its metrical forms, its elaborate scenery and machines, and, above all, that chastened elegance of the Attic dialect which the fastidiousness of an Athenian citizen required and exacted from the poets and orators. The comedy became a regular drama, recalling indeed a recollection of the old phallic comus by an extravagant obscenity of language and costume, but often presenting an elegance in the dialogues and a poetic refinement in the melic portions, which would have borne a comparison with the best efforts of the contemporary tragic muse. Upon this stock the mighty genius of Aristophanes grafted his own Pantagruelism, which has in every age, since the days of its reproducer Rabelais,

---

[1] *Scienza Nuova*, III. p. 638: "La satira serbò quest' *eterna propietà*, con la qual ella nacque, di dir villanie ed ingiurie."

[2] Aristot. *Poet.* 5.

found in some European country, and in some form or other, a more or less adequate representative—Cervantes, Quevedo, Butler, Swift, Sterne, Voltaire, Jean Paul, Carlyle, and Southey. By Pantagruelism we mean—in accordance with the definition which we have elsewhere given of the term[1]—an assumption of Bacchanalian buffoonery as a cloak to cover some serious purpose. Rabelais, who invented the word to express a certain literary development of the character sustained by the court-fools in the Middle Ages, must have been quite conscious that he was reproducing, as far as his age allowed, not only the spirit, but even the outward machinery of the Old Comedy. At any rate he adopts the disguise of low buffoonery for the express purpose of attacking some form of prevalent cant and imposture; and this was consistently the object of Aristophanes. Whether he professedly takes Aristophanes as his model, and as the lamp to light him on the way,[2] may be regarded as an open question; but there can be no doubt that the manner and the object of the curé of Meudon were identical with those of the great comedian of Athens, and that the name of Pantagruelist, invented by the one, accurately describes the leading characteristics of his main prototype. The chief difference between the Old Comedy of Athens, as represented by Aristophanes, and the modern manifestations of the same riotous drollery, as a cover for some serious purpose which it might be premature, unsafe, or generally inexpedient to disclose, must be sought in the peculiar relations which subsisted between the old comedian and his democratic audience during the short period of the Old Comedy's highest perfection, namely, the interval between the commencement of the Peloponnesian war and the Sicilian expedition, when the irritable Demos was so conscious of his power and was so exhilarated by his good fortune that, like the kings of the Middle Ages, he was

---

[1] In the *Quarterly Review*, No. CLXI. pp. 137 sqq.

[2] We have shown in the paper on Pantagruelism already cited that the reference to Aristophanes and Cleanthes as the lanterns of honour (Rabelais, v. c. 33) is derived from Varro (*L. L.* v. 9. p. 4, Müller), who is speaking of Aristophanes, the grammarian of Byzantium, and of the grammatical studies of the Stoics; but Rabelais, like his commentators, may have misunderstood Varro.

willing to tolerate any jokes at his own expense, if the
satirist would only pay him the compliment of adopting
the thin veil of caricature, and pretend to put forward as
an outpouring of privileged folly what he really meant to be
taken as the most serious remonstrance or the most biting
reproof.[1]

It is difficult, perhaps impossible, to draw a clearly
defined line of demarcation between the latest *writers* of the
Old and the earliest *writers* of the Middle Comedy. We
cannot say of them that this author was an old comedian,
that a middle comedian: they may have been both, as
Aristophanes certainly was, if the criterion was the absence
or presence of a *Parabasis*,[2] or speech of the chorus in
which the audience are addressed in the name of the poet,
and without, in many cases, any reference to the subject of
the play. Nor will the proper interpretation of the law
περὶ τοῦ μὴ ὀνομαστὶ κωμῳδεῖν[3] enable us to distinguish be-

---

[1] Aristophanes openly avows this mixture of the serious and the
ridiculous in his later comedies, when he no longer practised it with
the same objects. *Ran.* 391 : καὶ πολλὰ μὲν γελοῖά μ᾽ εἰπεῖν πολλὰ δὲ
σπουδαῖα. *Eccles.* 1200: σμικρὸν δ᾽ ὑποθέσθαι τοῖς κριταῖσι βούλομαι·
τοῖς σοφοῖς μὲν τῶν σοφῶν μεμνημένους κρίνειν ἐμέ· τοῖς γελῶσι δ᾽
ἡδέως διὰ τὸν γέλωτα κρίνειν ἐμέ.

[2] Τὰ τὰς παραβάσεις οὐκ ἔχοντα ἐδιδάχθη ἐξουσίας ἀπὸ τοῦ δήμου
μεθισταμένης καὶ ὀλιγαρχίας κρατούσης. Platonius. With regard to
the attempt of Meineke (*Quæstion. Scenicæ*, Sp. III. p. 50) to prove that
Antiphanes was a new comic poet because he mentioned the ματτύη
(Athen. XIV. p. 662 F), we may remark, that the word cannot be used
as a criterion to enable us to distinguish between two schools of
comedians, for it is mentioned by Nicostratus, the son of Aristophanes
(see Clinton in *Phil. Mus.* I. p. 560), and the dainty was not unknown
to Aristophanes himself, who uses the word ματτυολοιχός (*Nub.* 451).

[3] Mr. Clinton, in the Introduction to the second volume of his *Fasti
Hellenici* (pp. xxxvi, &c.) has shown that the generally received idea,
which would distinguish the Middle from the Old Comedy by its
abstinence from personal satire, is completely at variance with the
fragments still extant; and that the celebrated law—τοῦ μὴ ὀνομαστὶ
κωμῳδεῖν τινά—simply forbade the introduction of any individual on
the stage *by name as one of the dramatis personæ.* This prohibition,
too, might be evaded by suppressing the name and identifying the
individual by means of the mask, the dress, and external appearance
alone. "This law, then, when limited to its proper sense, is by no
means inconsistent with a great degree of comic liberty, or with those
animadversions upon eminent names with which we find the comic

tween the comedians as belonging to one class or the other. As to the *comedies* themselves, however, we may safely conclude, on the authority of Platonius, that the Middle Comedy was a form of the old, but differed from it in three particulars: it had no chorus, and therefore no parabasis—this deviation was occasioned by the inability of the impoverished state to furnish the comic poets with choragi: living characters were not introduced on the stage—this was owing to the want of energy produced by the subversion of the democratic empire: as a consequence of both these circumstances, the objects of its ridicule were general rather than personal, and literary rather than political. If, therefore, we were called upon to give to the Old and Middle Comedy their distinctive appellations, we should call one *Caricature* and the other *Criticism;* and if we wished to illustrate the difference by modern instances, we should compare the former to the Lampoon, the latter to the Review. The period to which the writers of the Middle Comedy belonged may be defined generally as that included between the termination of the Peloponnesian war and the overthrow of Athenian freedom by Philip of Macedon, from B.C. 404 to B.C. 340. The numerous comedies which appeared in this interval, especially those belonging to the latter half of the period, were chiefly occupied in holding up to light and not ill-natured ridicule the literary and social peculiarities of the day. The writers seized on what was ludicrous in the contemporary systems of philosophy. They parodied and travestied not only the language but sometimes even the plots of the most celebrated tragedies and epic poems. And, in the same spirit, they not unfrequently took their subjects directly from the old mythology. In their satires on society they attacked rather classes of men than prominent individuals of the class. Courtesans, parasites, and wanton revellers, with their pic-nic feasts, were freely represented in general types,[1] and the self-conceited

---

poets actually to abound " (*Fast. Hell.* p. xlii.). The date of the law is uncertain; probably about B.C. 404, during the government of the Thirty.

[1] See the anecdote about Antiphanes, Ath. XIII. pr.

cook, with his parade of culinary science, was a standing character in the Middle Comedy.[1] Athenian politics were generally avoided; but these poets did not scruple to make sport of foreign tyrants, like the Dionysii of Syracuse and Alexander of Pheræ.[2] Their style was generally prosaic,[3] and they usually confined themselves to the comic trimeter. But long systems of anapæstic dimeters were sometimes introduced, and in their parodies and travesties they imitated the metres of the poets whom they ridiculed.

The New Comedy commenced, as is well known, with the establishment of the supremacy of Philip,[4] and flourished at Athens during the period distinguished as that of the Macedonian rulers, who are called the *Diadochi* and *Epigoni;* it belongs, therefore, to the interval between the 110th and 130th Olympiads, i. e. between B.C. 340 and B.C. 260. We can see in Plautus and Terence, who translated or imitated the Greek writers of this class, satisfactory specimens of the nature of this branch of Comedy. It corresponded as nearly as possible to our own comic drama, especially to that of Farquhar and Congreve, which Charles Lamb calls the Comedy of *Manners*, and Hurd the Comedy of *Character*. It arose in all probability from a union of the style and tone of the Euripidean dialogue with the subjects and characters of the later form, the Middle Comedy. The particular circumstances of the time had given a new direction to the warlike tendencies of the Greeks. Instead of serving in the ranks of the national militia and fighting in free warfare at home, the active, restless, or discontented citizen found a ready welcome and good pay in the mer-

---

[1] This was the principal character in the *Æolosicon*, one of the latest plays of Aristophanes, and it is always re-appearing.

[2] As in the *Dionysius* of Eubulus and the *Dionysalexandrus* of the younger Cratinus.

[3] Anonym. *de Comm.* III.: τῆς δὲ μέσης κωμῳδίας οἱ ποιηταὶ πλάσματος μὲν οὐχ ἥψαντο ποιητικοῦ, διὰ δὲ τῆς συνήθους ἰόντες λαλιᾶς λογικὰς ἔχουσι τὰς ἀρετάς, ὥστε σπάνιον ποιητικὸν χαρακτῆρα εἶναι παρ' αὐτοῖς.

[4] Meineke says (*Hist. Crit. Com.* p. 435) that he dates the commencement of the new comedy from the period immediately preceding the battle of Chæronein, and that the anonymous writer on comedy (p. xxxii.) is not quite accurate in saying ἡ νέα ἐπὶ 'Αλεξάνδρου εἶχε τὴν ἀκμήν.

cenary armies kept up by the Greek sovereigns of Asia and Egypt. Such a soldier or leader of mercenaries, having returned from abroad with a full purse, an empty head, and a loud tongue, became a standing character in the New Comedy. The other characters, the greedy parasite, the clever and unprincipled slave, and the scheming or tyrannical courtesan, may have appeared in the Middle Comedy; but they are the new comedian's indispensable staff. And now for the first time the element of love becomes the main ingredient in dramatic poetry.[1] The object of the young man's passion is not the free-born Athenian maiden, but some accomplished ἑταίρα, or an innocent girl, who is ostensibly the slave or associate of the ἑταίρα, but turns out at the end of the piece to be the lost child of some worthy citizen.[2] A good deal of ingenuity is shown in the contrivance of these unexpected recognitions (ἀναγνωρίσεις), and here also the drama of Euripides had furnished the comedian with his model. The "heavy father," as he is called on our stage, is generally an indispensable personage, and in the intrigues of the piece he is often the dupe of the manœuvring slave, or led by some incidental temptations into the very vices and follies which he had reproved in his son. The greatest care is taken in the delineation of these characters, and there can be little doubt that they represented accurately the most prominent features of the later Attic society. The drama under such circumstances did not attempt to make men better than they were, and it is to be feared that the comic stage did little more than present in the most attractive colours the lax morality of the age.

It is not our intention to speak of the dramas and quasi-dramas of a later age; it may however be of some assistance to the student if we subjoin a general tabular view of the rise and progress of the proper Greek Drama.

---

[1] Ovid, *Fast.* II. 369: Fabula jucundi nulla est sine amore Menandri.
[2] See *Hist. of Gr. Liter.* Vol. III. pp. 2 sqq.

TABLE OF DRAMATIC CLASSIFICATION.

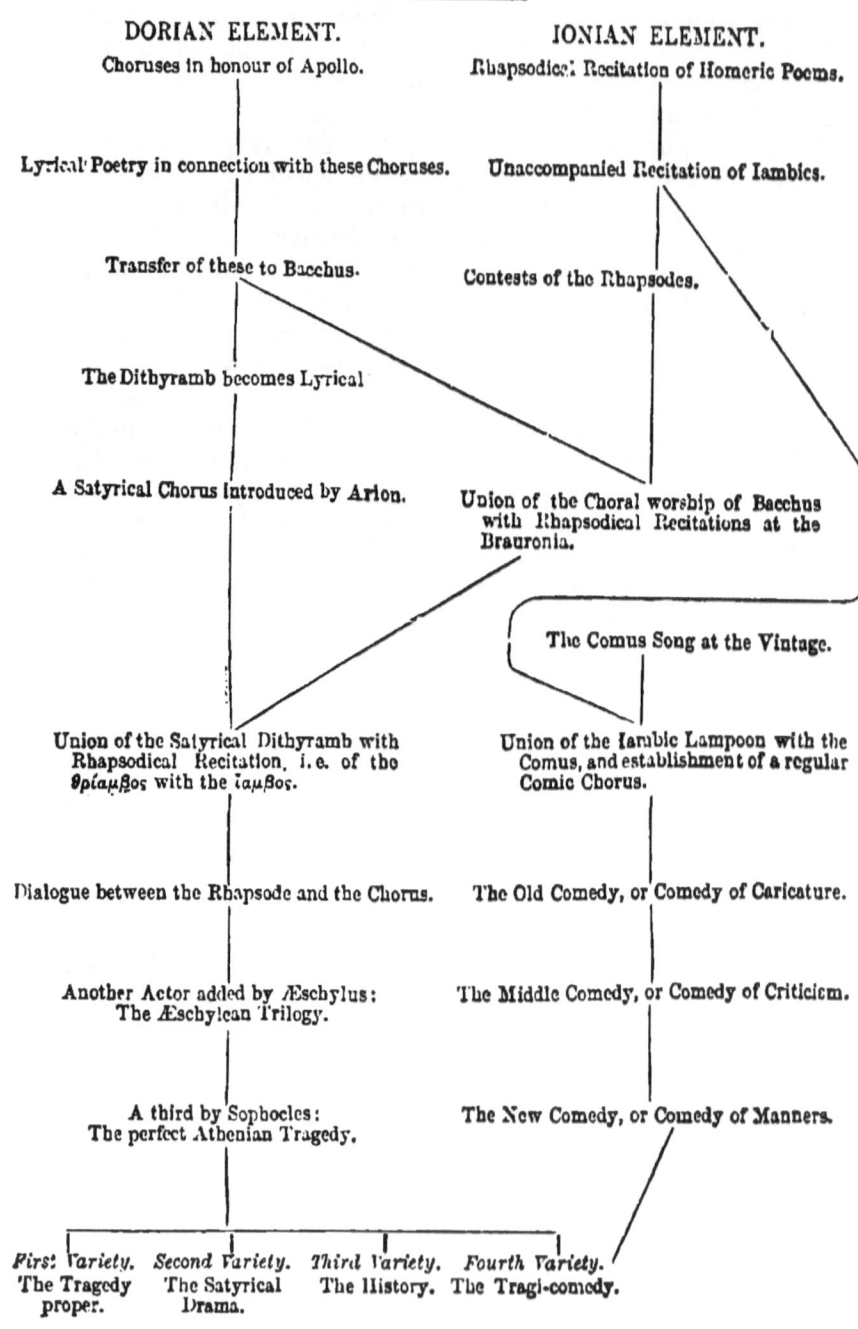

DORIAN ELEMENT.
Choruses in honour of Apollo.

IONIAN ELEMENT.
Rhapsodies: Recitation of Homeric Poems.

Lyrical Poetry in connection with these Choruses.

Unaccompanied Recitation of Iambics.

Transfer of these to Bacchus.

Contests of the Rhapsodes.

The Dithyramb becomes Lyrical

A Satyrical Chorus introduced by Arion.

Union of the Choral worship of Bacchus with Rhapsodical Recitations at the Brauronia.

The Comus Song at the Vintage.

Union of the Satyrical Dithyramb with Rhapsodical Recitation, i.e. of the θρίαμβος with the ἴαμβος.

Union of the Iambic Lampoon with the Comus, and establishment of a regular Comic Chorus.

Dialogue between the Rhapsode and the Chorus.

The Old Comedy, or Comedy of Caricature.

Another Actor added by Æschylus: The Æschylean Trilogy.

The Middle Comedy, or Comedy of Criticism.

A third by Sophocles: The perfect Athenian Tragedy.

The New Comedy, or Comedy of Manners.

First Variety. The Tragedy proper.　*Second Variety.* The Satyrical Drama.　*Third Variety.* The History.　*Fourth Variety.* The Tragi-comedy.

APPENDIX TO CHAPTER V.

A. W. SCHLEGEL'S GENERAL SURVEY OF THE DRAMA IN DIFFERENT AGES AND COUNTRIES.

*   *   *   *   *   *   *   *

IT is well known that about three and a half centuries ago the study of ancient literature was revived by the diffusion of the Greek language (the Latin never became extinct); the classical authors were brought to light and rendered universally accessible by the art of printing; the monuments of ancient genius were diligently disinterred. All this supplied manifold excitements to the human mind, and formed a marked epoch in the history of our mental culture; it was fertile in effects, which extend even to us, and will extend to an incalculable series of ages. But at the same time the study of the ancients was perverted to a deadly abuse. The learned, who were chiefly in possession of it, and were incompetent to distinguish themselves by works of their own, asserted for the ancients an unconditional authority; in fact with great show of reason, for in their kind they are models. They maintained that only from imitation of the ancient writers is true salvation for human genius to be hoped for; in the works of the moderns they appreciated only what was, or seemed to be similar to those of the ancients; all else they rejected as barbarous degeneracy. Quite otherwise was it with the great poets and artists. Lively as might be the enthusiasm with which the ancients inspired them, much as they might entertain the design of vying with them, still their independence and originality of mind constrained them to strike out into their own path, and to impress upon their productions the stamp of their own genius. Thus fared it, even before that revival. with Dante, the father of modern poetry; he avouched that he took Virgil as his teacher, but produced a work which, of all mentionable works, most differs in its make from the *Æneid*, and in our opinion very far surpassed his fancied master in power, truth, compass, and profoundness. So was it likewise, at a later period, with Ariosto, who has perversely been compared with Homer: nothing can be more unlike. So, in art, with Michel-Angelo and Raphael, who nevertheless were unquestionably great connoisseurs in the antiques. As the poets for the most part had their share of scholarship, the consequence was a schism in their own minds between the natural bent of their genius and the obligation of an imaginary duty. Where they sacrificed to the latter, they were commended by the learned; so far as they followed the bent of the former, they were favourites with the people. That the heroic lays of a Tasso and a Camoens still survive on the lips of their fellow-countrymen is assuredly not owing to their imperfect affinity with Virgil, or even with Homer; in Tasso it is the tender feeling of chivalrous love and honour, in Camoens the glowing inspiration of patriotic enthusiasm.

Those ages, nations, and ranks which found the imitation of the ancients most to their liking were precisely such as least felt the want of a self-formed poetry. The result was dead school-exercises, which at best can excite but a frigid admiration. Bare imitation in the fine arts is always fruitless of good: even what we borrow from others must, as it were, be born again within us if ever it is to issue forth in the nature of poetry. What avails the dilettantism of composing with other people's ideas? Art cannot subsist without Nature, and man can give his fellow-men nothing but himself.

Genuine successors of the ancients and true co-rivals with them, walking in their path and working in their spirit by virtue of congenial talents and cultivation of mind, have ever been as rare as your handi-craftsmanlike insipid copyists were and are numerous. The critics, bribed to their verdict by the mere extrinsicality of form, have for the most part very liberally sanctioned even these serviles. These were "correct modern classics," while the great and truly living popular poets, whom a nation, having once got them, would not consent to part with, and in whom moreover there were so many sublime traits that could not be overlooked, these they were fain at most to tolerate as rude wild geniuses. But the unconditional separation thus taken for granted between genius and taste is an idle evasion. Genius is neither more nor less than the faculty of electing, unconsciously in some measure, whatever is most excellent, and therefore is *taste* in its highest activity.

Pretty much in this way matters proceeded until, no long time since, some thinking men, especially Germans, set themselves to adjust the misunderstanding, and at once to give the ancients their due, and yet fairly recognise the altogether different peculiarity of the moderns. They did not take fright at a seeming contradiction. Human nature is indeed in its basis one and indivisible, but all investigation declares that this cannot be predicated in such a sense concerning any one elementary power in all nature, as to exclude a possibility of divergence into two opposite directions. The whole play of vital motion rests upon attraction and repulsion. Why should not this phenomenon recur on the great scale in the history of mankind likewise? Perhaps in this thought we have discovered the true key to the ancient and modern history of poetry and the fine arts. They who assumed this invented for the characteristic spirit of *modern* art, as contrasted to the *antique* or *classical*, the designation *romantic*. And not an inappropriate term either: the word is derived from *romance*, the name originally given to the popular languages which formed themselves by intermixture of the Latin with the dialects of the Old-German, in just the same way as modern culture was fused out of the foreign elements of the northern national character and the fragments of antiquity, whereas the culture of the ancients was much more of one piece.

This hypothesis, thus briefly indicated, would carry with it a high degree of self-evidence, could it be shown that the self-same contrast between the endeavour of the ancients and moderns does symmetrically, I might say systematically, pervade all the manifestations of the artistic and poetic faculty, so far as we are acquainted with the phases of ancient mind : that it reveals itself in music, sculpture, painting, architecture, &c., the same as in poetry: a problem which still remains to be worked out in its entire extent and compass, though much has been excellently well remarked and indicated in respect of the individual arts.

To mention authors who have written in other parts of Europe, and prior to the rise of this "School" in Germany,—in music, Rousseau recognised the contrast, and showed that rhythm and melody were the prevailing principle of the ancient, as harmony is of the modern music. But he is contracted enough to reject the latter ; in which we cannot at all agree with him. With respect to the arts of design, Hemsterhuys makes a clever apophthegm : "The ancient painters seem to have been too much sculptors, the modern sculptors are too much painters." This goes to the very heart of the matter ; for, as I shall more expressly prove in the sequel, the spirit of all ancient art and poetry is *plastic*, as that of the modern is *picturesque*.

I will endeavour, by means of an example borrowed from another art, that of architecture, to illustrate what I mean by this harmonious recognition of seeming opposites. In the Middle Ages there prevailed, and in the latter centuries of that era developed itself to the most perfect maturity, a style of architecture which has been denominated *Gothic*, but ought to have been called *Old-German*. When, upon the revival of classic antiquity in general, imitation of the Grecian architecture came up, which often indeed was but too injudiciously applied, without regard had to difference of climate and to the destination of the edifices, the zealots for this new taste condemned the Gothic style altogether, reviled it as tasteless, gloomy, barbarous. In the Italians, if anywhere, this was excusable : considering their many hereditary remains or ancient structures, and also their climatical affinity with the Greeks and Romans, partiality for ancient architecture lay, as it were, in their very blood. But we northern people are not to be so easily talked out of those powerful, solemn impressions which fall upon us at the very entering into a Gothic cathedral. Rather we will endeavour to account for these impressions, and to justify them. A very little attention will satisfy us that the Gothic architecture bespeaks not only extraordinary mechanical skill, but a marvellous outlay of inventive genius ; upon still closer contemplation we shall recognise its profound significance, and perceive that it forms a complete finished system in itself quite as much as does that of the Greeks.

To apply this to the matter in hand. The Pantheon is not more different from Westminster Abbey or St. Stephen's in Vienna than is the structure of a tragedy of Sophocles from that of a play of Shakespeare. The comparison between these miracles of poetry and architecture might be carried out still further. But really does admiration of the one necessitate us to have a mean esteem of the other ? Cannot we admit that each in its own kind is great and admirable, though *this* is and is meant to be, quite another thing from *that?* It were worth making the attempt. We do not wish to argue any man out of his preference for the one or the other. The world is wide, and has room enough in it for many things that differ, without their interfering with one another. But a preference originating in views directed to one side alone of the question, a preference conceived one knows not why nor wherefore, is not what makes a connoisseur. No: the true connoisseur is he who can suspend his mind, free and unconstrained, in liberal contemplation of discrepant principles and tendencies, renouncing the while his own individual partialities.

It might suffice for our present purpose to have thus barely indicated the existence of this striking contrast between the antique or classical and the romantic. But as exclusive admirers of the ancients still persist in maintaining that every deviation from these models is a mere whim of the "new school" of critics, who speak in a mysterious way about it, but cannot manage to make it dependent upon any valid idea, I will endeavour to give an explanation of the origin and spirit of the *romantic*, and then let it be determined whether the use of the term and recognition of the thing be thereby justified.

The mental culture of the Greeks was a finished education in the school of nature. Of a beautiful and noble race, gifted with impressible senses and a cheerful spirit, under a mild sky, they lived and bloomed in perfect health of being, and, favoured by a rare combination of circumstances, achieved all that could be achieved by the limitary creature man. Their whole system of art and poetry is the manifestation of this harmony of all powers. They invented the poetry of joy.

Their religion consisted in deification of nature in its various powers, and of the earthly life: but this worship, which fancy, among other nations, darkened with hideous shapes hardening the heart to cruelty, assumed among this people a form of grandeur, dignity, and mildness. Here superstition, elsewhere the tyrant of human endowments, seemed glad to lend a hand to their most free development; it cherished the art by which it was adorned, and out of idols grow *ideals*.

But greatly as the Greeks succeeded in the Beautiful, and even the Moral, we can concede to their culture no higher character than that of a refined and dignified sensuality. Of course this must be understood in the general and in the gross. Occasional dim forebodings of philosophers, lightning gleams of poetic inspiration, these form the exception. Man can never altogether turn his back upon the Infinite; some evanid recollections will testify of the home he has lost; but the point to be considered is, what is the predominant tendency of his endeavours?

Religion is the root of man's being. Were it possible for him to renounce all religion, even that which is unconscious and independent of the will, he would become all surface, no heart nor soul. Shift this centre in any degree, in the same degree will the system of the mind and affections be modified in its entire line of effect.

And this was brought about in Europe by the introduction of Christianity. This sublime and beneficent religion regenerated the decrepit worn-out old world, became the leading principle in the history of the modern nations, and at this day, when many conceit themselves to have out-grown its guidance, they are more influenced by it in their views of all human affairs than they are themselves aware.

Next to Christianity, the mental culture of Europe, since the commencement of the Middle Ages, was decidedly influenced by the German race of northern invaders, who infused new quickening into a degenerated age. The inclemency of northern nature drives the man more inward upon himself, and what is lost in sportive development of the sensitive being is amply compensated, wherever there are noble endowments, in earnestness of spirit. Hence the frank heartiness with which the old German tribes welcomed Christianity; so that among no other race of men has it penetrated so deeply into the inner man, approved itself so energetic in its effects, and so interwoven itself with all human sensibilities.

The rugged but honest heroism of the northern conquerors, by admixture of Christian sentiments, gave rise to *chivalry*, the object of which was to guard the practice of arms, by vows which were looked upon as sacred, from that rude and base abuse of force into which it is so apt to decline.

One ingredient in the chivalrous virtue was a new and more delicate spirit of love, considered as an enthusiastic homage to genuine female excellence, which was now for the first time revered as the acme of human nature, and, exalted as it was by religion under the form of virgin maternity, touched all hearts with an indefinable intimation of the mystery of pure love.

As Christianity did not, like the heathen worship, content itself with certain exterior performances, but laid claim to the whole inner man with all its remotest thoughts and imaginations, the feeling of moral independence took refuge in the domain of *honour;* a kind of secular morality which subsisted along with that of religion, and often came in collision therewith, but yet akin to it in so far as it never calculated consequences, but attached absolute sanctity to principles of action elevated as articles of faith above all inquisition of a misplaced ratiocination.

Chivalry, love, and honour are, together with religion itself, the subjects of that natural poetry which poured itself forth with incredible copiousness in the Middle Ages, and preceded a more conscious and thoughtful cultivation of the romantic spirit. This æra too had its mythology, consisting in chivalrous fables and religious legends, but its marvellous and its heroism formed a perfect contrast to those of the ancient mythology.

Some writers, in other respects agreeing with us in our conception and derivation of the peculiar character of the moderns, have placed the essence of the northern poetry in melancholy, and, rightly understood, we have no objection to this view of the matter.

Among the Greeks, human nature was self-satisfied; it had no misgiving of defect, and endeavoured after no other perfection than that which it actually could attain by the exercise of its own energies. A higher wisdom teaches us that human nature, through a grievous aberration, has lost the position originally assigned to it, and that the sole destination of its earthly existence is to struggle back thither, which, however, left to itself, it cannot.   The old religion of the senses did but wish to earn outward perishable blessings ; immortality, as far as it was believed, stood shadow-like in the obscure distance, a faded dream of this sunny waking life.   Under the Christian view it is just the reverse : the contemplation of the infinite has annihilated the finite ; life has become the world of shadows, the night of being ; the eternal day of essential existence dawns only beyond the grave. Under such a religion, that mysterious foreboding which slumbers in every feeling heart cannot but be wakened into distinct consciousness that we are in quest of a happiness which is unattainable here, that no external object will ever be altogether able to fill the capacity of the soul, that all enjoyment is a fleeting illusion.   And when the soul sits down, as it were, beside these waters of Babylon, and breathes forth its longing aspirations towards the home from which it has become estranged, what else can be the key-note of its songs but heaviness of heart?   And so it is.   The poetry of the ancients was that of possession, ours is that of longing desire ; the one stands firm on the soil of the present, the other wavers betwixt reminiscence of the past and bodeful intimations of the future.   Let not this be understood to imply that all must flow away in monotonous lamentation, the melancholy always uttering itself audibly, and drowning all besides.   As under that cheerful view of things which the Greeks took, that austere Tragedy of theirs was still a possible phenomenon ; so that romantic poetry, which originated in the different views I have been describing, could run along the whole scale of the feelings, even up to the highest note of joy ; but still there will always be an indescribable something in which it shall carry the marks of its origin.   The feeling of the moderns has, on the whole, become more deep and inward, the fancy more incorporeal, the thoughts more contemplative.   To be sure in nature, the boundaries run into one another, and the things are not so sharply defined as one is under the necessity of doing in order to eliminate a theoretical idea.

The Grecian ideal of human nature was, perfect unison and proportion of all powers, *natural harmony*.   The moderns, on the contrary, have arrived at the consciousness of the disunion there is within, which renders such an ideal no longer possible ; hence the endeavour of their poetry is to make these two worlds, between which we feel ourselves to be divided, the world of sense and the world of spirit, at one with each other, and to blend them indissolubly together.   The impressions of sense shall be hallowed, as it were, by their mysterious league with higher feelings, while the spirit will deposit its bodings or indescribable intuitions of the infinite in types and emblems derived from the phenomena of the visible world.

In Grecian art and poetry there is an original unconscious unity of form and matter ; the modern, so far as it has remained faithful to its own proper spirit, attempts to bring about a more thorough interpenetration of both, considered as two opposites.   The former solved its problem to perfection, the latter can satisfy its *ad infinitum* endeavour only in a way of approximation, and, by reason of a certain semblance of incompleteness, is the rather in danger of being misappreciated.

* * * * * * *

What is *dramatic?* To many the answer may seem obvious: "Where different persons are introduced speaking, but the poet himself does not speak in his own proper person." But this is no more than the exterior pre-requisite of the form; the form is that of dialogue. But the persons of a dialogue may express thoughts and sentiments without operating a change on each other, and so may leave off at last each in the same mind as at the beginning; in such a case, however interesting the matter of the discussion may be, it cannot be said to excite any dramatic interest. I will exemplify this in the *philosophic dialogue*, a quiet species of discussion not intended for the stage. In Plato, Socrates asks the inflated sophist Hippias, "What is the beautiful?" He is forthwith prepared with his shallow answer, but presently finds himself compelled by Socrates' ironical objections to abandon his first definition, and stumble about clutching after other ideas, and finally to quit the field, shamed by the exposure of his ignorance, and out of temper at finding more than his match in the philosopher. Now, *this* dialogue is not merely instructive in a philosophical point of view, but entertaining as a drama in miniature. And justly has this lively progress in the thoughts, this stretch of expectation for the issue, in one word, this dramatic character, been extolled in the dialogues of Plato.

Hence already we are in a condition to apprehend wherein the great charm of dramatic poetry consists. Activity is the true enjoyment of life, nay more, is life itself. Mere passive enjoyments may lull into a listless complacency, which, however, if there be any stirrings of interior sensibility, cannot long be free from the inroad of ennui. Now, most people by their position in life, or, it may be, from incapacity for extraordinary exertions, are tethered within a narrow round of insignificant engagements. Day follows day, one like another, under the sleepy rule of custom; life progresses without perceptible motion, the rushing stream of the youthful passions stagnating into a morass. From the self-dissatisfaction which this occasions they seek to make their escape in all kinds of games, which always consist in some occupation, some self-imposed task, in which there are difficulties to be overcome, but withal not troublesome. Now of all games the *play* is unquestionably the most entertaining. We see others act, if we cannot act to any great purpose ourselves. The highest subject of human activity is man, and in the play we see men measuring their powers upon each other as friends or foes; influencing each other in their capacity of rational and moral beings, through the medium of opinion, sentiment, and passion; definitely ascertaining their mutual relations, and bringing them to a decisive position. By abstraction and pretermission of all that is not essential to the matter in hand, namely, of all those daily wants and consequent petty distractions which in real life break in upon the progress of essential actions, the poet contrives to condense within small compass much that excites attention and expectation. Thus he gives us a picture of life that resuscitates the days of youth, an extract of what is moving and progressive in human existence.

But this is not all. Even in lively oral narration it is common to introduce the persons speaking, and to vary tone and expression accordingly. But the gaps which these speeches would leave in the hearers' mental picture of the story the narrator fills up by a description of the concomitant actions or other incidents, in his own name. The dramatic poet foregoes this assistance, but finds abundant compensation in the following invention. He requires that each of the characters of his story should be personated by a living individual; that this individual should, in sex, age, and form, come as near as may be to the fictitious individual of the story, nay, should assume his entire personality; that he should accompany every speech with the appropriate expression of voice, mien, and gesture, and moreover annex thereto those visible actions, of which otherwise the audience would need to be apprised by narrative. Still further: these vicegerents of the creatures of his imagination are required to appear in the costume belonging to their assumed rank, and to the times and country in which they lived: partly for the sake of closer resemblance: partly because even in dress there is something characteristic. Lastly, he requires that they should be environed by a locality in some measure similar to that in which he makes the incidents to have taken place, because this also helps to realise the fiction; that is to say, he will have scenery. Now here is a *theatre* complete. It is plain that the very form of dramatic poetry, that is, the exhibition of an action by dialogue without the aid of narrative, implies the theatre as the necessary complement. We grant, there are dramatic works not originally designed for the stage, and indeed not likely to be particularly effective there, which nevertheless read excellently. But I very greatly question whether they would make the same vivid impression upon a reader who had never witnessed a play nor heard one described. We are habituated, in reading dramatic compositions, to fancy to ourselves the acting.

The invention of the theatre and theatrical art seems a very obvious and natural one. Man has a great turn for mimic imitation; in all lively transposing of himself into the situation, sentiments, and passions of others, he assimilates himself to them in his exterior, whether he will or no. Children are perpetually going out of themselves; it is one of their favourite sports to copy the grown people they have opportunity of observing, or indeed whatever else comes into their heads; and with their happy pliancy of imagination, they can make all alike serve their turn, to furnish them with the insignia of the assumed dignity, be it that of a father, a schoolmaster, or a king. There remains but one step more to the invention of the Drama: namely, to draw the mimic elements and fragments clear off from real life, and confront the latter with these collectively in one mass; yet in many nations this step never was taken. In the very copious description of ancient Egypt in Herodotus and others, I do not recollect any indication of this. The Etruscans on the contrary, so like the Egyptians in many other particulars, had their theatrical games, and, singular enough, the Etruscan term for "actor," *histrio*, has survived in living languages even to the most recent times. The whole of Western Asia, the Arabians and Persians, rich as their poetical literature is in other departments, know not the Drama. Neither did Europe in the Middle Ages: upon the introduction of Christianity the old dramas of the Greeks and Romans were set aside, partly because they had reference to heathen ideas, partly because they had degenerated into shameless immorality; nor did they revive until nearly a thousand years later. So late as the fourteenth century we find in that very complete picture which Boccaccio has given of the then existing frame of society no trace whatever of plays. Instead of them they had simply their *Conteurs, Menestriers*, and *Jongleurs*. On the other hand, it must by no means be supposed that the invention of the Drama was made only once in the world, and was passed along from one nation to another. The English circumnavigators found among the islanders of the Southern Ocean (a people occupying so low a grade in point of intellectual capacity and civilisation) a rude kind of drama, in which a common incident of life was imitated well enough to be diverting. To pass to the other extremity of the world: that nation from which perhaps all the civilisation of the human race emanated, I mean the Indians, had their dramas for ages before that country was subjected to any foreign influence. They possess a copious dramatic literature, the age of which ascends backward nearly two thousand years. Of their plays (Nataks) we are at present acquainted with one specimen only, the charming *Sacontala*, which, with all the foreign colouring of its native climate, in its general structure bears such striking resemblance to our romantic drama, that we might suspect the translator, Sir William Jones, of having laboured to produce the resemblance, out of his partiality for Shakspeare, were not the fidelity of his translation attested by other scholars. In the golden times of India the exhibition of these Nataks delighted the splendid imperial court at Delhi; but under the misery of their many oppressions, dramatic art in that country seems at present to lie extinct. The Chinese, on the contrary, have their standing national theatre: *standing* indeed, it may be conjectured, in every sense: I make no question but in the establishment of arbitrary rules and nice observance of unimportant conventionalities they leave the most correct of the Europeans far behind them.

With all this extensive diffusion of theatrical entertainments, it is surprising to find what a difference there exists in point of dramatic talent between nations equally favoured in other respects. The talent for the Drama would seem to be a peculiar quality, essentially distinct from the gift of poetry in general. The contrast between the Greeks and Romans in this respect is not to be wondered at; for the Greeks were quite a nation of artists, the Romans a practical people. Among the latter, the fine arts were introduced only as a corrupting article of luxury, both betokening and accelerating the degeneracy of the times. This luxury they carried out on so large a scale, in respect of the theatre, that perfection in essentials must have been neglected in the rage for meretricious accessories.   Even among the Greeks dramatic talent was anything but universal: iu Athens the theatre was invented, in Athens it was exclusively brought to perfection.   The Doric dramas of Epicharmus form but an inconsiderable exception to this remark. All the great dramatic geniuses of Greece were born iu Attica, and formed their style at Athens.   Widely as the Grecian race diffused itself, felicitously as it cultivated the fine arts almost wherever it came, yet beyond the bounds of Attica it was fain to admire, without being able to compete with, the productions of the Attic stage.

*   *   *   *   *   *   *   *

BOOK II

LITERARY HISTORY OF THE GREEK DRAMA.

CHAPTER I.

THE GREEK TRAGEDIANS.

SECTION I.

CHŒRILUS, PHRYNICHUS, AND PRATINAS

Use begets Use.
GUESSES AT TRUTH.

As soon as Tragedy had once established itself in Greece, it made very rapid advances to perfection. According to the received dates, the first exhibition of Thespis preceded by ten years only the birth of Æschylus, who in his younger days contended with the three immediate successors of the Icarian. CHŒRILUS began to represent plays in the 64th Ol. 523 B.C.,[1] and in 499 B.C. contended for the prize with Pratinas and Æschylus. It is stated that he contended with Sophocles also, but the difference in their ages renders this exceedingly improbable, and the mistake may easily have arisen from the way in which Suidas mentions the book on the chorus which Sophocles wrote against him and Thespis.[2] It would seem that Tragedy had not altogether departed from its original form in his time, and that the chorus was still satyric, or *tragic* in the proper sense of the word.[3]

---

[1] Χοιρίλος, Ἀθηναῖος, τραγικός, ξδ' ὀλυμπιάδι καθεὶς εἰς ἀγῶνας καὶ ἐδίδαξε μὲν δράματα πεντήκοντα καὶ ρ'. ἐνίκησε δὲ ιγ'. Suidas.

[2] See Näke's *Chœrilus*, p. 7. Suidas : Σοφοκλῆς ἔγραψε λόγον καταλογάδην περὶ τοῦ χοροῦ πρὸς Θέσπιν καὶ Χοιρίλον ἀγωνιζόμενος.

[3] ἡνίκα μὲν βασιλεὺς ἦν Χοιρίλος ἐν Σατύροις. Anonym. *ap. Plotium de Theatris*, p. 2633.

Chœrilus is said to have written 150 pieces,[1] but no fragments have come down to us. The disparaging remarks of Hermeas and Proclus do not refer to him, but to his Samian namesake,[2] and he is mentioned by Alexis[3] in such goodly company, that we cannot believe that his poetry was altogether contemptible. One of his plays was called the Alope, and it appears to have been of a strictly mythical character.[4] Some improvements in theatrical costume are ascribed to him by Suidas and Eudocia.[5]

PHRYNICHUS was the son of Polyphradmon, and a scholar of Thespis.[6] The dates of his birth and death are alike unknown: it seems probable that he died in Sicily.[7] He gained a tragic victory in 511 B.C.[8] and another in 476, when Themistocles was his choragus:[9] the play which he produced on this occasion was probably the Phœnissæ, and Æschylus is charged[10] with having made use of this tragedy in the composition of his Persæ, which appeared four years after, a charge which Æschylus seems to rebut in "the

---

[1] The numbers in Suidas are, however, in this instance, not to bo depended on, as they are not the same in all the MSS.

[2] See Näke's *Chœrilus*, p. 92.

[3] Athen. iv. p. 164 c:

> Ὀρφεὺς ἔνεστιν, Ἡσίοδος, τραγῳδία,
> Χοιρίλος, Ὅμηρος, Ἐπίχαρμος, συγγράμματα
> Παντοδαπά.

[4] Pausan. I. 14, § 3: Χοιρίλῳ δὲ Ἀθηναίῳ δρᾶμα ποιήσαντι Ἀλόπην ἔστ᾽ εἰρημένα Κερκύονα εἶναι καὶ Τριπτόλεμον ἀδελφούς, κ. τ. λ.

[5] οὗτος κατά τινας τοῖς προσωπείοις καὶ τῇ σκευῇ τῶν στολῶν ἐπεχείρησεν.

[6] Φρύνιχος, Πολυφράδμονος, ἢ Μινύρου· οἱ δὲ Χοροκλέους· Ἀθηναῖος, τραγικός, μαθητὴς Θέσπιδος. Suidas in Φρύν.
The first of the names mentioned here for the father of Phrynichus i. the correct one. See *Schol. Arist. Av.* 750; Pausan. x. 31, 2. The name also appears under the form Phradmon. *Prol. Aristoph.* p. xxix.

[7] Clinton, *F. H.* Vol. II. p. xxxi., note (t).

[8] ἐνίκα ἐπὶ τῆς ξζ ὀλυμπιάδος. Suidas.

[9] Ἐνίκησε δὲ [Θεμιστοκλῆς] καὶ χορηγῶν τραγῳδοῖς, μεγάλην ἤδη τότε σπουδὴν καὶ φιλοτιμίαν τοῦ ἀγῶνος ἔχοντος. Καὶ πίνακα τῆς νίκης ἀνέθηκε, τοιαύτην ἐπιγραφὴν ἔχοντα.—Θεμιστοκλῆς Φρεάρριος ἐχορήγει, Φρύνιχος ἐδίδασκεν, Ἀδείμαντος ἦρχεν. Plutarch, in *Themist.* c. v.

[10] By Glaucus, in his work on the subjects of the plays of Æschylus: see *Arg. ad Persas.*

Frogs" of Aristophanes.[1] In 494 B.c. Miletus was taken by the Persians, and Phrynichus, unluckily for himself, selected the capture of that city as the subject of a historical tragedy. The skill of the dramatist, and the recent occurrence of the event, affected the audience even to tears, and Phrynichus was fined 1000 drachmæ for having recalled so forcibly a painful recollection of the misfortunes of an ally.[2] We have already mentioned the introduction of female characters into Tragedy by Phrynichus: he seems, however, to have been chiefly remarkable for the sweetness of his melodies,[3] and the great variety and cleverness of his figure-dances.[4] The Aristophanic Agathon speaks gene-

[1]   ἀλλ' οὖν ἐγὼ μὲν ἐς τὸ καλὸν ἐκ τοῦ καλοῦ
ἤνεγκον αὔθ', ἵνα μὴ τὸν αὐτὸν Φρυνίχῳ
λειμῶνα Μουσῶν ἱερὸν ὀφθείην δρέπων. Ran. 1294—1296.

[2] 'Αθηναῖοι μὲν γὰρ δῆλον ἐποίησαν ὑπεραχθεσθέντες τῇ Μιλήτου ἁλώσει, τῇ τε ἄλλη πολλαχῆ, καὶ δὴ ποιήσαντι Φρυνίχῳ δρᾶμα Μιλήτου ἄλωσιν, καὶ διδάξαντι, ἐς δάκρυά τε ἔπεσε τὸ θέητρον, καὶ ἐζημίωσάν μιν, ὡς ἀναμνήσαντα οἰκήϊα κακά, χιλίῃσι δραχμῇσι· καὶ ἐπέταξαν μηκέτι μηδένα χρᾶσθαι τούτῳ τῷ δράματι. Herod. VI. 21.

[3]   Ἔνθεν, ὡσπερεὶ μέλιττα,
Φρύνιχος ἀμβροσίων
μελέων ἀπεβόσκετο καρπόν, ἀεὶ
φέρων γλυκεῖαν ᾠδάν. Aristoph. Av. 748.

Philocleon, the old Dicast, as we are told by the chorus of his brethren,

ἡγεῖτ' ἂν ᾄδων Φρυνίχου· καὶ γάρ ἐστιν ἀνὴρ
φιλῳδός. Vesp. 269.

And a little before these fellow-dicasts are represented by Bdelycleon as summoning their aged colleague at midnight.

. . . μινυρίζοντες μέλη
ἀρχαιομελισιδωνοφρυνιχήρατα. V. 219.

Παρὰ τὰ μέλη καὶ τὴν Σιδῶνα καὶ τὸν Φρύνιχον καὶ τὰ ἐρατὰ ἔμιξεν, οἷον ἀρχαῖα μέλη Φρυνίχου ἐρατὰ καὶ ἥδεα. . . Φρύνιχος δὲ ἐγένετο τραγῳδίας ποιητής, ὃς ἔγραψε δρᾶμα Φοινίσσας, ἐν ᾧ μέμνηται Σιδωνίων. τὸ δὲ μέλη [τὸ δὲ μέλι?] εἶπε διὰ τὴν γλυκύτητα τοῦ ποιητοῦ. Schol. in loc. " Scribendum—μέλι—cum Suida in ἀρχαῖος et μινυρίζω. Quod Aristarchum in codice suo legisse ex annotatione Scholiastæ cognoscitur. Aves, 748: ἔνθεν ὡσπερεὶ μέλιττα Φρύνιχος κ. τ. λ."—Dindorf. See above, p. 71, note 3.

[4] Plutarch (Symp. III. 9) has preserved part of an epigram, said to have been written by the dramatist himself, in which he thus commemorates the fruitfulness of his fancy in devising figure-dances:

Σχήματα δ' ὄρχησις τόσα μοι πόρεν, ὅσσ' ἐπὶ πόντῳ
Κύματα ποιεῖται χείματι νὺξ ὀλοή.

rally of the beauty of his dramas,[1] though of course they fell far short of the grandeur of Æschylus,[2] and the perfect art of Sophocles. The names of seventeen tragedies attributed to him have come down to us, but it is probable that some of these belonged to the other two writers who bore the same name.

We learn from Suidas the following particulars respecting PRATINAS. He was a Phliasian, the son of Pyrrhonides or Encomius, a tragedian, and the opponent of Chœrilus and Æschylus, when the latter first represented. As we have already stated,[3] he was the first writer of satyrical dramas as a distinct species of entertainment; and we may connect this circumstance with the place of his birth; for Phlius was near Corinth and Sicyon, the cradles of the old tragedies of Arion and Epigenes. On one occasion, while he was acting, his wooden stage gave way, and in consequence of that accident, the Athenians built a stone theatre. He exhibited fifty dramas, of which thirty-two were satyrical. The Phliasians seem to have taken great delight in these performances of their countryman,[4] and according to Pausanias,[5] erected a monument in the market-place in honour of " Aristias, the son of Pratinas, who with his father excelled all except Æschylus in writing satyrical

---

[1] *Thesmophor.* 164 sqq.

[2] The difference between Phrynichus and Æschylus is distinctly stated in several passages of the *Ranæ:*

$$\ldots \tau o \grave{v} s \ \theta \epsilon a \tau \grave{a} s$$
ἐξηπάτα, μωροὺς λαβὼν παρὰ Φρυνίχῳ τραφέντας. 909.

Upon which the Scholiast remarks, ἀπατεὼν γάρ, ὡς ἀφελέστερος ὁ Φρύνιχος.

The same fact is also forcibly declared in the address of the Chorus to Æschylus in the same comedy :

ἀλλ' ὦ πρῶτος τῶν 'Ελλήνων πυργώσας ῥήματα σεμνὰ
καὶ κοσμήσας τραγικὸν λῆρον. 1004.

That the word λῆρος does not imply anything merely comical and ludicrous in the tragedies before Æschylus, is clear from the use of the word ληρεῖν, in v. 923.

[3] Above. p. 75.

[4] See Schneider, *De Orig. Trag.* p. 90.

[5] II. 13.

dramas." Pratinas also wrote Hyporchemes.[1] His son Aristias inherited his father's talents, and competed with Sophocles.[2]

[1] Athen. XIV. p. 617 C: Πρατίνας δὲ ὁ Φλιάσιος, αὐλητῶν καὶ χορευτῶν μισθοφόρων κατεχόντων τὰς ὀρχήστρας, ἀγανακτεῖν τινας ἐπὶ τῷ τοὺς αὐλητὰς μὴ συναυλεῖν τοῖς χοροῖς, καθάπερ ἦν πάτριον, ἀλλὰ τοὺς χοροὺς συνᾴδειν τοῖς αὐληταῖς· ὃν οὖν εἶχε θυμὸν κατὰ τῶν ταῦτα ποιούντων ὁ Πρατίνας ἐμφανίζει διὰ τοῦδε τοῦ ὑπορχήματος. Τίς ὁ θόρυβος ὅδε, κ. τ. λ.

Müller suggests (*Hist. Lit. Gr.* I. p. 295 [390]) that this Hyporcheme may have occurred in a satyrical drama. But we have seen above, pp. 36, 75, that the Satyric corresponded rather to the Pyrrhic than to the Hyporchematic dance.

[2] Auct. *Vit. Sophocl.*

CHAPTER I.

SECTION II.

ÆSCHYLUS.

Et digitis tria tura tribus sub limine ponit.

OVID.

ÆSCHYLUS, the son of Euphorion, was born at Eleusis,[1] in the fourth year of the 63rd Olympiad (B.C. 525). In his boyhood he was employed in a vineyard, and, while engaged in watching the grapes, with his mind full of his occupation, and inspired with reverence for the god of the vintage, felt himself suddenly called upon to follow the bent of his own genius, and contribute to the spectacles which had just been established at Athens in honour of Dionysus.[2]

[1] *Vit. Anonym.*, given in Stanley's edition of this poet, and the Arundel Marble. The invocation to the Eleusinian goddess, which he is made to utter by Aristophanes, may refer to the place of his birth :

Δήμητερ, ἡ θρέψασα τὴν ἐμὴν φρένα,

Εἶναί με τῶν σῶν ἄξιον μυστηρίων. *Ranæ*, 884.

These lines would seem to show that he had been initiated into the mysteries, which is quite at variance with the defence which he set up when accused before the Areopagus. See Clem. Al. quoted below.

[2] Ἔφη δὲ Αἰσχύλος μειράκιον ὂν καθεύδειν ἐν ἀγρῷ φυλάσσων σταφυλάς, καὶ οἱ Διόνυσον ἐπιστάντα, κελεῦσαι τραγῳδίαν ποιεῖν. ὡς δὲ ἦν ἡμέρα (πείθεσθαι γὰρ ἐθέλειν) ῥᾷστα ἤδη πειρώμενος ποιεῖν. οὗτος μὲν ταῦτα ἔλεγεν. Pausan. I. 21, 2.

To this employment of the poet were probably owing the habits of intemperance with which he has been charged, and also his introduction on the stage of characters in a state of drunkenness. Athenæus tells us (X. p. 428) : Καὶ τὸν Αἰσχύλον ἐγὼ φαίην ἂν τοῦτο διαμαρτάνειν· πρῶτος γὰρ ἐκεῖνος καὶ οὐχ, ὡς ἔνιοί φασιν, Εὐριπίδης παρήγαγε τὴν τῶν μεθυόντων ὄψιν εἰς τραγῳδίαν. ἐν γὰρ τοῖς Καβείροις εἰσάγει τοὺς περὶ τὸν Ἰάσονα μεθύοντας. ἃ δ' αὐτὸς ὁ τραγῳδιοποιὸς ἐποίει, ταῦτα τοῖς ἥρωσι περιέθηκε· μεθύων γοῦν ἔγραφε τὰς τραγῳδίας· διὸ καὶ Σοφοκλῆς αὐτῷ μεμφόμενος ἔλεγεν ὅτι, Ὦ Αἰσχύλε, εἰ καὶ τὰ δέοντα ποιεῖς, ἀλλ' οὖν οὐκ εἰδώς γε ποιεῖς· ὡς ἱστορεῖ Χαμαιλέων ἐν τῷ περὶ Αἰσχύλου. The same observation of Sophocles is given in the same words, I. p. 22, and is probably taken, as Welcker suggests (*Tril.* p. 254, note) from Sophocles' treatise on the chorus.

He made his first appearance as a tragedian in B.C. 499,[1] when, as we have already stated, he contended with Chœrilus and Pratinas. Nine years after this he distinguished himself in the battle of Marathon,[2] along with his brothers Cynegeirus and Ameinias, and the poet, who prided himself upon his valour more than upon his genius, looked back to this as to the most glorious action of his life.[3] In 484 B.C. he gained his first tragic victory, and in 480 B.C. took part in the battle of Salamis, in which Ameinias gained the ἀριστεῖα: he also fought at Platæa. He celebrated the glorious contests which he had witnessed in a tragic trilogy, with which he gained the prize (472 B.C.).[4] After all that has been written on the subject,[5] we are of opinion that Æschylus made only two journeys to Sicily. The first was in 468 B.C. according to the express testimony of Plutarch;[6] and took place immediately after his defeat

---

This failing is also mentioned by Plutarch : καὶ τὸν Αἰσχύλον φασὶ τραγῳδίας πίνοντα ποιεῖν καὶ διαθερμαινόμενον. *Symp.* I. 5 ; by Callisthenes : οἱ γάρ, ὡς τὸν Αἰσχύλον ὁ Καλλισθένης ἔφη που, λέγων τὰς τραγῳδίας ἐν οἴνῳ γράφειν, ἐξορμῶντα καὶ ἀναθερμαίνοντα τὴν ψυχήν. Lucian, *Encom. Demosth.* ; and by Eustathius, *Odyss.* θ'. p. 1598.

That he subsequently departed from his original reverence for the religion of Bacchus, we shall show in the text, and this was probably occasioned by his military connection with the Dorians, and the love which he then acquired for the Dorian character and institutions.

[1] Suidas in Αἰσχ.
[2] Ἐν μάχῃ συνηγωνίσατο Αἰσχύλος ὁ ποιητὴς [ἐτ]ῶ[ν] ὧν ΔΔΔΠ. *Marm. Arund.* No. 49; *Vit. Anonym.*
[3] Pausan. *Attic.* I. 4; Athenæus, XIV. p. 627. In the epitaph which he is said to have composed for himself, he makes no mention of his tragedies, and speaks only of his warlike achievements :

Αἰσχύλον Εὐφορίωνος Ἀθηναῖον τόδε κεύθει
Μνῆμα καταφθίμενον πυροφόροιο Γέλας.
Ἀλκὴν δ' εὐδόκιμον Μαραθώνιον ἄλσος ἂν εἴποι,
Καὶ βαθυχαιτήεις Μῆδος ἐπιστάμενος.

[4] Gruppe thinks (*Ariadne*, p. 154) that the Prometheus was acted first at Syracuse, and afterwards at Athens, under the poet's own superintendence : the Perscis, which we are here alluding to, first at Athens, and afterwards in Sicily.
[5] By Böckh, *de Græcæ Tragœdiæ Principibus*, c. IV. V.; Blomfield, *Præf. Pers.* pp. xvi. sqq.; Hermann, *de Eumen. Choro*, II. pp. 155 sqq.; Welcker, *Trilogie*, pp. 516 fol.; Lange, *de Æschyli Vitâ*, pp. 15 sqq.
[6] Plutarch, *Cimon*, VIII.

by young Sophocles, though it is difficult to believe Plutarch's assertion, that he left Athens in disgust at this indignity. As, however, it is stated that he went to the court of Hiero,[1] and brought out a play at Syracuse to please that king, who died in 467 B.C., he must, if he was at Athens to contend with Sophocles, have started for Sicily immediately after the decision; and he was then at Athens if Plutarch has given us correct information. He probably spent some time in Sicily on his first visit, as would appear from the numbers of Sicilian words which are found in his later plays.[2] The other journey to Sicily he is said to have made ten years after (458 B.C.), and for this a very sufficient reason has been assigned. In that year he brought out the Orestean trilogy; and in the Eumenides, the last play of the trilogy, showed so openly his opposition to the politics of Pericles and his abettor Ephialtes,[3] that his abode at Athens might easily have been made not only unpleasant, but even unsafe, especially as his fondness for the Dorian institutions, his aristocratical spirit, and his adoption of the politics of Aristeides, had doubtless made him long before obnoxious to the demagogues.

He died at Gela two years after the representation of the

---

[1] Ἀπῆρε δὲ εἰς Ἱέρωνα τὸν Σικελίας τύραννον. *Vit. Anonym.* So Pausanias: Καὶ ἐς Συρακούσας πρὸς Ἱέρωνα Αἰσχύλος καὶ Σιμωνίδης ἐστάλησαν, I. 2. Also Plutarch: Καὶ γὰρ καὶ οὗτος [Αἰσχύλος] εἰς Σικελίαν ἀπῆρε καὶ Σιμωνίδης πρότερον. *De Exilio.*

[2] Οὐκ ἀγνοῶ δέ, ὅτι οἱ περὶ τὴν Σικελίαν κατοικοῦντες ἀσχέδωρον καλοῦσι τὸν σύαγρον. Αἰσχύλος γοῦν ἐν Φορκίσι, παρεικάζων τὸν Περσέα τῷ ἀγρίῳ τούτῳ συΐ, φησίν

Ἔδυ δ' ἐς ἄντρον ἀσχέδωρος ὥς.

Ὅτι δὲ Αἰσχύλος, διατρίψας ἐν Σικελίᾳ πολλαῖς κέχρηται φωναῖς Σικελαῖς, οὐδὲν θαυμαστόν. Athen. IX. p. 402 B.—To the same effect Eustathius: Χρῆσις δέ φασιν ἀσχεδώρου παρ' Αἰσχύλῳ διατρίψαντι ἐν Σικελίᾳ καὶ εἰδότι. *Ad Odyss.* p. 1872.—And Macrobius: " Ita et Dii Palici in Siciliâ coluntur; quos primum omnium Æschylus tragicus, *vir utique Siculus*, in literas dedit," &c., &c. *Saturnal.* v. 19.

Some Sicilian forms are to be found in his extant plays: thus, πεδάρσιος, πεδαίχμιοι, πεδάοροι, μάσσων, μᾶ, &c., for μετάρσιος, μεταίχμιοι, μετέωροι, μείζων, μῆτερ, &c. See Blomfield, *Prom. Vinc.* 277, *Gloss.*, and Böckh, *de Trag. Græc. c.* v.

[3] See Müller's *Eumeniden*, § 35 fol.

Orestea, i. e. in B. C. 456.[1] It is said,[2] that an eagle having mistaken his bald head for a stone, dropped a tortoise upon it in order to break the shell, and that the poet was killed by the blow; but the story is evidently an invention, most unnecessarily devised to account for the natural death of a persecuted exile nearly seventy years old.

Another reason has been assigned for Æschylus' second journey to Sicily. It is founded on a statement, alluded to by Aristotle,[3] and given more distinctly by Clemens Alexandrinus and Ælian,[4] that Æschylus was accused of impiety before the Areopagus, and acquitted, as Ælian says, in consequence of the services of his brother Ameinias, or, according to Aristotle and Clemens, because he pleaded ignorance. Eustratius tells us[5] from Heraclides Ponticus that he would have been slain on the stage by the infuriated populace had he not taken refuge at the altar of Bacchus; and that he was acquitted by the Areopagus in consequence of his brother *Cynegeirus'* intercession. This reason for his second departure from Athens is quite in accordance with the former; for if he had incurred the ill-will of the people and the demagogues, nothing was more natural than that

[1] Ἀφ' οὗ Αἰσχύλος ὁ ποιητής, βιώσας ἔτη [Δ]ΔΠΙΙΙΙ, ἐτελεύτησεν ἐν [Γέλ]ᾳ τῆς [Σι]κελίας ἔτη Η[Δ]ΔΔΔΙΙΙ, ἄρχοντος Ἀθήνησι Καλλίου τοῦ προτέρου. *Mar. Arund.* No. 50.

[2] *Vit. Anonym.*; Suidas in Χελώνη μυῶν; Valer. Max. IX. 2; Ælian, *Hist. Animal.* VII. 16.

[3] *Ethic.* III. 1 : ὃ δὲ πράττει, ἀγνοήσειεν ἄν τις· οἷον λέγοντές φασιν ἐκπεσεῖν αὐτούς, ἢ οὐκ εἰδέναι ὅτι ἀπόρρητα ἦν, ὥσπερ Αἰσχύλος τὰ μυστικά.

[4] Αἰσχύλος (says Clemens) τὰ μυστήρια ἐπὶ σκηνῆς ἐξειπών, ἐν Ἀρείῳ πάγῳ κριθεὶς οὕτως ἀφείσθη, ἐπιδείξας αὐτὸν μὴ μεμυημένον. *Strom.* II.— Ælian tells the tale in a somewhat different way; a more romantic one of course: Αἰσχύλος ὁ τραγῳδὸς ἐκρίνετο ἀσεβείας ἐπί τινι δράματι. Ἑτοίμων οὖν ὄντων Ἀθηναίων, βάλλειν αὐτὸν λίθοις, Ἀμεινίας ὁ νεώτερος ἀδελφός, διακαλυψάμενος τὸ ἱμάτιον ἔδειξε τὴν πῆχυν ἔρημον τῆς χειρός. Ἔτυχε δὲ ἀριστεύων ἐν Σαλαμῖνι ὁ Ἀμεινίας ἀποβεβληκὼς τὴν χεῖρα, καὶ πρῶτος Ἀθηναίων τῶν ἀριστείων ἔτυχεν. Ἐπεὶ δὲ εἶδον οἱ δικασταὶ τοῦ ἀνδρὸς τὸ πάθος, ὑπεμνήσθησαν τῶν ἔργων αὐτοῦ καὶ ἀφῆκαν τὸν Αἰσχύλον. *Var. Hist.*, V. 19.

[5] In his commentary on Aristotle, *loc. cit.* fol. 40. He mentions the names of five plays on which these charges were founded, the Τοξότιδες, the Τερείας, the Σίσυφος πετροκυλιστής, the Ἰφιγένεια, and the Οἰδίπους. But we know nothing of the dates of these plays. Comp. Welcker, *Tril.* 106, 276.

he should have been made amenable to the same charges which a similar faction afterwards brought against Alcibiades.[1] And there is something in the intervention of the Areopagus between the people and their intended victim, which may at once account for the attempt to overthrow it, which, we conceive, shortly followed this trial, as also for the bold stand which Æschylus made on behalf of that tribunal.

There are great discrepancies respecting the number of plays written by Æschylus. The writer of the life prefixed to his remains assigns seventy plays to him, Suidas ninety, and Fabricius more than one hundred. Of these only seven remain.

The most remarkable improvements which Æschylus introduced into Tragedy are the following: he added a second actor, limited the functions of the chorus, and gave them a more artificial character: he made the dialogue, which he created by the addition of a second actor, the principal part of the drama:[2] he provided his Tragedy with all sorts of imposing spectacles,[3] and introduced the custom of contending with Trilogies, or with three plays at a time. He seems also to have improved the theatrical costumes, and to have made the mask more expressive and convenient, while he increased the stature of the performers by giving

---

[1] Thucyd. VI. 53; Andocid. *de Myster.* Comp. Droysen, in the *Rhein. Museum* for 1835, pp. 161 fol.

[2] These first three improvements are stated by Aristotle, *Poet.* c. IV. 16 (below, Part II.): καὶ τό τε τῶν ὑποκριτῶν πλῆθος ἐξ ἑνὸς εἰς δύο πρῶτος Αἰσχύλος ἤγαγε, καὶ τὰ τοῦ χοροῦ ἠλάττωσε καὶ τὸν λόγον πρωταγωνιστὴν παρεσκεύασε. The first is given also by Diogen. Laert. *Vit. Plat.*: Θέσπις ἕνα ὑποκριτὴν ἐξεῦρεν. . καὶ δεύτερον Αἰσχύλος. The names of his two actors are given in an old life prefixed to one of the editions. Ἐχρήσατο δὲ ὑποκριτῇ πρῶτον μὲν Κελάνδρῳ. . .δεύτερον αὐτῷ πρόσηψε Μιόνισκον τὸν Χαλκιδέα. Hermann has made an extraordinary blunder with regard to the latter part of the quotation from Aristotle: he has actually supposed that πρωταγωνιστήν is an epithet, though it is obvious from the position of the article that it is a tertiary predicate (Donalds. *Gr. Gr.* 489 sqq.), and is used tropically, just as Aristotle elsewhere uses χορηγεῖν, &c., metaphorically. Compare Plut. *Mus.* p. 667, Wyttenb.: πρωταγωνιστούσης τῆς ποιήσεως, τῶν δ' αὐλητῶν ὑπηρετούντων τοῖς διδασκάλοις.

[3] "Primum Agatharchus Athenis, Æschylo docente tragœdiam, scenam fecit, et de eâ commentarium reliquit." Vitruv. Præf. Lib. VII.

them thick-soled boots (ἀρβύλαι κόθορνοι[1]). In short he did so much for the drama, that he was considered as the father of Tragedy,[2] and his plays were allowed to be acted after his death.[3]

We shall find, in the remaining Tragedies of Æschylus, most ample confirmation of what we have said respecting

[1] " Post hunc [Thespin] personæ pallæque repertor honestæ
Æschylus, et modicis instravit pulpita tignis,
Et docuit magnumque loqui, nitique cothurno."

Horat. *Epist. ad Pis.* 279.

So Suidas: Αἰσχύλος εὗρε προσωπεῖα δεινὰ καὶ χρώμασι κεχρισμένα ἔχειν τοὺς τραγικούς, καὶ ταῖς ἀρβύλαις, ταῖς καλουμέναις ἐμβάταις, κεχρῆσθαι. The Aristophanic Æschylus alludes to these improvements in the costumes. *Ran.* 1060. Compare Athen. I. p. 21, and Philost. *Vit. Apoll.* VI. 11: ἐσθήμασί τε πρῶτος ἐκόσμησεν ἃ πρόσφορον ἥρωσί τε καὶ ἡρωῖσιν ἠσθῆσθαι. *Vit. Gorg.* I. 9: ἐσθῆτί τε τὴν τραγῳδίαν κατασκευάσας καὶ ὀκρίβαντι ὑψηλῷ καὶ ἡρώων εἴδεσιν. There are many allusions to the ἀρβύλαι of the actors in the Greek Tragedians themselves.

[2] —Ὅθεν Ἀθηναῖοι πατέρα μὲν αὐτὸν τῆς τραγῳδίας ἡγοῦντο. Philost. *Vit. Apoll.* VI. 11. And thus the Chorus in the *Ranæ* address him :

Ἀλλ' ὦ πρῶτος τῶν Ἑλλήνων πυργώσας ῥήματα σεμνά,
Καὶ κοσμήσας τραγικὸν λῆρον. v. 1004.

So Quintilian : "Tragœdias *primus* in lucem Æschylus protulit." x. 1.
[3] "Ἐκάλουν δὲ καὶ τεθνεῶτα εἰς Διονύσια. Τὰ γὰρ τοῦ Αἰσχύλου ψηφισαμένων ἀνεδιδάσκετο, καὶ ἐνίκα ἐκ καινῆς. Philostr. *Vit. Apoll.* VI. 11.—Also, *Vit. Anonym.*—Aristophanes alludes to this custom of re-exhibiting the dramas of Æschylus in the opening of the *Acharnians*, where Dicæopolis complains :

ἀλλ' ὠδυνήθην ἕτερον αὖ τραγῳδικόν,
ὅτε δὴ κεχήνη προσδοκῶν τὸν Αἰσχύλον,
ὁ δ' ἀνεῖπεν· 'εἴσαγ', ὦ Θέογνι, τὸν χορόν.' v. 9 &c.

Upon which the Scholiast remarks: τιμῆς δὲ μεγίστης ἔτυχε παρὰ Ἀθηναίοις ὁ Αἰσχύλος, καὶ μόνου αὐτοῦ τὰ δράματα ψηφίσματι κοινῷ καὶ μετὰ θάνατον ἐδιδάσκετο. The allegation of the poet (*Ranæ*, 868):

Ὅτι ἡ ποίησις οὐχὶ συντέθνηκέ μοι,

is also supposed by the Scholiast to refer to this decree. Quintilian assigns a very different reason for this practice, when, speaking of Æschylus as 'rudis in plerisque et incompositus,' he goes on, '*propter quod correctas* ejus fabulas in certamen deferre posterioribus poetis Athenienses permisere, suntque eo modo multi coronati.' x. 1. What authority he had for such an assertion does not now appear." Former Editor.

his political opinions, and also of Cicero's statement, that he was a Pythagorean.[1] Even the improvements which are due to him are so many proofs of his anti-democratical spirit. For though he seems to have first turned his attention to the drama, in consequence of his accidental connection with the country worship of Bacchus, yet in all his innovations we shall detect a wish to diminish the choral or Bacchic element of the Tragedy, and to aggrandise the other part, by connecting it with the old Homeric Epos, the darling of the aristocracy: indeed he used to say himself, that his dramas were but dry scraps from the great banquets of Homer,[2] and it was owing to this that he borrowed so little from the Attic traditions, or from the Heracleia and Theseis, of which Sophocles and Euripides afterwards so freely availed themselves.[3] We have another proof of his willingness to abandon all reference to the worship of Bacchus in his way of treating the dithyrambic chorus, which the state gave him as the basis of his Tragedy. He did not keep all this chorus of fifty men on the stage at once, but broke it up into subordinate choruses, one or more of which he employed in each play of his Trilogy.[4] Even his improvement of the costume was a part of the same plan; for the more appropriate he made the costumes

[1] "Veniat Æschylus, non poeta solum, sed etiam Pythagoreus; sic enim accepimus." Cicero. *Tusc. Disp.* II. 9.

"In philosophical sentiments, Æschylus is said to have been a Pythagorean. In his extant dramas the tenets of this sect may occasionally be traced; as deep veneration in what concerns the gods, *Agam.* 360; high regard for the sanctity of an oath and the nuptial bond, *Eumen.* 208; the immortality of the soul, *Choëph.* 320; the origin of names from imposition, and not from nature, *Agam.* 683; *Prom. V.* 85, 852; the importance of numbers, *Prom. Vinct.* 457; the science of physiognomy, *Agam.* 769; and the sacred character of suppliants, *Suppl.* 342; *Eum.* 226." Former Editor.

Comp. a paper in the *Class. Journal*, No. XXII. pp. 207 fol. "On the Philosophical sentiments of Æschylus."

[2] Athen. VIII. p. 347 E: τὰ τοῦ καλοῦ καὶ λαμπροῦ Αἰσχύλου ὃς τὰς αὑτοῦ τραγῳδίας τεμάχη εἶναι ἔλεγε τῶν Ὁμήρου μεγάλων δείπνων.

[3] See Welcker, *Trilogie*, p. 484. In style and representation, however, Sophocles was much more Homeric than Æschylus, who probably paid attention only to the mythical materials in general, and according to their Epic connection. *Trilogie*, p. 485.

[4] See Müller's *Eumeniden*, near the beginning of the first essay.

of his actors, the farther he departed from the dresses worn in the Bacchic processions; which, however, to the last kept their place on the tragic stage.[1] And may not the invention of the Trilogy have been also a part of his attempt to make the λόγος, or theatrical declamation,[2] the principal part in his tragedy (πρωταγωνιστής)? We think we could establish this, if our limits admitted a detailed examination of the principles which governed the composition of an Æschylean Trilogy:[3] at present we shall merely suggest that the invention of a πρόλογος and a ῥῆσις, attributed to Thespis, points to two entrances only of the Thespian actor; and that the τριλογία, in its old sense, may have been originally a πρόλογος, and two λόγοι or ῥήσεις, instead of one; consequently, an increase of business for the ὑποκριτής. Now, when Æschylus had added a second actor, each of these λόγοι became a διάλογος, or δρᾶμα: and it would be natural enough that Æschylus, if he had the intentions which we have attributed to him, should expand each of these διάλογοι into a complete play, and break up the chorus into three parts, assigning one to each dialogue, and subordinating the whole chorus to the action of the piece. There is something in favour of this view in the probable analogy between the first piece of a Trilogy and the prologue of Thespis, which we consider to have been certainly of less importance than the ῥῆσις. "It is credible," says an ingenious writer,[4] "that when the new Trilogy first came out, only the middle piece received an accurate dialogical and dramatic completion; whereas, on the contrary, the introductory and concluding pieces were less removed from the old form, and besides remained confined to a more moderate compass." This is borne out by all that we know of the earlier Trilogies of Æschylus, in which the first play has generally a prophetic reference to the second; and the

---

[1] *Ibid.* § 32.

[2] That this is the meaning of λόγος, in the passage of Aristotle, is sufficiently clear; for λογεῖον was the stage on which the actor as distinguished from the chorus, performed.

[3] Welcker has done a great deal towards settling this question æsthetically (*Trilogie*, pp. 482—540).

[4] Gruppe, *Ariadne*, p. 147; compare Welcker, *Trilogie*, p. 49c. Hermann (*Opusc.* II. p. 313) admits this of the musical importance.

I

third, though important in a moral and religious point of view, is little more than a finale,[1] whereas all the stirring interest is concentrated in the Middle Tragedy : παντὶ μέσῳ τὸ κράτος Θεὸς ὤπασεν, say the chorus in the Eumenides, and this principle is the key as well to the trilogy of Æschylus as to the morals of Aristotle. Besides, the leading distinction between the Æschylean Tragedy and the Homeric Epos is, that the latter contains an uninterrupted series of events, whereas the former éxhibits the events in detached groups.[2] In this also we are to seek for the relation subsisting between the drama of Æschylus and the plastic arts, of which he was always full, to which he often alludes,[3] and which perhaps he practised himself.[4] Now, in all ages of art the pyramidal group has been considered the most beautiful: the reader need only recall to his mind the Æginetan pediment, the Laocoon, and the most beautiful of Raphael's pictures ; for instance, the upper part of the Transfiguration, the Sistine Madonna, and the *Mater pulcræ dilectionis*. It may have been the object of Æschylus to realise this. But as he always subjoined a satyrical drama to the three Tragedies, and was very eminent in that species

---

[1] See Welcker, *Tril.* pp. 491, 492.

[2] *Ibid.* pp. 486 foll.

[3] For instance, *Agamem.* 233 : πρέπουσά θ' ὡς ἐν γραφαῖς.

405 : εὐμόρφων δὲ κολοσσῶν ἔχθεται χάρις ἀνδρί.

775 : κάρτ' ἀπομούσως ἦσθα γεγραμμένος.

Eumen. 50 : εἶδόν ποτ' ἤδη Φινέως γεγραμμένας

. . . .

. . . .

ῥέγκουσι δ' οὐ πλαστοῖσι φυσιά-
μασιν.

284 : τίθησιν ὀρθὸν ἢ κατηρεφῆ πόδα.

(Comp. Müller, *Eumeniden,* p. 112).

Supplices, 279 : Κύπριος χαρακτήρ τ' ἐν γυναικείοις τύποις
εἰκὼς πέπληκται τεκτόνων πρὸς ἀρσένων.

458 : νέοις πίναξι βρέτεα κοσμῆσαι τάδε.

[4] This is implied in the improvements which he made in the masks, dresses, &c.

of composition,[1] he must have aimed, in his Trilogies, rather at internal symmetry than at external completeness.

But, in addition to all these evidences, from the general form of the Tragedies of Æschylus, of a Dorian spirit warring against their once Dorian element, the chorus; there is no lack of passages in his plays which point directly to his fondness for the Dorians[2] and for Aristeides,[3] and which show that the maxims of Solon were deeply engraved on his memory.[4] It is also highly interesting to trace in his few remaining Tragedies the frequently occuring allusions to his military and other public employments. For as we easily detect in the writer of the Divina Commedia the stern Florentine, who charged in the foremost ranks of the Guelfian chivalry at the battle of Campaldino,[5] so may we at once recognise, in the tone of Æschylus' Tragedies, the high-minded Athenian, the brother of Ameinias and Cynegeirus, whose sword drank the blood of the dark-haired Medes at Marathon and Salamis. His poems are full of military and political terms;[6] he breathes an unbounded contempt for the barbarian prowess,[7] and he introduces on the stage the grotesque monsters whose images he had

[1] As the trilogies were acted early in the year, it is probable that the night began to close in before the last piece and the satyrical drama were over. This may account for Prometheus, the fire-kindler (which was probably a torch-race, Welcker, *Tril.* pp. 120, 507), being the satyrical drama of the *Perseis;* for the torch-procession at the end of the *Eumenides*, and for the conflagration at the end of the *Troades.* Comp. Gruppe, *Ariadne,* p. 361.

[2] Comp. *Pers.* 179, 803   [3] See Müller *Eumeniden,* § 138.

[4] The following is one of many passages in which the words of Solon are nearly repeated by Æschylus.

Solon, p. 80, Bach :

πλούτου δ' οὐδὲν τέρμα πεφασμένον ἀνδράσι κεῖται·
οἳ γὰρ νῦν ἡμῶν πλεῖστον ἔχουσι βίον
διπλάσιον σπεύδουσι· τίς ἂν κορέσειεν ἅπαντας;

Agamemn. 972 : μάλα γάρ τοι τᾶς πολλᾶς ὑγιείας
ἀκόρεστον τέρμα.

[5] "In quella battaglia memorabile e grandissima, che fu a Campaldino, lui giovane e bene stimato si trovò nell' armi combattendo vigorosamente a cavallo nella prima schiera. Aretin. *Vita di Dante,* p. 9.

[6] We allude to such phrases as μακάρων πρύτανις, βασιλῆς δίοποι, στρατιᾶς ἔφοροι, φιλόμαχοι βραβῆς.

[7] For instance, in the *Supplices,* 727, 8, 930 sqq.

often seen among the spoils of the Persians.[1] Even his
high-flown diction is a type of his military character, for
many of his words strike on the ear like trumpet-sounds.
The description given of his language by Aristophanes is
so vivid, and at the same time so true, that we must endeavour to lay it before our readers in an English dress. The
chorus of initiated persons is speaking of the prospect of a
contest between Æschylus and Euripides ; they express their
expectations thus :[2]

Surely unbearable wrath will rise in the thunderer's bosom,
When he perceives his rival in art, that treble-toned babbler,
Whetting his teeth: he will then, driven frantic with anger,
Roll his eye-balls fearfully.

Then shall we have plume-fluttering strifes of helmeted speeches,
Break-neck grazings of galloping words and shavings of actions,
While the poor wight averts the great geniusmonger's
Diction high and chivalrous.

Bristling the stiffened mane of his neck-enveloping tresses,
Dreadfully wrinkling his brows, he will bellow aloud as he utters
Firmly rivetted words, and will tear them up plankwise,
Breathing with a Titan's breath.

Then will that smooth and diligent tongue, the touchstone of verses,
Twisting and twirling about, and moving the snaffle of envy,
Scatter his words, and demolish, with subtle refinement,
Doughty labours of the lungs.

In addition to the many other allusions to nautical
matters in Æschylus, the importance which he attaches to

---

[1] Aristoph. *Ran.* 937 :

οὐχ ἱππαλεκτρυόνας, μὰ Δί, οὐδὲ τραγελάφους ἅπερ σύ,
ἃν τοῖσι περιπετάσμασιν τοῖς Μηδικοῖς γράφουσιν.

[2] Aristoph. *Ran.* 814. It may be as well to remind the student that
Æschylus is here compared to a lion, Euripides to a wild boar. Great
contempt for Euripides is expressed in l. 820, in the opposition of
φωτός applied to him, to ἀνδρός applied to Æschylus ; l. 824 intimates
the difficulty of pronouncing the long words of Æschylus, which are
afterwards compared to trees torn up by the root, as opposed to the
twigs and branches with which the rolling-places were generally
strewed. (904.)

τὸν δ' ἀνασπῶντ' αὐτοπρέμνοις
τοῖς λόγοισιν
ἐμπέσοντα συσκεδᾶν πολ-
λὰς ἀλινδήθρας ἐπῶν.

Zeus Soter, the god of mariners, is of itself a sufficient indication of his seafaring life.[1]

Though Æschylus does not seem to have had much relish for the Dionysian rites or for an elementary worship of Bacchus, he was a highly religious man, and strongly attached to the Dorian idolatry, on which Pythagoras founded his more spiritual and philosophical system of religion.[2]

It is an established fact, that Æschylus borrowed, in his later days, the third actor, and the other improvements of Sophocles. The time at which he adopted the modifications introduced by his younger contemporary is of importance with reference to the chronological arrangement of his extant plays, which it is our next business to consider.

Although it is certain that Æschylus exhibited his Tragedies in tetralogies or connected sets of three with a satyrical after-piece, we have only one of his trilogies, the latest of them, and the satyrical dramas are altogether lost. The other four plays which have come down to us seem to have been the center-pieces of the Trilogies to which they belonged. No one of them can be referred to the first twelve years of his dramatic career. But three of the four exhibit his Tragedy in its original form, with only two speaking persons on the stage; one of them, in the opinion of some critics, leaves it doubtful whether he had as yet adopted the Sophoclean extension of the stage-business; and the three constituting his Trilogy of the *Orestea* give us the Greek Tragedy in the fullest development to which it ever attained.

[1] See Müller, *Eumeniden*, § 94 foll. It appears to us, from the fact mentioned by Strabo (IX. p. 396), that there was a temple of Zeus Soter on the shore of the Peiræus, and from the words of Diphilus (Athen. p. 229 B):

ὑπὸ τοῦτον ὑπέμυξ' (we would read ὑπένυξ') εὐθὺς ἐκβεβηκότα,
τὴν δεξιὰν ἐνέβαλον ἐμνήσθην Διὸς
Σωτῆρος,

that this Zeus Soter was the god of mariners, to whom they offered up their vows immediately on landing. Comp. *Agamemn.* v. 650: τύχη δὲ σωτὴρ ναῦν θέλουσ' ἐφέζετο, and see our note on Pindar, *Olymp.* VIII. 20 sqq. p. 54.

[2] See Müller, *Eumeniden*, u. s. and elsewhere; and Klausen's *Theologumena Æschyli.*—And in connection with the remarks on Æschylus' love of sculpture, see above, p. 25, note 1.

The earliest extant play of Æschylus seems to have been the *Persæ*. It is expressly stated that the tetralogy, to which it belonged, and which consisted of the *Phineus*, the *Persæ*, the *Glaucus Potnieus*, and *Prometheus Pyrcœus*, was performed in the archonship of Menon, B.C. 472.[1] The direct reference to the great events, which had taken place some seven years earlier, places the *Persæ* in the same category with the Μιλήτου Ἅλωσις of Phrynichus; but while the latter commemorated a grievous disaster, Æschylus celebrated glorious victories, and he was enabled, as we may infer from the names of the other plays in the Trilogy, to connect these topics of contemporary interest with a wide field of mythology and vaticination.   The *Phineus*, who gave his name to the introductory drama, was the blind soothsayer, who predicted to the Argonauts the adventures which would befal them in that first attack upon Asia by the Greeks, and it would be easy for the·poet to interweave with this a series of prophecies referring to the glorious overthrow of the counter-expedition of Xerxes. The scene of the extant play, which forms the center-piece of the Trilogy, is laid at Susa, where the Queen-dowager Atossa, prepared for coming disaster by an ominous dream, receives from a Persian messenger the details of the battle of Salamis, and of the retreat of the defeated army across the Strymon. After this the shade of Darius appears, and predicts the battle of Platæa.   The piece concludes with the appearance of Xerxes himself in a most unkingly plight, and he and the chorus pour forth a κόμμος or dirge, deploring the sad consequences of his attempt to subjugate Greece. The third play was called *Glaucus*, and the didascalia states that it was the *Glaucus Potnieus*. There was also another play of Æschylus called the *Glaucus Pontius*, and some scholars have contended that this was the third Tragedy in the Trilogy under consideration.[2] We cannot recognise the necessity for such an alteration of the document as it has come down to us; for there is no more difficulty in con-

---

[1] *Argument. Pers.*: ἐπὶ Μένωνος τραγῳδῶν Αἰσχύλος ἐνίκα Φινεῖ, Πέρσαις, Γλαύκῳ Ποτνιεῖ, Προμηθεῖ.

[2] Welcker, *Tril.* pp. 311 sqq. 471; *Nachtrag*, p. 176; Müller, *Hist. Gr. Lit.* I. p. 425.

necting the *Glaucus Potnieus* with the *Persæ* than there is in establishing a correspondence of plot between the latter and the *Glaucus Pontius*. It is sufficient to remark that the apparition of Darius was evoked for the purpose, as it seems, of predicting the battle of Platæa (vv. 800 sq.). Now Potniæ was on the road from Thebes to Platæa,[1] and the few fragments of the play called *Glaucus Potnieus* certainly do not authorize us in denying that some of the many legends, of which Potniæ was the traditional home, might have been brought into connection with the battle of Platæa. The incident in the fate of Glaucus himself, namely, that he was torn to pieces by his own steeds, is undoubtedly referred to in one of the fragments;[2] and when we remember the dream of Atossa, and how Xerxes is overthrown by the visionary horses which he yokes to his chariot,[3] it is quite conceivable that some prophetical inferences may have been drawn from the downfall of Glaucus in the chariot-race at the funeral games of Pelias.[4] In any case, it is clear that the *Persæ* with its contemporary references stood between two plays which derived their names and probably their action and circumstances from the mythical traditions of ancient Hellas. With regard to the *Persæ* itself, it has been well remarked[5] that "in this instance the scene is not properly Grecian; it is referred by the mind to Susa, the capital of Persia, far eastward even of Babylon, and four months' march from Hellas. Remoteness of space in that case countervailed the proximity in point of time; though it may be doubted whether, without the benefit of the supernatural, it would, even in that case, have satisfied the Grecian taste. And it certainly would not, had the reference of the whole piece not been so intensely Athenian."

The next in point of date of the extant plays of Æschylus was the *Seven against Thebes*, which is stated to have been

[1] Pausan. IX. 8; Strabo, p. 409.
[2] e. g. *Fragm.* 30; see Hermann, *de Æschyli Glaucis*, Opusc. II. p. 63.
[3] *Pers.* 181.
[4] Pausan. VI. 20, § 19. As ταράξιππος, Glaucus may have been serviceable according to Greek superstition in the defeat of the cavalry of Mardonius.
[5] De Quincey, *Leaders in literature and traditional errors affecting them*, p. 66.

acted after the *Persæ*,[1] but must have appeared in the life-
time of Aristeides, who died not later than B.C. 468. For
the beautiful verses respecting Amphiaraus were considered
at Athens to refer to that upright statesman.[2] This play, as
Aristophanes makes its author call it, was truly full of warlike spirit,[3] but its construction is eminently simple. The
dialogue is mainly sustained by Eteocles, the young king
of Thebes, who receives intelligence of the seven champions
about to attack the seven gates of his city, and appoints a
warrior to meet each of them, reserving his brother Polyneices for himself. The play ends with an announcement
of the victory of Thebes ; and Antigone and Ismene, in conjunction with the chorus, pour forth a lament over their two
brothers who have fallen in the fratricidal strife. Antigone,
in particular, declares her resolve to bury Polyneices in
spite of the prohibition of the Theban senate (1017). And
while the first play of the Trilogy, probably the *Œdipus*,
must have developed the circumstances leading to the
paternal curses, to which Eteocles makes such emphatic
reference at the beginning of the *Seven against Thebes* (v. 70),
the fate of Antigone must have been introduced into the
last play, no doubt the *Eleusinians*, the main topic of which
was the interference of Theseus to procure the burial at
Eleutheræ and Eleusis of the Argives who fell before
Thebes.[4]

---

[1] Aristophanes says (*Ran.* 1058): εἶτα διδάξας Πέρσας μετὰ τοῦτο,
speaking of the *Seven against Thebes*, but the Schol. informs us : τὸ δὲ
εἶτα καὶ τὸ μετὰ τοῦτο, οὐ θέλουσιν ἀκούειν πρὸς τὰς διδασκαλίας, ἀλλ'
ἐν ἴσῳ τῷ καὶ τοῦτο ἐδίδαξα καὶ τὸ ἕτερον. And again (*ad v.* 1053): οἱ
Πέρσαι πρότερον δεδιδαγμένοι εἰσίν· εἶτα οἱ ἑπτὰ ἐπὶ Θήβας.

[2] Plut. *Apophthegm. Reg.* p. 186 B (739 Wyttenb.): Αἰσχύλου ποιή-
σαντος εἰς 'Αμφιάραον·

οὐ γὰρ δοκεῖν ἄριστος ἀλλ' εἶναι θέλει,
βαθεῖαν ἄλοκα διὰ φρενὸς καρπούμενος,
ἀφ' ἧς τὰ κεδνὰ βλαστάνει βουλεύματα·

καὶ λεγομένων τούτων πάντες εἰς 'Αριστείδην ἀπέβλεψαν.

[3] *Ran.* 1054: δρᾶμα ποιήσας "Αρεως μεστόν.

[4] Plutarch, *Thes.* c. 29: συνέπραξε δὲ (Θησεὺς) καὶ 'Αδράστῳ τὴν
ἀναίρεσιν τῶν ὑπὸ τῇ Καδμείᾳ πεσόντων, οὐχ, ὡς Εὐριπίδης ἐποίησεν ἐν
τραγῳδίᾳ, μάχη τῶν Θηβαίων κρατήσας, ἀλλὰ πείσας καὶ σπεισάμενος. . .
ταφαὶ δὲ τῶν μὲν πολλῶν ἐν 'Ελευθεραῖς δείκνυνται, τῶν δὲ ἡγεμόνων περὶ

The most contradictory opinions have been maintained
respecting the chronology of the *Prometheus*. For while one
critic contends that it is the oldest of the extant plays of
Æschylus, and was exhibited soon after Ol. 75, 2, B.C. 478,[1]
another eminent scholar says that it "was in all probability
one of the last efforts of the genius of Æschylus, for the
third actor is to a certain extent employed in it."[2] The
reason alleged for this late date of the play—namely, the
assumed employment of a third actor—falls to the ground
when we adopt the probable supposition[3] that Prometheus,
who does not speak during the dialogue between Vulcan
and his coadjutor, Strength, was represented by a lay figure
attached to the rock scenery, behind whose mask the protagonist spoke during the rest of the play. The reasons
which induce us to take a middle course between these con-
flicting opinions and to place the *Prometheus* third among
the extant plays of Æschylus are briefly as follows. The
references to Sicily, the Sicelisms of the language, and the
covert allusions to Sicilian affairs, especially the description
of the great eruption of Ætna,[4] seem to point to an epoch
subsequent to the poet's first visit to Sicily in B.C. 468. On
the other hand, the sarcastic allusions to tyrants and cour-
tiers[5] are not likely to have appeared in a play acted in

Ἐλευσῖνα, καὶ τοῦτο Θησέως Ἀδράστῳ χαρισαμένου. καταμαρτυροῦσι δὲ
τῶν Εὐριπίδου Ἱκετίδων οἱ Αἰσχύλου Ἐλευσίνιοι, ἐν οἷς καὶ ταῦτα λέγων
ὁ Θησεὺς πεποίηται.

[1] G. F. Schömann, *des Æschylos gefesselter Prometheus*, pp. 79 sqq.

[2] Müller, *Hist. Gr. Lit.* I. p. 432.

[3] Welcker, *Tril.* p. 30; Hermann, *Opusc.* II. p. 146; *ad. Æsch.* p. 55.
It is curious that Schömann, who argues for the oldest date of the
Prometheus, disallows this supposition, and imagines that one of the
choreutæ took the part of the third actor (u. s. pp. 85 sqq.). Such a
parachoregema cannot be imagined in the very earliest days of the Greek
Drama.

[4] vv. 367 sqq. :   ἔνθεν ἐκραγήσονταί ποτε
        ποταμοὶ πυρὸς δάπτοντες ἀγρίαις γνάθοις
        τῆς καλλικάρπου Σικελίας λευροὺς γύας.

It is true that this eruption took place B.C. 478, but the description
points to a recent view of the effects rather than to a recent hearsay of
the fact. For the Sicelisms in the *Prometheus* see Blomfield's *Gloss.* 277.
And for allusions to Hiero's affairs, see Droysen's *Translation*, p. 568.

[5] See e. g. 917: σέβου, προσεύχου, θῶπτε τὸν κρατοῦντ' ἀεί.

Sicily, or indeed during the life-time of Hiero, and this consideration will induce us to place the Tragedy after B.C. 467.
But it seems reasonable to conclude that the elaborate description of the subject of another Trilogy[1] would hardly have
been put into the mouth of Prometheus if that series of
plays had been already acted.   And as we shall see that the
Supplices, the center play of the Trilogy about the daughters
of Danaus, must have been performed about B.C. 461, we
must place the *Prometheus* at some time between that date
and the poet's return from Sicily.   If we must fix a particular date, we can suggest none better than the year B.C. 464,
when the news would reach Athens that Themistocles had
entered the service of the Persian king.[2]   The warrior of
Marathon and Salamis, and the friend of Aristeides, would
at such a time with peculiar force utter that abomination of
treason, which the poet puts into the mouth of his chorus.[3]
This noble Tragedy, the *Prometheus bound*, which exhibits
Prometheus fettered to the mountain side, but still defying
the power of Jove and refusing to divulge the oracle of
Themis, on which the continuance of that power depended,
was preceded by *Prometheus the fire-bringer*, in which the
labours of Prometheus on behalf of mankind were fully exhibited, and was followed by *Prometheus unbound*, in which
Prometheus is released by Hercules and reconciled to Jove,
to whom he now discloses the prophecy that Thetis would
give birth to a son more powerful than his father, and so
releases him from the consequences of his intended marriage
with that sea-goddess.

The remaining single play, the *Suppliants*, belonged to a
trilogy, which some have called the *Danais*, and which undoubtedly related to the wholesale murder of 49 of the 50
sons of Ægyptus on their marriage-night.   The first play,
which is supposed to have been the *Ægyptians*, represented
of course the circumstances which led to the flight of Danaus

---

[1] Cf. vv. 830 sqq., with the *Supplices* as it stands.
[2] Themistocles arrived in Persia soon after the death of Xerxes in
B.C. 465, during the influence of Artabanes.   See Clinton, *F. II.* II. p. 40.
[3] 1048 sqq.   τοὺς προδότας γὰρ μισεῖν ἔμαθον,
                         κοὐκ ἔστι νόσος
                         τῆσδ᾽ ἥντιν᾽ ἀπέπτυσα μᾶλλον.

and his 50 daughters from Egypt. The *Suppliants* exhibits the exiles seated before a group of altars at Argos, and shows how they were received by King Pelasgus and his people, and how the attempt of the Egyptian herald, to carry them back to Egypt by force, was resisted by the hospitable Greeks. In the last play, called the *Danaides*, Æschylus must have detailed the feigned reconciliation of the two brothers, the marriage of their two progenies, and its fatal consequences.[1] There is reason to believe that the piece ended, like the *Eumenides*, with a formal trial, or rather with two trials. On the one hand, it seems clear that the 49 homicidal daughters, together with their father, who instigated the deed, were publicly tried at the suit of Ægyptus;[2] and the feeling with which the poet regards their case in the *Suppliants*,[3] leaves it hardly doubtful that they were acquitted on the ground that they had no other means of escaping the incestuous marriage forced upon them by Ægyptus.[4] But if they were justified, Hypermnestra must have been culpable, and there seem to be good grounds for the inference that she was rescued from the dilemma by the intervention of Venus, who is known to have appeared in the play[5] and to have claimed a part of the blame for the universal ἵμερος, to which Hypermnestra yielded when the love for Lynceus made her disobey her father.[6] Whether the play introduced any reference to the device of a foot-race to determine the re-marriage of the

---

[1] See Hermann's paper, *de Æschyli Danaidibus*, Opusc. II. pp. 319 sqq.
[2] Eurip. *Orest.* 862:

οὖ φασὶ πρῶτον Δαναὸν Αἰγύπτῳ δίκας
διδόντ' ἀθροῖσαι λαὸν ἐς κοινὰς ἕδρας.

[3] *Suppl.* 38: πρίν ποτε λέκτρων ὧν Θέμις εἴργει
σφετεριξάμενον πατραδελφείαν
τήνδ' ἀεκόντων ἐπιβῆναι.

[4] Hermann, *Opusc.* II. p. 330.
[5] Athen. p. 600 A: καὶ ὁ σεμνότατος Αἰσχύλος ἐν ταῖς Δαναΐσιν αὐτὴν παράγει τὴν Ἀφροδίτην λέγουσαν·

ἐρᾷ μὲν ἁγνὸς οὐρανὸς τρῶσαι χθόνα, κ.τ.λ.
τῶνδ' ἐγὼ παραίτιος.

[6] *Prom.* 864: μίαν δὲ παίδων ἵμερος θέλξει τὸ μὴ
κτεῖναι σύνευνον.

homicidal widows,[1] there is no means of deciding. It is remarkable that the same verb is used in the *Supplices* to
denote the assignment of a handmaiden to each of the
chorus,[2] and in the story of the mythographer, to denote the
assignment of a husband to each of the 50 cousins.[3] With
regard to the former circumstance, we are not to suppose
that a crowd of 100 dancers appeared in the orchestra or on
the stage. But as the chorus was probably the same in all
three plays, and as reference is made to the number of 50[4]
it is not improbable that the whole number of choreutæ may
have been employed in each play, some of them sustaining
the action on the stage, and others executing dances in the
orchestra. The date of this Trilogy is approximately determined by distinct references in the *Suppliants* to amicable
relations between the popular party at Argos and the
Athenians,[5] and to the anticipated results of a conflict between Greeks and Egyptians.[6] And as the war with Egypt
began in B.C. 462, and the alliance between Athens and
Argos came into operation in B.C. 461, we may fix the latter
year for the performance of this Trilogy.[7]

In these separate plays we see no traces of the employment of a third actor. It has been shown already that a
simple expedient would enable two actors to perform the
introductory scene of the *Prometheus*. Even in the *Supplices*
the Protagonist had only to play Danaus and the Egyptian
herald, and the Deuteragonist had no character to sustain

[1] Pind. ix. *Pyth.* 116; Apollodor. I. 1, 5, § 12.

[2] *Suppl.* 984: τάσσεσθε, φίλαι δμωΐδες, οὕτως
ὡς ἐφ' ἑκάστῃ διεκλήρωσεν
Δαναὸς θεραποντίδα φέρνην.

[3] Apollod. II. 1, 5, § 1: ὡμολόγει τοὺς γάμους καὶ διεκλήρου τὰς κόρας.

[4] *Prometh.* 855; *Suppl.* 316.

[5] *Suppl.* 699: φυλάσσοι τιμίοισι τιμὰς
το δήμιον, τὸ πτόλιν κρατύνει,
προμαθεύς τ' εὐκοινόμητις ἀρχά·
ξένοισί τ' εὐξυμβόλους πρὶν ἐξοπλίζειν Ἄρη,
δίκας ἄτερ πημάτων διδυῖεν.

[6] Cf. 761: βύβλου δὲ κάρπος οὐ νικᾷ στάχυν.
953: ἀλλ' ἄρσενάς τοι τῆσδε γῆς οἰκήτορας
εὑρήσετ', οὐ πίνοντας ἐκ κριθῶν μέθυ.

[7] Müller, *Eumeniden*, p. 125.

except Pelasgus. And yet in the complete Trilogy, the *Orestea*, which is known to have been acted in B.C. 458,[1] and which has many dramatic features in common with the Trilogy to which the *Supplices* belonged, we have the three actors in every play. We do not of course know whether this extended machinery was employed in any earlier play, which is now lost. But it seems reasonable to conclude, from the specimens which we have, that Æschylus did not borrow this most characteristic improvement of his rival Sophocles till quite the close of his own dramatic career. And it is just possible that the *Orestea* may have been the first and last example of this condescension to the established fashion at Athens. In a subsequent chapter we will fully analyse the structure of this great effort of the genius of Æschylus, and will endeavour to indicate all the details of the stage business.[2] Here it will be sufficient to call attention to the connection of the Trilogy with the political principles of Æschylus. The four separate plays are, as we have seen, the middle pieces in the Trilogies to which they belonged. But the extant Trilogy makes everything work up to the final Tragedy. Clytæmnestra kills her husband on the plea that he had slain Iphigenia, but really because she had conspired with Ægisthus to usurp his throne. She is Lady Macbeth and Queen Gertrude of Denmark both in one. Having been guilty of this homicide, she ought, according to Greek usage, to have gone into exile, and this is the doom pronounced upon her by the senators of Argos.[3] This sentence she sets at nought, and reigns at Argos in spite of the laws of God and man. Outraged religion, then, speaking by the voice of Apollo, orders the son of Agamemnon, as the proper avenger of blood, to put her and Ægisthus to death. It is clear that this command, rather than any vindictive feeling, is the influencing motive with Orestes; and therefore when the Erinyes, as the avenging goddesses, who alone could prosecute Orestes, he being legally justified,

---

[1] *Argum.*: ἐδιδάχθη τὸ δρᾶμα ἐπὶ ἄρχοντος Φιλοκλέους ὀλυμπιάδι π' ἔτει β'· πρῶτος Αἰσχ. Ἀγαμ. Χοηφ. Εὐμεν. Πρωτεῖ σατυρικῷ· ἐχορήγει Ξενοκλῆς Ἀφιδνεύς.

[2] Book III. chapter II.   [3] *Choëph.* 900 sqq.

demand his punishment, Apollo, with the sanction of Zeus,
pleads his cause before the Areopagus at Athens; and while
his human judges, by an equality of votes, neither acquit nor
condemn him, Athena, or divine wisdom, who was also the
divine patroness of Athens, gives a casting vote in his favour,
and at the same time appeases the Eumenides by promising
them a perpetual seat in the Areopagus, where every one
who owned himself guilty of homicide would be *ipso facto*
condemned, without any liberty of pleading, as Orestes had
done, excuse or justification. This seems to have been in accordance with the practice of that venerable tribunal; whereas
the Ephetæ, when they sat at the Delphinium, or temple of
Apollo, the justifying advocate of Orestes, took cognisance
of those cases of admitted homicide which were defended on
some valid plea of justification; and when they sat at the
Palladium, or temple of Athena,—the presiding judge who
acquitted Orestes,—they took cognisance of those cases of
homicide, in which an accident or absence of malicious intention was pleaded by the culprit.[1]   Now at the time when
the *Orestea* was acted, the Areopagus, which, besides its
judicial functions, was an oligarchial tribunal exercising an
authority not unlike that of the censors at Rome, and
which especially claimed the right of passing sentence on
charges of impiety (ἀσέβεια), had just been reduced to its
jurisdiction in homicide by Pericles and his partisan
Ephialtes,[2] who not only objected generally to its senatorial
power, but had reason to fear its becoming an instrument of
the Lacedæmonian party in mooting that charge of inherited
sacrilege which was always hanging over the head of the
great democratic leader.[3]   Whether Æschylus, both by his
favourable reference to the Argive alliance, which was formed
at this time,[4] and by his prediction of the perpetuity of the
remaining privileges of the Areopagus, endeavoured to
conciliate the hatred of the contending factions,[5] or whether
he was engaged with Cimon in an attempt to rescind the

---

[1] Grote, *Hist. Gr.* III. pp. 103 sqq.
[2] Thirlwall, Vol. IV. pp. 22 sqq.   [3] Id. p. 24.
[4] *i. e.* in the year before the *Orestes* was acted.
[5] Grote, *Hist. Gr.* V. p. 499, note.

measures of Pericles and Ephialtes, which led to the ostracism of Cimon[1] and to the retirement of Æschylus from Athens, can perhaps hardly be determined with any certainty.[2] There can be no doubt, however, of the reference of the *Eumenides* to these contemporary incidents in the history of Athens.

[1] Plutarch, *Cimon*, c. 17.
[2] Müller's opinion, *Eumenid.* § 35 sqq., that the criminal jurisdiction of the Areopagus was taken away by Ephialtes, is controverted by Thirlwall and Grote.

CHAPTER. I.

SECTION III.

SOPHOCLES.

Τύν σε χοροῖς μέλψαντα Σοφυκλέα, παῖδα Σοφίλλου,
Τῆς τραγικῆς Μούσης ἀστέρα Κεκρόπιον,
Πολλάκις ἐν θυμέλῃσι καὶ ἐν σκηνῇσι τεθηλὼς
Βλαισὸς 'Αχαρνίτης κισσὸς ἔρεψε κόμην,
Γύμβος ἔχει καὶ γῆς ὀλίγον μέρος· ἀλλ' ὁ περισσὸς
Αἰὼν ἀθανάτοις δέρκεται ἐν σελίσιν.

SIMMIAS.

SOPHOCLES, the son of Sophilus or Sophillus, was born at
Colonus, an Attic deme about a mile from the city, in
(B.C.) 495. His father, who was a man of good family, and
possessed of considerable wealth,[1] gave him an excellent
education. His teacher in music was the celebrated Lamprus,
and he profited so much by his opportunities, that he gained
the prize both in music and in the Palæstra.[2] He was hardly
sixteen years old when he played an accompaniment on the
lyre to the Pæan, which the Athenians sang around the
trophy erected after the battle of Salamis; in other words,
he was the exarchus, and possibly, therefore, composed
the words of the ode.[3] His first appearance, as a tragedian,

---

[1] Lessing (Leben des Sophocles, sämmtlichte Schriften, Vol. VI. pp.
282 sqq.), to whom we are indebted for nearly all the particulars which
we have given in the text, quotes (note C) Plin. H. N. XXXVII. 11:
" principe loco genitum Athenis."

[2] Καλῶς τε ἐπαιδεύθη καὶ ἐτράφη ἐν εὐπορίᾳ. . . διεπονήθη δὲ ἐν παισὶ
καὶ περὶ παλαίστραν καὶ μουσικήν, ἐξ ὧν ἀμφοτέρων ἐστεφανώθη, ὥς φησιν
Ἵστρος. Ἐδιδάχθη δὲ τὴν μουσικὴν παρὰ Λάμπρῳ. Vit. Anonym.

[3] Σοφοκλῆς δὲ πρὸς τῷ καλὸς γεγενῆσθαι τὴν ὥραν ἦν καὶ ὀρχηστικὴν
δεδιδαγμένος καὶ μουσικὴν ἔτι παῖς ὢν παρὰ Λάμπρῳ. Μετὰ γοῦν τὴν ἐν
Σαλαμῖνι ναυμαχίαν περὶ τρόπαιον γυμνὸς ἀληλιμμένος ἐχόρευσε μετὰ
λύρας· οἱ δὲ ἐν ἱματίῳ φασί. Καὶ τὸν Θάμυριν διδάσκων αὐτὸς ἐκιθάρισεν.
Ἀκρως δὲ ἐσφαίρισεν, ὅτε τὴν Ναυσικάαν καθῆκε. Athen. I. p. 20.

Μετὰ τὴν ἐν Σαλαμῖνι ναυμαχίαν Ἀθηναίων περὶ τρόπαιον ὄντων, μετὰ
λύρας γυμνὸς ἀληλιμμένος τοῖς παιανίζουσι τῶν ἐπινικίων ἐξῆρχε. Vit.
Anon.

was attended by a very remarkable circumstance. Cimon removed the bones of Theseus from Scyrus to Athens (468 B.C.).[1] He arrived at Athens about the time of the tragic contests, and Æschylus and Sophocles were among the competitors. The celebrity of the former, and the personal beauty, rank, popularity, and known accomplishments of the latter, excited a great sensation. When therefore Cimon and his nine colleagues entered the theatre of Bacchus, to perform the usual libations, the Archon, Apsephion, instead of choosing judges by lot, detained the ten generals in the theatre, and having administered an oath to them, made them decide between the rival tragedians. The first prize was awarded to Sophocles, and, as we have seen, Æschylus departed immediately for Sicily.[2] This decision does not imply any disregard of the Æschylean Tragedy on the part of the Athenians. The contest was, as has been justly observed, not between two individual works of art, but between two species or ages of art :[3] and if, as we think has been fully demonstrated,[4] the *Triptolemus* was

---

[1] *Marm. Par.* No. LVII.: ἀφ' οὗ Σοφοκλῆς ὁ Σοφίλλου ὁ ἐκ Κολωνοῦ ἐνίκησε τραγῳδίᾳ, ἐτῶν ὢν ΔΔΠΙΙΙ, ἔτη ΗΗΠΙ, ἄρχοντος 'Αθήνησιν 'Αψηφίονος. "These were the greater Dionysia, or the Διονύσια τὰ ἐν ἄστει, in the month Elaphebolion ; because the *Archon Eponymus*, Apsephion, presided; and, ὁ μὲν ἄρχων διατίθησι Διονύσια, ὁ δὲ βασιλεὺς (conf. Aristoph. *Acharn.* 1224, et Schol. ad l.o.) προέστηκε Ληναίων. Pollux, VIII. 89, 50." Clinton, *F. H.* II. p. 39.

[2] 'Εθεντο δ' εἰς μνήμην αὐτοῦ, καὶ τὴν τῶν τραγῳδῶν κρίσιν ὀνομαστὴν γενομένην· πρώτην γὰρ διδασκαλίαν τοῦ Σοφοκλέους ἔτι νέου καθέντος, 'Αφεψίων (sic). ὁ ἄρχων, φιλονεικίας οὔσης καὶ παρατάξεως τῶν θεατῶν, κριτὰς μὲν οὐκ ἐκλήρωσε τοῦ ἀγῶνος· ὡς δὲ Κίμων μετὰ τῶν συστρατηγῶν προελθὼν εἰς τὸ θέατρον ἐποιήσατο τῷ θεῷ τὰς νενομισμένας σπονδάς, οὐκ ἀφῆκεν αὐτοὺς ἀπελθεῖν, ἀλλ' ὁρκώσας, ἠνάγκασε καθίσαι καὶ κρῖναι δέκα ὄντας, ἀπὸ φυλῆς, μιᾶς ἕκαστον· ὁ μὲν οὖν ἀγὼν καὶ διὰ τὸ τῶν κριτῶν ἀξίωμα τὴν φιλοτιμίαν ὑπερέβαλε. νικήσαντος δὲ Σοφοκλέους, λέγεται τὸν Αἰσχύλον περιπαθῆ γενόμενον, καὶ βαρέως ἐνέγκοντα, χρόνον οὐ πολὺν 'Αθήνησι διαγαγεῖν, εἶτ' οἴχεσθαι δι' ὀργὴν εἰς Σικελίαν. Plutarch, *Cimon*, c. VIII.
There is probably an allusion to this in Aristoph. *Ran.* 1109 sqq., where the chorus says, that the military character of the spectators fits them to be judges of the contest between Æschylus and Euripides, ἐστρατευμένοι γάρ εἰσι.

[3] Welcker, *Trilogie*, p. 513.

[4] By Lessing, *Leben des Sophocles* (note I), from a passage in Plin. *H. N.* XVIII. 7: *Sophoclis Triptolemus ante mortem Alexandri annis*

K

one of the plays which Sophocles exhibited on that occasion,
we can readily conceive that, when the minds of the people
were full of their old national legends, the subject which
the young poet had chosen, and the desire to encourage his
first attempt, would be sufficient to overweigh the reputation
of his antagonist, coupled as it was with anti-popular
politics, especially as the Æschylean Tragedy lacked that
freshness of novelty and loveliness of youth which hung
around the form and the poetry of the beautiful son of
Sophillus. Sophocles rarely appeared on the stage in
consequence of the weakness of his voice:[1] we are told,
however, that he performed on the lyre, in the character of
Thamyris, and distinguished himself by the grace with
which he played at ball in his own play called *Nausicaa*.[2]
Iu 440 B.C. he brought out the *Antigone*, and we are informed that it was to the political wisdom exhibited in that
play that he owed his appointment as colleague of Pericles
and Thucydides in the Samian war.[3] On this occasion he
met with Herodotus, and composed a lyrical poem for that

---

fere 145. But Alexander died 323 B.C., and 323 + 145 = 468. On the
Triptolemus in general, see Welcker, *Tril.* 514 (who thinks it was
certainly not a satyrical drama), and Niebuhr, *Hist. Rom.* Vol. I.
pp. 17, 18. The arguments adduced by Gruppe (*Ariadne*, pp. 358 foll.)
to prove that the *Rhesus* was the play which Sophocles exhibited on
this occasion, are all in favour of Lessing's opinion.

[1] Πρῶτον καταλύσας τὴν ὑπόκρισιν τοῦ ποιητοῦ διὰ τὴν ἰδίαν ἰσχνο-
φωνίαν. *Vit. Anonym.*

[2] See the passage of Athen. (I. p. 20) quoted above. " The Nausicaa
was, according to all appearances, a satyric drama. The Odyssee was
in general a rich storehouse for the satyrical plays. The character of
Ulysses himself makes him a very convenient satyrical impersonation."
Lessing, *Leben des Sophocles*, note K (Vol. VI. p. 342).

[3] Strabo, XIV. p. 446 ; Suidas, v. Μέλιτος; Athen. XIII. p. 603 F:
Scholiast, Aristoph. *Pax*, v. 696: Cic. *de Off.* I. 40; Plutarch, *Pericl.*
c. VIII.; Plin. *H. N.* XXXVII. 2, Val. Max. IV. 3 : all testify that the
true cause is assigned by Aristophanes of Byzantium in the argument
to the *Antigone*: Φασὶ δὲ τὸν Σοφοκλέα ἠξιῶσθαι τῆς ἐν Σάμῳ στρατηγίας
εὐδοκιμήσαντα ἐν τῇ διδασκαλίᾳ τῆς 'Αντιγόνης. A similar distinction
was conferred upon Phrynicus, Ælian, *V. H.* III. 8. It is probable that
Sophocles conciliated the favour of the more popular party by the way
in which he speaks of Pericles, v. 662, and they were perhaps willing
to take the hint in v. 175, where, we may observe iu passing, φρόνημα
signifies " political opinions," as in the phrases, ἐμπέδοις φρονήμασιν,

historian.¹ It does not appear that he distinguished himself in his military capacity.² He received many invitations from foreign courts, but loved Athens too well to accept them. He held several offices in his old age. He was priest of the hero Alon,³ and in the year 413 B.C. was elected one of the πρόβουλοι. This was a board of commissioners, all old men, which was established immediately after the disastrous termination of the Syracusan expedition, to devise expedients for meeting the existing emergencies.⁴ The constitution of such a committee was necessarily aristocratic,⁵ and two years after, 411 B.C., Sophocles, once the favourite of the people and the colleague of Pericles, fell into the plans of Peisander and the other conspirators, and consented in the temple of Neptune, at his own Colonus, to the establishment of a council of four hundred; in other words, to the subversion of the old Athenian constitution.⁶ He afterwards defended his policy on the grounds of expediency.⁷ Nicostrata had borne him a son, whom he

---

τοιόνδ' ἐμὸν φρόνημα, ἴσον χρονῶν, which occur in the same play. On the meanings of φρονεῖν and φρόνημα in Sophocles, see the notes on the translation of the *Antigone*, pp. 155, 168.

¹ Plutarch, *An seni*, &c., c. 3, IV. 153, Wyttenb. On this subject the student may consult the Introduction to the *Antigone*, p. xvii. and *Transactions of the Philol. Soc.* I. No. 15, where it will be seen that Herodotus was an imitator of Sophocles.

² At least if we may credit the tale told of him by Ion, a contemporary poet (Athenæus, XIII. 604), where he is made to say of himself: Μελετῶ στρατηγεῖν, ὦ ἄνδρες· ἐπειδήπερ Περικλῆς ποιεῖν μὲν ἔφη με, στρατηγεῖν δ'οὐκ ἐπίστασθαι.

³ Ἔσχε δὲ καὶ τὴν τοῦ Ἄλωνος ἱερωσύνην, ὃς ἥρως ἦν μετὰ Ἀσκληπιοῦ παρὰ Χείρωνι. *Vit. Anonym.*

⁴ Thucyd. VIII. 1 : καὶ ἀρχήν τινα τῶν πρεσβυτέρων ἀνδρῶν ἑλέσθαι οἵτινες περὶ τῶν παρόντων ὡς ἂν καιρὸς ᾖ προβουλεύσουσι. We consider these πρόβουλοι to have been most probably elected to serve as ξυγγραφῆς (Thucyd. VIII. 67), for it was the ξυγγραφῆς who brought about the revolution, and we learn from Aristotle (see below) that Sophocles contributed to it in his character of πρόβουλος.

⁵ Aristot. *Polit.* VI. 5, 10: δεῖ γὰρ εἶναι τὸ συνάγον τὸ κύριον τῆς πολιτείας. καλεῖται δ' ἔνθα μὲν πρόβουλοι διὰ τὸ προβουλεύειν. ὅπου δὲ τὸ πλῆθός ἐστι βουλὴ μᾶλλον.

⁶ Thucyd. VIII. 67: ξυνέκλησαν τὴν ἐκκλησίαν εἰς τὸν Κολωνόν (ἔστι δὲ ἱερὸν Ποσειδῶνος ἔξω πόλεως ἀπέχον σταδίους μάλιστα δέκα) κ.τ.λ.

⁷ Καὶ συμπεραινόμενον, ἐὰν ἐρώτημα πυιῇ τὸ συμπέρασμα, τὴν αἰτίαν

named Iophon: he had another son Ariston, by Theoris
of Sicyon, whose son, Sophocles, was a great favourite with
his grandfather and namesake. From this reason, or because, according to Cicero, his love for the stage made him
neglect his affairs, his son Iophon charged him with dotage
and lunacy, and brought him before the proper court, with
a view to remove him from the management of his property.
The poet read to his judges a part of the *Œdipus at Colonus*
which he had just finished, and triumphantly asked " if that
was the work of an idiot?" Of course the charge was
dismissed.[1] We are sorry to say that this very pretty story
is a mere fabrication, for the *Œdipus at Colonus* must have
been acted, at least for the first time, before the breaking
out of the Peloponnesian war.[2] Sophocles died in the very
beginning of the year 405 B.C.; according to Ister and
Neanthes he was choked by a grape, which the actor
Callippides brought him from Opus, at the time of the
Anthesteria. Satyrus tells us that he died in consequence
of exerting his voice too much while reading the *Antigone*
aloud:[3] others say that his joy at being proclaimed tragic
victor was too much for his decayed strength. His family
burial-place was Decelea, and as that town was in the
possession of the Lacedæmonians, it was not possible to bring
him there until Lysander, having heard from the deserters
that the great poet was dead, permitted his ashes to rest
with those of his ancestors. There is a legend, that Bacchus

εἰπεῖν· οἷον Σοφοκλῆς ἐρωτώμενος ὑπὸ Πεισάνδρου, " εἰ ἔδοξεν αὐτῷ, ὥσπερ
καὶ τοῖς ἄλλοις προβούλοις, καταστῆσαι τοὺς τετρακοσίους;" ἔφη.—" Τί δὲ
οὐ πονηρά σοι ταῦτα ἐδόκει εἶναι;" ἔφη. " Οὐκ οὖν σὺ ταῦτα ἔπραξας τὰ
πονηρά;" "Ναί," ἔφη, "οὐ γὰρ ἦν ἄλλα βελτίω." Aristot. *Rhet.* III. 18.

[1] *Vit. Anonym.*; Cicero, *de Senectute*, § 7; Val. Max. VIII.

[2] See Reisig, *Enarrat. Œd. Col.* pp. v. sqq.; J. W. Süvern, *On some
historical and political allusions in Ancient Tragedy*, pp. 6, 8; Lachmann, in the *Rhein. Mus.* for 1827, pp. 313 fol.: Hermann in Zimmer-
mann's *Zeitschrift*, 1837, No. 98, pp. 803 sqq., inclines to the opinion
that the *Œdip. Col.* was written before, but not published till after, the
Peloponnesian war.

[3] We have seen that ἰσχνοφωνία was attributed to Sophocles: if it
arose from delicate lungs, this account of his death is probable enough.
There are chronological objections to the other two statements. See
Clinton, *F. H.* II. p. 85.

appeared twice to Lysander in a dream, and enjoined him to allow the interment to take place.[1] According to one account, they placed the image of a Siren over his tomb, according to another, a bronze swallow. Ister informs us that the Athenians decreed him an annual sacrifice. He wrote, besides Tragedies, an elegy, pæans, and a prose work on the chorus, against Thespis and Chœrilus. Only seven of his Tragedies have come down to us; but an ingenious attempt has been made to show that the *Rhesus*, which is generally attributed to Euripides, was the first of the plays of Sophocles.[2]

With regard to the whole number of plays composed by Sophocles, we have the authority of Aristophanes, of Byzantium, that 130 were ascribed to him, of which seventeen were spurious. It has been objected [3] to this large number, that the *Antigone*, which was acted in 440, was the thirty-second play; and as Sophocles began to exhibit in 468, and died in 405, he would have written eighty-one pieces in the last thirty-six years of his literary life, and only thirty-two in the first twenty-seven years; whereas it is not likely that he would have written more in his declining years than in the vigour of his life: and it has been conjectured that he wrote only about seventy plays. Reasons have, however, been given,[4] which incline us to believe that Aristophanes is correct in assigning to him 113 genuine dramas. For, in the first place, the meaning of the words, on which this objection is founded, is not sufficiently clear: it is not certain that the grammarian is not referring to Tragedies only, and in that case, even supposing that Sophocles wrote five separate plays in that time, we should have to add nine satyrical dramas to make up the Tetralogies, and thus we should not have a very disproportionate

---

[1] See *Vita Anonym.* Pausanias, I. 21 § 1, gives a somewhat different story. Λέγεται δὲ Σοφοκλέους τελευτήσαντος ἐσβάλλειν εἰς τὴν Ἀττικὴν Λακεδαιμονίους, καὶ σφῶν τὸν ἡγούμενον ἰδεῖν ἐπιστάντα οἱ Διόνυσον κελεύειν τιμαῖς, ὅσαι καθεστήκασιν ἐπὶ τοῖς τεθνεῶσι, τὴν Σειρῆνα τὴν Νέαν τιμᾶν. καὶ οἱ τὸ ὄναρ Σοφοκλέα καὶ τὴν Σοφοκλέους ποίησιν ἐφαίνετο ἔχειν.

[2] Gruppe, *Ariadne*, pp. 285—305.

[3] By Böckh, *de Gr. Trag. Princip.* pp. 107—109.

[4] By Clinton, *Phil. Museum*, I. pp. 74 fol.

number of trilogies for the remaining thirty-six years. Besides, we have a list of 114 names of dramas attributed to Sophocles, of which ninety-eight are quoted more than once as his, and it is exceedingly unlikely that many of these should have been written by his son Iophon, or his grandson, the younger Sophocles. It will be recollected, too, that in the earlier part of his life Sophocles was much engaged in public affairs; he was a general, at least once,[1] and went on several embassies;[2] this, in addition to the greater facility in writing, which he might have acquired by long practice, would account for his pen being more prolific in the latter part of his life. He obtained the first prize eighteen,[3] twenty,[4] or twenty-four times,[5] and it is not probable that his first and second prizes taken together were much fewer than thirty. Now it seems that about twenty-four of the dramas, the names of which have come down to us, were satyrical: we may suppose that he wrote about twenty-seven satyrical dramas on the whole: this would give us twenty-seven Tetralogies, or 108 plays, and there remain five single plays to satisfy the statement of Suidas, that he contended with drama against drama. This statement we shall now proceed to examine. It certainly does not imply that he never contended with Trilogies, for it is known that he wrote satyrical dramas which in his time were never acted by themselves. One of the conjectures which have been proposed with respect to the meaning of the words of Suidas is, that Sophocles opposed to the Trilogies of Æschylus three Tragedies, not intimately connected with one another, like the Æschylean plays, but each complete in itself.[6] This presumes, however, that Suidas understood the word τετραλογία in a technical sense, as expressing the distinguishing peculiarity of the Æschylean Trilogy with its accompanying satyric drama. We cannot believe that the grammarian had any such accurate perception of the

---

[1] Justin says (lib. III. 6) that he served against the Lacedæmonians.

[2] καὶ ἐν πρεσβείαις ἐξητάζετο. *Vit. Anonym.*

[3] Diodor. XIII. 103.

[4] Νίκας ἔλαβεν εἴκοσιν ὥς φησι Καρύστιος· πολλάκις δὲ καὶ δευτερεῖα ἔλαβε. *Vit. Anonym.*

[5] Suidas.   [6] Welcker, *Trilogie.* p. 51.

real nature of the trilogy. Nevertheless, the fact may have been such, although Suidas did not know it, for nothing is more likely than that the custom of contending with single plays, which Sophocles, perhaps sparingly, adopted, arose from his having given to each of the plays in his Trilogies an individual completeness which the constituent parts of an Æschylean Trilogy did not possess. We shall derive some further reasons for believing this from a consideration of the general principles which guided the art of Sophocles.

That he did act upon general principles is sufficiently proved by the fact that he wrote a book on the dramatic chorus. The objection, which (according to Chamæleon) he made to Æschylus, that even when his poetry was what it ought to be, it was so only by accident,[1] is just such a remark as a finished artist would make to a self-taught genius. But we might conclude, without any extrinsic authority, from a moderate acquaintance with his remaining Tragedies, that he is never beautiful or sublime without intending to be so: we see that he has a complete apprehension of the proper means of arriving at the objects of tragical imitation: he feels that his success depends not upon his subject, but upon himself; he has the faculty of "making with right reason;" in short, he is an artist in the strictest sense of the word.[2] "Sophocles," says one who has often more than guessed at truth, "is the summit of Greek art; but one must have scaled many a steep before one can estimate his height: it is because of his classical perfection that he has generally been the least admired of the great ancient poets; for little of his beauty is perceptible to a mind that is not thoroughly principled and imbued with the spirit of antiquity."[3] The ancients themselves fully appreciated Sophocles: his great contemporary

---

[1] See Athen. I. 22, X. 428, quoted in the sect. on Æschylus.

[2] Aristot. Eth. Nicom. VI. p. 1140, l. 10, Bekker: ἔστι δὲ τέχνη πᾶσα περὶ γένεσιν καὶ τὸ τεχνάζειν, καὶ θεωρεῖν, ὅπως ἂν γένηταί τι τῶν ἐνδεχομένων καὶ εἶναι καὶ μὴ εἶναι καὶ ὧν ἡ ἀρχὴ ἐν τῷ ποιοῦντι ἀλλὰ μὴ ἐν τῷ ποιουμένῳ.——ἡ μὲν οὖν τέχνη ὥσπερ εἴρηται ἕξις τις μετὰ λόγου ποιητική ἐστι.

[3] Guesses at Truth, Vol. I. p. 267. Comp. Müller, Hist. Lit. Gr. c. XXIV. § 13.

Aristophanes will not expose Æschylus to the risk of a con
test with a man to whom he has voluntarily given up a part
of the tragic throne, and to whom he delegates his authority
when he returns to the upper world:[1] his numerous victories and the improvements which Æschylus found it necessary to borrow from him, are all so many proofs of the
estimation in which he was held by his countrymen: but it
is to be feared that few, if any, of his modern readers
will ever be able to divest themselves completely of all
their modern associations, and thus set a just value upon
productions so entirely and absolutely Greek as the Tragedies of Sophocles.　If we would understand them at all, we
must always bear in mind that he was the successor of
Æschylus; that he intended rather to follow up and im-
prove upon his predecessor and contemporary, than to create
an entirely new species for himself.　Art always follows at
the heels of genius.　Genius creates forms of beauty; art
marshals them, and sets them in order, forming them into
groups and regulating the order of their successive appearances.　Genius hews rude masses from the mines of thought,
but art gives form and usefulness to the shapeless ore.　Æschylus felt what a Greek Tragedy ought to be, as a religious
union of the two elements of the national poetry; and he
modelled bold, colossal groups, such as a Phidias might have
conceived, but not such as a Phidias would have executed.
Sophocles, with a highly cultivated mind, and a deep and
just perception of what is beautiful in art, was enabled to
effect an outward realisation of his great contemporary's
conceptions; and what was already perfected in the mind of
Æschylus, this he exhibited, in its most perfect form, before
the eyes of all Athens.　The Tragedy of Sophocles was not
generically different from that of Æschylus; it bore the same
relation to its forerunner that a finished statue bears to an
unfinished group.　For when Sophocles added a third actor
to the two of Æschylus,[2] he gave so great a preponderance to
the dialogue, that the chorus, or the base on which the three

---

[1] Comp. Aristoph. *Ran.* 790, 1515.

[2] Τρεῖς δὲ [ὑποκριτὰς] καὶ σκηνογραφίαν Σοφοκλῆς.　Arist. *Poet.* IV.
16.　Τὸν δὲ τρίτον [ὑποκριτὴν] Σοφοκλῆς, καὶ συνεπλήρωσεν τὴν τραγῳδίαν.　Diog. Laert. *in Plat.*

plays stood, was unable any longer to support them; in assigning to each of them a separate pedestal, he rendered
them independent, and destroyed the necessary connection
which had previously bound them together; so that it became from thenceforth a matter of choice with the poet
whether he represented with Trilogies or with separate plays.
As we have before said, we think Sophocles did both: the
number of his satyrical dramas shows that his exhibitions
were principally Tetralogies, and we are willing to accept
the statement in Suidas, that he sometimes brought out his
Tragedies one by one. What Æschylus, following his natural taste, practised in the internal economy of his pieces,
for instance, in the exclusion of everything beneath the dignity of Tragedy, this Sophocles adopted as a rule of art, to
be applied or departed from as the occasion might suggest.
The words which Landor puts into his mouth express what
appear to us to have been his general feelings.[1] "I am,"
says he, in reference to the master-works at Athens, "only
the interpreter of the heroes and divinities who are looking
down upon me." He felt himself called upon to make an
advance in the tragic art, corresponding to those improvements which Phidias had made upon the works of his immediate forerunners: he did so, and with reference to the
same objects. The persons who figured in the old legends,
and in the poems of the epic Cycle, were alone worthy in
his opinion of the cothurnus; and if ever an inferior or
ludicrous character appears in his Tragedies, he is but a
slavish instrument in the poet's hands to work out the
irony of the piece; a streak of bright colour thrown into
the picture, in order to render more conspicuous its tragic
gloom.

Besides the addition of a τριταγωνιστής,[2] some other
improvements are ascribed to this poet; he seems to have
made the costumes more appropriate, to have introduced
scene-painting, and to have altered the distribution of the
chorus.

The public character of Sophocles was, as we have seen,
rather inconsistent. In the earlier years of his political

---

[1] Landor's *Imaginary Conversations*, II. p. 142.
[2] Which is also attributed to Æschylus (Themistius, p. 316).

life he was a partisan of Pericles, and his plays contain many
passages evidently written with a view to recommend himself to that statesman. In the *Antigone* he advises the
Athenians to yield a ready and implicit obedience to the
man whom, for the time being, they had placed over themselves;[1] and if, as we believe, the *Œdipus at Colonus* was
written just before the breaking out of the Peloponnesian
war, it is more than probable that the refusal of Theseus to
deliver up Œdipus, though a polluted person, has reference
to the demand made by the confederates with regard to the
expulsion of Pericles.[2]

The private character of Sophocles was unfortunately very
far from faultless. He was a notorious sensualist,[3] and, in
his later days, rather avaricious.[4] He possessed, however,
those agreeable qualities which are very often found along
with habits of vicious indulgence; he was exceedingly goodnatured, always contented,[5] and an excellent boon companion.[6] His faults were due rather to his age and country
than to any innate depravity. His Tragedies are full of the
strongest recommendations of religion and morality; and
we know no ancient poet who has so justly and forcibly
described the infallibility and immortality of God, as opposed
to man's weakness, ignorance, and liability to error:[7] or

---

[1] 670.　　　'Αλλ' ὃν πόλις στήσειε τοῦδε χρὴ κλύειν
　　　　　　Καὶ σμικρὰ καὶ δίκαια καὶ τἀναντία.

See *Introduction to the Antigone*, p. xv.

[2] Comp *Œd. Col.* 943 sqq. with Thucyd. I. 126, 127. Lachmann in
the *Rhein. Mus.* for 1827, pp. 327 fol.

[3] Cic. *Offic.* I. 40; *de Senect.* 47; Athen. XII. p. 510; XIII. p. 592;
XIII. p. 603; Plato, I. *Resp.* p. 329 B.

[4] 'Ερμῆς.　　πρῶτον δ' ὅ τι πράττει Σοφοκλέης ἀνήρετο.
　'Τρυγαῖος.　εὐδαιμονεῖ· πάσχει δὲ θαυμαστόν.
　'Ερμῆς.　　　　　　　　　　　　　　Τὸ τί;
　'Τρυγαῖος.　ἐκ τοῦ Σοφοκλέους γίγνεται Σιμωνίδης.
　'Ερμῆς.　　Σιμωνίδης; πῶς;
　'Τρυγαῖος.　　　　　　"Οτι, γέρων ὢν καὶ σαπρός,
　　κέρδους ἕκατι κἂν ἐπὶ ῥιπὸς πλέοι. *Pax*, 695 sqq.

[5] Aristoph. *Ran.* 82.

[6] See the amusing anecdote from *Ion*, Athen. XIII. p. 603 E.

[7] We allude to *Antig.* 604, which is generally misunderstood. The
connection of ideas in the passage is as follows: " What mortal trans-
gression or sin is Jupiter liable to, Jupiter the sleepless and everlasting
god? But mortal men know nothing of the future till it comes upon

who has set the beauty of piety and righteousness, and the danger and folly of impiety and pride, in a stronger and clearer light than he has.[1]

To characterise the man and his works in one word, calmness is the prominent feature in the life and writings of Sophocles. In his politics, an easy indifference to men and measures; in his private life, contentment and good nature; in his Tragedies, a total absence of that wild enthusiasm which breaks down the barriers of common sense, are the manifestations of this rest of mind: his spirit was

> Like a breath of air,
> Such as is sometimes seen, and hardly seen,
> To brush the still breast of a crystal lake.[2]

He lived, as it were, in the stronghold of his own unruffled mind, and unmoved, heard the pattering storm without.[3] His very burial created peace out of war, and hostile armies held a truce, as the tomb closed upon one loved by all Athens, admired by all Greece, and destined to teach and delight the civilised world in ages yet to come.

Of the seven plays of Sophocles, which have come down to us, only two are referred by express testimony to fixed dates—the *Antigone*, which, as we have seen, was acted in

---

them." We should certainly read ὑπερβασία in the nominative case. Τὶς ὑπερβασία κατέχει τεὰν δύνασιν; is equivalent to τεὰ δύνασις κατέχει οὕτινα ὑπερβασίαν. Compare Theognis, 743—6, which Sophocles had in his head:

> Καὶ τοῦτ᾽, ἀθανάτων βασιλεῦ, πῶς ἐστι δίκαιον
> Ἔργων ὅστις ἀνὴρ ἐκτὸς ἐὼν ἀδίκων,
> Μή τιν᾽ ὑπερβασίην κατέχων, μηδ᾽ ὅρκον ἀλιτρόν,
> Ἀλλὰ δίκαιος ἐών, μὴ τὰ δίκαια πάθῃ;

[1] See the beautiful chorus in *Œd. Tyr.* 863 sqq.
[2] Wordsworth (*Excursion*, p. 9c).
[3] He says himself, in a fragment of the *Tympanistæ* (No. 563):

> Φεῦ, φεῦ, τί τούτου χάρμα μεῖζον ἂν λάβοις,
> τοῦ γῆς ἐπιψαύσαντα κᾆθ᾽ ὑπὸ στέγῃ
> πυκνῆς ἀκοῦσαι ψεκάδος εὐδούσῃ φρενί.

It is clear that this, like many other passages referring to escape from the sea, expresses the feelings, and in part the language, of those who were initiated into the Eleusinian mysteries. Cf. Eurip. *Bacch.* 900; Demosth. *Coron.* p. 516 A; Lucret. II. init.; Cic. *Att.* II. 7.

B.C. 440, and the *Philoctetes*, which appeared in B.C. 409.[1]
Although it is stated that the *Œdipus Coloneus* was first
acted, after the death of the poet, in B.C. 401, and though,
as we have seen, a pretty story refers its composition to the
end of the poet's life, it is almost generally agreed among
scholars that it belongs to the most vigorous period of his
life, though it may have received additions and modifications
at a later period.[2] With the exception then of the *Antigone*
and *Philoctetes*, we have only internal evidence to fix the
succession of the extant Tragedies. And here we cannot, as
in the case of Æschylus, divide the plays into distinct groups
indicating an earlier and a later period of dramatic art.
They all exhibit the tragic power of Sophocles in its full
maturity, and they all exemplify that wonderful power
of drawing upon the most recondite treasures of the Greek
language which made Sophocles a favourite with Virgil,
the only Latin poet who exhibits the same combination of
profound thought and elaborately chastened style.[3] It is
true that Sophocles, in an important citation of his words
preserved by Plutarch, recognised three epochs in his own
style—first, the tumid grandeur which he had borrowed
from Æschylus; secondly, a harsh and artificial employment
of terms, which he had introduced himself; and thirdly, the
style which he considered best and most suited to the representation of human character.[4] If we are right in supposing

---

[1] *Arg. Philoct.*: ἐδιδάχθη ἐπὶ Γλαυκίππου, πρῶτος ἦν Σοφοκλῆς.
[2] See Bernhardy, *Grundriss*, II. p. 788.
[3] Virgil says (*Eclog.* VIII. 10):

"Sola Sophocleo tua carmina digna cothurno."

And there are examples in his poetry of a very close imitation of the
peculiarities of the Sophoclean style. There are at least four imitations
of the line in the *Ajax*, 674:

δεινῶν ἄημα πνευμάτων ἐκοίμισε
στένοντα πόντον—

namely, *Eclog.* II. 26; *Georg.* IV. 484; *Æn.* I. 66, v. 763; and the
figure in *Georg.* III. 241, *nigramque* alte subjectat arenam, is clearly
borrowed from Soph. *Antig.* 590: κελαινὰν θῖνα καὶ δυσάνεμον.
[4] Plutarch, *de Profect. Virt. Sent.* p. 79 B: ὁ Σοφοκλῆς ἔλεγε, τὸν
Αἰσχύλου διαπεπαιχὼς ὄγκον, εἶτα τὸ πικρὸν καὶ κατάτεχνον τῆς αὑτοῦ
κατασκευῆς, εἰς τρίτον ἤδη τὸ τῆς λέξεως μεταβάλλειν εἶδος ὅπερ ἐστὶν
ἠθικώτατον καὶ βέλτιστον. The substitution of αὑτοῦ for αὐτοῦ, and the

that this citation really gives us the words of Sophocles, and that we must therefore take the participle διαπεπαιχώς in its old Attic rather than in its subsequent Hellenistic sense,[1] it will imply either that both the first two styles belonged to the very earliest period of his literary career,[2] or that he had merely amused himself with sporting in those styles;[3] and in either case we can hardly suppose that they are to be found in Tragedies subsequent to the *Antigone*. On the other hand, all the extant Tragedies, even the *Philoctetes*, which is known to have been produced by Sophocles in his old age, exhibit traces of that intentional obscurity with regard to which it has been well observed,[4] that "Sophocles often plays at hide-and-seek with the significations of words, in order that the mind, having exerted itself to find out his meaning, may comprehend it more vividly and distinctly when it is once arrived at." The claim which Sophocles makes for the style of his mature age, namely, that it is the best adapted for the delineation of human character, is combined, by the echo of an old and able criticism, with a recognition of his elaborate art and ingenuity.[5] And we are inclined to the belief that he never shook off entirely the peculiarities of his second style; but that, as he advanced in life, he combined with it more and more a readier flow of dramatic oratory, such as we find in his contemporary Euripides.[6] As far as this comparative

---

introduction of εἰς before τρίτον, are due to Müller, *Hist. Gr. Lit.* I. p. [340] 449. In a note to Müller we have explained κατασκευή in its opposition to λέξις, as above.

[1] Moeris, p. 158: ἐρεσχελεῖν Ἀττικῶς· διαπαίζειν, Ἑλληνικῶς. Cf. *Etym. M.* p. 621, 54: Πλάτων διαπαίζει τὴν λέξιν ὡς βάρβαρον.

[2] This is Müller's translation: "Having put away along with his boyish days."

[3] This seems to be in accordance with the only use of the word by an author of the classical age: Plato, *Leges*, VI. 769 A: καλῶς τοίνυν ἂν ἡμῖν ἡ πρεσβυτῶν ἔμφρων παιδιὰ μέχρι δεῦρ' ἂν εἴη τὰ νῦν διαπεπαισμένη.

[4] Müller, *Hist. Gr. Lit.* I. p. [356] 469.

[5] *Vit. Sophocl. ad fin.*: ἠθοποιεῖ δὲ καὶ ποικίλλει καὶ τοῖς ἐπινοήμασι τεχνικῶς χρῆται, Ὁμηρικὴν ἐκματτόμενος χάριν. οἶδε δὲ καιρὸν συμμετρῆσαι καὶ πράγματα ὥστ' ἐκ μικροῦ ἡμιστιχίου ἢ λέξεως μιᾶς ὅλον ἠθοποιεῖν πρόσωπον.

[6] Müller, I. p. [356] 470, refers especially to the speeches of

facility admits of recognition, it may help us to class with the *Antigone*, as his earliest extant play, the *Electra*, which is its counterpart in representing the contrast of two sisters, and so making the third actor play an important and essential character in the development of the drama. The *Trachiniæ* seems to claim the third place on account of the difficulty of the language, and other features of strong resemblance to the *Antigone*. Then we should class together the *Œdipus Tyrannus* and the *Œdipus Coloneus* with their connected subjects and not dissimilar mode of treatment. And we should associate the *Philoctetes* with the *Ajax*, in which also Ulysses appears as the leading instrument in the development of the plot. We will briefly characterise the separate plays considered in this order of succession.

In the *Antigone* the main object is to show the contrast between the heroine, who insists on burying her brother against the will of the state, represented by Creon, and the latter, who violates the laws of heaven by denying the rites of sepulture to Polyneices and burying Antigone alive. Both, in a certain sense, have justice on their side, and therefore both excite the sympathy of the audience; both, in another sense, are guilty of violating the law—the princess the law of man, and the king the law of God—and therefore the tragical results in both cases assume the form of a righteous doom. The plot is rendered more interesting by the contrast of the characters of the two sisters, Antigone and Ismene, and by the introduction of the love of Hæmon, Creon's son, for his cousin Antigone. In this latter incident the play approaches nearly to some of the characteristics of the romantic drama. And on the whole there is perhaps no Greek Tragedy which makes a stronger appeal to the feelings, and which is more exquisitely finished in all its parts, than the *Antigone* of Sophocles. If the *Agamemnon* of Æschylus approximates in some points to the grandeur of *Macbeth*, there is much in the *Antigone* to remind us of *Romeo and Juliet*.[1]

Menelaus, Agamemnon, and Teucer in the *Ajax*, and to Œdipus' defence in the *Œdipus Coloneus*.

[1] The present writer has endeavoured to exhibit all the character-

The *Electra*, which Dioscorides classes with the *Antigone* as exemplifying the highest perfection of the art of Sophocles,[1] is in many respects the counterpart of that play. The strongest emotion displayed is the sisterly love of the heroine for her brother Orestes, whom she supposes to have perished; and the contrast between Electra and Chrysothemis corresponds exactly to that between Antigone and Ismene. There is another strong sentiment in Electra's sorrow for her murdered father, and in the heroic resolve of the lonely and persecuted maiden to slay Ægisthus with her own hand. The highest point of tragic interest is reached when Electra, having uttered her beautiful address to the urn, which, as she supposes, contains the ashes of her brother, is raised from despair to overpowering joy by recognising him in the stranger who had himself given her the simulated remains of Orestes. The matricidal catastrophe at the end is terrible without being extravagant, and the manner in which Ægisthus, who had come home confidently hoping to hear that Orestes was dead, is obliged to lift the covering from the corpse of Clytæmnestra, produces a striking effect, without falling into melo-dramatic vulgarity.

If the *Electra* resembles the *Antigone* in the prominence which it gives to sisterly affection, and in the contrast between the pairs of sisters in each play, the *Trachiniæ* is not without very striking indications of a similarity in manner and conception which refers it to the same period of the poet's literary activity. Characters and descriptions in

---

istics of this masterpiece of Greek Tragedy in an edition and translation of the *Antigone*, published in 1848.

[1] *Anth. Pal.* VII. 37:

 α. τύμβῳς ὅδ' ἐστ', ὤνθρωπε, Σοφοκλέος, ὃν παρὰ Μουσῶν
  ἱρὴν παρθεσίην, ἱερὸς ὤν, ἔλαχον·
 ὅς με τὸν ἐκ Φλιοῦντος. ἔτι τρίβυλον πατέοντα,
  πρίνινον, ἐς χρυσέον σχῆμα μεθηρμόσατο,
 καὶ λεπτὴν ἐνέδυπεν ἀλουργίδα· τοῦ δὲ θανόντος
  εὔθετον ὀρχηστὴν τῇδ' ἀνέπαυτα πόδα.
 β. ὄλβιος ὡς ἀγαθὴν ἔλαχες στάσιν· ἡ δ' ἐνὶ χερσὶν
  κούριμος. ἐκ ποίης ἥδε διδασκαλίης;
 α. εἴτε σοι Ἀντιγόνην εἰπεῖν φίλον, οὐκ ἂν ἁμάρτοις,
  εἴτε καὶ Ἠλέκτραν· ἀμφότεραι γὰρ ἄκρον.

both plays seem to have a certain resemblance.[1]   Both plays
have an ὀρχηστικόν or dancing song instead of a stasimon.[2]
The exaltation of the power of love is similarly expressed in
both.[3]   And figures of speech,[4] and even phraseology[5] in the
one play, sound like echoes of something similar in the
other.   But while the *Antigone* is perhaps the most vigorous
and perfect of the plays of Sophocles, the *Trachiniæ* is
undoubtedly his feeblest effort.   It turns entirely on the
justifiable jealousy of Deianeira, who really loves her
husband Hercules, and, fearing that he had given his
affections to Iole, sends him the poisoned shirt of Nessus,
in the sincere belief that it will operate as a love-charm.   It
produces, as the treacherous Centaur intended, the most
exquisite sufferings, and Hercules is laid on the funeral pile
to consume his mortal frame, and so to escape his misery,
and to receive immortal life.   But Deianeira slays herself
on learning the consequences of an error which, as her son
declares, she had committed with the best intentions.[6]   And
Hercules, who had at first broken forth into the most
violent imprecations against his wife, recognises the decree
of fate in the calamity in which she had been the unwilling
agent.

There are none of the plays of Sophocles which exhibit
more strikingly than the two which bear the name of
Œdipus, that solemn irony which the genius of a modern
scholar has detected in the framework of this poet's Tragedies.[7]   This irony consists in the contrast, which the spectator, well acquainted with the legendary basis of the
tragedy, is enabled to draw between the real state of the

---

[1] Lichas reminds us of the Sentinel in the *Antigone*, and Hyllus
pleading with his father for Deianeira is the counterpart of Hæmon, as
the advocate of his bride.   The silence of Deianeira on hearing of
her husband's fate is paralleled by that of Eurydice, and the descriptive
speeches are framed on the same model.

[2] Cf. *Antig.* 1115 sqq.; *Trach.* 205 sqq.

[3] Cf. *Antig.* 781 sqq.; *Trach.* 497 sqq.

[4] Cf. *Antig.* 586 sqq.; *Trach.* 112 sqq.

[5] As in the almost unique examples of the tertiary predicate ἀδάκρυτος
(*Antig.* 881; *Trach.* 106) for ὥστε οὐ δακρύουσιν (*Greek Grammar*, art. 498).

[6] *Trach.* 1136: ἅπαν τὸ χρῆμ' ἥμαρτε, χρηστὰ μωμένη.

[7] Thirlwall, *On the Irony of Sophocles*, *Philol. Mus.* II. pp.
483 sqq.

case and the conceptions supposed to be entertained by the person represented on the stage. It is this contrast, regarded from different points of view, which makes the two plays about Œdipus the counterparts of one another, and induces us to think that, whether they were or were not written nearly at the same time,[1] they were intended by the poet to form constituent parts of one picture.

The *Œdipus Tyrannus* represents the king of Thebes, in the full confidence of his own glory[2] at the beginning of the play, but brought step by step to the consciousness of the horrible guilt in which he had unawares involved himself. "The wrath of heaven," says the expositor to whom we have referred,[3] "has been pointed against the afflicted city, only that it might fall with concentrated force on the head of a single man; and he who is its object stands alone calm and secure : unconscious of his own misery, he can afford pity for the unfortunate : to him all look up for succour : and, as in the plenitude of wisdom and power, he undertakes to trace the evil, of which he is himself the sole author, to its secret source." The greatest dramatic ingenuity is shown in the manner in which Œdipus investigates the dreadful reality, and the hearer, though acquainted with the plot, shudders when Œdipus becomes at last conscious that he is about to hear the whole extent of his calamity.[4] The powerful and self-confident king of the early part of the play becomes the blind and helpless outcast of the concluding scene; but his sins were involuntary,[5] and his punishment and humiliation are his own act; so that the sufferer leaves the stage an object of the spectator's compassion, and a fit hero for the drama which renders poetic justice to this poor child of fate.

In the *Œdipus Coloneus* the exiled king appears supported by his affectionate daughter Antigone, and dependent on the charity of strangers. His outward condition could not be more helpless and pitiable. But he is on the verge of his predicted resting-place. The sanctuary of the awful

---

[1] The silence of Jocasta (1075) brings this play into a connection of manner with the *Antigone* and *Trachiniæ*.

[2] 8: ὁ πᾶσι κλεινὸς Οἰδίπους καλούμενος.   [3] Thirlwall, p. 496.

[4] *Œd. Tyr.* 1169: πρὸς αὐτῷ γ' εἰμὶ τῷ δεινῷ λέγειν—κἄγωγ' ἀκούειν.

[5] *Œd. Col.* 266: τά γ' ἔργα μου πεπονθότ' ἐστὶ μᾶλλον ἢ δεδρακότα.

L

goddesses, who persecuted the voluntary matricide Orestes, is opened to him, the unwilling murderer of his father, as a place of repose in which he would exercise a protecting power over the land which received him. The Thebans, who had expelled him as a polluted person, strive in vain to get him back; his son Polyneices, whom he regarded as a parricide,[1] seeks his protection, but is rejected with imprecations; and Œdipus descends to his sacred tomb, summoned by thunder from on high,[2] and led by Hermes and the goddess of the shades,[3] to the spot where he would be for ever the protecting genius of the land of Attica.[4]

The *Ajax* represents the consequences of the frenzy into which that hero was driven by the disappointment of his claims to the armour of Achilles. Under the influence of a strong delusion, which Athena, in the prologue, states that she had brought upon him, he attacks the flocks and herds of the Greek army while he imagines that he is slaying or leading away captive his successful rival Ulysses and the chieftains who had slighted him. On coming to his senses he calmly resolves on self-destruction as the only means of withdrawing himself from the disgrace and punishment which he has incurred. After a fine scene, in which he takes leave of his son Eurysaces, he withdraws to a distant part of the camp, professedly for the purpose of purifying himself from the stains of his senseless bloodshed, and of burying the sword of Hector. The chorus rejoices in the hope that his temper is soothed and softened, and that all will be well. In the meantime his brother Teucer, who has passed through the camp on his return from an expedition, and has there seen the prophet Calchas, sends a messenger to insure the hero's detention at home, because the soothsayer has declared that Athena is persecuting Ajax for that day only, and that he will be saved if he survives it. The chorus proceed to search for him. The scene having changed, we see Ajax, who, after an energetic speech, falls upon his sword. And his body is found by his friends, whose lamentations are interrupted by the successive arrival of Menelaus and Agamemnon, who come to forbid his burial.

---

[1] 1361 : σοῦ φονέως μεμνημένος.
[2] 1456 sqq.   [3] 1547, 8.   [4] 1523, sqq.

The contest between Teucer and these chieftains is terminated unexpectedly by the intervention of Ulysses, the bitterest foe of the deceased warrior, who comes forward to proclaim his excellences, and to plead for the respect due to his remains. And in this way a Tragedy, on which the poet has expended all the resources of his art, is brought to a conclusion, which satisfies the prepossessions of the Athenian audience, by a proper apotheosis of their national hero.

In the *Philoctetes* Ulysses appears as the hated adversary of another great warrior; but though the issue of the play is in accordance with the object of his designs, the crafty and politic chieftain does not gain the character for generosity which is accorded to him at the end of the *Ajax*. It was by his advice that Philoctetes had been left on the island of Lemnos, because his wound had made him a noisome pest in the camp. But as it is declared that Troy will not fall without the arrows of Hercules, which Philoctetes possesses, Ulysses volunteers, in company with the young Neoptolemus, to bring him back to the army. Neoptolemus is at first persuaded to become the instrument in the deceit which Ulysses has determined to practise. But his young and generous nature recoils. He discloses the meditated treachery to Philoctetes, and the cunningly-laid plan for getting the wounded archer to Troy is utterly frustrated. Here is the *dignus vindice nodus;*[1] and Hercules descends from Olympus to command Philoctetes to go to Troy and share with Neoptolemus in the glory of its capture. The opposition between the three characters is thus reconciled, and they are all justified: Ulysses in his public-spirited policy, Neoptolemus in his straightforward veracity, and Philoctetes in his natural resentment. It is to be observed, however, that this use of the *Deus ex machinâ*, which is found only in the latest play of Sophocles, and which is considered to have been mainly due to Euripides, is in itself an indication of declining dramatic power.[2]

[1] Horace, *Ars Poet.* 191.
[2] Cic. *de Nat. Deor.* I. 20, § 52: "Ut tragici poetæ, quum explicare argumenti exitum non potestis, confugitis ad deum."

CHAPTER I.

SECTION IV.

EURIPIDES.

Aeschylus ruft Titaner herauf und Götter herunter ;
Sophocles führt anmuthig der Heldinnen Reih'n und Heroen ;
Endlich Euripides schwatzt ein sophistischer Rhetor am Markte.

A. W. SCHLEGEL.

οἱ μὲν γὰρ ἀρχαῖοι πολιτικῶς ἐποίουν λέγοντας, οἱ δὲ νῦν ῥητορικῶς.

ARISTOTELES.

Like as many substances in nature, which are solid, do putrify and
corrupt into worms ; so it is the property of a good and sound know-
ledge, to putrify and dissolve into a number of subtle, idle, unwholesome,
and, as I may term them, vermiculate questions which have indeed a
kind of quickness, and life of spirit, but no soundness of matter or
goodness of quality.

BACON.

EURIPIDES, the son of Mnesarchus, was born in the island
of Salamis, on the day of the glorious sea-fight (B.C. 480).[1]
His mother, Clito, had been sent over to Salamis with the
other Athenian women when Attica was given up to the
invading army of Xerxes ;[2] and the name of the poet, which
is formed like a patronymic from the Euripus, the scene of
the first successful resistance to the Persian navy, shows

---

[1] Diog. Laert. II. 45 : ἡμέρᾳ καθ' ἣν οἱ Ἕλληνες ἐναυμάχουν ἐν Σαλαμῖνι.
Plutarch, *Sympos.* VIII. I : ἐτέχθη καθ' ἣν ἡμέραν οἱ Ἕλληνες ἐτρέψαντο
τοὺς Πέρσας. Suidas. The Parian marble places his birth five years
earlier, and we shall see in the passage of Aulus Gellius, quoted below,
that his age was not known with certainty while he was yet alive.

[2] He belonged properly to the deme Phlya of the Cecropid tribe, but
he, perhaps, had some land in Salamis, and sometimes resided there.
"Philochorus refert," says Aulus Gellius, " in insulâ Salamine spe-
luncam esse tetram et horridam, quam nos vidimus, in quâ Euripides
tragœdias scriptitarit." *Noct. Att.* XV. 20. (Whenever we have quoted
no other authority, it will be presumed that we refer either to the life
of Euripides by Thomas Magister, or to the anonymous life published
by Elmsley, from the Ambrosian MS., and printed at the end of his
edition of the *Bacchæ*.)

that the minds of his parents were full of the stirring events of that momentous crisis. His father was certainly a man of property, else how could his son have been a pupil of the extravagant[1] Prodicus? It would appear that he was also born of a good family.[2] But this is no argument, as Philochorus supposes,[3] against the implications of Aristophanes[4] and the direct statement of Theopompus[5] that his mother was a seller of herbs; for it is quite possible that his father may have made a marriage of disparagement. Like Sophocles, he was well educated. He attended the lectures of Anaxagoras, Prodicus, and Protagoras; and was so well versed in the gymnastic exercises of the day, that he gained two victories in the Eleusinian and Thesean athletic games when only seventeen years old. Mnesarchus had intended that he should enter the lists of Olympia among the younger combatants, but some objection was raised against him on the score of age, and he was excluded from the contest.[6] To his other accomplishments he added a taste for painting, which he cultivated with some success; a few specimens of his talents in this respect were preserved

[1] See *Rhein. Mus.* for 1832, p. 22 foll.
[2] Athenæus, x. p. 424.   [3] Apud Suid. Εὐριπ.
[4]   Προπηλακιζομένας ὁρῶσ' ὑμᾶς ὑπὸ
Εὐριπίδου, τοῦ τῆς λαχανοπωλητρίας. *Thesmoph.* 386.
Again, speaking of Euripides, the female orator says—
    Ἄγρια γὰρ ἡμᾶς, ὦ γυναῖκες, δρᾷ κακά,
    Ἅτ' ἐν ἀγρίοισι τοῖς λαχάνοις αὐτὸς τραφείς. 455.
Dicæopolis, in the *Acharnians*, among his other requests, says to Euripides—
    Σκάνδικά μοι δός, μητρόθεν δεδεγμένος. 454.
The same insinuation is more obscurely conveyed in the *Equites*—
Νικ.   πῶς ἂν οὖν ποτὲ
    Εἴποιμ' ἂν αὐτὸ δῆτα κομψευριπικῶς;
Δημ. Μή μοι γε, μή μοι, μὴ διασκανδικίσῃς. 17.
And in the *Ranæ*:
Αἰσχ. Ἄληθες, ὦ παῖ τῆς ἀρουραίς θεοῦ; 839.
[5] "Euripidis poetæ matrem Theopompus agrestia olera vendentem victum quæsisse dicit.' *Noct. Att.* xv. 20.
[6] "Mnesarchus, roborato exercitatoque filii sui corpore, Olympiam certaturum inter athletas pueros deduxit. Ac primo quidem in certamen per ambiguam ætatem receptus non est. Post Eleusinio et Thesæo certamine pugnavit et coronatus est." Aul. Gell. *Noct. Att.* xv. 20.

for many years at Megara. He brought out his first
Tragedy, the *Peliades*, in (B.C.) 455,[1] consequently at an
earlier age than either of his predecessors. He was third
on this occasion, but gained the first prize fourteen years
after,[2] and also in 428 B.C., when the *Hippolytus* was represented,[3] though he does not appear to have been often so
successful.[4] His reputation, however, spread far and wide,
and if we may believe Plutarch, some of the Athenians, who
had survived the disastrous termination of the Syracusan
expedition, obtained their liberty or a livelihood by reciting
and teaching such passages from the poems of Euripides as
they happened to recollect.[5] We shall show by-and-by
that Euripides was one of the advocates for that expedition;
and we are told that he wrote a funeral poem on the

---

[1] *Arund. Marble*, No. 61. It appears, however, that he had applied
himself to dramatic composition before this. Aul. Gell. XV. 20. See
Hartung, *Euripides Restitutus*, I. pp. 6. sqq.

[2] *Arund. Marble*, 61.

[3] Argument to the *Hippol.*: ἐδιδάχθη ἐπὶ Ἀμείνονος ἄρχοντος ὀλυμπιάδι πζʹ ἔτει τετάρτῳ. πρῶτος Εὐριπίδης· δεύτερος Ἰοφῶν· τρίτος Ἴων.

[4] Suidas says he gained only five victories, one of which was with a
posthumous play.

[5] Ἔνιοι δὲ καὶ δι' Εὐριπίδην ἐσώθησαν. Μάλιστα γάρ, ὡς ἔοικε, τῶν ἐντὸς
Ἑλλήνων ἐπόθησαν αὐτοῦ τὴν μοῦσαν οἱ περὶ Σικελίαν· καὶ μικρὰ τῶν
ἀφικνουμένων ἑκάστοτε δείγματα καὶ γεύματα κομιζόντων ἐκμανθάνοντες,
ἀγαπητῶς μετεδίδοσαν ἀλλήλοις. Τότε γοῦν φασι τῶν σωθέντων οἴκαδε
συχνοὺς ἀσπάσασθαι τὸν Εὐριπίδην φιλοφρόνως, καὶ διηγεῖσθαι τοὺς μέν,
ὅτι δουλεύοντες ἀφείθησαν, ἐκδιδάξαντες, ὅσα τῶν ἐκείνου ποιημάτων
ἐμέμνηντο, τοὺς δ', ὅτι πλανώμενοι μετὰ τὴν μάχην, τροφῆς καὶ ὕδατος
μετέλαβον τῶν μελῶν ᾄσαντες. Οὐ δεῖ δὴ θαυμάζειν, ὅτι τοὺς Καυνίους
φασί, πλοίου προσφερομένου τοῖς λιμέσιν, ὑπὸ λῃστρίδων διωκομένου, μὴ
δέχεσθαι τὸ πρῶτον ἀλλ' ἀπείργειν· εἶτα μέντοι διαπυνθανομένους, εἰ
γινώσκουσιν ᾄσματα τῶν Εὐριπίδου, φησάντων, ἐκείνων, οὕτω παρεῖναι
καταγαγεῖν τὸ πλοῖον. Plutarch, *Nicias*, cxxix. We have perhaps an
additional proof of the lasting popularity of Euripides in Syracuse in
the fact that Archomelus, who composed an epigram in B.C. 220, on the
great ship of Hiero (*Anth. Pal.* Appendix 15), and who was therefore
more or less connected with Sicily, writes thus on the poet's inimitable
excellence (*Anth. Pal.* VII. 50, p. 321):

τὴν Εὐριπίδεω μήτ' ἔρχεο μήτ' ἐπιβάλλου,
    δύσβατον ἀνθρώποις οἶμον, ἀοιδοθέτα.
λείη μὲν γὰρ ἰδεῖν καὶ ἐπίκροτος· ἢν δέ τις αὐτὴν
    εἰσβαίνῃ, χαλεποῦ τρηχυτέρη σκόλοπος·
ἢν δὲ τὰ Μηδείης Αἰητίδος ἄκρα χαράξῃς,
    ἀμνήμων κείσῃ νέρθεν· ἔα στεφάνους.

EURIPIDES. 151

Athenian soldiers who fell in Sicily. Late in life he retired
to Magnesia, and from thence proceeded to Macedonia,
where his popularity procured him the protection and
friendship of King Archelaus. It is not known what
induced him to quit Athens, though many causes might be
assigned. The infidelity of his two wives, Melito and
Chœrila, which is supposed to have occasioned the miso-
gynism for which he was notorious, may perhaps have made
him desirous of escaping from the scenes of his domestic
discomforts, especially as his misfortunes were continually
recalled to his remembrance by the taunts and jeers of his
merciless political enemy, Aristophanes.[1] Besides, he appears
to have been very intimate with Socrates and Alcibiades, the
former of whom is said to have assisted him in the composition of his Tragedies;[2] and when Alcibiades won the chariot-
race at Olympia, Euripides wrote a song in honour of his
victory.[3] That Socrates was, even at this time, very un-

[1] *Ran.* 1045 :
Eurip. Οὐδὲ γὰρ ἦν τῆς Ἀφρυδίτης οὐδέν σοι·
Æschyl. μηδέ γ᾽ ἐπείη.
Ἀλλ᾽ ἐπὶ σοί τοι καὶ τοῖς σοῖσιν πολλὴ πολλοῦ ᾽πικαθῆτο.
Ὥστε γε καὐτόν σε κατ᾽ οὖν ἔβαλεν.
Bacchus. Νὴ τὸν Δία τοῦτο γέ τοι δή·
Ἃ γὰρ ἐς τὰς ἀλλοτρίας ἐποίεις, αὐτὸς τύτοισιν ἐπλήγης.

[2] "Laertius (in Socrat.) has preserved a couplet which cunningly
brings this charge :
Φρύγες, ἐστὶ καινὸν δρᾶμα τοῦτ᾽ Εὐριπίδου,
Ὧι καὶ τὰ φρύγαν᾽ ὑποτίθησι Σωκράτης.

"Allusion is made to the same imputation in a line of Antiphanes
(Athen. IV. 134):
Ὁ τὰ κεφάλαια συγγράφων Εὐριπίδη,
where κεφάλαια are the sententious sayings which Socrates was reputed
to have furnished. Ælian (*Var. Hist.* II. 13) states that Socrates
seldom went to the theatre except to see some new Tragedy of
Euripides performed.
"This philosophising in his dramas gave Euripides the name of the
stage philosopher: 'Euripides, auditor Anaxagoræ, quem philosophum
Athenienses scenicum appellaveruut.' Vitruv. VIII. in præf."—Former
Editor. See Dindorf, in *Poet. Scen.* p. 574.

[3] Plutarch, *Alcibiad.* c. XI. : Λέγει δ᾽ ὁ Εὐριπίδης ἐν τῷ ᾄσματι ταῦτα·
Σὲ δ᾽ ἀείσομαι, ὦ Κλεινίου παῖ·
Καλὸν ἁ νίκα· κάλλιστον δ᾽ ὃ
Μηδεὶς ἄλλος Ἑλλάνων

popular, is exceedingly likely;[1] and Alcibiades was a condemned exile. Perhaps, then, Euripides only followed the
dictates of prudence in withdrawing from a country where
his philosophical,[2] as well as his political sentiments, exposed him to continual danger. At the court of Archelaus,
on the contrary, he was treated with the greatest distinction, and was even admitted to the private counsels of
the king. He wrote some plays in Macedonia, in one of
which (the *Bacchæ*) he seems to have been inspired by the
wild scenery of the country[3] where he was residing; and
the story, according to which he is torn to pieces by dogs,[4]
just as his hero Pentheus is rent asunder by the infuriated
Bacchanals, arose perhaps from a confusion between the
poet and the last subject on which he wrote. It is clearly
a fabrication, for Aristophanes in *the Frogs* would certainly
have alluded to the manner of his death, had there been anything remarkable in it. He died B.C. 406, on the same day
on which Dionysius assumed the tyranny.[5] He was buried
at Pella, contrary to the wishes of his countrymen, who
requested Archelaus to send his remains to Athens, where
however a cenotaph was erected to his memory with this
inscription :

Μνᾶμα μὲν Ἑλλὰς ἅπασ’ Εὐριπίδου· ὀστέα δ’ ἴσχει
  Γῇ Μακεδών· ᾗ γὰρ δέξατο τέρμα βίου.
Πατρὶς δ’ Ἑλλάδος Ἑλλάς, Ἀθῆναι· πλεῖστα δὲ Μούσας
  Τέρψας, ἐκ πολλῶν καὶ τον ἔπαινον ἔχει.

Euripides was the last of the Greek Tragedians properly

"Αρματι πρῶτα δραμεῖν καὶ δεύτερα
Καὶ τρίτα βῆναι δ’ ἀπονητί,
Τρὶς στεφθέντ’ ἐλαίᾳ
Κάρυκι βοᾶν παραδοῦναι.

[1] Archelaus invited Socrates also to his court. Aristot. *Rhet.* II. 23.
[2] Aristot. *Rhet.* III. 15.
[3] See Elmsley on the argument, p. 4. In v. 400 we should read
Πέλλαν for Πάφον.
[4] Hermesianax Colophonius (Athen. XIII. 598); Ovid, *Ibis*, 595;
Aul. Gell., *Noct. Attic* XV. 20; Val. Max., IX. 12.—Pausanias (I. p. 3)
seems to doubt the truth of the common account. Dionysius Byzantius
expressly denies it (*Anthol.* III. 36).
[5] See Clinton, *F. H.* II. p. 81.

so called. "The sure sign of the general decline of an art," says an able writer, "is the frequent occurrence, not of deformity, but of misplaced beauty. In general Tragedy is corrupted by eloquence, and Comedy by wit."[1] This symptom of the decline of Tragedy is particularly conspicuous in Euripides, and so much of tragical propriety is given up for the sake of rhetorical display, that we sometimes feel inclined to doubt whether we are reading the works of a poet or a teacher of elocution.[2] It is this quality of Euripides which has in all ages rendered him a much greater favourite than either Æschylus or Sophocles; it is this also which made the invention of Tragi-comedy by him so natural and so easy; it is this which recommended him to Menander as the model for the dialogue of his New Comedy; and it is for this that Quintilian so strongly recommends him to the notice of the young aspirant after oratorical fame.[3] In the Middle Ages, too, Euripides was infinitely better known than the two other great Tragedians; for the more un-Greek and common-place and rhetorical and hair-splitting

[1] Lord Macaulay in the *Edinburgh Review*, No. xc. p. 278.

[2] Euripides seems to have been quite prepared to defend the long speeches which he introduces into his plays. In the *Orestes*, where there is a complete rhetorical ἀντιλογία, he makes his hero say (640):

λέγοιμ' ἂν ἤδη· τὰ μακρὰ τῶν σμικρῶν λόγων
ἐπίπροσθέν ἐστι καὶ σαφῆ μᾶλλον κλύειν.

[3] "Sed longe clarius illustraverunt hoc opus Sophocles atque Euripides; quorum in dispari dicendi viâ uter sit poeta melior, inter plurimos quaeritur. Idque ego sane, quoniam ad praesentem materiam nihil pertinet, injudicatum relinquo. Illud quidem nemo non fateatur necesse est, iis, qui se ad agendum comparant, utiliorem longe Euripidem fore. Namque is et in sermone (quod ipsum reprehendunt, quibus gravitas et cothurnus et sonus Sophoclis videtur esse sublimior) magis accedit oratorio generi: et sententiis densus, et in iis, quae a sapientibus tradita sunt, paene ipsis par, et in dicendo ac respondendo cuilibet eorum, qui fuerunt in foro diserti, comparandus. In affectibus vero cum omnibus mirus, tum in iis, qui miserationc constant, facile praecipuus. Hunc et admiratus maxime est (ut saepe testatur) et secutus, quamquam in opere diverso, Menander." *Inst. Orat.* X. I. 67. C. J. Fox remarks (*Correspondence*, edited by Lord John Russell, III. 178) that of all poets Euripides appeared to him the most useful for a public speaker.

the former was, the more attractive was he likely to prove in an age when scholastic subtleties were mistaken for eloquence, minute distinctions for science, and verbal quibbles for sure evidences of proficiency in the *ars artium*.[1] We cannot wonder then that Dante, who calls his Latin Aristotle "the master of those that know,"[2] and an Italian version of Moralia "his own Ethics,"[3] should make no mention of Æschylus and Sophocles in his survey of the shades of departed poets, but should class the rhetorical Euripides and the no less quibbling Agathon among the greatest of the poets of Greece.[4] But if it be easy to explain how the quasi-philosophical character of Euripides gained him so much popularity among his less civilised contemporaries, the Sicilians and Macedonians, and among the semi-barbarous Europeans of the Middle Ages, we shall have still less difficulty in explaining how he came to be so unlike the two great

---

[1] In one form of verbal quibbling, the habit of punning on similar sounds, Euripides is not more responsible than Æschylus and Sophocles, and Shakspere has followed them in this respect. Valckenaer says (*ad Phœn.* p. 187): "Amat Tragicus noster ἐτυμολογεῖν, atque ob eam insaniam merito quoque fuit a comicis irrisus." This exclusive censure of Euripides is answered by Lobeck (*ad Soph. Aj.* 430); see also Elmsley on Eurip. *Bacch.* 508. And the practice is so common in all the tragedians that it furnishes a constant problem for the ingenuity of translators, who are not always very happy in their substitutions of English for Greek in reproducing this play upon words. For instance, it is absurd in Æsch. *Agam.* 671, to translate the play upon the name of Helen in the epithets ἑλέναυς, ἕλανδρος, ἑλέπτολις, by "a Hell to ships, a Hell to men, and a Hell to cities;" for this does not really recall the proper name: if we said "a knell to ships," &c., we should at any rate have a reference to a common abbreviation of the name *Helen* (*Nell*). Similarly in Euripides, *Bacchæ*, 367: Πενθεὺς δ' ὅπως μὴ πένθος εἰσοίσει δόμοις τοῖς σοῖσι, might be rendered: "Take heed, lest Pentheus makes your mansion a penthouse of grief," instead of seeking a longer paraphrase. And a similar rendering might apply to v. 508.

[2] *Inf.* IV. 131.

[3] *Inf.* XI. 80, referring to Aristot. *Eth.* VII. 1. That Dante read Aristotle's Ethics in the Italian translation of *Taddeo d'Alderotto*, surnamed *l'Ippocratista*, may be inferred from the *Convito*, I. 10, p. 39.

[4] *Purgat.* XXII. 106:

> "*Euripide* v' è nosco e Anacreonte,
> Simonide, *Agatone*, e altri piùe
> Greci che già di lauro ornar la fronte."

writers who preceded him; one of whom was in his later days the competitor of Euripides. We have already insisted at some length upon the connection between the actors of Sophocles, Æschylus, and their predecessors, and the Homeric rhapsode. Now the rhapsodes were succeeded by a class of men whom, for want of a more definite name, it has been customary to call sophists,[1] and sometimes the sophist and the rhapsode were united in the same person: indeed so completely were they identified in most cases, that Plato makes Socrates treat Hippias the sophist, who was also a rhapsode, and Ion the rhapsode, who seems to have been a sophist too, with banter and irony of precisely the same kind. Since, then, Euripides was nursed in the lap of sophistry, was the pupil and friend of the most eminent of the sophists, and perhaps to all intents a sophist himself, we cannot wonder that he should turn the rhapsodical element of the Greek Drama into a sophistical one: in fact, the transition was not only natural, but perhaps even necessary. It may, however, be asked, how is this reconcilable with the statement that Socrates assisted Euripides in the composition of his Tragedies? for Socrates was, if we can believe Plato's representation of him, the sworn foe of the sophists. We answer that Socrates was, in the more general sense of the word, himself a sophist; his opposition to the other sophists, which has probably been exaggerated by his pupils and apologists, to whom we owe nearly all we know about him, is no proof of a radical difference between him and them: on the contrary, it is proverbial that there are no disagreements so rancorous and implacable as those between persons who follow the same trade with different objects in view. That Socrates was the least pernicious of the sophists, that if he was not a good citizen, he was at least an honest man, we are very much disposed to believe; but in the eyes of his contemporaries he differed but little from the rest of the tribe: Aristophanes attacks him as the head of the school, and perhaps some of the comedian's animosity to Euripides may have arisen

[1] The young student will find some interesting remarks on these personages in Coleridge's *Friend*, vol. III. p. 112 foll. See also the articles on Prodicus in Nos. I. and IV. of the *Rhein. Mus.* 1832.

from his belief that the tragedian was only a Socrates and a sophist making an *epideixis* in iambics.[1]

Euripides was not only a rhetorical sophist. He also treated his audience to some of the physical doctrines of his master Anaxagoras.[2] For instance, he goes out of his way to communicate to them the Anaxagorean discovery, that the sun is nothing but an ignited stone:[3] he tells them that the overflowing of the Nile is merely the consequence of the melting of the snow in Æthiopia,[4] and that the æther is an embodiment of the Deity.[5]

In his political opinions Euripides was attached to Alcibiades and to the war party; and in this again he was opposed to Aristophanes, and, we may add, to the best interests of his country. He endeavours to inspire his countrymen with a contempt for their formidable enemies the Spartans,[6] and with a distrust of their good faith;[7] in order that the Athenians might not, through fear for their prowess, scruple to continue at war with them, and might, through suspicion, be as unwilling as possible to make peace. We find him also united with the sophist Gorgias and the profligate Alcibiades in urging the disastrous expedition to Sicily; for he wrote the Trilogy to which the *Troades* belonged, in the beginning of the year 415,[8] in which that expedition started, manifestly with a view to encourage the gaping *quidnuncs* of the Agora to fall into the ambitious schemes of Alcibiades, by recalling the recollection of the success of a similar expedition, undertaken in the mythical ages; and it has been conjectured that his

[1] Aristophanes speaks of him thus:

ὅτε δὴ κατῆλθ' Εὐριπίδης ἐπεδείκνυτο
τοῖς λωποδύταις, κ.τ.λ. *Ranæ*, 771.

[2] On the allusions which Euripides makes to the philosophy of Anaxagoras, the reader of this poet should consult Valckenaer's *Diatribe*. pp. 25—58.

[3] *Orest.* VI. 984, and the fr. of the *Phaëthon*.

[4] *Helen.* 1—3, fr. of the *Archelaus*.

[5] *Troad.* 878 sqq.

[6] For instance, in his ridiculous exhibition of Menelaus in the *Troades*, and in the *Orestes*. See particularly *Orest.* 717 sqq.; *Androm.* 590.

[7] *Andromache*, 445 sqq.

[8] See Clinton, *F. H.* II. p. 75.

wiser opponent wrote the *Birds* in the following year to ridicule the whole plan and its originators.[1]

Besides obliterating the genuine character of the Greek Tragedy, by introducing sophistry and philosophy into the dialogue, Euripides degraded it still further by laying aside all the dignity and καλοκἀγαθία which distinguished the costumes and the characters of Æschylus and Sophocles, by vulgarising the tragic style,[2] by introducing rags and tatters on the stage,[3] by continually making mention of the most trivial and ordinary subjects,[4] and by destroying the connection which always subsisted, in the perfect form of the drama, between the chorus and the actors.[5] With regard to his system of prologues, which Lessing most paradoxically considers as showing the perfection of the drama, we need only mention that Menander adopted it from him, and point to the difference between this practice and that of Æschylus, Sophocles, and Shakspere, in order to justify the ridicule which Aristophanes unsparingly heaps upon them as factitious and unnecessary parts of a Tragedy.

Like the other sophists, Euripides was altogether devoid of religious feelings; his moral character will not bear a searching scrutiny; and, unlike the good-tempered, cheerful Sophocles, he displayed the same severity of manner which distinguished his never-smiling preceptor Anaxagoras. On the whole, were it not for the exceeding beauty of many of his choruses, and for the proof which he occasionally exhibits of really tragic power, we should be unable to understand the admiration with which he has inspired the most cultivated men in different ages; and looking at him from the point of view occupied by his contemporaries, we must join with Aristophanes, not only in calling him, what he

---

[1] See J. W. Süvern's interesting Essay on the *Birds* of Aristophanes.

[2] See Müller, *Hist. Lit. Gr.* I. p. 336 [483]. In *Hercul. Fur.* 859, it is clear that στάδια δραμοῦμαι, the reading of Flor. 2, is a gloss on the genuine σταδιοδρομήσω, which ought to be restored. And in *Electr.* 841, we ought certainly to read ἠλάλαξε δ' ὡς θνῄσκων φόνῳ.

[3] *Ran.* 841 sqq.   [4] *Ib.* 980 sqq.

Καὶ τὸν χορὸν δὲ ἕνα δεῖ ὑπολαβεῖν τῶν ὑποκριτῶν καὶ μόριον εἶναι τοῦ ὅλου, καὶ συναγωνίζεσθαι, μὴ ὥσπερ Εὐριπίδης, ἀλλ' ὥσπερ Σοφοκλῆς. Aristot. *Poёt.* XVIII. 21.

undeniably was, a bad citizen[1] and an unprincipled man, but also in regarding him as a dramatist who degraded the moral and religious dignity of his own sacred profession. At the best, he is one of those poets who appear to the greatest advantage in selections of elegant extracts. " His works," says an eminent critic,[2] "must be regarded less in their entirety than in detail. In single passages there is much that in itself is excellent, deeply moving, and masterly, which, if part of a whole, is liable to censure. We might almost maintain that, with Euripides, those very parts are most beautiful which he introduced as superfluous additions, merely because he could not resist the temptations offered by certain situations; though indeed it sometimes happens that the overabundant heaping-together of materials impedes the development of the individual parts, and that the episodes fail in making their due impression from a want of proper extension. Tragic effect to be perfect requires completeness in preparation, development, and solution; but for this there is frequently a want of room with Euripides. In the *Troades*, for instance, there is such a quantity of matter that the death of Polyxena can only be narrated in a few words. Thus, in this Tragedy the effect of the tragic incidents is destroyed by the overabundance which makes them neutralise each other." In accordance with these remarks the same author has very ably contrasted the feebler art of Euripides with the rude vigour of Æschylus and the graceful dignity of Sophocles. "If," he says,[3] "we take a comparative view of the heroes of Greek Tragedy, we find that in Æschylus the mighty subject-matter is not always satisfactorily developed—that in Euripides the luxuriance of the matter often predominates over the form—that in Sophocles, on the contrary, the matter is so completely proportionate to the form that, with all its abundance, it adapts itself without constraint, and, as it were, of its own

---

[1] On the connection of Euripides and Socrates with the mischievous Girondism of the middle-class party at Athens, we have written elsewhere (*Quarterly Review*, No. CLXI. vol. 71, p. 116; continuation of Müller's *Hist. Lit. Gr.* vol. II. p. 165, new ed.).

[2] F. Jacobs, *Hellas, or the home, history, literature, and art of the Greeks.* Translated by J. Oxenford, p. 235.

[3] *Hellas*, p. 236.

accord, to the law of order. With the first nature is grand and powerful, but art is somewhat unwieldy; with the second art is somewhat too lax and pliant; with Sophocles art rules over a free and beautiful nature. Æschylus pays homage to grandeur without grace : Euripides only seeks the fascinating: Sophocles combines dignity and beauty in intimate union. The first fills us with words, the second with compassion, Sophocles with noble admiration. The whole plan of their works corresponds to their different aims. Æschylus, at the very commencement, often raises himself to a height which only his own gigantic mind can hope to surmount; Sophocles leads us on gradually; Euripides, through successive sections, repeats the same tones of touching sorrow. Æschylus proceeds rapidly from his preparation to the catastrophe; Sophocles, as he approaches the catastrophe retards his steps ; Euripides, with uncertain tread, pursues an uncertain goal, rather heaping up misfortune than rendering it more intense. Æschylus is simple without art : with Sophocles simplicity is a result of art: with Euripides variety often predominates to the injury of art. The mighty and extraordinary events which are the focus of the action with his predecessors, are often with Euripides no more than strengthening rays, and the incidents are not unfrequently more tragical than the catastrophe. The immolation of a daughter torn from her mother's arms, the murder of an innocent boy, the voluntary death of a wife on her husband's funeral-pile, the sacrifice of a youth for his country, of a maiden for her family,—all these with Euripides are mere incidents of the action."[1]

Thanks to accident, or the corrupted taste of those to whom we owe all of ancient literature that we possess, the remaining plays of Euripides are more than all the extant dramas of Æschylus and Sophocles taken together. Of his many compositions fifteen Tragedies,[2] two Tragi-comedies,[3]

---

[1] There is a severe criticism on Euripides in the *Foreign Quarterly Review*, No. XLVIII. Professor Blackie refers to this article as his own (*Æschylus*, I. p. xxxvii). Schlegel's comparison of the related plays of the three Tragedians is given in an Appendix to this chapter.

[2] Or 16, if the *Rhesus* is reckoned one of his.

[3] The *Orestes* and the *Alcestis*.

and a satyrical drama[1] have come down to us; and the fragments of the lost plays are very numerous.

It appears that Euripides, like the other two great tragedians, exhibited his dramas in Tetralogies, and in more
than one instance we have among his extant plays those
which formed a portion of the same theatrical representation.
We do not, however, derive much advantage from this.
His Tetralogies were not, like those of Æschylus, bound
together by a community of subject and treatment, and
except as a chronological fact, the juxtaposition of particular
dramas is quite unimportant to the reader of his works.

The order in which the extant plays of Euripides were
produced may be ascertained to a certain extent either
from direct statements resting on the didascaliæ or from
internal evidence. In making a few remarks on the particular plays we shall be content in the main with the
results of the most recent and elaborate investigation of
the subject.[2]

The earliest extant play of Euripides is the *Rhesus*,
which, as we have already mentioned, has been attributed to
Sophocles, and regarded as one of his earliest dramas.[3] On
the other hand, it has been supposed that four actors are
required in the scene in which Paris appears immediately
after Diomedes and Ulysses have left the stage, and while
Athena is still there; and it has been suggested accordingly that it belongs to the later Athenian stage, perhaps
to the school of Philocles.[4] It must be confessed that there
are serious objections to its genuineness;[5] but Euripides
certainly wrote a play called the *Rhesus*, which Attius
imitated in his *Nyctegersis*,[6] and it is expressly stated that
this was one of his earliest efforts.[7] That the present play
was this juvenile production has been warmly maintained

---

[1] The *Cyclops*.
[2] J. A. Hartung, *Euripides Restitutus*, vol. I. 1843; vol. II. 1844.
[3] Gruppe, *Ariadne*, pp. 285 sqq.
[4] Müller, *Hist. Lit. Gr.* I. p. 501, note.
[5] Valckenaer, *Diatribe*, 9, 10; Hermann, *Opusc.* III. pp. 262 sqq.
[6] Hartung, l. p. 15.
[7] Crates, *ap. Schol. Rhes.* 575: Κράτης ἀγνοεῖν φησὶ τὸν Εὐριπίδην
τὴν περὶ τὰ μετέωρα θεωρίαν διὰ τὸ νέον ἔτι εἶναι, ὅτε τὸν 'Ρῆσον
ἐδίδασκε.

by two of the admirers of Euripides,[1] and it has been referred to the year B.C. 466.[2]

The undoubtedly genuine Drama, which bears the name of *Alcestis*, was acted as the after-piece to the Trilogy of the *Cressæ*, the *Alcmæon in Psophide*, and the *Telephus*, in B.C. 438.[3] Though the main incident, the voluntary death of Alcestis as a vicarious substitute for her husband Admetus, is eminently pathetic and tragical, the character of Hercules is conceived in the spirit of comedy, and the rescue of Alcestis from the grave nullifies all the emotions excited by the first part of the play.

The *Heracleidæ* is referred to the period immediately before the Peloponnesian war B.C. 434, and is supposed to allude in many passages to the divine assistance on which the Athenians could rely, and to the probable discomfiture of any presumptuous invaders.[4] It is conjecturally placed in the same Tetralogy with the *Peleus* and *Ægeus*, and the satyrical drama *Eurystheus*.[5] The subject of the play is the generous protection which the Athenians accorded to the Heracleidæ, and the incident of the sacrifice of Macaria is introduced to give some special pathos to a piece which is otherwise somewhat tame and common-place.

It is known that the *Medea* was acted in the archonship of Pythodorus, B.C. 431, and that it was the first play of a Tetralogy which included the *Philoctetes*, *Dictys*, and the satyrical drama of "the Reapers" (Θερισταί).[6] The *Medea* is the most faultless of the dramas of Euripides, and has really many excellences. Its object is to depict the jealousy of a divorced and outraged wife, and the dreadful vengeance which she exacts on the rival who has superseded her. It has been well remarked[7] that "the scene which paints the struggle in Medea's breast between her plans of revenge and her love for her children will always be one of the most touching and impressive ever represented on the

---

[1] Vater, *Vindiciæ Rhesi*, and Hartung.

[2] Hartung, I. p. 8.

[3] See the didascalia in *Cod. Vatic.* quoted above, p. 82, note 4.

[4] Hartung, I. pp. 288 sqq. Müller, *Hist. Gr. Lit.* I. p. 488 (new ed.), refers it to the time of the battle of Delium, B.C. 421.

[5] Hartung, p. 289.   [6] *Argum. Med.*

[7] Müller, *Hist. Lit. Gr.* I. p. 485 (new ed.).

M

stage." Its dramatic value is proved by the success of
the modern plays and operas in which the injured wife
murders, or intends to murder her children, as an appropriate punishment of a faithless husband.[1]

Euripides obtained the first prize with his *Hippolytus
Crowned* in the archonship of *Ameinon* or *Epameinon*, B.C.
428.[2] This play, like the *Medea*, has been revived with
great success on the modern stage,[3] and in spite of great
faults, it produces a considerable effect on the reader. The
plot turns on the criminal love of Phædra for her step-son
Hippolytus, the Joseph of classical mythology. As in the
similar cases of Bellerophon and Peleus, the scorned and
passionate woman seeks the ruin of the chaste young man,
but in this instance she also commits suicide. The father,
Theseus, is induced to believe in his son's guilt. And the
innocent hero is torn to death by his own steeds, who are
frightened by sea-monsters sent against them by Neptune,
and his death having been thus effected by the malice of
Aphrodite and the blind compliance of the sea-god, the
chaste goddess Artemis appears *ex machinâ* to do poetic
justice to the innocent victim.

It has been conjectured that the *Cyclops*, our only remaining satyrical drama, belonged to the same Tetralogy
as the *Hippolytus*, which also, it is supposed, contained the
Bellerophontes and the *Antigone*.[4] The *Bellerophontes* is
recommended for this juxta-position by its similarity of
subject, with of course a difference of treatment. The
Antigone of Euripides had a fortunate termination, as
far as Hæmon and the heroine were concerned,[5] and the

---

[1] It is only necessary to mention the Tragedy *Médée* and the operas
Medea and *Norma*.

[2] *Argum. Hippol.*

[3] In Racine's *Phèdre*. The great French dramatist says, in the
preface to his play: "Je ne suis point étonné que ce caractère (de
Phèdre) ait eu un succès si heureux du temps d'Euripide, et qu'il ait
encore si bien réussi dans notre siècle, puisqu'il a toutes les qualités
qu'Aristote demande dans le héros de la tragédie, et qui sont propres à
exciter la compassion et la terreur."

[4] Hartung, I. pp. 385 sqq.

[5] Aristoph. Byz. *in Argum. Antig. Soph.*; κεῖται δὲ ἡ μυθοποιΐα καὶ
παρ' Εὐριπίδῃ ἐν 'Αντιγόνῃ· πλὴν ἐκεῖ φωραθεῖσα μετὰ τοῦ Αἵμονος δίδοται
πρὸς γάμου κοινωνίαν καὶ τίκτει τὸν Μαίμονα.

fragments seem to point to a tyranny of love, which is quite
at variance with the moral of the *Hippolytus*.[1] In general
there is very little reason for connecting the two plays.
The *Cyclops* is placed at the same epoch with the *Hippolytus*,
because it seems to have been acted before the expedition to
Syracuse;[2] but this is a very slender argument. The plot
of the *Cyclops*, of which we have given an analysis in a subsequent chapter, is merely a dramatic version of the adventure
with Polyphemus in the ninth book of the *Odyssey*.

The *Ion* is referred[3] to about B.C. 427, because it alludes
unmistakably to the porch at Delphi, which the Athenians
decorated as a memorial of Phormio's victories,[4] and actually
mentions Rhium, where the trophy stood;[5] it probably
alludes also to the relations between Athens and their
colonists on the coast of Asia Minor,[6] which had become very
critical in the 88th Ol. The plot of the *Ion* is interesting,
and ingeniously developed. It turns on the recognition by
Creusa of her own son by Apollo in the young priest Ion,
whom she had endeavoured to poison by the instrumentality
of a faithful domestic, under the belief that he was the
child of her husband Xuthus, and a bastard intruder on
the ancient honours of her family. That the *Ion* was exhibited in the same Tetralogy with the *Ino* and *Erechtheus*,
and the satyrical drama *Sciron*, is inferred from considerations more or less precarious.[7]

The date of the *Hecuba* is fixed to B.C. 424 by two
parodies of its language in the *Nubes* of Aristophanes,[8]
which show that it must have appeared before B.C. 423,
and by a reference in the play itself[9] to the sacred rites of
Delos, which the Athenians took into their own hands in

---

[1] See *Fragments*, VI. and VII.　　　[2] Hartung, I. p. 388.
[3] By Böckh, *de Gr. Trag. Princ.* p. 191.
[4] *Ion*, 184 sqq.　　　[5] v. 1592.
[6] v. 1581:　　　οἱ τῶνδε δ' αὖ
παῖδες γενόμενοι ξὺν χρόνῳ πεπρωμένῳ
κυκλάδας ἐποικήσουσι νησαίας πόλεις
χερσούς τε παράλους ὃ σθένος τἠμῇ χθονὶ
δίδωσιν.

[7] Hartung, I. pp. 451 sqq.　　　[8] 718, 1165.
[9] 466 sqq.

M 2

B.C. 425. So that the play must have fallen between these two years.[1] And it is conjectured[2] that the other plays of the Tetralogy were the *Alcmena* or *Licymnius*, *Pleisthenes*, or the *Pelopidæ*, and the satyrical drama called *Theseus*, the latter of which must have been of similar import to the *Sciron* of the immediately previous Tetralogy.

The *Hecuba*, which has always been one of the most popular plays of Euripides, introduces the aged queen of Troy as a marked and vigorous character. After her daughter Polyxena has been torn from her to be sacrificed at the tomb of Achilles, the corpse of her only remaining son Polydorus is cast up by the waves, and she learns that he has been murdered by the treacherous king of Thrace, Polymestor, to whom he had been intrusted along with some treasure. She entices the perfidious wretch and his children into her tent, and there slays them and puts out his eyes; and she then successfully defends her act when called to an account before Agamemnon. Besides the character of Hecuba, who appears as a sort of philosopher of the Euripidean school, the noble resignation of Polyxena is made to interest the spectators by a display similar to that which we find in the *Heracleidæ* and the *Iphigenia at Aulis*.

Some allusions to the inconveniences of old age[3] place the *Hercules Furens* among the later compositions of Euripides, and certain references to his wish for peace with Thebes and Sparta[4] strengthen the hypothesis that the play was acted about B.C. 422. It is conjectured[5] that the other plays of the Tetralogy were the *Temenides*, the *Cresphontes*,[6]

---

[1] It is also supposed that there is an allusion to the Spartan disaster at Pylos in v. 649:

στένει δὲ καὶ τις ἀμφὶ τὸν εὔροον Εὐρώταν
Λάκαινα πολυδάκρυτος ἐν δόμοις κόρα.

[2] Hartung, I. pp. 542, 546.

[3] See v. 639 sqq., especially v. 678: ἔτι τοι γέρων ἀοιδὸς κελαδεῖ μναμοσύναν, which may be compared with Æschylus, *Agam.* v. 104.

[4] vv. 471, 1135, 1303.   [5] Hartung, II. p. 21 sqq.

[6] The *Cresphontes* refers in one of the choral fragments both to the advancing age of the poet and his longing for peace (*Fragm.* xv.):

εἰράνα βαθύπλουτε . . .
ζῆλός μοι σέθεν, ὡς χρονίζεις,

and a satyrical drama called *Cercyon.* In many parts the
Hercules is singularly vigorous and effective, but its dramatic
merits are seriously compromised by its want of unity in
the subject and action. The first part of the play is occupied
with the liberation of the family of Hercules from the
persecutions of Lycus; and then *Lyssa* or madness appears
as the only explanation of the frenzy, in which Hercules
slays his wife and children.

The reference, which the chorus of the *Iphigenia at
Tauri,* supposed to consist of Delian women, makes to the
island of Delos and to the worship of Apollo there,[1] may
have been prompted by the restoration of the Delians to
their island, which the Athenians carried out in B.C. 421 in
obedience to an oracle;[2] and if so, the play may have been
performed about this time. It is conjectured[3] that the
Phrixus, Epopeus, and *Alope* were the other plays of the
Tetralogy. The *Iphigenia at Tauri* exhibits happier situations and greater taste in the execution than perhaps any
play of Euripides. The poet avoids the awkwardness of
making the pure and elevated priestess a sacrificer of her
unfortunate countrymen. The duty of Iphigenia is only to
consecrate the victims,[4] and it has so happened that no Greek
has been driven to the inhospitable coast before the arrival
of Orestes.[5] The mutual recognition of the brother and
sister, the plan of flight, and the deep devotion of Orestes to
his friend Pylades, sustain the interest of the piece, which has
furnished materials for the greatest Tragedy of Pacuvius,[6]
and for a singularly beautiful reproduction by Goethe.[7]

The *Supplices* makes the Argive ruler contract an alliance
with Athens, by which all his descendants are to be bound.[8]
This must surely refer to the treaty between Athens and
Argos, brought about by Alcibiades in B.C. 420. For
Euripides and Alcibiades were in some sort of connection
with one another. A few years previously (B.C. 424)

δέδοικα δὲ μὴ πρὶν πόνοις
ὑπερβάλῃ με γῆρας
πρὶν σὰν προσιδεῖν χαρίεσσαν ὥραν, κ.τ.λ.

[1] 1096 sqq.   [2] Thucyd. v. 32, cf. c. 1.   [3] Hartung, II. p. 142.
[4] v. 617 sqq.   [5] v. 244 sqq.   [6] The *Duloresles.*
[7] The *Iphigenie auf Tauris.*   [8] v. 1192 sqq.

Alcibiades had won the prize at Olympia, and Euripides had
written the ode for him.[1]　It is probable therefore that
Euripides might use his stage opportunities for recommending the political action of Alcibiades; and the general
subject of the play, the services rendered by Theseus in
procuring from the Thebans the interment of the Argive
warriors, may have been intended to promote the newly
established relations between Argos and Athens.　The reference to the three classes in the state is quite in the
spirit of Alcibiades himself.[2]

The *Andromache* describes the persecution of the widow
of Hector, now married to Neoptolemus, by Menelaus and
his daughter Hermione, the intervention of Peleus to pro-
tect her, the abduction of Hermione by Orestes, and the
assassination of Neoptolemus by the latter.　At the end
Thetis appears *ex machinâ* to promise the deification of
Peleus, and the future sovranty of Andromache's descendants
among the Molossi.　There is a distinct reference in this
play to the deceit into which the Spartan ambassadors were
led by Alcibiades during the negotiations of B.C. 420,[3] and
there seems little doubt that, as the *Supplices* recommends
the alliance with Argos, the *Andromache* favours the rupture
with Sparta, both brought about by Alcibiades in the same
year; and both plays have been accordingly referred, with
the *Œnomaus* and the former *Autolycus*, to a Tetralogy
produced in B.C. 419.[4]

It is known that the *Troades* was brought out in B.C. 415
with the *Alexander*, the *Palamedes*, and the satyrical drama
Sisyphus.[5]　The play refers distinctly to the expedition to
Sicily, which sailed in this year;[6] and it is not improbable
that the whole Tetralogy was filled with allusions which
would be transferred from the successful attack on Troy to
the expected capture of Syracuse.　There is no play even of
Euripides which exhibits such a want of dramatic concen-

---

[1] Plut. *Vit. Alcibiad.* c. 11.
[2] Comp. *Suppl.* 247 with Thucyd. VI. 18, § 7.
[3] Comp. Thucyd. v. 45 with *Androm.* 445 : λέγοντες ἄλλα μὲν γλώσσῃ,
φρονοῦντες δ' ἄλλα.
[4] Hartung, II. p. 76 sqq.
[5] Ælian, *V. H.* II. 8.　　　　　[6] v. 220.

tration. It is rather a series of incidents than the proper development of one leading idea. The allotment of Cassandra to Agamemnon, and her prophecies; the sacrifice of Polyxena, dismissed with a few words, because it had previously appeared in the *Hecuba;* the flinging of Astyanax from the walls of the city, and the sorrow of Andromache; the singular argumentation of Hecuba and Helen before Menelaus; and the final picture of the conflagration of Troy, form an unconnected succession of scenes, any one of which might have been worked up by dramatic genius into a complete play.

The six remaining Tragedies may be grouped in pairs.

That the *Electra* and the *Helena* were acted together with the *Andromeda* in B.C. 412, seems to be established by an adequate induction. For the *Andromeda* was acted eight years before the *Ranœ* of Aristophanes,[1] i. e. in B.C. 412. Then again, the *Helena* was acted with the *Andromeda.*[2] Finally, the conclusion of the *Electra* prepares the hearer for the new version of the history of Helen, which is given in the play of that name,[3] and the *Thesmophoriazusœ* of Aristophanes, which was brought out in B.C. 411, speaks of " the new Helen " with distinct reference to this play.[4] It is therefore tolerably certain that the *Electra* and *Helena* were connected plays, and were acted in B.C. 411. There is less reason for the supposition[5] that the *Busiris* was the satyrical drama of this Tetralogy. In the *Electra*, as in the *Helena*, Euripides departs from the established traditions. The former heroine is married to a common countryman, and is exhibited as a good economical housewife. The motives for the murder of Ægisthus by Clytæmnestra are purely vindictive, and instead of being justified on religious

---

[1] Schol. Aristoph. *Ran.* 53 : ἡ γὰρ ᾿Ανδρομέδα ὀγδόῳ ἔτει προῆκται.

[2] Schol. *Thesmoph.* 1012 : συνδεδίδακται γὰρ (ἡ ᾿Ανδρομέδα) τῇ ῾Ελένῃ.

[3] 1280 :   Πρωτέως γὰρ ἐκ δόμων
ἥκει λιποῦσ᾿ Αἴγυπτον, οὐδ᾿ ἦλθεν Φρύγας·
Ζεὺς δ᾿, ὡς ἔρις γένοιτο καὶ φόνος βροτοῖς,
εἴδωλον ῾Ελένης ἐξέπεμψ᾿ ἐς ῎Ιλιον.

In v. 1347 there is probably an allusion to the fresh expedition to Syracuse under Demosthenes.

[4] 850 : τὴν καινὴν ῾Ελένην μιμήσομαι.

[5] Hartung, II. p. 360.

grounds, the Dioscuri, who appear *ex machinâ* at the end, insinuate that Apollo, in recommending the deed, uttered an unwise oracle.[1] The *Helena* of Euripides gives us a modification of the view of Stesichorus,[2] which is quite at variance with that of Euripides himself in the *Troades.* The plot is occupied with the elopement of the innocent and injured heroine from Egypt, where she had resided, while the Greeks were fighting for her at Troy, and Menelaus, with the help of Theonoe, the prophetic sister of the Egyptian king, effects the escape of his wife from the Pharaoh who wished to marry her.

The *Orestes,* which was a tragi-comedy of the same class as the *Alcestis,*[3] was acted in the archonship of Diocles, B.C. 408,[4] and must have been the fourth play of the Tetralogy to which it belonged. The third play was the *Phœnissæ.*[5] The other two were the *Antiope* and the *Hypsipyle.*[6] In the *Phœnissæ* we have the same subject as that of the *Seven against Thebes* exhibited in the Euripidean style. At the same time there are unmistakable indications of the writer's acquaintance with the *Œdipus Coloneus.* The introduction of Polyneices, the expulsion of Œdipus, and Antigone's resolve to accompany her father, were perhaps suggested by Sophocles; the determination to bury Polyneices comes from Æschylus. But Euripides has involved himself in a contradiction by making the expulsion of Œdipus subsequent

---

[1] *Electra,* 1244:

δίκαια μέν νῦν ἥδ' ἔχει· σὺ δ' οὐχὶ δρᾶς,
Φοῖβός τε Φοῖβος, ἀλλ' ἄναξ γάρ ἐστ' ἐμός,
σιγῶ· σοφὸς δ' ὦν οὐκ ἔχρησέ σοι σοφά.

[2] According to Stesichorus Helen never left Greece, but it was her εἴδωλον, φάσμα, which went to Troy. According to Euripides the gods formed a false Helen who went to Troy, while the true one was carried to the Egyptian king Proteus by Hermes.

[3] *Argum. Alc.:* τὸ παρὸν δρᾶμα ἐκ τραγικοῦ κωμικόν. *Cod. Παυν. ap. Matth.* VII. p. 114: παρὰ τοῖς τραγικοῖς ἐκβάλλεται ὅ τε Ὀρέστης καὶ ἡ Ἄλκηστις. . . ἔστι μᾶλλον κωμῳδίας ἐχόμενα.

[4] Schol. *Orest.* 371; cf. ad. 772.

[5] *Ibid.* 1481: ἐν τῷ τρίτῳ δράματι οὗτός φησιν ἐν τῷ χορῷ τῷ "Κάδμος ἔμολε" (*i.e. Phœniss.* 638).

[6] Schol. Arist. *Ran.* 53: διὰ τί μὴ ἄλλο τι τῶν δι' ὀλίγου διδαχθέντων καὶ καλῶν, Ὑψιπύλης, Φοινισσῶν, Ἀντιόπης; ἐπειδὴ οὐ συκοφαντητὰ ἦν τὰ τοιαῦτα.

to the mutual fratricide, so that one hardly sees how
Antigone can perform the double part, which Sophocles has
arranged for her, without any such inconsistency. There
are some fine scenes in the play. The altercation between
the two brothers is spirited. The view of the besieging host
from the roof of the palace is well conceived. And the
death of Menœceus would be affecting, if it were not a mere
repetition of the self-sacrifice of Macaria in the *Heracleidæ*.
There is hardly any real Tragedy in the *Orestes*. The
crazy matricide, about to be freed by the Argives and
deserted by Menelaus on whom he had placed his reliance,
seeks to avenge himself on Helen; and when she vanishes
to heaven, he takes her daughter Hermione as a substitute,
and is about to slay her, when the Dioscuri appear and
command him to marry the damsel. The cowardice of the
Phrygian slave is positively ludicrous, and was perhaps
intended to excite the mirth of the audience.

After the death of Euripides in B.C. 406, the plays which
he wrote for representation in Macedonia—the *Iphigenia at
Aulis*, the *Alcmæon at Corinth*, the *Bacchæ*, and the *Archelaus*
—were produced as new Tragedies at Athens by the
younger Euripides, who was probably the nephew of the great
Tragedian.[1] It is not improbable that they had been
already performed at Pella, for the *Bacchæ* is full of allusions
to Macedonian scenery,[2] and the *Iphigenia* may have been
suggested to him during his stay in Magnesia on his route
to the north.[3] These two plays, which have come down to
us, not without considerable mutilations, may be reckoned
among the happiest dramatic efforts of Euripides. In the
Iphigenia Euripides excites our interest and touches our
feelings by a very lively picture of the circumstances attending the sacrifice of the princess. Agamemnon's vain
attempts to save his daughter, the knightly courage of
Achilles, who is willing to fight the whole army on her

---

[1] Schol. Arist. *Ran.* 67, where the younger Euripides is called the
son of his namesake. The Ἀλκμαίων διὰ Κορίνθου is so called to distinguish it from the Ἀλκμαίων διὰ Ψωφῖδος acted together with the
Alcestis.
[2] Cf. vv. 400 where read Πέλλαν. 565 sqq.
[3] *Vit. cod. Mediol. coll. Ambros.* Hartung, II. p. 510.

behalf, the indignation of Clytæmnestra, and the self-
devotion of Iphigenia, who, after pleading in the prettiest
and most pathetic speech for her life, at last solves all the
difficulties by offering herself as a voluntary sacrifice, form
a dramatic development which is found in few of the poet's
earlier plays, and which has made this Tragedy a model both
for Ennius, and for Racine and Schiller. The text unfortunately is not only mutilated but deformed by tasteless
interpolations. The prologue, as it stands, is in a great
state of confusion. It begins with a dialogue in anapæsts
(vv. 1—48), then follows a monologue of the usual Euripidean
style (vv. 49—114), after which the dialogue in anapæsts is
resumed until the entrance of the chorus (v. 164).[1]　On
the other hand, it appears, from a quotation by Ælian,[2] that
we have lost the epilogue, in which Artemis appeared and
promised to make the sacrifice of Iphigenia illusory, and it
has long been held that the concluding scene, as we have it,
is an interpolation.[3]　There are besides many corruptions
in detail.[4]　With the exception of some lacunæ in the last
scene, the *Bacchæ* is in a much better state of preservation
than the sister Tragedy. It details the miserable end of
Pentheus, who stands alone in obstinate resistance to the

---

[1] Hartung, in his edition of this play, Erlang. 1837. begins the first
scene with Agamemnon's speech (v. 47), omitting the five concluding
lines.

[2] *De Animal.* VII. 29 : ὁ δὲ Εὐριπίδης ἐν τῇ 'Ιφιγενείᾳ·
　　ἔλαφον δ' 'Αχαιῶν χερσὶν ἐνθήσω φίλαις [l. λάθρᾳ]
　　κερούσσαν, ἣν σφάζοντες αὐχήσουσι σὴν
　　σφάζειν θυγάτερα.

From the use of the futures ἐνθήσω and αὐχήσουσι it has been supposed
by some critics that these words must have been part of the prologue ;
but σὴν must refer to Clytæmnestra, who could not have been so addressed till the conclusion of the play.

[3] Porson, *Præf. Hec.* p. xxi. [18], speaking of the two readings of
Iph. Aul. 1579, says: "si me rogas, utra harum vera sit lectio,
respondeo, neutra. Nec quicquam mea refert; quippe qui persuasus
sim, totam cam scenam abusque versu 1541 spuriam esse, et a recentiore
quodam, nescio quando, certe post Æliani tempora, suppositam."

[4] See Böckh, *Gr. Tr. Princ.* c. XVII.; the editions of Hermann, Lips.
1831; Hartung, Erlang. 1837; Monk, Cantabr. 1840; also W. Dindorf,
Zeitsch. f. d. Alterthumswiss. Nov. 1839 ; Seyffert, *de dupl. rec. Iph. A.*,
Hal. 1831 ; Bartsch, *de Eur. Iph. A.* Vrat. 1837; Zirndorfer, *Diss. de
Iph. A.* Marburg, 1838.

worship of Bacchus, when all his family have yielded a willing assent to the new religion. This solemn warning against the dangers of a self-willed θεομαχία seems to have made this drama highly suggestive to those intelligent and educated Jews who first had a misgiving with regard to the wisdom of their opposition to Christianity.[1] And the devout and religious tone of the play would almost make us suppose that Euripides himself, at the close of his life, had become converted from the sophistic scepticism of his earlier years.[2] It is probable that the *Bacchœ* was always a favourite play in Macedonia, where it was first produced. Olympias, the mother of Alexander the Great, openly played the part of the mother of Pentheus,[3] and Alexander himself was able to make an apposite quotation from the text of this Tragedy.[4]

[1] This important reference was first made by the writer of these pages in a work entitled *Christian Orthodoxy reconciled with the conclusions of modern Biblical Learning*, Lond. 1857, pp. 291–294.

[2] cf. vv. 200: οὐδὲν σοφιζόμεσθα τοῖσι δαίμοσι, κ.τ.λ.
    v. 393: τὸ σοφὸν δ' οὐ σοφία,
    τό τε μὴ θνητὰ φρονεῖν
    βραχύς αἰών.
    v. 880: ὁρμᾶται μόλις ἀλλ' ὅμως
    πιστὸν τό γε θεῖον σθένος, κ.τ.λ.

[3] Plutarch, *Vit. Alex.* c. 2.
[4] Id. *Ibid.* c. 53: εἰπεῖν οὖν τὸν 'Αλέξανδρον ὅτι κατ' Εὐριπίδην· τὸν λαβόντα τῶν λόγων
    καλὰς ἀφορμὰς οὐ μέγ' ἔργον εὖ λέγειν.
See *Bacch.* vv. 266, 267.

A. W. SCHLEGEL'S COMPARISON OF THE CHOËPHORŒ OF ÆSCHYLUS WITH THE ELECTRAS OF SOPHOCLES AND EURIPIDES.

THE relation which Euripides bears to his two great predecessors will be set in the clearest light by a comparison between their three plays, which happily are still extant, upon the same subject, namely, Clytæmnestra's death by the avenging hand of Orestes.

The scene of Æschylus' Choëphorœ is laid in front of the royal palace; the tomb of Agamemnon appears on the stage. Orestes enters with his trusty Pylades, and opens the play (which unhappily is somewhat mutilated at the beginning) with a prayer to Mercury and a promise of revenge to his father, to whom he consecrates a lock of his hair. He sees a procession of females clad in mourning attire issuing from the palace, and thinking he recognises his sister among them, he steps aside with Pylades, to reconnoitre them before he shows himself. The Chorus, consisting of captive Trojan maidens, in a speech accompanied by gestures of woe, reveal the occasion of their mission to Agamemnon's tomb, namely, a frightful dream of Clytæmnestra's: they add their own dark presentiments of vengeance impending over the blood-guilty pair, and bewail their lot in being obliged to serve unrighteous lords. Electra consults the Chorus whether she shall do the bidding of her hostile mother, or pour out the offering in silence, and then by their advice she too addresses a prayer to infernal Mercury and the soul of her father, for herself and the absent Orestes, that he may appear as the avenger. During the pouring-out of the libation, she and the Chorus make a lament for the departed hero. Presently discovering the lock of hair, of a colour resembling her own, and footprints round about the tomb, she lights upon the conjecture that her brother has been there; and while she is beside herself with joy at the thought, he steps forward, and makes himself known. Her doubts he completely overcomes by producing a garment woven by her own hand; they abandon themselves to their joy; he addresses a prayer to Jupiter, and makes known how Apollo, under most terrible menaces of persecution by his father's Furies, has called upon him to destroy the authors of Agamemnon's death, in the same manner as they had destroyed him, namely, by subtilty. Now follow odes of the Chorus and Electra, consisting partly of prayers to the deceased king and to the infernal deities, partly calling to mind all the motives to the act enjoined upon Orestes, and, above all, the murder of Agamemnon. Orestes inquires about the vision which induced Clytæmnestra to send the offerings, and is informed that she dreamed she had a child in the cradle, which child was a dragon, which she laid to her breast, and suckled with her own blood. He, then, will be this dragon; and he explains more particularly how he will steal into the house as a disguised stranger, and take both Ægisthus and herself at unawares. With this intention he departs, accompanied by Pylades. The subject of the ensuing ode is the boundless audacity of mankind, and especially of women, in their unlawful passions; which it confirms with dreadful examples from mythic story, and shows how avenging Justice is sure to overtake them at last. Orestes, returning as a stranger with Pylades, craves admission into the palace; Clytæmnestra comes out, and being informed by him that Orestes is dead, at which tidings Electra makes a show of lamentation, she invites him to enter and be her guest. After a short prayer of the Chorus, enters Orestes' nurse, and makes a lament for her nursling; the Chorus inspires her with a hope that he yet lives, and advises her to send Ægisthus, for whom Clytæmnestra has despatched her, not with, but without, his body-guard. As the moment of danger draws near, the Chorus offers a petition to Jupiter and Mercury that the deed may prosper. Ægisthus enters, holding conversation with the messenger, cannot yet quite persuade himself of an event so joyful to him as Orestes' death, and therefore hastens into the house, where, after a short prayer of the Chorus, we hear his dying cry. A servant rushes out and gives the alarm before the door of the women's abode, to warn Clytæmnestra. She hears it, comes out, calls for a hatchet to defend herself; but as Orestes without a moment's delay advances upon her with the bloody sword, her courage fails, and most affectingly she holds before him the breast at which she, his mother, suckled him. Hesitatingly he asks counsel of Pylades, who in a few lines urges him on by the most powerful considerations: after a brief dialogue of accusation and self-vindication, he drives her before him into the palace, to slay her beside the corpse of Ægisthus. The Chorus, in a solemn ode, exults in the consummated retribution. The great doors of the palace are thrown open, and disclose, in the chamber, the slain pair laid together on a bed. Orestes orders the servants to unfold, that all may see it, the long trailing garment in which his father, as he drew it on and was muffled in its folds, received the murderous stroke of the axe: the Chorus beholds on it the stains of blood, and breaks out into a lamentation for Agamemnon's murder. Orestes, feeling that his soul is already becoming confused, avails himself of the time that is still left to vindicate his act: he declares that he will repair to Delphi, there to be purified from his blood-guiltiness, and forthwith flees, full of horror, before his mother's Furies, whom the Chorus does not yet see, and deems a phantom of his brain, but who leave him no more rest. The Chorus concludes the play with a reflection on the scene of murder thrice repeated in that royal house since the Thyestean banquet.

The scene of Sophocles' *Electra* is also laid in front of the palace, but without Agamemnon's tomb. At day-break enter as from abroad Pylades, Orestes, and his keeper, who on that bloody day had been his preserver. The latter gives him instructions, as he introduces him to the city of his fathers: Orestes replies with a speech upon the commission given him by Apollo, and the manner in which he means to execute it, and then addresses a prayer to the gods of his native land, and to the house of his fathers. Electra is heard sobbing within; Orestes wishes to greet her immediately, but the old man leads him away to present an offering at the grave of his father. Electra comes out; in a pathetic address to heaven she pours forth her griefs, and in a prayer to the infernal deities her unappeased longing for revenge. The Chorus, consisting of virgins of the land, approaches to administer consolation. Electra, alternating song and speech with the Chorus, makes known her unabatable sorrow, the contumely of her oppressed life, her hopelessness on account of Orestes' many lingerings, notwithstanding her frequent exhortations, and gives faint hearing to the encouraging representations made by the Chorus. Chrysothemis, Clytæmnestra's younger, more submissive, and favourite daughter, comes with a grave-offering, which she is commissioned to bear to her father's sepulchre. An altercation arises between the sisters concerning their different sentiments: Chrysothemis tells Electra that Ægisthus, now absent in the country, has come to the severest resolutions respecting her; to which the other bids defiance. Then she proceeds to relate how Clytæmnestra has had a dream that Agamemnon was come to life again, and planted his sceptre in the floor of the house, whence there sprang up a tree that over-shadowed the whole land; whereby she was so terrified, that she commissioned her to be the bearer of this grave-offering. Electra advises her not to regard the commands of her wicked mother, but to offer at the tomb a prayer for herself, her brother and sister, and for the return of Orestes to take vengeance: she adds to the oblation her own girdle and a lock of her hair. Chrysothemis promises to follow her advice, and departs. The Chorus augurs from the dream that retribution is nigh, and traces back the crimes committed in this house to the arch-sin of its first founder, Pelops. Clytæmnestra chides her daughter, to whom, however, perhaps from the effect of the dream, she is milder than usual: she justifies what she did to Agamemnon; Electra attacks her on that score, but without violent altercation on either side. After this Clytæmnestra, standing beside the altar in front of the house, addresses her prayer to Apollo for welfare and long life, and secretly for the destruction of her son. Now enters the keeper of Orestes, and, in the character of messenger from a Phocian friend, announces the death of Orestes, entering withal into the most minute details how he lost his life at the chariot-race in the Pythian games. Clytæmnestra scarcely conceals her exultation, although at first a touch of maternal feeling comes over her, and she invites the messenger to partake of the hospitality of her house. Electra, in touching speeches and songs, abandons herself to her grief; the Chorus in vain attempts to console her. Chrysothemis returns from the tomb overjoyed, with the assurance that Orestes is near at hand, for she has found there the lock of his hair, his drink-offering, and wreaths of flowers. Electra's despair is renewed by this account; she tells her sister the dreadful tidings which have just arrived, and calls upon her, now that no other hope is left them, to take part with her in a daring deed, and put Ægisthus to death; this proposal Chrysothemis, not possessing the courage, rejects as foolish and, after a violent altercation, goes into the house. The Chorus bewails Electra now so utterly desolate; Orestes enters with Pylades and some servants, who bear the urn which, it is pretended, contains the ashes of the dead youth. Electra prevails upon him by her entreaties to give it into her hands, and laments over it in the most touching speeches; by which Orestes is so overcome, that he can no longer conceal himself; after some preparation, he makes himself known to her, and confirms the discovery by showing her the signet-ring of their father. She gives vent, in speech and song, to her unbounded joy, until the old man comes out, rebukes them both for their imprudence, and warns them to refrain themselves. Electra with some difficulty recognises in him the faithful servant to whom she had entrusted Orestes for preservation, and greets him thankfully. By the old man's advice Orestes and Pylades hastily betake themselves with him into the house to surprise Clytæmnestra while she is yet alone. Electra offers a prayer in their behalf to Apollo: the ode of the Chorus announces the moment of retribution. From within the house is heard the shriek of the dismayed Clytæmnestra, her brief entreaties, her wailings under the death-blow. Electra, from without, calls upon Orestes to finish the deed: he comes out with bloody hands. The Chorus sees Ægisthus coming, and Orestes hastes back into the house to take him by surprise. Ægisthus inquires about the death of Orestes, and from Electra's equivocal replies is led to believe that his corpse is within the house. He therefore orders the doors to be thrown open to convince those among the people who bore his sway with reluctance, that there is no more hope from Orestes. The middle entry is thrown open, and discloses in the interior of the palace a covered body lying on a bed. Orestes stands beside it, and bids Ægisthus uncover it: he suddenly beholds the bloody corpse of Clytæmnestra, and finds himself lost past redemption. He desires to be allowed to speak, which, however, Electra forbids. Orestes compels him to go into the house, that he may slay him on the selfsame spot where Ægisthus had murdered his father.

The scene of Euripides' *Electra* lies, not in Mycenæ, but on the borders of the Argolic territory, in the open country, in front of a poor solitary cottage. The inhabitant, an old peasant, comes out, and in the prologue tells the audience how matters stand in the royal house: partly what was known already, but moreover, that not content to treat Electra with ignominy and leave her unwedded, they had married her beneath her rank to him; the reasons he assigns for this procedure are strange enough, but he assures the audience he has too much respect for her to debase her in reality to the condition of his wife. They are therefore living in virgin wedlock. Electra comes out before it is yet day-break, bearing on her head, which is shorn in servile fashion, a pitcher, with which she is going to fetch water; her husband conjures her not to trouble herself with such unwonted labours, but she will not be kept from the performance of her housewifely duties, and the two depart, he to his work in the field, she upon her errand. Orestes now enters with Pylades, and in a speech to his friend states that he has already sacrificed at his father's grave, but that he does not venture into the city, but wishes to look about for his sister (who, he is aware, is married and lives here-about on the frontier), that he may learn from her the posture of affairs. He sees Electra coming with the water-pitcher, and retires. She strikes up a song of lamentation over her own fate and that of her father. The Chorus, consisting of rustic women, comes and exhorts her to take part in a festival of Juno, which she however, in the dejection of her sorrow, and pointing to her tattered garments, declines. They offer to lend her a supply of holiday gear, but she is fixed in her purpose. She espies Orestes and Pylades in their lurking-place, takes them for robbers, and is about to flee into her cottage; upon Orestes coming forth and stopping her, she thinks he is going to kill her; he pacifies her, and gives her tidings that her brother lives. Hereupon he inquires about her situation, and then the whole matter is drilled into the audience once more. Orestes still forbears to make himself known, but merely promises to do Electra's commission to her brother, and testifies his sympathy as a stranger. The Chorus thinks this too good an opportunity to be lost of gratifying their own ears also with a little news from town; whereupon Electra, after describing her own miserable condition, depicts the wanton and insolent behaviour of her mother and Ægisthus: this wretch, she says, capers upon Agamemnon's grave, and pelts it with stones. The peasant returns from his work, and finds it not a little indecorous in his wife to be gossiping with young men; but when he hears they are bearers of intelligence from Orestes, he invites them into his house in' the most friendly manner. Orestes, at sight of this worthy man, enters into a train of moral reflections, how often it does happen that the most estimable men are found in low families, and under an unpromising exterior. Electra reproves her husband for inviting them, knowing as he does that they have nothing in the house; he is of opinion that even were it so, the strangers would good-naturedly put up with it; but a good housewife can always manage to get together all sorts of dishes, her stores will surely hold out for one day. She sends him to Orestes' old keeper and former preserver, who lives hard by in the country, to bid him come and bring along with him something for their enter-tainment. The peasant departs with saws upon riches and moderation. Off flies the Chorus into an ode upon the expedition of the Greeks against Troy, prolixly describes all that was graven on the shield of Achilles, which his mother Thetis brought him, but winds it up, however, with the wish that Clytæmnestra may be punished for her wickedness.

The old keeper, who finds it right hard work to climb up-hill to the house, brings Electra a lamb, a cheese, and a skin of wine; hereupon he falls a-weeping, not forgetting, of course, to wipe his eyes with his tattered garments. In replying to Electra's questions, he relates how at the grave of Agamemnon he had found traces of an oblation, together with a lock of hair, and therefore he conjectures that Orestes has been there. Hereupon ensues an allusion to the mode of recognition used by Æschylus, namely by the resemblance of the hair, the size of the foot-marks, the garment, which are demonstrated, all and several, to be absurd. The seeming improbability of the Æschylean anagnorisis perhaps admits of being cleared up; at all events one may easily let it pass; but a reference like this to another author's treatment of the same subject is the most annoying interruption, the most alien from genuine poetry that can possibly be. The guests come out; the old keeper reconnoitres Orestes with a scrutinising eye, knows him, and convinces even Electra that it is he, by a scar on his eyebrow received from a fall in his childhood—so this is the superb invention for which Æschylus' is to be cashiered!—they embrace, and abandon themselves to their joy during a short ode of the Chorus. In a lengthy dialogue Orestes, the old man, and Electra concert their plans. Ægisthus, the old man knows, has gone into the country to sacrifice to the Nymphs: there Orestes will steal in as a guest and fall upon him by surprise. Clytæmnestra, for fear of evil tongues, has not gone with him: Electra offers to entice her mother to them by the false intelligence of her being in childbed. The brother and sister now address their united prayers to the gods and their father's shade for a happy issue. Electra declares she will make away with herself if it should miscarry, and for that purpose will have a sword in readiness. The old man departs with Orestes to conduct him to Ægisthus, and afterwards to betake himself to Clytæmnestra. The Chorus sings the Golden Ram, which Thyestes stole from Atreus by the help of the treacherous wife of the latter, and how he was punished for it by the feast made for him with his own children's flesh, at the sight of which the Sun turned out of his course: a circumstance, however, concerning which the Chorus, as it sapiently adds, is very sceptical. From a distance is heard a noise of tumult and groans, Electra thinks her brother is overcome, and is going to kill herself. But immediately there comes a messenger, who, prolixly and with divers jokes, relates the manner of Ægisthus' death. Amidst the rejoicing of the Chorus, Electra fetches a wreath, with which she crowns her brother, who holds in his hand the head of Ægisthus by the hair. This head she in a long speech upbraids with its follies and crimes, and says to it, among other things, " it is never well to marry a woman with whom one has lived before in illicit intercourse; that it is an unseemly thing when a woman has the mastery in the family," &c. Clytæmnestra is seen approaching, Orestes is visited by scruples of conscience concerning his purpose of putting a mother to death, and concerning the authority of the oracle, but is induced by Electra to betake himself into the cottage, there to accomplish the deed. The queen comes in a superb chariot hung with tapestry, and attended by her Trojan female slaves. Electra would help her to descend, but this she declines. Thereupon she justifies what she had done to Agamemnon by reference to the sacrifice of Iphigenia, and requires her daughter to make her objections; all which is in order to give Electra an opportunity of holding a captious, quibbling harangue, in which, among other things, she

N

upbraids her mother with having sat before her mirror, and studied her toilette too much while Agamemnon was away. Clytæmnestra is not angry, although Electra plainly declares her purpose of putting her to death if ever she should have the power; she inquires about her daughter's confinement, and goes into the cottage to perform the ceremonies of purification. Electra accompanies her with a sarcastic speech. Then we have a choral ode upon retribution, the cry of the murdered woman within the house, and the brother and sister return stained with blood. They are full of remorse and despair at what they have done, afflict themselves by repeating to each other their mother's lamentable speeches and gestures; Orestes will flee into foreign lands, Electra asks "who will marry me now?" The Dioscuri, their uncles, appear in the air, vituperate Apollo for his oracle, command Orestes, in order to secure himself from the Furies, to go and have himself tried by the Areopagus: they also prophesy his further destinies. They then ordain a marriage between Electra and Pylades, her first husband to be taken with them to Phocis and handsomely provided for. After reiterated wailings the brother and sister take a lifelong farewell of each other, and the play comes to an end.

It is easy to perceive that Æschylus has grasped the subject on its most terrific side and borne it back into the domain of the gloomy deities, in which he so much delights to take up his abode. Agamemnon's grave is the murky centre, whence the avenging retribution emanates; his gloomy ghost the soul of the whole poem. The very obvious exterior imperfection, of the play's dwelling too long on one point without perceptible progress, becomes in fact a true interior perfection: it is the hollow stillness of expectation before a storm or earthquake. It is true there is much repetition in the prayers, but their very accumulation gives the impression of a great unheard-of purpose, to which human powers and motives alone are inadequate. In the murdering of Clytæmnestra and in her heart-rending speeches, the poet, without disguising her crimes, has gone to the utmost verge of all that he had a right to demand of our feelings. The crime which is to be punished is kept in view from the very first by the tomb, and at the conclusion is brought still nearer to the eye of memory by the unfolding of the fatal garment: thus Agamemnon, even after full revenge, is murdered, as it were, afresh before the mental eye. Orestes' betaking himself to flight betrays no undignified remorse or weakness: it is only the inevitable tribute which he must pay to offended Nature.

How admirably Sophocles has managed the subject I need only remark in general terms. What a beautiful preface he has made, in those introductory scenes to that mission of Clytæmnestra's to the tomb, with which Æschylus begins at once! With what polished ornament he has invested the whole, for example in the story of the games! How skilfully he husbands the pathos of Electra—first general expressions of woe, then hopes derived from the dream, their annihilation by the intelligence of Orestes' death, new hopes suggested by Chrysothem is only to be rejected, and, last of all, the mourning over the urn! The noble spirit of Electra is finely set off by the contrast with her tamer sister. Indeed the poet has given quite a new turn to the subject by directing the interest principally to Electra. A noble pair he has made of this brother and sister; allotting to the female character invincible constancy and devotedness, the heroism of endurance; to the male, the beautiful vigour of a hero's youthful prime. To this the old man in his turn opposes thoughtfulness and experience: the circumstance that both poets leave Pylades silent[1] is an instance how greatly ancient art disdained all useless redundancy.

But what especially characterises the tragedy of Sophocles, is the heavenly serenity amid a subject so terrific, the pure breath of life and youth which floats through the whole. The radiant god Apollo, who enjoined the deed, seems to shed his influence over it; even the daybreak at the opening of the play is significant. The grave and the world of shades are kept afar off in the distance; what in Æschylus is effected by the soul of the murdered monarch proceeds here from the heart of the living Electra, which is gifted with equal energy for indignant hatred and for love. Remarkable is the avoidance of every gloomy foreboding in the very first speech of Orestes, where he says he feels no concern at being thought to be dead, so long as he knows himself to be alive in sound health and strength. Nor is he visited either before or after the deed by misgivings and compunctions of conscience; so that all that concerns his purpose and act is more sternly sustained in Sophocles than in Æschylus; the terrific stroke of theatrical effect in the person of Ægisthus, and the reserving this person to await an ignominious execution at the end of the play, is even more austere than anything in Æschylus' play. The most striking emblem of the relation the two poets bear to each other is afforded by Clytæmnestra's dreams: both are equally apt, significant, ominous; Æschylus' is grander, but horrible to the senses; that of Sophocles terrible, and majestically beautiful withal.

Euripides' play is a singular instance of poetical or rather unpoetical obliquity: to expose all its absurdities and contradictions would be an endless undertaking. Why, for instance, does Orestes badger his sister by keeping up his incognito so long? How easy the poet makes his labour, when, if anything stands in his way, he just shoves it aside without further ceremony—as here the peasant, of whom, after he has sent up the old keeper, nobody knows where he is all this while! The fact is, partly, Euripides wanted to be novel, partly he thought it too improbable that Orestes and Pylades should despatch the king and his wife in the midst of their capital city: to avoid this he has involved himself in still grosser improbabilities. If there be in the play any relish whatever of the tragic vein, it is not his own, it belongs to the fable, to his predecessors, and to tradition. Through his views it has ceased at least to be a tragedy; he has laboured every way to lower it down to the level of a "family-picture," as the modern phrase is. The effect attempted in Electra's indigence is sad claptrap: he betrays the

---

[1] [Pylades speaks in the *Choeph.* 900 sqq.]

knack of his craft in her complacent ostentation of her own misery. In
all the preparatives to the deed there is utter levity of mind and want
of inward conviction : it is a gratuitous torturing of one's feelings that
Ægisthus with his expressions of goodnatured hospitality, and Clytæmnestra with her kindly compassion towards her daughter, are set in an
amiable point of view, just to touch us in their behalf: the deed is no
sooner accomplished but it is obliterated by a most despicable repentance,
a repentance which is no moral feeling at all, but a mere animal revulsion.
Of the calumniations of the Delphian oracle I shall say nothing. As
the whole play is annihilated thereby, I cannot see for what end Euripides wrote it at all, except it were that a comfortable match might be got
up for Electra, and that the old peasant might make his fortune as a
reward for his continency. I could only wish Pylades were married out
of hand, and the peasant fingered a specified sum of money told out to
him upon the spot in hard cash : in that case all would end to the
audience's satisfaction like a common comedy.

Not to be unjust, however, I must add the remark that the Electra
is perhaps of all Euripides' extant plays the very vilest. Was it rage
for novelty that led him here into such vagaries? No doubt it was a
pity that in this subject two such predecessors had forestalled him. But
what forced him to measure himself with them, and to write an Electra
at all?

CHAPTER I.

SECTION V.

AGATHON AND THE REMAINING TRAGEDIANS.

'Επιφυλλίδες ταῦτ' ἐστὶ καὶ στωμύλματα,
Χελιδόνων μουσεῖα, λωβηταὶ τέχνης,
*Α φροῦδα θᾶττον, ἢν μόνον χορὸν λάβῃ.

ARISTOPHANES.

IN addition to the seven Tragedians, of whom we have attempted to give some account, a list of thirty-four names of tragic poets, so called, has been drawn up.[1] Of these very few are worthy of even the slightest mention, and we have but scanty information respecting those few, of whom we might have wished to know more.

ION, the son of Orthomenes of Chios, was, according to Suidas, not only a tragedian, but a lyric poet and philosopher also. He began to exhibit in B.C. 451, and wrote twelve, thirty, or forty dramas. The names of eleven have been collected.[2] He gained the third prize when Euripides was first with the *Hippolytus* in B.C. 428.[3] He wrote not only Tragedies, but elegies,[4] dithyrambs,[5] and an account of the visits paid by eminent men to his native island.[6] Though he did not exhibit till after Euripides had commenced his dramatic career, and though he was, like that poet, a friend of Socrates,[7] we should be inclined to infer, from his having written dithyrambs, that he belonged to an earlier age of the dramatic art, and that his plays were free from the corruptions which Euripides had introduced into Greek Tragedy; it is, indeed, likely that a foreigner would copy rather from the old models, than from modern innovations. He died before Euripides, for he was dead when Aristophanes brought

---

[1] By Clinton, *F. H.* II. pp. xxxii.—xxxv.
[2] By Bentley (*Epistola ad Millium.*)
[3] *Argum. Hippolyti.*
[4] Athenæus, x. p. 436.
[5] Aristoph. *Pax*, 798.
[6] Athenæus, III. p. 93.
[7] Diogenes Laert. II. p. 23.

out the *Peace*[1] (B.C. 419). From an anecdote mentioned
by Athenæus, that he presented each Athenian citizen with
a Chian vase on one occasion when he gained the tragic
prize,[2] we may infer that he was a man of fortune.

ARISTARCHUS, of Tegea, who first exhibited in B.C. 454,
deserves to be mentioned as having furnished models for the
imitations of Ennius.

ACHÆUS, of Eretria, must also be considered as belonging
to an earlier age of the tragic art than Euripides, whose
senior he was by four years. He wrote forty-four, thirty, or
twenty-four dramas, but only gained one tragic victory.[3] His
countryman Menedemus considered him the best writer of
satyrical dramas after Æschylus.[4]

AGATHON was, like his friend Euripides, a dramatic sophist.
He is best known to us from his appearance in the *Banquet*
of Plato, which is supposed to have been held at his house
on the day after the celebration of his tragic victory. This
appears to have taken place at the Lenæa, in the archonship
of Euphemius, B.C. 416.[5] He is introduced to us by Plato
as a well-dressed, handsome young man, courted by the
wealth and wisdom of Athens, and exercising the duties of
hospitality with all the ease and refinement of modern po-
liteness. In the *Epideixis*, in praise of love, which he is
there made to pronounce, we are presented with the artificial
and rhetorical expressions which his friend[6] Aristophanes
attributes to his style,[7] and which we might have expected

---

[1] Schol. *Pac.* 837 : ὅτι ὁ μὲν Ἴων ἤδη τέθνηκε, δῆλον.
[2] Athenæus, I. p. 4.   [3] Suidas.
[4] Diog. Laert. II. p. 133.
[5] Athenæus, V. p. 217 A : ἐπὶ ἄρχοντος Εὐφήμου στεφανοῦται
Ληναίοις.
[6] It will be recollected that Aristophanes is introduced at Plato's
Banquet among the other intimates of Agathon.
[7]
        Μέλλει γὰρ ὁ καλλιεπὴς Ἀγάθων
        Δρυόχους τιθέναι, δράματος ἀρχάς.
        Κάμπτει δὲ νέας ἀψῖδας ἐπῶν·
        Τὰ δὲ τορνεύει, τὰ δὲ κολλομελεῖ,
        Καὶ γνωμοτυπεῖ, κἀντονομάζει,
        Καὶ κηροχυτεῖ, καὶ γογγύλλει,
        Καὶ χοανεύει. *Thesmoph.* 49.

from a pupil of Gorgias.[1] Aristotle tells us[2] that he was the first to introduce into his dramas arbitrary choral songs, which had nothing to do with the subject; and it appears from the same author that he sometimes wrote pieces with fictitious names, which Schlegel justly concludes were something between the idyl and the newest form of Comedy.[3] He was residing at the court of Archelaus when Euripides died :[4] the cause of his departure from Athens is not known. He is represented as a delicate and effeminate person in Aristophanes' play, called the Θεσμοφοριάζουσαι ;[5] and it is, perhaps, only the intimacy subsisting between Aristophanes and him which has gained for him the affectionate tribute of esteem which the comedian puts into the mouth of Bacchus,[6] and has saved him from the many strictures which he deserved both as a poet and as a man. The time of his death is not recorded.

XENOCLES, though he is called an execrable poet,[7] gained a tragic prize with a Trilogy, over the head of Euripides, in B.C. 415.[8] He was the son of CARCINUS, a tragedian of whom nothing is known, and is continually ridiculed by Aristophanes. His brothers, Xenotimus and Demotinus or Xenoclitus, were choral dancers.

[1] It appears from the *Banquet* that he was Gorgias' pupil: his imitation of Gorgias is mentioned by Philostratus, *de Soph.* I. : 'Ἀγάθων ὁ τῆς τραγῳδίας ποιητὴς ὃν ἡ κωμῳδία σοφόν τε καὶ καλλιεπῆ οἶδε (in allusion to the last quotation) πολλαχοῦ τῶν ἰαμβείων γοργιάζει: and by the Clarkian Scholiast on Plato (Gaisford, p. 173): ἐμιμεῖτο δὲ τὴν κομψότητα τῆς λέξεως Γοργίου τοῦ ῥήτορος.

[2] Τοῖς δὲ λοιποῖς τὰ ᾀδόμενα οὐ μᾶλλον τοῦ μύθου, ἢ ἄλλης τραγῳδίας ἐστί· δι' ὃ ἐμβόλιμα ᾄδουσι, πρώτου ἄρξαντος 'Αγάθωνος τοιούτου. Aristot. *Poet.* XVIII. 22.

[3] Lect. v. ad fin. One of these was called the *Flower*. Aristot. *Poet.* IX. 7.

[4] Schol. ad Aristoph. *Ran.* 85 ; Ælian, *V. H.* II., 21, XIII. 4 ; Clark, *Schol. Plato*, p. 173.

[5] *Thesmoph.* 29 sqq. 191, 192.

[6] *Ran.* 84 :
'Ηρ. 'Αγάθων δὲ ποῦστιν; Δι. ἀπολιπών μ' ἀποίχεται,
'Αγαθὸς ποιητὴς καὶ ποθεινὸς τοῖς φίλοις.

[7] Aristoph. *Ran.* 86 ; *Thesm.* 169.

[8] Ælian, *V. H.* II. II. 8. On 'the son of Cleomachus' (Athen. XIV. 638 F) who defeated Sophocles, see Meineke, *Fragm. Com. Ant.* p. 28 ; Müller, *Hist. Lit. Gr.* I. p. 505 (new ed.).

IOPHON, the son of Sophocles, is described by Aristophanes[1] as a man whose powers were, at the time of his father's death, not yet sufficiently proved to enable a critic to determine his literary rank. He appears, however, to have been a creditable dramatist, and gained the second prize in B.C. 428, when Euripides was first and Ion third.[2]

EUPHORION, the son of Æschylus, deserves to be mentioned as having obtained the first prize, when Sophocles gained the second, and Euripides the third. He probably produced on this occasion one of his father's posthumous Tragedies, with which he is said to have conquered four times. He did, however, occasionally bring out Tragedies of his own composing.[3]

EURIPIDES and SOPHOCLES, the nephew and grandson respectively of their namesakes, are said to have exhibited, either for the first or for the second time, some of the dramas of their relatives. The younger Sophocles reproduced the *Œdipus at Colonus*, in B.C. 401;[4] and first contended in his own name B.C. 396[5]. Euripides the younger is said to have published an edition of Homer.[6]

MELETUS, the accuser of Socrates, is stated to have been a tragedian,[7] and a writer of drinking songs.[8] Œdipus was the subject of one of his plays.[9]

CHÆREMON, who flourished about B.C. 380, was celebrated for his *Centaur*, in which he mixed up the drama with the styles of epic and lyric poetry then fashionable.[10] He had a great talent for description, but his works were better suited for the closet than for the stage.[11]

---

[1] *Ran.* 73 sqq.   [2] *Arg. Hippolyti.*
[3] Suidas, v. Εὐφορίων. *Argument. Medeæ.*
[4] Elms. *ad Bacch.* p. 14, and Suidas.
[5] Diodor. Sic. XIV. 53.   [6] Suidas.
[7] Schol. *Ran.* 1337: τραγικὸς ποιητὴς ὁ Μέλητος· οὗτος δέ ἐστιν ὁ Σωκράτῃ γραψάμενος· κωμῳδεῖται δὲ ὡς ψυχρὸς ἐν τῇ ποιήσει καὶ ὡς πονηρὸς τὸν τρόπον.
[8] *Ran.* 1297.   [9] Gaisford, *Lect. Platon.* p. 170.
[10] Aristot. *Poet.* I.; Athenæus, XIII. p. 608.
[11] Aristot. *Rhet.* III. 12.

SOSICLES, of Syracuse, gained seven victories, and wrote seventy-three Tragedies. He flourished in the reigns of Philip and Alexander of Macedon.[1]

The tyrants CRITIAS and DIONYSIUS the elder, and the rhetorician THEODECTES obtained some eminence as Tragedians.

In the reign of Ptolemy Philadelphus, seven tragic poets flourished at Alexandria, who were called the *Pleias ;*[2] their names were HOMERUS, SOSITHEUS, LYCOPHRON, ALEXANDER ETOLUS, ÆANTIDES, SOSIPHANES, and PHILISCUS.[3] It is quite uncertain, however, how far their works possessed an independent and original character; it is probable that the best of these tragedies were servile imitations of the great Attic models,[4] and some of them may have been mere *centos*, not altogether unlike the *Christus Patiens* of Gregorius Nazianzenus.[5]

---

[1] Suidas. He is not in Clinton's list.

[2] The Alexandrian custom of making *Pleiads* or groups of seven for " the stars" of the day is shown also by the well-known enumeration of the seven wonders of the world.

[3] The authorities do not agree in their lists of these tragedians. There are four different catalogues (Clinton, *F. H.* III. p. 502): Homerus, Philiscus, and Lycophron appear in all four ; Alexander Ætolus and Sositheus in three ; Æantides has three testimonies, and Sosiphanes has two ; and Dionysides, who is substituted for Sosiphanes in one of the lists, is attested by Strabo, XIV. p. 675.

[4] In the list of Lycophron's tragedies we have two plays entitled *Œdipus*, and others called *Æolus, Andromeda, Hercules, Supplices, Hippolytus, Pentheus.*

[5] " The Alexandrine scholars also took to manufacturing tragedies ; but if we may form a judgment from the only extant specimen, Lycophron's *Alexandra*, which consists of an interminable monologue, full of vaticination and lumbered with obscure mythology, these productions of a would-be-poetical dilettantism were utterly lifeless, untheatrical, and every way flat and unprofitable. The creative power of the Greeks in this department was so completely defunct, that they were obliged to content themselves with repetitions of the old masterpieces." On the *Alexandra*, which was not a tragedy, as Schlegel supposes, see *Hist. Lit. Gr.* II. pp. 437 foll.

CHAPTER II.

ON THE GREEK COMEDIANS.

SECTION I.

THE COMEDIANS WHO PRECEDED OR WERE CONTEMPORARY WITH ARISTOPHANES.

Quorum Comœdia prisca virorum est.

HORATIUS.

FROM the first exhibition of Epicharmus to the last of Posidippus, the first and last of the Greek comedians, is a period of about 250 years; and between these two poets, one hundred and four authors are enumerated,[1] who are all said to have written Comedies. The claims of some of these, however, to the rank of comedians are very doubtful, and two who are contained in the list, Sophron and his son Xenarchus, were mimographers, and as such, were not only not comedians, but hardly dramatists at all, in the Greek sense of the word.

It has been already mentioned that Greek Comedy did not attain to a distinct literary form until it became Athenian; and that, in its Attic form, it presents itself in three successive varieties—the Old, the Middle, and the New Comedy. The Sicilian Comedy, which, in some of its features, resembled the Middle rather than the Old Comedy, found its origin in the same causes as the latter, being immediately connected with the old farces of Megara and the rustic buffooneries which were common to the whole of Greece. The absence, indeed, of a distinct political reference deprived it of that ingredient which gave its greatest significance to the plays of Aristophanes and his principal Athenian contemporaries during the first half of the Peloponnesian war, and on this account we cannot class the dramatic efforts of the Siceliotes with those of the Attic poets. But the Sicilian Comedy comes first in chronological order, and Aristotle

---

[1] By Clinton, *F. H.* II. pp. xxxvi.—xlvii.

connects Crates with Epicharmus. Before therefore we speak of the Attic comedians, we must give some account of Epicharmus and his school.

EPICHARMUS, the son of Helothales, whom Theocritus calls the inventor of Comedy,[1] and who, according to Plato,[2] bore the same relation to Comedy that Homer did to Tragedy, was a native of Cos,[3] and went to Sicily with Cadmus, the son of Scythes, about the year B.C. 488. After residing a short time at the Sicilian Megara,[4] he was removed to Syracuse along with the other inhabitants of that town, when it was conquered by Gelo in B.C. 484. Diogenes Laertius states that Epicharmus was only three months old when he first went to Sicily; but this is contradicted by his own statement, that the poet was one of the auditors of Pythagoras,[5] who died in B.C. 497, by the statement of Aristotle,[6] that he was long before Chionides and Magnes, and by the fact that he was a man of influence in the reign of Hiero, who died eighteen years after the date of Epicharmus' arrival in Sicily. Besides being a Pythagorean and a comic poet, he is said to have been a physician, as was also his brother. This has been considered an additional proof of his Coan origin.[7] He was ninety or ninety-seven

[1]   "Α τε φωνὰ Δώριος, χώνήρ, ὁ τὰν κωμῳδίαν
          Εὑρὼν 'Επίχαρμος·
       "Ω Βάκχε, χάλκεόν νιν ἀντ' ἀλαθινοῦ
          Τὶν ὧδ' ἀνέθηκαν,
       Τοὶ Συρακόσσαις ἐνίδρυνται Πελωρεῖς τᾷ πόλει,
          Οἷ' ἀνδρὶ πολίτᾳ,
       Σωρὸν γὰρ εἶχε χρημάτων, μεμναμένοι
          Τελεῖν ἐπίχειρα
       Πολλὰ γὰρ ποττὰν ζοάν τοῖς παισὶν εἶπε χρήσιμα.
          Μεγάλα χάρις αὐτῷ. Epig. XVII.

[2] Theætet. p. 152 E: οἱ ἄκροι τῆς ποιήσεως ἑκατέρας, κωμῳδίας μὲν 'Επίχαρμος. τραγῳδίας δὲ "Ομηρος.   [3] Diog. Laert. VIII. 78.
[4] See Müller, Dorians, I. 8, §5, note (q), and IV. 7, §2.
[5] Diog. u. s.; καὶ οὗτος ἤκουσε Πυθαγόρου.
[6] 'Εκεῖθεν [ἐκ Σικελίας] γὰρ ἦν 'Επίχαρμος ὁ ποιητὴς, πολλῷ πρότερος ὢν Χιωνίδου καὶ Μάγνητος. Arist. Poet. III. 5.—Chionides, on the authority of Suidas and Eudocia, began to exhibit B.C. 487: Aristotle's expression, πολλῷ πρότερος ὢν Χιωνίδου, would therefore almost induce us to carry back the date of Epicharmus' first Comedy still higher than B.C. 500.   [7] Müller, Dor. IV. 7, §2.

years old when he died.[1]   The Comedies of Epicharmus[2] were partly parodies of mythological subjects, and as such not very different from the dialogue of the satyrical drama; partly political, and in this respect may have furnished a model for the dialogue of the old Athenian Comedy. He must have made some advance towards the Comedy of Character, if it be true that the *Menœchmi* of Plautus was founded upon one of his plays,[3] and Müller has therefore well remarked,[4] that although "the Sicilian Comedy in its artistic development preceded the Attic by about a generation, yet the transition to the *middle* Attic Comedy, as it is called, is easier from Epicharmus than from Aristophanes, who appears very unlike himself in the play which tends towards the form of the Middle Comedy." It is not stated expressly that he had choruses in his Comedies; it seems, however, probable from the title of one of them (the Κωμασταί) that he had.[5] His style was not less varied than his subjects; for while, on the one hand, he indulged in the wildest buffoonery, he was fond, on the other hand, of making his characters discourse most philosophically on all topics, and we may discern in many of his remaining lines that moral and gnomic element which contributed so much to the formation of the dialogue in the Attic Tragedy.[6]   Aristotle charges him with using false antithesis,[7] the effect perhaps of his acquaintance with the forced and artificial rhetoric of the Sicilians.   The titles of thirty-five of his Comedies are known.[8]

[1] Diog. Laert. (VIII. 78) gives the former number; Lucian (Macrob. XXV.) the latter.
[2] On the nature of the Comedy of Epicharmus, see Müller, *Dor.* IV. 7, §§ 2, 3, 4; *Hist. Lit. Gr.* II. pp. 44 [56 new ed.] sqq.
[3] *Prolog. Menæchm.* 12.
[4] *Hist. Lit. Gr.* II. p. 46 [59 new ed.].   [5] See above, p. 77.
[6] See the passages in Clinton, *F. H.* II. p. xxxvi. note (g).
[7] *Rhetoric*, III. 9.
[8] These titles are as follows:

1. Ἀλκυών, 2. Ἄμυκος, 3. Ἀταλάνται, 4. Βάκχαι, 5. Βούσιρις, 6. Γᾶ καὶ Θάλασσα, 7. Διόνυσοι, 8. Ἐλπὶς ἢ Πλοῦτος, 9. Ἥβας γάμος, 10. Ἡρακλῆς Παράφορος, 11. Κύκλωψ, 12. Κωμασταὶ ἢ Ἥφαιστος, 13. Μέγαρις, 14. Μοῦσαι, 15. Νιόβης γάμος, 16. Ὀδυσσεὺς αὐτόμολος, 17. Ὀδυσσεὺς ναυαγός, 18. Προμηθεὺς Πυρκαεύς, 19. Σειρῆνες, 20. Σκίρων, 21. Σφίγξ, 22. Τρῶες, 23. Φιλοκτήτης, 24. Ἀγρωστῖνοι, 25. Ἁρπαγαί, 26. Δίφιλος, 27. Ἑορτή, 28. Θεωροί, 29. Λόγος ἢ Λογική, 30. Νᾶσοι, 31. Ὀρύα, 32. Περίαλλος, 33. Πέρσαι, 34. Πίθων, 35. Χύτραι.   See

Although Epicharmus is mentioned as the inventor of Comedy, it is probable that PHORMIS,[1] or Phormus,[2] preceded him by a few Olympiads; for he was the tutor to the children of Gelon, Hiero's predecessor. He is supposed to have been the same with the Phormis of Mænalus, who distinguished himself in the service of Gelo and Hiero in a military capacity.[3] From the titles of his plays it is presumed that they were mythological parodies.[4] He is said to have been the first to cover the stage with purple skins.[5]

DINOLOCHUS, according to Suidas the son, according to others the scholar of Epicharmus, flourished about B.C. 487. He was a native of Syracuse or Agrigentum: probably he was born at the latter place, and represented at Syracuse. Ælian says he contended with Epicharmus.[6]

While the Doric Comedy was rapidly advancing to perfection in Sicily, a comic drama, originally perhaps of much the same kind, sprang up in Attica. This was the old Comedy, which was represented by a list of forty poets, and some three hundred plays, including in the calculation the great name of Aristophanes. Reserving him and his works for a separate chapter, we shall here enumerate the leading poets of the old Comedy, who were his predecessors or contemporaries.

CHIONIDES, who is called the first writer of the old Athenian Comedy, was a contemporary of the Sicilian comedians.[7] T judge from the three titles which have come down to us—the Ἥρωες, Πέρσαι ἢ Ἀσσυριοί, and the Πτωχοί, we

---

Fabricius, II. p. 300, Harles, where, however, there are some repetitions of names.

[1] Aristot. *Poet.* III. 5; V. 5.
[2] Athenæus, XIV. 652 A; Suidas Φόρμος.
[3] Pausan. V. 27, I. Bentley thinks he is the same with the poet: not so Müller, *Dor.* IV. 7, § 2, note (g).
[4] Three of them were called Ἀκφαῖος, Ἀλκυόνες, and Ἰλίου πόρθησις.
[5] Suid. Comp. Aristot. *Ethic.* IV. 2, 20.   [6] Ælian, *H. A.* VI. 51.
[7] Suidas, s. v. Χιωνίδης, says that he was the πρωταγωνιστὴς τῆς ἀρχαίας κωμῳδίας, and that he exhibited eight years before the Persian war, i. e. in B.C. 488. Aristotle, therefore, or rather, his interpolater (*Poet.* III. 5), must be misinformed when he says that Epicharmus flourished long before Chionides and Magnes.

should conclude that his Comedies had a political reference, and were full of personal satire; and, from an allusion in Vitruvius,[1] we may infer that they were gnomic like those of Epicharmus. The same appears to have been the character of the Comedies of his countryman and contemporary MAGNES, from whom Aristophanes borrowed the titles of two of his plays, the Βάτραχοι and Ὄρνιθες, and perhaps the form of all of them. Magnes gained many victories in his younger days; but when he was old, says Aristophanes,[2] he was cast aside, merely because the edge of his satire was blunted.

Of ECPHANTIDES we know little more than that for some doubtful reason he was called Καπνίος,[3] and that he was one of the oldest and most celebrated of the early comedians. We have the title of only one of his plays, the Σάτυροι.[4] The Πύραυνος, mentioned as a play of Ἐμφάνης, has been assigned to him; but the true reading is probably Ἀντιφάνης.[5]

CRATINUS, the son of Callimedes, was born at Athens, B.C. 519.[6] It is stated that he succeeded Magnes; he must, therefore, have commenced his dramatic career late in life.[7] We do not know the date of any of his Comedies earlier than the Ἀρχίλοχοι: and since allusion was made in that Comedy to the death of Cimon (B.C. 449), it must have been represented after that event.[8] By a decree prohibiting Comedy, which was passed in the year B.C. 440, and was not repealed till the year B.C. 436, he was prevented from

---

[1] " Hæc ita esse plures philosophi dixerunt, non minus etiam poetæ, qui antiquas comœdias Græcè scripserunt, et easdem sententias versibus in scena pronuntiaverunt, Eucrates, *Chionides*, Aristophanes," &c. Vitruv. Præf. in lib. VI.

[2] *Equit.* 520:

Τοῦτο μὲν εἰδὼς ἄπαθε Μάγνης ἅμα ταῖς πολιαῖς κατιούσαις,
Ὃς πλεῖστα χορῶν τῶν ἀντιπάλων νίκης ἔστησε τρόπαια,
Πάσας δ' ὑμῖν φωνὰς ἱείς, καὶ ψάλλων, καὶ πτερυγίζων,
Καὶ λυδίζων, καὶ ψηνίζων, καὶ βαπτόμενος βατραχείοις,
Οὐκ ἐξήρκεσεν· ἀλλὰ τελευτῶν ἐπὶ γήρως, οὐ γὰρ ἐφ' ἥβης,
Ἐξεβλήθη πρεσβύτης ὤν, ὅτι τοῦ σκώπτειν ἀπελείφθη. 518.

[3] Meineke, *Hist. Crit. Com.* I. p. 36.

[4] Athen. I, p. 96 c.   [5] Meineke, l. c. p. 37.

[6] He died in B.C. 422, at the age of ninety-seven. Lucian, *Macrob.* c. XXV.   [7] See Clinton, *F. H.* II. p. 49.   [8] See Plutarch, *Cimon*, c. X.

producing any Comedies or plays in that interval.[1] After the repeal of this decree in B.O. 436, Cratinus gained three comic victories. In B.C. 425 he was second with the Χειμαζόμενοι, Aristophanes being first with the 'Αχαρνῆς, and Eupolis third with the Νουμηνίαι.[2] In B.C. 424 he gained the second prize with the Σάτυροι, Aristophanes being first with the 'Ιππῆς, and Aristomenes third with the Ὑλοφόροι or 'Ολοφυρμοί.[3] In B.C. 423 Cratinus gained the first prize with the Πυτίνη: Ameipsias was second with the Κόννος, and Aristophanes third with the Νεφέλαι.[4] The old poet died the year after this victory.[5] The names of forty of his Comedies are known.[6] He appears to have been an exceedingly bold satirist,[7] and was so popular that his choruses were sung at every banquet by the *comus* of revellers.[8] The model for his iambic style was doubtless Archilochus,[9] whom he regarded as a type of his own profession, and whom he multiplied as he might have done any other ideal, in the chorus of one of his plays (the 'Αρχίλοχοι). To his audacious frankness even Aristophanes appeared to be infected with the mincing rhetoric of Euripides.[10] There is

[1] Schol. Aristoph. *Acharn.* 67.
[2] *Argum. Acharn.*   [3] *Argum. Equit.*   [4] *Argum. Nub.*
[5] Lucian, *Macrob.* xxv.; *Proleg. Küst.* p. xxix.
[6] Fabric. II. p. 431, Harles.
[7] Comp. Horat. I. *Serm.* iv. 1 sqq. with Persius, I. 123.
[8] Aristoph. *Equit.* 526 sqq.

Εἶτα Κρατίνου μεμνημένος, ὃς πολλῷ ῥεύσας ποτ' ἐπαίνῳ
Διὰ τῶν ἀφελῶν πεδίων ἔρρει, καὶ τῆς στάσεως παρασύρων
'Εφόρει τὰς δρῦς καὶ τὰς πλατάνους καὶ τοὺς ἐχθροὺς προθελύμνους·
Ἆσαι δ' οὐκ ἦν ἐν συμποσίῳ πλὴν ΔΩΡΟΙ ΣΥΚΟΠΕΔΙΛΕ,
Καὶ ΤΕΚΤΟΝΕΣ ΕΥΠΑΛΑΜΩΝ ΥΜΝΩΝ· οὕτως ἤνθησεν ἐκεῖνος.
Νυνὶ δ' ὑμεῖς αὐτὸν ὁρῶντες παραληροῦντ' οὐκ ἐλεεῖτε,
'Εκπιπτουσῶν τῶν ἡλέκτρων, καὶ τοῦ τόνου οὐκ ἔτ' ἐνόντος,
Τῶν θ' ἁρμονιῶν διαχασκουσῶν· ἀλλὰ γέρων ὢν περιέρρει,
Ὥσπερ Κόννας, στέφανον μὲν ἔχων αὖον, δίψει δ' ἀπολωλώς,
Ὃν χρῆν διὰ τὰς προτέρας νίκας πίνειν ἐν τῷ Πρυτανείῳ,
Καὶ μὴ ληρεῖν, ἀλλὰ θεᾶσθαι λιπαρὸν παρὰ τῷ Διονύσῳ.
Comp. Buttm. *Mythol.* II. 345 foll.

[9] His fragments abound in direct imitations of the great iambographer. See Cratin. *Archiloch.* Fr. VIII. IX.; *Pytine*, Fr. XI. &c. The verb συγκεραυνόω in *Pyt.* Fr. VIII. is Archilochian; see above, p. 30.
[10] He asks this question of his rival (*Fragm. Incert.* CLV.):

Τί δὲ σύ; κομψός τις ἔροιτο θεατής,
Ὑπολεκτολόγος, γνωμιδιώκτης, εὐριπιδαριστοφανίζων. · [Τὸ

reason to believe that Cratinus, in imitation of Sophocles, increased the number of comic actors to three.[1] Of his private character we know nothing, save that he was a great tippler, and recommended the use of wine both by precept and by example.[2]

CRATES is said to have been originally an actor in the plays of Cratinus;[3] he could not, however, have followed this profession very long, for we learn from Eusebius that he was well known as a comedian in B.C. 450, which was not long after Cratinus, if he could be called in any sense the successor of Magnes, began to exhibit. He was the first comedian at Athens who departed from the satyrical form of Comedy, and formed his plots from general stories.[4] The names of twenty-six of his Comedies are known.[5] Aristophanes speaks in the highest terms of his wit and ingenuity.[6] His brother EPILYCUS was an epic poet and comedian.[7]

PHERECRATES is mentioned as an imitator or rival of Crates, whose actor he is said to have been; and an admirable emendation of the corrupt passage, which is our chief account of him, assigns his first victory to the archonship of Theodorus, B.C. 438.[8] Although the same authority

To which Aristophanes answers (*Fragm.* CCCXCVII.):

Χρῶμαι γὰρ αὐτοῦ τοῦ στόματος τῷ στρογγύλῳ,
Τοὺς νοῦς δ' ἀγοραίους ἧττον ἢ κεῖνος ποιῶ.

[1] *Anon. de Com.* p. xxxii. Comp. Meineke, *Quæstiones Scenicæ*, I. p. 19.
[2] Comp. Horat. I. *Epist.* XIX. 1; Aristoph. *Pax*, 687 (700) and Schol.; Meineke, *Fragm. Com.* vol. II. p. 119.
[3] Schol. Aristoph. *Equit.* (p. 567, Dindorf).
[4] Τῶν δὲ 'Αθήνησιν Κράτης πρῶτος ἦρξεν ἀφέμενος τῆς ἰαμβικῆς ἰδέας, καθόλου ποιεῖν λόγους ἢ μύθους. Aristot. *Poet.* IV. 7.
[5] Fabricius, II. p. 429, Harles.
[6] Aristoph. *Equit.* 537:

Κράτης
*Ος ἀπὸ σμικρᾶς δαπάνης ὑμᾶς ἀριστίζων, απ'πεμπεν
'Απὸ κραμβοτάτου στόματος μάττων ἀστειοτάτας ἐπινοίας.
[7] Suid. Κράτης.
[8] *Anon. de Com.* p. xxix.: Φερεκράτης 'Αθηναῖος νικᾷ ἐπὶ θεάτρου (1. ἐπὶ Θεοδώρου Dobree) γενόμενος ὁ δὲ (om. ὁ Dobr.) ὑποκριτὴς ἐζήλωκε Κράτητα.

says that he abstained from personal vituperation,[1] the
fragments of his plays show that he attacked Alcibiades, the
tragic poet Melanthius, Polytion, and others. He was
distinguished by the elegance of his style, and is called
'Αττικώτατος.[2] Perhaps his name is most familiar to scholars
as the inventor of the Pherecratean metre, which he calls
a contracted anapæstic verse,[3] and which he probably
formed by omitting the first two times in the parœmiac.[4]
We have the names of between 15 and 20 of his Comedies.

PHRYNICHUS, the comic poet, who must be carefully distinguished from the tragedian of the same name, exhibited first
in the year B.C. 435.[5] He was attacked as a plagiarist in the
Φορμοφόροι of Hermippus, which was written before the death
of Sitalces, i.e. before B.C. 424.[6] In B.C. 414 when Ameipsias
was first with the Κωμασταί, and Aristophanes second with
the *Ορνιθες, Phrynichus was third with the Μονότροπος.[7] In
B.C. 405 Philonides was first with the Βάτραχοι of Aristophanes, Phrynichus second with the Μοῦσαι, and Plato third
with the Κλεοφῶν.[8] He is ridiculed by Aristophanes in the
Βάτραχοι for his custom of introducing grumbling slaves on
the stage.[9] The names of ten of his pieces are known to us.[10]

[1] τοῦ μὲν λοιδορεῖν ἀπέστη.
[2] Athen. VI. p. 268 E; Suid. s. v. 'Αθηναία; Phrynichus Sophist. ap.
Steph. Byz. s. v. 'Αθῆναι, p. 34, Meineke.
[3] Ap. Hephæst. X. 5; XV. 15; Schol. Ar. Nub. 564:
   ἄνδρες πρόσσχετε τὸν νοῦν
   ἐξευρήματι καινῷ
   συμπτύκτοις ἀναπαίστοις.
[4] As the parœmiac is itself catalectic, the omission of a syllable at
the beginning makes it σύμπτυκτος, i. e. "folded in at both ends."
[5] Suid. Φρύν.—ἐδίδαξε τὸ πρῶτον ἐπὶ ποστ' ὀλυμπιάδος. Clinton would
read πζ'.
[6] Clinton, F. H. II. p. 67. [7] Arg. Av. [8] Arg. Ran.
[9] Aristoph. Ran. 12 sqq.
  Ξανθίας. τί δῆτ' ἔδει με ταῦτα τὰ σκεύη φέρειν,
      εἴπερ ποιήσω μηδὲν ὧνπερ Φρύνιχος
      εἴωθε ποιεῖν, καὶ Λύκις, κ' 'Αμειψίας,
      σκεύη φερούσ' ἑκάστοτ' ἐν κωμῳδίᾳ·
  Διόνυσος. μὴ νῦν ποιήσῃς· ὡς ἐγὼ θεώμενος,
      ὅταν τι τούτων τῶν σοφισμάτων ἴδω,
      πλεῖν ἢ 'νιαυτῷ πρεσβύτερος ἀπέρχομαι.
[10] Fabricius, II. p. 483, Harles.

O

Of HERMIPPUS, the son of Lysis, we know nothing save that he was opposed to Pericles,[1] and on one occasion prosecuted Aspasia for impiety.[2] His brother MYRTILUS was also a comedian.[3]

EUPOLIS was not much older than Aristophanes. It is stated by Suidas that he was seventeen years old when he began to exhibit; and if we may conclude from another statement,[4] that he produced his first Comedy in the archonship of Apollodorus, he must have been born about the year B.C. 446.[5] The success of his Comedy, called Νουμηνίαι in B.C. 425, has been already mentioned. Two of his Comedies, the Μαρικᾶς and the Κόλακες, appeared in B.C. 421. The Αὐτόλυκος came out in the following year, when perhaps he wrote the Ἀστράτευτοι also, for that play appears to have preceded the Εἰρήνη of Aristophanes, which was acted in B.C. 419.[6] According to one account he was thrown overboard by Alcibiades on his way to Sicily in B.C. 415, in consequence of some invectives against that celebrated man, which he had introduced into one of his Comedies. This story is improbable in itself; and it is, besides, refuted by two circumstances: Eratosthenes adduced some Comedies which he had written after the year B.C. 415,[7] and Pausanias tells us that his tomb was on the banks of the Asopus in the territory of the Sicyonians.[8] According to another account, he fell in a sea-fight in the Hellespont; and Ægina is said to have been the place of his burial. The titles of twenty-four of his Comedies have been preserved.[9] Eupolis

---

[1] See the Anapæsts in Plutarch, *Pericles*, xxxiii.

[2] Plutarch, *Pericles*, cxxxi. cxxxii. This was about the year B.C. 432.   [3] Suid. Μυρτίλος.

[4] *Prolegom. Aristoph.* p. xxix.   [5] Clinton, *F. H.* ii. p. 63.

[6] See Clinton, under these years. Autolycus was a sort of Agathon; like Agathon he obtained a victory at the public games, and is the hero of a symposium (Athen. v. 187 F, 217 D, and Xenoph. *Symposium*); and, like Agathon, he was courted for his personal attractions. Athen. p. 188 A.

[7] "Quis enim non dixit, Εὔπολιν, τὸν τῆς ἀρχαίας, ab Alcibiade, navigante in Siciliam, dejectum esse in mare? Redarguit Eratosthenes. Adfert enim, quas ille post id tempus fabulas docuerit."—Cicero *ad Att.* vi. i.

[8] Pausan. ii. 7, 3.   [9] Fabricius, ii. p. 445, Harles.

was very personal and scurrilous, and almost every one of his plays seems to have been written to caricature and lampoon some obnoxious individual. The Μαρικᾶς was a professed attack upon the demagogue Hyperbolus;[1] in the Αὐτόλυκος he ridiculed the handsome pancratiast of that name[2] in the Ἀστράτευτοι, which was probably a pasquinade, directed against the useless and cowardly citizens of Athens, Melanthius was denounced as an epicure;[3] the Βάπται dealt very hardly with Alcibiades;[4] and in the Λάκωνες he inveighed against Cimon, both in his public and private character, because that statesman was thought to incline too much to the Spartans, and showed in every action a desire to counteract the democratical principle, which was at work in the Athenian constitution.[5] Aristophanes, too, seems to have been on bad terms with Eupolis, whom he charges with having pillaged the materials for his Μαρικᾶς from the Ἱππῆς,[6] and with making scurrilous jokes on his premature baldness.[7]

[1] Schol. *Nub.* 591 : ἐδιδάχθη καθ' Ὑπερβόλου μετὰ τὸν Κλέωνος θάνατον. See also the passage from the Ἱππῆς quoted below.

[2] Athen. v. 216, where Eupolis is said to have brought out this piece under the name of Demostratus, probably the same as Demopœcetus, a comic poet mentioned by Suidas, v. χάραξ. There were two editions of the *Autolycus*. [3] Schol. Aristoph. *Pax*, 808.

[4] Themist. p. 110 B. The words of Juvenal, II. 91, if they refer to this Comedy, would imply that the obscene rites of Cotytto were the objects of his censure—

"Talia secretâ coluerunt orgia tædâ
Cecropiam soliti *Baptæ* lassare Cotytto."

On the Cotyttia and the Baptæ, see Buttmann, *Mythol.* II. p. 159 sqq. and Meineke, *Hist. Crit.* p. 119 sqq.

[5] Plutarch. *Cim.* XV. With regard to the name of the Comedy, we may remark, that Cimon had called his son Lacedæmonius (see Thucyd. I. 45), and that the name of the son was often an epithet of the father. Müller, *Dor.* I. 3, § 10, note (f).

[6]
Οὗτοι δ' ὡς ἅπαξ παρέδωκεν λαβὴν Ὑπέρβολος,
Τοῦτον δείλαιον κολετρῶσ' ἀεὶ καὶ τὴν μητέρα.
Εὔπολις μὲν τὸν Μαρικᾶν πρώτιστον παρείλκυσεν
Ἐκστρέψας τοὺς ἡμετέρους Ἱππέας κακὸς κακῶς,
Προσθεὶς αὐτῷ γραῦν μεθύσην, τοῦ κόρδακος εἴνεχ', ἣν
Φρύνιχος πάλαι πεποίηχ', ἣν τὸ κῆτος ἤσθιεν. *Nubes*, 551 sqq.

Eupolis, however, had reasons for recriminating. See Meineke, *Hist. Crit.* p. 101, and below, Section II.

[7] See the Schol. on *Nub.* 532:
οὐδ' ἔσκωψε τοὺς φαλακρούς.

Eupolis appears to have been a warm admirer of Pericles as a statesman and as a man,[1] as it was reasonable that such a Comedian should be, if it is true that he owed his unrestrained licence of speech to the patronage of that celebrated minister. We may form an idea of the style of Eupolis from the *Horsemen* and *Frogs* of Aristophanes, which had many points in common with the *Maricas* and *Demi* of this poet. For as in the *Maricas* Hyperbolus, so in the *Horsemen* Cleon is represented as an intriguing and influential slave of the people, and in both Comedies the worthy Nicias appears as an undervalued and superseded domestic. As in the *Frogs* of Aristophanes, Bacchus visits the lower world to seek out and restore to Athens one of the older and better Tragedians, so in the *Demi* of Eupolis, Myronides is made to bring back Solon, Miltiades, and Pericles, to their unworthy and degenerate countrymen.

Other writers of the Old Comedy are mentioned as the predecessors or contemporaries of Aristophanes; but we know little more of them than their names; though it is probable that many of them (for instance, AMEIPSIAS, who twice conquered Aristophanes) were (at least in the opinion of their contemporaries) by no means deficient in merit.

Of those poets of the Old Comedy, who survived the full vigour of Athenian democracy and lived till the period of transition to the Middle Comedy, the most eminent were PLATO, THEOPOMPUS, and STRATTIS.

PLATO, commonly known as ὁ κωμικός, to distinguish him from his great namesake the philosopher, first exhibited in B.C. 427,[2] and as he alluded in one of his plays to the appoint-

---

[1] Eupolis, Δῆμοις.

Κράτιστος οὗτος ἐγένετ' ἀνθρώπων λέγειν.
'Οπότε παρέλθοι, ὥσπερ ἀγαθοὶ δρομῆς,
'Εκ δέκα ποδῶν ᾕρει λέγων τοὺς ῥήτορας.
B. Ταχὺν λέγεις μέν, πρὸς δέ γ' αὐτοῦ τῷ τάχει
Πειθώ τις ἐπεκάθιζεν ἐπὶ τοῖς χείλεσιν·
Οὕτως ἐκήλει, καὶ μόνος τῶν ῥητόρων
Τὸ κέντρον ἐγκατέλειπε τοῖς ἀκροωμένοις.

Schol. Aristoph. *Acharn.* p. 794, Diudorf. See Meineke, *Fragm.* II. 458.
[2] Cyrill. *ad Julian.* I. p. 13 B.

ment of Agyrrhius as general of the army at Lesbos,[1] he must have been flourishing in B.C. 389. In his *Peisander* he described himself as having laboured for others, like an Arcadian mercenary.[2] And this has been interpreted as indicating his poverty.[3] It may, however, simply mean that Plato did not at first represent under his own name; but, like Aristophanes and Ameipsias, published his dramas anonymously, until in the *parabasis* to the *Peisander* he thought it expedient to assert his literary claims.[4] There seems to be little doubt that Plato was one of the most distinguished of the contemporaries of Aristophanes. His style is described as " brilliant."[5] Though he inclined to the type of Middle Comedy in his later years, his earlier plays were full of political satire, and Dio Chrysostom mentions him, along with Aristophanes and Cratinus, as a specimen of the abusive personalities to which the Athenians were willing to listen.[6] His attacks were directed against demagogues like Cleon, Hyperbolus, Cleophon, Peisander, and Agyrrhius, against the general Leagrus, and the rhetoricians Cephalus and Archinus. And, like Eupolis, he ventured to ridicule Aristophanes himself.[7] He left twenty-eight Comedies,[8] some of which bore the names of the persons against whom they were directed.[9]

THEOPOMPUS, the son of Theodectes, Theodorus, or Tisamenus, is said to have been a contemporary of Aristophanes, but, if we may judge from the titles of twenty of

---

[1] Plutarch, *Præc. resp. ger.* p. 801 B. For Agyrrhius and his appointment see Xen. *Hell.* IV. 8, 31: Diod. Sic. XIV. 99. Cf. Schol. *Ec les.* 102.

[2] Suidas, s. v. Ἀρκάδας μιμούμενοι.

[3] Suidas says διὰ πενίαν Ἀρκάδας μιμεῖσθαι ἔφη, but there is nothing to show that this was the assertion of Plato himself.

[4] Meineke, *Hist. Crit. Com.* p. 162.

[5] Bekker, *Anecd.* p. 1461: ὁ τὸ χαρακτῆρα λαμπρότατος. Cf. Suidas, s. v. Πλάτων. [6] *Orat.* XXXIII. p. 4, Reiske.

[7] *Schol. Plat.* p. 331, Bekker: κωμῳδεῖται δὲ ὅτι τὸ τῆς Εἰρήνης κολοσσικὸν ἐξῆρεν ἄγαλμα Εὔπολις Αὐτολύκῳ, Πλάτων Νίκαις.

[8] *Anon. de Com.* p. xxxiv.; Bekker, *Anecd.* u. s. Suidas enumerates 30, but two of these, the Λάκωνες and Μαμμάκυθος, were merely two editions of the same play.

[9] As the Κλεοφῶν, the Ὑπέρβολος and the Πείσανδρος.

his plays, which have been preserved, his style must have been chiefly that of the Middle Comedy.

STRATTIS, who began to exhibit about B.C. 412, and wrote about twenty plays, two of which, the *Medea* and *Phœnissœ*, derived their titles and probably their subjects from tragedies by Euripides, is chiefly interesting from the fact that he entertained a warm admiration for the tragi-comedies of that poet, especially the *Orestes* which he called δρᾶμα δεξιώτατον,[1] a circumstance which tends to confirm our belief that Euripides exercised a paramount influence over the later writers of Attic Comedy.

Besides the fifteen names which we have mentioned, the following poets are assigned to the Old Comedy.

1. TELECLEIDES, a contemporary and opponent of Pericles.

2. PHILONIDES, a friend and coadjutor of Aristophanes.

3. ARCHIPPUS, who gained the prize in B.C. 415, and was chiefly celebrated for a play called the *Fishes* in which he ridiculed the fish-dinners of Athens.

4. ARISTOMENES, who competed with Aristophanes in B.C. 424 and 392.

5. CALLIAS, a younger contemporary of Cratinus.

6. LYSIPPUS, who won the prize in B.C. 435, and whose play called the *Bacchœ* gained some reputation.

7. LEUCON, who competed with Aristophanes and Eupolis in B.C. 422 and 421.[2]

8. METAGENES, who is known by the names of some five or six Comedies, and seems to have enjoyed a considerable reputation.

9. ARISTAGORAS, who edited the Αὖραι of Metagenes with the new title Μαμμάκυθος, to which Aristophanes alludes.

[1] Schol. Eurip. *Orest.* 278.   [2] Meineke, *Hist. Crit. Com.* p. 217.

10. ARISTONYMUS, a contemporary of Aristophanes, best known by his play called *The Shivering Sun*, ('Ήλιος ῥιγῶν).

11. ALCÆUS, a writer of mythological Comedies.

12. EUNICUS (or ÆNICUS), whose Comedies *Anteia* or *Anthcia* and *The Cities* are attributed to other writers.[1]

13. CANTHARUS, a contemporary of Plato the Comedian, to whom one of his plays is attributed.

14. DIOCLES of Phlius, of the same age as Cantharus.

15. NICOCHARES, son of Philonides, wrote mythical Comedies, and belonged to the Middle Comedy as well as to the Old.

16. NICOPHON, a younger contemporary of Aristophanes, but a poet of the mythical school.

17. PHILYLLIUS,[2] a careless poet, inclining to the style of the Middle Comedy.

18. POLYZELUS, a poet of mythical Comedy.

19. SANNYRION, a contemporary of the later poets of the Old Comedy, by whom he is ridiculed.

20. APOLLOPHANES, a contemporary of Strattis.

21. EPILYCUS, author of the *Coraliscus*.

22. EUTHYCLES, author of the *Profligates* and *Atalanta*.

23. DEMETRIUS, wrote after the Peloponnesian war.

24. CEPHISODORUS, author of the *Amazons*, *Antilais*, *Trophonius* and the *Hog*.

25. AUTOCRATES, author of the *Tympanistæ*.

---

[1] Meineke, *Hist. Crit. Com.* pp. 250, 260.
[2] Philyllius is said to have been the first to introduce torches on the stage (Schol. Aristoph. *Plut.* 1195); and it is remarkable that he used the word ἀναλφάβητος as a synonym for ἀμάθητος γραμμάτων (*Anti-atticista*, p. 83).

CHAPTER II.

SECTION II.

ARISTOPHANES.

Ie suys, moyennant ung peu de Pantagruelisme (vous entendez que c'est certaine guayeté desperit conficte en mepriz des choses fortuites) sain et degourt; prest a boyre, si voulez.　　　　　RABELAIS.

OF the works of the other comedians we possess only detached fragments; but eleven of the plays of ARISTOPHANES have come down to us complete. This alone would incline us to wish for a fuller account of the writer, even though the intrinsic value of his remaining Comedies were not so great as it really is. Unfortunately, however, we know much less about Aristophanes than about any of his distinguished contemporaries, and the materials for his biography are so scanty and of so little credit, that we willingly turn from them to his works, in which we see a living picture of the man and his times. The following are the few particulars which are known regarding his personal history.[1] His father's name was Philippus,[2] not Philippides, as has been inferred from the inscription on a bust supposed to represent him.[3] Of the rank and station of his father we know nothing; it is presumed, however, from his own silence, and that of his enemies, that it was respectable. More

---

[1] The reader will find a full and accurate discussion of all questions relating to the life of Aristophanes down to the representation of the *Clouds* in Ranke's *Commentatio de Aristophanis Vitâ*, prefixed to Thiersch's edition of the *Plutus*. See also Bergk in Meineke's *Fragm.* II. pp. 893—940.

[2] This is stated by all the authorities of his life—namely, his anonymous biographer, the writer on Comedy in the Greek prolegomena to Aristophanes, the Scholiast on Plato, and Thomas Magister.

[3] The inscription is Ἀριστοφάνης Φιλιππίδου. That this statue is not genuine is now generally agreed. See Winckelmann, II. p. 114. The fact that his son's name was Philippus is an evidence that it was also the grandfather's name. Ranke, clxxxiv.

than one country claims the honour of being his birthplace.
The anonymous writer on Comedy says merely that he was
an Athenian; the author of his life, and Thomas Magister
add that he was of the Cydathenæan Deme, and Pandionid
Tribe. Suidas tells us, that some said he was from Lindus
in Rhodes, or from Camirus; that others called him an
Egyptian,[1] and others an Æginetan. All this confusion
seems to have arisen from the fact, that Cleon, in revenge
for some of the invectives with which Aristophanes had
assailed him, brought an action against the poet with a view
to deprive him of his civic rights (ξενίας γραφή). Now the
defence, which Aristophanes is said to have set up on this
occasion, shows the object of Cleon was to prove that he
was not the son of his reputed father Philippus, but the
offspring of an illicit intercourse between his mother and
some person who was not an Athenian citizen. Consequently his nominal parents are tacitly admitted to have
been Athenian citizens, and, as Cleon failed to prove his
illegitimacy, he must have been one likewise. That he
was born at Athens cannot but be evident to every one who
has read his Comedies. Would a mere resident alien have
laboured so strenuously for the good of his adopted country?
Would one who was not a citizen by birth have ventured to
laugh at all who did not belong to the old Athenian
φρατρίαι?[2] and how are we otherwise to account for the
purely Athenian spirit, language, and tone which pervade
every line that he wrote? It would not be difficult to
explain why these different countries have been assigned as
the birthplaces of Aristophanes. With regard to the
statement that he was a Rhodian; he is very often confounded with Antiphanes and Anaxandrides, the former of
whom was, according to Dionysius, a Rhodian, and the
latter, according to Suidas, was born at Camirus. The
notion that he was an Ægyptian may very well have arisen
from the many allusions which he makes to the people of
that country, and their peculiar customs. With regard to
the statement of Heliodorus that he was from Naucratis,
it is possible that writer may be alluding to some com-

[1] Heliodorus περὶ Ἀκροπόλεως (apud Athen. VI. p. 229 E) says that
he was of Naucratis in the Delta. [2] Ran. 418; Aves, 765.

mercial residence of his ancestors in that city, but his words do not imply that either Aristophanes or his parents were born there. His Æginetan origin has been presumed from the passage in the *Acharnians*, in which his actor Callistratus (who was the nominal author of the play) alludes to his being one of the κληροῦχοι, to whom that island had been assigned.[1] We have positive evidence that he was one of them, and the fact that these κληροῦχοι were generally poor[2] would show that Callistratus is alluding to himself, and not to Aristophanes ; and even if he were, this would be no proof, that Aristophanes was not a citizen, for all the κληροῦχοι continued to enjoy their civic rights.[3] The remains of Aristophanes are sufficient to show that he had received a first-rate education. There is no positive evidence for the opinion,[4] that he was a pupil of Prodicus. The three passages in his remaining Comedies,[5] in which he mentions that sophist, do not show the usual respect of a disciple for his master, and the coincidence in name, and probable similarity of subject, between the Ὧραι of Aristophanes and *The Choice of Hercules* by Prodicus, are perhaps a proof that the comedian parodied and ridiculed, rather than admired and imitated, the latter.[6]

The literary career of Aristophanes naturally divides itself into three periods, defined by the corresponding changes of social and political life at Athens. As Attic Comedy rose and fell with the democratic domination of the state, even the genius of its greatest representative could not control the outward influences to which he was exposed. The waning vigour of popular freedom necessarily affected the political character of Comedy, and deprived the *parabasis*

---

[1] Thucyd. II. 27; Diod. XII. 44. Callistratus was one of them, Aristophanes not. Schol. *Acharn.* 654, p. 801, Dind.: οὐδεὶς ἱστόρηκεν ὡς ἐν Αἰγίνῃ κέκτηταί τι Ἀριστοφάνης, ἀλλ᾽ ἔοικε ταῦτα περὶ Καλλιστράτου λέγεσθαι, ὃς κεκληρούχηκεν ἐν Αἰγίνῃ μετὰ τὴν ἀνάστασιν Αἰγινητῶν ὑπὸ Ἀθηναίων.

[2] Böckh, *Econ. of Ath.* Vol. II. p. 172, note 521, Engl. Tr.

[3] Böckh, *Ec.* II. p. 174.

[4] Of Rückert on Plat. *Symp.* pp. 280 sqq.

[5] *Aves*, 692; *Nubes*, 360; fr. *Tragonist.* No. 418, Dindorf.

[6] On the Ὧραι of Aristophanes and Prodicus, see Welcker in the *Rhein. Mus.* for 1833, p. 576. He thinks that the connection between the Ὧραι of these two authors is merely accidental, p. 592.

or address to the audience of its unconstrained liberty of speech. On the other hand, the fatal catastrophe of Syracuse, while it destroyed the flower of the citizens, so seriously diminished the resources of the state, that the dramatic entertainments could no longer be exhibited with the same lavish expenditure. From both causes, the chorus of Comedy became insignificant, till, at last, there was the literary paradox of a κωμῳδία without its κῶμος. The eleven extant Comedies of Aristophanes may be arranged in three groups, corresponding to the three periods to which we refer. In the first period, which extends to the time of the Sicilian expedition, we have six Comedies, all of which represent the unimpaired genius of the poet, and the complete machinery of the comic stage. These are the *Acharnians*, the *Horsemen*, the *Clouds*, the *Wasps*, the *Peace*, and the *Birds*. The second period, which corresponds to the later years of the war, is represented by three dramas, in which the political element and the chorus are both diminished in prominence and importance. These are the *Lysistrata*, the *Thesmophoriazusæ*, and the *Frogs*. The third and concluding period, which followed the downfall of the Athenian empire, exhibits the genius of Aristophanes in its feeblest form, and has transmitted to us only two Comedies, the *Ecclesiazusæ* and the *Plutus*, in which the choral element is altogether insignificant, and the plots are derived from the ideal world rather than from the actualities of Athenian life, which furnished the materials for the Comedies of the first period.

Aristophanes brought out his first Comedy, the *Banqueters*, (Δαιταλεῖς) in B.C. 427 :[1] and it is from the known date of this play that we must infer his birth-year. It is stated[2] that he was at this time little more than a boy (σχεδὸν μειράκισκος). We are told, indeed,[3] that he was thirty years of age when the *Clouds* was acted. This would place his birth-year at B.C. 453, if the first edition, or at 452, if

[1] See the passages in Clinton, *F. H.* II. p. 65.
[2] Schol. *Ran.* 504. Müller thinks (*Hist. Lit. Gr.* II. p. 19, new ed.) that this statement is an exaggeration, and that Aristophanes was at least twenty-five in B.C. 427.
[3] Schol. *Nub.* p. 237, Dindorf.

the second edition of that play is referred to.[1]   But could a
man born so early as B.C. 452 be called σχεδὸν μειράκισκος at
the time of the great plague ? We think he could not.
If, then, these two authorities of the same kind contradict
one another, which are we to adopt?   Now there is no
reason to doubt the first statement, that Aristophanes was
very young at the time when his first Comedy appeared ;
and there is reason to believe that the second statement is
merely an inference drawn from a misinterpretation of a
passage in the *Clouds*.   We feel inclined, therefore, to
reject the latter altogether, and take the former as the only
means we have of approximating to the birth-year of
Aristophanes, which if he was σχεδὸν μειράκισκος or nearly
seventeen in B.C. 427, must have been about the year
B.C. 444.

The *Banqueters*, which was acted in the name of Philonides,[2] was an exposition of the corruptions which had
crept into the Athenian system of education.   A father was
introduced with two sons, one of them educated in the
old-fashioned way, the other brought up in all the new-
fangled and pernicious refinements of sophistry ; and by
drawing a comparison between the two young men to the
disadvantage of the latter, the poet hoped to attract the
attention of his countrymen to the dangers and inconveniences of the new system.[3] The second prize was awarded
to Philonides, and the play was much admired.[4]   In B.C. 426
he brought out the *Babylonians*, and, in the following spring,
the *Acharnians*, both under the name of his actor Callistratus.[5] The latter gained the first prize, the second and
third being adjudged to Cratinus and Eupolis.   The chorus
of the *Babylonians* consisted of barbarian slaves employed in

---

[1] Unless we adopt Ranke's conjecture with regard to the date of the
second edition, which would make the two accounts nearly agree.   See
below, p. 184.

[2] Dindorf, *fr. Aristoph.* p. 527, Oxford edition.   Ranke (p. cccxx)
thinks it was Callistratus.   If there is truth in the statement that he
handed over to Callistratus his political dramas, and to Philonides
those which related to private life, the Δαιταλεῖς was probably transferred to the latter.

[3] See Süvern, *über die Wolken*, pp. 26 foll.

[4] Schol. *Nub.* 529.   [5] Clinton, *F. II.* under those years.

the mills :[1] this is all that we know of the plot of the piece.
It appears to have been acted at the great Dionysia, and to
have been an attack upon the demagogues ; for Cleon, who
was then (Pericles having recently died) at the head of
affairs,[2] brought an εἰσαγγελία before the senate against
Callistratus, on the grounds that he had satirized the public
functionaries in the presence of their allies, who were then
at Athens to pay the tribute.[3] This accusation has been
confounded with the indictment of ξενία, brought by Cleon
against Aristophanes himself.

It does not appear that Cleon was successful in establishing his charge, for we find Callistratus again upon the stage
the following year, when the *Acharnians* was performed at
the Lenæa. The object of this play, the earliest of the
Comedies of Aristophanes which have come down to us
entire, is to induce the Athenians, by holding before them
the blessings of peace, and by ridiculing the braggadocios of
the day, to entertain any favourable proposals which the
Lacedæmonians might make for putting an end to the
disastrous war in which they were engaged ; and while he
ventured to utter the well-nigh forgotten word *Peace*, he
boldly told his countrymen that they had sacrificed, without

[1] See Hesych. s. vv. Βαβυλώνιοι.—Σαμίων ὁ δῆμος. And Suid. s. v.
Βαβυλωνία κάμινος.
[2] Thucydides, writing of the year before the performance of *The
Babylonians*, says (III. 36), that Κλέων was τῷ δήμῳ παρὰ πολὺ ἐν τῷ
τότε πιθανώτατος.
[3] Comp. *Acharn.* 355 foll. :

Αὐτός τ᾽ ἐμαυτὸν ὑπὸ Κλέωνος ἅπαθον
Ἐπίσταμαι διὰ τὴν πέρυσι κωμῳδίαν.
Εἰσελκύσας γάρ μ᾽ εἰς τὸ βουλευτήριον
Διέβαλλε καὶ ψευδῆ κατεγλώττιζέ μου,
Κἀκυκλοβόρει κἄπλυνεν ὥστ᾽ ὀλίγου πάνυ
Ἀπωλόμην μολυνοπραγμονούμενος·

with vv. 476 foll. :

Ἐγὼ δὲ λέξω δεινὰ μὲν δίκαια δέ·
Οὐ γάρ με νῦν γε διαβαλεῖ Κλέων ὅτι
Ξένων παρόντων τὴν πόλιν κακῶς λέγω,
Αὐτοὶ γάρ ἐσμεν οὑπὶ Ληναίῳ τ᾽ ἀγών,
Κοὔπω ξένοι πάρεισιν·

and the Scholiasts. On the relations between Aristophanes and Cleon,
and on the character of the latter, the student will find some striking
remarks in Grote, *Hist. Gr.* Vol. VI. pp. 657 sqq.

any just or sufficient cause, the comforts which he painted to them in such vivid colours.

Aristophanes, having conferred upon the nominal authors of his plays much, not only of reputation, but also of danger, now thought it right to appropriate to himself both the glory and the hazard of his undertaking, and in B.C. 424 demanded a chorus in his own name. The Comedy, which he exhibited on this occasion, and in the composition of which Eupolis claimed a share, was the *Horsemen*; it was acted at the Lenæa, and gained the first prize: Cratinus was second, and Aristomenes third.[1] The object of this play is to over-throw Cleon, who was then flushed with his undeserved success at Sphacteria in the preceding year, and had excited the indignation of Aristophanes and all the Athenians who wished well to their country, by his constant opposition to the proposals of the Lacedæmonians for an equitable arrangement of the terms of peace. The demagogue was considered at that time so formidable an adversary, that no one could be found to make a mask to represent his features, so that Aristophanes, who personated him on the stage, was obliged to return to the old custom of smearing the face with wine-lees;[2] and, as Cleon is represented in the play as a great drunkard, the substitute was probably adequate to the occasion. The Comedy is an allegorical caricature of the broadest kind, showing how the eminent generals and states-men, Nicias and Demosthenes, with the aid of the καλοὶ κἀγαθοί among the citizens, delivered the Athenian John Bull from the clutches of the son of Cleænetus, and effected a marvellous change in the temper and external appearance of their doting master. This is expressed in a wonderfully ingenious manner. The instrument they use is one Agora-critus, who is called a sausage-seller (ἀλλαντοπώλης). Now there lived, at this time, a celebrated sculptor of that name, who, having made for the Athenians a most beautiful statue

---

[1] *Argum. Eqq.* The reference of this piece to the Lenæa is sup-ported by the allusion in vv. 881—3, to the wintry weather, which prevailed in the month Lenæon, according to Hesiod. On the claims of Eupolis to a share in this Comedy, see Bernhardy, *Grundriss*, II. p. 973; and for the passage attributed to him, Meineke, *Fragm.* II. 1, p. 577.   [2] Schol. *Eqq.* 230. See above, p. 80.

of Venus which they could not buy, transformed it into a representation of Nemesis, and sold it to the Rhamnusians.[1] It is this Agoracritus, who, by a play upon the words ἀλλάσσειν and ἀλλᾶς, is called a transformation-monger in regard to the People : he changes the easy good-tempered old man into a punisher of the guilty—a laughing Venus into a frowning Nemesis ;—he metamorphoses the ill-clad unseemly Demus of the Pnyx into a likeness of the beautiful Demus, the son of Pyrilampes the Rhamnusian, just as Agoracritus transferred to Rhamnus a statue destined for Athens. It seems to have been in consequence of this attack that Cleon made the unsuccessful attempt (to which we have already alluded) to deprive Aristophanes of his civic rights.

The next recorded Comedy of Aristophanes is the *Clouds*, the most celebrated and perhaps the most elaborately finished, as it is certainly the most serious, of his remaining plays. When he first submitted it to the judges, the plays of Cratinus and Ameipsias, who were his competitors, were honoured with the first and second prizes. This was in the year B.C. 423; and it is probable that Aristophanes, indignant at his unexpected ill-success, withdrew the play, and did not bring it out till some years afterwards, when he added something to the *parabasis*, and perhaps made a few other alterations. The author of the argument and the Scholiast refer the second edition to the year B.C. 422, but it has been shown from the mention of the *Maricas* of Eupolis, and other internal evidences, that it could not have been acted till some years after the death of Cleon ; and it is conjectured that it did not appear till after the exhibition of the *Lysistrata* in B.C. 411.[2] It will not be expected that we should here enumerate the various opinions which have been entertained of the object of Aristophanes in writing this Comedy,[3] or that we should enter upon a

---

[1] Plin. *H. N.* xxxvi. 4.   [2] Ranke, chapters xxviii. and xL.
[3] We refer the reader who wishes to study this subject minutely and accurately to Hermann, *Præfat. ad Nubes*, xxxii—liv ; Wolf's Introduction to his German translation of the play ; Reisig. *Præfat. ad Nubes*, viii—xxx, and his Essay in the *Rheinisches Museum* for 1828, pp. 191 and 464 ; Mitchell's and Welcker's Introductions to their

new and detailed examination of the piece. We must, on
the present occasion, be content with stating briefly and
generally, what we conceive to have been the design of the
poet. In the *Wasps*, which was written the year after the
first ill-success of the *Clouds*, he calls this Comedy an
attack upon the prevailing vices of the young men of his day.[1]
Now, if we turn to the *Clouds*, we shall see that he not only
does this, but also investigates the causes of the corrupt
state of the Athenian youth; and this he asserts to have
arisen from the changes introduced into the national education by the sophists, by the substitution of sophistical for
rhapsodical instruction. The hero of the piece is Socrates,
who was, in the judgment of Aristophanes, a sophist to all
intents and purposes. We do not think it necessary to deny
that Socrates was a well-meaning man, and in many respects
a good citizen; we are disposed to believe that he was, not
because Plato and Xenophon have represented him as such
(in their justification of his character, each of them is but
ἰατρὸς ἄλλων αὐτὸς ἕλκεσι βρύων), but because Aristophanes
has brought no specific charges against him, as far as his
intentions are concerned. But Socrates was an innovator
in education; he approved, perhaps assisted in the corruptions which Euripides introduced into Tragedy; he was the
pupil and the friend of several of the sophists; it was in his
character of dialectician that he was courted by the ambitious young men; he was the tutor of Alcibiades; his singular manners and affected slovenliness had every appearance
of quackery; and, if we add, that he was the only one of the
eminent sophists who was an Athenian-born, we shall not

Translations of Aristophanes; Ranke. *Comment.* chapters XLI.—XLIV.;
Süvern's *Essay*; and Müller, *Hist. Lit. Gr.* II. pp. 33, new ed. sqq.
Rötscher has given a general statement of some of these opinions in
his *Aristophanes und sein Zeitalter*, pp. 294—391, which he follows up
with his own not very intelligible view of the question.

[1] vv. 1037 foll. :

> Ἀλλ' ὑπὲρ ὑμῶν ἔτι καὶ νυνὶ πολεμεῖ. φησίν τε μετ' αὐτοῦ
> Τοῖς ἠπιάλοις ἐπιχειρῆσαι πέρυσιν καὶ τοῖς πυρετοῖσιν
> Οἳ τοὺς πατέρας τ' ἦγχον νύκτωρ καὶ τοὺς πάππους ἀπέπνιγον,
> Κατακλινόμενοί τ' ἐπὶ ταῖς κοίταις ἐπὶ τοῖσιν ἀπράγμοσιν ὑμῶν
> Ἀντωμοσίας καὶ προσκλήσεις καὶ μαρτυρίας συνεκόλλων, κ.τ.λ.

able opinion, which Aristophanes everywhere expresses respecting the dramatic merits of Euripides, could not have left his audience in any doubt as to the results of a comparison which he undertook to make, between the great founder of Greek tragedy, and the rhetorical poet, who had so entirely altered its character. Accordingly, Æschylus is carried back to the city, where his Tragedies were still alive; for he is made to say, with considerable humour, that his poetry had not died with him, and that Euripides, who had brought his works down to Hades, was better prepared for the literary contest.[1]

The exhibition of the *Frogs* was speedily followed by the battle of Ægos-Potami, the fall of Athens, and the subversion of the democracy. For some years there was no possibility for any display of the literary genius of such a poet as Aristophanes, and we do not hear of him until some years after the return of Thrasybulus. From the concluding period of his literary history, only two Comedies have come down to us complete; and both of these present to us a very different state of things from that which had prevailed during the Peloponnesian war. While democracy had revived with some of its worst abuses, and while demagogues, like Agyrrhius, were leading the populace into the most whimsical extravagances, the educated class had learned to express with boldness the feelings of disgust and contempt with which this wild republicanism had inspired them. This anti-democratic tendency was fostered by the writings of some able men attached to the government of the thirty tyrants, among whom the most eminent was Plato. Connected with Critias by the ties of blood, and a near relation of the Charmides, who fell fighting against the party of Thrasybulus, he had but little sympathy with the restored democracy at Athens; and when his teacher Socrates had been put to death in B.C. 399, after a prosecu-

---

[1] vv. 866 sqq.:

Αἰ. ἐβουλόμην μὲν οὐκ ἐρίζειν ἐνθάδε·
      οὐκ ἐξ ἴσου γάρ ἐστιν ἀγὼν νῷν.
Δι.   τί δαί;
Αἰ. ὅτι ἡ ποίησις οὐχὶ συντέθνηκέ μοι,
      τούτῳ δὲ συντέθνηκεν, ὥσθ' ἕξει λέγειν.

tion instituted by men connected with the popular party,
Plato retired to Megara, and did not return to Athens till
after some four years spent in foreign travel. The feelings
of despair with which he regarded all existing forms of
government are recorded in an epistle written about this
time,[1] and it has been fairly argued[2] that he must have
published soon afterwards at least the first sketch of his
Republic, in which his object is to maintain by the elaborate
picture of an ideal government the thesis laid down in the
epistle, namely that the only remedy for the miseries of
mankind must be sought in the establishment of a truly
philosophical aristocracy.   One of the most offensive
features in Plato's ideal *Republic* is his proposal for a community of property and wives, and the supposition that the
original edition, containing the first six books,[3] was given
to the public soon after B.C. 395, is strongly supported by
the statement of the old grammarians,[4] that this work is
ridiculed by Aristophanes in his *Ecclesiazusæ* which
appeared in B.C. 392, and in which Plato is mentioned, as
he is also in the *Plutus*, by a diminutive of his original name
Aristocles.[5]   In this comedy the women assume the male
attire, steal into the assembly, and by a majority of votes
carry a new constitution,[6] which realizes, in part at least,
the Platonic Utopia; for there is to be a community of
goods and women, and with regard to the latter the rights
of the ugly are to be protected by special enactment.   The
play has a good deal of the old Aristophanic energy, and
its indecency is as extravagant as its drollery and humour.
It has the literary characteristics as well as the phallic

[1] Plato, *Epist.* VII. pp. 324 B, sqq., especially 326 A, B.
[2] By Professor Thompson. See our *History of the Literature of
Greece*, Vol. II. pp. 211 sqq.
[3] *History of the Literature of Greece*, II. p. 245.
[4] Diog. Laert. III. 23; Herodian, *apud Etym. M.* p. 142 F.
[5] *Ecclesiaz.* 646; *Plutus*, 313.
[6] It is intimated, with a good deal of point, that this transference
of the government to the women was the only expedient which had
not been tried among the many changes of constitution at Athens
(v. 456):

ἐδόκει γὰρ τοῦτο μόνον ἐν τῇ πόλει
οὔπω γεγενῆσθαι.

grossness of the oldest Attic Comedy. But it is manifestly
deficient in the outward apparatus which had set out the
Comedy in its best days. The chorus is poorly equipped,
and it has little to do in any respect which would have
required careful training. There is no *parabasis*; but instead of this a mere *plaudite* is addressed to the audience
before the chorus go to supper.[1]

The *Plutus*, in its extant form, is the second edition of the
play, which appeared in B.C. 388. The first edition was
performed in B.C. 408. In the play, which has come down
to us, we have only here and there a reminiscence of what
the Old Comedy had been. The chorus is altogether insignificant. There is no political satire, and the personal
attacks are directed against individuals capriciously
selected. The plot is the development of a very simple and
perfectly general truth of allegorical morality—that if the
god of riches were not blind, he would have bestowed his
favours with more discrimination. In this play Plutus falls
into the hands of Chremylus, a poor but most worthy
citizen, who contrives to restore the blind god to the use of
his eyes. The natural consequences follow. The good
become rich, and the bad are reduced to poverty. There
is a slight dash of the old Aristophanic humour in the
successive pictures of these alterations in the condition of
the different classes of men. But on the whole the play
exhibits many symptoms, not only of the change which had
come over the whole spirit of Greek comic poetry, but also
of the decay of the poet's vigour and vivacity. The *Plutus*
is not yet a play of the Middle Comedy, but it has lost
all the characteristic features of the ancient comic drama of
Athens.

The last two Comedies which Aristophanes wrote were
called *Æolosicon* and *Cocalus*; they were brought out about
the time of the peace of Antalcidas by Araros, one of the
sons of the poet, who had been his principal actor at the

---

[1] vv. 1154 sqq.:

σμικρὸν δ' ὑποθέσθαι τοῖς κριταῖσι βούλομαι·
τοῖς σοφοῖς μὲν τῶν σοφῶν μεμνημένους κρίνειν ἐμέ·
τοῖς γελῶσι δ' ἡδέως διὰ τὸν γέλων κρίνειν ἐμέ,
κ.τ.λ.

representation of the second edition of the *Plutus*. They both belonged to the second variety of Comedy; namely, the Comedy of Criticism. The *Æolosicon* was a parody and criticism of the *Æolus* of Euripides.[1] The *Cocalus* was, perhaps, a similar criticism of a Tragedy or Epic Poem, the hero of which was Cocalus, the fabulous king of Sicily, who slew Minos;[2] it was so near an approach to the third variety of Comedy, that Philemon was able to bring it again on the stage with very few alterations.[3]

It is altogether unknown in what year Aristophanes died; it is probable, however, that he did not long survive the commencement of the 100th Olympiad, B.C. 380.[4] He left three sons, Philippus, Araros, and Nicostratus, who were all poets of the Middle Comedy, but do not appear to have inherited any considerable portion of their father's wonderful abilities. Their mother was not a very estimable woman; at all events, the poet is said to have declared, in one of his Comedies, that he was ashamed of her and his two foolish sons; meaning, we are told, the two first mentioned.[5]

The number of Comedies brought out by Aristophanes is not known with certainty: the reader will see in the note a list of forty-four names of Comedies attributed to him.[6]

---

[1] See Grauert, in the *Rhein. Mus.* for 1828, pp. 50 fol. The name Αἰολοσίκων is a compound (like Ἡρακλειοξανθίας, &c.) of the name of Euripides's tragic hero, and Sicon, a celebrated cook. Grauert, p. 60. And for this reason the whole Comedy was full of cookery terms. Grauert, pp. 499 fol.

[2] Grauert, p. 507.

[3] Clemens Alex. *Strom.* VI. p. 628: τὸν μέντοι Κώκαλον τὸν ποιηθέντα Ἀραρότι τῷ Ἀριστοφάνους υἱεῖ, Φιλήμων ὁ κωμικὸς ὑπαλλάξας ἐν Ὑποβολιμαίῳ ἐκωμῴδησεν.

[4] Ranke, p. cxcix.

[5] *Vit. Anonym.* p. xvii: (Ἀριστοφάνης) μετήλλαξε τὸν βίον παῖδας καταλιπὼν τρεῖς, Φίλιππον ὁμώνυμον τῷ πάππῳ καὶ Νικόστρατον καὶ Ἀραρότα.—τινὲς δὲ δύο φασί, Φίλιππον καὶ Ἀραρότα, ὧν καὶ αὐτὸς ἐμνήσθη·

Τὴν γυναῖκα δὲ
αἰσχύνομαι τώ τ' οὐ φρονοῦντε παιδίω·
ἴσως αὐτοὺς λέγων.

[6] I. Δαιταλῆς. II. Βαβυλώνιοι. III. Ἀχαρνῆς. IV. Ἱππῆς. V. Νεφέλαι πρότεραι. VI. Προάγων. VII. Σφῆκες. VIII. Εἰρήνη προτέρα. IX. Ἀμ-

In the very brief sketch which we have given of the general objects of Aristophanes' Comedies, we have confined ourselves to their external and political references. It must not, however, be supposed, because Aristophanes was a Pantagruelist, a fabricator of allegorical caricatures, giving vent at times to the wildest buffoonery, and setting no bounds to the coarseness and plain-spokenness of his words, that his writings contain nothing but a political *gergo;* on the contrary, we find here and there bursts of lyric poetry, which would have done honour to the sublimest of his Tragical contemporaries. The fact is, that Aristophanes was not merely a wit and a satirist; he had within himself all the ingredients which are necessary to form a great poet; the nicest discrimination of harmony, a fervid and active imagination drawing upon the stores of an ever-creating fancy, and a true and enlarged perception of ideal beauty. This was so notorious even in his own time, that Plato, who had little reason to speak favourably of him, declared that the Graces, having sought a temple to dwell in, found it in the bosom of Aristophanes,[1] and it is very likely in consequence of Plato's belief in the real poetical power of Aristophanes, that he makes Socrates convince him in the *Banquet,* that the real

---

φιάρaος. Χ. Ὄρνιθες. XI. Λυσιστράτη. XII. Θεσμοφοριάζουσαι πρότεραι. XIII. Πλοῦτος πρότερος. XIV. Βάτραχοι. XV. Ἐκκλησιάζουσαι. XVI. Πλοῦτος δεύτερος. XVII. Αἰολοσίκων πρότερος. XVIII. Αἰολοσίκων δεύτερος. XIX. Κώκαλος. These are arranged in the supposed order of their appearance. The remaining names are alphabetically arranged. I. Ἀνάγυρος. II. Γεωργοί. III. Γῆρας. IV. Γηρυτάδης. V. Δαίδαλος. VI. Δαναΐδες. VII. Δράματα ἢ Κένταυρος. VIII. Δράματα ἢ Νίοβος. IX. Εἰρήνη δευτέρα. X. Ἥρωες. XI. Θεσμοφοριάζουσαι δεύτεραι. XII. Λήμνιαι. XIII. Ναυαγός, or Δὶς Ναυαγός. XIV. Νεφέλαι δεύτεραι. XV. Νῆσοι. XVI. Ὁλκάδες. XVII. Πελαργοί. XVIII. Ποίησις. XIX. Πολύειδος. XX. Σκηνὰς καταλαμβάνουσαι. XXI. Ταγηνισταί. XXII. Τελμισσῆς. XXIII. Τριφάλης. XXIV. Φοίνισσαι. XXV. Ὧραι. See Dindorf's *Collection of the Fragments.* Bergk, p. 901. On the Γῆρας, see Süvern's essay on that play; and on the Τριφάλης, Süvern, *über die Wolken,* pp. 62—65.

[1] Apud Thom. Mag.:

Αἱ χάριτες τέμενός τι λαβεῖν ὅπερ οὐχὶ πεσεῖται
Ζητοῦσαι, ψυχὴν εὗρον Ἀριστοφάνους.

artists of Tragedy and Comedy are one and the same.[1] Of
the private character of Aristophanes we know little, save
that he was, like all other Athenians, fond of pleasure; and
it is intimated by Pluto[2] that he was not distinguished by
his abstinence and sobriety. That coarseness of language
was in those times no proof of moral depravity, has already
been sufficiently shown by a modern admirer of Aristophanes:[3] the fault was not in the man, but in the manners
of the age in which he lived, and to blame the Comedian
for it, is to give a very evident proof of that unwillingness
to shake off modern associations which we have already
deprecated.[4] The object of Aristophanes was one most
worthy of a wise and good man; it was to cry down the
pernicious quackery which was forcing its way into Athens,
and polluting, or drying up, the springs of public and
private virtue; which had turned religion into impudent
hypocrisy, and sobriety of mind into the folly of word-
wisdom; and which was the cause alike of the corruption
of Tragedy, and of the downfall of the state. He is not
to be blamed for his method of opposing these evils: it was
the only course open to him; the demagogues had introduced the *comus* into the city, and he turned it against
them, till it repented them that they had ever used such
an instrument. So far, then, from charging Aristophanes
with immorality, we would repeat, in the words which a
great and a good man of our own days used when speaking
of his antitype Rabelais, that the morality of his works is of
the most refined and exalted kind, however little worthy of
praise their manners may be,[5] and, on the whole, we
would fearlessly recommend any student, who is not so
imbued with the lisping and drivelling mawkishness of the
present day as to shudder at the ingredients with which the
necessities of the time have forced the great Comedian to
dress up his golden truths, to peruse and re-peruse Aristophanes, if he would know either the full force of the Attic

---

[1] *Sympos.* p. 223 D.   [2] For instance, see *Symp.* 176 B.
[3] Porson's Review of Brunck's Aristophanes, *Mus. Criticum*, II. pp.
114, 115.
[4] Above, pp. 7, 8.
[5] Coleridge's *Table Talk*, I. p. 178.

dialect, or the state of men and manners at Athens, in the most glorious days of her history.[1]

[1] The admiration which all true scholars have felt and expressed for Aristophanes, will survive the attacks of certain modern detractors. Among these, Hartung, in his *Euripides restitutus*, has endeavoured to exalt that tragedian at the expense of the great author of the *Frogs*, whom he assails in the most abusive language (I. 380, 476). The disapprobation of the poetry and politics of Euripides, which Aristophanes so strongly avowed, is not incompatible with the imitation of his style, which he frankly admitted in his Σκηνὰς καταλαμβάνουσαι (above, p. 191). And with regard to another charge, it is quite impossible with the fragmentary evidence before us, to strike the balance of mutual obligation between Eupolis and Aristophanes. See Bernhardy, *Grundriss*, II. p. 973.

CHAPTER II.

SECTION III.

THE COMEDIANS WHO SUCCEEDED ARISTOPHANES.

I coltivatori della commedia seguirono l'esempio di questi primi, come essi aveano pur seguito quello degli antichi, senza che nè gli uni nè gli altri, impediti da una servile imitazione, avessero soffocato il proprio genio o negletto i costumi del paese e del tempo loro.

SALFI.

ALTHOUGH, as we have already remarked,[1] the writers of the Old and Middle Comedy are not easily distinguished, and although we have been obliged to indicate several of the old comedians as having tended rather to the middle form of Comedy, writers on the subject have always attempted a distinct classification of the comedians rather than of their plays; and perhaps it may be said with truth that those who never wrote in the flourishing period of Athenian democracy, and whose earliest plays exhibit the characteristics of the final efforts of Aristophanes, may be regarded as belonging distinctively to the Middle Comedy.

According to this distinction, the Middle Comedy is represented by a list of thirty-seven writers,—nearly as many as those of the Old Comedy,—and by more than double the number of the plays attributed to the former school—Eubulus, Antiphanes, and Alexis having among them contributed more than 600 plays to the catalogue! The following are the names of the Middle Comedians:

1. ANTIPHANES. 2. EUBULUS. 3. ANAXANDRIDES. 4. ALEXIS. 5. ARAROS, son of Aristophanes. 6. PHILIPPUS, brother of the preceding. 7. NICOSTRATUS. 8. PHILETÆRUS.

---

[1] On these authors and their works, see Meineke, *Quæstiones Scenicæ* Spec. III. and his *Historia Critica*, pp. 303 sqq. and 445 sqq.; also Müller, *Hist. Lit. Gr.* II. ch. xxix.

9. AMPHIS.   10. ANAXILAS.   11. EPHIPPUS.   12. CRATINUS, the younger. 13. EPIGENES. 14. ARISTOPHON. 15. OPHELION. 16. ANTIDOTUS.   17. DIODORUS of Sinope.   18. DIONYSIUS, a countryman of the preceding.   19. HENIOCHUS. 20. ERIPHUS.   21. SIMYLUS.   22. SOPHILUS.   23. SOTADES. 24. PHILISCUS.   25. TIMOTHEUS.   26. THEOPHILUS. 27. AUGEAS. 28. DROMON. 29. EUBULIDES, the philosopher. 30. HERACLEIDES.   31. CALLICRATES.   32. STRATON. 33. EPICRATES, of Ambracia,   34. AXIONICUS.   35. MNESI-MACHUS.   36. TIMOCLES.   37. XENARCHUS.

The anonymous grammarian, who is our oldest authority for the history of the Greek comic stage, says that there were sixty-four writers of New Comedy.[1]   But we have only the following twenty-seven names which we can with certainty assign to this age of the drama.   They are given in alphabetical order : ANAXIPPUS, APOLLODORUS of Carystus, APOLLODORUS of Gela, ARCHEDICUS, BATHO, CRITO, DAMOXENUS, DEMETRIUS, DIPHILUS, EPINICUS, EUDOXUS, EUPHRON, HEGESIPPUS, HIPPARCHUS, LYNCEUS, MACHON, MENANDER, PHILEMON and his son, PHILIPPIDES, PHŒNI-CIDES, POSEIDIPPUS, SOSIPATER, SOSIPPUS, STEPHANUS, THEOGNETUS.

Other names are occasionally mentioned, though it cannot be determined whether they belonged to the Middle Comedy or not.   Thus we have DEMOPHILUS, from whom Plautus derived some of his plots; CLEARCHUS and CROTYLUS, to each of whom three Comedies are assigned CHARICLEIDES, CALLIPPUS, DEMONICUS, DEXICRATES, ÉVAN-GELUS, LAON, MENECRATES, NAUSICRATES, who has two comedies assigned to him, NICON, NICOLAUS, NICOMACHUS, PHILOSTEPHANUS, POLIOCHUS, SOSICRATES, two of whose plays are mentioned, THUGENIDES, TIMOSTRATUS, to whom four comedies are attributed, and XENON.

In these lists of writers of the Middle and New Comedy there are only a few who deserve or require any special notice.

Of the authors of the Middle Comedy we may mention the following :

_____
[1] περὶ κωμῳδίας, xxx. 20, p. 537, Meineke.

It appears from the words of Suidas,[1] that EUBULUS, the son of Euphranor, who was an Athenian, and flourished about the year B.C. 375, stood on the debateable ground between the middle and new Comedy, and to judge from the fragments in Athenæus, who quotes more than fifty of his comedies by name, he must have written plays of both sorts. He composed in the whole 104 comedies.

ANTIPHANES was born in Rhodes in B.C. 404, began to exhibit about B.C. 383 and died in Chios in B.C. 330. He composed 260 or 280 comedies, and the titles of 130 of these have come down to us. It appears from these names and from the numerous fragments, that the Comedies of Antiphanes were generally of the critical kind, but sometimes approximated to the Comedy of Manners.[2]

ANAXANDRIDES, of Camirus in Rhodes, flourished about the year B.C. 376.[3] He wrote sixty-five Comedies. To judge from the twenty-eight titles which have come down to us, we should infer that they were all of the second class; as, however, we are told that he introduced intrigues and love-affairs on the stage, we must presume that, like his countryman Antiphanes, he made an advance towards the third class of Comedy. Chamæleon tells us,[4] that he was a tall handsome man, and fond of fine dresses; he gives us a proof of his want of temper, that he used to destroy, or sell for waste paper, all his unsuccessful comedies. He lived to a good old age.

ALEXIS, of Thurium, wrote 245 Comedies; the titles of 113 of them are known to us. The *Parasite*, one of his Comedies, seems from the name to belong to the New Comedy. He flourished from the year 356 to the year 306, and was more than one hundred years old when he died.[5]

---

[1] Εὔβουλος—ἐδίδαξε δράματα ρδ' ἦν δὲ κατὰ οα' ὀλυμπιάδα, μεθόριος τῆς μέσης κωμῳδίας καὶ τῆς νέας.

On Antiphanes and his fragments, see Clinton, *Phil. Mus.* I. pp. 558 fol.

[3] Parian Marble, No. 71, and Suidas.   [4] Athenæus, IX. p. 374 A.

[5] Clinton, *F. H.* II. p. 175.

We know nothing of him, except that he was an epicure,[1] and the uncle and instructor of Menander.[2]

TIMOCLES, to whom twenty-seven Comedies are attributed, was a writer of very considerable vigour, and occasionally recurred to the political invective of the older Comedy. Demosthenes was sometimes the object of his attacks. He was still exhibiting in B.C. 324.[3]

Of the authors of the New Comedy it will be sufficient to mention the following.

PHILIPPIDES, the son of Philocles of Athens, is one of the six poets generally selected as specimens of the New Comedy.[4] He flourished about the year B.C. 335, and wrote forty-five Comedies; of the twelve titles preserved, one at least, the *Amphiaraus*,[5] seems to belong to the Middle or Old Comedy. The intimacy which existed between him and Lysimachus was of great service to Athens.[6] As that prince did not assume the title of king till B.C. 306, and as it appears from the words of Plutarch,[7] that Lysimachus was king at the time of his acquaintance with Philippides, the poet must have lived after that year; besides, we know that he ridiculed the honours paid by the Athenians to Demetrius, in 301 B.C.[8] There is, therefore, every reason to believe the statement of Aulus Gellius, that he lived to a very advanced age,[9] though perhaps the cause assigned for his death, excessive joy on account of an

---

[1] Athenæus, VIII. p. 334 C.

[2] Prolegom. Aristoph. p. xxx, and Suidas, where we must read πάτρως.

[3] See the passages in Clinton, *F. H.* II. p. 161.

[4] Prol. Aristoph. p. xxx: ἀξιολογώτατοι Φιλήμων, Μένανδρος, Δίφιλος, Φιλιππίδης, Ποσείδιππος, Ἀπολλόδωρος.

[5] Quoted by Athenæus, III. p. 90.   [6] Plutarch, *Demetr.* c. XII.

[7] Φιλοφρονουμένου δέ ποτε τοῦ Λυσιμάχου πρὸς αὐτὸν καὶ εἰπόντος, "Ὦ Φιλιππίδη, τίνος σοι τῶν ἐμῶν μεταδῶ;" "Μόνον," ἔφη, "ὦ βασιλεῦ, μὴ τῶν ἀπορρήτων."

[8] Clinton, *F. H.* II. p. 177.

[9] III. 15: "Philippides comœdiarum poëta haud ignobilis, ætate jam editâ, cum in certamine poëtarum præter spem vicisset, inter illud gaudium repente mortuus est."

Q

unexpected victory, is, like the similar story respecting Sophocles, a mere invention.

PHILEMON was, according to Strabo,[1] a native of Soli, though Suidas makes him a Syracusan, probably because he resided some time in Sicily. He began to exhibit about the year B.C. 330, and died at the age of ninety-seven, some time in the reign of Antigonus the second.[2] According to Diodorus,[3] he lived ninety-nine years, and wrote ninety-seven Comedies. Various accounts are given of the manner of his death.[4] Lucian tells us, he died in a paroxysm of laughter at seeing an ass devouring some figs intended for his own eating. The names of fifty-three of his Comedies have come down to us.[5] Philemon was considered as superior to Menander;[6] and Quintilian, while he denies the correctness of this judgment,[7] is nevertheless willing to allow Philemon the second place. We may see a favourable specimen of his construction of plots, in the *Trinummus* of Plautus, which is a translation from his Θησαυρός.[8] His plays, like those of Menander, contained many imitations of Euripides; and he was so ardent an admirer of that poet, that he declared he would have hanged himself for the prospect of meeting Euripides in the other world, if he could have convinced himself that the departed spirits were really capable of recognizing one another.[9]

---

[1] XIV. p. 671.   [2] Clinton, *F. H.* II. p. 157.
[3] *Eclog. Lib.* XXIII. p. 318.
[4] Plutarch, *An seni, &c.* p. 785; Lucian, *Macrob.* c. XXV. (Vol. VIII. p. 123, Lehm.); Apuleius, *Florid.* XVI. Suidas says he was ninety-four when he died, and gives nearly the same description of his death as Lucian.
[5] Fabricius, II. p. 476, Harles.
[6] Aul. Gell. XVII. 4; Quintil. III. 7, 18.
[7] X. 1, 72: "*Philemon*, qui ut pravis sui temporis judiciis Menandro sæpe prælatus est, ita consensu tamen omnium meruit credi secundus."
[8] *Prol. Trinummi*, 18:
   "Huic nomen Græce est Thesauro fabulæ;
   Philemo scripsit; Plautus vortit barbare,
   Nomen Trinummo fecit."
[9] *Fragm.* 40 A, p. 48, Meineke; *Anthol. Pal.* Vol. II. p. 161:
   Εἰ ταῖς ἀληθείαισιν οἱ τεθνηκότες
   Αἴσθησιν εἶχον, ἄνδρες, ὥς φασίν τινες,
   Ἀπηγξάμην ἂν ὡς ἰδεῖν Εὐριπίδην.

MENANDER, the son of Diopeithes, the well-known general, and Hegesistrata,[1] and the nephew of the comedian Alexis,[2] was born at Athens in B.C. 342,[3] while his father was absent on the Hellespont station.[4] He spent his youth in the house of his uncle, and received from him and from Theophrastus instructions in poetry and philosophy:[5] he may have derived from the latter, in some measure, the knowledge of character for which he was so eminent. In B.C. 321 his first comedy came out;[6] it was called 'Οργή.[7] He wrote in the whole 105[8] or 108[9] Comedies, and gained the prize eight times : 115 titles of Comedies ascribed to him have come down to us ; it is not certain, however, that all these are correctly attributed to him.[10] He died at Athens in the year B.C. 291.[11] According to one account he was drowned while bathing in the harbour of the Peiræus.[12] It appears from the encomiums which are heaped upon him,[13] that he was by far the best writer of the Comedy of Manners among the Greeks. We have a few specimens of the ingenuity of his plots in some of the plays of Terence, whom Julius Cæsar used to call a demi-Menander.[14] He was an imitator of Euripides,[15] and we may infer from what

[1] Suidas, Μένανδρος.   [2] Suidas, Ἄλεξις.

[3] Clinton, F. H. II. p. 143.

[4] Comp. Ulpian and Demosth. p. 54, 3, with Dionys. Dinarch. p. 666.

[5] Proleg. Aristoph. p. xxx; Diogen. Laërt. v. 36.

[6] Proleg. Aristoph. p. xxx.   [7] Euseb. ad Olyn. 114, 4.

[8] Apollod. ap. Aul. Gell. xvII. 4 :

> Κηφισιεὺς ὢν ἐκ Διοπείθεος πατρός,
> Πρὸς τοῖσιν ἑκατὸν πέντε γράψας δράματα
> 'Εξέλιπε, πεντήκοντα καὶ δυοῖν ἐτῶν.

[9] Suidas, γέγραφε κωμῳδίας ρη'.

[10] Fabricius, II. pp. 460, 468, Harles.   [11] Clinton, F. H. II. p. 181.

[12] A line in the Ibis attributed to Ovid, is supposed by some to allude to this (591):

> "Comicus ut mediis periit dum nabat in undis."

[13] Quintil. x. 1, 69; Plutarch, Tom. IX. pp. 387 sqq. Reiske; and Dio Chrysost. XVIII. p. 255.   [14] Donatus, Vit. Terentii.

[15] See the passages compared by Meineke, Fragm. Com. Gr. Vol. IV. pp. 705 foll. It is interesting to know that it is still doubtful whether the Senarius quoted by St. Paul in I Corinth. xv. 33, was not borrowed by Menander, in his Thais, from some lost play of Euripides. It is quoted in Latin by Tertullian, ad Uxor. 1. 8.

Quintilian says of him,[1] that his comedies differed from the
Tragi-comedies of that poet only in the absence of mythical
subjects and a chorus. Like Euripides, he was a good
rhetorician, and Quintilian is inclined to attribute to him
some orations published in the name of Charisius.[2] The
every-day life of his countrymen, and manners and characters
of ordinary occurrence, were the objects of his imitation.[3]
His plots, though skilfully contrived, are somewhat monotonous; there are few of his comedies which do not bring on
the stage a harsh father, a profligate son, and a roguish
slave.[4] In his person Menander was foppish and effeminate.[5] He wrote several prose works.[6] A statue was
erected to his memory in the theatre at Athens.[7]

The date of the birth of DIPHILUS is unknown; it is
stated that he exhibited at the same time with Menander.[8]

[1] x. 1, 69.   [2] x. 1, 70.

[3] Aristoph. Byz. ap. Schol. Hermogenis, p. 38:

$$\text{Ὦ Μένανδρε καὶ βίε,}$$
$$\text{Πότερος ἄρ' ὑμῶν πότερον ἐμιμήσατο;}$$

Manilius, v. 472:

"Ardentes juvenes, raptasque in amore puellas,
Elusosque senes, agilesque per omnia servos,
Quis in cuncta suam produxit saecula vitam
Doctor in urbe sua linguae sub flore Menander,
Qui vitae ostendit vitam, chartisque sacravit."

[4]   "Dum fallax servus, durus pater, improba laena,
Vivent, dum meretrix blanda, Menandrus erit."

Ovid, 1. Amorum, xv. 13.

[5]   "In quis Menander, nobilis comoediis,"

Unguento delibutus, vestitu affluens,
Veniebat gressu delicato et languido.

Quisnam cinaedus ille in conspectu meo
Audet venire? Responderunt proximi:
Hic est Menander scriptor."

Phaedrus, v. 1, 9.

"Prorsus si quis Menandrico fluxu delicatam vestem humi protrahat."
—Tertullian, c. iv. de Pallio.

[6] Suidas, Μένανδρος.   [7] Pausan. 1. 21, 1.

[8] Δίφιλος Σινωπεύς, κατὰ τὸν αὐτὸν χρόνον ἐδίδαξε Μενάνδρῳ, τελευτᾷ
ἐν Σμύρνῃ, δράματα δὲ αὐτοῦ ρ'. Proleg. Arist. p. xxxi.

He was born at Sinope,[1] and died at Smyrna. Of one hundred Comedies, which he is said to have written, the names of forty-eight are preserved.[2] The *Casina* of Plautus is borrowed from his Κληρούμενοι,[3] and the *Rudens* from some other play;[4] and Terence tells us, that he introduced into the *Adelphi* a literal translation of part of the Συναπο-θνήσκοντες of Diphilus.[5] It appears from the *Casina* and *Rudens*, and from a fragment of Machon,[6] that he wrote prologues to his dramas, which were probably very like the prologues of the Latin comedians, though they were, we think, originally borrowed (like all the New Comedy) from the tragedies of Euripides.

APOLLODORUS, of Gela in Sicily,[7] is also called a contemporary of Menander. He is often confused with APOLLODORUS of Carystus in Euboea, whom Suidas calls an Athenian, probably because he had the Athenian franchise, but who flourished between B.C. 300 and 260. For he is said to have been a contemporary of MACHON, who was a

[1] Strabo, XII. p. 546.   [2] Fabricius, II. p. 438, Harles.

[3]   "*Clerumenæ* vocatur hæc comœdia
        Græce; Latine *Sortientes*. Diphilus
        Hanc Græce scripsit, post id rursum denuo
        Latine Plautus cum latranti nomine."
                              Prolog. Casinæ, 30—32.

[4] *Prolog. Rud.* 32 :
        "Primum dum huic esse nomen urbi Diphilus
        Cyrenas voluit."

[5]   "*Synapothnescontes* Diphili comœdia 'st :
        Eam *Commorientes* Plautus fecit fabulam.
        In Græca adolescens est, qui lenoni eripit
        Meretricem in primâ fabulâ : eum Plautus locum
        Reliquit integrum, cum hic locum sumpsit sibi
        In *Adelphos*, verbum de verbo expressum extulit."
                              Prol. Adelph. 6—11.

[6] Athen. XIII. p. 580 A :
                    ὁ Δίφιλος,
        "νὴ τὴν 'Αθηνᾶν καὶ θεοὺς ψυχρόν γ'," ἔφη,
        "Γναθαῖν', ἔχεις τὸν λάκκον ὁμολογουμένως."
        ἡ δ' εἶπε, "τῶν σῶν δραμάτων γὰρ ἐπιμελῶς
        εἰς αὐτὸν ἀεὶ τοὺς προλόγους ἐμβάλλομεν."

[7] On the two comedians of this name see Clinton, *F.H.* III. pp. 521, 2; Meineke, *Hist. Crit. Com.* pp. 459 sqq.

Corinthian or Sicyonian by birth, who resided at Alexandria, and gave instructions in Comedy to Aristophanes of Byzantium, and whose Comedies obtained for him a place among the Alexandrian poets immediately after those of the Pleiad.[1] Of twenty-four Comedies, which are mentioned under the name of Apollodorus, four are ascribed to the earlier poet, six to the latter, and four to both. The remaining ten are quoted under the name of Apollodorus without any ethnic distinction.[2] The later Apollodorus was much the more distinguished writer of the two, and there can be little doubt that it is he, and not the Geloan, who is mentioned as one of the six chief poets of the New Comedy.[3] The *Phormio* of Terence is a translation from his Ἐπιδικαζόμενος, and the *Hecyra*, which is said in the didascalia to have been taken from Menander, was, according to a recently discovered fragment, also borrowed from this poet.[4]

POSIDIPPUS, the son of Cyniscus of Cassandreia, wrote thirty comedies; the titles of fifteen of these are known, and some of them were Latinized like those of the three last-mentioned poets.[5] He began to exhibit in B.C. 289, two years after the death of Menander.[6]

The Greek Comedy properly ends with Posidippus, but there are some writers of a later date called comedians. RHINTHON, of Tarentum, is called a comedian by Suidas, but his plays seem to have been rather *phlyacographies*, or Tragi-comedies, and of those he left thirty-eight. He flourished in the reign of the first Ptolemy.[7] The titles of

---

[1] Athenæus, p. 664 A (cf. VI. p. 241 F): ἦν δ' ἀγαθὸς ποιητὴς εἴ τις ἄλλος τῶν μετὰ τοὺς ἑπτά. The author of the article on Apollodorus of Caryatus, in Smith's *Dictionary of Biography*, applies to Apollodorus what Athenæus says of Machon.

[2] Clinton's *F. H.* III. pp. 521, 2.   [3] Meineke, p. 462.

[4] Mai, *Fragm. Plaut. et Terent.* p. 38: "Fabulæ ejus [Terentii] exstant quatuor e Menandro translatæ, Andria, Eunuchus, Adelphi et Heautontimorumenos; duæ ex Apollodoro Caricio [sic] Hecyra et Phormio."

[5] Aul. Gell. II. 23.   [6] Suidas, Ποσείδιππος.

[7] Suidas: Ῥίνθων, Ταραντῖνος, κωμικός, ἀρχηγὸς τῆς καλουμένης Ἱλαροτραγῳδίας ὅ ἐστι Φλυακογραφία. υἱὸς δὲ ἦν κεραμέως καὶ γέγονεν ἐπὶ τοῦ πρώτου Πτολεμαίου. Δράματα δὲ αὐτοῦ κωμικὰ τραγικὰ λη'.

six of his plays are known.[1] SOPATER, of Paphos, was a writer of the same kind; and also SOTADES, of Crete, who flourished under Ptolemy Philadelphus, and wrote in the Ionic dialect,[2] and in the so-called *Ionic a minore* metre. From the extravagant indecency of the Sotadean poems the name has become a by-word of reproach.[3]

[1] Clinton, *F. H.* III. p. 486.   [2] *Ibid.* p. 500.
[3] See *History of Greek Literature*, II. p. 464.

CHRONOLOGY OF THE GREEK DRAMA.

B.C.	Olympiad.	The Drama.	Contemporary Persons and Events.
708	XVIII. 1.	*Archilochus*	*Gyges* of Lydia.
693	XXI. 4.	*Simonides* of Amorgus	
610	XLII. 3.	*Arion* and *Stesichorus* fl.	*Pisander* of Corinth.
594	XLVI. 3.	*Solon* fl.	
562	LIV. 3.	*Susarion*	Usurpation of *Pisistratus*, B.C. 560.—The accession of *Cyrus*, B.C. 559.
549	LVII. 4.		Death of *Phalaris*.
544	LIX. 1.	*Theognis*	
535	LXI. 2.	*Thespis* first exhibits .	*Anacreon, Ibycus, Hipponax,—Pythagoras.*
525	LXIII. 4.	*Æschylus* born . . .	*Cambyses* conquers Egypt.
524	LXIV. 1.	*Chœrilus* first exhibits	
519	LXV. 2.	*Cratinus* born	
518	—— 3.		*Pindar* born.
511	LXVII. 2.	*Phrynichus* first exhibits.	Expulsion of the *Pisistratidæ*, B.C. 510—of the *Tarquins*, B.C. 509.
508	LXVIII. 1.	Institution of the Χορὸς ἀνδρῶν. *Lasus* of Hermione, the dithyrambic poet.	*Heraclitus* and *Parmenides*, the philosophers.— *Hecatæus*, the historian.
500	LXX. 1.	*Epicharmus* perfects Comedy.	Birth of *Anaxagoras*.
499	—— 2.	*Æschylus* first exhibits, and contends with *Chœrilus* and *Pratinas*.	Ionian war commences, and Sardis is burnt.
495	LXXI. 2.	Birth of *Sophocles* . .	Miletus taken, B.C. 494.
490	LXXII. 3.	*Æschylus* at Marathon .	*Miltiades.*

B.C.	Olympiad.	The Drama.	Contemporary Persons and Events.
487	LXXIII. 2.	*Chionides* first exhibits .	
484	LXXIV. 1.	*Æschylus* gains his first tragic prize.	Birth of *Herodotus.*
480	LXXV. 1.	*Euripides* born . . .	Thermopylæ, Salamis.— *Leonidas, Aristides, Themistocles.* — *Pherecydes,* the historian.—*Gelon* of Syracuse.
477	—— 3.	*Epicharmi* Νᾶσοι . . .	*Hiero* succeeds *Gelon,* B.C. 478.
476	LXXVI. 1.	*Phrynichus* victor with his Φοίνισσαι. *Themistocles* choragus.	*Simonides* gains the prize Ἀνδρῶν Χορῷ.
472	LXXVII. 1.	*Æschyli* Πέρσαι, Φινεύς, Γλαῦκος Ποτνιεύς, Προμηθεὺς Πυρφόρος.	Birth of *Thucydides,* B.C. 471.
468	LXXVIII. 1.	*Sophocles* gains his first tragic prize. *Æschylus* goes to Sicily.	*Socrates* born. — Mycenæ destroyed by the Argives.—Death of *Simonides,* B.C. 467.
458	LXXX. 3.	*Æschyli* Ὀρεστεία. *Æschylus* again retires to Sicily.	*Anaxagoras.* Birth of *Lysias.*
456	LXXXI. 1.	*Æschylus* dies . . .	*Herodotus* at Olympia.
455	—— 2.	*Euripides* exhibits the *Peliades.*	End of the Messenian and Egyptian wars.—*Empedocles* and *Zeno.*—*Pericles.*
454	—— 3.	*Aristarchus,* of Tegea, the tragedian, and *Cratinus,* the comic poet, flourish.	
451	LXXXII. 2.	*Ion* of Chios begins to exhibit.	
450	—— 3.	*Crates* exhibits . . .	*Bacchylides,* the lyric poet. —*Archelaus,* the philosopher.
443	LXXXIII. 1.	*Cratini* Ἀρχίλοχοι . .	Death of *Cimon,* B.C. 449.

B.C.	Olympiad.	The Drama.	Contemporary Persons and Events.
447	LXXXIII 2.	*Achæus Eretriensis*, the tragedian.	Battle of Coronea.
441	LXXXIV. 4.	*Euripides* gains the first tragic prize.	*Herodotus* and *Lysias* go with the colonists to Thurium, B.C. 443.
440	LXXXV. 1.	Comedy prohibited by a public decree.	The Samian war, in which *Sophocles* is colleague with *Pericles*.
437	—— 3.	The prohibition of Comedy repealed.	*Isocrates* born, B.C, 436.
435	LXXXVI. 2.	*Phrynichus*, the comic poet, first exhibits.	Sea-fight between the Corinthians and Corcyræans.
434	—— 3.	*Lysippus*, the comic poet, is victorious.	*Andocides, Meton, Aspasia.*
431	LXXXVII. 2.	*Euripidis* Μήδεια, Φιλοκτήτης, Δίκτυς, Θερισταί.	Attempt of the Thebans on Platæa.
		Aristomenes, the comic poet.	*Hippocrates.*
430	—— 3.	*Hermippus*, the comic poet.	Plague at Athens.
429	—— 4.	*Eupolis* exhibits . . .	Siege of Platæa.—Birth of *Plato*.
428	LXXXVIII. 1.	*Euripidis* Ἱππόλυτος .	*Anaxagoras* dies.
		Plato, the comic poet	
427	—— 2.	*Aristophanis* Δαιταλεῖς .	Surrender of Platæa.—*Gorgias of Leontium.*
426	—— 3.	*Aristophanis* Βαβυλώνιοι .	*Tanagra.*
425	—— 4.	*Aristophanes* first with the Ἀχαρνεῖς: *Cratinus* second with the Χειμαζόμενοι: *Eupolis* third with the Νουμηνίαι.	*Cleon* at Sphacteria.
424	LXXXIX. 1.	*Aristophanes* first with the Ἱππεῖς; *Cratinus* second with the Σάτυροι: *Aristomenes* third with the Ὀλοφυρμοί.	*Xenophon* at Delium.—Amphipolis taken from *Thucydides* by *Brasidas*.

B.C.	Olympiad.	The Drama.	Contemporary Persons and Events.
423	LXXXIX. 2.	*Cratinus* first with the Πυτίνη: *Ameipsias* second with the Κόννος: *Aristophanes* third with the Νεφέλαι.	The year's truce with Lacedæmon. — *Alcibiades* begins to act in public affairs.
422	—— 3.	*Aristophanis* Σφῆκες et ai δεύτεραι Νεφέλαι. (Sed vide supra.) *Cratinus* dies.	*Brasidas* and *Cleon* killed at Amphipolis.
421	—— 4.	*Eupolidis* Μαρικᾶς et Κόλακες.	Truce for fifty years with Lacedæmon.
420	XC. 1.	*Eupolidis* Αὐτόλυκος et 'Αστράτευτοι.	Treaty with the Argives.
419	—— 2.	*Aristophanis* Εἰρήνη.	
416	XCI. 1.	*Agathon* gains the tragic prize.	Capture of Melos.
415	—— 2.	*Xenocles* first; *Euripides* second with the Τρῳάδες, 'Αλέξανδρος, Παλαμήδης, and Σίσυφος. *Archippus*, the comic poet, gains the prize.	Expedition to Sicily.
414	—— 3.	*Aristophanis* 'Αμφιάραος (εἰς Λήναια). *Ameipsias* first with the Κωμασταί: *Aristophanes* second with the 'Ορνιθες: *Phrynichus* third with the Μονότροπος (εἰς ἄστυ).	
413	XCI. 4.	*Hegemonis* Γιγαντομαχία.	Destruction of the Athenian army before Syracuse.
412	XCII. 1.	*Euripidis* 'Ανδρομέδα .	Losbos, Chios, and Erythræ revolt.
411	—— 2.	*Aristophanis* Λυσιστράτη et Θεσμοφοριάζουσαι.	The 400 at Athens.
409	—— 4.	*Sophocles* first with the Φιλοκτήτης.	

B.C.	Olympiad.	The Drama.	Contemporary Persons and Events.
408	XCIII. 1.	*Euripidis* 'Ορέστης.	
406	—— 3.	*Euripides* dies . . .	*Arginusæ.*—*Dionysius* becomes master of Syracuse. — *Philistus,* the Sicilian historian.
405	—— 4.	Death of *Sophocles* . .	*Ægospotami.*—*Conon.*
		Aristophanis Βάτραχοι, first; *Phrynichi* Μοῦσαι, second; *Platonis* Κλεοφῶν, third.	The *Thirty* at Athens.
404	XCIV. 1.	*Antiphanes* born.	
401	—— 3.	*Sophoclis* Οἰδίπους ἐπὶ Κολώνῳ exhibited by the *younger Sophocles;* who first represented in his own name, B.C. 396.	*Xenophon,* with *Cyrus.*—*Ctesias,* the historian.—*Plato.*
392	XCVII. 1.	*Aristophanis* 'Εκκλησιάζουσαι.	*Agesilaus.*
388	XCVIII. 1.	*Aristophanis* Πλοῦτος β'.	
387	—— 2.	•	Peace of *Antalcidas.*
386	—— 3.	*Theopompus,* the last poet of the Old Comedy.	
383	XCIX. 2.	*Antiphanes* begins to exhibit.	
376	CI. 1.	*Eubulus, Araros,* and *Anaxandrides,* the comic poets, flourished.	
368	CIII. 1.	*Aphareus,* the tragedian	
356	CVI. 1.	*Alexis,* the comic poet .	*Alexander* born.—Expulsion of *Dionysius.*—Death of *Timotheus,* the musician.
348	CVIII. 1.	*Heraclides,* the comic poet.	*Demosthenes* against *Midias.*—*Philip* and the Olynthian war.
/ 342	CIX. 3.	Birth of *Menander* . .	*Timoleon* at Syracuse.—*Isocrates.*—*Aristotle.*

B.C.	Olympiad.	The Drama.	Contemporary Persons and Events.
336	CXI. 1.	*Amphis*, the comic poet, still exhibits.	*Philip* assassinated.
335	—— 2.	*Philippides*, the comedian.	
332	CXII. 1.	*Stephanus*, the comic poet.	Siege of Tyre.
330	—— 3.	*Philemon* begins to exhibit.	*Darius* slain.
324	CXIV. 1.	*Timocles* still exhibits .	*Alexander* dies. — *Demosthenes* dies, B.C. 322.
321	—— 4.	*Menandri* 'Οργή.	
		Diphilus.	
307	CXVIII. 1.	*Demetrius*, the comic poet.	*Epicurus.—Agathocles.*
304	CXIX. 1.	*Archedippus, Philippides,* and *Anaxippus,* the comic poets, flourish.	*Demetrius Poliorcetes.*
291	CXXII. 2.	Death of *Menander* . .	*Arcesilaus.*
289	—— 4.	*Posidippus* begins to exhibit—*Rhinthon* flourishes.	
280	CXXV. 1.	*Sotades*	War with Pyrrhus.
230	CXXXVII. 3.	*Macho*, the comedian.	
200	CXLV. 1.	*Apollodorus,* the Carystian.	*Plautus* dies.

BOOK III.

EXHIBITION OF THE GREEK DRAMA.

CHAPTER I.

ON THE REPRESENTATION OF GREEK PLAYS IN GENERAL.

*Dass man auf das ganze Verhältniss der Orchestra zur Bühne keine vom
heutigen Theater entnommenen Vorstellungen übertragen, und die alte
Tragödie nicht* MODERNISIREN *dürfe, ist ja wohl eine der ersten Regeln,
die man bei der Beurtheilung dieser Dinge zu beobachten hat.*—K. O.
MUELLER.

IF the Greek plays themselves differed essentially from
those of our own times, they were even more dissimilar in
respect of the mode and circumstances of their representation. We have theatrical exhibitions of some kind every
evening throughout the greater part of the year, and in
capital cities many are going on at the same time in different
theatres. In Greece the dramatic performances were carried
on for a few days in the spring; the theatre was large
enough to contain the whole population, and every citizen
was there, as a matter of course, from daybreak to sunset.[1]
With us a successful play is repeated night after night, for
months together : in Greece the most admired dramas were
seldom repeated, and never in the same year. The theatre
with us is merely a place of public entertainment; in
Greece it was the temple of the god, whose altar was the
central point of the semicircle of seats or steps, from which
some 30,000[2] of his worshippers gazed upon a spectacle
instituted in his honour. Our theatrical costumes are

---

[1] Æsch. κατὰ Κτησ. p. 488, Bekker : καὶ ἅμα τῇ ἡμέρᾳ ἡγεῖτο τοῖς
πρέσβεσιν εἰς τὸ θέατρον.
The torch-races in the last plays of a trilogia (above, p. 102) seem to
show that the exhibitions were not over till dark.
[2] Plato, *Sympos.* p. 175 E.

intended to convey an idea of the dresses actually worn by
the persons represented, while those of the Greeks were
nothing but modifications of the festal robes worn in the
Dionysian processions.[1] Finally, the modern playwright
has only the approbation or disapprobation of his audience
to look to; whereas no Greek play was represented until it
had been approved by a board appointed to decide between
the rival dramatists, It will be worth our while, then, to
consider separately the distinguishing peculiarities of a
Greek dramatic exhibition. We shall discuss the points of
difference successively, as they relate to the *time*, the *means*,
the *place*, and the *manner* of performance? to which we shall
add a few remarks on the audience and the actors. And
first with regard to the *time*.

Theatrical exhibitions formed a part of certain festivals of
Bacchus; in order, then, to ascertain at what time of the
year they took place, we must inquire how many festivals
were held in Attica in honour of that God, and then
determine at which of them theatrical representations were
given. There have been great diversities of opinion in
regard to the number of the Attic Dionysia:[2] it appears,
however, to be now pretty generally agreed among scholars

---

[1] Müller, *Eumeniden*, § 32, and *Hist. Gr. Lit.* I. p. 393 new ed.

[2] The reader who wishes to investigate the question fully is referred
to Scaliger (*Emendat. Temp.* I. p. 29), Paulmier (*Exercitat. in Auctores
Græcos*, pp. 617—619), Petit (*Legg. Atticæ*, pp. 112—117), Spanheim
(*Argum. ad Arist. Ran.* Tom. III. pp. 122 sqq. ed. Beck), Oderici
(*Dissert. de Didasc. Marmorea*, Rom. 1777, and in Marini, *Iscriz.
Albane*, Rom. 1785, pp. 161—170), Kanngiesser (*Kom. Bühne*, pp.
161—170), and Hermann (Beck's *Aristoph.* Tom. v. pp. 11—28), who
infer from the Scholiast, on Aristoph. *Ach.* 201 and 503, that the
Lenæa were identical with the rural Dionysia; to Selden (*ad Marm.
Oxon.* pp. 35—39), Corsini (*F. A.* II. 325—329), Ruhnken (in Alberti's
Hesych. *Auctar.* to Vol. I. p. 1000), Barthélemy (*Mém. de l'Acad. des
Inscr.* XXXIX. pp. 172 sqq.), Wyttenbach (*Biblioth. Crit.* II. 3, pp. 41
sqq.), Spalding (*Abhandl. d. Berl. Academie*, 1804—1811, pp. 70—82),
Blomfield (in *Mus. Crit.* II. pp. 75 sqq.), and Clinton (*F. H.* II. p. 332),
who identify the Lenæa and Anthesteria; finally to Böckh (*Abhandl.
d. Berlin. Acad.* 1816, pp. 47—124), Buttmann (*ad Dem. Mid.* p. 119),
and Dr. Thirlwall (in the *Phil. Mus.* II. pp. 273 fol.), who adopt the
opinion stated in the text. Some arguments in favour of the second
hypothesis have been brought forward by a writer in the *Classical
Museum*, No. XI. pp. 70 sqq.

that there were four Bacchic feasts; In the sixth, seventh, eighth, and nine months respectively of the Attic year.

I. The "country Dionysia" (τὰ κατ' ἀγροὺς Διονύσια) were celebrated all over Attica, in the month Poseidon, which included the latter part of December and the beginning of January. This was the festival of the vintage, which is still in some places postponed to December.[1]

II. The festival of the wine-press (τὰ Λήναια) was held in Gamelion, which corresponded to the Ionian month Lenæon, and to part of January and February. It was, like the rural Dionysia, a vintage festival, but differed from them in being confined to a particular spot in the city of Athens, called the Lenæon, where the first wine-press (ληνός) was erected.

III. The "Anthesteria" (τὰ 'Ανθεστήρια, τὰ ἐν Λ.μναῖς) were held on the eleventh, twelfth, and thirteenth days of the month Anthesterion. This was not a vintage festival, like the former two. The new wine was drawn from the cask on the first day of the feast (Πιθοίγια), and tasted on the second day (Χόες): the third day was called Χύτροι, on account of the banqueting which went on then.[2] At the *Choës* each of the citizens had a separate cup, a custom which arose, according to the tradition, from the presence of Orestes at the feast, before he had been duly purified;[3] it has been thought, however, to refer to a difference of castes among the worshippers at the time of the adoption of the Dionysian rites in the city.[4] The "Anthesteria" are called by Thucydides the more ancient festival of Bacchus.[5]

IV. The "great Dionysia" (τὰ ἐν ἄστει, τὰ κατ' ἄστυ, τὰ ἀστικά) were celebrated between the eighth and eighteenth of Elaphebolion.[6] This festival is always to be understood when the Dionysia are mentioned without any qualifying epithet.

---

[1] *Philol. Mus.* II. p. 296.
[2] See the end of the *Acharnians*, and Aul. Gell. VIII. 24.
[3] See Müller's *Eumeniden.* § 50. [4] See above p. 60. [5] II. 15.
[6] Æschin. περὶ παραπρεσβ. p. 36: μετὰ τὰ Διονύσια ἐν ἄστει καὶ τὴν ἐν Διονύσου ἐκκλησίαν προγράψαι δύο ἐκκλησίας, τὴν μὲν τῇ ὀγδόῃ ἐπὶ δέκα, τὴν δὲ τῇ ἐνάτῃ ἐπὶ δέκα: and κατὰ Κτησ. p. 63: εὐθὺς μετὰ τὰ Διονύσια τὰ ἐν ἄστει, τῇ ὀγδόῃ καὶ ἐνάτῃ ἐπὶ δέκα.

At the first, second, and fourth of these festivals, it is known that theatrical exhibitions took place. The exhibitions at the country Dionysia were generally of old pieces;[1] indeed, there is no instance of a play being acted on those occasions for the first time, at least after the Greek Drama had arrived at perfection. At the Lenæa and the great Dionysia, both Tragedies and Comedies were performed;[2] at the latter the Tragedies at least were always new pieces; the instances in the *didascaliæ*, which have come down to us, of representations at the Lenæa are indeed always of new pieces,[3] but from the manner in which the exhibition of new Tragedies is mentioned in connexion with the city festival,[4] we must conclude that repetitions were allowed at the Lenæa as well as at the country Dionysia. The month Elaphebolion may have been selected for the representation of new Tragedies, because Athens was then full of the dependent allies, who came at that time to pay the tributes,[5] whereas

---

[1] Thus Demosthenes twits Æschines with his wretched performances in some of the characters of Sophocles and Euripides at the deme Cotyttus. *De Coronâ*, p. 288. Comp. Æschin. c. *Timarch.* p. 158. There appear to have been dramatic exhibitions at Phlya, in the time of Isæus: καὶ οὐ μόνον εἰς τὰ τοιαῦτα παρεκαλούμεθα, ἀλλὰ καὶ εἰς Διονύσια εἰς ἀγρὸν ἦγεν ἀεὶ ἡμᾶς, καὶ μετ' ἐκείνου τε ἐθεωροῦμεν καθήμενοι παρ' αὐτόν, &c.—Isæus, *de Ciron. Hæred.* Vol. I. p. 114, *Orator. Attic.* Oxford.

[2] Law in Demosth. *Mid.* p. 517. ἡ ἐπὶ Ληναίῳ πομπὴ καὶ οἱ τραγῳδοὶ καὶ οἱ κωμῳδοί, καὶ τοῖς ἐν ἄστει Διονυσίοις ἡ πομπὴ καὶ οἱ παῖδες καὶ ὁ κῶμος καὶ οἱ κωμῳδοί καὶ οἱ τραγῳδοί.

[3] See above, pp. 182, 206, 211, 213.

[4] See the decree, Demosthenes περὶ στεφάνου, p. 264, Bekker: ἀναγορεῦσαι τὸν στέφανον ἐν τῷ θεάτρῳ Διονυσίοις τραγῳδοῖς καινοῖς. *Lexicon Sangerm.* p. 309. Bekker: τραγῳδοῖσι; τῶν τραγῳδῶν οἱ μὲν ἦσαν παλαιοὶ οἱ παλαιὰ δράματα εἰσάγοντες· οἱ δὲ καινοί, οἱ καινὰ καὶ μηδέποτε εἰσαχθέντα. See Hemsterhuis on Lucian's *Timon.* Vol. I. p. 463, Lehmann.
This custom continued down to the times of Julius Cæsar, when a similar decree was passed in favour of Hyrcanus the high-priest and Ethnarch of the Jews. See Josephus, *Antiq. Jud.* XIV. 8.

[5] Οὐ γάρ με καὶ νῦν διαβαλεῖ Κλέων, ὅτι
Ξένων παρόντων τὴν πόλιν κακῶς λέγω.
Αὐτοὶ γὰρ ἐσμέν, οὑπὶ Ληναίῳ τ' ἀγών,
Κοὔπω ξένοι πάρεισιν· οὔτε γὰρ φόροι
Ἥκουσιν, οὔτ' ἐκ τῶν πόλεων οἱ ξύμμαχοι.

R

the Athenians alone were present at the Lenæa.   It does
not clearly appear that there were any theatrical exhibitions
at the Anthesteria; it is, however, at least probable that
the Tragedians read to a select audience at the Anthesteria
the Tragedies which they had composed for the festival in
the following month, or, perhaps, the contests took place
then, and the intervening month was employed in perfecting
the actors and chorus in their parts.[1]

In considering the *means* of performance, we must recall
to mind the different origins of the two constituent parts
of a Greek drama—the chorus and the dialogue.   Choruses
were, as we have seen,[2] originally composed of the whole
population.   When, however, in process of time, the fine
arts became more cultivated, the duties of this branch of
worship devolved upon a few, and ultimately upon one who
bore the whole expense, when paid dancers were employed.[3]
This person, who was called the *Choragus*, was considered as
the religious representative of the whole people,[4] and was
said to do the state's work for it (λειτουργεῖν[5]).   The

Ἀλλ' ἐσμὲν αὐτοὶ νῦν γε περιεπτισμένοι·
Τοὺς γὰρ μετοίκους ἄχυρα τῶν ἀστῶν λέγω.

Aristoph. *Acharn.* 477 : see the Scholiast.

Hence Æschines takes occasion to reproach Demosthenes with being
too vain to be content with the applause of his own fellow-citizens,
since he must needs have the crown decreed him proclaimed at the
great Dionysia, when all Greece was present: οὐδὲ ἐκκλησιαζόντων
Ἀθηναίων ἀλλὰ τραγῳδῶν ἀγωνιζομένων καινῶν, οὐδ' ἐναντίον τοῦ δήμου,
ἀλλ' ἐναντίον τῶν Ἑλλήνων ἵν' ἡμῖν συνειδῶσιν ἄνδρα τιμῶμεν.—
Contra Ctesiph. Vol. III. p. 469, *Orat. Att.* Oxford.

[1] *Philol. Mus.* II. pp. 292 foll.
[2] Above, p. 27.   [3] See Buttmann on Dem. *Mid.* p. 37.
[4] Hence his person and the ornaments which he procured for the
occasion were sacred.   See Demosth. *Mid.* p. 519, *et passim.*
[5] On this word, see Valckenaer on *Ammon.* II. 16; Ruhnken, *Epist.
Crit.* I. p. 54; Hesychius, s. v. p. 463, Vol. II.   It is formed from λέως,
λεῖτον, λήϊτον (see Herod. VII. 197: λήϊτον καλέουσι τὸ πρυτανήϊον οἱ
Ἀχαιοί).   The best notion of the meaning of a liturgy may be derived
from Æschyl. *Eumen.* 340 :

Σπευδόμενος δ' ἀφελεῖν τινα τάσδε μερίμνας
Θεῶν δ' ἀτέλειαν ἐμαῖς λείταις ἐπικραίνειν,

if the emendations which we have introduced, or adopted from Müller,
are to be received.

Choragia, the Gymnasiarchy, the feasting of the Tribes, and the Architheoria, belonged to the class of regularly recurring state burthens (ἐγκύκλιοι λειτουργίαι), to which all persons whose property exceeded three talents were liable. It was the choragus' business[1] to provide the chorus in all plays, whether Tragic or Comic, and also for the lyric choruses of men and boys, Pyrrhichists, Cyclian dancers, and others; he was selected by the managers of his tribe (ἐπιμεληταὶ φυλῆς) for the choragy which had come round to it. His first duty, after collecting his chorus, was to provide and pay a teacher (χοροδιδάσκαλος), who instructed them in the songs and dances which they had to perform, and it appears that the choragi drew lots for the first choice of teachers. The choragus had also to pay the musicians and singers who composed the chorus, and was allowed to press children, if their parents did not give them up of their own accord. He was obliged to lodge and maintain the chorus till the time of performance, and to supply the singers with such aliments as conduce to strengthen the voice. In the laws of Solon the age prescribed for the choragus was forty years; but this rule does not appear to have been long in force. The relative expense of the different choruses, in the time of Lysias, is given in a speech of that orator.[2] We learn from this that the tragic chorus cost nearly twice as much as the comic, though neither of the dramatic choruses was so expensive as the chorus of men, or the chorus of flute-players.[3]

The actors were the representatives not of the people, but of the poet; consequently the choragus had nothing to do with them.[4] If he had paid for them, the dramatic choruses would surely have exceeded in expensiveness all the others; besides, the actors were not allotted to the choragi, but to

[1] On the choragia, see Böckh's *Public Economy*, Vol. II. pp. 207 foll. Engl. Transl., or Stuart's *Athens*.

[2] Lysias, Ἀπολ. δωροδ. p. 698. Translated by Bentley (*Phalaris*, p. 360). [3] Demosth. *Mid.* p. 565.

[4] This is shown by Böckh, after Heraldus (*Public Economy*, III. ch. 22, p. 455, Engl. Tr.). Notwithstanding, however, what Böckh has said about the passage in Plutarch, *Phocion*, 19, it seems that the choragus had something to do with the costume of the actors, or at least of the supernumeraries who appeared on the stage or in the orchestra.

the poets; and were therefore paid either by these, or, as we rather think, by the state.

When a dramatist had made up his mind to bring out a play, he applied, if he intended to represent at the Lenæa, to the king-archon, and, if at the great Dionysia, to the chief archon[1] for a chorus, which was given to him[2] if his piece was deemed worthy of it.[3] Along with this chorus he received three actors by lot,[4] and these he taught independently of the choragus, who confined his attention to the chorus. The most important personage in the formation of every chorus was the actual leader, precentor, or fugleman, whose voice and movements the choreutæ followed in all the songs and evolutions of the orchestra.[5] This functionary was called κορυφαῖος, χοροῦ ἡγεμών, χοροποιός,[6] also χοροστάτης,[7] and corresponded no doubt to the ἐξάρχων of the old choruses. It is probable that there were two other fuglemen to take charge of the subordinate divisions of the chorus, when it was broken up into sections,[8] and perhaps the passage in the *Eumenides*, which led to the absurd supposition that the chorus in that play consisted of three only, refers to the coryphæus and his two immediate subalterns.[9] When the whole chorus was drawn up in three lines, these two subalterns stood immediately behind the coryphæus in the second and third ranks respectively, and were called παραστάτης and τριτοστάτης with reference to their leader.[10]

[1] See above, p. 129, note (1).

[2] There is some difference of opinion as to the person "who gave the chorus." Some think it was the choragus who was applied to (see Küster on Aristoph. *Eq.* 510; Ducker on Aristoph. *Ran.* 94); others that it was the archon: this opinion is in itself the most likely to be true, and appears to be confirmed by the words of Aristotle quoted above, p. 76, note (4).

[3] Hence χορὸν διδόναι signifies generally to approve or praise a poet. See Plato, *Resp.* II. p. 383 c, and Aristoph. *Ran.* in p. 181 supra.

[4] This practice subsisted to the last: see Plotinus, III. 2, p. 484, Creuzer.

[5] Aristot. *de Mundo*, c. 6: καθάπερ ἐν χορῷ κορυφαίου κατάρξαντος συνεπηχεῖ πᾶς ὁ χορός. [6] J. Pollux, IV. § 106.

[7] Himerius, p. 558; Theodor. Prodr. *Rhod.* IV. p. 170.

[8] Buttmann, *Index in Dem. Mid.* s. v. κορυφαῖος, p. 178.

[9] v. 135: ἔγειρ' ἔγειρε καὶ σὺ τήνδ' ἐγὼ δὲ σέ.

[10] Aristot. *Polit.* III. 4. 6: ἀνάγκη μὴ μίαν εἶναι τὴν τῶν πολιτῶν πάντων ἀρετήν, ὥσπερ οὐδὲ τῶν χορευτῶν κορυφαίου καὶ παραστάτου.

It is clear that the three actors, who were termed πρωτ-αγωνιστής, δευτεραγωνιστής, and τριταγωνιστής respectively,[1] were always regarded as a distinct troop or company, and that each retained his relative rank. Thus Ischander was regularly a δευτεραγωνιστής of the πρωταγωνιστής Neoptolemus,[2] and Æschines never rose to a higher rank than that of a τριτ-αγωνιστής.[3] The first actor was regarded as the representative and manager of his troop; he carried the inferior actors with him, received for himself the prize of victory, and, though he may have given a share of this and of the other honours of the performance to his second performer, it is probable that the tritagonist was obliged to be contented with his pay.[4] Before a troop could be regarded as generally entitled to perform, it must have gained a prize. Otherwise it was obliged to encounter some previous scrutiny, which was waived in the case of any actor who had succeeded in a competition.[5] It is reasonable also to conclude that the protagonist of a successful troop was free from the risk of drawing lots for his poet. At least we hear that the eminent actors Cleander and Myniscus attached themselves almost exclusively to Æschylus;[6] that Sophocles almost monopolized the services of Tlepolemus and Cleidemides;[7] and that the latter poet sometimes composed his plays with a special reference to the qualities of the actors who had to

---

Metaph. IV. 11, p. 1018 b. 28: οἷον παραστάτης τριτοστάτου πρότερον καὶ παρανήτη νήτης· ἔνθα μὲν γὰρ ὁ κορυφαῖος, ἔνθα δὲ ἡ μόνη ἀρχή. Jul. Pollux, IV. § 106, seems to call the παραστάτης δευτεροστάτης.

[1] Above, p. 59, note 2.

[2] Dem. *de Fals. Legat.* p. 344, 7.

[3] See the passage quoted at the end of this chapter.

[4] Dem. *de Coron.* p. 314; Lucian, *Navig.* ad fin., *Icaromen.* 29; Plutarch, *Præcept. Polit.* p. 816 ad fin.

[5] Hesychius and Suidas, s. v.: νεμήσεις ὑποκριτῶν· οἱ ποιηταὶ ἐλάμ-βανον τρεῖς ὑποκριτὰς κλήρῳ νεμηθέντας· ὧν ὁ νικήσας εἰς τοὐπιὸν ἀκρίτως (-τος Suid.) παρελαμβάνετο. Where Hemsterhuis conjectures παρελάμβανε and renders the passage (*ad Luciani Tim.* c. 51): "quorum poetarum qui superior discessit, in posterum sine discrimine suos sibi actores legebat." But the context shows that the relative refers to the actors and not to the poets.

[6] Hermann *in Aristot. Poet.* p. 193.

[7] Bernhardy, *Grundriss*, p. 642.

perform in them,[1] just as modern composers will sometimes
write an opera for a particular singer. The control which
the protagonist exercised over his conadjutors is shown in
many ways. If the inferior actors had finer voices than
their chief, they were sometimes obliged to do themselves
imperfect justice in order that he might shine the more.[2]
And though the protagonist had sometimes to appear in a
humble character by the side of his crowned and sceptred
hireling, the tritagonist,[3] the great actor Theodorus always
took care to sustain any part, even that which belonged to
the tritagonist, if this involved the first entry on the stage,
in order to make sure of the first impression on the
audience.[4] That the poet would undertake to teach a
protagonist how to act his play seems very improbable, and
the phrase διδάσκειν δρᾶμα must refer only to the general
superintendence, which the poet, in conjunction with the
choragus, exercised during the rehearsals of the play.

When the day appointed for the trial came on, all parties
united their efforts,[5] and endeavoured to gain the prize by a
combination of the best-taught actors with the most sump-
tuously dressed and most diligently exercised chorus.[6]

---

[1] *Vit. Sophocl.* p. x.: καὶ πρὸς τὰς φύσεις αὐτῶν (τῶν ὑποκριτῶν)
γράψαι τὰ δράματα.

[2] Cic. *div. in Cæcil.* 15, 48: "ut in actoribus Græcis fieri videmus,
sæpe illum qui est secundarum vel tertiarum partium, quum possit
aliquoties clarius dicere quam ipse primarum, multum submittere ut
ille princeps quam maxime excellat."

[3] Plut. *Præcept. Polit.* p. 816 F: ἄτοπον μὲν γάρ ἐστιν τὸν μὲν ἐν
τραγῳδίᾳ πρωταγωνιστὴν Θεόδωρον ἢ Πῶλον ὄντα μισθωτῷ τῷ τὰ τρία
(τρίτα?) λέγοντι πολλάκις ἕπεσθαι ἢ προσδιαλέγεσθαι ταπεινῶς ἂν ἐκείνος
ἔχῃ τὸ διάδημα καὶ τὸ σκῆπτρον.

[4] Aristot. *Polit.* IV. (VII.) 17, p. 1336: ἴσως γὰρ οὐ κακῶς ἔλεγε τὸ
τοιοῦτον Θεόδωρος ὁ τῆς τραγῳδίας ὑποκριτής· οὐθένι γὰρ πώποτε παρῆκεν
ἑαυτοῦ προεισάγειν οὐδὲ τῶν εὐτελῶν ὑποκριτῶν, ὡς οἰκειουμένων τῶν
θεατῶν ταῖς πρώταις ἀκοαῖς.

[5] The contending choragi were called ἀντιχόρηγοι (Demosth. *Mid.*
p. 595, Bekker), the rival dramatists ἀντιδιδάσκαλοι (Aristoph. *Vesp.*
1410), and their performers ἀντίτεχνοι (Alciphron, III. 48), a name
which is also given to Euripides as the rival of Æschylus in the
dramatic contest between them in the *Ranæ*, 815.

[6] For the harmony and equality of voice required in the chorus see
Aristotle, *Polit.* III. 113, § 21: οὐδὲ δὴ χοροδιδάσκαλος τὸν μείζον καὶ
κάλλιον τοῦ παντὸς χοροῦ φθεγγόμενον ἐάσει συγχορεύειν.

That the exertions of the choragus and the actors were often as influential with the judges as the beauty of the poem cannot be doubted,[1] when we have so many instances of the ill-success of the best dramatists. The judges were appointed by lot, and were generally,[2] but, as we have seen, not always,[3] five in number. The archon administered an oath to them; and, in the case of the cyclian chorus, partiality or injustice was punishable by fine.[4] The successful poet was crowned with ivy (with which his choragus and performers were also adorned),[5] and his name was proclaimed before the audience. The choragus who had exhibited the best musical or theatrical entertainment generally received a tripod as a reward or price. This he was at the expense of consecrating, and in some cases built the monument on which it was placed.[6] Thus the beautiful choragic monument of Lysicrates, which is still standing at Athens, was undoubtedly surmounted by a tripod; and the statue of Bacchus, in a sitting posture, which was on the top of the choragic monument of Thrasyllus, probably supported the tripod on its knees. Such, at least, seems to have been the

Fig. 1.

<hr />

[1] It is expressly stated by Aristotle, *Rhet.* III. 1, § 4. Cf. Terence, *Phormio, Prolog.* vv. 9, 10.

[2] See Maussac, *Diss. Crit.* p. 204; Hermann, de quinque judicibus poetarum, *Opusc.* VII. p. 88.

[3] Above, p. 129. [4] Æschin. κατὰ Κτησιφ. § 85.

[5] See the passages quoted by Blomfield (*Mus. Crit.* II. p. 88), and the lines of Simmias, in p. 128, supra.

[6] Lysias ubi supra, p. 202. Comp. Wordsworth's *Athens and Attica*, pp. 153, 4.

intention of the holes drilled in the lap of the figure. From the inscriptions on these monuments, the *didascaliæ* of Aristotle, Carystius Pergamenus, Dicæarchus, and Callimachus, were probably compiled.[1] The choragus in Comedy consecrated the equipments of his chorus,[2] and was expected to provide his choreutæ with a handsome entertainment, an expectation which, to judge from the complaints of the comic poets themselves, he did not always fulfil in a satisfactory manner.[3] It is probable that the tragic chorus also looked for a similar conclusion of their labours. The successful poet, as we see from Plato's *Banquet*, commemorated his victory with a feast. As, however, no prize-drama was permitted to be represented for a second time (with an exception in favour of the three great dramatists, which was not long in operation),[4] the poet's glory was very transient; so much so, that when Thucydides wished to predict the immortality of his work, he sought for an apt antithesis in the once-heard dramas of the contemporary poets.[5] The time allowed for the representation was portioned out by the clepsydra, and seems to have been dependent upon the number of pieces represented.[6] What this number was is not known. It is probable, however, that about three trilogies might have been represented on one day.[7]

---

[1] Böckh's *Corpus Inscript.* i. p. 350.

[2] Lysias ubi supra. Comp. Theophrastus, *Charact.* XXII.

[3] See Eupolis, ap. Jul. Poll. III. § 115, (p. 551 Meincke):

ἤδη χορηγὸν πώποτε
ῥυπαρώτερον τοῦδ' εἶδες;

Aristoph. *Acharn.* 1120:

ὅς γ' ἐμὲ τὸν τλήμονα Λήναια χορηγῶν ἀπέκλεισ'
ἄδειπνον.

Cf. Arist. *Av.* 88 and the Scholiast: τοῦτο εἰς διαβολὴν τοῦ χορηγοῦ ὅτι μικρὸν δέδωκεν ἱερεῖον.

[4] Above, p. 110; Aul. Gell. VII. 5; Plutarch, *Rhetorum Vitæ.*

[5] I. 22: κτῆμα δὲ ἐς ἀεὶ μᾶλλον ἢ ἀγώνισμα ἐς τὸ παραχρῆμα ἀκούειν ξύγκειται.

[6] Τοῦ δὲ μήκους ὅρος, πρὸς μὲν τοὺς ἀγῶνας καὶ τὴν αἴσθησιν, οὐ τῆς τέχνης ἐστίν. Εἰ γὰρ ἔδει ἑκατὸν τραγῳδίας ἀγωνίζεσθαι, πρὸς κλεψύδρας ἂν ἠγωνίζοντο, ὥσπερ ποτὲ καὶ ἄλλοτέ φασιν. Aristot. *Poet.* c. VII.

[7] "Yet that number seems to have been a fixed thing: so Aristotle speaks of it: εἴη δ' ἂν τοῦτο, εἰ τῶν μὲν ἀρχαίων ἐλάττους αἱ συστάσεις

The *place* of exhibition was, in the days of the perfect Greek drama, the great stone theatre erected within the Lenæon, or inclosure sacred to Bacchus. The building was commenced in the year B.C. 500, but not finished till about B.C. 381, when Lycurgus was manager of the treasury. In the earlier days of the drama the theatre was of wood, but an accident having occurred at the representation of some plays of Æschylus and Pratinas, the stone theatre was commenced in its stead.[1]

The student who wishes to entertain an adequate notion of the Greek Theatre must not forget that it was only an improvement upon the mode of representation adopted by Thespis, which it resembled in its general features. The two original elements were the θυμέλη, or altar of Bacchus, round which the cyclian chorus danced,[2] and the λογεῖον or stage from which the actor or exarchus spoke;[3] it was

---

εἶεν, πρός τε τὸ πλῆθος τῶν τραγῳδιῶν τῶν εἰς μίαν ἀκρόασιν τιθεμένων παρήκοιεν. *Poet.* § 40. See Tyrwhitt's note. If each tribe furnished but one choragus, and not, as some appear to have supposed, one for each different kind of contest, the number of tragic candidates could scarcely have exceeded three. For there seem never to have been less than three or four distinct kinds of choruses at the great Dionysian festivals: which, when portioned out amongst the ten choragi, could not by any chance allow of more than three or four choragi to the tragic competitors; which agrees very well with all that is elsewhere mentioned on this head, for we seldom meet with more than three candidates recorded, and probably this was in general the whole number of exhibitors. Aristophanes, indeed, had on one occasion *four* rival comedians to oppose (*Argum.* III. in Plut.); but this was, in all likelihood, at the *Lenæa*, when, perhaps, not a single tragedy had been offered for representation, and, consequently, a large proportion of choruses would be left disengaged for comic candidates.

"If the custom of contending with tetralogies was still retained, Aristotle, in the passage above, most probably intended by τῶν τραγῳδιῶν τῶν εἰς μίαν ἀκρόασιν τεθεμένων the exhibition of one such tetralogy. This supposition is in some measure supported by the fact, that there were three or four separate hearings in the day; since four tetralogies would occupy from twelve to sixteen hours: and if, as is natural, each competitor took up a whole hearing, this will confirm our former induction with regard to the number of candidates."
—*Former Editor.*

[1] Libanius's *Argument. Demosth. Olynth.* I. and Suidas, Πρατίνας.
[2] See Müller, *Anhang zum Buch*, Æsch. *Eumeniden*, p. 35.
[3] Above, p. 113, note 2

the representative of the wooden table from which the earliest actor addressed his chorus,[1] and was also called ὀκρίβας.   But in the great stone theatres, in which the perfect Greek dramas were represented, these two simple materials for the exhibition of a play were surrounded by a mass of buildings, and subordinated to other details of a very artificial and complicated description.   That part of the structure, which was set apart for the audience, and was more properly called the θέατρον, may be discussed without any doubt or difficulty; for not only are the authorities explicit in their accounts, but we have many remains which are sufficiently complete to serve as a safe basis for architectural restorations; and the theatre at Aspendus in Pamphylia, which has come down to us without a single defect of any consequence in the stone-work, enables us to restore, with very slight risk of error, all the details of the proscenium and orchestra which were presented to the eyes of a Greek audience.   With regard, however, to the minor arrangements of the stage, such as the painted scenes and the other machinery of exhibition, we are left in a great measure to an interpretation of the ancient descriptions; for the more fragile materials of which these parts of the theatre were constructed have yielded to the stress of time, and so left us without any tangible evidence to support the scattered statements of ancient writers.   It will be desirable, therefore, before we proceed to give a general description of a Greek theatre, based on an examination of all the authorities, and including all the particulars for which we have any evidence, either monumental or literary, to present to the student the actual form of the best preserved of the ancient theatres, and to make this ocular demonstration the basis and starting-point of the more theoretical reconstructions.

The theatre at Aspendus belongs unquestionably to the times of the Roman domination in Asia Minor.   An inscription over the eastern door informs us that two brothers, A. Curtius Crispinus Arruntianus and A. Curtius Auspicatus Titinnianus, in accordance with their father's will, had

---

[1] Above, p. 60; Pollux, IV. 123: ἐλεὸς δὲ ἦν τράπεζα ἀρχαία, ἐφ' ἣν ποὸ Θέσπιδος εἶς τις ἀναβὰς τοῖς χορευταῖς ἀπεκρίνετο.

contributed to the repairs or adornment of the theatre in
honour of their ancestral gods and the imperial house ;[1] and
it has been conjectured[2] from an inscription at Præneste,
which one of the two brothers had set up to P. Ælius Pius
Curtianus, that these persons lived in the time of M.
Antoninus. Be that as it may, other inscriptions, placed on
a pedestal in the interior, and over the door leading to the
seats, inform us that the architect was a Greek, Zeno, the
son of Theodorus.[3] And we may infer that the theatre at
Aspendus, though it belongs in its present state to the time
of the Roman Cæsars, was probably built on the foundations, and perhaps to a certain extent according to the
model of a previously existing Greek theatre. In its
general features it corresponds to the restorations which
have been made, with the aid of the fragments, of the *cavea*
of the theatre at Catana as seen from the stage,[4] and of the
stage of the theatre at Tauromenium, as seen from the
cavea.[5] It contains all that was required for the representation of a Greek play in the best period of the drama; and
though, as we shall see, Vitruvius makes certain distinctions
between the Greek and Roman theatres, it does not follow
that all theatres built in Greek cities during the Roman
period departed from the ancient model, which, after all,
was the point of departure for the Roman architects themselves.

It will be observed that the theatre at Aspendus, as represented in the accompanying ground-plan (Plate opposite
p. 252), elevation of the lower front (fig. 2), and view of the

---

[1] Böckh, *C. I.* III. p. 1163:

"Dis patriis et domui Augustorum
ex testamento A. Curtii Crispini A. Curtius Crispinus Arruntianus et A. Curtius Auspicatus Titinnianus fecerunt."

Θεοῖς πατρίοις καὶ δόμῳ Σεβαστῶν
ἐκ διαθήκης Α. Κουρτίου Κρεισπείνου Α. Κούρτιος Κρεισπεῖνος 'Αῤῥουν-
τιανὸς καὶ Α. Κούρτιος Αὐσπικᾶτος Τιτιννιανὸς ἐποίησαν.

[2] Henzen, *Annali dell' Instituto di Corr. Arch.* 1852, p. 165.
[3] Böckh, III. pp. 172, 1161.
[4] Serradifalco, *Antich. della Sicilia,* Vol. v. Taf. III.; Wieseler,
Theatergebäude, Taf. III. 12.
[5] Serradifalco, Vol. v. Tav. XXII.; Wieseler, Taf. III. 6.

interior (see Frontispiece),[1] is externally a plain building, with three complete rows of windows, besides sixteen other openings of the same kind. In the interior, the *theatrum*, or part allotted to the spectators, is a hemicycle composed of

Fig. 2.

[1] These illustrations are taken from Texier, *Description de l'Asie Mineure*, Paris, 1849, Vol. III. Pl. 232 sqq. The description is due to Schönborn (*Scene der Hellenen*, pp. 26—28, 83—94), who saw the theatre about the same time as Texier.

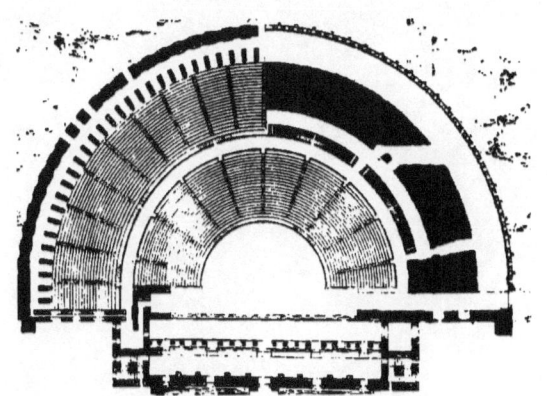

two *præcinctiones* or divisions separated by a *diazoma* or lobby, and there are nineteen tiers of seats in each of these separate halves of the theatre. The whole is crowned by a portico or gallery with fifty-eight arches. The great majority of the audience must have got to their places through the *parodi* of the orchestra, from which there are steps leading to the rows of seats, or through the gallery at the upper end, which had doors behind it. It was, however, possible to reach the upper seats by a door at the north end of the seats leading to the *diazoma*. The scene-front is connected with the spectators' seats by walls on either side rising to the full height of the theatre, and there can be no doubt that this part of the building was covered in by a roof. There are three stories in the scene. In the first story there are five doors. A cubical basement of stone appears in each angle of the scene, and these are continued by the sides of the doors, so that there are twenty of them in all. Those in the corners have each of them an unfluted column, reaching to the second story, and these columns are still found in the Greek theatre at Myra in Lycia. The other basements by the doors were probably the distances from the proscenium at which the moveable scenery hung from the balconies above. Besides the five doors the first story has nine windows, of which the four larger stand between the doors, and the other five over the doors. These windows, like those in the upper story, are merely ornamental, as they do not go through the wall. In the second story, immediately over the cubical basements of the *podium*, there is a corresponding number of little balconies, each consisting of a slab resting on two supports projecting at right angles from the wall. The faces of the latter are ornamented, like the frieze of a building, with the skulls of victims connected by garlands. On each of the balconies there is a low pedestal, and they are all connected by a narrow ledge, which may have served as the support of the planks laid across from one balcony to the other, when the exigencies of the performance required that the whole should be used as a continuous upper stage. It is to be remarked that Vitruvius, as we shall see, speaks of the *pluteum* in the singular; and there is no reason why these little balconies should not be regarded as really connected by the ledge to which reference has been made. There are no traces of balustrades. But the upper part of the scene served, no doubt, as a sufficient protection for the actors, when they had to appear on the second story. There are three little doors in the second story, leading to the gallery formed by the series of balconies; also eight windows corresponding to those of the lower story, the place of the ninth being occupied by one of the doors. The third story has no doors or windows, and instead of a practicable gallery, it has a series of ornamental pediments, triangular or semicircular, standing over the projections below, and similarly supported. That in the centre, which is much the largest, is adorned with a female figure, surrounded by ramifications of foliage. There are traces in the third story both of the supports of the roof, and of the orifices, in which stage machinery rested. The two wings of the theatre are divided by a party wall, in continuation of the proscenium, and the outer half of each, i.e., that which is bounded by the front wall of the theatre, constitutes in each case a staircase to the upper stories of the building.

We now proceed to show how exactly this well-preserved theatre corresponds in all essential features to the general descriptions which have come down to us.

A formal description of an ancient theatre necessarily rests on the geometrical rules of Vitruvius. The Roman theatre was arranged, he tells us,[1] according to the following scheme: describe a circle (*abcdefghiklm*) with a radius corresponding to the intended size of the orchestra, and in this inscribe four equilateral triangles, *aei*, *bfk*, *cgl*, *dhm*, the angles of which shall touch the circumference at equal distances. Let any side, *mh*, of an included triangle be taken to represent the direction of the *scena*, and parallel to this draw the line *ag* through the centre of the circle. The line *mh* produced to *o* on one side and to *n* on the other, so as to make it double the diameter, or four times the radius of the circle, gives the front of the scene; and the line *ag* marks the limits of the pulpitum on the side of the orchestra.

[1] Vitruvius, v. 6 7.

The five angles, which fall within the scene, indicate the positions of the five doors opening on the stage; and the other seven angles define the directions of the steps leading to the seats of the spectators.

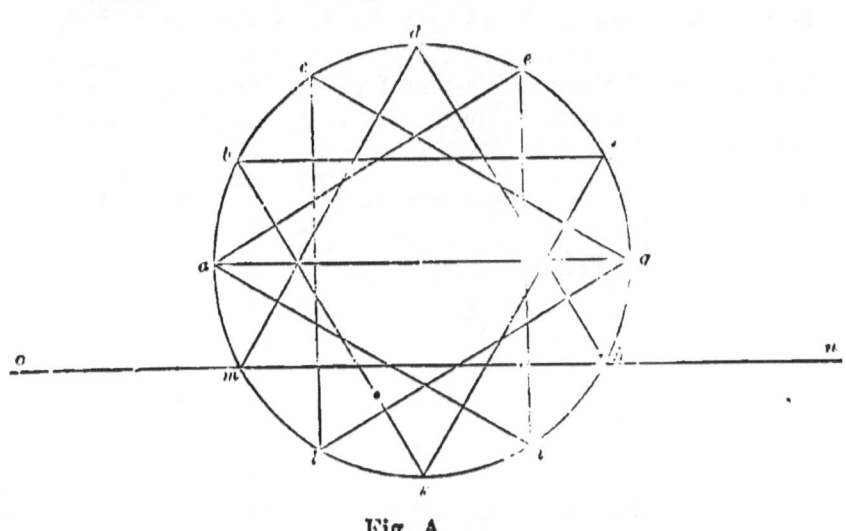

Fig. A.

From this it appears that the orchestra in a Roman theatre formed a semicircle of which the furthest point was one radius from the front of the stage, and one radius and a half from the front of the scene; the scene was four radii in length, and the stage half a radius in breadth.

The Greek theatre was arranged according to the follow ing scheme.[1] Taking a circle *agy*, inscribe in it three squares *nkfc*, *mieb*, *lgdy*, so that the angles touching the circumference may be equidistant from one another. As before, let any side, *nk*, of an included square be taken to represent the boundary of the proscenium on one side of the spectators; then a tangent *pr*, drawn parallel to this side, will represent the front of the scene. Let *o* be the centre of the circle, and *q* the centre of the orchestra thus defined; through *q* draw *ah* parallel to *nk*; and from *a* and

[1] Vitruvius, v. 8.

h, with the radius of the original circle, draw the arcs *st, uv,* cutting the produced line *nk* in the points *w* and *x.* The length of the scene shall be equal to the line *wx.*

From this it appears that the orchestra in a Greek theatre was more than a semicircle, the furthest point being one radius and five-sevenths from the front of the stage, and a whole diameter from the front of the scene. The breadth of the stage is therefore $\frac{4}{7}$ of the radius.

These proportions, though differing in special cases,

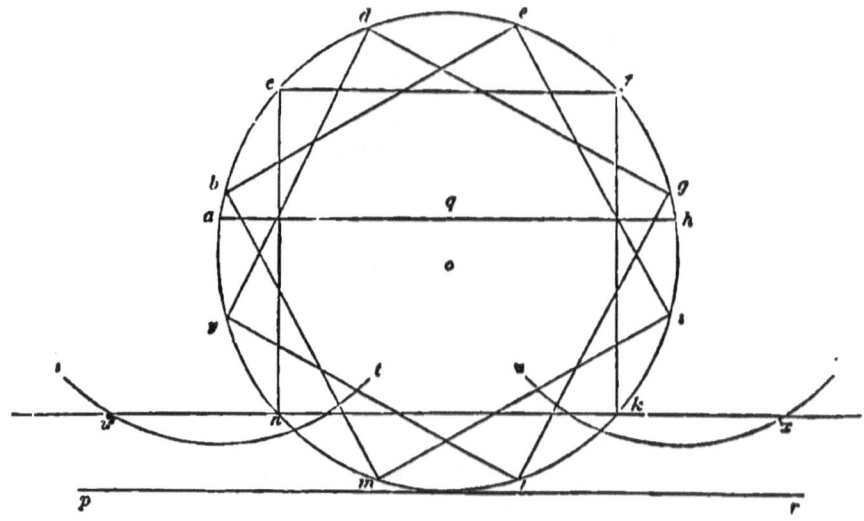

Fig. B.

correspond in the main to those of the existing theatres, and may be assumed as the basis of the following description, and of the plan (Plate opposite fig. B) by which it is illustrated.[1]

In building a theatre, the Greeks always availed them-

[1] This plan, with the exception of the stage, is derived from that which was published by Mr. T. L. Donaldson in the supplemental volume to Stuart's *Antiquities of Athens,* 1830, p. 33. It has also appeared in the *Library of Entertaining Knowledge,* "Pompeii," Vol. I. p. 232, where the woodcut preserves the engraver's error of OPKHΣTPA for ΘPΧHΣTPA, by way of identification; for the author of the plan is not mentioned.

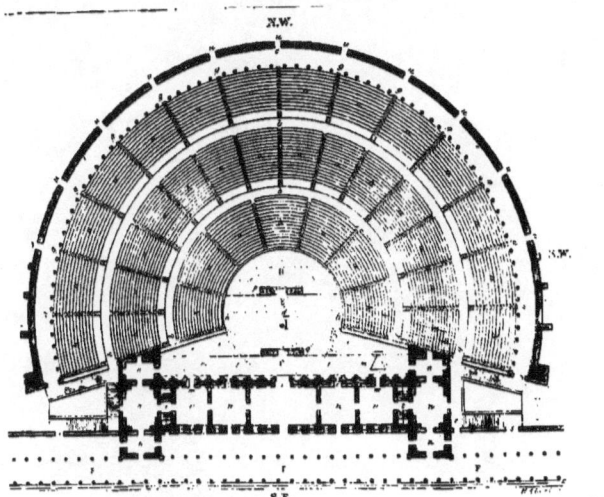

selves of the slope of a hill, which enabled them to give the
necessary elevation to the back rows of seats, without those
enormous substructions which we find in the Roman
theatres. If the hill-side was rocky, semicircles of steps,
rising tier above tier, were hewn out of the living material.
If the ground was soft, a semicircular excavation of certain
dimensions was made in the slope of the hill, and afterwards
lined with rows of stone benches. Even when the former
plan was practicable, the steps were frequently faced with
copings of marble. This was the case with the theatre of
Bacchus at Athens, which stood on the south-eastern side
of the rocky Acropolis. This semicircular pit, surrounded
by seats on all sides but one, and in part filled by them,
was called the κοῖλον or *cavea* (ᴀ ᴀ ᴀ), and was assigned
to the audience. At the top it was enclosed by a lofty
portico and balustraded terrace (*c*). Concentric with this
circular arc, and at the foot of the lowest range of seats,
was the boundary line of the orchestra, ὀρχήστρα, or
"dancing-place" (ʙ), which was given up to the chorus.
If we complete the circle of the orchestra (compare fig. B),
and draw a tangent to it at the point most removed from
the audience, this line will give the position of the scene,
σκηνή, or "covered building"[1] (ᴅ ᴅ), which presented to
the view of the spectators a lofty façade of hewn stone,
susceptible of such modifications as the different plays
rendered suitable. In front of this scene was a narrow
stage, called, therefore, the προσκήνιον (ᴄ), which was
indicated by the parallel side of a square,[2] inscribed in the
orchestral circle, but extended to the full length of the
scene on both sides (i.e. to ᴅ ᴅ). Another parallel at a
certain distance behind the scene gave the portico (ꜰ ꜰ),
which formed the lower front of the whole building.

We are not to suppose that a Greek theatre exhibited in

[1] "*Scene* properly means a tent or hut, and such was doubtless
erected of wood by the earliest beginners of dramatic performances, to
mark the dwelling of the principal person represented by the actor."
—Müller, *Hist. Lit. Gr.* I. p. 301.

[2] The angles of this square, and of two others inscribed in the
orchestral circle as indicated in the accompanying plan, point out the
divisions of the *cunei*, the commencements of the *iter* (at *h h*), and the
width of the *eccyclema* (at *i*).

its architecture any elaborate or superfluous ornamentation.
It was constructed for a special purpose—the adequate
representation of dramatic entertainments of a certain kind
before a very considerable multitude of spectators,—and if
it effected this purpose, the architect and his employers
were quite satisfied.   He was not inspired with the unprofitable ambition of an eminent and successful member
of the same profession in our own time, of whom it has
been said at once pointedly and truly, that being employed
to build a house of Parliament, which was to accommodate a
certain number of members and to admit of the speakers
being well heard, he contrived it so that the persons, for
whom it was intended, could not all be present, while those
who spoke were, except under very favourable circumstances,
inaudible to the reporters and their proper audiences ; and
who being also employed to build a picture gallery for a
nobleman, so contrived it that scarcely one of the paintings
could be seen in a good light; though in both cases he
erected stately buildings very pleasing to the eye when
seen from without.   Very different was the performance
of the architect who constructed a Greek theatre.   If the
seats of the spectators did not run on the side of a hill
they were surrounded by a wall without ornaments or
windows, and resembling the tower of a fortress rather
than a splendid edifice.   And the front of the theatre was
so devoid of all decorations that it would have suggested to
a modern spectator the idea of a barrack or a manufactory,
rather than of a place consecrated to the Muses.[1]

   The κοῖλον or *cavea* (A) was divided into two or more flights
of steps by the διαζώματα or *præcinctiones* (bbb), which were
broad belts, concentric with the upper terrace and with
the boundary line of the orchestra, and served both as
lobbies and landings.[2]   The steps of the κοῖλον were again
subdivided transversely into masses called κερκίδες, *cunei*, or

---

[1] Schönborn, *Scene der Hellenen*, p. 22, and compare the elevation of
the theatre at Aspendus (Fig. 2).

[2] The view which has been given of the theatre at Aspendus shows
the corresponding parts of these *præcinctiones*; but in the theatre at
Herculaneum there is no proper *diazoma* to separate the rows of seats,
which run above each other in distinct galleries.

"wedges" ($a a a$), by stairs κλίμακες ($g g g$), running from one διάζωμα to another, and converging to the centre of the orchestra. These stairs were called σελίδες, or gangways, from their resemblance, *mutatis mutandis*, to the passage across the σέλματα or ζυγά of a trireme,[1] for they were flanked on both sides by spectators seated before and below one another, just as the σελίς running fore and aft in a galley passed between the rowers, the highest of the three benches being always behind the middle tier, and this again being behind the lowest. As it seems that there were eleven tiers of seats between each διάζωμα in the theatre at Athens, the diazoma itself being counted as the twelfth row, we shall understand the allusion in Aristophanes (*Equites*, 546) :

αἴρεσθ' αὐτῷ πολυ τὸ ῥόθιον, παραπέμψατ' ἐφ' ἕνδεκα κώπαις
θόρυβον χρηστὸν ληναΐτην—

"raise for him a plash of applause in good measure, and waft him a noble Lenæan cheer with eleven oars," for each κερκίς would suggest the idea of eleven benches of rowers, and the applause demanded by the chorus would come like the plash of eleven oars striking the water[2] at once.

Different parts of the theatre received different names from the class of the spectators to whom they were appropriated. Thus, the lower seats, nearest to the orchestra, which were assigned to the members of the council (βουλή) and others who had a right to reserved seats (προεδρία), were called βουλευτικὸς τόπος, and the young men sat together in the ἐφηβικὸς τόπος.[3] The spectators entered either from

---

[1] There is no doubt that the primary sense is the nautical, as given by Hesychius: σελίδες· τὰ μεταξὺ διαφράγματα τῶν διαστημάτων τῆς νεώς. Eustathius also and Julius Pollux connect σελίς with σέλμα. Phrynichus says (*Anecd. Bekk.* 62, 27): σελὶς βιβλίου· λέγεται δὲ καὶ σελὶς θεάτρου; but the use of σελίς to denote the intercolumnar space of a manuscript, and hence to signify the page of a book in general, is the latest use of the three, and is probably derived from the resemblance between the lines of seats in the theatre divided by gangways, and the lines of writing separated by intercolumnar spaces of blank paper.

[2] See our paper "On the Structure of the Athenian Trireme," *Camb. Phil. Soc.* Vol. x. Part i.

[3] κ̓τ̓θ̓ ὁρᾷ τὸν ἄνδρα τῆς γυναικὸς ἐν βουλευτικῷ. Aristoph. *Aves*, 794.

the hill above by doorways in the upper portico, (uuu), or by staircases in the wings of the lower façade (ss).[1]

The orchestra (B) was a levelled space twelve feet lower than the front seats of the κοῖλον, by which it was bounded. Six feet above this was a boarded stage (E), which did not cover the whole area of the orchestra, but terminated where the line of view from the central *cunei* was intercepted by the boundary line. It ran, however, to the right and left of the spectators' benches (et, et), till it reached the sides of the scene. The main part of this platform, as well as an altar of Bacchus in the centre of the orchestral circle (d), was called the θυμέλη.[2] The segment of the orchestra not covered by this platform was termed the κονίστρα, *arena*, or "place of sand." In front of the elevated scene, and six feet higher than the platform in the orchestra (i. e. on the same level with the lowest range of seats) was the προσκήνιον,

---

On which the Scholiast remarks: οὗτος τόπος τοῦ θεάτρου, ὃ ἀνειμένος τοῖς βουλευταῖς, ὡς καὶ ὁ τοῖς ἐφήβοις Ἐφηβικός.

Allusion is made to these reserved seats, in the *Equites*, 669:

Κλέων.   Ἀπολῶ σε νὴ τὴν προεδρίαν τὴν ἐκ Πύλου.
Ἀλλαντοπώλης. Ἰδοὺ προεδρίαν· οἶον ὑψομαί σ' ἐγὼ
               Ἐκ τῆς προεδρίας ἔσχατον θεώμενον.

From whence and elsewhere we may infer, that eminent public services were rewarded by this highly-prized προεδρία. It is a great matter with the vain-glorious man in Theophrastus: τοῦ θεάτρου καθῆσθαι, ὅταν ᾖ θέα, πλησίον τῶν στρατηγῶν. *Char.* II.

[1] Kolster maintains (*Sophokleische Studien*, p. 25) that at Athens the only entrances for the spectators were those to the right and left of the orchestra, for that the stage lay to the south; and to the north, at the back of the theatre, where the rocks of the Acropolis rose, there could have been no entrance.

[2] The student should remark the successive extensions of meaning with which this word is used. At first it signified the *altar* of Bacchus, round which the cyclic chorus danced the dithyramb. Then it signified the *platform*, on which this altar stood, and which served for the limited evolutions of the chorus. Lastly it denoted any platform for musical or dramatic performances, so that in the later writers the *thymele* is identified with the *proscenium*, which extended as far as the centre of the orchestral circle in the Roman theatres (see *Jahrb. f. Phil. u. Pädag.* LI. 1, pp. 22—32). We believe that in the time of Euripides, at all events, the thymele signified the platform for the chorus, and not merely the altar which stood upon it: see Eurip. *Electr.* 712 sqq.

mentioned above (c), and called also the λογεῖον, or "speaking-stage." There was a double flight of steps (κλιμακτῆρες) from the *arena* (κονίστρα) to the platform in the orchestra (*p*), and another of a similar description from this orchestral platform to the προσκήνιον or real stage (*q*). There were also two other flights of steps leading to the orchestral platform from the chambers below the stage (*fh, fh*). These were called the χαρώνιοι κλίμακες, or "Charon's stairs," and were used for the entrance of spectres from the lower world, and for the ghostly apparitions of the departed. There was another entrance to the thymelic platform, which led to the outer portico of the theatre by passing under the seats of the spectators (*hbr*). This may have been used when there was no regular *parodos* of the chorus (of which more presently), and when the choreutæ made their exit in an unusual manner, as in the last scene of the *Eumenides*. The regular entrances of the chorus were by the πάροδοι (*tn, tn*), and along the δρόμος or *iter* (*te, te*).

The scene itself was a façade of masonry consisting regularly of two stories (whence it is called διστεγία)[1] divided by a *pluteum* or continuous balcony, either made throughout of a platform of stone, or consisting of a series of projections with balustrades, which might be made continuous by laying a flooring of planks from one to the other. If there was a third story, it was called the *episcenus;* but this was not essential. The scene was adorned by columns, and Vitruvius gives their regular dimensions; namely, those in the lower story, with their pedestals and capitals, were one-fourth of the diameter of the orchestra; over these the epistyles and entablatures were one-fifth of the columns below; in the second story we have the *pluteum* with its entablature or balcony half the height of the *pulpitum* or stage, which Vitruvius designates as "the lower balcony,"[2] and above the pluteum we have the columns of the second story less by one-fourth than those of the lower story, the epistylium with the entablature being as before one-fifth of the columns below. If there

---

[1] Vitruv. v. 7: "*pluteum* insuper cum unda et corona inferioris plutei limidia parte." See Schönborn, p. 82; and below, part II.
[2] Pollux, IV. § 13c.

is an *episcenos*, its *pluteum* is half the *pluteum* below it, and
its columns less by one-fourth than the columns of the
second story, the epistylium and entablature bearing the
same proportion, namely, one-fifth, to the corresponding
columns.   These measurements of course varied with the
tastes of different epochs, and the size of the theatre in the
particular case.   The distinctive and indispensable features
of the scene were the *pluteum* or balcony, and the five doors by
which the actors made their different entrances on the stage.
On these particulars it will be necessary to make some remarks.

It seems more than probable that in the most flourishing
period of the Greek drama, the mere front of the scene was
never used to indicate by itself the place of the action, but
that this was always depicted on a painted curtain or some
similar representation.   That these pictures were suspended
from the pluteum seems to be the most natural supposition,
and if the scene represented a mountain, as in the *Prometheus*, a watch-tower, as in the *Supplices*, or a palace, as in
the *Agamemnon*, on the top of which an actor had to appear,
it is obvious that the pluteum would furnish him with the
necessary footing; and there can be no doubt that there
were approaches to it by doors in the scene, as in fact we
see in the theatre at Aspendus.   It is also evident that the
pluteum must have furnished a basis for certain machines,
which were worked above the stage.   For example, the
θεολογεῖον,[1] which was apparently a platform surrounded
by clouds, and contrived for the introduction of divine
personages, was of course moved from the side of the
scene along the pluteum.   The whole of the action in the
Peace of Aristophanes from v. 178, when Trygæus is
raised on his monster beetle to the second story of the
scene, by means of a machine (v. 174), to v. 728, when
he returns to the stage,—having lost his beetle,—by
means of the staircase behind the scene, must have taken
place in sight of the spectators on the upper balcony of
the pluteum.

Every one of the five doors in the scene had its appropriate destination.   The centre door (*i*), or *valvæ regiæ* of

---

[1] Pollux, IV. § 130 : ἀπὸ δὲ θεολογείου ὄντος ὑπὲρ τὴν σκηνὴν ἐν ὕψει
ἐπιφαίνονται θεοί, ὡς ὁ Ζεὺς καὶ οἱ περὶ αὐτὸν ἐν Ψυχοστασίᾳ.

Vitruvius, was the regular entrance of the *protagonist*, and represented, according to the scenery hung before it, a palace, a cavern, or other abode of the chief actor for the time being; the door to the spectators' right of this (*k*) was the abode of the *deuteragonist*, and the door to the spectators' left (*l*) was appropriated to the *tritagonist*. Pollux says, perhaps referring to a particular play, the *Bacchæ* of Euripides, that the right door indicated the strangers' apartment (ξενών), and the left a prison (εἰρκτή). Vitruvius terms both of the doors near the centre *hospitalia*. In Comedy Pollux calls the adjacent space to the centre κλίσιον, "the out-buildings," with reference of course to some particular Comedy; and the scenery represented wide entrances called κλισιάδες θύραι, adapted for the ingress of cattle and wagons. Towards either side of the scene were two other doors which Vitruvius calls *itinera* and *aditus*, and these, with the περίακτοι, or triangular prisms moving on pivots, which were fixed beside or in them (*m, m*), indicated to the spectators whether the actors entering by these doors were to be supposed as coming from the city or the harbour in the immediate neighbourhood of the locality represented, or from a distance. The student will remember that these five entrances led to the stage, and belonged to the actors only. And the distinction between the two elements in the ancient drama, on which we have so often insisted, must be borne in mind here. For in addition to these five εἴσοδοι for the entrances of the actors, there were two πάροδοι, one on each side, for the chorus. These πάροδοι did not lead to the stage, but either opened at once from the wings into the orchestra, as we see in the theatre at Aspendus, or, to favour the idea that the side entrances of the chorus and actors corresponded, the chorus passed under the stage, and came out by doors (*t, t*), on a line with the *periacti* (*m, m*), which are often mentioned in connection with the *parodi*. If any one, who so entered the orchestra, had afterwards to mount the stage, as Agamemnon in the play of that name, he was obliged to ascend by a flight of steps.[1] Now we are told that while,

---

[1] It is clear that the doors on the stage were always used for the entrances and exits of the actors, except in the few cases in which they made their first appearance on horseback or in a chariot, like Ismeno

with regard to the side-doors on the stage, the *right* door
indicated that the actor so entering came from a distance, but
the *left* that he came from the city or the harbour, and that
if the *right*-hand περίακτος was turned, it indicated that the
road leading to the distant object was different, but that if
both περίακτοι were turned, with of course a change in the
decorations of the scene itself, the place of action was
different, or there was a total change of scene. But, on
the other hand, it is said that, with regard to the πάροδοι or
entrances of the chorus, that on the *right* was supposed to
lead from the market-place (if we read ἀγορῆθεν for ἀγρόθεν)
or from the harbour or from the city, but that those who came
on foot (i.e. not floating in the air like the chorus of Oceanides
in the *Prometheus*) from any other quarter entered by the
left πάροδος.[1] As it is quite impossible that the entrances
of the chorus and the actors should not have had the same

---

in the *Œdipus Coloneus*, and Agamemnon and Cassandra in the first
play of the *Orestea*. See Schönborn, *Scene der Hellenen*, pp. 17 sqq.;
Kolster, *Sophokleische Studien*, Pref. p. xii.

[1] This is Schönborn's explanation of the difficulty (*Scene der Hellenen*, pp. 72 sqq.). Kolster, on the contrary (*Sophokleische Studien*,
pp. 24 sqq.), understands the words of Pollux (IV. 126) of the actors,
and reads them as follows : τῶν μέντοι παρόδων ἡ μὲν δεξιὰ ἀγρόθεν ἢ
ἐκ λιμένος ἢ ἐκ πόλεως ἄγει, οἱ δ' ἀλλαχόθεν πέζοι ἀφικνούμενοι κατὰ
τὴν ἑτέραν εἰσίασιν· εἰσελθόντες δὲ [ἐφ' ἵππου ἢ ἐφ' ἁμαξῶν] εἰς τὴν
ὀρχήστραν ἐπὶ τὴν σκηνὴν διὰ κλιμάκων ἀναβαίνουσι. He supposes that,
as the theatre at Athens was on the south slope of the Acropolis, the
city and the harbour would lie on the right and the country of Attica
on the left: consequently, the spectators would imagine that the
right-hand door, by which they had entered the theatre along with
their foreign visitors, led to distant parts, and that the left-hand door,
by which the countrymen from Rhamnus, Marathon, &c., had made
their way to the seats, led to the home district. In order to reconcile
this view with the text of Pollux, Kolster understands ἀγρόθεν as
meaning *peregre*, though he owns that he cannot produce any example
of such a meaning. He supports his view by the statement that the
ξενών was on the right and the prison on the left of the centre door;
for he argues that the prisoner was originally also the slave, who was
connected with the labours of the field, and must therefore have his
ergastulum on the home-side, on which also, as Kolster thinks, the
κλίσιον, or stall for the cattle, was placed. It does not appear to us
that this interpretation is in accordance with the principles of sound
criticism.

reference to the quarters from which they were supposed to
enter, this apparent inconsistency must be explained by the
fact that the scene and the θέατρον, properly so called, were
regarded as distinct buildings, the orchestra belonging to
the latter; and while the entrances on the stage were
designated according to the right and left hands of the
actors, the entrances of the chorus, which faced the stage,
were denoted according to the right and left hands of the
spectators. Consequently, the spectators looked to their
right when they expected a new entrance, whether of actor
or chorus, from the neighbourhood of the scene of action,
but to their left when they expected to see an arrival from
a distance. Thus in the *Agamemnon*, the chorus enters by
the right parodos ; the herald, and the king with Cassandra
come from the left of the audience; and Ægisthus, on the
other hand, from the right side door.

It seems clear, from the original meaning of the word
σκηνή, i.e. covered building, that the scene had a roof of some
kind. There are but few traces of this in the existing
monuments. But as far as the evidence is available it may
be concluded that the roof was flat, and that it had a coping
with battlements.

The stage (λογείον, ὀκρίβας, ἴκρια, *pulpitum*) was a long
narrow platform extending to the whole length of the scene,
and elevated to a height of ten or twelve feet above the
orchestra.[1] Its breadth, according to Vitruvius, was one-
seventh of the diameter of the orchestra, but its length was
nearly double the orchestral diameter. It was therefore a
mere ledge at the foot of the scene, and was appropriately
called the *podium*, according to the original application of
that term. As we have already mentioned,[2] the stage was
a representative of the wooden table from which the
exarchon spoke to his chorus, and to the end it seems to
have a movable wooden structure, sometimes, however,
resting on supports of masonry. In several of the ancient
theatres, especially in that at Aspendus, we still see flights
of steps leading from the stage-doors to the level of the

---

[1] In the Roman theatre the stage was at most five feet higher than
the level of the orchestra.

[2] Above, p. 66.

orchestra; and this alone is sufficient to indicate the fact that the λογεῖον was taken down, whenever, as was frequently the case, the theatre was required for public meetings or other purposes not strictly theatrical.[1]

In its original meaning the word προσκήνιον was no doubt synonymous with λογεῖον, for it signified that which was before the scene, and it is used in this sense by Virgil and other writers.[2] It is equally clear, however, that the word was used improperly to denote the scene itself, or rather the face of the scene, which was turned towards the spectators,[3] and with a stricter reference to the form of the word, it denoted the curtain or hanging before the scene.[4]

There are two other derivatives from σκηνή, which have occasioned no little difficulty and misconception. These are παρασκήνιον and ὑποσκήνιον.

In the singular number, παρασκήνιον denotes what was sung by a member of the chorus instead of a fourth actor.[5] But in the plural, παρασκήνια undoubtedly means the lateral projections of the scene, by the sides of the δρόμος with the

---

[1] Schönborn, p. 29.

[2] Virg. *Georg.* II. 382: *veteres ineunt proscenia ludi.* Where Servius says: *proscenia...sunt pulpita ante scenam, in quibus ludicra exercentur.* Plut. *Moral.* p. 1096 B: χαλκοῦν Ἀλέξανδρον ἐν Πέλλῃ βουλόμενον ποιῆσαι τὸ προσκήνιον οὐκ εἴασεν ὁ τεχνίτης ὡς διαφθεροῦν τῶν ὑποκριτῶν τὴν φωνήν. Polybion (?) *apud Suid.* s. v.: ἡ τύχη παρελκομένη τὴν πρόφασιν κάθαπερ ἐπὶ προσκήνιον, παρεγύμνωσε τὰς ἀληθεῖς ἐπινοίας.

[3] The προσκήνιον and λογεῖον are mentioned separately in the inscriptions at Patara (Böckh, *C. I.* No. 4283, Vol. III. p. 151): καθιέρωσεν τό τε προσκήνιον, ὃ κατεσκεύασεν ἐκ θεμελίων ὁ πατὴρ αὐτῆς ... καὶ τὴν τοῦ λογείου κατασκευὴν καὶ πλάκωσιν ἃ ἐποίησεν αὐτή (where πλάκωσις means "pargetting" or "rough-casting"). And the grammarian published by Cramer (*Anecd. Paris.* I. p. 19) must have meant the scene itself when he attributed to Æschylus the προσκήνια καὶ διστεγίας. Hence Vitruvius (v. 6) speaks of the *proscenii pulpitum,* and Suetonius (*Nero,* cc. 12, 26) of the *proscenii fastigium* and *pars proscenii superior.*

[4] Suidas s. v.: τὸ πρὸ τῆς σκηνῆς παραπέτασμα. Duris, *ap. Athen.* XII. p. 536 A: ἐγράφετο ἐπὶ τοῦ προσκηνίου ἐπὶ τῆς οἰκουμένης ὀχούμενος. *Id.* XIII. p. 587, et Harpocrat. s. v. Νάννιον: προσκήνιον ἐκαλεῖτο ἡ Νάννιον, ὅτι πρόσωπόν τε ἀστεῖον εἶχε καὶ ἐχρῆτο χρυσίοις καὶ ἱματίοις πολυτέλεσι, ἐκδῦσα δὲ ἦν αἰσχροτάτη. Cf. Synesius, p. 128 C.

[5] Pollux, IV. § 109: ὁπότε μὲν ἀντὶ τετάρτου ὑποκριτοῦ δέοι τινὰ τῶν χορευτῶν εἰπεῖν ἐν ᾠδῇ, παρασκήνιον καλεῖται τὸ πρᾶγμα, ὡς ἐν Ἀγαμέμνονι Αἰσχύλου.

apartments which they contained, and the doors or openings
by which the chorus entered the orchestra. Modern
writers on the subject, with the exception of C. O. Müller
and Sommerbrodt,[1] have allowed themselves to be misled by
the confused descriptions of the grammarians, who suppose
that the *parascenia* were entrances to the stage rather
than to the orchestra, and buildings behind the scene
itself, and not those behind the lateral projections only.[2]
That the παρασκήνια were separate from the scene and
beside it, is clear from the form of the word,[3] from
the definition given by Theophrastus,[4] and from the
phraseology of Aristeides.[5] And that the doors from them
led to the orchestra and not to the stage, and were used by
the chorus and not by the actors, is proved by the passage
in Demosthenes, where he charges Meidias with barricading
and nailing up the παρασκήνια;[6] in order, as Ulpian
justly remarks, that the chorus might be obliged to go
round by the outer entrance, instead of passing at once
through the πάροδος to the orchestra.[7]

[1] Müller (*Handb. d. Arch.* § 289, 5) understands the παρασκήνια as
the *versuræ procurrentes;* and Sommerbrodt (*de Æsch. re Scen.* p. 23)
says distinctly: "Demosthenis ætate παρασκήνια ædificia fuisse in
utroque scenæ latere extructa, per quæ chorus posset in orchestram
intrare."

[2] See the passages quoted by Meineke, *Fragm. Com. Gr.* Vol. IV.
Epimetrum VII. pp. 722 sqq.; Schönborn, *Scene d. Hellenen,* pp. 98, 99.

[3] This may be inferred from the proper sense of the preposition παρά,
which we also find in the word πάροδος, and with a like signification.
For the actors were said εἰσιέναι, and their entrances were called
εἴσοδοι; but the entrance of the chorus was a πάροδος (Jul. Poll. IV.
108: καὶ ἡ μὲν εἴσοδος τοῦ χοροῦ πάροδος καλεῖται, ἡ δὲ κατὰ χρείαν
ἔξοδος, ὡς πάλιν εἰσιόντων μετάστασις· ἡ δὲ μετ' αὐτὴν εἴσοδος ἐπι-
πάροδος· ἡ δὲ τελεία ἔξοδος ἄφοδος), and Ulpian calls the παρασκήνια
—τὰς ἐπὶ τῆς σκηνῆς (not ἐπὶ τὴν σκηνὴν) εἰσόδους, which indicates
that they were not *on* the stage, but only *towards* the stage (Donalds.
Gr. Gr. 483).

[4] Harpocrat. s. v.: ἔοικε παρασκήνια καλεῖσθαι, ὡς ὁ Θεόφραστος ἐν
εἰκοστῷ νόμων ὑποσημαίνει, ὁ περὶ τὴν σκηνὴν ἀποδεδειγμένος τόπος ταῖς
ἐν τὸν ἀγῶνα παρασκευαῖς. ὁ δὲ Δίδυμος τὰς ἑκατέρωθεν τῆς ὀρχήστρας
εἰσόδους οὕτω φησὶ καλεῖσθαι.

[5] II. p. 397, 3: σὺ τὴν σκηνὴν θαυμάζων τὰ παρασκήνια ᾐτιάσω καὶ τοὺς
λόγους ἀφεὶς ἑτέρεις τὰ παραφθέγματα· οὕτω πόρρω τοῦ νόμου βαίνεις.

[6] *Mid.* p. 520, 18: τὰ παρασκήνια φράττων, προσηλῶν.

[7] *Schol. ad Dem.* Tom. IX. p. 547, Dind.: τουτέστιν ἀποφράττων τὰς

The ὑποσκήνιον has generally been understood as indicating the front of the stage itself, and the chambers below the stage.[1] This opinion has been derived from the words of Pollux.[2] But if this had been the case, the name would surely have been ὑπολογεῖον, not ὑποσκήνιον, and the analogy of ἐπισκήνιον, which denotes the third story of the scene, when there was one, would lead at once to the conclusion that ὑποσκήνιον must denote the lower story of the scene itself. Besides Pollux is here speaking of the scene, for he immediately afterwards mentions the three doors; and, as he says that the ὑποσκήνιον was adorned with columns and images, he could hardly have been speaking of the temporary substructure of the λογεῖον. In the monuments which represent the λογεῖον during the performance of a piece, it seems to be ornamented with candelabra and fillets of wool, or such other decorations as might be painted on the wood (see Fig. 3).[3] That the lower part of the scene itself was adorned with images and columns we know from Vitruvius and from the inscription at Patara.[4] It is also clear that

---

ἐπὶ τῆς σκηνῆς εἰσόδους, ἵνα ὁ χορὸς ἀναγκάζηται περιιέναι διὰ τῆς ἔξωθον εἰσόδου, καὶ οὕτω βραδύνοντος ἐκείνου συμβαίνῃ καταγελᾶσθαι τὸν Δημοσθένην. Kolster supposes that Meidias nailed up the *periacti*, and barricaded what remained of the space after the withdrawal of the height of the right-angled triangle in the circle, i.e. a quarter of the diameter (*Sophokleïsche Studien*, p. 37). This presumes, with Overbeck (*Pompeii*, pp. 119—130), that the *periacti* were the *versuræ* of Vitruvius. But he says distinctly, v. 7, after having mentioned the three middle doors: "secundum autem ea (i.e. hospitalia) (sunt) spatia ad ornatus comparata (quæ loca Græci περιάκτους vocant;" and then follows an explanation of the περίακτοι), "secundum ea loca versuræ sunt procurrentes, quæ efficiens una a foro, altera a peregre aditus in scenam." From which it is quite clear that the *versuræ* were the παρασκήνια and not the περίακτοι.

[1] This view is taken by Sommerbrodt, *de Æsch. re Scen.* p. 25; Geppert, *Altgr. Bühne*, p. 100; Strack, *Altgr. Theat.* p. 4; Streglitz, *Beitr. zur Gesch. d. Bank.* i. p. 178; Genelli, *Theat. z. Ath.* p. 47. The right view is taken by Schönborn, p. 101.

[2] IV. § 124: τὸ δὲ ὑποσκήνιον κίοσι καὶ ἀγαλματίοις κεκόσμητο πρὸς τὸ θέατρον τετραμμένον, ὑπὸ δὲ λογεῖον κειμένον.

[3] Wieseler, *Theatergeb.* Taf. III. 18, IX. 14.

[4] Vitruv. v. 6; Böckh, *C. I.* No. 4283: τὴν τῶν ἀνδριάντων καὶ ἀγαλμάτων ἀνάστασιν.

Pollux uses ὑπό with the accusative to signify " behind " rather than " under,"[1] so that ὑπὸ λογεῖον κείμενον means " lying behind the stage." And for the same reason we must understand a chamber in the lower story of the scene, where we read that Asopodorus heard the applause given to one of the flute-players, being himself in the ὑποσκήνιον,[2] or that Phocion used to walk behind the scene when the audience was assembling.[3]

Fig. 3.

As a general rule the action in a Greek drama was sup- posed to take place in the open air. In the earliest and

[1] IV. § 128: δείκνυσι τὰ ὑπὸ τὴν σκηνὴν ἐν ταῖς οἰκίαις ἀπόῤῥητα πραχθέντα. Cf. Schol. Æsch. Eumen. 47: τὰ ὑπὸ τὴν σκηνήν, " what is going on behind the scene."

[2] Athen. XIV. p. 531 F: διατρίβων αὐτὸς ἐν τῷ ὑποσκηνίῳ.

[3] Plutarch, V. Phoc. V.: τὸν Φωκίωνά φασι πληρουμένου τοῦ θεάτρου περιπατεῖν ὑπὸ σκηνήν.

rudest exhibitions the hero came forth from a wooden tent or hut (σκηνή) to the stage before it, which was originally and properly termed " the space before the tent " (προσκήνιον), and there narrated his adventures or conversed with the chorus. This condition was imposed on the dramatist in the most perfect state of his art, and all the dialogue, in the regular development of an ancient play, is supposed to be carried on in some place more or less public. It might, however, be necessary to display to the eyes of the spectators some action which belonged to the interior, or had just taken place behind the scene. For example, in the *Agamemnon* of Æschylus, the chorus on hearing the death-cry of the king proposes to rush in at once, and bring the matter to the proof while the sword is still wet (v. 1318). And immediately afterwards we see Clytæmnestra standing where she had slain her husband (v. 1346). This change of scene to the interior was not effected as it is with us, and as other changes of scene were effected by the Greeks,

namely, by substituting a fresh pictorial background, but by pushing forward the chamber itself to the stage. Had they merely removed the curtain and shown a recess, such as seems to have been constructed in the smaller Roman theatres,[1] the interior would have appeared dark in comparison with the daylight of the stage, and the spectators in the great theatres, especially those seated at the side, could not have seen what was going on. To obviate this difficulty, Æschylus[2] contrived a moveable chamber, corresponding to the size of the door in the scene which was opened to exhibit the interior, and this chamber,

Fig. 4.

[1] This recess is clearly indicated in the remains of the theatre at Pompeii, as given in the subjoined illustration (Fig. 4).
[2] Cramer, *Anecd. Paris.* I. p. 19: εἰ μὲν δὴ πάντα τις Αἰσχύλῳ βούλεται τὰ περὶ τὴν σκηνὴν εὑρήματα προσνέμειν, ἐκκυκλήματα καὶ περιάκτους καὶ μηχανάς, ἐξώστρας τε καὶ προσκήνια καὶ διστεγίας.

according as it was merely pushed out or rolled out on wheels, was called the ἐξώστρα or ἐκκύκλημα.[1] These words are often used as synonyms.[2] But as the word ἐξώστρα, in its military sense, denoted one of those boarding-bridges, which were thrust forth from the besiegers' tower to the battlements of the enemy,[3] and as the same word in later Greek denoted a balcony projecting from the upper story of a house,[4] it may be inferred that, as distinguished from the ἐκκύκλημα, the ἐξώστρα was generally used in those cases when the interior of an upper chamber was exhibited. It may, however, have been used also on the level of the stage, when a complete development of the interior was not required. With regard to the ἐκκύκλημα in particular, it is clear from the description in the grammarians, that it was a machine which moved on wheels,[5] and which might be rolled out through any one of the three principal doors on the stage, according to the interior which it was intended to display.[6] It is said to have been lofty, i.e. as high as the doorway through which it moved, and to have had a seat upon it, in order, of course, that the actor, who was thus produced, might ride safely during the evolution.[7] It was probably a semicircular stage, the diameter being equal to the breadth of the door through which it moved,

[1] The most complete essay on these contrivances is that by C. O. Müller, *Ersch u. Gruber's Encyclop.* s. v. *Ekkyklema, Kleine Schriften,* I. p. 524.

[2] Pollux, IV. § 122: τὴν δὲ ἐξώστραν ταὐτὸν τῷ ἐκκυκλήματι νομίζουσιν. Hesych.: ἐξώστρα ἐπὶ τῆς σκηνῆς τὸ ἐκκύκλημα. Schol. Aristoph. *Thesm.* 276: ἱερὸν ὠθεῖται. Schol. Ravenn. *ibid.*: ἐκκυκλεῖται ἐπὶ τὸ ἔξω τὸ Θεσμοφόριον.

[3] Vegetius, *de re Militari,* IV. 21.

[4] "᾽Εξώστρα et ᾽Εξώστης, Moeniorum Projectio." Vide Ducange and Schleusner.

[5] Schol. Aristoph. *Acharn.* 415: ἐκκύκλημα λέγεται μηχάνημα ξύλινον τρόχους ἔχον. Schol. Clem. Alex. p. 11, Potter: ἐκκύκλημα ἐκάλουν σκεῦός τι ὑπότροχον ἐκτὸς τῆς σκηνῆς, οὗ στρεφομένου ἐδόκει τὰ ἔσω τὰ ἔξω φανερὰ γίγνεσθαι.

[6] Pollux, IV. § 128: χρὴ τοῦτο νοεῖσθαι καθ' ἑκάστην θύραν, οἱονεὶ καθ' ἑκάστην οἰκίαν.

[7] Id. ibid.: καὶ τὸ μὲν ἐκκύκλημα ἐπὶ ξύλων ὑψηλὸν βαθρόν, ᾧ ἐπίκειται θρόνος· δείκνυσ δὲ -ὰ ὑπὸ σκηνὴν ἐν ταῖς οἰκίαις ἀπόρρητα πραχθέν-α.

i.e. about sixteen feet in the case of the middle door, and it moved on hinges like that door, to which for the moment it corresponded. From various allusions, in which the action of the ἐκκύκλημα or ἐξώστρα is metaphorically applied to the revelation or unveiling of those things which generally are or ought to be hidden behind a curtain,[1] it may be inferred that the παραπέτασμα or hanging scene was always removed before this evolution was performed. The change of scene to the interior was supposed to affect the chorus as well as the actors, as we see from the passage in the *Agamemnon*, to which reference has already been made.[2]

With regard to the exterior, the changes of scene were effected, as we have already mentioned, by the περίακτοι (scil. θύραι) or revolving doors in the form of a triangular prism, which stood before the side doors on the stage, and by turning round on a pivot (*m, m*), not only indicated the different regions supposed to lie in the neighbourhood of the scene, but were also made use of as machines for introducing suddenly sea and river-gods, and other incidental

---

[1] Cicero, *de Provinciis Consularibus*, 6, § 14: "quibuscum jam in exostra heluatur, antea post siparium solebat." Polyb. XI. 16, 18: τῆς τύχης ὥσπερ ἐπίτηδες ἐπὶ τὴν ἐξώστραν ἀναβιβαζούσης τὴν ὑμετέραν ἄγνοιαν. Clem. Alex. *Protrept.* p. 11, Potter: τὴν γοητείαν τὴν ἐγκεκρυμμένην αὐτοῖς οἷον ἐπὶ σκηνῆς τοῦ βίου τοῖς τῆς ἀληθείας ἐκκυκλήσω θεαταῖς. Id. *Strom.* VII. p. 886: οὐ γὰρ ἐκκυκλεῖν χρὴ τὸ μυστήριον. Cf. Æsch. *Agam.* 1145: ὁ χρησμὸς οὐκέτ' ἐκ καλυμμάτων ἔσται δεδορκώς, where we have the same thought, with a different allusion.

[2] The Scholiast on Aristophanes, *Nubes*, 218, where Socrates is introduced as sitting or walking (225: ἀεροβατῶ) on a κρεμάθρα, or shelf, says in explanation: παρεγκύκλημα· δεῖ γὰρ κρεμᾶσθαι τὸν Σωκράτην ἐπὶ κρεμάθρας καθημένον καὶ τοῦτον εἰσελθόντα καὶ θεασάμενον αὐτὸν οὕτω πυθέσθαι. κρεμάθρα δὲ λέγεται, διὰ τὸ οὕτως αὐτὴν ἀεὶ μετέωρον εἶναι κρεμαμένην. νῦν μέντοι τὰ περιττεύοντα [ὄψα] εἰς αὐτὴν εἰώθαμεν ἀποτίθεσθαι (i.e. such as cheeses and other stores). And on v. 132, on the words ἀλλ' οὐχὶ κόπτω τὴν θύραν, he remarks: τοῦτο δὲ παρεγκύκλημα· δεῖ γὰρ αὐτὸν ἐλθεῖν καὶ κόψαι τὴν θύραν τοῦ Σωκράτους. From these passages it is concluded, and reasonably, as we think, by Schönborn (*Scene der Hellenen*, p. 347), that the παρεγκύκλημα was a practicable projection at the side of the stage. In a secondary application it meant anything inserted in a play, as a mimic gesticulation between the speeches (Schol. *Nub.* 18, 22). or a person arbitrarily introduced (Heliodorus, *Æthiop.* p. 265, 5: ἕτερον ἐγίγνετο παρεγκύκλημα τοῦ δράματος ἡ Χαρίκλεια). But it cannot have denoted a simple ἐκκύκλημα, as Müller contends (*Kleine Schriften*, I. p. 538).

apparitions.[1]   As the right-hand δρόμος represented the
country road, and the left-hand that which led to the city,
the changes of scene effected by the revolutions of the
right-hand περίακτος were distant views painted in perspective; while those on the left were pictures of single
objects supposed to be close at hand. The scenery, which
was regularly placed before the main scene, was apparently
painted on canvas, the framework being of solid wood.   In
the *Œdipus Coloneus*, the grove of the Eumenides was thus
represented, and perhaps some evergreens were actually
placed on the stage. If the
scene had to be changed,
which was rarely the case
in Tragedy, the operation
was concealed by a cur-
tain (αὐλαία), which was
drawn up through a slit
between the stage and
the scene, and not, like
ours, allowed to drop from
above. This receptacle for
the curtain and the cy-

Fig. 5.

linder, round which it was rolled, is plainly seen in the

---

[1] The following are authorities respecting the περίακτοι.   Vitruv.
v. 7: "secundum ea spatia ad ornatus comparata (quæ loca Græci
περίακτους dicunt) ab eo, quod machinæ sunt in iis locis, *versatiles
trigonos* habentes."   Jul. Pollux, IV. 126: παρ' ἑκάτερα δὲ τῶν δύο
θυρῶν τῶν περὶ τὴν μέσην, ἄλλαι δύο εἶεν ἄν, μία ἑκατέρωθεν, πρὸς ἃς
αἱ περίακτοι συμπεπήγασιν· ἡ μὲν δεξιὰ τὰ ἔξω πόλεως δηλοῦσα, ἡ δ'
ἀριστερὰ τὰ ἐκ πόλεως· μάλιστα τὰ ἐκ λιμένος· καὶ θεούς τε θαλαττίους
ἐπάγει καὶ πάνθ' ὅσα ἐπαχθέστερα ὄντα ἡ μηχανὴ φέρειν ἀδυνατεῖ· εἰ δὲ
ἐπιστρέφοιεν αἱ περίακτοι ἡ δεξιὰ μὲν ἀμείβει τόπον· ἀμφότεραι δὲ χώραν
ὑπαλλάττουσι. ἐπὶ τὴν σκηνὴν διὰ κλιμάκων ἀναβαίνουσι.   From the use
of the *periacti* as *side*-scenes, it seems most probable that they were
not let into the wall (for it is πρὸς ἅς, not πρὸς αἷς or ἐν αἷς), and from
the analogy between the employments of the περίακτος and the μηχανή,
which was placed in the left πάροδος, it may be inferred that these
triangular prisms stood as represented in the plan, between the side-
entrances to the stage and the orchestra.   Kolster suggests (*Sophokleische Studien*, Pref. p. viii) that the axis of the cylinder was fixed in
the lintel and threshold of the side-door, so that the apex of the
triangle stood within the wall.   This would have prevented the
audience from seeing the whole of the side-scene.

T

small theatre at Pompeii, as represented in the annexed illustration. This difference between the ancient practice and our own must be remembered by the student, who would understand such passages as the following (Ovid, *Metamorphoses*, III. 111—114):

> "Sic, ubi tolluntur festis aulæa theatris,
> Surgere signa solent, primumque ostendere vultum,
> Cetera paullatim, placidoque educta tenore
> Tota patent, imoque pedes in margine ponunt."

Here the reference is to the drawing up of the curtain at the end of an act, when the figures which were embroidered on it (Virgil, *Georg.* III. 25), were gradually displayed to the audience, the head rising first, just as the armed men rose from the ground when Cadmus sowed the serpent's teeth. Conversely, Horace says (2 *Epist.* I. 189):

> "Quattuor aut plures aulæa premuntur in horas,
> Dum fugiunt equitum turmæ peditumque catervæ:"

that is, the curtain was down, as the play was going on for four hours or more, while the spectacle, as in one of Mr. Charles Kean's revivals, went on as an episode in the play.

Scene-painting (σκηνογραφία, σκιαγραφία) in the days of Agatharcus became a distinct and highly-cultivated branch of art. When the scene exhibited its most usual representation,—that of a house,—the altar of Apollo Agyicus was invariably placed on the stage near the main entrance. There are many allusions to this both in Tragedy and Comedy.[1]

The theatre at Athens was well supplied with machinery calculated to produce startling effects. Besides the *periacti*, which were used occasionally to introduce a sea-deity on his fish-tailed steed, or a river-god with his urn, there was the θεολογεῖον, a platform surrounded by clouds, and suspended from the top of the central scene, whence the deities conversed with the actors or chorus. Sometimes they were introduced near the left *parodos*, close to the *periactos*, by means of a crane turning on a pivot, which

---

[1] See *e.g.* Æschyl. *Agam.* 1051, 6.

was called the μηχανή.[1] The γέρανος was a contrivance for snatching up an actor from the stage and raising him to the θεολογεῖον; and by the αἰῶραι, an arrangement of ropes and pullies, Bellerophon or Trygæus could fly across the stage.

Then there was the βροντεῖον, a contrivance for imitating the sound of thunder. It seems to have consisted of bladders full of pebbles, which were rolled over sheets of copper laid out in the ὑποσκήνια. Again, the appearance of lightning was produced by means of a *periactos* or triangular prism of mirrors placed in the θεολογεῖον. This was called the κεραυνοσκοπεῖον. It may be inferred too that either the orchestra or the stage was occasionally supposed to represent water. Thus in the *Frogs*, Bacchus rows either on or in front of the λογεῖον to the melodious croakings of the chorus which swims around his boat.

From the enormous size of the theatre at Athens, which is said to have contained 30,000 spectators,[2] it became necessary to employ the principles of acoustics to a considerable extent. All round the κοῖλον were placed bell-shaped vessels of bronze, called ἠχεῖα, placed in an inverted position, and resting on pedestals, which received and distributed the vibrations of sound.

The influence of the situation and peculiar construction of the Greek theatre upon the imagination of the dramatist has been fully shown by an accomplished scholar who visited Athens some years since.[3]

Our conceptions of the *manner* of representation also depend upon the twofold division of the Attic drama. We must recollect the military origin of the chorus,[4] its employment in the worship of Bacchus,[5] the successive adoption of the lyre and the flute as accompaniments,[6] the nature of

---

[1] Jul. Poll. IV. 128: ἡ μηχανὴ δὲ θεοὺς δείκνυσι καὶ "Ηρωας τοὺς ἐν ἀέρι, Βελλεροφόντας, ἢ Περσεῖς· καὶ κεῖται κατὰ τὴν ἀριστέραν πάροδον ὑπὲρ τὴν σκηνὴν τὸ ὕψος. Hence the phrase *Deus ex Machina*.

[2] Plato, *Sympos.* 175 E. See, however, Wordsworth's *Athens and Attica*, pp. 92 sqq.

[3] See Wordsworth's *Athens and Attica*, pp. 94 foll.

[4] Above, pp. 27 foll.   [5] Above, p. 37.

[4] Above, p. 36.

T 2

the cyclic chorus,[1] and the improvements of Stesichorus,[2] in order to understand fully the peculiar and otherwise unaccountable evolutions of the dramatic chorus. We must remember also that the actor was originally a rhapsode who succeeded the Exarchus of the Dithyramb,[3] that he was the representative of the poet,[4] who was the original Exarchus, that he acted in a huge theatre at a great distance from the spectators, and that he often had to sustain more than one part in the same piece; all this we must recollect, if we would not confound the functions of Polus with those of Macready.

The first remark with regard to the chorus will explain to us the order and manner in which the choreutæ made their entry. The chorus was supposed to be a lochus of soldiers in battle array.[5] In the dithyrambic or cyclic chorus of fifty, this military arrangement was not practicable; but when the original choral elements had become more deeply inrooted in the worship of Bacchus, and the three principal Apollonian dances were transferred to the worship of that god,[6] the dramatic choruses became like them quadrangular, and were arranged in military rank and file.[7] The number of the tragic chorus for the whole Trilogy appears to have been fifty; the comic chorus consisted of twenty-four. The chorus of the Tetralogy was broken into four sub-choruses, two of fifteen, one of twelve, and a satyric chorus of eight, as appears from the distribution in the remaining Trilogy.[8] When the chorus of fifteen entered in ranks three abreast, it was said to be divided κατὰ ζυγά: when it was distributed into three files of five, it was said to be κατὰ στοίχους. The same military origin explains the fact that the anapæstic metre was generally, if not always, adopted for the opening choral song; for this metre was also used in the Greek marching songs.[9] The muster of the chorus round the Thymele, shows that the chorus was Bacchic as well as military; the mixture of lyric and flute music points

---

[1] Above, p. 38.
[2] Above, p. 40, note (1).
[3] Above, p. 66, and elsewhere.
[4] Above, p. 65.
[5] Müller, *Eumeniden*, § 12.
[6] Above, p 28.
[7] Müller, *Eumeniden*, § 5.
[8] Id. *ibid.* § 1 foll.
[9] Id. *ibid.* § 16.

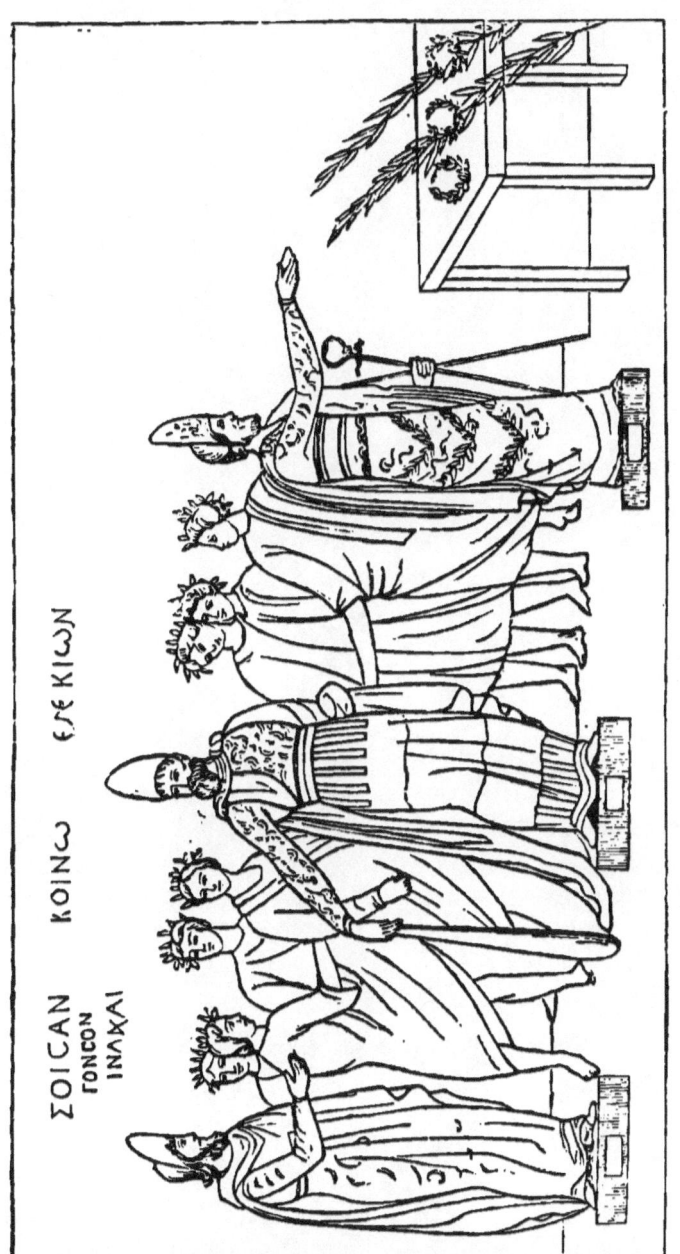

THE CYRENAIC PICTURE.

to the same union of two worships;[1] and in the strophic and antistrophic form of most of the choral odes, we discern the traces of the choral improvements of Stesichorus.

Again, with regard to the actor, when we remember that he was but the successor of the Exarchus, who in the improvements of Thespis spoke a πρόλογος before the chorus came on the stage, and held a ῥῆσις, or dialogue, with them after they had sung their choral song,[2] we shall see why there was always a soliloquy or a dialogue, in the first pieces of the more perfect Tragedies, before the chorus came on.[3] The actor's connexion with the rhapsode is also a reason for the narrative character of the speeches and dialogues, and for the general absence of the abrupt and vehement conversations which are so common in our own plays.

But, independently of any peculiarities of a literary nature, the great size of the theatre,[4] and the religious character of the festival, gave occasion for some very remarkable differences between the outward appearance and costume of the ancient actors, and those who sustain parts in the performances of the modern drama. These differences consisted mainly in the two following particulars : (a) the tragic actor was always raised on soles of enormous thickness, which gave additional height to his person, while his body and limbs were also stuffed and padded to a corresponding size, and his head was surmounted by a colossal mask, suited to the character which he bore; and (b) every performer, whatever his character might be, was uniformly arrayed in the gay and gaudy attire of the Dionysian festival. We will consider these peculiarities separately, because they spring from distinct causes; for the thick soles and the mask were due to the size of the theatre, and the festal dress to the religious nature of the solemnities. With regard to both of these peculiarities we have abundant authorities in ancient works of art. Masks of every de-

---

[1] Müller, *Eumeniden*, § 18.   [2] See above. p. 66, and p. 113.
[3] The *Supplices* and *Persæ* of Æschylus, which are the only two plays that begin with an anapæstic march, were not the first plays of the Trilogies to which they belonged.
[4] See Dr. Wordsworth's *Athens and Attica*, p. 92.

scription are repeated in pictures and sculptures, and figures arrayed in the theatrical dress are to be met with everywhere. We have also representations of complete scenes from the different kinds of dramas, especially, however, from Comedies ; and, by great good fortune, we have rescued from the ruins of time, in all the brightness of the original colouring, not only a series of twenty-two pairs of figures representing performers in Tragedies, followed by a similar pair from a Satyric drama, but also the three actors accompanied by the chorus. The former are given in a number of hexagonal Mosaics, which were found at Lorium in Etruria, where Antoninus Pius was brought up, and where he died, and which are now let into the modern Mosaic pavement of an octagonal room of the Pio-Clementine Museum at Rome called the Saloon of the Muses.[1] The latter representation was discovered in a grotto, on one side of the Necropolis of Cyrene, the four walls of which are covered with well-preserved paintings representing the dramatic and other entertainments, which the deceased had exhibited in his lifetime, or which had been given on occasion of his funeral.[2] By the aid of these ancient authorities we can describe the attire of a Greek actor as accurately as if we were detailing the costume of a performer on the modern stage.

We shall first discuss (a) those peculiarities of the theatrical costume, which were designed to increase the stature of the actor, and to give greater distinctness to his features when seen from a distance, and then (b) illustrate the festal attire in which he walked the stage.

(a) The thick-soled boot, worn by hunters and others, who had to walk over rough and tangled ground, was

---

[1] This mosaic is fully described by Millin, *Description d'une Mosaïque Antique du Musée Pio-Clémentine à Rome représentant des Scènes de Tragédies*, Paris, 1829. See also Müller, *Gött. Gel. Anz.* 1831, pp. 1234 sqq. ; Wieseler, *Theatergeb.* pp. 48 sqq. Some specimens of the figures are given in the accompanying plate, p. 281.

[2] See J. R. Pacho, *Relation d'un Voyage dans la Marmorique, la Cyrénaïque,* &c. Paris, 1827, Pl. XLIX. and L. cf. Müller, *Handbuch d. Arch.* § 425, 2; Creuzer, *Deutsch. Schrift. zur Archäol.* Vol. III. 499 ; Wieseler, *Theatergeb.* pp. 99 sqq. The figures are given in plate, p. 278.

I (See p. 292).

II (See p. 292).

III (See p. 292).

IV (See p. 294).

V (See p. 293).

VI (See p. 295).

FIGURES FROM THE PIO-CLEMENTINE MOSAIC.

called the *cothurnus* (κόθορνος), and does not appear to have been different from the ἀρβύλη or *pero*. At least Agamemnon, who enters the orchestra in a mule-car, has his ἀρβύλαι taken off before he mounts the stage by the πορφυρόστρωτος πόρος, laid for him by Clytæmnestra,[1] and Hippolytus is said to have stept into his chariot all booted as he was (αὐταῖσιν ἀρβύλαισιν).[2] The adoption of this form of boot was not primarily occasioned by the necessity of giving the actor a more elevated stature. The incident mentioned by Herodotus[3] shows that the cothurnus was an effeminate chaussure, and it is clear that it formed a part of the costume of the worshippers of Bacchus, who imitated the half-womanly character of their divinity. The upper leather was highly ornamented[4] and laced down the front, but the thickness of the sole seems to have required that for ordinary purposes the buskin should not fit closely to the foot,[5] so that the name κόθορνος was adopted as a designation of Theramenes, who was regarded as a turn-coat or trimmer in politics.[6]

Fig. 6.

But although the ordinary κόθορνος or ἀρβύλη had a very thick sole against which stones and other obstacles struck with a ringing sound as the passenger stumped along the road,[7] it bore no comparison in this respect to the tragic

[1] Æsch. *Agam.* 917:
> ἀλλ' εἰ δοκεῖ σοι ταῦθ' ὑπαί τις ἀρβύλας
> λύοι τάχος πρόδουλον ἔμβασιν ποδός.

[2] Eurip. *Hippol.* 1188:
> μάρπτει δὲ χερσὶν ἡνίας ἀπ' ἄντυγος,
> αὐταῖσιν ἀρβύλαισιν ἁρμόσας πόδας.

[3] I. 125. Hence Aristoph. *Ran.* 47: τί κόθορνος καὶ ῥόπαλον ξυνηλθέτην;

[4] See Fig. 6; and compare Fig. 15, p. 291.

[5] See the story of Alcmæon, who made his cothurni, like the jackboots of Hudibras, serve as an additional pocket for his gold. Herod. VI. 125.

[6] Xen. *Hell.* II. 3, § 31: ὅθεν δήπου καὶ κόθορνος ἐπικαλεῖται· καὶ γὰρ ὁ κόθορνος ἁρμόττειν μὲν τοῖς ποσὶν ἀμφοτέροις δοκεῖ, ἀποβλέπει δ' ἐπ' ἀμφότερον.

[7] Theocrit. VII. 25, 26:
> ὡς τεῦ ποσὶ νεισσομένοιο
> πᾶσα λίθος πταίοισα ποτ' ἀρβυλίδεσσιν ἀείδει.

buskins. Their enormous and extravagant height may be
seen in the accompanying figure of the Tragic Muse, and
is singularly shown in the two monuments which are our
principal authorities for the costume of the Greek drama.
In the Pio-Clementine Mosaic, as Millin well remarks,[1] the

figures seem at first sight to have no
feet, but resemble the marionettes
which are worked from below. On
a closer examination, however, we
observe that the feet of the actors
are covered by their long robes, and
that we only see the high soles on
which they are elevated. For in one
of the figures (No. IV, see the accompanying plate, p. 281), where
a woman in a state of great agita-
tion is rushing in to announce some
dreadful intelligence, one of her feet
is lifted from the stage, so that we
see the bottom of the sole : and in
two others (also given in the accompanying plate), the toe of.the buskin
projects beyond the bottom of the
robe. In the Cyrenaic picture the
three figures of the actors are raised
on little pedestals, if Pacho's copy
is correctly drawn, and Müller has

Fig. 7.

supposed[2] that the picture represents statues of actors
and not the actors themselves, a supposition which is set
aside by the whole composition. There can be little doubt
that these basements merely depict the soles of their
buskins, the square space in the middle being perhaps
intended to indicate the divisions between the two soles in
each case.[3] In a painting on a wall at Pompeii[4] the

---

[1] P. 16: "On diroit qu'ils n'ont pas de pieds; ils ont l'air de ces
marionettes que l'on promène à travers les fentes des planches d'un
théâtre, et dont les fils qui les font mouvoir sont dessous, au lieu
d'être dessus."

[2] *Handb. d. Arch.* § 425, 2.

[3] This is Wieseler's opinion, *Theatergeb.* p. 100.

[4] Gell, *Pompeii*, Vol. II. Pl. LXXV.

peculiar shape of the soles conveyed to Sir W. Gell the idea that the figures were Scythian Hippopodæ! but a more exact copy, which has subsequently been made by Wieseler,[1] shows that the figures merely wear a sort of sabot or wooden shoe. That these soles of the cothurnus, which seem to have been called ἐμβάται or ἔμβατα,[2] were made of wood, probably of some very light wood, if not occasionally of cork, is distinctly stated by the Scholiast on Lucian;[3] and the Pio-Clementine Mosaic shows us that they were generally painted so as to harmonize with the robe of the actor. On account both of its connection with the Dionysiac attire, and of its special use in giving height and dignity to the tragic actor, the *cothurnus* was an emblem of Tragedy, as the *soccus* was of Comedy;[4] the Tragic Muse is equipped with this clumsy buskin;[5] and the word itself is used by the Latin poet as a synonym for *tragœdia.*[6]

In addition to the cothurnus, and the padded figure,[7] the tragedian was increased to a colossal stature by his mask (προσωπεῖον), which not only represented a set of features much larger than those of any ordinary man, but was raised to a great height above the brow by a sort of elevated frontlet or foretop (ὄγκος, *superficies*),[8] rising in the shape of the letter Λ,[9] which formed the frame of a tire or periwig

---

[1] Wieseler, *Theatergeb.* p. 51, and Taf. Δ, No. 23.

[2] See Valckenaer, *Ammon.* p. 49.

[3] *Ad Jov. Trag.* p. 13: ἐμβάτας μὲν τὰ ξύλα ἃ βάλλουσιν ὑπὸ τοὺς πόδας οἱ τραγῳδοί, ἵνα φανῶσι μακρότεροι.

[4] Horace, *Ars Poetica,* 80:

"Hunc *socci* cepere pedem grandesque *cothurni.*"

[5] Wieseler, *Theatergeb.* p. 52, Taf. IX. 2. See Fig. 7, p. 284.

[6] Horace, 2 *Carm.* I. 13:

" grande munus
Cecropio repetes *cothurno.*"

Virgil, *Eclog.* VIII. 10:

" Sola Sophocleo tua carmina digna *cothurno.*"

[7] Lucian, *Jupiter Tragœdus,* II. 44; *de Gymnas.* 23; *de Saltat.* II. 27.

[8] The word ὄγκος (cf. ἄγχι, ἄγκος, ἄγκυρα, &c.) refers to the curve at the top; the Latin *superficies,* which also means a roof, indicates that it was over the face.

[9] Pollux, IV. § 133: λαβδοειδὲς τῷ σχήματι.

(πηνίκη, φενάκη),[1] attached to the mask. When this head-piece was fitted on, there was only one outlet for the voice, sometimes represented as a square, but more generally as a round opening (*os rotundum*),[2] so that the voice

Fig. 8.   Fig. 9.

might be said to sound through it—hence the Latin name for a mask (*persona a personando*);[3] hence also the strong expressions (βομβῶν, περιβομβῶν) used by the grammarians in speaking of the voice of the tragic actor. As the holes for the eyes must have been opposite to those of the actor, the mouth would fall below his chin, and some contrivance must have been adopted, after the manner of a speaking-trumpet, to produce this striking effect. The *persona muta*, or dumb actor, was furnished with a mask in which the lips

---

[1] Hence φενακίζειν, "to deceive." See Hemsterhuis on Julius Pollux, x. § 170.

[2] The mouth is square in the figures on the Pio-Clementine Mosaic, Nos. 1, 3, 4, 5, Plates II. III. IV. The size of the mouth is alluded to by Persius, v. 3: "fabula seu mœsto ponatur hianda tragœdo;" and Juvenal, III. 175: "personæ pallentis *hiatum*."

[3] Gabius Bassus, apud Aul. Gell. v. 7. Barth derives the word from περὶ σῶμα, Voss from πρόσωπον, Döderlein from παρασαίνω, Mr. Talbot from Persephone, and an English theologian from περιζώνιον!

were closed, as in the accompanying illustration from a painting at Pompeii.

The greatest possible care was bestowed on the fabrication of masks; and the manufacturer of stage costume got his name from this part of the actor's equipment.[1] It is not certainly known of what material the mask was composed. The ὄγκος in the Cyrenaic picture seems, in the case of all the three actors, to be a metal plate, and it is not improbable that this connexion of the mask

Fig. 10.

and wig, on which they both depended, was of some stiff and solid substance. Bötticher has supposed,[2] on the strength of a passage in Lucretius,[3] that the masks were made of clay; but a mask of *terra cotta* would have been much too heavy, and it is more reasonable to infer that the poet refers to the coating of chalk with which the surface was overlaid in order to receive the colouring, or perhaps to the colours themselves.[4] The lighter the mask the more convenient it would be for the performer, and though the description in Lucretius seems to be inconsistent with Millin's conjecture that it was made of cork,[5] there is no reason why it should not have been moulded from the bark of some other tree[6] moistened in water, and then modelled in a bust. The *oscilla*, or heads of Bacchus, which were imitations of the

---

[1] Pollux, IV. 115: καὶ σκευὴ μὲν ἡ τῶν ὑποκριτῶν στολή (ἡ δ' αὐτὴ καὶ σωμάτιον ἐκαλεῖτο), σκευοποιὸς δὲ ὁ προσωποποιός.

[2] *Funemaske*, p. 12.

[3] IV. 296 sqq.:

"Ut si quis, prius arida quam sit
Cretea persona, adlidat pilæve trabive,
Atque ea continuo rectam si fronte figuram
Servet, et elisam retro sese exprimat ipsa,
Fiet ita, ante oculos fuerit qui dexter, ut idem
Nunc sit lævus, et e lævo sit mutua dexter."

It is quite clear from this that the mask was made of some substance fitted by maceration for receiving an impression and capable of being turned inside out, which would hardly be possible with a clay mould.

[4] As in Petronius:

"Dum sumit creteam faciem Sestoria, cretam
Perdidit illa simul, perdidit et faciem."

[5] *Descr. d'un Mos.* p. 6.

[6] Virgil, *Georg.* II. 387:

"Oraque corticibus sumunt horrenda cavatis."

tragic mask, and which were suspended from the pine-trees near a vineyard,[1] in order that the district might become fruitful, whereon the face of the god was directed by the wind,[2] were most probably made of bronze or copper; for the lighter substance would not have stood the effects of the weather.   One of the *oscilla* preserved in the British Museum is of marble, and has a ring on the top, for the

Fig. 11.

purpose of suspension. The masks in the Pio-Clementine Mosaic are mostly of a swarthy colour; those in the Cyrenaic picture are quite natural; and it is probable that a resemblance to nature was preserved, though of course the colours were strongly pronounced and exaggerated.   It is obvious, as Müller says,[3] that the masks were sometimes changed between the acts, and that a difference of complexion was introduced to mark the change in the condition of the character, as when Œdipus or Polymnestor returns to the stage after the loss of his eyes.[4]   The masks of female characters were furnished with the ὄγκος, as in the figure of the tragic Muse (Fig. 7), in the parody of the *Antigone* (Fig. 17), and in the Pompeian picture already cited,[5] but the features were less exag-

[1] Virgil, *Georg.* II. 389:
"Oscilla ex alta suspendunt mollia pinu."
[2] Id. *ibid.* 390:
"Hinc omnis largo pubescit vinea fetu
    Complentur vallesque cavæ saltusque profundi,
    Et quocunque Deus circum caput egit honestum."
Creuzer supposes (*Symbol.* IV. 93) that this practice referred to the purifying influence of the wind, indicated by the worship of Bacchus Lichnites.   [3] *Hist. of Gr. Lit.* I. p. 395.
[4] These were called ἔκσκευα πρόσωπα. Pollux, iv. § 141.

[5] Gell, *Pompeii*, Vol. II. Pl. LXXV., of which the annexed is a copy, as far as concerns the female head in question.

gerated, and they had sometimes caps of a peculiar colour, with hanging ribands kept down by a knob or tassel of gilded metal called ῥοΐσκος, i.e., " a little pomegranate."[1]

There was a different kind of mask for almost every character. Julius Pollux divides the tragic masks alone into twenty-six classes :[2] and while he informs us that the comic masks were much more numerous,[3] he specifies only four kinds of satyric masks, two portraying satyrs with grey hair or a long beard, and two representing Sileni, as youthful or aged respectively.[4] The last of these is depicted in the Pio-Clementine Mosaic, as a bald-headed, grey-bearded mask, crowned with ivy (Pl. v. No. vii.), and the last group on that mosaic (Pl. xxviii.) represents the Silenus in full costume, bald-headed and crowned with ivy, though dressed in the tragic robe like the other figures. The accompanying groups (Fig. 12, 13, 14) show the tragic, comic, and satyric masks in contrast with one another.

Fig. 12.

(b) It has been already remarked that the dress of the tragic actors was derived from the gay festal costume of the

---

[1] Millin, Mosaïque, Pl. v. No. viii.; Monum. Antiq. inéd. ii. 249.
[2] iv. § 133 sqq.
[3] Jul. Poll. iv. §§ 143—154.
[4] Id. § 142.

U

worshippers of Bacchus. The performers, says Müller,[1] wore "long striped garments reaching to the ground (χιτῶνες ποδήρεις, στολαί) over which were thrown upper robes (ἱμάτια, χλαμύδες) of purple or some other brilliant colour, with all sorts of gay trimmings and gold ornaments, the

Fig. 13.

Fig. 14.

ordinary dress of Bacchic festal processions and choral dances. Nor was the Hercules of the stage represented as the sturdy athletic hero, whose huge limbs were only concealed by a lion's hide ; he appeared in the rich and gaudy dress we have described, to which his distinctive attributes, the club and the bow, were merely added."

The accompanying illustration (Fig. 15) contains all the elements of this Dionysiac costume.[2] It represents an actor dressed in the character of Bacchus. He does not wear the mask with its lofty fore-top, but he is shod with the cothurnus, which has the usual high sole, and the upper leather, which

[1] Müller, *Hist. Lit. Gr.* I. p. 296. For the details and minutiæ of the Greek theatrical costume, see also Müller's *Eumeniden*, § 32 ; Schön, *De Personarum in Euripidis Bacchabus Habitu scenico Commentatio*, Lips. 1831 ; and Millin's *Description of the Pio-Clementine Mosaic.* On the different styles of dress adopted by the different characters, see Jul. Pollux, IV. 18, and for examples, compare the Introduction to the *Antigone*, pp. xxxii sqq.

[2] It is taken from Buonarroti, *Osservazioni sopra alcuni Medagli Antichi*, p. 447; Bellori, *Pictur. Ant. Crypt. Rom.* T. xv.; Panofka, *Cabinet de Pourtalès-Gorgier*, Pl. xxxviii.

is visible, is adorned with the most elaborate lacing. He wears on his head a chaplet of ivy. The mutilated staff in his hand is undoubtedly a fragment of the thyrsus.[1] Over a syrma, with sleeves reaching to his wrists, he wears the usual upper robe of Bacchus fastened by a girdle. The long garland of flowers, which hangs round his neck, is one of the regular Bacchic adornments. By his left side is a statuette, unfortunately mutilated, which probably represents

Fig. 15.

Melpomene; and the female figure, also imperfect, to which he turns his head, is probably a representation of Victory, who is about to place a crown on the head of the successful actor.[2] On the other side is a boy playing the ἐπινίκιον, and probably the same as the performer who accompanied him on the stage. The curtain in the background seems to

---

[1] Pollux, IV. 117: ὁ δὲ κροκωτὸς ἱμάτιον· Διόνυσος δὲ αὐτῷ ἐχρῆτο καὶ μασχαλιστῆρι ἀνθίνῳ καὶ θύρσῳ.

[2] Müller, Handb. d. Arch. § 425, 2.

indicate that the actor is receiving this public recognition as he sits enthroned on the proscenium.

As the general costume of the tragic performers was thus fixed by the conventions of the Bacchic festival, the discrimination of the character represented depended on the expression of the mask, on certain adjuncts, and partly on the colour of the dress. It was only Euripides who ventured to allow his tragic heroes to appear in rags, and he incurred by this departure from Bacchic magnificence, the keenest ridicule of his comic contemporaries. The other dramatists contrived that every character should be consistent with the dignity and splendour of the festal occasion, with which the exhibition was connected. The adjuncts, which marked the different characters, were very simple, and might be recognized at once. Of the attributes of Hercules we have already spoken. He has both the club and the bow in the

Pio-Clementine Mosaic (No. I, Pl. p. 281), but the club alone in the same Mosaic (Millin, Pl. VIII. Wieseler, No. 3), in the Cyrenaic picture, and in the following illustration from a bas-relief in the Villa Albani. Mercury has simply a caduceus in the Pio-Clementine Mosaic (Millin, Pl. X.) and in the Cyrenaic picture. The figure in the act of shooting with a bow and arrow at a man bearing an unsheathed poignard (No. III, Pl. p. 281) probably represents Hercules in the act of slaying Lycus.[1] The royal tragic costume is

Fig. 16.   marked by the long sceptre borne in the left hand,[2] and by a sword with its

μύκης[3] at the end of the scabbard (No. II, Pl. p. 281). It

---

[1] The drawn dagger indicates the murderous purpose of the person about to be slain. See Eurip. *Herc. F.* 735 sqq.

[2] Ovid, *Amorum*, III. 1, 11 sqq.:

> "Venit et ingenti violenta Tragœdia passu:
>   Fronte comæ torva; palla jacebat humi;
> Lœva manus sceptrum late regale tenebat;
>   Lydius alta pedum vincla cothurnus erat."

[3] Herod. III. 64.

is difficult to say what is the distinguishing object in some of the figures in the Mosaic,[1] but the first is obviously a young female figure with a torch[2] in each hand; and may fairly be identified with the Cassandra of the *Troades*. In one group (Millin, Pl. xxv. Wieseler, VIII. 3) a figure is introduced bearing a branch of olive as a suppliant, and it is not improbable, as Millin has suggested (p. 28), that the scene represented is that in the *Supplices* of Euripides, when Adrastus appeals to Æthra the mother of Theseus. In the picture from Pompeii, to which reference has been already made (Wieseler, VIII. 12), a heroine bearing a child in swaddling clothes, is addressing a female domestic, who

Fig. 17.

carries a water-jug in her right hand. That Antigone, both in the prologue and when she is brought before Creon, carries in her hand the *prochus* or pitcher, with which she poured forth the triple libations round the dead body of her

---

[1] In No. v, Pl. p. 281, the male figure seems to carry in his left hand the red sheath of the dagger which he bears in his right; and the female figure, who is bending her knee in the act of supplication, is perhaps Clytæmnestra, at the moment when Orestes threatens her with death.

[2] vv. 308 sqq.:

ἄνεχε, πάρεχε, φῶς φέρε σέβω, φλέγω,
ἰδού, ἰδού
λαμπάσι τόδ᾽ ἱερόν.

brother,[1] is most probable in itself, and is confirmed by a ludicrous parody of the latter scene, in which an old and bald-headed man, dressed up as Antigone, and bearing an exaggerated hydria, pulls off his female mask at the moment when Creon is about to sentence the supposed culprit to death.[2] (See Fig. 17.) With regard to the colours of the tragic dress, the three figures in the Cyrenaic painting are mainly attired in blue and yellow. The protagonist, who represents Hercules, has his garments elaborately ornamented, the Mercury has his blue robe adorned with rings of gold and sprigs of olive, and the third figure, besides the admixture of blue and yellow in his dress, has some pink figures embroidered on it. They have all girdles in which pink is the prevailing colour. Both the female characters in the scene with the child ἐν σπαργάνοις have garments of a bluish-green.[3] There is more variety in the colours on the Pio-Clementine mosaic, but most of them have transversal bars of purple or gold (called ῥάβδοι παρυφαί[4]) on the sleeves and bodies of their upper garments. This band sometimes appears also as the πεζίς[5] or lower border of the chiton. In one of the groups, where a tyrant with threatening mien, is addressing a prisoner, who stands before him with drooping head and his hands bound behind his back, the former has a bright red dress without any stripes, bound round his waist with a golden girdle.[6] The attire of mourning, when the character was represented as suffering under some special calamity, was for a woman a black gown with a pale

---

[1] *Introduction to the Antigone*, p. XXXII.

[2] Gerhard, *Ant. Bildwerke*, Taf. LXXIII.; Panofka, *Annali dell' Inst. Arch.* Vol. XIX. pp. 216 sqq.; Welcker, *Gerhard's Arch. Ztg.* N. F. 1846, pp. 333 sqq.; Wieseler, *Theatergeb.* p. 55, Pl. IX. No. 7.

[3] Wieseler, *Theatergeb.* p. 52: "Beide Personen haben einen blaugrünlichen Chiton."

[4] Pollux, VII. § 53: αἱ μέντοι ἐν τοῖς χιτῶσι πορφυραῖ ῥάβδοι παρυφαὶ καλοῦνται. Hesych. παρυφή· ἡ ἐν τῷ χιτῶνι πορφύρα.

[5] Pollux, VII. § 62: ὧα δὲ τὸ ἐξωτάτω τοῦ χιτῶνος ἑκατέρωθεν,—αἱ δὲ παρὰ τὰς ὥας παρυφαὶ καλοῦνται πέζαι καὶ πεζίδες.

[6] Like the philosopher Lysias, who being elected crowned priest of Hercules, became ἐξ ἱματίου τύραννος, i. e. as soon as he laid aside his ordinary upper garment and assumed the tragic chlamys; for he is described as πορφυροῦν μὲν μεσόλευκον χιτῶνα ἐνδεδυκώς, χλαμύδα δὲ ἐφεστρίδα περιβεβλημένος πολυτελῆ (Athenæus, V. p. 215, B, C).

green or quince-yellow upper robe,[1] and for a man, if he was an exile, soiled white robes, or generally garments of black or dark brown, or quince-yellow, or with a shade of olive-green.[2] The black or at least a very dark robe is plainly seen in the Mosaic (No. VI, Pl. p. 281), and the pale green upper robe in the figure, which Mercury is conducting to the grave (Pl. X. Wieseler, VII. 5). Pollux mentions especially a net-like woollen robe (ἀγρηνόν) as worn by Teiresias and other soothsayers,[3] and a bulging robe (κόλπωμα) as worn by kings over their variegated under-dress,[4] which from the word used must have been confined by the girdle,[5] and may have been the projec-tions before the breast and the stomach men-tioned by Lucian.[6] The upper garment was not properly an ἱμάτιον thrown over the left shoulder and brought back under the right arm according to the ἡ ἐπὶ δέξια ἀναβολή, but a sort of χλαμύς, ἐφαπτίς, ἐφεστρίς, or ἐπιπόρπαμα fastened with a clasp on the shoulder like a soldier's cloak or wrapper. The general name for it was ἐπίβλημα, and the clasp on the shoulder was one of its special marks.[7] There are many allusions in the classical Tragedies to this feature in the dramatic attire. When an actor divests himself of his upper garment he is said to throw off his clasped robe.[8] It is with the tongues

Fig. 18.

[1] Pollux, IV. § 118: τῆς ἐν συμφορᾷ ὁ μὲν συρτὸς μέλας, τὸ δὲ ἐπίβλημα γλαυκὸν ἢ μήλινον.

[2] § 117: οἱ δ' ἐν δυστυχίαις ὄντες ἢ λευκὰ δυσπινῆ εἶχον, μάλιστα οἱ φυγάδες, ἢ φαιὰ ἢ μέλανα ἢ μήλινα ἢ γλαύκινα.

[3] § 116: τὸ δ' ἦν πλέγμα ἐξ ἐρίων δικτυῶδες περὶ πᾶν τὸ σῶμα, ὃ Τειρεσίας ἐπεβάλλετο ἤ τις ἄλλος μάντις.

[4] Ibid.: κόλπωμα ὃ ὑπὲρ τὰ ποικίλα ἐνεδέδυντο οἱ Ἀτρεῖς καὶ οἱ Ἀγαμέμνονες καὶ ὅσοι τοιοῦτοι.

[5] As in the epithet βαθύκολπος.

[6] De Sallat. 27: ἐῶ λέγειν προστερνίδια καὶ προγαστρίδια. The whole of Lucian's description of the tragic actor is worth reading by the student.

[7] Athenæus, XII. p. 535 E: ὁ δὲ Σικελίας τύραννος Διονύσιος ξυστίδα καὶ χρυσοῦν στέφανον ἐπὶ περόνῃ μετελάμβανε τραγικόν.

[8] Eurip. Herc. F. 959: γυμνὸν σῶμα θεὶς πορπαμάτων. Electr. 820: ῥίψας ἀπ' ὤμων εὐτρεπῆ πορπάματα.

of the buckles from his wife's dress that Œdipus puts out his own eyes,[1] and with the same instrument Hecuba and her attendants blind Polymnestor.[2]

The dress of the chorus was in accordance with the personages represented; and although it was different in kind from that of the actors, the choragus took care that it was equally splendid. But as the actors represented heroic characters, whereas the chorus was merely a deputation from the people at large, and in fact stood much nearer to the audience, the mask was omitted, and while the actors wore the *cothurnus*, the chorus appeared either bare-footed as in the Cyrenaic picture, or in their usual sandals.

The comic actors for the same reason were content with the *soccus* or thin-soled buskin (Fig. 19, 20), and their

Fig. 19.   Fig. 20.   Fig. 21.   Fig. 22.

mask had no ὄγκος (Fig. 21, 22); but the προσωποποιός made up for the lack of this exaggeration by an extravagant ugliness in the features of most of the characters, which set nature completely at defiance.[3] In the Old Comedy, as Pollux tells

---

[1] Sophocles, *Œd. T.* 1269.
[2] Eurip. *Hec.* 1170:

> ἐμῶν γὰρ ὀμμάτων
> πόμπας λαβοῦσαι τὰς ταλαιπώρους κόρας
> κεντοῦσιν, αἱμάσσουσιν.

[3] The most accessible specimen of the old comic costume is furnished by the puppet "Punch." It has not been noticed that his name, as well as his form, may be traced to a classical origin. "Punch" and

us,[1] the mask was for the most part a caricature of the person represented; but in the New Comedy there was a regular mask for every conventional character, the old man in particular having no less than ten types of countenance.[2] There is a superabundance of monuments representing the scenes of the New Comedy. Indeed, there is an illustrated manuscript of Terence,[3] which is probably at least as old as the sixth century, and may have been copied from one still more ancient, and statues, reliefs, and paintings exhibit the comic actors of the later stage in every character and in all varieties of posture. In a marble bas-relief, sup-

Fig. 23.

posed to represent the second scene of the fifth act of Terence's *Andria*,[4] an angry master, who is about to commit his slave to the tender mercies of a *lorarius*, is pacified by a friend of similar age. The figure of the supposed Simo is given in the annexed illustration.

The slave is always distinguished by a singular deformity in the mouth. The sitting figure, which is here subjoined, is frequently repeated in ancient statues,[5] and exhibits the

---

"Punchinello" are corruptions of the Italian *Pulcino* and *Pulcinello*, which are representatives of the contemptuous diminutive *pulchellus*. This epithet may be applied to little figures (Cic. *Fam.* VII. 23), and our own phrase "pretty Poll," addressed to the parrot, may show how easily such a ὑποκόρισμα may be suggested by the pleasure which results from petty imitations. In the same way, the Greeks called the ape καλός, or καλλίας (Böckh *ad Pind. P.* II. v. 72), and it is not improbable that the same or a similar epithet was given to the masked and padded actors in the pantomimic shows of ancient Greece and Italy.

[1] IV. § 143: τὰ δὲ κωμικὰ πρόσωπα, τὰ μὲν τῆς παλαιᾶς κωμῳδίας ὡς τὸ πολὺ τοῖς προσώποις ὧν ἐκωμῴδουν ἀπεικάζετο ἢ ἐπὶ τὸ γελοιότερον ἐσχημάτιστο.   [2] Pollux, IV. §§ 143 sqq.

[3] See Wieseler, *Theatergeb.* pp. 63 sqq. Taf. X. Nos. 2—7, from a MS. in the Vatican at Rome; No. 8, from a MS. in the Ambrosian Library at Milan.

[4] *Mus. Borb.* Vol. IV. T. XXIV.; Wieseler, Taf. XI. No. 1.

[5] See Wieseler, *Theaterg.* Taf. XI. Nos. 8, 9, 10, 11, and Taf. XII. No.

peculiarity of the slave's mask, to which we refer.

From the ring on the finger of one of the repetitions of this comic character, and from the crown on his head, it is inferred that he represents a drunken slave, probably in the Δακτύλιος of Menander, or in the *Condalium* of Plautus,[1] which was borrowed from it; and this inference is strengthened by the appearance of a similar figure in a scene represented on a terra-cotta relief, which is found in two private collections at Rome. Here a bearded figure, in an attitude like that in the above illustration, is seated on an altar, and two other figures, resembling the conventional old man of the New Comedy, appear to have been in angry altercation with him. It is natural then to conclude that we have some such scene as that in the *Mostellaria* (v. 1. 45):

Fig. 24.

Ego interim hinc aram occupabo,

and (v. 54):

Sic tamen hinc consilium dedero; nimio plus sapio sedens;
Tum consilia firmiora sunt de divinis locis.

---

5. The accompanying figure (24) is in the British Museum, and is engraved in *Anc. Marb. in the Br. Mus.* Part x. Pl. XLIII.

[1] Varro, *L. L.* VII. § 77. Accius says it was not written by Plautus, A. Gell. *N. A.* III. 3. The *condalium* seems to have been a kind of ring peculiar to slaves, Plaut. *Trin.* IV. 3, 7. The word is derived from κόνδυλος.

And the ring, if it does not refer to the *Condalium*, on which the play of Menander turned, may have been stolen like that in the *Curculio* of Plautus (ii. 3. 81).[1]

Of the dresses in the Old Comedy we have no monumental illustrations,[2] but the allusions in Aristophanes tell us how extravagant they must have been, and in what unrestrained obscenity the poet and his patrons indulged. The numerous scenes from the New Comedy, which are still preserved in ancient works of art, show that though the language became more reserved and better regulated, the eyes of the audience were not treated with much respect. The actors often wore harlequinade dresses, with trousers fitting close to the leg, and with protuberances and indecent appendages, indicating clearly enough the phallic origin of Greek Comedy.

The most interesting examples of the costume of Comedy are furnished by two pictures representing scenes of a very similar character, one of which has been referred to a φλύαξ τραγικός, or tragic foolery of Rhinthon[3]; and the other to the *Althœa* of Theopompus, a poet of the Middle Comedy[4]; In the former of these, Jupiter, attended by Mercury, is about to climb to the chamber of Alcmena, who is looking out of a window in full dress as an *Hetœra*.[5] Jupiter, who

---

[1] This interpretation is due to Visconti, *Mus. Pio-Clem.* Tom. III. p. 37.

[2] The representation of the first scene of the *Frogs* of Aristophanes, on a painted vase (Gerhard, *Denkm. n. Forsch.* 1849, Taf. III. No. 1; Wieseler, *Theater geb.* A, 25), is hardly an exception, for it does not correspond to the text, and is obviously a later production.

[3] Winckelmann, *Monum. inéd.* P. I. No. 190; Müller, *Denkmäler d. alt. Kunst*, II. Pl. III. No. 49; Wieseler, Taf. IX. 11.

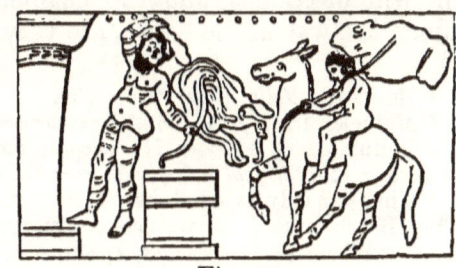

Fig. 25.

[4] Panofka, *Cab. Pourtalès*, Pl. X.; Wieseler, Taf. IX. 12.

[5] She wears an ornamented cap or μίτρα, which is referred to this character by Pollux, IV. § 154: ἡ δὲ διάμετρος (ἑταίρα) μίτρᾳ ποικίλῃ τὴν κεφαλὴν κατείληπται. Cf. Servius *ad Verg. Æn.* IV. 216; Juvenal, *Sat.* III. 66: "ite quibus grata est picta lupa barbara mitra."

has a bearded mask with a modius on his head like Serapis, is bearing a ladder, with his head between the steps. Mercury has his caduceus in his left hand, and bears a lamp in his right. He is also distinguished by his *petasos* and his *chlamys*. All the details of the picture point to circumstances of common occurrence in Greek comedies, with whom the μοιχὸς Ζεύς was a favourite character.[1] The ladder is expressly mentioned by Xenarchus, a poet of the Middle Comedy,[2] and the window which in correct drawing should be at a much greater height from the ground, represents the opening in the upper story of the stage from which the *hetæra* was frequently represented as looking down upon her lover.[3] It is worthy of remark that both Jupiter and Mercury are represented as bare-footed. In the other picture, which probably represents a similar nocturnal visit paid by Bacchus to Althæa in the Comedy of Theopompus,[4] a female dressed like the Alcmena of the other scene, is looking out of a window, while a comic figure with mask, socci, and other appendages, is climbing the ladder to reach her. He wears a chaplet on his head, and while he presents Althæa with "the apples of Dionysus,"[5] i.e. quinces, as an offering of love, he carries in his other hand a red band for her hair.[6] His bare-footed attendant has in his left hand a flambeau and a crown of myrtle, and in his right a little box (καδίσκος), containing some present for the lady. Althæa was the wife of Œneus, and the chaplets of vine-leaves, which adorn the wall of the house, are very appropriate to his name

---

[1] Bergk, *de Reliq. Com. Att.* p. 287.

[2] Meineke, III. p. 617: μὴ κλίμακα στησάμενον εἰσβῆναι λάθρᾳ.

[3] Pollux, IV. § 130: ἐν δὲ κωμῳδίᾳ ἀπὸ τῆς διστεγίας πορνόβοσκοί τι κατοπτεύουσι ἢ γρᾴδια ἢ γύναια καταβλέπει. Cf. Vitruv. V. 6, 9.

[4] This Comedy is cited by Athen. XI. p. 501 F; Pollux, IX. § 180. That Bacchus used to go as comast or reveller to the house of Althæa is known from Eurip. *Cyclops*, 37 sqq.:

> μῶν κρότος σικιννίδων
> ὅμοιος ὑμῖν νῦν τε χὤτε Βακχίῳ
> κώμοις συνασπίζοντες 'Αλθαίας δόμους
> προσῆτ' ἀοιδαῖς βαρβίτων σαυλούμενοι;

[5] Theocr. II. 120: μᾶλα μὲν ἐν κύλποισι Διωνύσοιο φυλάσσων. III. 10: ἠνίδε τοι δέκα μᾶλα φέρω.

[6] Müller, *Handb. d. Arch.* § 340, 4.

as the man of the vineyard. The colours of the picture are an interesting feature in the costume. The crowns on the heads of the figures are white.[1] The σωμάτιον of the man on the ladder is a brownish-red, his sleeves and leggings are of a bright brown. The other man is dressed entirely in yellow, and this is the colour of the robe in the picture, which represents a comic performer in the act of being masked and dressed by Bacchus.[2] The soccus as a general rule seems to have been yellow.[3]

The choruses of Aristophanes were arrayed in fantastic costumes more or less expressive of the allegorical caricature which they represented. Thus the *Birds* had masks with huge open beaks, and the *Wasps* flitted about the orchestra protruding enormous stings.

That the dresses of the actors in the satyrical drama did not differ in kind from those of the performers of the chief parts in the Tragedies, which they followed, is an obvious inference, and the fact is established by the last group in the Pio-Clementine Mosaic, which represents an actor accompanied by one of the chorus of satyrs, seen at a distance or in a diminutive form. There is also a painting on a vase in the Museo Borbonico at Naples,[4] which gives us not only the three actors in a satyrical drama, but a chorus of eleven, two musicians, one playing on the flute, the other a citharist, and the leader of the chorus, who is called Demetrius. In the midst Bacchus is reclining on a bed, with Kora-Ariadne in his arms; and the Muse, with a mask in her hand, is sitting at the end of the bed, attended by Himeros. Of the three actors, one is attired in the full tragic costume; another, who represents Hercules, has a highly decorated tunic, which, however, is shorter than the usual syrma; the third actor, who represents Silenus, has a closely-fitting, hairy dress, and bears a panther's skin on his left shoulder. The choreutæ, with the exception of one who is handsomely

---

[1] This was the proper colour for a loving serenader; Theocr. II. 121: κρατὶ δ' ἔχων λεύκαν, Ἡρακλέος ἱερὸν ἔρνος.

[2] *Mus. Borbon.* Vol. III. Tav. IV.; Wieseler, Taf. x. 1.

[3] Müller, *Handb. d. Arch.* § 388, 2.

[4] *Monum. ined. dell' Inst. di Corrisp. Arch.* Vol. III. T. XXI.; Wieseler, Taf. VI. No. 2, p. 47.

dressed, and another, who has ornamented drawers, like our mountebanks,[1] have goat-skins about their loins with phallic appendages, but are otherwise naked. The same fashion of dressing the choreutæ in nothing except shaggy aprons is observable in a very beautiful Mosaic found at Pompeii, a copy of which is subjoined.[2] This picture introduces us to

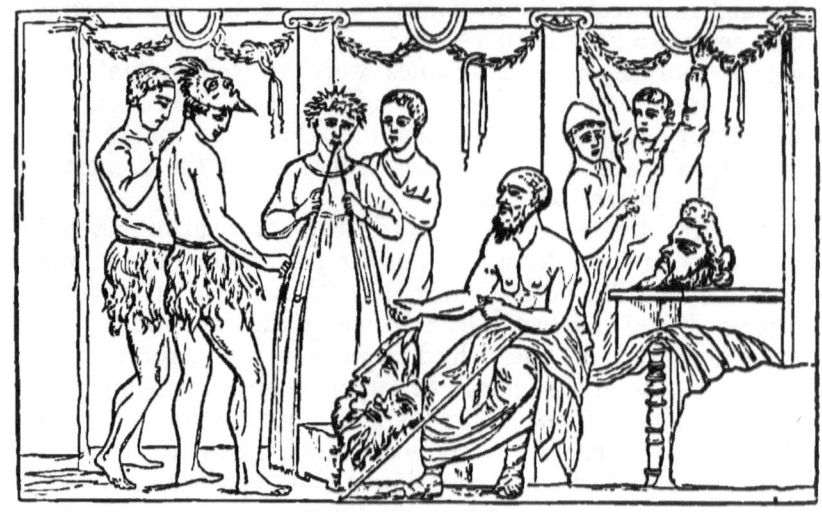

Fig. 26.

the χορήγιον or διδασκαλεῖον, which was probably in one of the *parascenia* or green-rooms of the theatre,[3] just as the

---

[1] These drawers are worn by the satyric choreutæ on Tischbein's vase (Wieseler, VI. 3), and by the satyric citharist on Laborde's vase (Wieseler, VI. 5).

[2] Gell, *Pompeii*, New Series, Vol. I. Pl. XLV.; *Mus. Borbon.* Vol. II. T. LVI.; Wieseler, Taf. VI. I. The accompanying engraving (Fig. 26), which is taken from the *Museo Borbonico*, is not quite accurate; for there are only two masks before the teacher, the third being on the table behind him.

[3] Pollux, IV. § 106: χορήγιον ὁ τόπος οὗ ἡ παρασκευὴ τοῦ χοροῦ. Cf. IX. §§ 41, 42. *Bekk. Anecd.* 72, 17: χορηγεῖον: ὁ τόπος ἔνθα ὁ χορηγὸς τούς τε χοροὺς καὶ τοὺς ὑποκριτὰς συνάγων συνεκρότει. We learn from Antiphou (*de Choreut.* § 11, p. 143) that the διδασκαλεῖον was sometimes in the choragus' own house: πρῶτον μὲν διδασκαλεῖον ᾖ ἦν ἐπιτηδειότατον τῆς ἐμῆς οἰκίας κατεσκεύασα. But we are disposed to agree with Magnin (*Revue d. d. Mond.* T. XXII. p. 257): "quelque fût

chorodidascalus is giving the last instructions to the choreutæ
and actors, before the commencement of the satyric drama
for which they are dressing. Seated on a chair he is
addressing one of the two choreutæ before him, and apparently teaching him how to manage his hands. One of
these choreutæ has not yet put on his mask, the other has
raised it that he may the better observe his teacher. As
the roll of paper, which the chorodidascalus holds in his
left hand, is folded up, we infer that he has already gone
through the text of the play. Near the centre of the
picture we have a flute player tuning his double flute. He
is probably the χοραύλης, who accom-
panied the chorus, and this name was
inscribed on the base of the statue (Fig.
27) found on the Appian way. This instrumental performer is crowned with
green and yellow leaves, and his long
gown is white, with blue stripes running
from the top to the bottom. Over his
breast and shoulders and down to his
lips he has a trimming of violet with
reddish crosses or stars. This trimming
is probably the ὀχθοιβοί mentioned by
Photius.[1] By the side of the flute-player

Fig. 27.

one of the actors is advancing probably to take the mask,
which the teacher is raising with his right hand. Another
actor, who has already received his mask which lies beside
him on the table, is fitting on his chiton with the aid of a
servant. The mask of the Silen, which lies at the foot of
the teacher, indicates a third part; and unless we suppose
that this part is to be undertaken by one of the two actors
already present, we must conclude that, as only two of the
choreutæ are still in the room, the third actor has not yet
made his appearance. The gowns of both the actors are bright

---

d'ailleurs le lieu où l'on commençât des exercices, on les terminait au
théâtre, dans une pièce des parascenia ou du postscenium appelée
χοραγεῖον."

[1] P. 566, 5, Porson: Ὀχθοιβούς: τὰ λώματα· ἔστι δὲ περὶ τὸ στῆθος
τοῦ χιτῶνος ἁλουργὲς πρόσραμμα.

blue with stripes of some different colour, which is not very distinct.   The red mantle, which is thrown over the chair with gilded legs immediately to the right of the chorodi-dascalus, is, no doubt, intended to form part of the costume of one of the actors.   The wall of the apartment is adorned with Ionian pilasters, between which are suspended gar-lands and tæniæ.   The latter are perhaps indications of success in the dramatic competition.

This examination of the details of the costume in the three great classes of the ancient drama will suffice to show how entirely conventional and unreal the performance of a Greek play must have been when contrasted with our modern notions.   It is of course an open question, whether it is more in accordance with the principles of dramatic art to

> " let gorgeous Tragedy
> In sceptred pall come sweeping by,"

according to a fixed system of representation, or to ransack the stores of illuminated missals, monumental brasses, and even Assyrian monuments, in order to put on the stage an exact resemblance of the times to be exhibited : whether it is better to let Comedy revel in the grotesque exaggerations of our pantomimes, or to place on the stage a carpeted boudoir with all the details of modern comfort.   It is at least certain that the present method of putting plays on the stage, which seems to have reached its ultimate development under the management of Mr. Macready and Mr. Charles Kean, is quite a modern innovation.   It began with Le Kain and Talma in France, and has been fully perfected in this country under the Kembles.   But Shakspere was content to apologize for disgracing the name of Agincourt

> " With four or five most vile and ragged foils,
> Right ill-disposed in brawl ridiculous."

Garrick played ancient Romans in bag-wigs and ruffles ; until the last few years Falstaff fought at Shrewsbury with a highlander's target, and a white coat with red and gold facings of the time of George the First; and it was at the beginning of the present century that the French per-

former, who was arrayed for the first time in an approximation to the classic costume of Agamemnon, demanded of
Talma, with much indignation, where he was expected to
carry his snuff-box.

Aristotle, or the grammarian by whom his treatise on
Poetry has been interpolated, informs us [1] that every Greek
Tragedy admitted of the following subdivisions; the *prologue*,
the *episodes*, the *exode*, which applied to the performances
of the actors, and the *parodus* and *stasima*, which belonged
to the chorus. The songs from the stage (τὰ ἀπὸ σκηνῆς)
and the dirges (κομμοί) are peculiar to some Tragedies only.
Besides these, it seems that there was occasionally a dancing
song or canzonet of a peculiar nature.[2] The proper entrance of the chorus was from the parascenia by one of the
parodi (*nte*). The *parodus* was the song which the choreutæ sang as they moved, probably in different parties,
along these side entrances of the orchestra.[3] It was generally either interspersed with anapæsts, as is the case in the
Antigone; or preceded by a long anapæstic march, as in the
case of the *Supplices* and *Agamemnon*. Sometimes this anapæstic march was followed by a system of the cognate[4] Ionics
à minore. This we find in the *Persæ*. In some Tragedies
there was no *parodus*, but the opening of the play found the
chorus already assembled on the Thymele, and prepared
to sing the first *stasimon*. Such is the case in the *Œdipus
Tyrannus*. It seems probable that they then entered by the
passage under the seats (*rbh*). The *stasima* were always
sung by the chorus when it was either stationary or moving
on the same limited surface around the altar of Bacchus, and
with its front to the stage. The places of the choreutæ
were marked by lines on the stage (διαγράμματα). The two
circles round the altar, indicated in the plan, give the maxi-
mum and minimum range of their evolutions. When those
evolutions amounted to a dance,[5] it was of the nature of the
emmeleia, which, as we have seen, was a staid and solemn
form of the *gymnopædic* gesticulations. The satyric chorus
danced the rapid *pyrrhic*, or some form derived from it, and

[1] Chap. XII. below, Part II.   [2] Introd. to *Antigone*, p. xxxi.
[3] Ibid. p. xxx.   [4] Donaldson's *Gr. Gr.* art. 650, p. 620.
[5] Böckh, *Antigone*, pp. 280 sqq.

we may infer that it involved a great deal of tramping back-
wards and forwards, with high steps and lively movements
of the hands, like the morris-dance in England, or the
tarantella in Italy. Although the *cordax*, derived from the
hyporcheme, was the original form of dance adopted by the
phallic comus, it was so grossly indecent, that Aristophanes
claims credit for its omission in *The Clouds*.[1] The comic
chorus sang its *parodus* and its *stasima* in the same manner as
the tragic; but they were, as pieces of poetry, much less
elaborate, and generally much shorter. The main performance of the chorus in Comedy was the *parabasis*. It
was an address to the audience in the middle of the play
and was the most immediate representative of the old
trochaic or anapæstic address by the leader of the phallic song,
for which the personal lampoons of Archilochus furnished the
model, and to which the Old Comedy of Athens was mainly
indebted for its origin. This *parabasis*, or "countermarch,"
was so called, because the chorus which had previously stood
facing the stage, and on the other side of the central altar
wheeled about and made a movement towards the spectators,
who were then addressed by the coryphæus in a short
system of anapæsts or trochees, called the κομμάτιον, and
this was followed by a long anapæstic system, termed
πνῖγος ("suffocation"), or μακρόν ("long"), from the effort
which its delivery imposed upon the reciter. In the extant
remains of Greek lyric poetry, those parts of the *epinikia*
of Pindar, which allude to the professional rivalries and
literary pretensions of the poet, are the nearest approxi-
mations to this function of the choral comus. The parabasis is often followed by a lyrical song in honour of some
divinity, and this by a short system, properly of sixteen
trochaic tetrameters, which is called the *epirrhema* or
"supplement." The French would term it *l'envoi*. It
contains some joking addition to the main purport of the
parabasis. The lyric poem generally consisted of strophe
and antistrophe; and the *epirrhema* had its *antepirrhema*.
These divisions confirm the supposition that the lyric poem
was derived from the mutual λοιδορίαι of the phallic singers,

---

[1] See vv. 537 sqq.

and the *epirrhema* from the interchange of ribaldry in which the comus indulged.

There were regularly never more than three actors (ὑπο-κριταί, ἀγωνισταί), who, as we have seen, were designated as respectively the *first*, *second*, and *third* actor (πρωταγωνισ-τής, δευτεραγωνιστής, τριταγωνιστής[1]). The third actor in Tragedy was first added by Sophocles ;[2] and it is said that Cratinus was the first to make this addition in Comedy.[3] Any number of mutes might appear on the stage. If children were introduced as speaking or singing on the stage, the part was undertaken by one of the chorus, who stood behind the scene, and it was therefore called a παρα-σκήνιον, from his position, or παραχορήγημα, from its being something beyond the proper functions of the chorus.[4] It has been concluded[5] that a fourth actor was indispensable to the proper performance of the *Œdipus Coloneus*. But we cannot admit that this innovation was necessary in the particular case,[6] and in all others it is tolerably easy to see how all the parts might have been sustained without inconvenience by three actors. The protagonist regularly undertook the character in which the interest of the piece was thought to centre ; and it was so arranged that he could also give those narratives of what was supposed to have taken place off the stage, which constituted to the last the most epic portion of the Tragedy, and which probably, in the days of Thespis and Phrynichus, comprised all the chief efforts of the original rhapsode or exarchus.[7] By a great stroke of comic humour

[1] Above, pp. 59, 245.
[2] Above, p. 136.   [3] *Anonym. de Comœdia*, p. xxxii.
[4] Pollux, IV. § 109, says that it was παρασκήνιον if one of the chorus said anything in a song instead of a fourth actor (above, p. 266), but παραχορήγημα εἰ τέταρτος ὑποκριτής τι παραφθέγξαιτο; and he cites the *Agamemnon* of Æschylus for the former, and the *Memnon* of the same poet for the latter. See C. F. Hermann, *Disput. de Distribut. Personarum in Trag. Græcis*, Marburg, 1840, pp. 39, 40, 64, 66.
[5] By Müller, *Hist. Lit. Gr.* I. p. 305.
[6] The difficulty raised by Müller, namely, that the part of Theseus must have been divided between two actors, if there were only three in all, does not seem to be a very formidable one. The mask and the uniformity of tragic declamation would make it as easy for two actors to represent one part, as for one actor to sustain several characters.
[7] Introduction to the *Antig.* p. xx.

Aristophanes makes Agoracritus, the hero of *The Knights*, appear as the narrator of his own adventures,[1] an office which a tragedian would have assigned to some messenger from the scene of action. The deuteragonist and tritagonist seem to have divided the other characters between them, less according to any fixed rule than in obedience to the directions of the poet, who was guided by the exigencies of his play.[2] The actors took rank according to their merits, and the tritagonist was always considered as inferior to the other two.

The narrowness and distance of the stage rendered any elaborate grouping unadvisable. The arrangement of the actors was that of a processional bas-relief.[3] Their movements were slow, their gesticulations abrupt and angular, and their delivery a sort of loud and deep-drawn sing-song, which resounded throughout the immense theatre.[4] They probably neglected everything like *by-play*, and *making points*, which are so effective on the English stage. The distance at which the spectators were placed would prevent them from seeing those little movements, and hearing those low tones which have made the fortune of many a modern actor. The mask too precluded all attempts at varied expression, and it is probable that nothing more was expected from the performer than was looked for from his predecessor the rhapsode,—namely, good recitation.[5] The

---

[1] vv. 624 sqq.   [2] Introd. to the *Antig.* pp. xx sqq.

[3] "As ancient sculpture," says Müller (*Hist. of Gr. Lit.* I. p. 398), "delighted above all things in the long lines of figures which we see in the pediments and friezes, and as even the painting of antiquity placed single figures in perfect outline near each other, but clear and distinct, and rarely so closely grouped as that one intercepted the view of another; so also the persons on the stage, the heroes and their attendants (who were often numerous) stood in long rows on the long and narrow stage." It is to be remarked, however, that numerous retinues, especially if they appeared with horses or chariots, were often introduced into the orchestra.

[4] This is pretty evident from the epithets, which, as Pollux tells us, might be applied to the actor, IV. 114: εἴποις δ' ἂν βαρύστονος ὑποκριτής, βομβῶν, περιβομβῶν, ληκυθίζων, λαρυγγίζων, φαρυγγίζων, κ. τ. λ.

[5] Professor Blackie, after quoting these words (*The Lyrical Dramas of Æschylus translated from the Greek*, Lond. 1850, Vol. I. p. xlvi), adds: "These observations, flowing from a realization of the known

rhythmical systems of the tragic choruses were very simple, and we may conclude that the music to which they were set was equally so. The dochmiac metre, which is regularly found in the κομμοί and τὰ ἀπὸ σκηνῆς, would admit of the most inartificial of plaintive melodies. The comic choral songs very frequently introduce the easy asynartete combinations,[1] which were so much used by Archilochus; and we find in Aristophanes a very curious form of the antispastic metre, the invention of which is attributed to Eupolis.[2]

We shall conclude with a few observations on the audience, and on the social position of the actors. For the first few years after the commencement of theatrical performances no money was paid for admission to them; but after a time (probably about the year B.C. 501) it was found convenient to fix a price for admission, in order to prevent the crowds and disturbances occasioned by the gratuitous admission of every one who chose to come.[3] The charge was two obols;[4] but lest the poorer classes should be excluded, the entrance money was given to any person who might choose to apply

---

circumstances of the case, will sufficiently explain to the modern reader the extreme stiffness and formality which distinguishes the tragic dialogue of the Greeks from that dexterous and various play of verbal interchange which delights us so much in Shakspere and the other masters of English tragedy. Every view, in short, that we can take, tends to fix our attention on the musical and the religious elements, as on the life-blood and vital soul of the Hellenic τραγῳδία; forces us to the conclusion, that, with a due regard to organic principle, its proper designation is *sacred opera*, and not *tragedy*, in the modern sense of the word, at all; and leads us to look on the dramatic art altogether in the hands of Æschylus, not as an infant Hercules strangling serpents, but as a Titan, like his own Prometheus chained to a rock, whom only after many ages a strong Saxon Shakspere could unbind."

[1] Donaldson's *Gr. Gr.* 666, p. 628. [2] Id. *ibid.* 677, p. 633.

[3] It is probable that at Athens, as well as Rome, each person entitled to admission was furnished with a ticket indicating his place in the theatre. A ticket of admission to the *Casina* of Plautus has been found at Pompeii.

[4] This account of the Theoricon is taken from Böckh's *Publ. Econ.* I. pp. 289 foll. Engl. Tr.

for it, provided his name was registered in the book of the
citizens (ληξιαρχικὸν γραμματεῖον). The lowest and best seats
were set apart for the magistrate, and for such persons as had
acquired or inherited a right to front seats (προεδρία).[1] It
is probable that those who were entitled to reserved places
at the theatre had also tickets of admission provided for
them. Foreigners on the contrary were obliged generally
to be contented with the back seats.[2] The entrance-money
was paid to the lessee of the theatre (θεατρώνης, θεατροπώλης,
ἀρχιτέκτων), who defrayed the rent and made the necessary
repairs out of the proceeds. The distribution of the ad-
mission-money, or θεωρικόν, as it was called, out of the
public funds, was set on foot by Pericles, at the suggestion
of Demonides of Œa; its application was soon extended till
it became a regular largess from the demagogues to the
mob at all the great festivals; and well might the patriot
Demosthenes lift up his voice against a practice which was
in the end nothing but an instrument in the hands of the
profligate orators, who pandered to the worst passions of
the people. The lessee sometimes gave a gratis exhibition,
in which cases tickets of admission were distributed.[3] Any
citizen might buy tickets for a stranger residing at Athens.[4]
We have no doubt that women were admitted to the
dramatic exhibitions, at least to the Tragedies;[5] and boys

---

[1] See Aristoph. *Equ.* 704; Demosth. *Mid.* p. 572.

[2] See Alexis *ap. Poll.* IX. 44:

    ἐνταῦθα περὶ τὴν ἐσχάτην δεῖ κερκίδα
    ὑμᾶς καθιζούσας θεωρεῖν, ὡς ξένας.

[3] Καὶ ἐπὶ θέαν ἡνίκα ἂν δέῃ πορεύεσθαι, οὐκ ἐᾶν τοὺς υἱεῖς [ἀλλ'] ἡνίκα
προῖκα ἀφιᾶσιν οἱ θεατρῶναι. Theophrast. *Charact.* XI.
"Theophrastus mentions this as one of the marks of ἀπόνοια in a
person, Καὶ ἐν θεάμασι δὲ τοὺς χαλκοῦς ἐκλέγειν, καθ' ἕκαστον παριών·
καὶ μάχεσθαι τοῖς τὸ σύμβολον φέρουσι, καὶ προῖκα θεωρεῖν ἀξιοῦσι.
Charact. VI. Among the relics from Pompeii and Herculaneum
preserved in the Studii at Naples, is an oblong piece of metal about
three inches in length, and one in breadth, inscribed Αἰσχύλος. This
was perhaps the σύμβολον of Theophrastus."—*Former Editor.*

[4] Καὶ ξένοις δὲ αὑτοῦ θέαν ἀγοράσας, μὴ δοὺς τὸ μέρος, θεωρεῖν. Theophrast. *Charact.* IX.

[5] Pollux uses the same term θεατρία (II. § 56, IV. § 121), which is
alone some evidence of the fact. It is stated, however, expressly by
Plato, *Gorgias*, 502 D; *Legg.* II. 658 D; VII. 817 C; and by Aristoph.

as well as men were present at all performances of plays,[1] nor were slaves excluded.[2] It seems probable however that the women sat by themselves in a particular part of the theatre; for in the theatre at Syracuse there are still inscriptions on the nine different κερκίδες, or compartments, from which it would appear that the centre and four western compartments (namely those to the left of the spectator) were assigned to the men, while the four eastern compartments were reserved for the female spectators.[3] The conduct of the audience was much the same as that of the spectators at our own theatres, and they seem to have had little scruple in expressing their approbation or disapprobation, as well of the poet[4] as of the actors.[5] Their mode of doing this was sometimes very violent, and even in the time of Machon it was customary to pelt a bad performer with stones.[6]

The Athenian performers were much esteemed all over Greece; they took great pains over their bodily exercises,[7] and dieted themselves in order to keep their voices clear and strong.[8] Their memory must have been cultivated with assiduous care, for they never had the assistance of a prompter, like the performers on the modern stage.[9] We

---

Eccles. 21—23; Satyrus ap. Athen. p. 534. See Bekker's Charicles, pp. 403 sqq.

[1] For their appearance at tragedies, see the passages of Plato quoted in note 3. That they were allowed to see comedies also is clear from Aristoph. Nub. 537; Pax, 50, 766; Eupolis ap. Aristot. Eth. Nic. IV. 2.

[2] Plato, Gorg. p. 502.

[3] This is inferred from the female names on the eastern κερκίδες; see Göttling, über die Inschriften im Theater zu Syrakus, Rhein. Mus. 1834, pp. 103 sqq.

[4] Athenæus, XIII. p. 583 F.

[5] Demosth. De Coronâ (p. 345 and 346, Bekker). Comp. Milton's imitation of the passage. (Prose Works, p. 80, in the Apology for Smectymnuus.)

[6] Athen. VI. p. 245.   [7] Cicero, Orat. c. IV.

[8] Plato, Legg.

[9] Hermann (Opusc. V. 304) says: "In theatro ὑποβολεύς dictus est, qui histrioni verba subjiciebat, quem nos Gallico vocabulo souffleur appellamus. Sic Plutarchus in Præc. ger. resp. 17, p. 813 E: μιμεῖσθαι τοὺς ὑποκριτάς, πάθος μὲν ἴδιον καὶ ἦθος καὶ ἀξίωμα τῷ ἀγῶνι προστιθέντας, τοῦ δὲ ὑποβολέως ἀκούοντας, καὶ μὴ παρεκβαίνοντας τοὺς ῥυθμοὺς

believe that the protagonist at all events was generally paid by the state; in the country exhibitions, however, two actors would occasionally pay the wages of their τριταγω-νιστής.[1] The salary was often very high,[2] and Polus, who generally acted with Tlepolemus in the plays of Sophocles,[3] sometimes earned a talent by two days' performances.[4] The histrionic profession was not thought to involve any degradation. The actors were of necessity free Athenian citizens, and by the nature of the case had received a good education. The actor was the representative of the drama-tist, and often the dramatist himself. Sophocles, who sometimes performed in his own plays, was a person of the highest consideration; the actor Aristodemus went on an embassy,[5] and many actors took a lead in the public assembly.[6] Theodorus, who was a contemporary of Aristo-demus, and to whose mastery over his art both Aristotle, who had seen him on the stage,[7] and later writers, to whom his fame had descended,[8] bear ample testimony, was honoured by a monument, which was a conspicuous object on the sacred road to Eleusis even in the time of Pausanias.[9] It is true that Demosthenes, among the exaggerated contumelies which he heaps on his opponent Æschines, lays a particular stress on his connexion with the stage. But it must be

---

καὶ τὰ μέτρα τῆς διδομένης ἐξουσίας ὑπὸ τῶν κρατούντων." But, as Bernhardy remarks (*Griech. Litterat.* II. p. 648), we have here only a reference to the φωνάσκος, who kept C. Gracchus within bounds by the tone of his instrument (Plut. *Tib. Gracchus*, c. 2; Aul. Gellius, *N. A.* I. 11).

[1] Demosth. *de Coronâ*, p. 345, Bekker.
[2] See Böckh, *Public Econ.* Book I. c. XXI. p. 120, Engl. Tr.
[3] Comp. Aul. Gell. VII. 5, with Schol. Ar. *Nub.* 1269.
[4] Plutarch, *Rhet. Vitæ.*
[5] Æsch. περὶ παραπρ. p. 347, Bekker.
[6] Demosth. περὶ παραπρ. p. 377; Bekker, *de Coronâ*, p. 281.
[7] See, for example, *Rhet.* III. 2, § 4: οἷον ἡ Θεοδώρου φωνὴ πέπονθε πρὸς τὴν τῶν ἄλλων ὑποκριτῶν· ἡ μὲν γὰρ τοῦ λέγοντος ἔοικεν εἶναι· αἱ δ' ἀλλότριαι.
[8] It is said that he actually extorted tears from the savage tyrant, Alexander of Pheræ; Ælian, *V. H.* XIV. 14; cf. Plut. *Pelop.* 29.
[9] I. 37, § 3: πρὶν δὲ ἢ διαβῆναι τὸν Κηφισόν. Θεοδώρου μνῆμά ἐστι τραγῳδίαν ὑποκριναμένου τῶν καθ' αὑτὸν ἄριστα.

remembered that in all this he does not attempt to depreciate the profession itself. He is at great pains to indicate not only that Æschines never rose beyond the rank of a τριταγωνιστής,[1] and that he was merely the subordinate partner of Theodorus and Aristodemus,[2] just as Ischander was the regular δευτεραγωνιστής of Neoptolemus,[3] but that he utterly failed even in that humble capacity. On one occasion, when Æschines was performing at Collytus the part of Œnomaus in the play of Sophocles which bore that name, and was pursuing Ischander, who as deuteragonist took the part of Pelops, in the death-race for Hippodameia, which was probably represented in the orchestra, it is stated the future statesman fell in a very unseemly manner, had to be set on his feet again by Sannio, the teacher of the chorus, and was hissed off the stage by the offended spectators.[4] It is also intimated that at one time in his dramatic career, whether before or after this mishap does not appear, Æschines was content to be tritagonist to ranting actors named Simylus and Socrates, in whose company he was so pelted by the audience with figs, grapes, and olives, that it was worth his while to collect these missiles, and to find some compensation for the wounds which he had received in this way by living on the fruits of other men's orchards.[5] These insulting allusions, which were afterwards repeated in part by Demochares, the nephew of Demosthenes,[6] had in all probability little more than a foundation on fact.[7] But if they were sustained in

---

[1] De Coroná, pp. 270, 11; 297, 25; 315, 9.

[2] De Fals. Legat. pp. 418, 420, 2.

[3] De Fals. Legat. p. 344, 7: Ἴσχανδρον τὸν Νεοπτολέμου δευτεραγωνιστήν.

[4] De Coroná, p. 288, 19: ὃν ἐν Κολλυτῷ ποτε Οἰνόμαον κακῶς ἐπέτριψας. Anonym. Vit. Æsch. pp. 11 sq.: Δημοχάρης φησὶν Ἰσχάνδρου τοῦ τραγῳδοῦ τριταγωνιστὴν γενέσθαι τὸν Αἰσχίνην καὶ ὑποκρινόμενον Οἰνόμαον διώκοντα Πέλοπα αἰσχρῶς πεσεῖν καὶ ἀναστῆναι ὑπὸ Σαννίωνος τοῦ χοροδιδασκάλου. Apoll. Vit. Æsch. pp. 13 sq.: Αἰσχίνης τριταγωνιστὴς ἐγένετο τραγῳδιῶν καὶ ἐν Κολλυτῷ ποτε Οἰνόμαον ὑποκρινόμενος κατέπεσεν.

[5] De Coroná, p. 314, 10. The true explanation of this passage is that given by Mr. C. R. Kennedy, in the note to his translation, p. 97.

[6] Apud Harpocrat. s. v. Ἴσχανδρος. Anonym. Vit. Æsch. p. 11.

[7] The theatrical career of Æschines has been carefully examined by

every respect by the dramatic history of Æschines, it is clear that they affect only his personal reputation as an actor, and do not derogate from the general respectability of the histrionic art. In some cases, the actors were not only recognized by the state, but controlled and directed by special enactments. Thus, according to the law brought forward by the orator Lycurgus, the actors were obliged to compare the acting copies of the plays of the three great tragedians, with the authentic manuscripts of their works, preserved in the state archives; and it was the duty of the public secretary to see that the texts were accurately collated.[1]

<hr />

Arnold Schaefer, *Demosthenes und seine Zeit*, I. pp. 213—226. He falls into the old mistake of supposing that Æschines himself habitually imitated the manner of Solon (p. 225, note). More accurate scholarship would have led him to notice that Demosthenes uses the aorist ἐμιμήσατο, and that an imperfect would have been employed had he meant to imply habitual imitation. We have shown elsewhere that the statue from Herculaneum represents Solon, and not Æschines ("On the Statue of Solon mentioned by Æschines and Demosthenes," *Transactions of the Cambridge Philosophical Society*, Vol. x. Part 1). On the exaggerations or fabrications of Demosthenes in these attacks on Æschines, see *Hist. Lit. of Gr.* Vol. II. p. 365.

[1] *Vitæ X. Oratorum*, p. 841 D, p. 377 Wyttenb.: ὡς χαλκᾶς εἰκόνας ἀναθεῖναι τῶν ποιητῶν, Αἰσχύλου, Σοφοκλέους, Εὐριπίδου, καὶ τὰς τραγῳδίας αὐτῶν ἐν κοινῷ γραψαμένους φυλάττειν, καὶ τὸν τῆς πόλεως γραμματέα παραναγιγνώσκειν τοῖς ὑποκρινομένοις· οὐκ ἐξεῖναι γὰρ αὐτὰς [ἄλλως] ὑποκρίνεσθαι.

CHAPTER II.

Veteres ineunt proscenia ludi.
VERGILIUS.

HAVING fully considered all the circumstances connected
with the representation of a Greek play in general, we must
now apply the results of this inquiry to an investigation of
the manner in which these arrangements were practically
applied in particular cases. And as our space will not
allow us to examine with sufficient minuteness the details
which probably attended the exhibition of every extant
Tragedy and Comedy, it will be desirable to select those
dramas which furnish the most decisive and distinctive examples of the scenic ingenuity of the Greeks. The most
prominent peculiarity is undoubtedly the complete or partial
change of the indications of locality. And this is of very
rare occurrence. In the seven plays of Æschylus there is a
complete change of scene only in the second and third
plays of the extant Trilogy; and the left *periactos*, which,
as we have seen, indicates the direction of the foreign or
distant regions from which the visitant is supposed to enter
the stage, is not turned once in all the remains of the oldest
dramatist. Sophocles has only one example of a complete
change of scene, that in the *Ajax*; and only one of the
turning of the left *periactos*, that in the *Œdipus Tyrannus*,
when the road to Corinth is substituted for that to Delphi
with, perhaps, a distant view of Parnassus. In the numerous plays of Euripides we have no example of a complete change of place, but several of his plays require a
change of the left *periactos*. The scene is completely
changed in five of the eleven plays of Aristophanes; but
the left *periactos* is turned only in the *Acharnians* and in
the *Lysistrata*; and in the latter there are four or five of
these indications of a different point of approach to the
stage from a distance.

In making a selection from the extant Greek plays, we shall commence with the only complete Trilogy, the *Orestea*, or, as it may have been once called, the *Agamemnonia* of *Æschylus*, and shall then take those of the other plays which furnish the most various examples of a complete theatrical exhibition.

The scene of the *Agamemnon* of Æschylus represents the palace of the Atreidæ, and the open space immediately before it. The front of the palace is adorned with altars of various gods, especially those to whom the herald addresses himself on entering the stage (vv. 503 sqq.), and that of Apollo *Agyieus* was of course one of them (v. 1085). The palace was represented as rising to a considerable height, for the watchman, who speaks the prologue to the Tragedy, is able to command from his elevated position a view of the surrounding country, as far at least as the Arachnæan mountains (v. 309). As Pollux mentions the σκοπή and φρυκτώριον among the parts of the theatre, the question has been raised whether the watchman is posted on the roof of the palace or on some detached elevation. But it is clear from the words of the poet that the sentinel must have been on the palace itself (v. 3 : στέγαις Ἀτρειδῶν. v. 301 : Ἀτρειδῶν ἐς τόδε σκήπτει στέγος), and the balcony of the διστεγία would furnish the proper elevation. That a flat roof without battlements is intended is shown by the statement that he gazed lying down and leaning on his elbows like a dog (vv. 2, 3 : κοιμώμενος ἄγκαθεν κυνὸς δίκην), i.e. in the attitude familiar to us from the posture of the sphinx, which is the conventional form of the watchful guardian. The right-hand *periactos* represented the city of Argos, and the left the road to the coast.

The watchman, who introduces the play, speaks the prologue from his post on the roof and then makes his exit by a door supposed to lead into the palace, for he had already summoned the inmates of the royal house (v. 26).

The chorus then enters (v. 39) by the right-hand parodos, and the anapæsts are recited while they are moving to the thymele and taking their post around it. During these evolutions Clytæmnestra with her attendants enters the stage by the centre door (v. 83), and, after making her offerings at the

altars before the palace, goes off by the right-hand side-door
(v. 103) to repeat these offerings at the temples in the city;
and she does not reappear till the end of the first choral
song (v. 254), when she comes forward to the front of the
stage and enters into colloquy with the leaders of the
chorus. She explains to the chorus why she has offered a
sacrifice of thanksgiving, and after a vivid description of
the manner in which the message of the capture of Troy
was transmitted by a series of beacons, and of the contrast
between the victors and the vanquished in the captured city,
she again retires by the centre door into her palace. Hereupon follows the first stasimon of the chorus (vv. 357—448).
And a considerable lapse of time is supposed to intervene.
In the most of the editions it is supposed that Clytæmnestra
returns to the stage at the commencement of the next
episode, and that she speaks the words which indicate the
approach of the herald (vv. 489—500); but it is generally
the business of the chorus to announce the entrance of a
new character, the herald addresses himself to the chorus
down to v. 582, and the name of Clytæmnestra is mentioned
first in v. 585; it seems therefore clear that Hermann is
right in assigning the first words of the episode to the
chorus, and whether Clytæmnestra re-enters from the house
at v. 587, or a few verses before, it is obvious that she takes
no part in the dialogue till she makes that speech, where
the word πάλαι must be understood in its largest sense.
The herald, who is probably the Homeric Talthybius, had
entered of course by the side-door on the left, behind the
periactos representing the road to Nauplia; and he withdraws
by the same door, for the queen charges him with a message to her husband. After the second stasimon (vv. 681—
781), a few anapæstic lines introduce the triumphal procession of Agamemnon, who drives into the orchestra in a
mule-chariot, accompanied by the captive Casandra, and
followed by a retinue of attendants. He does not mount
the stage till v. 957, when he reluctantly sets his foot on
the costly carpets and follows his treacherous wife into the
palace. It is clear from v. 1054 (πείθου λιποῦσα τόνδ᾽ ἁμα-
ξήρη θρόνον) that Casandra remains in the orchestra, seated
still in the mule-chariot. It is probable that the armed

attendants of Agamemnon also remain in the orchestra.
The address in v. 1651, εἶα δὴ ξίφος πρόκωπον πᾶς τις εὐτρε-
πιζέτω, would hardly apply to the aged chorus consisting, as
we shall see, of only twelve persons.   After the gloomy
strains of the third stasimon (vv. 975—1032), Clytæmnestra
comes forth from the palace and endeavours fruitlessly to
induce Casandra to enter the royal apartments.   Casandra,
who had remained silent while the queen was on the stage,
breaks forth, immediately after her exit, into the most
impassioned strains, and the dialogue between her and the
chorus constitutes one of the finest scenes in the whole
body of the extant Tragedies of the Greeks.   After having
declared to the chorus, with increasing distinctness, the
impending murder of Agamemnon and herself, she rushes
into the house to meet her doom.   We should infer from
the conventional καὶ μήν that she leaves the orchestra at
the end of her interchange of songs with the chorus (v.
1178).

When Casandra leaves the stage (v. 1330), the chorus
recites a few anapæsts, which probably indicate a movement
of the whole body to take up a new position.   The death-
cry of Agamemnon is heard (v. 1343), and each of the
twelve choreutæ expresses his opinion as to what ought to
be done.   The proposal to rush into the palace and convict
the murderer while the fresh-dripping sword is still in his
hand (v. 1350: ὅπως τάχιστά γ᾽ ἐμπεσεῖν καὶ πρᾶγμ᾽ ἐλέγχειν
ξὺν νεορράντῳ ξίφει) seems to be generally adopted, and as
Clytæmnestra is immediately afterwards discovered on the
spot where she had slain her husband (v. 1379: ἔστηκα δ᾽
ἔνθ᾽ ἔπαισ᾽ ἐπ᾽ ἐξειργασμένοις), it may fairly be concluded
that the eccyclema, which exposes the interior of the palace,
is supposed to include the chorus also, and the whole of
the κόμμος which follows, down to the anapæsts (vv. 1567
—1576), which indicate a movement of the parties, is to be
understood as taking place within the palace.

The eccyclema is withdrawn, and the chorus is again in
the open place before the house of the Atreidæ, when
Ægisthus, attended by an armed escort (v. 1650), enters
the stage by the right-hand side-door (v. 1577), as though
he had come from the city on learning that Clytæmnestra

had consummated his plot with her (vv. 1608—1611). A lively altercation ensues between Ægisthus and the chorus, assisted probably by the attendants of Agamemnon, and the two parties are about to come to blows, when they are parted by the hasty re-appearance of Clytæmnestra, and the play ends as the guilty pair enter the palace to assume the sovereign power, and the chorus leaves the orchestra by the right-hand parodos.

It will be observed that in this grand Tragedy there is no deviation from the unity of place; for the eccyclema, which displays the interior of the palace, is only a partial change of scene. The unity of time, however, is conspicuously violated. For Clytæmnestra's speech before the first stasimon is supposed to be spoken on the day of the capture of Troy (v. 320 : Τροίαν Ἀχαιοὶ τῆδ' ἔχουσ' ἐν ἡμέρᾳ), and the herald, who enters after the stasimon, details circumstances referring to a long passage from Troy, interrupted by a dreadful storm which dispersed the fleet. Several days must therefore be supposed to have elapsed between the two acts of the play.

The distribution of the parts among the three actors in the *Agamemnon* may be very easily arranged, so as to allow the same actor (i.e. the tritagonist) to perform the same part in all three plays of the Trilogy, and at the same time to retain the leading characters for the best performer :[1]

Protagonist, Agamemnon, the guard, the herald.

Deuteragonist, Casandra, Ægisthus.

Tritagonist, Clytæmnestra.

The middle play of the *Orestea*, which is known as the *Choëphorœ* or "bearers of funeral libations," is divided by a total change of scene into two distinct parts. The scene of the first act, which terminates at v. 651, is a desolate tract of country at some distance from the city, perhaps hilly, and certainly provided with brushwood for the concealment of Orestes and Pylades. The central object is the mound which indicates the tomb of Agamemnon. The play begins with the entrance of Orestes and his friend from the left side-door, and the former speaks the prologue, which has come down to us considerably mutilated. The

See Müller, *Hist. Lit. Gr.* i. p. 406.

chorus enters from the right parodos at v. 10. In the
present state of the text we cannot say whether they sang
any anapæsts as they advanced to the thymele, but the
commencement of their first choral song (vv. 22 sqq.) seems
to imply that they had previously been silent. Although
Orestes is made to suppose (v. 16) that he sees Electra along
with the chorus, it is clear that this is only intended to
indicate a natural illusion on his part. For Electra must
enter by the right-hand side-door, where the *periactos*
perhaps represented a distant view of the royal palace, and
her entrance is marked by her address to the chorus in
vv. 84 sqq. The maidens of the chorus are sent to accompany Electra (v. 23: χοᾶν πρόπομπος. v. 85: τῆσδε προσ-
τροπῆς ἐμοὶ πομποί) and to perform certain acts of public
mourning (vv. 24, 423 sqq.), but they do not themselves
make the offering; this is performed by Electra (v. 129),
who is therefore alone on the stage. She is joined by
Orestes (v. 212), who appears suddenly from his place of
concealment, and although Pylades is not mentioned till
v. 561, there is no reason to doubt that he re-enters with
his friend. They both leave the stage by the right-hand
door before the first stasimon (vv. 585 sqq.). For it seems
absurd to refer τούτῳ in v. 583,

τὰ δ' ἄλλα τούτῳ δεῦρ' ἐποπτεῦσαι λέγω
ξιφηφόρους ἀγῶνας ὀρθώσαντί μοι,

to Pylades. The very terms of the phraseology, compared
with the address at the beginning of the play,

Ἑρμῆ χθόνιε, πατρῷ' ἐποπτεύων κράτη,

show that the necropolis was adorned with a statue of the
infernal Mercury, to whom there are frequent allusions in
the course of the Tragedy. It is probable that Electra does
not accompany her brother and his friend, but that she and the
chorus make their exit at the end of the stasimon (v. 651).
Both the stage and the orchestra being now clear, the
scene is entirely changed, and both the periacti are turned.
That on the left represents a distant view of the grave of
Agamemnon, that on the right the city of Argos; and the
scene itself shows us the royal palace, with a lodging for

strangers to the left. Orestes and Pylades enter by the left side-door. Clytæmnestra comes forth to greet them from the centre door of the palace, and sends them into the strangers' lodgings. The re-entrance of the chorus by the left-hand parodos,—for they must be supposed to come directly from the grave to which they refer (v. 722),—is indicated by a few anapæsts (vv. 719—733). As Clytæmnestra manifestly returns to the palace after her brief conversation with Orestes, and as she sends Cilissa to Ægisthus (v. 734), the old nurse must come forth from the centre door, and make her exit by the right-hand side-door leading to the city. By the same door Ægisthus enters after the second stasimon (v. 838), and betakes himself to the strangers' apartments, where he is at once put to death by Orestes. From the words of the chorus in vv. 872, 873,

$$\text{ἀποσταθῶμεν πράγματος τελουμένου}$$
$$\text{ὅπως δοκῶμεν τῶνδ' ἀναίτιαι κακῶν}$$
$$\text{εἶναι. μάχης γὰρ δὴ κεκύρωται τέλος,}$$

it may fairly be inferred that the choreutæ take refuge and conceal themselves in the parodos until the end of the interview between Clytæmnestra and the matricide. The servant of course comes forth from the strangers' apartments and knocks at the centre door, and Clytæmnestra comes from the house at his summons, just as Orestes rushes out in pursuit of her (v. 892). After Orestes has dragged his mother into the strangers' lodging in order to slay her beside Ægisthus (vv. 894, 904), the chorus reappears and sings the stasimon (vv. 931—972) at the thymele. It is clear that the corpses of the queen and her paramour are exhibited to the spectators, when Orestes reappears, and says (v. 973),

$$\text{.ἴδεσθε χώρας τὴν διπλῆν τυραννίδα—}$$

but it is not so certain in what manner this is effected. As no mention is made of the chorus entering the guests' chambers, where the murders have been perpetrated, and as Orestes clearly intends a public display, we must infer that the eccyclema was not used, but that the bodies were

brought out on a bier, as the bodies of Eteocles and
Polyneices were paraded in the *Seven against Thebes*. It is
not only clear from the question of the chorus (v. 1051) and
from the words of Orestes (v. 1061) that the phantom forms
of the Erinyes are visible to Orestes alone; but the care,
which is taken in the following play, not to exhibit the
Eumenides until the audience have been wound up to the
highest point of expectation, precludes the supposition that
the effects of that play would be anticipated by the premature
introduction of the chorus, from which it bears its name.
Orestes leaves the stage by the left side-door, and the
chorus proceeds to the right-hand parodos, reciting the concluding anapæsts.

In the *Eumenides*, as in the *Choëphoræ*, there are two
distinct acts, each with its appropriate scenery. The scene
of the first act (vv. 1—234) is the temple of Apollo at
Delphi. The centre door on the stage represents the main
entrance of the temple, the interior of which is displayed by
the eccyclema after v. 93. The right-hand door is marked
by a sacred grove, through which Apollo retires after
dismissing Orestes. On the other side there may have been
the dwelling of the Pythia, from which she enters at the
beginning of the play, and to which she returns after the
prologue. It is probable that the neighbourhood of Delphi,
to which the Pythia alludes in her opening address, is
depicted in the scenery. And there is every reason to
conclude that the altars or statues of the deities mentioned
by her also adorned the stage. The time intended is the
morning after the arrival of Orestes, who has come straight
from Argos (cf. v. 282: ποταίνιον γὰρ ὄν κ.τ.λ.), followed by
the Furies, and whom Apollo has purified while his
persecutors slept. After the prologue, the eccyclema rolls
out the chorus who are sleeping round the altar,[1] the hero
appears on the stage between Apollo and Hermes, and the
latter accompanies him, as he sets forth on a long journey
by sea and land, before he reaches Athens the object of his

---

[1] Bötticher has made the costume of the chorus in this play the
subject of a special dissertation (*die Furienmaske im Trauerspiel und
auf den Bildwerken der alten Griechen*, Weimar, 1801, *Kleine Schriften,*

wishes (vv. 75 sqq.). While Orestes and Hermes leave the stage by the left-hand side-door, Apollo retires into the grove, for of course he cannot appear in his temple till v. 179, when he expels the intruders. After the stage is cleared (v. 94), the ἀναπίεσμα immediately exhibits the apparition of Clytæmnestra's ghost. That the sleeping chorus had been visible while Apollo was speaking is clear from the words of the god (v. 67: τάσδε τὰς μαργοὺς ὁρᾷς); and that the interior was shown by the eccyclema, perhaps by a two-fold evolution, is distinctly stated by the scholiast, who says, δευτέρα γίνεται φαντασία· στραφέντα γὰρ μηχανήματα ἔνδηλα ποιεῖ τὰ κατὰ τὸ μαντεῖον ὡς ἔχει. The words of Apollo, v. 201, τοσοῦτο μῆκος ἔκτεινον λόγου, show that they were still in the temple in spite of his order to quit it, and it is plain that they do not depart until they have said (229, 230):

> ἐγὼ δ', ἄγει γὰρ αἷμα μητρῷον δίκας,
> μέτειμι τόνδε φῶτα κακκυνηγέτις.

And they immediately leave the stage in single file by the left-hand door by which Orestes and Hermes had made their exit. Apollo, after reciting his three lines (232—234), returns to his temple, the eccyclema is withdrawn, and the whole scene is changed.

Between the first and second acts we must suppose a considerable interval of time, during which Orestes has traversed many a region by land and sea (v. 240: ὅμοια χέρσον καὶ θάλασσαν ἐκπερῶν, cf. v. 77), and has visited many nations as a purified suppliant (vv. 284—286). It has generally been supposed that the scene represents the temple of Minerva

---

1. pp. 189—277), and he has given two pictures of the theatrical Fury, one representing all the repulsive and loathsome features which seem to have belonged to the Æschylean chorus, and the other exhibiting the usual type of theatrical beauty and splendid costume, but indicated as a minister of vengeance by the serpent-locks, and by the serpent and torch which she carries in her hands. He believes (p. 138 [271]) that the latter was the only personification of the Fury admitted on the stage after the time of Pericles and Phidias.

Polias at Athens.[1] But it is manifest that during the
latter part of the act the scene is the Areopagus, and there
is no indication of another change of scene.   There must,
however, have been a temple and statue of Minerva in the
Areopagus.   For Minerva is made to say to Orestes (v. 474),
ἱκέτης προσῆλθες καθαρὸς ἀβλαβὴς δόμοις, Apollo's injunction
to the fugitive is (v. 80), μολὼν δὲ Παλλάδος ποτὶ πτόλιν ἵζου
παλαιὸν ἄγκαθεν λαβὼν βρέτας, and he is described by the
goddess (v. 409) as βρέτας τοὐμὸν τῷδ' ἐφημένῳ ξένῳ.   The
most probable solution is that the poet supposes Orestes to
have reached the temple of Ἀθηνᾶ Ἀρεία, to whom he was
said to have consecrated an altar in the Areopagus on his
acquittal.[2]   The scene then represents the Areopagus, with
a distant view of Athens, certainly with a statue, and probably with a temple of Minerva.   As Orestes says (v. 256)
ἥκω, " I am come," it is reasonable to conclude that he is
seen near the statue of the goddess as soon as the scene is
shifted, and the chorus re-enters by the left-hand parodos
as soon as he has uttered his short prayer (v. 244).   After
the stasimon, preceded by a few anapæsts, as the chorus pass
from the part of the orchestra immediately below the stage
to the thymele (vv. 307—396), Minerva appears on the
balcony of the stage, as though borne through the air on a
chariot of clouds.   This is shown by her own words (vv.
403—405) :

> ἦλθον ἄτρυτον πόδα
> πτερῶν ἄτερ ῥοιβδοῦσα κόλπον αἰγίδος
> κώλοις ἀκμαίοις τόνδ' ἐπιζεύξασ' ὄχον.

If she had come in an ordinary chariot it would have been
needless to say that she came without wings, or that she
used her ægis to make a flapping as birds do with their
wings (cf. Soph. Antig. 1004: πτερῶν γὰρ ῥοῖβδος οὐκ ἄσημος
ἦν).   She clearly means that she rode upon the wings of the
wind.   After the explanation with the chorus and Orestes,
Minerva, who had descended to the stage, proceeds on foot

---

[1] This is the opinion of Droysen, Donner, Genelli, Müller, Schömann
and Hermann.   Geppert and Schönborn maintain the view adopted in
the text.

[2] Pausan. I. 28, § 5: καὶ βωμός ἐστιν Ἀθηνᾶς Ἀρείας ὃν ἀνέθηκεν
ἀποφυγὼν τὴν δίκην.

by the right-hand door to summon the judges for the trial·
(v. 489). The stasimon follows (vv. 490—505). And
then Minerva returns from the right with the twelve judges
who take their seats either on the steps of her temple or on
seats before the centre door, while Apollo appears from the
left to support his suppliant. The judges give their votes
separately in the twelve intervals of the couplets spoken by
the chorus and Apollo (vv. 711—733). Orestes is acquitted,
and departs by the left-hand door, as soon as he has expressed his gratitude and bound his countrymen by a promise of future friendliness (vv. 754—777). As he takes
no notice of Apollo, that divinity must have departed after
the declaration of the verdict in 752, 753. It may be presumed that the Areopagus retain their places till the procession at the end of the play. When Minerva has succeeded in allaying the wrath of the Eumenides, she takes
leave of the chorus (v. 1003 : χαίρετε χύμεῖς), and says that
she must go before to prepare their abode for them; and
she leaves the stage by the right-hand door after making
her concluding speech (vv. 1021—1031). The πρόπομποι
then make their appearance through the right-hand parodos,
and lead the chorus from the orchestra by the same door.
As they depart, the Areopagites leave the stage in solemn
procession.

The distribution of the parts in the second and third
plays of the Trilogy must have been as follows:

Choëphorœ.

Protagonist, Orestes.
Deuteragonist, Electra, Ægisthus, Pylades.
Tritagonist, Clytæmnestra.

Eumenides.

Protagonist, Orestes.
Deuteragonist, Apollo.
Tritagonist, Pythia, Clytæmnestra, Minerva.

The Trilogy was succeeded by a satyrical drama, the *Proteus*
which had some reference to the adventures of Menelaus,
alluded to in the *Agamemnon* (vv. 674 sqq.). The manner in

which the complete chorus of forty-eight was made available for the separate choruses of the four plays, is thus stated by C. O. Müller.[1] The *Agamemnon* had a chorus of twelve senators, as appears from their conference in vv. 1319—1342; the *Eumenides* had a chorus of fifteen, as appears from the most probable arrangement of the μυγμὸς διπλοῦς of v. 125, as seven repetitions of the word λαβέ, each spoken by a pair of choreutæ, the imperative φράζου being uttered by the coryphæus; the chorus of the *Choëphorœ* had probably this larger number; and this would leave two ζυγά, or ranks of three each, for the satyric drama. It is probable that the chorus of old men from the *Agamemnon* appeared as the Areopagites in the *Eumenides*, and the chorus of the *Choëphorœ* constituted the festive procession at the end of the last play in the Trilogy.

We have examined the details of the representation of these three plays at some length, because, taken together they furnish the most complete specimen of a Greek dramatic entertainment which has come down to us. Indeed, with the exception of the satyrical drama, which served as an after-piece to the Trilogy, we have here before us a perfect sample of the elaborate theatrical exhibitions, which were provided for the amusement of the Athenians at their Bacchic festivals. It will be seen that no regard was paid to the unities of time and place. The second and third plays are respectively broken into two distinct parts by the change of the scene, and the first play, which has no change of scene, supposes, like the third, a considerable interval of time between the first and second acts. And while Æschylus has thus allowed himself a full latitude in dealing with space and time, he exhibits in this, the last of his dramatic works, a full acquaintance with all the improvements of the stage. The three actors are all put in requisition, and the chorus, originally one and undivided, is broken up into sections for the sake of the separate plays.

Of the other tragedies of Æschylus, the *Prometheus* alone requires a special notice of its mode of representation. It differs from all other plays by making no use of the stage. The action proceeds entirely on the balconies above the first

[1] *Eumeniden*, pp. 75 sqq.

story. The scene represents a desolate and rocky region, not far from the shore of Ocean at the extremity of the world. The centre door is blocked up by the representation of a craggy mountain. To the summit of this (v. 142 : τῆσδε φάραγγος σκοπέλοις ἐν ἄκροις) Vulcan, attended by Strength and Force, is engaged in fastening the form of Prometheus. On the right-hand *periactos* there is a representation of the sea, and a more distant part of the coast is represented on the left. There can be little doubt[1] that Prometheus himself was represented by a lay figure, so contrived that an actor standing behind the pictorial mountain could speak through the mask. No protagonist could have been expected to submit to the restraint of such an attitude throughout the whole of the play, to say nothing of the catastrophe at the end, when the rocks fall asunder, and Prometheus is dashed down into Tartarus.[2]

Vulcan and his attendants leave the balcony by one of the doors in the διστεγία which lead to it (v. 87), and Prometheus is left alone till the entrance of the chorus indicated by the anapæsts recited by him (vv. 120 sqq.). A question arises, whether the chorus, which comes through the air, borne on clouds, like Minerva in the *Eumenides* (cf. v. 135 with *Eumen.* 405), and which must have appeared at first on the balcony, remains there throughout the play,[3] or descends to its proper place in the orchestra at v. 277, where their anapæsts indicate a movement on their part. We have no hesitation in adopting the latter view of the case, for the following reasons. (1) The balcony would not suffice for the regular evolutions of a chorus, which in this, as in other plays, has to perform antistrophic songs. (2) As Oceanus appears in the same way and from the same side as the chorus, there would be no room for both of the machines on the balcony. (3) A Greek play in which the chorus never entered the orchestra would be an unparalleled solœcism. If it is urged on the contrary that Prometheus on the top of the rock would be too distant to

<hr />

[1] See Hermann's note, p. 55.
[2] Schömann, *des Æschylos gefesselter Prometheus*, p. 87, believes that Prometheus was represented by an actor throughout the play.
[3] This is Schönborn's opinion, p. 292.

converse with the chorus at the thymele, it may be answered that the audience are still more distant, and yet they are supposed to hear all his words. And if reference is made to the warning of Mercury (v. 1060),

$$\mu\epsilon\tau\acute{a} \ \pi ov \ \chi\omega\rho\epsilon\hat{\iota}\tau' \ \acute{\epsilon}\kappa \ \tau\hat{\omega}\nu\delta\epsilon \ \tau\acute{o}\pi\omega\nu$$
$$\mu\grave{\eta} \ \phi\rho\acute{\epsilon}\nu as \ \acute{\upsilon}\mu\hat{\omega}\nu \ \acute{\eta}\lambda\iota\theta\iota\acute{\omega}\sigma\eta$$
$$\beta\rho ov\tau\hat{\eta}s \ \mu\acute{\upsilon}\kappa\eta\mu' \ \acute{a}\tau\acute{\epsilon}\rho a\mu\nu ov,$$

as showing that they must have been near Prometheus, we reply that it indicates, on the contrary, that they were not within the immediate sphere of the danger, for he would not have used the plural τόπων in that case, and he would have indicated even a worse risk than that of losing their senses owing to the crash of the thunder.

But although the chorus must be placed in the orchestra, all the actors speak from the upper platform. Oceanus remains seated on his courser in the clouds, and rides away upon it when his selfish fears are excited (v. 396). Io, who had been wandering on the sea-shore near the mountain (v. 575 : πλανᾷ τε νῆστιν ἀνὰ τὰν παραλίαν ψάμμον), enters from the left on the balcony which represents the summit of these rugged rocks ; for she speaks of casting herself down from them in her despair (vv. 747 sqq.) :

$$\tau\acute{\iota} \ \delta\hat{\eta}\tau' \ \acute{\epsilon}\mu o\grave{\iota} \ \zeta\hat{\eta}\nu \ \kappa\acute{\epsilon}\rho\delta os, \ \grave{a}\lambda\lambda' \ o\grave{\upsilon}\kappa \ \acute{\epsilon}\nu \ \tau\acute{a}\chi\epsilon\iota$$
$$\acute{\epsilon}\rho\rho\iota\psi' \ \acute{\epsilon}\mu a\upsilon\tau\grave{\eta}\nu \ \tau\hat{\eta}\sigma\delta' \ \grave{a}\pi\grave{o} \ \sigma\tau\acute{\upsilon}\phi\lambda ov \ \pi\acute{\epsilon}\tau\rho as ;$$

In the same manner Mercury enters from the same side ; for there is no reference whatever, as in the case of Oceanus and the chorus, to his having flown thither through the air, and he is expressly called " the running-footman of Jove" (v. 941: τὸν Διὸς τρόχιν) ; and as Prometheus sees him at once, he cannot be on the stage below. It is clear that the chorus leaves the orchestra by the right-hand parodos, just as Mercury quits the balcony by a side-door to the left, probably veiled by a peak of the mountain, and Prometheus is left alone to describe the coming storm in the splendid anapaests which conclude the play and accompany the exodus of the chorus. Then, it may be presumed, scenic rocks fall asunder, and the figure representing Prometheus descends with them below the stage.

As a specimen of the manner in which Sophocles, the perfecter of the Greek drama, placed his Tragedies on the stage, it will be sufficient to examine the latest of his plays, the *Œdipus at Colonos*.

The scene, which remains the same throughout the play, is minutely described in the opening verses. Œdipus entering from behind the left-hand *periactos*, which represents the road to Thebes, asks his guide Antigone (vv. 1, 2):

> τέκνον τυφλοῦ γέροντος 'Αντιγόνη, τίναˉ
> χώρους ἀφίγμεθ', ἢ τίνων ἀνδρῶν πόλ·

"Child of a blind old man, Antigone,
What lands, what city are we come unto?"

and she replies (vv. 14—20):

> πάτερ ταλαίπωρ' Οἰδίπου, πύργοι μέν, οἳ
> πόλιν στέγουσιν, ὡς ἀπ' ὀμμάτων, πρόσω·
> χῶρος δ' ὅδ' ἱρός, ὡς σάφ' εἰκάσαι, βρύων
> δάφνης, ἐλαίας, ἀμπέλου· πυκνόπτεροι δ'
> εἴσω κατ' αὐτὸν εὐστομοῦσ' ἀηδόνες·
> οὗ κῶλα κάμψον τοῦδ' ἐπ' ἀξέστου πέτρου.
> μακρὰν γάρ, ὡς γέροντι, προὐστάλης ὁδόν.

"O woe-worn father Œdipus, the towers
That girt the city, as mine eyes inform me,
Are still far off: but where we stand the while
A consecrated grove displays itself,
Thick set with bay-trees, olive-trees, and vines;
And from within, with closely ruffled plumes,
The nightingales make sweetest melody.
Then sit thee down on this rough stone: thine age
May hardly brook such lengthened pilgrimage."

From this it is clear, that the centre of the stage represents this grove of the Eumenides as surrounded by a low dry-stone dyke, on which the blind wanderer takes his seat (v. 19). The entrance to the grove substitutes brazen steps for the stones of the wall (v. 57 : ὃν δ' ἐπιστείβεις τόπον χθονὸς καλεῖται τῆσδε χαλκόπους ὁδός. v. 192 : αὐτοῦ· μηκέτι τοῦδ' ἀντιπέτρου βήματος ἔξω πόδα κλίνῃς). In the immediate neighbourhood of the grove was seen the pool, against which Œdipus is warned by the chorus (vv. 155, sqq.). The right-hand *periactos* exhibited a view of Colonos, and near it was seen, probably as a picture, the statue of the hero of the place (v. 59: τόνδ' ἱππότην Κολωνόν). In the interval between this and the grove the scenery gave a distant view of Athens. To the left of the grove we may presume that there was a perspective representation of the country of Attica between Colonos and the Theban borders, from which Œdipus and his daughter have travelled. All five doors of the stage must have been used in the course of the piece.

After Œdipus has taken his seat on the fence of the sacred enclosure, a man of Colonos enters from the right, and informs him that he has violated holy ground. The stranger, however, does not venture to remove him, but departs by the door by which he had entered, to summon the chorus, and to bear the tidings to Theseus (v. 298). When he has made his exit, Antigone leads her father quite within the grove (v. 113: καί μ' ἐξ ὁδου πόδα κρύψον κατ' ἄλσος). The chorus then enters by the right-hand parodos, and though in search of Œdipus, it does not mount the stage. For when the blind king comes forth from the grove (v. 138), the chorus is engaged in spying round the outside of the enclosure (v. 55: λεύσσων περὶ πᾶν τέμενος), and it addresses him as, still at a distance, though he is standing on the narrow stage (v. 162: μετάσταθ', ἀπόβαθι· πολλὰ κέλευθος ἐρατύει· κλύεις, ὦ πολύμοχθ' ἀλᾶτα). The conference between Œdipus and the chorus is interrupted by the unexpected arrival of Ismene (v. 310), who comes mounted on horseback (v. 312), and accompanied by a faithful domestic (v. 334). It may be considered doubtful whether the horse is seen by the audience.[1] The mention of the servant seems to be introduced because he is there to hold the horse after she has dismounted, and the interval between v. 310 when she is first seen, and v. 324 when she first speaks, together with the momentary difficulty in recognizing her (v. 315 sqq.), may be best explained by the supposition that she rides into the orchestra, leaves her horse with the servant,

---

[1] Schönborn says (p. 280): "Den Anblick des Rosses den Zuschauern zu gewähren, dazu liegt kein Motiv vor." Kolster, on the other hand, justly remarks (*Pref.* p. xi): "Schönborn musste wenigstens sagen warum der Dichter denn Ismene von der Schwester zu Ross *sehen* lässt, wenn sie nicht so auftreten soll; Sophokles wirft doch dergleichen Worte nicht umsonst hin."

(who leads it out) and then mounts the stage. It may fairly be inferred that when Ismene retires from the stage to pour forth the libations on the other side of the grove (v. 505 : τοὔκειθεν ἄλσος τοῦδε), she makes her exit by the middle door on the left. For she is seized by Creon on his way from Thebes, though the ordinary route to Bœotia is not that which Ismene is supposed to have taken, otherwise she would not have needed the guidance of the chorus. Now it is expressly intimated that the road from Thebes branched off in two directions not far from Colonos (v. 900). And it is to be understood that Creon had diverged from the straight road on his approach to the sacred grove in search of Œdipus, so as to pass through the spot where Ismene was occupied in her pious offices.

As Theseus leaves Œdipus to the care of the chorus (v. 653), it is quite clear that the old men of Colonos cannot be passive spectators of Creon's outrage, and the text shows that some at least of the choreutæ mount the stage and lay hands on the Theban prince ; for he says to them (v. 855), μὴ ψαύειν λέγω, and the choir-leader replies, οὔτοι σ' ἀφήσω.[1]

---

[1] Kolster maintains that the struggle takes place on the steps leading to the orchestra, through which Creon had to return. He says (p. 60): "If any one denies his appearance in the orchestra because he does not come on horseback or in a chariot, he ought to remark, first, that he comes not alone, but accompanied by numerous attendants, v. 723, οὐκ ἄνευ πομπῶν; and then, that though he comes expressly to carry off Œdipus, he does not at once address him, whom he would have been close to, if he had appeared on the stage, but speaks to the chorus in twelve long trimeters, and obviously opens a safe way to the stage by his conciliatory expressions. It is not till v. 740 that he directs his speech to Œdipus; and when his overtures are rejected, he changes his tone, and Œdipus learns with horror that Creon has already got possession of Ismene and is intending to carry off his other daughter also. Hereupon Œdipus implores the aid of the chorus, which at once forbids the meditated violence; Creon however beckons to his attendants to carry off the maiden, whom he has obviously seized with his own hands; these followers, who had been left in the orchestra, mount the steps and compel the chorus to give way, in spite of their protestations against a wrong which they are unable to prevent (v. 839: μὴ 'πίτασσ' & μὴ κρατεῖς). It is therefore a case in which the chorus and actors come into personal contact (Geppert, Ueb. d. Eingänge, p. 30). It is possible to explain particular expressions of the chorus by the supposition that different choreutæ are

The main body of the chorus, remaining in the orchestra, call loudly for Theseus, and he comes hastily from sacrificing in the neighbouring temple of Neptune, and therefore through the middle door on the right. The armed attendants of Creon have already left the stage with Antigone, probably by the door by which they had entered. And while Theseus enters into angry conversation with Creon, who had been detained by the choreutæ, he sends word to his followers to march off to the meeting of the road to Thebes and there to intercept the runaways. There is no reason to suppose that the horsemen and foot-soldiers of Theseus (v. 899) pass over the stage. It would be more natural to imagine them as pursuing their march on the other side of the sacred grove which forms the centre of the scene. As Creon is to be the guide of Theseus (v. 1025), they must leave the stage by the middle door on the left by which the former had entered, and of course Theseus re-enters (v. 1099) by the same opening.

It is stated (v. 1158) that Polyneices was a suppliant at the altar of Neptune, where Theseus was sacrificing when he was interrupted by the outrage of Creon. He therefore

---

speaking; but the only way to conceive the character of the separate words is to consider them as induced by the course of the action. How could we explain the decided expressions of v. 824

χώρει, ξέν, ἔξω θᾶσσον· οὔτε γὰρ τὰ νῦν
δίκαια πράσσεις, οὔθ' ἃ πρόσθεν εἴργασαι,

immediately followed by the helpless τί δρᾶς, ξένε; of v. 829, and by the feeble declaration of v. 831, ὦ ξέν' οὐ δίκαια δρᾶς? How incongruous would be the threat of v. 839,

τί δρᾶς, ὦ ξέν'; οὐκ ἀφήσεις; τάχ' εἰς βάσανον εἶ χερῶν,

if Antigone had not been conducted through the orchestra. The silence of the chorus during the act of violence, vv. 844—847, is the consequence of their flight before Creon's myrmidons. After these have withdrawn (v. 856) Creon is left alone face to face with the chorus, and the words ἐπίσχες αὐτοῦ, ξένε, are easily explained, if the chorus thinks it can cut off his retreat (v. 857: οὔτοι σ' ἀφήσω). At this point the chorus must either be on the stage, of which I can find no trace, or by occupying the steps from the orchestra is cutting off Creon's retreat, in which case he must be intending to depart by way of the orchestra."

enters (v. 1249) by the middle door on the right, and makes his exit by the same way (v. 1447).

The three peals of thunder (vv. 1456, 1462, 1479) accompanied by lightning, which presage the death of Œdipus, must have been audible and visible to the spectators, and the βροντεῖον and κεραυνοσκοπεῖον could not have been used with greater effect. The mirrors of the latter may have been so arranged as to throw a glare of light on the chorus (v. 1477).

It is obvious that, with Œdipus leading the way, the two princesses, Theseus, and his attendants entered the sacred grove by the main doorway (v. 1555). Some little time is supposed to elapse before the messenger returns with his account of all that had happened (v. 1579). When his speech is ended, Theseus returns to the stage with the two princesses (v. 1670). And though Theseus promises (v. 1773) to comply with the request of Antigone to send her to Thebes, in order, if possible, to prevent the fratricidal strife of his two brothers, it does not follow that she and her sister leave the stage by the left-hand side-door, as though they departed immediately for their native city. It is more reasonable to suppose that they go with Theseus to Athens, and therefore make their exit in his company, by the middle door on the right.

It has been already mentioned that the remaining plays of Sophocles furnish only one example of a complete change of scenery, and only one of a partial change by the revolution of the left-hand *periactos*. The former case is that of the *Ajax*. In the first act of this play, the scene is laid in that part of the Greek encampment, which lies between the tent of Ajax and the shore (v. 192 : ἐφάλοις κλισίαις). The interior of the tent of Ajax is displayed by means of the eccyclema, and he is seen surrounded by the cattle which he had slain in his delusion (vv. 346 sqq.). He is rolled off the stage by the same means, for he says (x. 579), δῶμα πάκτου, and (v. 581), πύκαζε θᾶσσον. After the stasimon of the chorus (596—645), Ajax comes forth from his tent, and then departs by the right-hand side-door as though he was going to the sea (v. 654: πρός τε λουτρὰ καὶ παρακτίους λειμῶνας). The messenger enters (v. 719) by the left-hand side-door as

coming from the distant camp of the Greeks. Tecmessa
goes forth to meet him with Eurysaces (v. 787) from the
right-hand middle door, representing her own tent, and the
child re-enters by the same door, when Tecmessa leaves the
stage in pursuit of Ajax by the right-hand side-door. The
messenger of course returns through the left side-door, and
the chorus breaking up into the two hemichoria, in which
they reappear in the second act, leave the orchestra by both
parodi. The stage being cleared, the scenery is completely
changed, and we have now an unfrequented spot partially
covered with trees, which renders the search for the body of
Ajax more difficult. Tecmessa stumbles upon it (v. 891)
immediately on her re-entrance, and it may be presumed
therefore that Ajax falls before the centre door, probably
behind a tree which masked that entrance. The other
persons who enter in the second act, Teucer, Menelaus,
Agamemnon, and Ulysses, come and return by the left-hand
side-door. It is clear from v. 1115 that Menelaus is accompanied by at least one herald, and this functionary attends
Agamemnon, whom he goes to fetch. This appears from
vv. 1116 and 1319, and justifies Martin's conjectures of σοῦ
τοῦδ' ὁμαίμονος for τοῦ σοῦ θ' ὁμαίμονος, in v. 1312. With
regard to the only change of the left-hand *periactos*, of which
Sophocles furnishes an example, and which occurs in the
Œdipus Tyrannus, it is obvious that in the first part of the
play the left-hand entrance must indicate the road to Delphi,
and probably the left-hand *periactos* gave a distant view of Parnassus, to which the chorus alludes (vv. 463 sqq.). But as the
messenger from Corinth enters by the same door on the left
(v. 924), it is clear that the *periactos* must be turned, so as
to exhibit a view of Cithæron or some other indications of
the road to the Isthmus.

It has been already mentioned that, in the extant plays of
Euripides, there is no instance of a complete change of scene,
and it would almost seem as though he had wished to make
up for that complication of incident, that succession of
plots to which reference has been made in a former chapter,
by a more rigid adherence to the unity of place than his
great contemporaries had thought necessary. There are,
however, several examples of a change of the left-hand

periactos, which indicated the region from which the actor, coming from a distance, was supposed to enter the stage. For instance, in the *Orestes*, the left-hand *periactos* must, in the first instance, represent generally the road to foreign parts by which Menelaus enters on his return from Troy (v. 356); but it must be turned so as to exhibit a view of part of the city, when Pylades enters (v. 729), for he says:

θᾶσσον ἤ μ' ἐχρῆν προβαίνων ἱκόμην δι' ἄστεως.

In the *Andromache* the left-hand *periactos* must have represented at the beginning of the play the road to Pharsalus, for Peleus is supposed to dwell there (v. 22); it must have represented a different direction, the road to Lacedæmon, in 746, 879, 1000, for Menelaus departs for Sparta, Orestes is on his way from the south to the shrine of Dodona, and Hermione departs in the same direction; and in 1069 the messenger comes from Delphi, so that there must have been an exhibition of all three faces of the *periactos*. In the *Supplices* the left *periactos* indicates the road to Thebes from which the herald comes and to which he returns (v. 584); thither Theseus goes (v. 597 cf. 637); from thence come the messenger (v. 639) and the seven corpses; also Theseus on his return (cf. 838). This *periactos*, however, is turned to indicate the road to Argos by which Iphis comes in search of Evadne (v. 1034). In the *Electra*, the left-hand *periactos* at first represents the road to Delphi by which Orestes and Pylades make their appearance; but as Electra's husband makes his exit by the same side in order to go to Lacedæmon, there must be a change of the side-scene for that purpose.

As a sample of the manner in which Euripides put his Tragedies on the stage, it will be sufficient to examine the *Bacchæ*, which is not only the most Dionysiac, but also one of the latest and most elaborate of his plays. Euripides, however, has left us, in addition to his Tragedies, a regular Satyric drama, and two tragi-comedies, which served the same purpose in a Tetralogy; and we must consider also the mode of representation in these two cases.

The scene in the *Bacchæ* represents the palace of Pentheus (vv. 60, 646) in the citadel at Thebes (653). Although there may have been some indications of towers and other

fortifications as this last passage shows (cf. v. 172 : ἐπύργωσ'
ἄστυ Θηβαίων τόδε), it is clear that the centre of the scene
representing the palace itself exhibited a Doric façade with
columns (591) and a frieze (1214). On the right of the
palace, i.e. on the side leading to the city, there may have
been a distant view of the oracular seat of Teiresias (347 :
ἐλθὼν δὲ θάκους τοῦδ' ἵν' οἰωνοσκόπει), and on the other side
was seen the sacred memorial of Semele, namely, the spot
where the smouldering ruins of her house stood, which
Cadmus had surrounded with a fence and made sacred, and
which Bacchus had enveloped in clusters of the mantling
vine :

> v. 6 : ὁρῶ δὲ μητρὸς μνῆμα τῆς κεραυνίας
> τόδ' ἐγγὺς οἴκων καὶ δόμων ἐρείπια
> τυφόμενα Δίου πυρὸς ἔτι ζῶσαν φλόγα
> ἀθάνατον "Ηρας μητέρ' εἰς ἐμὴν ὕβριν.
> αἰνῶ δὲ Κάδμον, ἄβατον ὃς πέδον τόδε
> τίθησι, θυγατρὸς σηκόν· ἀμπέλου δέ νιν
> πέριξ ἐγὼ 'κάλυψα βοτρυώδει χλόῃ.
>
> 596 : πῦρ οὐ λεύσσεις οὐδ' αὐγάζεις
> Σεμέλας ἱερὸν ἀμφὶ τάφον.

On the left of the palace, but in close contiguity to it (Jul.
Poll. IV. § 125 : εἱρκτὴ δὲ ἡ λαιά), and between it and a
κλίσιον representing the stable (v. 509 : ἱππικαῖς πέλας
φάτναισιν), was seen the entrance to a dark and gloomy
dungeon (v. 550 : σκοτίαις ἐν εἱρκταῖς. v. 611 : ἐς σκοτεινὰς
ὁρκάνας). On the extreme left the *periactos* indicated the
road to foreign and distant parts, and on the right the
periactos showed a view of Cithæron. If the city of Thebes
was at all indicated it must have been between the right-
hand *periactos* and the palace, in the same part of the scene
where the auspicial abode of Teiresias was represented. That
the road to Cithæron did not pass through the city is clear
from v. 840, where Pentheus asks,

> καὶ πῶς δι' ἄστεως εἶμι Καδμείους λαθών;

and Dionysus answers,

> ὁδοὺς ἐρήμους ἴμεν· ἐγὼ δ' ἡγήσομαι.

If the city was seen at all it must have been that part of
Thebes which lay in the direction of the gate called *Electra*

(v. 781 : στεῖχ' ἐπ' Ἠλέκτρας ἰὼν πύλας). The only change in this scenery which is required by the action of the play is the downfal and conflagration of the εἰρκτή in which Dionysus is imprisoned. It has been mentioned already that this εἰρκτή and the adjoining κλίσιον stood immediately to the left of the palace, and therefore between it and the monument of Semele. According to the description in the play, the architrave of this building falls asunder, and the columns are thrown down by the god as he rushes forth (590 : ἴδετε λάϊνα κίοσιν ἔμβολα διάδρομα τάδε). At the same time a flame rises from the sacred tomb of Semele and seems to consume the adjoining edifice (vv. 596 sqq., and cf. 623 : καὶ μητρὸς τάφῳ πῦρ ἀνῆψεν). How this was managed does not appear. Probably some light woodwork was allowed to fall, and a smoke was raised at the same time. We are not to conclude from the expectations of the chorus (v. 588 : τάχα τὰ Πενθέως μέλαθρα διατινάξεται πεσήμασιν), that the central building, the palace of Pentheus himself, is involved in this ruin and conflagration. On the contrary, we must conclude that, though shaken, it remains standing. For Dionysus summons Pentheus to come forth from his palace (v. 914 : ἔξιθι πάροιθε δωμάτων), and, at the end of the play, distinct reference is made to the triglyphs of the frieze to which the head of the supposed lion is to be affixed according to the oldest mode of adorning the Zophorus (v. 1212 sqq.).

> αἱρέσθω λαβὼν
> πηκτῶν πρὸς οἴκους κλιμάκων προσαμβάσεις
> ὡς πασσαλεύσῃ κρᾶτα τριγλύφοις τόδε
> λέοντος, ὃν πάρειμι θηρεύσας ἐγώ.

Cf. 1238 sqq. :

> φέρω δ' ἐν ὠλέναισιν, ὡς ὁρᾷς, τάδε
> λαβοῦσα τἀριστεῖα σοῖσι πρὸς δόμοις
> ὡς ἂν κρεμάσθῃ.

When therefore Dionysus says (v. 633), δώματ' ἔρρηξεν χαμᾶζε συντεθράνωται δ' ἅπαν, he refers only to the prison, for at the very time he makes this statement he says that he has come forth from the house (636 : ἥσυχος δ' ἐκβὰς ἐγὼ δωμάτων ἥκω πρὸς ὑμᾶς); that he hears the foot-fall of Pentheus within his palace (638 : ψοφεῖ γοῦν ἀρβύλη δόμων

z

ἔσω); and that he will soon come forth to the vestibule (ἐς προνώπι᾽ αὐτίχ᾽ ἥκει).

The progress of the action and the entrances and exits of the performers are easily described. At the opening of the play Dionysus is supposed to come from distant regions; he enters by the left-hand *periactos*, and the chorus, who came from Asia with him, appear after the prologue, by the corresponding *parodos* (v. 65). As the god says that he is going to Cithæron to join his worshippers there, he must cross the stage and make his exit (64) by the right-hand *periactos*. After the first choral song (170) Teiresias enters from the city, i. e. by the right side-door, and summons Cadmus, who comes forth from the middle door, or from the palace (178). As Pentheus has been abroad, he must make his first entrance, like Dionysus, from the left *periactos* (215). Cadmus and Teiresias leave the stage by the right *periactos* (369), and by the same entrance the satellites of Pentheus, who had remained on the stage during the chorus, appear (434), bringing Dionysus with them. At the end of the act (518) the god is conveyed to the prison, which, as has been mentioned, was to the left of the palace. And it appears from v. 616 that Pentheus accompanies him for the purpose of putting on the chains with his own hands. There was obviously a passage from the prison to the palace, and Dionysus (603, cf. 635), and afterwards Pentheus (652) come forth from the centre door. By the same door the king (846) and afterwards the god (861, cf. 929), leave the stage to equip Pentheus in his bacchic attire. Of course they reappear by the centre door (912), and depart by the right-hand *periactos* (976) on their way to Cithæron. The messenger naturally enters (1025) by the same *periactos*, and it may be concluded that he goes into the palace (1152). From the right *periactos*, we have the successive entrances of Agave with the head of her son (1166), and of Cadmus with the corpse of Pentheus borne after him by his attendants (1216). As Dionysus declares himself at the end of the play in his divine character, it is obvious that he must appear surrounded by clouds on the balcony of the scene (1332). There is a lacuna in the text at this part, but there can be no doubt as to the nature of

the theophany. The god vanishes as he appeared; Agave
flees from the stage in the opposite direction to Cithæron
(v. 1383); and the rest of the actors enter the palace by
the middle door. The chorus, consisting of the Asiatic
followers of Dionysus leave the orchestra as they had entered
it, by the parodos on the left.

The following was obviously the distribution of the parts
among the three actors :

Protagonist : Dionysus, Teiresias, and the second messenger.

Deuteragonist : Cadmus, servant, first messenger.

Tritagonist : Pentheus, Agave.

The chorus, which consisted of fifteen women, was perhaps
intended to represent the fourteen γεραιραί of the Anthesteria, with the King-Archon's wife at their head.[1] They
were dressed in Asiatic style,[2] with bare feet,[3] and the Lydian
head-tire;[4] and they performed their dances, which, according to the metres of the choruses, had a peculiarly martial
character, to the accompaniment of some flute-players, and
probably beat time with timbrels and cymbals which they
carried in their hands.[5]

As the *Cyclops* of Euripides is the only complete satyrical
drama which has come down to us, we must briefly consider the distinctive features of its representation. The
scene of the play is the coast of Sicily near mount Ætna,
which was probably shown in the background. The middle
door was the entrance to the cavern in the rock, which
served as the dwelling of Polyphemus. The right-hand
periactos indicated a road leading to the interior of the
island, and that to the left showed the approach from the
coast. Between the latter and the cavern was the κλίσιον,
in this case representing the stable for the cattle and sheep
of the Cyclops—the αὖλις (v. 363) from which Ulysses and
his companions were about to furnish themselves with pro-

---

[1] F. G. Schoen, *de Person. Habitu in Eurip. Bacch.* p. 73.
[2] Id. p. 130.
[3] *Bacch.* 860: ἆρ' ἐν παννυχίοις χοροῖς θήσω ποτὲ λευκὸν πόδ' ανα-
βακχεύουσα.   Cf. *Cyclops,* 72: λευκόποδας Βάκχας ; see Schoen, pp.
155, 6.   [4] Schoen, p. 141.   [5] Id. p. 121.

z 2

visions (v. 222, cf. 188). It does not appear that any doors
were used except the centre door and the two *periacti ;* in
all probability a large portion of the centre of the stage was
occupied by the rocky abode of the Cyclops; and it is clear
that at the end Polyphemus climbs to the top of the rock,
i. e. to the balcony, by a narrow passage between his own
cavern and the left of the stage, so as to make his exit by
the left-hand door on the balcony, while Ulysses and his
friends leave the stage as they had entered it by the left-
hand *periactos.* For Ulysses says, v. 702, ἐγὼ δ᾽ ἐπ᾽ ἀκτὰς
εἶμι, and the Cyclops, threatening to smash his ship with a
fragment of the rock on which he was (v. 704: τῆσδ᾽
ἀποῤῥήξας πέτρας), adds (706) :

<blockquote>
ἄνω δ᾽ ἐπ᾽ ὄχθον εἶμι καίπερ ὢν τυφλός,
δι᾽ ἀμφιτρῆτος τῆσδε προσβαίνων ποδί.
</blockquote>

At the beginning of the piece Silenus comes forth from the
middle door to which he returns (in 174), to make his
second entry from the same place (188). Ulysses and his
sailors come in from the left, where the *periactos* gave a view
of the coast and of their ship (v. 85). The Cyclops enters
from the extreme right, and is some time in reaching the
centre of the stage, for he is seen at v. 193, and does not
speak till v. 203. The chorus of satyrs had of course
entered by the right-hand *parodos,* but the concluding
words show that they follow Ulysses by the left-hand exit
from the orchestra. The centre door serves for the exits
of the Cyclops (346), and Ulysses (355). The latter (375)
and the Cyclops with Silenus (503) come forth from the
middle door, and leave the stage by it at 607 and 590 respectively. By the same door Ulysses returns (624), goes in
(653), and reappears with the Cyclops and his sailors (663).

The chorus of satyrs, although it seems to take an active
part in the progress of the plot, manifestly does not leave the
orchestra, its proper place. The allusions in the *parodos* to
the pastoral employments of the satyrs, who had left the
service of Bacchus for that of the Cyclops, are probably
connected with the mimic action introduced into their *sicinnis.*
It is clear, however, that living sheep were introduced on
the stage (vv. 188, 224), and certain supernumeraries, who

acted as servants of the chorus and were perhaps also in
part at least attired as satyrs, drive the cattle into the side-
cavern or κλίσιον after the entrance of the chorus, for Silenus
says to the satyrs (v. 82),

σιγήσατ᾽, ὦ τέκν᾽, ἄντρα δ᾽ εἰς πετρηρεφῆ
ποίμνας ἀθροῖσαι προσπόλοις κελεύσατε,

and these mutes are dismissed from the stage with the order
χωρεῖτε. As only two or three of such attendants would
be required for the purpose of driving the sheep, it is unnecessary to suppose with Schönborn that the same supernumeraries reappeared as the sailors of Ulysses. There
would certainly not have been time for the complete change
of costume required, during the four lines spoken by Silenus
before he directly addresses the new-comers, who appear
with κρωσσοί suspended from their necks immediately after
the departure of the shepherds. The words of Ulysses
(100), Σατύρων πρὸς οἴκοις τόνδ᾽ ὅμιλον εἰσορῶ, are quite
intelligible on the supposition that the chorus was in the
orchestra near the front of the stage. And although he says
in the plural ἐκφέρετε (137, 162), it is clear that Silenus
alone enters the cavern, for he promises in his own person
(163: δράσω τάδ᾽, ὀλίγον φροντίσας γε δεσποτῶν), and claims
the reward for himself (192). The Cyclops on entering from the right addresses the chorus, because Silenus
has slunk away to the left with the Greek sailors. It is
true that the chorus offers to take a part in the good work
of blinding Polyphemus (471: φόνου γὰρ τοῦδε κοινωνεῖν
θέλω), but it is clear that they do not leave the orchestra
(635: ἡμεῖς μέν ἐσμεν μακρότερον πρὸ τῶν θυρῶν ἑστῶτες);
they excuse themselves with undisguised pusillanimity;
and Ulysses is obliged to rely on his own companions (650:
τοῖσι δ᾽ οἰκείοις φίλοις χρῆσθαί μ᾽ ἀνάγκη). When the deed
is done, the chorus, at a safe distance, gives ludicrous misdi-
rections to the blinded Cyclops, who knocks his head against
the rock as he turns suddenly to the right at their bidding
(v. 683).[1]

---

[1] Nauck reads οὐκέτι for οὐκ ἐμέ, in v. 564; but even without this
alteration there is no necessity for supposing that one of the satyrs is
on the stage.

That Polyphemus appeared as a giant is necessary to the plot of the piece, and something more than a cothurnus was required to give him such a height as would justify him in addressing Ulysses as ἀνθρωπίσκε (316). How the exaggeration of stature was managed does not appear, but the experience of our own pantomimes shows that a very little ingenuity would produce all the necessary results. One thing seems quite clear — that his enormous mask was rather of the comic than of the tragic pattern, and that he was represented with a ludicrously extravagant mouth, like an ogre as he was. The chorus says to him (356), εὐρείας φάρυγγος, ὦ Κύκλωψ, ἀναστόμου τὸ χεῖλος, and the comic masks show that no limits were imposed on the dramatic artist in this respect.

The gluttony of Hercules in the *Alcestis*, which, as we have seen, took the place of the satyric drama in the Tetralogy to which it belonged, places that hero on a footing not altogether unlike that of Polyphemus in the *Cyclops*, and it is not improbable that his mask also partook of the comic character. A Hercules in this capacity is represented on a vase with a great loaf in one hand and a club in the other, and in full pursuit of a handmaiden who is running from him with a pitcher of wine.[1] Without being quite so ridiculous as this picture makes him, the Hercules of the *Alcestis* is represented as a wine-bibber and a gourmand in the house of mourning (747 sqq.), and must have reminded the spectators of the same demi-god as he had appeared in many Comedies. For the rest, the *Alcestis* is tragic enough, and the representation did not differ essentially from that of a regular Tragedy. The scene represents the palace of Admetus at Pheræ, which occupies the centre. The guest-chambers stand by themselves to the left of the palace (543 : χωρὶς ξενῶνές εἰσιν, cf. 546 sqq.). The corresponding door to the right indicates the road to Larissa and the tomb of Alcestis (835 : ὀρθὴν παρ' οἶμον, ἣ 'πὶ Λάρισσαν φέρει, τύμβον κατόψει ξεστὸν ἐκ προαστίου). And while the left-hand *periactos* represents the approach from distant parts the other side-scene shows us the neighbouring

[1] Panofka, *Mus. Blacas*, Pl. XXVI. B; Wieseler, *Supplement*, Taf. A,. No. 26.

city of Pheræ, from which the chorus, which enters the orchestra by the corresponding *parodos*, is supposed to come.

Apollo comes forth from the middle door (23 : λείπω
μελάθρων τῶνδε φιλτάτην στέγην), and probably leaves the
stage by the left *periactos* (76), from whence also Thanatos
had entered sword in hand (28); for as his functions were
confined to the earth, there is no reason for the supposition
that he ascended by the Charonian steps. From the middle
door the handmaiden comes forth (137 : ἀλλ' ἥδ' ὀπαδῶν
ἐκ δόμων τις ἔρχεται), and returns by the same opening
(see v. 209), to announce that the chorus is at hand. This
is of course the entrance for Admetus, Alcestis, and their
children (244, cf. 410), who retire as they came (434). The
same door is used for the entrances of Admetus (509) and
the dead Alcestis (606), and for the exit of the former.
Pheres comes and retires by the right-hand *periactos* (614,
733). By the same way the funeral procession leaves the
stage, for it is supposed to be accompanied by the chorus,
who depart of course by the corresponding *parodos* (740,
746). Hercules enters by the left-hand *periactos* (476), and
is conducted to the ξενῶνες at the left of the middle door
(550). From this the servant (747) and he (773) reappear;
and Hercules goes straight to the tomb by the right-hand
door (860), by which he returns with the veiled figure of
Alcestis (1006). He does not meet the funeral procession,
which re-enters the stage, as it had left it, by the *periactos*
on the right (861). At the end of the play, Admetus returns to his palace; Hercules goes forth by the left *periactos*
to encounter his Thracian adventure; and the chorus departs by the right-hand *parodos*. Although the chorus
undoubtedly takes a part in the obsequies of Alcestis,
there is no reason to suppose that it joins the procession by
mounting the stage. A departure by the right *parodos*
which was close to the right *periactos*, would suffice to
indicate the junction of the choreutæ with the actors and
their attendants.

We now pass on to the representation of the ancient
Comedies.

The most opposite opinions have been entertained
respecting the scenery of the *Acharnians*; for while one

critic considers it necessary to suppose a total change of
scenery from the Pnyx at Athens to the farm of Dicæopolis,
from this to the house of Euripides, and then again to the
farm in the country;[1] while another writer suggests that the
Pnyx is represented by the orchestra, and that the curtain is
not dropt till the assembly breaks up and the chorus enters
v. 204), so that the scenery is entirely confined to the
country;[2] while a third concludes that the country place of
Dicæopolis was so near to Athens that it and the city might
both be represented on the stage;[3] it is held by the most
recent authority that the scene is from first to last confined
to Athens.[4] This view of the matter seems to us to be
supported by the words of the poet himself. At the point
where the scene must change, if it changes at all, from
Athens to the country, Dicæopolis says distinctly that he
will *go within* (εἰσιών) and celebrate the rural festival of
Bacchus (v. 22). This can only mean that he enters the
house already seen on the stage. Then it is clear that he
is at Athens (ἐν ᾿Αθηναίοις, v. 492), and at the Lenæa (v. 504),
when he makes his final defence in answer to the chorus.
Finally, it is expressly intimated that the market, which
Dicæopolis opens, is in the city itself, for the Megarian says
on entering (v. 730): ἀγορὰ 'ν ᾿Αθάναις χαῖρε, Μεγαρεῦσιν
φίλα, "All hail! Market of Athens, dear to the Megarians."
We have no doubt then that the scene is from first to last
at Athens. The centre represents the house of Dicæopolis,
whose part is played by the *protagonist*, and the balcony
above the centre door serves for the flat roof of the house
from which his wife views the festive procession (v. 262: σὺ
δ᾿, ὦ γύναι, θεῶ μ᾿ ἀπὸ τοῦ τέγους). Dicæopolis performs the
ceremonies of the rural Dionysia at Athens, because, like
the other country proprietors, he has been obliged to take
up his abode in the city, and to acquiesce in the utter ruin
of his farm, as he expressly says (v. 512: κἀμοὶ γάρ ἐστιν
ἀμπέλια κεκομμένα). Of the two other main doors, that on the
right represents the house of Euripides, that on the left of
the house of Lamachus, who must be a near neighbour of
Dicæopolis (see vv. 1071 sqq.). The right-hand *periactos*

---

[1] Geppert, pp. 161 sqq.   [2] Genelli, pp. 257 sqq.
[3] Böckh, *über die Lenäen*, p. 91.   [4] Schönborn, pp. 307 sqq.

gave a view of Athens in the neighbourhood of the Pnyx, and the benches (ξύλα) are placed on that side of the stage for the committee-men and the other representatives of the assembly (see v. 25). The left-hand *periactos* represents first the road to Lacedæmon (v. 175) and Megara (v. 728), and it is turned to represent the road to Thebes (v. 860). At the beginning of the play, Dicæopolis enters from the centre door and proceeds towards the right where he takes his place in the Pnyx. The herald, with the committee-men (πρυτάνεις), Amphitheus and the other citizens, enter (v. 40) from the door behind the right-hand *periactos*. From the same side the ambassadors appear (v. 61), and after them the ridiculous figure of Pseudartabas (v. 94), who, as "the king's eye," has a monstrous orifice in his mask, resembling the port-hole of an Athenian trireme with the leather-bag below to prevent it from shipping water (v. 97: ἄσκωμ' ἔχεις που περὶ τὸν ὀφθαλμὸν κάτω). These are followed by the Thracian mercenaries (v. 155), who steal the garlick of Dicæopolis; and Amphitheus, who had been ejected by the Prytanes (v. 58), reappears from the right (v. 129), in order to cross the stage to the left (v. 132) with the commission to buy eight shillings' worth of peace for Dicæopolis. From the left *periactos* he returns (175) pursued by the Acharnians, who of course enter by the left-hand *parodos* (v. 204); Amphitheus continues his flight into the city, and Dicæopolis retires to his own house, from whence he reappears with his family (237). The chorus interrupt the festivities by actually throwing stones on the stage (284). The Acharnians are brought to terms by the production of the basket of charcoal, made to resemble a child ἐν σπαρ-γάνοις, which Dicæopolis fetches from his house (v. 331); and he also goes in to procure the chopping-block on which he is to plead his cause (v. 359: ἐπίξηνον ἐξενεγκὼν θύραζε). A question arises as to the scene with Euripides. Many com-mentators, and even the latest writers on this play,[1] suppose that Euripides and his servant appear on the balcony or second story of the scene. But in this, as we think, they have been misled by the Scholiast, who has not

---

[1] See Brunck on v. 411, and Schönborn, p. 311.

understood the Greek of his author, and we conceive that the direct reference to the ἐκκύκλημα must be accepted as a proof of the fact that Euripides is shown in the interior of his house, but on the level of the stage. The words of the original run thus (vv. 394 sqq.) :

ΔΙΚ. παῖ παῖ. ΚΗΦ. τίς οὗτος ; ΔΙΚ. ἔνδον ἔστ᾿ Εὐριπίδης ;
ΚΗΦ. οὐκ ἔνδον ἔνδον ἐστίν, εἰ γνώμην ἔχεις.
ΔΙΚ. πῶς ἔνδον, εἶτ᾿ οὐκ ἔνδον ; ΚΗΦ. ὀρθῶς, ὦ γέρον.
  ὁ νοῦς μὲν ἔξω συλλέγων ἐπύλλια
  οὐκ ἔνδον, αὐτὸς δ᾿ ἔνδον ἀναβάδην ποιεῖ
  τραγῳδίαν. ΔΙΚ. ὦ τρισμακάρι᾿ Εὐριπίδη,
  ὅθ᾿ ὁ δοῦλος οὑτωσὶ σοφῶς ὑποκρίνεται.
  ἐκκάλεσον αὐτόν. ΚΗΦ. ἀλλ᾿ ἀδύνατον.
ΔΙΚ.   ἀλλ᾿ ὅμως.
  οὐ γὰρ ἂν ἀπέλθοιμ᾿, ἀλλὰ κόψω τὴν θύραν.
  Εὐριπίδη, Εὐριπίδιον,
  ὑπάκουσον εἴπερ πώποτ᾿ ἀνθρώπων τινί.
  Δικαιόπολις καλεῖ σε, Χολλείδης, ἐγώ.
ΕΥΡ. ἀλλ᾿ οὐ σχολή.
ΔΙΚ. ἀλλ᾿ ἐκκυκλήθητ᾿. ΕΥΡ. ἀλλ᾿ ἀδύνατον.
ΔΙΚ.   ἀλλ᾿ ὅμως.
ΕΥΡ. ἀλλ᾿ ἐκκυκλήσομαι· καταβαίνειν δ᾿ οὐ σχολή.
ΔΙΚ. Εὐριπίδη. ΕΥΡ. τί λέλακας. ΔΙΚ. ἀναβάδην ποιεῖς,
  ἐξὸν καταβάδην ; οὐκ ἔτος χωλοὺς ποιεῖς.

The meaning of this must be as follows :

Dic. What ho! Ceph. Who's there? Dic. Euripides within?
Ceph. Within and not within, if you can think.
Dic. How can he be within and not within?
Ceph. Rightly, old man. His mind collecting scraps,
  Is all abroad, and so is not within;
  But he himself is making tragedy
  With feet reposed upon his couch at home.
Dic. Thrice-blest Euripides, whose very slave
  Can act so well his master's character!
  But call him out.
Ceph.   It cannot be.
Dic.   It must;
  For I will not depart, but go on knocking.
  Euripides! Euripides, my boy!
  List to my words, if ever mortal man
  Secured your ear. 'Tis Dicæopolis
  By demo Cholleides, who is calling you.
Eur. But I've no time.
Dic.   Well, let them wheel you round.

Eur. It cannot be.
Dic.   It must.
Eur.   Well, I'll allow them
To wheel me round, but I can't leave my couch.
Dic. Euripides!
Eur.   What say'st thou?
Dic.   Do you write
With feet laid up, when you might set them down?
You're just the man to be the cripples' poet.

This passage is plain enough to any one, who knows Greek; but the Scholiast, who did not see that καταβαίνειν is to be explained by καταβάδην opposed to ἀναβάδην, and means merely to get off the couch or sofa, on which the tragedian was reclining, substitutes κατελθεῖν, and adds that Euripides φαίνεται ἐπὶ τῆς σκηνῆς μετέωρος. Independently of the plain construction of the Greek, the context shows that this was not the case. For first the *eccyclema* was not and could not be used on the balcony or second story of the stage; secondly, Dicæopolis knocks at the door until the interior is opened by the *eccyclema*; thirdly, Euripides gives the rags to his visitor, who must have been on a level with him to take them from his hands; and fourthly, when he wishes to relieve himself from the intruder he says (479), κλεῖε πηκτὰ δωμάτων, which is the same sort of order as that by which Ajax in Sophocles (*Ajax*, 581: πύκαζε θᾶσσον. 593: οὐ ξυνέρξεθ' ὡς τάχος;) directs the closing of the inner view of his tent by wheeling round the *eccyclema*. We have no doubt therefore that the interior is similarly displayed on the level of the stage in the *Acharnians*. After his apologetic speech and the scene with Lamachus, Dicæopolis retires into his house (625), and the *parabasis* follows. He then returns by the centre door and sets up the boundaries of his market (ὅροι ἀγορᾶς—probably ropes or poles) in the centre of the stage. The Megarian (729), the Bœotian (860), and the Attic farmer (1018) enter from the left: the sycophant (818), Nicarchus (908), the herald (1000), bridesman (1048) and the herald (1071) enter from the right. Lamachus and his servant (1179, 1190) of course return to the stage from the left. There seems to be no reason to suppose[1] that

---

[1] This is Schönborn's opinion, p. 311.

there is another use of the eccyclema in order to exhibit the
culinary preparations of Dicæopolis. It is clear that he is
outside, for he says (v. 1098), φέρ' ἔξω δεῦρο, and (v. 1102),
ὀπτήσω δ' ἐκεῖ, so that his directions about the fire (v. 1014)
are addressed to his servants within, who are not necessarily
visible.   As Dicæopolis is to sup with the Priest of Bacchus
(v. 1887), he goes off to the city, i.e. by the right-hand door
(v. 1142), and returns by the same way, supported by the
dancing-girls (1198), having won the prize in the ἅμιλλα τοῦ
χοός (1202).   Lamachus is carried off to the right to the
house of Pittacus, the surgeon, (1226); and shortly after
Dicæopolis makes his exit by the same door, for he is going
to the King-Archon to receive his prize; and at the same
time the chorus, whom he invites to follow him, go off by
the right-hand parodos.

After this specimen of the manner in which a Comedy
was put on the stage, it is not necessary to discuss the
performance of all the plays of Aristophanes. It is only
necessary to mention that the upper story of the scene, or
the balcony, is freely used in some of the plays, especially
in the *Birds* and the *Peace*, and that there is a complete
change of scenery in the following Comedies—in the *Birds*
at v. 1565, where the city of *Nephelococcygia* is seen for the
first time; in the *Ecclesiazusæ* at v. 877, where it is clear
that we are no longer in the neighbourhood of the house of
Praxagora (see vv. 1125, 1128), which had formed the
centre of the scene in the previous part of the play; in the
Frogs, where the first act represents the house of Hercules
and the Acherusian lake (1—270), and the second act the
subterraneous regions with the palace of Pluto; in the
Thesmophoriazusæ, where the first act gives us the house of
Agathon (1—279), and the second act the Thesmophorion;
and in the *Lysistrata*, where the first act gives us a street in
Athens with the heroine's house in the centre (1—253),
and the second act exhibits the Acropolis with its propylæa.
In the last-mentioned play, as has been already intimated,
there are four or five changes of the left-hand *periactos*.
There is no change of scene in the *Clouds;* but Strepsiades
and his son are shown in their beds at the beginning of the
Comedy by means of an *eccyclema*, and it is expressly stated

that the phrontisterion of Socrates is managed by a *parency-clema*, that is, by a practicable building projected at the side of the stage,[1] which admits of being destroyed at the end of the play. The κρεμάθρα, on which Sophocles is first seen (v. 218), was not a basket, for he says (225), ἀεροβατῶ, but a sort of shelf, connected no doubt with the balcony of the scene.

---

[1] See above, p. 271.

APPENDIX.

ON THE ROMAN THEATRE.

(*From Schlegel's Eighth Lecture.*)

Roman Theatre. Native varieties, Atellane Fables, Mimes, Comœdia Togata. Greek Tragedy transplanted to Rome. Tragedians of the more ancient epoch, and of the Augustan age. Idea of a kind of Tragedy peculiarly Roman, but which never was realized. Why the Romans were never particularly happy in Tragic Art. Seneca.

In treating of the Dramatic Literature of the Romans, whose Theatre is every way immediately attached to that of the Greeks, we have only to remark, properly speaking, one vast chasm, partly arising from the want of proper creative genius in this department, partly from the loss of almost all their written performances, with the exception only of a few fragments. The only extant works of the good classical age are those of Plautus and Terence, of whom I have already spoken as imitators of the Greeks.

Poetry in general had no native growth in Rome. It was not till those later times, in which the original Rome, by aping foreign manners, was drawing nigh to her dissolution, that poetry came to be artificially cultivated among the other devices of luxurious living. In the Latin we have an instance of a language modelled into poetical expression, altogether after foreign forms of grammar and metre. This approximation to the Greek was at first effected with much violence; the Græcism extended even to rude interpolation of foreign words and phrases. Gradually the poetic style was softened: of its former harshness we may perceive in Catullus the last vestiges, which however are not without a certain rugged charm. The language rejected these syntactical constructions, and especially the compounds, which were too much at variance with its own interior structure, and could not be lastingly agreeable to Roman ears; and at last the poets of the Augustan age succeeded in effecting the happiest possible incorporation between the native and the borrowed elements. But scarcely was the desired equipoise obtained, when a pause ensued: all free development was impeded, and the poetical style, notwithstanding its apparent elevation into a bolder and more learned character, had irretrievably imprisoned itself within the round of the phraseology it had once adopted. Thus the Latin language in poetry enjoyed but a brief interval of bloom between its unfashioned state and its second death. With the spirit also of their poetry it fared no better.

It was not by the desire to enliven their holiday leisure by exhibitions, which bear away one's thoughts from the real world, that the Romans were led to the invention of theatrical amusements: but in the dis-

consolateness of a dreary pestilence, against which all remedies seemed
unavailing, they first caught at the theatrical spectacle, as an experi-
ment to propitiate the wrath of the gods, the exercises and games of
the circus having till then been their only public exhibitions. But
the *Histriones*, whom for this purpose they called in from Etruria,
were only dancers, and probably not mimetic dancers, but merely such
as endeavoured to amuse by the adroitness of their movements. Their
oldest spoken dramas, those which were called the *Atellane Fables*,[1] the
Romans borrowed from the Oscans, the original inhabitants of Italy.
With these *Saturæ* (so called because they were at first improvisatory
farces, without dramatic coherence, for *Satura* means a *medley*) they
rested satisfied till Livius Andronicus, more than five hundred years after
the building of Rome, began to imitate the Greeks, and introduced the
regular kinds of drama, namely, Tragedy, and New Comedy, for
the Old was from its nature incapable of being transplanted.

Thus the Romans were indebted to the Etruscans for the first notion
of the stage-spectacle, to the Oscans for the effusions of sportive
humour, to the Greeks for a higher cultivation. In the comic department, however, they showed more original genius than in Tragedy.
The Oscans, whose language, early extinct, survived only in those farces,
were at least so near akin to the Romans, that their dialect was immediately intelligible to Latin hearers: for how else could the Atellane
Fables have afforded them any entertainment? So completely indeed
did they naturalize this diversion among themselves, that noble Roman
youths exhibited the like performances at the festivals: on which
account the actors, whose regular profession it was to exhibit the
Atellane Fables, stood exempt, as privileged persons, from the infamy
attached to other theatrical artists, namely, exclusion from the tribes,
and likewise enjoyed an immunity from military service.

Moreover the Romans had their own *Mimes*. The unlatin name of
these little pieces certainly seems to imply an affinity to the Greek
Mimes; but in their form they differed considerably from these,
and doubtless they had local truth of manners, and the matter was
not borrowed from Greek exhibitions.

It is singular, that Italy has possessed from of old the gift of a very
amusing though somewhat rude buffoonery, in extemporaneous speeches
and songs with accompanying antics, though it has seldom been coupled
with genuine dramatic taste. The latter assertion might easily be
justified by examination of what has been achieved in that country in
the higher departments of the drama down to the most recent times.
The former might be substantiated by many characteristic traits, which
at present would carry us too far from our subject into the Saturnalia
and the like. Even of the wit which prevails in the speeches of
Pasquino and Marforio, and the well-aimed popular satire on events of
the day, many vestiges may be found even in the times of the emperors,
who were not generally favourable to such liberties. More to our
present purpose is the conjecture, that in the Mimes and Atellane
Fables we perhaps have the earliest germ of the *Commedia dell' Arte*,

---

[1] [On the *Atellanæ*, see *Varronianus*, pp. 156 foll. ed. III.]

of the improvisatory farce with standing masks. A striking affinity
between these and the Atellanes appears in the employment of dialects
to produce a droll effect. But how would Harlequin and Pulcinello
be astonished to learn that they descend in a straight line from the
buffoons of the old Romans, nay of the Oscans![1] How merrily would
they thank the antiquarian who should trace their glorious genealogical
tree to such a root! From the Greek vase-paintings, we know that
there belonged to the grotesque masks of the Old Comedy a garb very
much resembling theirs; long trousers, and a doublet with sleeves,
articles of dress otherwise strange both to Greeks and Romans. To
this day, *Zanni* is one of Harlequin's names; and *Sannio* in the
Latin farces was the name of a buffoon, who, as ancient writers testify,
had his head shorn and wore a dress pieced together out of gay party-
coloured patches. The very image and likeness of Pulcinello is said
to have been found among the fresco-paintings of Pompeii. If he
derives his extraction originally from Atella, he has his local habitation
still pretty much in the old land of his nativity. As for the objection,
how these characters could be traditionally kept up notwithstanding a
suspension of all theatrical amusements for many centuries together,
a sufficient answer may be found in the yearly licenses of the carnival,
and the fools'-holidays of the middle ages.

The Greek mimes were dialogues written in prose, and not intended
for the stage. Those of the Romans were composed in verse, were
acted, and often delivered extempore. The most famous authors in
this department were *Laberius* and *Syrus*, contemporaries of Julius
Cæsar. He, as dictator, by his courtly request compelled Laberius, a
Roman knight, to exhibit himself publicly in his mimes, though the
scenic profession was branded with the loss of civil rights. Laberius
made his complaint of this in a prologue which is still extant, and in
which the painful feeling of annihilated self-respect is nobly and
touchingly expressed. It is not easy to conceive how in such a state
of mind he could be capable of cracking ludicrous jokes, and how the
audience, with so bitter an example of a despotic act of degradation
before their eyes, could find pleasure in them. Cæsar kept his word:
he gave Laberius a considerable sum of money, and invested him anew
with the equestrian rank, which however could not reinstate him
in the opinion of his fellow-citizens. But he took his revenge for the
prologue and other allusions,[2] by awarding the prize against Laberius
to Syrus, once the slave, and afterwards the freedman and pupil of
Laberius in the art of composing mimes. Of Syrus's mimes there are
still extant a number of sentences, which in matter and terse concise-
ness of expression deserve to be ranked with Menander's. Some of
them even transcend the moral horizon of serious Comedy itself, and
assume an almost stoic sublimity. How could the transition be effected
from vulgar jokes to such sentiments as these? And how could such

[1] [*Varronianus*, p. 163; above, p. 297.]
[2] What an inward humiliation for Cæsar, could he have foreseen, that after a few
generations, his successor in the despotism, Nero, out of a lust for self-dishonour,
would expose himself repeatedly to infamy in the same manner as he, the first despot,
had exposed a Roman of the middle order, not without exciting general indignation!

maxims be at all introduced, without a development of human relations as considerable as that exhibited in the perfect Comedy? At all events, they are calculated to give one a very favourable idea of the mimes. Horace indeed speaks disparagingly of Laberius' mimes, considered as works of art, either on account of the arbitrary manner in which they were put together, or their carelessness of execution. Yet this ought not of itself to determine our judgment against them, for this critical poet, for reasons which it is easy to conceive, lays much greater stress upon the diligent use of the file, than upon original boldness and fertility of invention. A single entire mime, which time however has unfortunately denied us, would clear up the matter much better than the confused notices of grammarians, and the conjectures of modern scholars.

The regular Comedy of the Romans was mostly *palliata*, that is, exhibited in the Grecian costume, and representing Grecian manners. This is the case with all the Comedies of Plautus and Terence. But they had also a *Comœdia togata*, so called from the Roman garb usually worn in it. *Afranius* is mentioned as the most famous author in this way. Of these Comedies we have nothing whatever remaining, and find so few notices on the subject, that we cannot even decide with certainty, whether the *togatæ* were original Comedies of home growth, or only Grecian Comedies recast with Roman manners. The last is more probable, as Afranius lived in the older epoch, when Roman genius had not even begun to stir its wings towards original invention; and yet on the other hand it is not easy to conceive how the Attic Comedies could have been adapted, without great violence, to a locality so entirely different. The tenour of Roman life was in general earnest and grave, though in personal intercourse they had no small turn for wit and joviality. The difference of ranks among the Romans had its political boundaries very strongly marked, the wealth of private persons was often almost regal; their women lived much more in society, and played a much more important part there than the Grecian women did; by virtue of which independence they also took their full share in the profligacy which went hand-in-hand with exterior refinement. The differences being so essential, an original Roman Comedy would be a remarkable phenomenon, and one that would exhibit this sovereign nation in quite a new point of view. That this was not effected in the *Comœdia togata*, is proved by the indifference with which the ancients express themselves on the subject. Quintilian does not scruple to say, that Latin literature limps worst in Comedy. This is his expression, word for word.

To come to Tragedy; we must remark in the first place, that in Rome, the acting of the borrowed Greek Tragedy was considerably dislocated by the circumstance, that there was no place for the Chorus in the Orchestra, where the principal spectators, the Knights and Senators, had their seats: the Chorus therefore appeared on the stage. Here then was the very incongruity, which we alleged as an objection to the modern attempts to introduce the Chorus. Other deviations also, scarcely for the better, from the Greek style of acting, were favourably

2 A

received.   At the very first introduction of regular plays, Livius Andronicus, a Greek by birth and Rome's first tragic poet and actor, in his monodies (viz. those lyric parts which were to be sung by a single person and not by the Chorus) separated the song from the mimetic dance, only the latter being left to the actor, while the singing part was performed by a boy stationed beside the flute player.   Among the Greeks in their better times, both the tragic song and the rhythmical gesticulation which accompanied it were certainly so simple, that a single individual might do ample justice to both.   But the Romans, it seems, preferred isolated excellence to harmonious union.   Hence, at a later period, their avidity for the pantomimes, which attained to great perfection in the times of Augustus.   To judge from the names of the most famous performers in this kind, *e.g.* Pylades and Bathyllus, it was by Greeks that this dumb eloquence was exercised in Rome, and the lyric parts, which were expressed by their gesticulative dance, were delivered in Greek.   Lastly, Roscius, and probably not he alone, frequently played without a mask : of which procedure there never was an instance, so far as we know, among the Greeks.   It might further the display of his art ; and here again, the satisfaction which this gave the Romans proves, that they had more taste for the disproportionately conspicuous talent of a virtuoso, than for the harmonious impression of a work of art considered as a whole.

In the Tragic Literature of the Romans, two epochs may be distinguished ; the older epoch of Livius Andronicus, Nævius, Ennius, also of Pacuvius and Attius, both which last flourished awhile later than Plautus and Terence ; and the polished epoch of the Augustan age.   The former produced none but translators and remodellers of Greek works, yet probably succeeded better and with more fidelity in the tragic than in the comic department.   Sublimity of expression is apt to turn out somewhat awkwardly in an untutored language : it may be reached, however, by an effort ; but to hit off the careless gracefulness of social wit requires natural humour and fine cultivation. We do not possess (any more than in the case of Plautus and Terence) even a fragment of a version from an *extant* Greek original, to help us to a judgment of the accuracy and general success of the copy : but a speech of some length from Attius' *Prometheus Unbound* is nowise unworthy of Æschylus ; its metre[1] also is much more careful than that of the Latin comedians usually is.   This earlier style was brought to great perfection by Pacuvius and Attius, whose pieces seem to have stood their ground alone on the tragic stage in Cicero's times and even later, and to have had many admirers.   Horace directs his jealous criticism against these, as he does against all the other more ancient poets.

[1] But in what metres may we suppose these tragedians to have translated the Greek Choral Odes?   Pindar's lyric metres, which have so much resemblance to the tragic, Horace declares to be inimitable in Latin.   Probably the labyrinthine structure of the Choral Strophes was never attempted : indeed neither Roman language nor Roman ears were calculated for it.   Seneca's Tragedies never take a higher flight from the anapæsts, than to a Sapphic or choriambic verse, the monotonous reiteration of which is very disagreeable.

The contemporaries of Augustus made it their ambition to compete with the Greeks in a more original manner; not with equal success, however, in all departments. The rage for attempting Tragedy was particularly great; works of this kind by the Emperor himself are mentioned. There is therefore much to favour the conjecture, that Horace wrote his *Epistle to the Pisos*, principally with a view of deterring these young men, who perhaps without any true call to such a task were bitten by the mania of the day, from so critical an undertaking. One of the chief Tragedians of this age was the famous *Asinius Pollio*, a man of a violently impassioned character, as Pliny says, and who was partial to the same character in works of fine art. He it was who brought with him from Rhodes and set up in Rome the well-known group of the Farnese Bull. If his Tragedies bore but about the same relation to those of Sophocles, as this bold, wild, but somewhat overwrought group does to the still sublimity of the Niobe, their loss is still very much to be lamented. But Pollio's political greatness might easily dazzle the eyes of his contemporaries as to the true value of his poetical works. Ovid tried his hand upon Tragedy, as he did upon so many other kinds of poetry, and composed a *Medea*. To judge from the drivelling common-places of passion in his *Heroïdes*, one would expect of him in Tragedy, at best an overdrawn Euripides. Yet Quintilian asserts, that here he showed for once what he might have accomplished, if he had but kept himself within bounds, rather than give way to his propensity to extravagance.

These and all the other tragic attempts of the Augustan age have perished. We cannot exactly estimate the extent of our loss, but to all appearance it is not extraordinarily great. In the first place, the Greek Tragedy laboured there under the disadvantage of all transplanted exotics: the Roman worship indeed was in some measure allied to that of the Greeks (though not nearly so identical with it as many suppose), but the heroic mythology of the Greeks was altogether indebted to the poets for its introduction into Rome, and was in no respect interwoven with the national recollections, as it was in such a multitude of ways among the Greeks. There hovers before my mind's eye the Ideal of a genuine Roman form of Tragedy, dimly indeed and in the back-ground of ages, as one would figure to one's self a being, that never issued into reality from the womb of possibility. In significance and form, it would be altogether distinct from that of the Greeks, and religious and patriotic in the old-Roman sense of the words. Truly creative poetry can only issue from the interior life of a people, and from religion, which is the root of that life. But the Roman religion was originally, and before they endeavoured to conceal the loss of its intrinsic substance by varnishing its outside with borrowed finery, of quite a different spirit from the religion of the Greeks. The latter had all the plastic flexibility of Art, the other the unchangeable fixity of the Priesthood. The Roman faith, and the ceremonies established on it, were more earnest, more moral, and pious,—more penetrating in their insight into Nature, more magical and mysterious than the Grecian religion—than that part of it at least which was exoteric to the mysteries. As the

2 A 2

Grecian Tragedy exhibits the free man struggling with destiny, so the spirit of a Roman Tragedy would be the prostration of all human motives beneath that hallowing binding force, *Religio*,[1] and its revealed omnipresence in all things earthly. But when the craving for poetry of a cultivated character awoke in them, this spirit had long been extinct. The Patricians, originally an Etruscan school of priesthood, had become merely secular statesmen and warriors, who retained their hereditary sacerdotal character only as a political form. Their sacred books, their Vedas, were become unintelligible to them, not so much by reason of the obsolete letter, as because they no longer possessed that higher science which was the key to the sanctuary. What the heroic legends of the Latins might have become under an earlier development, and what the colouring was that properly belonged to them, we may still see from some traces in Virgil, Propertius, and Ovid, though even these poets handled them only as matters of antiquarian interest.

Moreover, though the Romans now at last were for hellenizing in all things, they wanted that milder spirit of humanity which may be traced in Grecian History, Poetry, and Art, from the Homeric age downwards. From the severest virtue, which, Curtius-like, buried all personal inclinations in the bosom of native land, they passed with fearful rapidity to an equally unexampled profligacy of rapacity and lust. Never were they able to belie in their character the story of their first founder, suckled, not at the mother's breast, but by a ravening she-wolf. They were the Tragedians of the World's History, and many a drama of deep woe did they exhibit with kings led in fetters and pining in the dungeon: they were the iron necessity of all other nations; the universal destroyers for the sake of piling up at last from the ruins the mausoleum of their own dignity and freedom, amid the monotonous solitude of an obedient world. To them it was not given to touch the heart by the tempered accents of mental anguish, and to run with a light and forbearing hand through the scale of the feelings. In Tragedy, too, they naturally aimed at extremes, by overleaping all intermediate gradations, both in the stoicism of heroic courage, and in the monstrous rage of abandoned lusts. Of all their ancient greatness nothing remained to them save only the defiance of pain and death, if need were that they should exchange for these a life of unbridled enjoyment. This seal, accordingly, of their own former nobility they stamped upon their tragic heroes with a self-complacent and vain-glorious profusion.

Lastly, in the age of cultivated Literature, the dramatic poets, in the midst of a people fond of spectacle, even to madness, nevertheless wanted a public for Poetry. In their triumphal processions, their gladiatorial games and beast-fights, all the magnificence in the world, all the marvels of foreign climes were led before the eye of the spectator; he was glutted with the most violent scenes of blood. - On nerves thus steeled what effect could be produced by the finer gradations of tragic pathos? It was the ambition of the grandees to display to the people,

---

[1] [Schlegel adopts the old, but incorrect derivation of *relligio* from *religare;* see *Varron.* p. 482.]

in a single day, the enormous spoil of foreign or civil wars, on stages which were generally destroyed immediately after the use so made ot them. What Pliny relates of the architectural decorations of that erected by Scaurus borders on the incredible. When pomp could be carried no further, they tried to stimulate by novelty of mechanical contrivance. Thus a Roman at his father's funeral solemnity had two theatres built with their backs resting on each other, each moveable on a single pivot in the middle, in such a manner, that at the end of the play they were wheeled round with all the spectators sitting in them, and formed into a circus, in which games of gladiators were exhibited. In the gratification of the eyes that of the ears was wholly swallowed up: rope-dances and white elephants were preferred to every kind of dramatic entertainment; the embroidered purple robe of the actor, Horace tells us, was received with a general clapping, and so far from attentive and quiet was the great mass of the people, that he compares their noise to the roar of the ocean or of a forest-covered mountain in a storm.

Only one specimen of the talents of the Romans for Tragedy has come down to us : but it would be unfair to form a judgment from this of the lost works of better times : I mean, the ten Tragedies which pass under the name of *Seneca*. Their claim to his name seems to be very ambiguous : perhaps it is grounded only on a circumstance which ought rather to have led to a contrary conclusion, viz. that Seneca himself is one of the dramatis personæ in one of them, the *Octavia*. The learned are divided in their opinions on the subject. Some assign them partly to the philosopher, partly to his father the rhetorician : others assume the existence of a poet Seneca distinct from both. In this point all are agreed, that the plays are not all from one hand, but belong to different ages even. For the honour of Roman taste, one would fain hold them to be after-births of a very late æra of antiquity : but Quintilian quotes a verse from the *Medea*,[1] which we actually find in the extant piece of that name, so that the plea will not hold good for this play, which seems, however, to be no great deal better than the rest. We find also in Lucan, a contemporary of Nero, the very same style of bombast, which distorts everything great into nonsense. The state of constant outrage in which Rome was kept by a series of blood-thirsty tyrants, led to similar outrages upon nature in rhetoric and poetry. The same phenomenon has been observed in similar epochs of modern history. Under the wise and mild government of a Vespasian and a Titus, and still more of a Trajan, the Romans returned to a purer taste. But to whatever age these Tragedies of Seneca may belong, they are beyond all description bombastic and frigid, utterly devoid of nature in character and action, full of the most revolting violations of propriety, and so barren of all theatrical effect, that I verily believe they were never

---

[1] The author of this *Medea* makes his heroine strangle her children *coram populo*, in spite of Horace's warning, who probably when he uttered it had a Roman example before his eyes, for a Greek would hardly have committed this error. The Roman tragedians must have had a particular lust for novelty and effect to seek them in such atrocities.

meant to leave the schools of the rhetoricians for the stage. With the old Tragedies, those highest of the creations of Grecian poetical genius, these have nothing in common but the name, the exterior form, and the mythological matter : and yet they set themselves up beside them in the evident intention of surpassing them, in which attempt they come off like a hollow hyperbole contrasted with a most heartfelt truth. Every commou-place of Tragedy is worried out to the last gasp; all is phrase, among which even the simplest is forced and stilted. An utter poverty of mind is tricked out with wit and acuteness. They have fancy too, or at least a phantom of it; of the abuse of that faculty, one may look to these plays for a speaking example. Their persons are neither ideal nor real men, but misshapen giants of puppets; and the wire that sets them a-going is at one time an unnatural heroism, at another a passion alike unnatural, which no atrocity of guilt can appal.

In a history, therefore, of Dramatic Art, I might have wholly passed by the Tragedies of Seneca, but that the blird prejudice in favour of all that remains to us from antiquity has attracted many imitators to these compositions. They were earlier and more generally known than the Greek Tragedies. Not merely scholars destitute of poetical taste have judged favourably of them, nay, have preferred them to the Greek Tragedies, but even poets have deemed them worth studying. The influence of Seneca on Corneille's notion of Tragedy is too plain to be overlooked; Racine has deigned to borrow a good deal from him in his Phædra (as may be seen in Brumoy's enumeration), and nearly the whole of the scene in which the heroine declares her passion.

And here we close our disquisitions on the productions of Classical Antiquity.

SUPPLEMENTARY TREATISE ON THE LANGUAGE, METRES AND PROSODY

OF

THE GREEK DRAMATISTS.

ON THE LANGUAGE, METRES AND PROSODY

GREEK DRAMATISTS.

I. LANGUAGE.

ATTENTION has been already directed to the fact that the different origin of the dialogue and chorus in a Greek play is indicated by a corresponding difference of dialect, and that, while the dialogues represent the spoken language of the poet's age and country, with some few traditions derived from the Ionic of the rhapsodes, the choruses are more or less tinged with the conventional Doric of lyric poetry. The basis, however, of the whole dramatic style of the Greeks was the Attic dialect of the period during which the great dramatists flourished; and while we have the older Attic in Æschylus, we find in Sophocles, Euripides, and Aristophanes all the characteristics of the middle Attic of Thucydides, and in the fragments of Menander and the other poets of the New Comedy we have the language of Athens as it was spoken by Demosthenes or written by Aristotle. In briefly noticing the successive changes of the tragic style, we shall begin with those Epic, Æolic, and Doric peculiarities which are found in the dramatists, and then examine the standard of their Atticism.

I.—*Epic Forms in the Dramatists.*

Besides the common forms ξένος, μόνος, γόνατα, κόρος, δόρι, Θρᾷκες, ζωή, the dramatists wrote ξεῖνος, μοῦνος, γούνατα, κοῦρος, δουρί, Θρῆκες, ζοή. We also find οὔνομα (Soph. *Phil.* 251), εἰλίσσω, εἴνεκα (*New Cratylus*, § 277), εἰνάλιος (Eurip. *Phœn.* 6), καίω, κλαίω, ἐλαία (see Porson, *Præf. Hec.* p. 4; Hermann, *Præf. Ajac.* p. 18), αἰετός, αἰεί or αἰέν (Pors. *Præf. Hec.* p. 4, and Herm. *Præf. Hec.* p. 21), ἔσσομαι, μέσσος, πολλός, by the side of the Attic ὄνομα, ἐλίσσω, ἕνεκα, ἐνάλιος, κάω, κλάω, ἐλάα, ἀετός, ἀεί, ἔσομαι, μέσος, πολύς. The dative plural in -σι or -σιν is used whenever the metre requires it. Æschylus does not hesitate to substitute *a* for *ν* in the 3 pers. pl. of the optative middle, as in ἐκσωζοίατο for ἐκσώζοιντο (Pers. 449). We have also occasional Ionisms like νηός for νεώς (Æsch. *Pers.*

424), ἤμην (Soph. *Trach.* 24), κεινόν (*ibid.* 495), κίεις (Æsch. *Choëph.* 678), ἴκμενος (Soph. *Phil.* 494), κουλεῶν (Soph. *Aj.* 730), ἤλυθον (Eurip. *Electr.* 593).   The pronoun generally used as the article appears in the oblique cases as a substitute for the relative (Æsch. *Agam.* 628, 642; *Choëph.* 596; *Eumen.* 322, 878, 919; *Suppl.* 262, 301, 516, 579; Soph. *Phil.* 1112; *Œd. Col.* 35; *Œd. R.* 1379), and in the demonstrative use we have even τοὶ δέ for οἱ δέ (Æsch. *Pers.* 424). The use of νιν for αὐτόν is common enough, and we even find μιν (Soph. *Trach.* 388).   The reflexive σφέ is a perfectly general pronoun of reference in Æschylus (e. g. it is=αὐ-τόν, *Sept. c. Theb.* 451; αὐτοῦ, *Suppl.* 502; αὐτάς, *Sept. c. Theb.* 846). It is extremely doubtful if σφιν can be used for οἱ. In Æsch. *Pers.* 759, Soph. *Œd. C.* 1490, it may be understood as for σφίσιν. It is also an open question whether such a form as ἐλεεινός is allowable in the Greek dramatists (Pors. *Præf. Hec.* p. 7 ; Lobeck *ad Soph. Aj.* 421). The rare forms ἡσυχώτερος (Soph. *Antig.* 1089) and φίλιστος (Soph. *Aj.* 842) may perhaps be regarded as Ionic. Also κρυφείς for κρυβείς (*Aj.* 1124).   There can be little doubt that an epic tradition suggested the occasional omission of the augment in the speeches of the messengers (Matthiä, *Gr. Gr.* § 160, *Obs.*, see below, IV. 1). Uncontracted forms such as εὔροος, νόος, ῥέεθρον, are sometimes though very rarely found in the dramatists. Valckenaer rejects the particle ἠδέ for καί (*ad Phœn.* 1683), but it occurs more than ten times in Æschylus, in two fragments of Sophocles (345, 493, Dind.), and in Euripides, *Hec.* 323, *Herc. Fur.* 30.

II.—*Æolic Forms in the Dramatists.*

The most common Æolism is the substitution of πεδά for μετά in compounds, such as πεδάρσιος, πεδάορος, πεδαίχμιος, and this occurs even in dialogue (Æsch. *Prom.* 711; *Choëph.* 843; see Valcken. *ad Eurip. Phœniss.* 1034).   We have also μάσσων (Æsch. *Pers.* 432, 694; *Agam.* 584), γλύσσων (Aristoph. *ap. Etym. M.* p. 235), and similar forms, if these are to be regarded as Æolisms. A more decided instance is supplied by ὀρανίαν, which the metre requires in the *Suppl.* 788; cf. Alcæus: ὔει μὲν ὁ Ζεύς, ἐκ δ' ὀρανῶ μέγας χειμών.   And see Buttmann, *Lexil.* p. 200, Engl. Tr.

III.—*Doric Forms in the Dramatists.*

In the choruses, for the reasons already given, a certain amount of Dorism is invariably found, such as the substitution of *a* for η, e. g. νεότας for νεότης, μάτηρ for μήτηρ, πατριώταν for πατριώτην, διδύμαν for διδύμην; also νυμφᾶν for νυμφάων, νυμφῶν, βαρυβρεμέτα for βαρυβρεμέταο, βαρυβρεμέτου, and the like.

In the dialogue we have Ἀθάνα, δαρός, ἕκατι, κάρανον, ἄραρε, γάμορος, γάποτος, γαθοῦσα, ἑκαβόλος, κυναγός, ποδαγός, λοχαγός, ξυναγός, ὀπαδός (Pors. *ad Orest.* 26; Valcken. *ad Phœniss.* 11, 1113; *Hippol.* 1092, &c.), ἄραρε (Pors. *ad Orest.* 1323; Valcken. *ad Hippol.* 1090). Some Doric forms peculiar to Æschylus have been ascribed to his familiarity with the dialect of Sicily (above, p. 97).

IV.—*The Attic Dialect of the Tragedians, and Aristophanes.*

(1) As a general rule the augment is always prefixed in the indefinite tenses of the indicative mood in the dialogue of Tragedy (vide Porson, *Præf. Hec.* p. iv., cf. Wellauer *ad Æsch. Pers.* 302). There are some few exceptions, as in the case of χρῆν, ἄνωγα, καθεζόμην, καθήμην, &c. (Pors. *Suppl. Præf. Hec.* p. xvi.) When the verb begins with the diphthong ευ- the temporal augment is rarely expressed; thus εὗρον and εὕρηκα are more common than ηὗρον, ηὕρηκα (see Donaldson, *Gr. Gr.* p. 196, note). We have both εἴκασα and ἤκασα, and the forms εἴκαζον, ἐξεικασμένα, &c. are supported by the best authorities. We have also both ἀνήλωσα and ἀνάλωσα (cf. Valcken. *ad Phœn.* p. 222; Hermann, *ad Soph. Aj.* 1049). It has been suggested by Matthiä (§ 160, *Obs.*) that the occasional omission of the augment in long speeches by the messengers may be explained by the narrative and epic character of these descriptions, but even here it is limited to the beginning of a line or of a new sentence; and Hermann (*Præf. Bacch.* pp. L—LV) has given the following special rules for the cases in which the augment may be omitted:

" Prima est : verbum fortius, in quo augmenti accessio anapæstum facit, in principio versus positum, addi augmentum postulat:

ἐγένοντο Λήδᾳ Θεστιάδι τρεῖς παρθένοι.

"Secunda : verbum fortius, in quo augmenti accessio non facit anapæstum, in principio versus positum, carere potest augmento;

σίγησε δ' αἰθήρ·
κτύπησε μὲν Ζεὺς χθόνιος·
παίοντ', ἔθραυον·
πῖπτον δ' ἐπ' ἀλλήλοισιν·

" Tertia : ejusdemmodi verbum, si incipit sententiam, videtur etiam iu medio versu carere augmento posse: quale foret illud, ea, qua, supra dictum est, conditione:

γυμνοῦντο δὲ
πλευραὶ σπαραγμοῖς.

"Quarta: verbum minus forte, sive facit augmenti accessio anapæstum, sive non facit, in principio versus positum, si ultra primum pedem porrigitur, caret augmento: γοᾶτο· θώϋξεν.

"Quinta: ejusdemmodi verbum si non ultra primum pedem porrigitur, ut detracto augmento parum numerosum, aut vitatur, ut κάνες, aut cum alia forma commutatur, ut κάλει cum καλεῖ."

There can be no doubt that the omission of the augment in the choruses is an incident of the dialect in which they are supposed to be written (see Monk *ad Alcest.* 599). On the augment in general, see Donaldson's *Greek Grammar*, pp. 194, 201, 248.

(2) The more genuine forms in -σσ, as πράσσω, ἐλάσσων, are preferred to the later forms in -ττ, as πράττω, ἐλάττων, though the more recent form is occasionally found; thus we have πράττω (Soph. *Ant.* 564), ἔλαττον (Soph. *Electr.* 998), κρείττων (*ibid.* 1465), ἥττων (Eur. *Hec.* 274) (see Valcken. *ad Eurip. Phœn.* 406, 1388).

(3) Similarly, ἄρσην and θαρσῶ are preferred to the later assimilation ἄρρην and θαρρῶ (see Porson *ad Eurip. Hec.* 8; *Phœn.* 54).

(4) The second person singular of the pres. and fut. indic. middle or passive is generally contracted from -εαι into -ει in the older Attic, and this form is invariably found in the fut. ὄψει, and in the pres. βούλει and οἴει, which are thus distinguished from the subj. βούλῃ and οἴῃ; the form -ει is also to be preferred in Aristophanes; but -ῃ is most common in the MSS. of the tragedians (Donaldson, *Gr. Gr.* p. 253).

(5) In the past tense of οἶδα, the forms ᾔδειν, ᾔδεις, ᾔδει or ᾔδειν are more common in the tragedians than ᾔδη, ᾔδης, or ᾔδησθα. The dual and plural are ᾖστον, ᾖστην, ᾔδειμεν or ᾖσμεν, ᾖστε, ᾔδεισαν or ᾖσαν. The perfect ἔοικα makes in the plur. ἔοιγμεν and εἴξασι.

(6) Porson remarks (*ad Med.* 744) that the tragedians never substitute the verb in -ύω for that in -υμι, and that this change very rarely occurs in the Old Comedy. He also denies (*ad Orest.* 141) that the dramatic style admits of such forms as τιθεῖς, ξυνιεῖς, &c. for τίθης, ξυνίης, &c. But in order to sustain this rule it is necessary to alter the text in several passages (see Buttmann, *Ausführl. Gr. Spr.* p. 523; Matth. *Gr. Gr.* § 201, 1, note; cf. § 212, 7).

(7) In the imperf. of the substantive verb, the tragedians used to write ἦ, ἦσθα, ἦν (Cobet, *Novæ Lectiones*, p. 187).

(8) The forms κλῇς, κλῇθρον, κλῄω, &c. are more common in the dramatists than κλείς, κλεῖθρον, κλείω, &c. Similarly, nouns in -ευς, as βασιλεύς, ἱππεύς, form their nom. pl. in ῆς, as βασιλῆς, ἱππῆς. The accus. pl. of these nouns ends in -έας, but we have τούς τε δισσάρχας ὀλέσσας βασιλεῖς in Soph. *Aj.* 383, and it seems not improbable that we ought to restore φονεῖς for φονέας in Æsch. *Ag.* 1296.

(9) The following is the declension of ναῦς in the dramatists:

	Sing.	Pl.
N. V.	ναῦς	νᾶες, νῆες
G.	ναός, νηός, νεώς	ναῶν, νηῶν, νεῶν
D.	ναΐ, νηΐ	ναῦσι
A.	ναῦν, νῆα, νέα	νῆας, νέας, ναῦς

(10) In the second declension we have often -εως for -αος, as in νεώς for ναός, ἵλεως for ἵλαος, Μενέλεως for Μενέλαος, &c.

(11) Both πλέος and πλέως are common in the dramatists.

(12) The gen. pl. of γόνυ is not only γονάτων or γουνάτων, but also γούνων; δόρυ has gen. δορός, dat. δορί, Ion. δουρί; χείρ has both χειρός and χερός, &c.

(13) The proper names Ἀπόλλων and Ἄρης have the following peculiarities of inflexion: Ἀπόλλων, acc. Ἀπόλλωνα and Ἀπόλλω; Ἄρης, gen. Ἄρεος, dat. Ἄρει, accus. Ἄρην and Ἄρη.

(14) There are many passages in Sophocles where δύο is required by an elision or the necessity for a short syllable; none, excepting about four, where the word occurs at the end of a line, in which the form δύω would be admissible. The form δυοῖν, on the other hand, seems preferable to δυεῖν.

(15) In the pronouns we have κεῖνος as well as ἐκεῖνος; σέθεν as well as σοῦ; and ὅτου, ὅτῳ, ὅτοις are preferred to οὕτινος, ᾧτινι, οἷστισι.

(16) In the verbs the genuine forms of the imperative plural are retained; thus we have δρώντων instead of δράτωσαν, ἐπιχαιρόντων instead of ἐπιχαιρέτωσαν, ἀφαιρείσθων instead of ἀφαιρείσθωσαν, τυπτέσθων instead of τυπτέσθωσαν, &c.

(17) Verbs of which the future ends in -άσω, -εσω, -ισω, -οσω drop the σ and contract the resulting syllables. Thus we have σχεδῶ, καλῶ, οἰκτιῶ, ὁμοῦμαι, for σχεδάσω, καλέσω, οἰκτίσω, ὁμόσομαι. But this contraction does not take place when the syllable preceding the -άσω, -εσω, &c. is long by nature or position. Thus we never adopt this contracted form for ἀτῑμάσω, ἀρκέσω, αἰνέσω, &c.

(18) The genuine forms of the reduplication are preserved in γίγνομαι and γιγνώσκω, and there seems to be no sufficient reason for ever substituting the later γίνομαι and γινώσκω in the texts of the dramatists.

(19) Verbals in -τος retain or omit the σ between the root and termination, according to the caprice of the poet: thus we have ἀδάματος in Soph. Œd. T. 205, 1315, but ἀδάμαστος in Aj. 445, seemingly from the exigencies of the metre in the former cases. There is a distinction of meaning in γνωστός, "intelligible," and

γνωτός, "known;" but we have ἄγνωστος, ἄκλαυστος, εὔγνωστος, ἀκόρεστος, πάγκλαυστος without any difference of signification by the side of ἄγνωτος, ἄκλαυτος, εὔγνωτος, ἀκόρετος, πάγκλαυτος, which are also supported by MS. authority. Some of these verbals, as μεμπτός, πιστός, ὕποπτος, are used with an active as well as a passive signification (see Porson *ad Hec.* 1117).

(20) Both ἀνύω and ἀνύτω are found in the dramatists, the former more frequently, though Porson prefers the latter (*ad Phœn.* 463, *Hec.* 1157, cf. Hermann *ad Soph. Electr.* 1443).

(21) In the particles we may notice the forms ξύν for σύν, ἐς for εἰς, ἔσω for εἴσω, ἐνί for ἐν, ἀπαί, διαί, ὑπαί for ἀπό, διά, ὑπό, as occurring either regularly or occasionally in the dramatists. We have εἰν Ἅιδου δόμοις in Soph. *Antig.* 1226, and εἰνάλιος, *ib.* 346. For ἐνταυθοῖ, which is sometimes found in the text, we should read ἐντεῦθεν or ἐνταυθί (see *New Cratylus*, § 139); and when οὕνεκα appears as a preposition, it should be changed into εἵνεκα (*N. Crat.* § 277). For αὖθις we have both αὖτις and αὖτε. It is doubtful whether μέχρις occurs in Greek Tragedy (see the commentators on Soph. *Aj.* 568).

(22) Porson lays it down that the tragic writers preferred ἐχθαίρω to ἐχθραίνω and ἰσχαίνω to ἰσχναίνω (*ad Orest.* 292; *Med.* 555); but the MSS. sometimes give such forms as ἐχθρανεῖ (Soph. *Antig.* 93), ἐχθραντέος (*Aj.* 664), ἰσχναίνω (Æsch. *Prom.* 269, 380; *Eum.* 267, &c.) It is also proposed to substitute πνεύμων for πλεύμων in those passages in which the MSS. give the latter (Pors. *ad Eur. Orest.* 271); κνάπτω is considered more Attic than γνάπτω, though the MSS. vary (see commentators on Soph. *Aj.* 1010); and though μικρός is sometimes required by the metre, there can be no doubt that σμικρός is much more common in the dramatists (see Hermann *ad Soph. Electr.* 1113; Elmsley *ad Eur. Med.* 361).

(23) Compound adjectives in -ος are generally of two genders only, and the same is frequently the case with adjectives in -ιμος; but if there is any possibility of a doubt as to the gender, the feminine inflexion is used; thus we have ἀλκίμα θεός when a goddess is intended (Soph. *Aj.* 395); but it would have been ἀλκίμος θεά. Adjectives in -άς, -άδος, are properly feminine only; but they are used even with neuter nouns, as μανιάσιν λυσσήμασι, δρομάσι βλεφάροις (see Pors. *ad Orest.* 264).

(24) The -ι of the dative must not be elided in dramatic poetry (see Lobeck *ad Soph. Aj.* 802, p. 350, ed. 2). The same rule applies to τί, ὅτι, and περί.

(25) The elision of -ε in a verbal termination before the particle ἄν is extremely rare (Elmsley *ad Eurip. Med.* 416).

(26) Diphthongs are not elided, but form a crasis with the following vowel; except οἴμ' ὡς for οἴμοι ὡς.

(27) The following are the most usual crases in Attic Greek poetry:

(a) Crasis of the Article.

ο + α = ᾱ, as ὁ ἀνήρ = ἁνήρ, τὸ ἄλλο = τἆλλο, τὸ ἀργύριον = τἀργύριον.

ο + ε = ου, as ὁ ἐξ = οὑξ, ὁ ἐπιβουλεύων = οὑπιβουλεύων, τὸ ἔντερον = τοὔντερον.

ο + η = η, as τὸ ἥμισυ = θἤμισυ (Arist. Lys. 115).

ο + ι = οι, as τὸ ἱμάτιον = θοἰμάτιον (which is the only example of this crasis).

ο + ο = ου, as τὸ ὄνομα = τοὔνομα.

ο + υ = υ, as τὸ ὕδωρ = θὔδωρ (Crates ap. Meinek. II. 238).

ο + αι = αι, as τὸ αἷμα = θαἷμα, τὸ αἴτιον = ταἴτιον.

ο + αυ = αυ, as ὁ αὐτός = αὑτός, τὸ αὐτό = ταὐτό.

ο + οι = ω, as ὁ οἰζυρός = ᾡζυρός.

η + α = ᾱ, as ἡ ἀρετή = ἁρετή, τῇ ἀρετῇ = τᾱρετῇ.

η (or η) + ε = η, as ἡ ἐμή = ἠμή, ἡ εὐσέβεια = ηὐσέβεια, τῇ ἐμῇ = τῆμῇ.

ου + α = α, as τοῦ ἀνδρός = τἀνδρός, τοῦ αὐτοῦ = ταὐτοῦ, τοῦ Ἀγαμέμνονος = τἀγαμέμνονος.

ου + ε (or ο or υ) = ου, as τοῦ ἐμοῦ = τοὐμοῦ, τοῦ ἐκεῖθεν = τοὔκειθεν, τοῦ ὀνείδους = τοὐνείδους, τοῦ ὕδατος = θοὔδατος (but some read θὔδατος, see Arist. Lys. 370).

ου + η = η, as, τοῦ ἡλίου = θἠλίου.

ου + ου = ου, as τοῦ οὐρανοῦ = τοὐρανοῦ.

ῳ + α = α, as τῷ ἄνακτι = τἄνακτι.

ω + ε (or ο) = ω, as τῷ ἐμῷ = τῷμῷ, τῷ ὀνείρῳ = τῳνείρῳ.

ω + ι = ῳ, as τῷ ἱματίῳ = θῳματίῳ.

αι or οι + α = α, as οἱ ἄνδρες = ἅνδρες, αἱ ἀρεταί = ἁρεταί, οἱ αὐτοί = αὑτοί.

οι + ε = ου, as οἱ ἐμοί = οὑμοί, οἱ ἐν = οὑν.

αι + ε = αι, as αἱ ἐκκλησίαι = αἱκκλησίαι.

α + α (or ε or αι) = α, as τὰ ἄλλα = τἄλλα, τὰ αὐτά = ταὐτά, τὰ ἐκ = τἀκ, but τὰ αἰσχρά = ταἰσχρά, for which some read τᾱσχρά (Eurip. Troad. 384; Hippol. 505).

η + ο (or ω or οι or ου) = ω, as τὰ ὅπλα = θὤπλα, τὰ ὤρνεα = τὤρνεα, τὰ οἰζυρά = τῳζυρά, τὰ οὐράνια = τωράνια, τὸ οἰκίδιον = τῳκίδιον.

The crasis of the article with ἕτερος exhibits the following forms:
Sing. ἅτερος, ἁτέρα, θάτερον, θατέρου, θατέρῳ, θατέρᾳ.
Plur. ἅτεροι, ἅτεραι, θάτερα.

(b) Crasis of καί.

Before α, αι, αυ, ει, ευ, ι, η, οι, ου, υ, ω, the crasis of καί is formed by striking out αι; as κἀγαθός, καἰσχύνη, καὐτός, κεἰς, κεὐθύς, χἰκετεύετε, χἴλεως, χἠ, χοἰ, κοὐ, χὔδατος, χὑπέρ, χᾧτινι. But καὶ εἶτα = κᾆτα.

καί + ε = κα or χα, as καὶ ἔτι = κᾱτι, καὶ ἕτερος = χᾱτερος.
καί + ο = κω (or χω), as καὶ ὀξύ = κὠξύ, καὶ ὅσα = χῶσα, καὶ ὁ = χῶ, καὶ ὅστις = χῶστις; but this crasis does not take place with the simple relative ὅς.

(c) In other words the crasis is generally regulated by the forms given under the crasis of the article; thus we have ἀξιῶ ἐγώ = ἀξιῶ 'γώ, ὦ ἄνθρωπε = ὦνθρωπε, ἀγορὰ ἐν = ἀγορὰ 'ν, ἐγὼ οἶδα = ἐγῷδα, ἐγὼ οἶμαι = ἐγῷμαι, τοι ἄρα = τᾱρα, τοι ἄν = τᾱν, μοι ἔστι = μοῦστι, περιόψομαι ἀπελθόντα = περιοψομἀπελθόντα (Aristoph. Ran. 509), ὃ ἐξερῶ = οὐξερῶ, δήξομαι ἄρα = δήξομαρᾱρα (Acharn. 325), εἰ ἐπιταξόμεσθα = εἰ 'πιταξόμεσθα, Ἑρμᾶ ἐμπολαῖε = Ἑρμᾶ 'μπολαιε, μοῦ ἀφέλῃς = μἀφέλῃς (Soph. Phil. 903), μακροῦ ἀποπαύσω = μακροῦ 'ποπαύσω.

(28) Synizesis, which is incipient contraction or crasis, and produces the effect of one of these without representing it to the eye, occurs either in the same word or between two words.

(a) In the same word, as in

εα　pronounced ya in φονέας, &c.
εο　.........　yo .. θεοί, &c.
εω　.........　yo .. πόλεως, &c.
υο　.........　wo .. δυοῖν, &c.

(b) Between two words, as in ἦ οὐ, μὴ οὐ, ἐπεὶ οὐ, μὴ εἰδέναι, ἦ εἰδότως, ἐγώ εἰμι, ἐγὼ οὐ, ἴττω Ἡρακλῆς, ὦ Εὐριπίδη, in which the effect is that of an improper crasis.

(29) There are a few instances of arbitrary ἀποκοπή in the Greek dramatists; thus we have παῦ for παῦε (Arist. Equ. 821), δίαιν for δίαινε (Æsch. Pers. 1083), ἄμ for ἄμα (Arist. Vesp. 570).

(30) The syntax of the dramatists is that of the best Attic writers, and must be learned in extenso from a good Greek grammar.

II. TRAGIC AND COMIC METRES.[1]

The principal verses of a regular kind are Iambic, Trochaic, and Anapestic.

The scansion in all of them is by dipodias or sets of two feet. Each set is called a Metre.

The structure of verse is such a division of each line by the words composing it as forms a movement most agreeable to the ear.

---

[1] [This account of the ordinary metres of the Greek drama was drawn up in 1827 by the late Rev. James Tate, for many years the earnest and successful master of Richmond School, Yorkshire. If the student desires to see my views on the subject, together with all that I have to say respecting the choral metres of the Greeks, I can only refer him to the Sixth Part of my Greek Grammar.—J. W. D.]

The metrical ictus, occurring twice in each dipodia, seems to have struck the ear in pairs, being more strongly marked in the one place than in the other. Accordingly, each pair was once marked by the percussion of the musician's foot. *Pede ter percusso* is Horace's phrase when speaking of what is called Iambic Trimeter.

Those syllables which have the metrical ictus are said also to be in *arsi*, and those which have it not, in *thesi*, from the terms ἄρσις and θέσις : the latter is sometimes called the *debilis positio*.

I.—*The Tragic Trimeter.*

1. The Iambic Trimeter Acatalectic (i.e. consisting of three entire metres), as used by the tragic writers, may have in every place an Iambus, or, as equivalent, a Tribrach in every place but the last; in the odd places, 1st, 3rd, and 5th, it may have a Spondee, or, as equivalent, in the 1st and 3rd a Dactyl, in the first only it may have an Anapest.

This initial Anapest of the Trimeter is hardly perceptible in its effect on the verse : in the short Anacreontic,

> Μεσονυκτίοις ποθ᾽ ὥραις
> Στρέφεται ὅτ᾽ Ἄρκτος ἤδη, κ. τ. λ.

it evidently produces a livelier movement.

A Table of the Tragic Trimeter.

Verses containing pure Iambi (*a*), Tribrachs in 1st, 2nd, 3rd, 4th, and 5th places (*b*, *c*, *d*, *e*, *f*), Spondees in 1st, 3rd, and 5th (*g*), Dactyls in 1st and 3rd (*h*, *i*), Anapest in 1st (*j*), are given by Gaisford in his *Hephæstion*, p. 241, or may be read in the following line of the *Œdipus Rex* :

a. 8. ὁ πᾶσι κλεινὸς Οἰδίπους καλούμενος.
b. 112. πότερα δ᾽ ἐν οἴκοις ἤ 'ν ἀγροῖς ὁ Λάϊος.
c. 26. φθίνουσα δ᾽ ἀγέλαις βουνόμοις, τόκοισί τε.
d. 568. πῶς οὖν τόθ᾽ οὗτος ὁ σοφὸς οὐκ ηὔδα τάδε;
e. 826. μητρὸς ζυγῆναι, καὶ πατέρα κατακτανεῖν.
f. 1496. τί γὰρ κακῶν ἄπεστι; τὸν πατέρα πατήρ.

g.   30. Ἄιδης στεναγμοῖς καὶ γόοις πλουτίζεται.

h.   270. μήτ' ἄροτον αὐτοῖς γῆν ἀνιέναι τινά.

i.   257. ἀνδρός γ' ἀρίστου βασιλέως τ' ὀλωλότος.

j.   18. ἱερῆς· ἐγὼ μὲν Ζηνός· οἵδε τ' ἠθέων...

2. The last syllable in each verse appears to be indifferently
short or long: and even where one line ends with a short vowel, a
vowel is often found at the beginning of the next, as in *Œd. R.*
vv. 2, 3; 6, 7; 7, 8.

Sometimes, however, one verse with its final vowel elided passes
by scansion into the next, as *Œd. Col.* vv. 1164–5.

> Σοὶ φασὶν αὐτὸν ἐς λόγους ἐλθεῖν μολόντ'
> Αἰτεῖν, ἀπελθεῖν τ' ἀσφαλῶς τῆς δεῦρ' ὁδοῦ.

The case is thus restricted by Porson *ad Med.* 510: *Vocalis in
fine versus elidi non potest, nisi syllaba longa præcedat.* (On this
curious subject, consult Hermann's *Elementa Doctrinæ Metricæ,*
Lips. 1816, Glasg. 1817, p. 36 = 22, 3.)

3. Besides the initial Anapest (restricted, however, as below[1]) in
common words, in certain proper names, which could not else be
introduced, the Anapest is admitted also into the 2nd, 3rd, 4th and
5th places of the verse.

(2nd.) *Iph. A.* 416. ἦν Ἰφιγένειαν ὠνόμαζες ἐν δόμοις.
(3rd.) *Œd. Col.* 1317. τέταρτον Ἱππομέδοντ' ἀπέστειλεν πατήρ.
(4th.) *Œd. R.* 285. μάλιστα Φοίβῳ Τειρεσίαν, παρ' οὗ τις ἄν.
(5th.) *Antig.* 11. ἐμοὶ μὲν οὐδεὶς μῦθος, Ἀντιγόνη, φίλων.

In all these the two short syllables of the Anapest are inclosed
betwixt two longs in the same word, and show the strongest as well
as the most frequent case for the admission of such a licence. (The
nature of this licence will be considered in a note (C) ch. XVII. on
the admission of Anapests into the Iambic verse of Comedy).

In the few instances where the proper name begins with an
Anapest, as Μενέλαος, Πριάμου, &c., those names might easily, by
a different position, come into the verse like other words similarly
constituted. Elmsley, in his celebrated critique on Porson's *Hecuba,*
ed. 1808, considers all such cases as corrupt. (Vid. *Edinburgh
Review,* Vol. XIX. p. 69.) Porson's judgment seems to lean

---

[1] This Anapest in the tragic is generally included in the s me word;
except where the line begins either with an article or with a preposition
followed immediately by its case.   Monk, *Mus. Crit.* I. p. 63.

> *Philoct.* 754.   τὸν ἴσον χρόνον...
> *Orest.* 888.   ἐπὶ τῷδε δ' ἠγόρευον...
> *Iph. A.* 646.   παρ' ἐμοί...

the other way. At all events, the whole Anapest must be contained in the same word. (Vide *Hecub. Porsoni*, London, 1808, p. xxiii=p. 18; *Euripid. Porsoni* a Scholefield, Cantabr. 1826. To these editions only any references hereafter will be regularly made.)

II.—*The Comic Trimeter,*

besides the initial Anapest which it takes with less restriction, admits the Anapest of common words in all the other places but the last: it admits also the Dactyl in 5th.

Vesp. 979. κατάβα, κατάβα, | κατάβα, κατάβα, | καταβήσομαι.
Plut. 55. πυθοίμεθ᾽ ἂν | τὸν χρησμὸν ἡ | μῶν ὅτι νοεῖ.

In the resolved or trisyllabic feet one limitation obtains: the concurrence of $-\smile\smile$ or $\smile\smile\smile$ and $\smile\smile-$ in that order never takes place. The necessity for this will hereafter be seen, note (A), ch. xv.

A Table of Scansion for the Trimeter, both Tragic and Comic.

III.—*The Structure of the Iambic Trimeter.*

is decidedly Trochaic.

1. The two principal divisions of this verse, which gave the Trochaic movement to the ear, and continue it more or less to the close, take place after two feet and a half (M), or after three feet and a half (N), with the technical name of *Cæsura*. One or other of these divisions may be considered as generally necessary to the just constitution of the verse, the form M however being more frequent than the form N, nearly as four to one:

(M) *Œd. R.* 2. τίνας ποθ᾽ ἕδρας | τάσδε μοι θοάζετε.
(N) ———— 3. ἱκτηρίοις κλάδοισιν | ἐξεστεμμένοι;

The four cases of the Cæsura (M), and the eight cases of the Cæsura (N), as exemplified by Porson, are given below from the *Suppl. ad Præfat.* pp. xxvi, xxvii=21, 22.[1]

2. The two minor divisions, which give or continue the Trochaic movement, frequently occur after the first foot and a half (L) of the verse, and before the last foot and a half (R), called the final Cretic (—◡—).

(L) *Œd. R.* 120. τὸ ποῖον ; | ἐν γὰρ πόλλ᾽ ἂν ἐξεύροι μαθεῖν,
(R) ———— 121. ἀρχὴν βραχεῖαν εἰ λάβοιμεν | ἐλπίδος.

The former of these divisions (L), though not necessary, is always agreeable. The latter (R) requiring ◡— and rejecting —— in 5th, takes place not only in such a simple structure of words as that above given, but under circumstances more complex, which will be explained in note (B), ch. xvi., on the Cretic termination. This delicacy of structure was discovered by Porson, who gave the name of *pausa* to it, p. xxxii = 27.

---

[1] Nunc de Cæsuris videamus. Senarius, ut notum est, duas præcipuas cæsuras habet, penthemimerim, et hephthemimerim, id est, alteram quam voco *A*, quæ tertium pedem, alteram, quæ quartum dividat. Prioris cæsuræ quatuor sunt genera: primum est quod in brevi syllaba fit; secundum, quod in brevi post elisionem; tertium in longa, quartum in longa post elisionem.

> *Hec.* 5. (*A a*) Κίνδυνος ἔσχε | δορὶ πεσεῖν Ἑλληνικῷ.
> 11. (*A b*) Πατὴρ ἵν᾽ εἴ ποτ᾽ | Ἰλίου τείχη πέσοι.
> 2. (*A c*) Λιπὼν ἵν᾽ Ἅιδης | χωρὶς ᾤκισται θεῶν.
> 42. (*A d*) Καὶ τεύξεται τοῦδ᾽ | οὐδ᾽ ἀδώρητος φίλων.

Alterius cæsuræ, quam voco *B*, plura sunt genera.

Primum, cum in fine disyllabi vel hyperdisyllabi occurrit sine elisione; secundum, post elisionem; tertium, cum brevis syllaba est enclitica vox; quartum, cum non est enclitica, sed talis quæ sententiam inchoare nequeat; quintum, cum vox ista ad præcedentia quidem refertur, potest vero inchoare sententiam; sextum, cum syllaba brevis post elisionem fit. Duo alia cæsuræ hujus genera ceteris minus jucunda sunt, ubi sensus post tertium pedem suspenditur, et post distinctionem sequitur vox monosyllaba, vel sine elisione, vel per elisionem facta.

> *Hec.* 1. (*B a*) Ἥκω νεκρῶν κευθμῶνα | καὶ σκότου πύλας.
> —— 248. (*B b*) Πολλῶν λόγων εὑρήμαθ᾽ | ὥστε μὴ θανεῖν.
> —— 266. (*B c*) Κείνη γὰρ ὤλεσέν νιν | εἰς Τροίαν τ᾽ ἄγει.
> —— 319. (*B d*) Τύμβον δὲ βουλοίμην ἂν | ἀξιούμενον.
> Soph. *El.* 530. (*B e*) Ἐπεὶ πατὴρ οὗτος σὸς | ὃν θρηνεῖς ἀεί.
> —— *Phil.* 1304. (*B f*) Ἀλλ᾽ οὔτ᾽ ἐμοὶ καλὸν τόδ᾽ | ἐστὶν οὔτε σοί.
> Æsch. *Theb.* 1055. (*B g*) Ἀλλ᾽ ὃν πόλις στυγεῖ, σὺ | τιμήσεις τάφῳ ;
> Soph. *El.* 1038. (*B h*) Ὅταν γὰρ εὖ φρονῇς τόθ᾽ | ἡγήσει σὺ νῷν.

3. The following lines may serve to exhibit all the divisions connected with the structure of the verse :

(L)   (M)   (N)   (R)

Œd. R. 81.   σωτῆρι | βαίη | λαμπρὸς | ὥσπερ | ὄμματι.
Prom. V. 1005. ἢ πατρὶ | φῦναι | Ζηνὶ | πιστὸν | ἄγγελον.

4. When the line is divided in medio versu with the elision of a short vowel in the same word, or in the little words added to it, such as δέ, μέ, σέ, γέ, τέ, that division is called by Porson the *quasi-cæsura*, p. xxvii = 22.

Œd. R. 779. ἀνὴρ γὰρ ἐν δείπνοις μ' | ὑπερπλησθεὶς μέθης.
Hecub. 355. γυναιξὶ παρθένοις τ' | ἀπόβλεπτος μέτα.
Aj. Fl. 435. τὰ πρῶτα καλλιστεῖ | ἀριστεύσας στρατοῦ.
Hecub. 387. κεντεῖτε, μὴ φείδεσθ'· | ἐγὼ "τεκον Πάριν.

Verses of this latter formation Elmsley ingeniously defends, by an hypothesis that the vowel causing the elision might be treated as appertaining to the precedent word, and be so pronounced as to produce a kind of hephthemimeral cæsura (in this treatise marked by the letter N) :

τὰ πρῶτα καλλιστεία | ριστεύσας στρατοῦ.

Vid. Notes on the *Ajax, Mus. Crit.* I. p. 477.

5. Several instances, however, are found of the line divided in medio versu without any such clision, a worse structure still.

Aj. Fl. 1091. Μενέλαε, | μὴ γνώμας | ὑποστήσας | σοφάς.
Pers. 509 = 515. Θρῄκην | περάσαντες | μόγις | πολλῷ πόνῳ.

On this latter verse, vid. the Note of Blomfield, and Hermann's remark in the work already quoted, p. 110 = 70.

6. But though the verse sometimes does occur with its 3rd and 4th feet constructed as in the instances above, yet there is a structure of the words which the tragic writers never admit; that structure which divides the line by the dipodias of scansion like the artificial verse preserved by Athenæus :

Σὲ τὸν βόλοις | νιφοκτύποις | δυσχείμερον.

The following line, scarcely less objectionable as it stood in the former editions of Æschylus, *Pers.* 501 = 507,

Στρατὸς περᾷ | κρυσταλλοπῆγα | διὰ πόρον,

has been corrected by an easy transposition :

Κρυσταλλοπῆγα | διὰ πόρον στρατὸς περᾷ.

Vide Porson, u. s. pp. xxix, xxx. = 24, 25.

IV.—*The Structure of the Comic Trimeter,*

1. frequently admits such lines as are divided in medio versu without the quasi-cæsura, and, though somewhat rarely, such also as divide the line by the dipodias of scansion.

Plutus, 68. ἀπολῶ τὸν ἄνθρωπον | κάκιστα τουτονί.
Acharn. 183. σπονδὰς φέρεις | τῶν ἀμπέλων | τετμημένων;

2. It readily admits also a Spondee in the 5th foot, without any regard to the law of Cretic termination; as

Plut. 2. Δοῦλον γενέσθαι παραφρονοῦντος | δεσπότου.
—— 29. Κακῶς ἔπραττον καὶ πένης ἦν. | Οἶδά τοι.
—— 63. Δέχου τὸν ἄνδρα καὶ τὸν ὄρνιν | τοῦ θεοῦ.

3. And even when a Dactyl occupies the 5th foot, the modes of concluding the verse which usually occur are those most directly unlike to the tragic conclusion: as

Plut. 55. πυθοίμεθ' ἂν τὸν χρησμὸν ἡμῶν, | ὅ τι νοεῖ.

while forms of this kind are comparatively rare:

Plut. 823. Ἔνδον μένειν ἦν· ἔδακνε γὰρ | τὰ βλέφαρά μου.
—— 1149. Ἔπειτ' ἀπολιπὼν τοὺς θεοὺς | ἐνθάδε μενεῖς;

V.—*The Iambic Tetrameter Catalectic,*

1. peculiar to Comedy, consists of eight feet all but a syllable; or may be considered as two dimeters, of which the first is complete in the technical measure, the second is one syllable short of it.

This tetrameter line, the most harmonious of Iambic verses, is said to have its second dimeter catalectic to its first: the same mode of speaking prevails as to Trochaic and Anapestic tetrameters.

The table of scansion below, exhibiting all the admissible feet, is drawn up in every point agreeably to Porson's account of the feet separately allowable; except that Elmsley's plea for the admission (but very rarely) of ∪∪— of a common word in 4th is here received as legitimate. See his able argument on that question, *Edinb. Rev.* u. s. p. 84.

2. In the resolved or trisyllabic feet one restriction obtains; that the concurrence of the feet —∪∪ or ∪∪∪ and ∪∪— in that order never takes place; a rule which even in the freer construction of the Trimeter (ch. II.) is always strictly observed from its essential necessity.

1	2	3	4	5	6	7 8
⏑ – ⏑ –	⏑ – ⏑ –	⏑ – ⏑ –		⏑ – ⏑ –		⏑ – ⏑̆
⏑⏑⏑ ⏑⏑⏑	⏑⏑⏑ ⏑⏑⏑	⏑⏑⏑ ⏑⏑⏑		⏑⏑ ⏑⏑		
– – ⏑ –		– – ⏑ –		– – ⏑ –		
– ⏑⏑ ⏑ –		– ⏑⏑ ⏑ –		– ⏑⏑ ⏑ –		
⏑⏑ – ⏑⏑ –		⏑⏑ –		⏑⏑ – ⏑ –		
		(P. F. ⏑⏑ –	recipit.)			
		Proprii ⏑⏑ –	Nominis.			⏑⏑ –

3. From the first appearance of the scansional table here exhibited, it might be supposed that the varieties of this verse would be exceedingly numerous. Two considerations, however, for which we are indebted to the acuteness and diligence of Elmsley, show sufficient cause why the actual number of those varieties is comparatively small:

"All the trisyllabic feet which are admissible into Comic Iambics are employed with much greater moderation in the catalectic tetrameters than in the common trimeters." *Edinb. Rev.* u. s. p. 83.

"The Comic Poets admit Anapests more willingly and frequently into 1st, 3rd, and 5th places, than into the 2nd, 4th, and 6th of the tetrameter." *Edinb. Rev.* u. s. p. 87.

4. In the verses quoted below from Porson (xliii = 38) examples of the less usual feet will be found: of (*a*) ⏑⏑⏑ in 4th, of (*b*) ⏑⏑ – in 6th, and of (*c*) and (*d*) ⏑⏑ – proprii nominis in 4th and 7th.

The ⏑⏑ – (*e*) of a common word in 4th is given in deference to the judgment of Elmsley (*Nub.* 1059):

(*a*) πρώτιστα μὲν γὰρ ἕνα γε τινὰ καθεῖσεν ἐγκαλύψας.
(*b*) οὐχ ἧττον ἢ νῦν οἱ λαλοῦντες ἠλίθιος γὰρ ἦσθα.
(*c*) Ἀχιλλέα τιν' ἢ Νιόβην, τὸ πρόσωπον οὐχὶ δεικνύς.
(*d*) ἐγένετο, Μεναλίππας ποιῶν, Φαίδρας τε, Πηνελόπην δέ.
(*e*) πολλοῖς· ὁ γοῦν Πηλεὺς ἔλαβεν διὰ τοῦτο τὴν μάχαιραν.

5. The structure generally agrees with the scansion, and divides the verse into two dimeters. In the *Plutus*, those lines which have this division are to those lines which divide the verse in the middle of a word or after an article, &c. nearly as four to one:

Plut. 257, 8. οὔκουν ὁρᾷς ὁρμωμένους | ἡμᾶς πάλαι προθύμως,
        ὡς εἰκός ἐστιν ἀσθενεῖς | γέροντας ἄνδρας ἤδη ;
—— 284, 5. ἀλλ' οὐκέτ' ἂν κρύψαιμι· τὸν | Πλοῦτον γάρ, ὦ 'νδρες, ἥκει
        ἄγων ὁ δεσπότης, ὃς ὑ | μᾶς πλουσίους ποιήσει.

And very often the verse is even so constructed as to give a successsion of Iambic dipodias separately heard:

Plut. 253, 4. Ὦ πολλὰ δὴ | τῷ δεσπότῃ | ταὐτὸν θύμον | φαγόντες,
ἄνδρες φίλοι | καὶ δημόται | καὶ τοῦ πονεῖν | ἐρασταί.

After these pleasing specimens of the long Iambic, it is proper to state that the Comedy from which they are taken exhibits in all respects a smoothness and regularity of versification unknown to the earlier plays of Aristophanes. (Elmsley, u. s. p. 83.)

N.B. Of the nature of that licence which admits the Anapest, whether more or less frequently, into any place of the comic verse but the last, some account may be reasonably demanded. A probable solution of the difficulty will be offered in the note (C), ch. XVII., subjoined.

VI.—*The Trochaic Tetrameter Catalectic of Tragedy,*

1. consists of eight feet all but a syllable, or may be considered as made up of two dimeters, of which the second is catalectic (vide ch. v. § 1) to the first.

Its separate feet are shown in the scansional table below; and the Dactyl of a proper name, admissible only in certain places, is marked by the letters P. N.

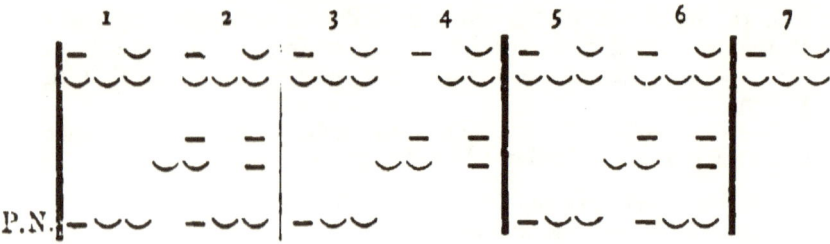

The Dactyl of a proper name is admitted chiefly where its two short syllables are inclosed between two longs in the same word; very rarely where the word begins with them; under other circumstances, never.

Iph. A. 882. εἰς ἄρ' Ἰφιγένειαν Ἑλένης | νόστος ἦν πεπρωμένος.
———— 1331. πάντες Ἕλληνες, στρατὸς δὲ | Μυρμιδόνων οἵ σοι
παρῆν;
Orest. 1549. Ξύγγονόν τ' ἐμὴν, Πυλάδην τε | τὸν τάδε ξυνδρῶντά μοι.

On the Dactyl or Anapest of proper names in the Trochaic or Iambic verse of Tragedy a suggestion will be offered in the note (C), ch. XVII.

In the two following lines will be found specimens of the pure Trochaic verse and of the Trochaic Spondee in all its places:

Phœn. 631. ἀντιτάξομαι κτενῶν σε. | κἀμὲ τοῦδ' ἔρως ἔχει.
———— 609. κομπὸς εἶ, σπονδαῖς πεποιθώς, | αἴ σε σώζουσιν θανεῖν.

2. As to scansion, one limitation only obtains, that —— (or ◡◡—) in the 6th never precedes ◡◡◡ in the 7th. Even in Comedy a verse like the following is exceedingly rare: (*R. P.* xlviii.=43.)

Οὔτε γὰρ ναυαγός, ἂν μὴ γῆς λάβηται | φερόμενος.

whereas of —◡ or ◡◡◡ in the 6th preceding ◡◡◡ in the 7th instances in Tragic verse are not at all uncommon. (The following line exhibits also ◡◡◡ in the 1st and 5th.)

Phœn. 618. Ἀνόσιος πέφυκας· ἀλλ' οὐ πατρίδος, ὡς σύ, | πολέμιος.

3. In structure, the most important point is this; that the first dimeter must be divided from the second after some word which allows a pause in the sense; not after a preposition, for instance, or article belonging in syntax to the second dimeter. (The following lines exhibit also ◡◡— in 2nd and 6th.)

Orest. 787. ὥς νιν ἱκετεύσω με σῶσαι. | τό γε δίκαιον ὧδ' ἔχει.
Phœn. 621. καὶ σύ, μῆτερ; οὐ θέμις σοι | μητρὸς ὀνομάζειν κάρα.

4. If the first dipodia of the verse is contained in entire words (*and so as to be followed at least by a slight break of the sense*), the second foot is a Trochee (*or may be a Tribrach*):

Phœn. 636. ὡς ἄτιμος, | οἰκτρὰ πάσχων, ἐξελαύνομαι χθονός.
Orest. 788. μητέρος δέ | μηδ' ἴδοιμι μνῆμα. πολεμία γὰρ ἦν.
Bacch. 585=629. κᾆθ' ὁ Βρόμιος, | ὡς ἔμοιγε φαίνεται, δόξαν λέγω.

This nicety of structure in the long Trochaic of Tragedy was first discovered by Professor Porson; not an idea of such a canon seems ever to have been hinted before. (Vid. Kidd's *Tracts and Misc. Criticisms of Porson,* p. 197; *Class. Journ.* No. XLV. pp. 166, 7; Maltby's *Lexicon Græco-Prosodiacum,* p. lxvii.)

In the following lines, apparently exceptions to the rule, the true sense marks the true structure also:

Orest. 1523. πανταχοῦ | ζῆν ἡδὺ μᾶλλον ἢ θανεῖν τοῖς σώφροσιν.

Here πανταχοῦ belongs to the whole sentence, and not to ζῆν exclusively.

Iph. Δ. 1318. τό γε τῆς θεᾶς παῖδα, | τέκνον, ᾧ γε δεῦρ' ἐλήλυθας.

Here no pause of sense takes place after θεᾶς, (which is a monosyllable,) but the words from τὸν to παῖδα are inclosed, as it were, in a vinculum of syntax.

The two following verses, the first with an enclitic after the four initial syllables, the second with such a word as is always subjoined to other words, have their natural division after the fifth syllable, and all is correct accordingly :

Iph. A. 1354. κατθανεῖν μέν μοι | δέδοκται· τοῦτο δ᾽ αὐτὸ Βούλομαι.
———— 897. ἀλλ᾽ ἐκλήθης γοῦν | ταλαίνης παρθένου φίλος πόσις.

Nor does the following verse,

Orest. 794. τοῦτ᾽ ἐκεῖνο κτᾶσθ᾽ ἑταίρους, μὴ τὸ συγγενὲς μόνον,

contain any real exception to the canon : for the first dipodia does not end with a word marked by any pause of utterance. Quite the contrary indeed ; for ἐκεῖνο is pronounced in immediate contact with κτᾶσθε :

τοῦτ᾽ ἐκεινοκτᾶσθ᾽ ἑταίρους, κ. τ. λ.

otherwise the 2nd foot would not be a spondee at all. (Something more on this head will be found in note (B), ch. XVI., where lines like the following are considered :

Hecub. 723. Ἡμεῖς μὲν οὖν ἑῶμεν, οὐδὲ ψαύομεν.)

5. If the verse is concluded by one word forming the Cretic termination (— ᴗ —), or by more words than one to that amount united in meaning, so that after the sixth foot that portion of sense and sound is separately perceived, then the sixth foot is — ᴗ or ᴗ ᴗ ᴗ, i. e. may not be — — or ᴗ ᴗ —.

Phœn. 616. ἐξελαυνόμεσθα πατρίδος. καὶ γὰρ ἦλθες | ἐξελῶν.
———— 643. ἐλπίδες δ᾽ οὔπω καθεύδουσ᾽, αἷς πέποιθα | σὺν θεοῖς.

It is unnecessary to remark, that, in verses like that below, the words at the close naturally go together, to form a quadrisyllabic ending, and have nothing to do with the rule here laid down.

Iph. A. 1349. σῷ πόσει· τὰ δ᾽ ἀδύναθ᾽ ἡμῖν καρτερεῖν | οὐ ῥᾴδιον.

The same is true of similar dissyllabic, quinquesyllabic, and other endings ; which, however, in Tragic verse rarely takes place.

VII.—In *the Comic Tetrameter,*

1. the *Scansion* agrees with the Tragic, except only that the — —

in 6th sometimes, though very rarely, precedes the ⏑⏑⏑ in 7th (ch. VI. § 2), as in the line from Philemon :

Οὔτε γὰρ ναυαγός, ἂν μὴ γῆς λάβηται φερομενος.

The Comic, like the Tragic Tetrameter, admits the —⏑⏑ only in the case of a proper name, and not otherwise.

2. But, in respect of *Structure*, the nice points of Tragic verse are freely neglected. Neither the great division in medio versu (ch. VI. § 3), nor the rules (ch. VI. §§ 4, 5), concerning those divisions which sometimes take place after the first dipodia, or before the final Cretic, appear to have been regarded in the construction of comic verse. Lines like the following occur in great abundance :

Nubes, 599. πρῶτα μὲν χαίρειν 'Αθηναί|οισι καὶ τοῖς ξυμμάχοις.

—— 580. ἅττ' ἂν ὑμεῖς | ἐξαμάρτητ', ἐπὶ τὸ βέλτιον τρέπειν.

—— 568. πλεῖστα γὰρ θεῶν ἁπάντων ὠφελούσαις—τὴν πόλιν.

VIII.—*Anapestic Verses.*

1. The Anapestic Dimeter of Tragedy is so named from the striking predominance of the Anapestic foot, though it frequently admits the Dactylic dipodia. In a regular System, it consists of Dimeters with a Monometer (or *Anapestic base*), sometimes interposed, and is concluded by a Dimeter Catalectic, technically called the Paremiac verse.

The separate feet of the Dimeter Acatalectic are shown in the scansional table below:

2. In the predominant or Anapestic dipodia the Anapest and Spondee are combined without any restriction,

Prom. V. 93—5. δέρχθηθ' οἷαις | αἰκίαισιν |
διακναιόμενος | τὸν μυριετῆ |
χρόνον ἀθλεύσω. |

3. In the occasional or Dactylic dipodia, the Dactyl most usually precedes its own Spondee, as in three instances which the following verses contain :

Prom. V. 292—5. ἥκω δολιχῆς | τέρμα κελεύθου |
διαμειψάμενος | πρὸς σὲ, Προμηθεῦ, |
τὸν πτερυγωκῆ | τόνδ' οἰωνὸν |
γνώμη στομίων | ἄτερ εὐθύνων. |

4. Sometimes the Dactyl is paired with itself:

Med. 161, 2. Ὦ μεγάλα Θέμι | καὶ πότνι' Ἄρτεμι, |
      λεύσσεθ' ἃ πάσχω. |

—— 167, 8. ὦ πάτερ, ὦ πόλις, | ὧν ἀπενάσθην
      αἰσχρῶς τὸν ἐμὸν | κτείνασα κάσιν. |

(Dactyli sæpissime substituuntur Anapæstis, nec tantum unus
aliquis, sed sæpe etiam plures continui. Quinque continuavit
Æschylus *in Agam.* 1561 = 1529.

        τοῦτο· πρὸς ἡμῶν
     κάππεσε, κάτθανε, καὶ καταθάψομεν,
     οὐχ ὑπὸ κλαυθμῶν τῶν ἐξ οἴκων.

Septum Euripides *in Hippolyt.* 1361 = 1358.

     πρόσφορά μ' αἴρετε, σύντονα, δ' ἕλκετε
     τὸν κακοδαίμονα, καὶ κατάρατον
     πατρὸς ἀμπλακίαις.   Hermann, p. 377 = 240.)

5. Very rarely, and perhaps not agreeably, in the Dactylic dipodia,
the Spondee is found to precede the Dactyl: of the two following
instances, the first presents the more objectionable form; the second,
succeeded by a Dactyl and Spondee, can hardly be said to offend
at all:

Androm. 1228 = 1204. δαίμων ὅδε τίς, | λευκὴν αἰθέρα
               πορθμενόμενος, | ......
Iph. A. 161 = 159.   θνητῶν δ' ὄλβιος | εἰς τέλος οὐδείς.

On this curious subject, in all its minutiæ, vide the acute and
diligent Elmsley, *ad Med.* 1050, note g, and *Œd. Colon.* 1766.

6. The Dactyl, when in any way it precedes the Anapest, appears
to be considered by metrical scholars as a case of great awkwardness
and difficulty. The following statement, reprinted with a few
verbal alterations from the *Museum Criticum*, (Vol. I. p. 333), may
suffice perhaps for all practical purposes.

The concurrence of Dactyl with Anapest, in that order, is not
very often found between one dimeter and another.

Eurip. *Electr.* 1320, 1.   ξύγγονε φίλτατε·
              διὰ γὰρ ξευγνῦσ' ἡμᾶς πατρίων·

(vid. *S. Theb.* vv. 827, 8. 865, 6, for two more instances.)

The combination is very rare where one dipodia closes with a
Dactyl, and the next begins with an Anapest, thus:

Eurip. *Electr.* 1317.   θάρσει· Παλλάδος—ὁσίαν ἥξεις
            πόλιν· ἀλλ' ἀνέχου.
    Hecub. 144.   ἴζ' Ἀγαμέμνονος | ἱκέτις γονάτων.

Within the same dipodia, we may venture to assert that such a combination never takes place.

7. Thus far of the Anapestic Dimeter, when the first dipodia, as most usually it does, ends with a word.

This, however, is not always the case: and of such verses as want that division those are the most frequent, and the most pleasing also, which have the first dipodia after an Anapest (sometimes after a Spondee) overflowing into the second, with the movement Anapestic throughout.

Agam. 52.   πτερύγων ἐρετμοῖσιν | ἐρεσσόμενοι.
——— 794 = 766.   καὶ ξυγχαίρουσιν | ὁμοιοπρεπεῖς.

(vide Gaisford, Πephœst. pp. 279, 80.   Maltby, *Lex. Grœco-Pros.* xxviii. xxix. for a large collection of miscellaneous examples.)

The following rare, perhaps singular, instance:

Prom. V. 172 = 179.   καί μ' οὔτε | μελιγλώσσοις πειθοῦς,

comes recommended at least by the uniform movement; whereas this line, if the reading be correct, from the Πippolytus,

v. 1376 = 1357.   τίς ἐφέστηκ' ἐνδέξια πλευροῖς ;

within the same word, ἐνδέξια, suffers the transition from Anapestic movement to Dactylic; a transition perhaps not entirely illegitimate, but one of very rare occurrence.

In the second line of those quoted below, the structure, though exceedingly rare, is recommended by the continuity of Dactylic feet before and after it.

Agam. 1557 = 1504. . . .τὴν πολυκλαύτην
                    Ἰφιγένειαν | ἀνάξια δράσας,
                    ἄξια πάσχων, κ. τ. λ.

8. The *synaphea*, (or συνάφεια,) that property of the Anapestic System which Bentley first demonstrated, is neither more nor less than *continuous scansion*: that is, scansion continued with strict exactness from the first syllable to the very last, but not including the last itself, as that syllable, and only that in the whole System, may be long or short indifferently.

In this species of verse one hiatus alone is permitted, in the case of a final diphthong or long vowel so placed as to form a short syllable. The following instances may serve (Hermann, p. 373=237):

Pers. 39.   καὶ ἐλειοβάται ναῶν ἐρέται.
—— 548.   ποθέουσαι ἰδεῖν ἀρτιζυγίαν.
—— 60.   οἴχεται ἀνδρῶν.
Hecub. 123.   τὼ Θησείδα δ', ὅζω Ἀθηνῶν.

With this point of prosody premised, two passages may suffice to exemplify the *Synaphea;*

 Prom. V. 199, 200. εἰς ἀρθμὸν ἐμοὶ καὶ φιλότητα
   σπεύδων σπεύδοντί ποθ' ἥξει.

The last syllable of v. 199 becomes long from the short vowel *a* being united with the consonants σπ at the beginning of v. 200. Had a single consonant, or any pair of consonants like κρ, πλ, &c. followed in v. 200, the last syllable of v. 199 would have been short, in violation of the metre.

 Again, *Med.* 161, 2. ὢ μεγάλα Θέμι καὶ πότνι' Ἄρτεμι,
   λεύσσεθ' ἃ πάσχω,......

If after v. 161, ending with a short vowel, any vowel whatever had followed in v. 162, that would have violated the law of hiatus observed in these verses. And if a double consonant, or any pair of consonants like κτ, σπ, δμ, μν, &c. had followed in v. 162, Ἄρτεμι, necessarily combined with those consonants, would have formed the Pes Creticus, and not the Dactyl required. But λεύσσω follows with λ initial, and all is correct.

 9. The Versus Parœmiacus has its table of scansion as follows:

One limitation as to the concurring feet obtains, that —◡ ◡ in 1st never precedes ◡◡— in 2nd.

 10. In the common dimeter, as must have already appeared, those dipodias form the most pleasing verse which end in entire words: but this law does not equally obtain in the Paremiac, which then comes most agreeably to the ear when it forms the latter hemistich of the dactylic hexameter,

whether with the first dipodia distinctly marked, as

 Prom. V. 127. πᾶν μοι φοβερὸν | τὸ προσέρπον

or with any other variety of structure, as

 Prom. V. 146. φρουρὰν ἄζηλον ὀχήσω.
 ———— 164. ἐχθροῖς ἐπίχαρτα πέπονθα.
 ————1106. τῆσδ', ἥντι ν' ἀπέπτυσα μᾶλλον.
 ———— 305. φίλος ἐστὶ βεβαιότερός σοι.

Sometimes, however, the Paremiac is differently formed, admitting (with restriction § 9) the Dactyl in the 1st:

Med. 1085. οὐκ ἀπόμουσον τὸ γυναικῶν.

(Vide *Museum Criticum,* Vol. I. pp. 328, 9, 332, 3.)

11. The following may serve as a short specimen of an Anapestic System with all its usual parts:

Med. 757—761. 'Αλλά σ' ὁ Μαίας πομπαῖος ἄναξ
    πελάσειε δόμοις,
    ὧν τ' ἐπίνοιαν σπεύδεις κατέχων,
    πράξειας, ἐπεὶ γενναῖος ἀνήρ,
    Αἰγεῦ, παρ' ἐμοὶ δεδόκησαι.

IX.—*The Anapestic Tetrameter Catalectic,*

1. peculiar to Comedy, consists of eight feet all but a syllable; or may be considered as made up of two dimeters, of which the second is catalectic to the first. Its scansional table is given below:

One restriction as to the feet separately admissible obtains, that the two feet —◡◡ ◡◡—, in that order, nowhere concur in the long Anapestic.

2. In the long as in the short Anapestic verse Dactyls are admitted much more sparingly into the second than into the first place of the dipodia. (Elmsley, p. 93.)

3. In the 1200 (or more) Tetrameter Anapestics of Aristophanes only nineteen examples occur of a Dactyl in 2nd, the only *second* place of a dipodia which it can occupy.

In thirteen of those verses the preceding foot is also a Dactyl, as in *Nub.* 400:

οὐδὲ Κλεώνυμον, οὐδὲ Θέωρον; | καίτοι σφόδρα γ' εἴσ' ἐπίορκοι.

In the remaining six of those verses four have the Dactyl after a Spondee, as *Nub.* 408:

ὤπτων γαστέρα τοῖς συγγενέσιν, | κᾆτ' οὐκ ἔσχων ἀμελήσας.

The other two have the Dactyl after an Anapest, as *Nub.* 351:

τί γάρ, ἦν ἅρπαγα τῶν δημοσίων | κατίδωσι Σίμωνα, τί δρῶσιν;
                                (Elmsley, p. 93.)

4 The last quoted verse exhibits the transition (in long Anapestics) from Anapestic movement to Dactylic in separate words. The following verses show within the same word the transition from Dactylic movement to Anapestic.   Both cases are very rare :

$$\overset{\|\;\;\;\;|}{}$$

Vesp. 706. εἰ γὰρ ἐβούλοντο βίον πορίσαι | τῷ δήμῳ, ῥᾴδιον ἦν ἄν.

$$\overset{|\;\;\;\;\;\;\;\;\;\;\;\bowtie\;\;|\;\;\;\;\;\;\;\;\;\;\;\|}{}$$

Ran. 1044. Οὐκ οἶδ᾽ οὐδεὶς ἥντιν᾽ ἐρῶσαν | πωποτ᾽ ἐποίησα γυναικα.

5. Of all those nineteen Tetrameters described in § 3, one only is destitute of the division (or *cæsura* technically so called) after the first dipodia :

Nubes, 353. ταῦτ᾽ ἄρα, ταῦτα Κλε|ώνυμον αὗται | τὸν ῥίψασπιν χθὲς
ἰδοῦσαι.   (Elmsley, p. 94.)

6. This division after the first dipodia is indispensable, if the 2nd foot be a Dactyl and the 3rd a Spondee: therefore the last syllable of the Dactyl may not begin an Iambic or ($\smile$——) Bacchean word.

The following verses, faulty on that account,

Eccl. 514. ξυμβούλοισιν ἁπάσαις | ὑμῖν χρήσωμαι. καὶ γὰρ ἐκεῖ μοι—
Equit. 505. ἠνάγκαζεν ἔπη | λέξοντάς γ᾽ ἐς τὸ θέατρον παραβῆναι—

have been corrected, the one by Brunck, the other by Porson, and by both from the same delicacy of ear, thus :

ξυμβούλοισιν | πάσαις ὑμῖν | χρήσωμαι. καὶ γὰρ ἐκεῖ μοι.
ἠνάγκαζεν λέξοντας ἔπη πρὸς τὸ θέατρον παραβῆναι.
                                         (Vide Porson, lix. ix.=53, 54.)

7. The division after the first dimeter is as strictly observed in the long Anapestic as in the long Trochaic verse (ch. vi. § 3); and, as in that, cannot take place after a preposition merely, or article belonging in Syntax to the second dimeter :

Plut. 487, 8. ἀλλ᾽ ἤδη χρῆν | τι λέγειν ὑμᾶς | σοφόν, ᾧ νικήσετε τηνδί,
        ἐν τοῖσι λόγοις | ἀντιλένοντες· | μαλακὸν δ᾽ ἐνδώσετε
        μηδέν.

These lines exhibit, beside the one necessary division after the first dimeter, that after the first dipodia also, which always gives the most agreeable finish to the verse.

8. It has been remarked, on the authority of Elmsley (vide ch. v. § 5), that the *Plutus* was written after the versification of the comic stage had assumed an appearance of smoothness and regularity quite unknown before.

The following analysis of 110 long Anapestic verses from v. 486

of the *Plutus* to v. 597 (there being no v. 566 in Dobree's edition) may very happily illustrate the truth of that remark.

In 104 of those lines, that which is here regarded as the most harmonious structure of the verse uniformly prevails.

Of the six which remain, three verses (517, 555, 586) differ only 'by having the Dactyl in quinto:

555. ὡς μακαρίτην, | ὦ Δάματερ, | τὸν βίον αὐτοῦ κατέλεξας.

And the other three verses (519, 570, 584), though wanting the division after the first dipodia, yet present the continuous flow of Anapestic movement throughout:

570. ἐπιβουλεύουσι τε τῷ πλήθει, καὶ τῷ δήμῳ πολεμοῦσιν.

N.B. In the Tetrameter Anapestic verse the very same hiatus of a long vowel or diphthong sometimes occurs as in the Dimeter. (Vide ch. VIII. § 8.)

For instance,

Plut. 528. Οὔτ' ἐν δάπισιν· τίς γὰρ ὑφαίνειν ἐθελήσει, χρυσίου ὄντος;
—— 549. Οὐκοῦν δήπου τῆς Πτωχείας Πενίαν φαμὲν εἶναι ἀδελφήν;

X.—*The Ictus Metricus of Anapestic Verse.*

1. The metrical ictus has been briefly explained at the beginning of this Introduction. Its application to the dipodias of Anapestic verse is quite clear and perspicuous: the ictus falls on the last syllable of the ⌣⌣— and its companion ——, and on the first of the —⌣⌣ and its accompanying ——.

First, in a line of pure Anapests, all but one Spondee in the 5th, which there seems to predominate:

Aves, 503. οβολον κατεβροχθισα, κᾳτα κενον τον θυλακον οικαδ'
αφειλκον.

Secondly, in a line of Anapests and Spondees:

Plutus, 536. και παιδαιριων ὑποπεινωντων και γραϊδιων κολοσυρτον;

Thirdly, in a line with Dactyls and Spondees in the first dimeter:

Plutus, 575. αλλα φλυαρεις και πτερυγιζεις. και πως φευγουσι σε παντες;

Fourthly, in lines of mixed movement Anapestic and Dactylic:

2 c

      | || | || | || |

Ibid. 508. δυο πρεσβυτα ξυνθιασωτα του ληρειν και παραπαιειν.

      | || | || | || |

   529. ουτε μυροισιν μυρισαι στακτοις, οποταν νυμφην αγαγησθον.

2. After this, the ictuation of the short Anapestic verse of Tragedy is very simple:

               | || | ||

     Med. 129, 30. μειζους δ' ατας, οταν οργισθη

                | || |

              δαιμων, οικοις απεδωκεν.

Ibid. 1080—85 (with — ⏑ ⏑ ⏑ in first of the Paremiac).

              | ||

       . . . αλλα γαρ εστιν

         | || | ||

       μουσα και ημιν, η προσομιλει

        | || | ||

       σοφιας ενεκεν· πασαισι μεν ου·

        | || | || ||

       παυρον γαρ δη γενος εν πολλαις

           | ||

        ευροις αν ισως

        | || |

       ουκ απομουσον το γυναικων.

3. Of course, we are not ignorant that Dawes has given a different Ictuation to the Dactylic parts of Anapestic verse so called.

Assuming that the Anapestic movement is necessarily kept up through the whole System, to preserve that uniformity he lays the

ictus on the middle syllable of the Dactyl, — ⏑ ⏑, and on the

second of the Spondee, — —. (*Miscell. Crit.* pp. 189, 122 = 354, 357 of Kidd's last edition.) Five lines marked by himself may suffice to show his mode of ictuation in the Dactylic dipodias.

              | | | |

     Equit. 496. Αλλ' ιθι χαιρων, και πραξειας

             | | | |

         κατα νουν τον εμον· και σε φυλαττοι

           | | |

         Ζευς αγοραιος· και νικησας

           | | | |

         αυθις εκειθεν παλιν ως ημας

           | | |

         ελθοις στεφανοις καταπαστος.

No scholar since that day appears to have doubted or discussed Dawes's account of this matter, much less to have approved and defended it. With great reluctance one dissents from so masterly a critic, whose contributions to metrical knowledge can never be estimated too highly: but much careful thought bestowed on the subject has led to that very different result which is here (§ 1) and above (ch. VIII. § 1) candidly stated, and not without some confidence proposed as the plain and practical truth.

XI.—*The Ictus of the long Trochaic verse of Tragedy.*

4. In the ictus of Trochaic and in that of Iambic verse, which for the greater clearness, as will be seen, are taken in that order, there is no doubt or difficulty, so long as the simple feet, and the Spondees when paired with one or the other, alone are concerned.

Every Trochee has the ictus on its first, every Iambus on its second syllable; and the Spondee, as it is Trochaic or Iambic, is marked accordingly.

Phœn. 609. κομπος ει, | σπονδαις πεποιθως, αἱ σε σωζουσιν θανειν.

——— 76. | πολλην αθροισας ασπιδ᾽ Αργειων αγει.

5. Of all the resolved feet, the Tribrach in Trochaic verse with its ictus on the first syllable ᴗ ᴗ ᴗ is most readily recognized by the ear as equivalent to the Trochee :

Phœn. 618. ανοσιος πεφυκας. αλλ᾽ ου πατριδος ὡς συ πολεμιος.

6. What the Tribrach is to the Trochee, the *nominal* Anapest is to the Trochaic Spondee, as its equivalent or substitute ; and this Anapest of course has its ictus on the first syllable ᴗ ᴗ — :

Orest. 1540. αλλα μεταβουλευσομεσθα. τουτο δ᾽ ου καλως λεγεις.

——— 1529. ου γαρ, ἡτις 'Ελλαδ᾽ αυτοις Φρυξι διελυμηνατο.

7. The following lines, formed artificially (like Bentley's *Commodavi*, &c. in his metres of Terence,) are calculated merely to afford an easy praxis for the ictuation of Trochaic verse :

ηλθεν οὑτος ηλθεν οὑτος | ηλθεν οὑτος ηλθε δη.

αδικος ηλθεν αδικος ελθων | αδικος ηλθεν ηλθε δη.

| 　 ‖ 　 | 　 ‖ 　 | 　 ‖ 　 | 　 ‖

ηλθεν αδικος ηλθεν αδικων | ηλθεν αδικος ηλθε δη.

| 　 ‖ 　 | 　 ‖ 　 | 　 ‖ 　 | 　 ‖

ποτερα δεδιε, ποτερα δεδιε, | ποτερα δεδιε δεδιοτα;

8. Instances frequently occurring of words like those now given,

| 　 |

αδικος, αδικων, &c. ictuated on the antepenult, may be considered, if not as positively agreeable to the ear, yet at any rate as passing without objection or offence.

But where the penultima of words like αμφοτερα or θορυβος is marked with the ictus, something awkward and hard, or so fancied at least, has even led to violations of the genuine text under pretence of improving the metre.

For example, the following genuine verse, *Iph. A.* 875 = 886,

| 　 ‖ 　 | 　 ‖ 　 | 　 ‖ 　 | 　 ‖

ω θυγατερ ηκεις επ᾽ ολεθρω και συ και μητηρ σεθεν,

has on that very plea been disfigured (vid. ch. VI. § 4) by this alteration:

| 　 ‖ 　 | 　 ‖ 　 | 　 ‖ 　 | 　 ‖

θυγατερ, ηκεις | επ᾽ ολεθρω σω και συ και μητηρ σεθεν.

In v. 1324 = 1345, the word θυγατερ occurs with the more usual, and it may be the pleasanter, ictuation:

| 　 ‖ 　 | 　 ‖ 　 | 　 ‖ 　 | 　 ‖

ω γυναι ταλαινα, Ληδας θυγατερ, ου ψευδη θροεις.

A similar difference is found in the ictus of Αρτεμιδι:

Iph. A. 872 = 883.

| · 　 ‖ 　 | 　 ‖ 　 | 　 ‖ · 　 | 　 ‖

παντ᾽ εχεις. Αρτεμιδι θυσειν παιδα σην μελλει πατηρ.

| 　 ‖ 　 | 　 ‖ 　 | 　 ‖ 　 | 　 ‖

348 = 359. Αρτεμιδι, και πλουν εσεσθαι Δαναϊδαις, ησθεις φρενας.

The two following lines from the *Persæ* also exhibit that peculiar ictus:

| 　 ‖ 　 | 　 ‖ 　 | 　 ‖ 　 | 　 ‖

739. ω μελεος, οιαν αρ᾽ ηβην ξυμμαχων απωλεσε.

| 　 ‖ 　 | 　 ‖ 　 | 　 ‖ 　 | 　 ‖

176. τουδε μοι γενεσθε, Περσων γηραλεα πιστωματα.

Other varieties, and not of very rare occurrence, may be remarked in these lines:

| 　 ‖ 　 | 　 ‖ 　 | 　 ‖ 　 | 　 ‖

Agam. 1644. δεχομενοις λεγεις θανειν σε· την τυχην δ᾽ ερωμεθα.

| 　 ‖ 　 | 　 ‖ 　 | 　 ‖ 　 | 　 ‖

Iph. A. 852 = 863. ως μονοις λεγοις αν, εξω δ᾽ ελθε βασιλικων δομων.

| 　 ‖ 　 | 　 ‖ 　 | 　 ‖ 　 | 　 ‖

—— 900 = 911. ουκ εχω βωμον καταφυγειν αλλον η το σον γονυ.

XII.—*The Ictus of Iambic Verse in Tragedy.*

9. In the Iambic dipodia (supra 4) the Iambus and the Spondee have the ictus on the second syllable. When the Tribrach stands in the place of the Iambus, and the *nominal* Dactyl in that of the Spondee, each of those feet has the ictus on the middle syllable,

᷉᷉᷉, ᷉᷉᷉.

The ictuation therefore of Iambic verse in its resolved feet may be readily shown:

Œd. R. 112. ποτερα δ' εν οικοις η 'ν αγροις ὁ Λαϊος.

—— 26. φθινουσα δ' αγελαις βουνομοις τοκοισι τε.

—— 508. πως ουν τοθ' οὑτος ὁ σοφος ουκ ηυδα ταδε ;

Med. 1173. ειτ' αντιμολπον ἡκεν ολολυγης μεγαν.

Œd. R. 719. ερριψεν αλλων χερσιν εις αβατον ορος.

Phœn. 40. ω ξενε, τυραννοις εκποδων μεθιστασο.

Œd. R. 257. ανδρος τ' αριστου βασιλεως τ' ολωλοτος.

Orest. 288. και νυν ανακαλυπτ' ω κασιγνητον καρα.

10. It has been truly asserted (ch. III.) that the structure of the Iambic Trimeter is decidedly Trochaic. And though every principal point in the constitution of that verse has been here separately stated and explained, yet the correspondence betwixt the Iambic Trimeter and a certain portion of the Trochaic Tetrameter (as hinted above, § 4) may be advantageously employed to illustrate the common properties of both. With this view, then, to any Trimeter (except only those very few with Anapests initial) let the Cretic beginning δηλαδή or ἀλλὰ νῦν be prefixed, and every nicety of ictuation, more clear, as it is, and more easily apprehended in Trochaic verse, will be immediately identified in Iambic.

For instance, the lines already quoted, *Œd. R.* 112, *Orest.* 288, *Œd. R.* 719, with the Cretic prefixed, become long Trochaics, and admit the Trochaic analysis:

δηλαδη. ποτερα δ' εν οικοις η 'ν αγροις ὁ Λαϊος.

δηλαδη. και νυν ανακαλυπτ', ω κασιγνητον καρα.

| | ‖ | | ‖ | | ‖ | | ‖ |

αλλα νυν ερριψεν αλλων χερσιν εις αβατον ορος.

By a similar process, the identity of the Cretic termination in both verses (ch. III. § 2. R. and ch. VI. § 5) as subject to the same canon is instantly discovered :

Orest. 762. δεινὸν οἱ πολλοὶ, κάκουργοὺς | ὅταν ἔχωσι | προστάτας.
—— 541. ..... ἀπελθέτω δὴ τοῖς λόγοισιν | ἐκποδών.
'Αλλὰ νῦν ἀπελθέτω δὴ | τοῖς λόγοισιν | ἐκποδών.

The correspondence, however, of the Iambic Trimeter with that portion of the Trochaic Tetrameter is then only quite perfect when the former verse has the predominant division, M. (ch. III. § 1), as in the Senarius quoted above.

XIII.—*The Ictus of the long Trochaic Verse of Comedy.*

11. The scansion of the Comic Tetrameter agrees with that of the Tragic, except in one point, that it admits, though very rarely, the —— in the 6th before the ◡ ◡ ◡ in the 7th; and the ictuation is the very same in both verses. Of that exception the line already quoted may afford a sufficient example :

| | ‖ | | ‖ | | ‖ | | ‖ |

ουτε γαρ ναυαγος, αν μη γης λαβηται φερομενος.

XIV.—*The Ictus of Iambic Verse in Comedy.*

12. The Comic Trimeter in Scansion differs from the Tragic by admitting the —◡◡ in the 5th, and the ◡◡— in the 2d, 3d, 4th, and 5th.

The Dactyl in the 5th of the Comic has the same ictus —◡◡ as it has in the 1st and 3rd of the Tragic Senarius, thus:

| | ‖ | | ‖ | | ‖ |

Plut. 55. πυθοιμεθ' αν τον χρησμον ἡμων, ὁτι νοει.
—— 1149. επειτ' απολιπων τους θεους ενθαδε μενεις.

Whatever be the real nature of that licence which admits the Anapest so freely into Comic verse, no doubt can exist as to the place of its ictus on the last syllable ◡◡— ; and the following lines may serve as examples :

| | ‖ | | ‖ | | ‖ |

Nub. 2. ω Ζευ βασιλευ, το χρημα των νυκτων οσον.
—— 24. ειθ' εξεκοπην προτερον τον οφθαλμον λιθῳ.

$$\overset{|}{} \quad \overset{||}{} \quad \overset{|}{} \quad \overset{||}{} \quad \overset{|}{} \quad \overset{||}{}$$

Nub. 20. ὁποσοις οφειλω, και λογισωμαι τους τοκους.

$$\overset{|}{} \quad \overset{||}{} \quad \overset{|}{} \quad \overset{||}{} \quad \overset{|}{} \quad \overset{||}{}$$

—— 11. αλλ' ει δοκει, ρεγκωμεν εγκεκαλυμμενοι.

13. The Tetrameter of Comedy admits no feet but those which are found, and with more frequency, in the Trimeter. The ictuation on the feet in each verse is the very same, as the following lines may serve to exemplify : (Porson, xli. = 38).

$$\overset{|}{} \quad \overset{||}{} \quad \overset{|}{} \quad \overset{||}{} \quad \overset{|}{} \quad \overset{||}{} \quad \overset{|}{}$$

Plut. 253. ω πολλα δη τω δεσποτη ταυτον θυμον φαγοντες.

$$\overset{|}{} \quad \overset{||}{} \quad \overset{|}{} \quad \overset{||}{} \quad \overset{|}{} \quad \overset{||}{} \quad \overset{|}{}$$

Ranœ 911. πρωτιστα μεν γαρ ἑνα γε τινα καθεισεν εγκαλυψας.

$$\overset{|}{} \quad \overset{||}{} \quad \overset{|}{} \quad \overset{||}{} \quad \overset{|}{} \quad \overset{||}{} \quad \overset{|}{}$$

—— 917. ουχ ηττον η νυν οἱ λαλουντες· ηλιθιος γαρ ησθα.

$$\overset{|}{} \quad \overset{||}{} \quad \overset{|}{} \quad \overset{||}{} \quad \overset{|}{} \quad \overset{||}{} \quad \overset{|}{}$$

Thesm. 549. εγενετο Μελανιππας ποιων Φαιδρας τε Πηνελοπην δε.

In this verse, generally, the Iambic structure so clearly pre-dominates, that little advantage can be gained by submitting it to the Trochaic analysis; as, against the judgment of Bentley, has been lately recommended by Ilgenius. (Vide Maltby, *Lex. Gr. Pros.* p. xxxvi.)

And yet in some cases, perhaps, of resolved feet, and in verses too wanting the regular cæsura, the law of ictuation may be more correctly apprehended by applying the Trochaic scale than otherwise.

It is worth the while to observe, that of 37 Tetrameters in the *Plutus*, vv. 253—289, containing only two resolved feet, one a Tribrach, and one a Dactyl, (vid. Elmsley, u. s. p. 83,) the versification is remarkably smooth; and if those lines be read with the proper ictus, the Iambic movement cannot fail to be pleasantly and distinctly felt on the ear.

XV.—Note A. *On the Concurrences.*

In ch. II., where the occurrence of ⏑⏑⏑ or —⏑⏑ before ⏑⏑— in the Trimeter of Comedy is condemned, a promise is given that the necessity for that limitation should be made to appear.

The true constitution of the Comic Senarius (in all its bearings) was first discerned by Dawes. In his Emendations on the *Acharnians* (*Misc. Crit.* 253—463, &c.) at v. 146,

Εν τοισι τοιχοις εγραφον Αθηναιοι καλοι,

he condemns as unlawful the concurrence of feet above mentioned, and claims the credit not only of discovering that canon, but of assigning the true reason also as derived from the laws of Iambic ictuation.

As the verse stands at present, he says,

$$\overset{|}{}\qquad\overset{|}{}$$

$$Εν\ τοισι\ τοιχοις\ εγραφον\ Αθηναιοι\ καλοι,$$

you have, with gross offence to the ear, the interval of four syllables from ictus to ictus, when the lawful extent of that interval can only be three. His emendation, demanded no less by the syntax of the whole passage than by the metre of that line, has since been sanctioned by the authority of the Ravenna MS.

$$Εν\ τοισι\ τοιχοις\ εγραφ',\ Αθηναιοι\ καλοι.$$

On the Trochaic Scale of Scansion, it is obvious to remark, that the redundance of a syllable in the vulgar text would be instantly detected :

$$αλλα\ νυν\ εν\ |\ τοισι\ τοιχοις\ |\ εγραφον\ Αθηναιτοι\ καλοι.$$

One illustration more, from a false reading in Tragedy, may not be deemed superfluous.

In the *Orestes*, 499 = 505, the text of the old editions stands thus :

$$αὐτὸς\ κακίων\ ἐγένετο\ μητέρα\ κτανών,$$

which in the Iambic Scansion presents the concurrence of the $—\cup\cup$ and the $\cup\cup—$. Here again the Trochaic scale affords the ready test ; it instantly detects the redundant syllable :

$$αλλα\ νυν\ αυ|τος\ κακιων\ |\ εγενετο\ μητε|ρα\ κτανων.$$

The just and simple emendation of Porson need hardly be given :

$$αὐτὸς\ κακίων\ μητέρ'\ ἐγένετο\ κτανών.$$

XVI.—Note B. *On the Pause or Cretic Termination.*

(Vide ch. III. § 2. ch. VI. § 5.)

1. In the Iambic Trimeter, if the slightest pause or break in the sense cause the word or words which give to the verse a Cretic ending ($—\cup—$) to be separately uttered, then the fifth foot may not be $——$, but must be $\cup—$ or $\cup\cup\cup$.

The different modes of concluding the line which reject the $——$ in 5th shall be first exhibited.

a. The simplest structure which rejects the —— there is the following, when the Cretic consists of a single detached word :

Hecub. 343. κρύπτοντα χεῖρα καὶ πρόσωπον | ἔμπαλιν.
Ion. 1.   Ἄτλας ὁ νώτοις χαλκέοισιν | οὐρανόν.

which lines in the old editions stand thus :

κρύπτοντα χεῖρα καὶ πρόσωπον | τοὔμπαλιν.
Ἄτλας ὁ χαλκέοισι νώτοις | οὐρανόν.
(Vide Porson, xxx. = 27.)

β. In the next case, the Cretic consists of —◡ and a syllable, thus :

Orest. 1079. κῆδος δὲ τοὐμὸν καὶ σὸν οὐκέτ᾿ | ἐστὶ | δή.
——— 1081. χαῖρ᾿, οὐ γὰρ ἡμῖν ἐστι τοῦτο, | σοί γε | μήν.

or the Cretic consists of an article or preposition (—) attached (in syntax or collocation) to the subsequent word :

Hecub. 382. καλῶς μὲν εἶπας, θύγατερ, ἀλλὰ | τῷ καλῷ.
——— 397. δεινὸς χαρακτήρ, κἀπίσημος | ἐν βροτοῖς.

Under this head of monosyllables are embraced τίς, πῶς, when interrogative, with ὡς, οὐ, καί, and the like. (Vide Porson, xxxi. = 27.)

2. Many semblances of the Cretic termination occur, to which the Canon bears no application. Those cases, admitting the —— in 5th, may be commodiously classed under the following heads :

Where a monosyllabic word before the final Iambus belongs by collocation to the preceding word ; as in enclitics :

Hec. 505. σπεύδωμεν, ἐγκονῶμεν· ἡγοῦ μοι, | γέρον.
Prom. V. 669. τί παρθενεύει δαρόν, ἐξόν σοι | γάμου.
Agam. 1019. ἔσω φρενῶν λέγουσα πείθω νιν | λόγῳ.
Rhes. 717. βίον δ᾿ ἐπαιτῶν εἱρπ᾿ ἀγύρτης τις | λάτρις.
Philoct. 801. ἔμπρησον, ὦ γενναῖε· κἀγώ τοι | ποτέ.

Or in such words, not enclitic, as cannot begin a sentence or a verse :

Prom. V. 107. οἷόν τέ μοι τάσδ᾿ ἐστί· θνητοῖς γὰρ | γέρα.
Trach. 718. πῶς οὐκ ὀλεῖ καὶ τόνδε ; δόξῃ γοῦν | ἐμῇ.
Prom. V. 846. λέγ᾿· εἰ δὲ πάντ᾿ εἴρηκας, ἡμῖν αὖ | χάριν.
Œd. T. 142. ἀλλ᾿ ὡς τάχιστα παῖδες, ὑμεῖς μὲν | βάθρων.
Soph. *Electr.* 413. εἴ μοι λέγοις τὴν ὄψιν, εἴποιμ᾿ ἄν | τότε.

In the numerous instances of ἄν so placed, it deserves remark, that ἄν is always subjoined to its verb, and that with elision, as in the line quoted. (Vide Porson, xxvi. = 28.)

3. Where words like οὐδείς and μηδείς so given, ought in Attic orthography to be written thus: οὐδ' εἶς and μηδ' εἶς:

Phœn. 759. ἀμφότερον· ἀπολειφθὲν γὰρ οὐδ' ἐν θάτερον.
Alc. 687.   ἦν δ' ἐγγὺς ἔλθῃ θάνατος, οὐδ' εἶς βούλεται.

(Vide Porson, xxxiv. v. = 31.)

4. And where in the plays of Sophocles, the dative cases plural of ἐγώ and σύ are exhibited as Spondees, thus, ἡμῖν, ὑμῖν, when that Tragedian, however strange it may appear, employed those pronouns in his verse actually as Trochees. In that pronunciation, they are by some Grammarians written, ἡμίν, ὑμίν, but ἡμιν, ὑμιν, more generally:

Electr. 1328. ἢ νοῦς ἔνεστιν οὔτις ὑμιν ἐγγενής;
Œd. Col. 25. πᾶς γάρ τις ηὔδα τοῦτό γ' ἡμιν ἐμπόρων.

In which two lines ὑμῖν and ἡμῖν would vitiate the metre.

(Vide Porson, xxxv. = 32.)

5. One particular case seems to have created a very needless perplexity : namely, where the verse is concluded by a trisyllabic word with certain consonants initial which do not permit the short vowel precedent to form a short syllable. (Vide Porson, xxxviii. = 34, 5.)

The following verses, as being supposed to labour under the vicious termination, are recommended by the Professor to the sagacity of young Scholars for correction :

Hecub. 717. ἡμεῖς μὲν οὖν ἐῶμεν, οὐδὲ ψαύομεν.
Androm. 347. φεύγει τὸ ταύτης σῶφρον· ἀλλὰ ψεύσεται.
Iph. A. 531. κἄμ' ὡς ὑπέστην θῦμα, κᾆτα ψεύδομαι.

(In these verses, also, from Euripides, the very same difficulty, if it be one, is involved :

Bacchæ 1284. 'Ωιμωγμένον γε πρόσθεν ἤ σε γνωρίσαι.
Electr. 850. τλήμων 'Ορέστης· ἀλλὰ μή με κτείνετε.)

Here the word preceding the final Cretic must be either a Trochee or a Spondee. If it is a Trochee, all is well : nothing more need be said. If it is not a Trochee, but a Spondee, what causes it to be so ? Evidently the final short vowel of each word being touched in utterance by the initial π of ψ, or πσ, with which the next word commences.

Then, so far from any pause or break of the sense intervening, on which condition alone the Canon operates, there is an absolute continuity of sound and sense together; and the verse ends with a quinquesyllabic termination, as complete as in *Phœn.* 32. 53, where ἐξανδρούμενος and συγκοιμωμένη terminate the line: even so, οὐδέπσαύομεν, ἀλλάπσεύσεται, κᾶταπσεύδομαι. (This was stated so long ago as 1802. Vide Dalzel, *Collect. Græc. Maj.* t. ii. Nott. p. 164.)

6. Several modifications of the line, according to the connexion of the words by which it is concluded, come next to be considered. Some of these cases, when the words are duly separated, present a dissyllabic, some a quadrisyllabic ending; in others the combination is such as to exhibit a collective termination of five syllables, or more:

a. *Œd. R.* 435. ἡμεῖς τοιοίδ' ἔφυμεν, ὡς μέν σοι δοκεῖ·

This line, even so read, would not violate the Canon; for it does not present a Cretic separately pronounced. But it stands far more correctly thus in Elmsley's Edition,—ὡς σοὶ μὲν | δοκεῖ, with an ending clearly dissyllabic.

β. The following line again as clearly presents a termination of four syllables:

Œd. R. 1157. ἔδωκ'· ὀλέσθαι δ' ὤφελον | τῇδ' ἡμέρᾳ.

The three following instances are taken from Elmsley, *ad Œd. Col.* 115.

γ. *Iph. A.* 858. δοῦλος, οὐχ ἁβρύνομαι τῷδ'· ἡ τύχη γάρ μ' οὐκ ἐᾷ.

Here the ending is not trisyllabic; for μ' οὐκ go together, and the enclitic μέ hangs upon γάρ : and as γάρ in collocation is attached to the precedent ἡ τύχη, the accumulation of syllables in continuity amounts to seven.

δ. *Ion.* 808. δέσποινα, προδεδόμεσθα· σὺν γὰρ σοὶ νοσῶ.

Here the words σὺν γὰρ σοί, being under the vinculum of Syntax, cannot be disjoined. And σὺν σοὶ γάρ, if so read, from the law of collocation in words like γάρ, must go together. Either way the structure of the verse is legitimate, with a dissyllabic ending.

ε. Eur. *Electr.* 275. ἤρου τόδ'; αἰσχρόν γ' εἶπας· οὐ γὰρ νῦν ἀκμή.

Here οὐ negatives νῦν, and of course must be uttered in the same breath with it, —— οὐ γὰρ νῦν | ἀκμή.
Elmsley himself, (*ad Œd. Col.* 115) on the two following lines,

ζ. *Œd. Col.* 265. ὄνομα μόνον δείσαντες· οὐ γὰρ δὴ τό γε,
η. *Electr.* 432. τύμβῳ προσάψῃς μεδέν· οὐ γάρ σοι θέμις,

justly remarks, that neither line contains anything wrong: for the words σοί and δή, the one enclitic, the other by collocation attached to the word precedent, make a slight dissyllabic ending, as far as any separate termination exists.

7. The following line may serve to represent several others of similar construction:

Aj. Fl. 1101. ἔξεστ' ἀνάσσειν, ὧν ὅδ' ἡγεῖτ' οἴκοθεν.

(Vide Elmsley, *Mus. Crit.* Vol. I. pp. 476—480, et *ad Heracl.* 371. 530.)

"If we suppose the first syllable of οἴκοθεν to be attracted by the elision to the preceding word, the verse will cease to be an exception to Porson's Canon." At the same time, he frankly confesses, that he is not satisfied with this solution of the difficulty, and goes on with great acuteness to state his objections to it.

Now, on the other hand, we are told of Hegelochus, who acted the part of Orestes in the play so named, that when he came to v. 273, ἐκ κυμάτων γὰρ αὖθις αὖ γαλήν' ὁρῶ, wanting breath to pronounce γαλήν' ὁρῶ with the delicate synalepha required, he stopped between the words, and uttered these sounds instead, γαλῆν ὁρῶ. (Vide Porson, *ad Orest.* 273.)

From this anecdote have we any right to conclude, that in cases like that of......ἡγεῖτ' οἴκοθεν, at the close of the verse, the first syllable of οἴκοθεν was by the elision attracted to the preceding word ἡγεῖτο? and in all similar cases may we suppose the two words to have been so closely connected in sound as to leave no perceptible suspension of the sense whatsoever?

It is enough perhaps to have thrown out the suggestion; and there let the matter rest for the present.[1]

XVII.—Note C. *On the Anapest Proprii Nominis in the Tragic Senarius and on other licences of a similar description.*

Before we engage in the direct discussion of the point here proposed, let a few remarks be premised.

1. In the first place, there is a well-known distinction in music betwixt common time and triple time. To this musical distinction there exists something confessedly analogous in the difference betwixt the time of Anapestic and Dactylic verse, and that of Iambic and Trochaic.

Agreeably then to this analogy, we may be allowed for the sake of illustration to use the terms common and triple time in the pages which follow.

2. In the next place, the terms Anapest and Dactyl have been already used on two occasions palpably different.

---

[1] It is quite clear that the aspirate at the beginning of a word was not pronounced in a synalepha unless it could be transferred to the preceding consonant, e.g. ταῦθ' ὁρῶ. While then γαλήν ὁρῶ would be distinctly given as *galèn horó*, the articulation of γαλήν' ὁρῶ must have been *galè-noró*, which would make a very perceptible difference.—J. W. D

First, as the names of the natural feet in the triple time of Anapestic and Dactylic verse, with their ictus thus, ‿‿–́, –́‿‿.

| | || | ||
Med. 167, 8. ω πατερ, ω πολις, ων απενασθην.

| || | ||
αισχρως τον εμον κτεινασα κυσιν.

Secondly, as the names of two short syllables before or after a long one, in the common time of Trochaic or Iambic verse, with a different ictus thus, ‿‿–́, –́‿‿.

| || | || | ||
Œd. R. 257. ανδρος γ' αριστου βασιλεως τ' ολωλοτος.

| || | || | || |
Phœn. 621. και συ μητερ; ου θεμις σοι μητρος ονομαζειν καρα.

In future, it may be safe and useful to call the first of these the *natural*, and the second the *nominal*, Dactyl and Anapest.

3. Thirdly, the terms Anapest and Dactyl have a different use still, to denote certain feet admissible in certain kinds of Iambic and Trochaic verse, as equivalent to the proper feet of each metre, being admitted not only into the Spondaic places of the dipodia, but into the Iambic and Trochaic likewise.

In the pronunciation of those peculiar feet, it is probable there was something correspondent to the slurring, so called, of musical notes; and since necessity demands a third name for a third character, it may justify our adoption of *slurred* Anapest and *slurred* Dactyl, as terms not inappropriate for that purpose.

Let the marks then, ‿ (‿) – and – (‿) ‿, be permitted to represent each of those peculiarities, when each requires to be separately represented. But for reasons of convenience, which will be found very striking when we come to the practical part of the subject, we beg leave to introduce a more comprehensive method, equally suited to Iambic and Trochaic verse; and that is, to make –‿‿– the sign of the apparent syllables involved in the discussion, and – (‿) ‿– or –‿– the sign of the real sounds as they are supposed to have been uttered.

Nubes 131. λόγων ἀκριβῶν σχινδαλάμους μαθήσομαι ;

    – ‿   ‿ –

Iph. A. 882. εἰς ἄρ’ Ἰφιγένειαν Ἑλένης νόστος ἦν πεπρωμένος ;

    – ‿ ‿ –

4. Whatever truth or probability may be found in the following attempt to account for the – ‿ ‿ – Proprii Nominis in the Trochaic or Iambic verse of Tragedy, (and for the admission of that licence with common words also into the Iambics of Comedy,) the whole merit of the discovery, if any, is due to S. Clarke, whose suggestion (*ad Il. B.* v. 811) is here pursued, enforced, and developed.

Clarke, after quoting instances of ‿ ‿ – Proprii Nominis, but only in the 4th foot of the Trimeter, proceeds to argue thus. If the Iambic verse of Tragedy, under other circumstances, rejects in the 4th the ‿ ‿ – as equal in time to – –, and admits only the ‿ – or equivalent ‿ ‿ ‿, then it is clear that the proper names which exhibit ‿ ‿ – to the eye could never have been pronounced at full length in three distinct syllables, but must have been hurried in utterance, so as to carry only ‿ – to the ear.

And since long proper names (as Clarke justly observes) are from their nature liable to be rapidly spoken ; in the following verses,

Phœn. 764 = 769. γάμους δ’ ἀδελφῆς Ἀντιγόνης παιδός τε σοῦ.
Androm. 14.   τῷ νησιώτῃ Νουπτολέμῳ δορὸς γέρας,

and in that above,

    εἰς ἄρ’ Ἰφιγένειαν Ἑλένης νόστος ἦν πεπρωμενος ;

naturally enough the names Ἀντιγόνης and Νουπτολέμῳ and Ἰφιγένειαν might be slurred into something like Ἀντ’γόνης. Νουπτ’λέμῳ, Ἰφ’γένειαν : the ear of course would find no cause of offence, and the eye takes no cognizance of the matter.

5. If this mode of solution be allowed as probable at least in the department of proper names in Tragic verse to which it bears direct application, by parity of argument perhaps it may be extended to the similar case of common words used in Comic verse also.

Take for instance the line above quoted ;

    λόγων ἀκριβῶν σχινδαλάμους μαθήσομαι ;

What was the objection to the old and vulgar reading, σχινδαλμούς ? Clearly this : that it placed a – – in 4th. What then does σχινδαλάμους place there ? Either ‿ ‿ – is pronounced as three distinct syllables, in what is called triple time, while the metre itself is in common, or by rapid utterance σχινδ’λάμους comes to the ear, and so the verse proceeds with its own regular movement.

Briefly, we have either σχινδαλμούς, a molossus, — — —, which murders the metre entirely;

or σχινδαλάμους, a full-sounded choriambus, —◡◡—, which contrary to the law of the verse mingles triple with common time;

or σχινδ(α)λάμους, i. e. in effect, the pes Creticus, —◡—, that very quantum of sound which the metre requires.

Obs. It may be necessary to remark, that Clarke's reasoning about the ◡◡— Proprii Nominis in the 4th is just as applicable to the 2nd place also with that foot as to the 4th. And if his argument, as here stated, be sufficient to account for the licence in the 2nd and 4th places, of course, where the same licence occurs in the 3rd and 5th, its admission there also must be considered in the very same light.

For examples of the ◡◡— (or —◡◡—) Proprii Nominis in all the four places, see ch. I. § 3.

6. Before advancing a step farther, it is but right to avow, that all which we at present propose is to set this question fairly a-going on its apparently reasonable and very probable ground.

High probability then favours the idea, that the Anapests (and Choriambi) of Greek Comedy (under all combinations of words and syllables) were passed lightly over the tongue without trespassing on the time allowed betwixt ictus and ictus in verses not containing those feet, i. e. in metres of common time.

Anything like a perfect enumeration of particulars commodiously classed would be found to demand a serious sacrifice of leisure and labour. The classes which are here given in specimen only, while they undoubtedly embrace a very great majority of the facts, may serve to show the nature of that extensive survey which would be necessary to make the induction complete.

7. Instances like σχινδαλάμους, it might à priori be calculated, are not likely to be very numerous; hardly 10 in every 100 of the Comic Trimeters: nor do all the words of similar dimensions with σχινδαλάμους present a choriambus so readily obedient to our organs at least for running four syllables into three.

Nubes 16. ὃν | ειροπολεῖ | θ' ἵππους· ἐγὼ δ' ἀπόλλυμαι,
Plutus 25. εὔνους γὰρ ὦν σοι | πυνθάνομαι | πάνυ σφόδρα.

Besides the instances of —◡◡— in one word, which afford the strongest case for the admission of the licence, some other principal modes in which that apparent foot is made up may be classed under four heads.

A. Where a long monosyllable, from its nature more or less adhering to the word which it precedes, may be supposed to form a coalescence of this kind, | —|◡◡—|.

Plutus   45. εἶτ' οὐ ξυνίης | τὴν ἐπίνοι|αν τοῦ θεοῦ ;
Acharn. 52. σπονδὰς ποιεῖσθαι | πρὸς Λακεδαι|μονίους μόνῳ.
Nubes   12. ἀλλ' | οὐ δύναμαι | δείλαιος εὕδειν δακνόμενος.

| **B**. Where either a monosyllable precedes, having from the law of collocation less adherence to what follows; or some longer word precedes, not particularly attached to the word which follows, or by syntax united to it :

Plut.   56. ἄγε | δὴ πρότερον | σὺ σαυτόν, ὅστις εἶ, φράσον.
Nub.   25. Φίλ|ων, ἀδικεῖς· | ἔλαυνε τὸν σαυτοῦ δρόμον.
Plut. 148. δοῦλ|ος γεγένη|μαι διὰ τὸ μὴ πλουτεῖν ἴσως.

C. Where, after an elision, concurrences of this kind take place :

Plut.   12. μελαγχο|λῶντ' ἀπέπεμ|ψε μου τὸν δεσπότην.
——   16. οὗ|τος δ' ἀκολου|θεῖ, κἀμὲ προσβιάζεται.
—— 195. κἂν | ταῦτ' ἀνύσῃ|ται, τετταράκοντα βούλεται.

D. Where a monosyllable by its natural position follows a longer word :

Plut. 688. τὸ γρᾴδιον δ' ὡς | ᾔσθετο δὴ | μου τὸν ψόφον.
—— 943. καὶ ταῦτα πρὸς τὸ μέτωπον | αὐτίκα δὴ | μάλα.

N.B. From the very close connection of the article with its noun, τὸ μέτωπον may be fairly taken as one word ; and so, in the following line, we may consider τὰ νοσήματα :

Plut. 708. δείσας· ἐκεῖνος δ' ἐν κύκλῳ τὰ νοσήματα.

Thus v. 943 will become referable to the class A, and v. 708 to the class B, along with many combinations of the very same kind.

8. If the idea of this inquiry had struck the mind of Elmsley as worthy at all of his careful research, little or nothing would have been afterwards left for investigation. The topic was not without interest to him as an Editor of Aristophanes : and on the *Acharnians*, ad v. 178, and in reference to v. 531,

Τί ἐστιν ; ἐγὼ μὲν δεῦρό σοι σπονδὰς φέρων—
Ἤστραπτεν, ἐβρόντα, ξυνεκύκα τὴν Ἑλλάδα—

in a note of great and successful acuteness, he examines and settles a curious point in the main subject itself.

"178. Hodie hic τί ἐστ' malim, et ᾔστραπτ', v. 531. Nam longe rarius, quam putaram, anapaestum in hoc metri genere inchoat ultima vocis syllaba." The whole note will amply repay the trouble of perusal.

III. PROSODY.

On Syllabic Quantity, and on its Differences in Heroic and Dramatic Verse.

1. By *syllabic quantity* is here meant the quantity of a syllable under these circumstances : the vowel, being unquestionably short, precedes a pair of consonants of such a nature that it may anywhere be pronounced either distinctly apart from them, or in combination with the first of the two.

If the vowel be pronounced apart from those consonants, as in πε-τρας, that syllable is said to be *short* by *nature*.

If the vowel be pronounced in combination with the first of those consonants, as in πετ-ρας, the syllable then is said to be *long* by *position*.

2. The subjoined list comprises all the pairs of consonants which may *begin* a word, and also *permit* a short vowel within the same word to form a short syllable.

i. πρ, κρ, τρ : φρ, χρ, θρ : βρ, γρ, δρ.

ii. πλ, κλ, τλ : φλ, χλ, θλ.—iii. πν, κν : χν, θν.—iv. τμ.

The only remaining pairs, βλ, γλ : δμ : and μν, which are at once *initial*, and in very few cases *permissive*, may on account of that rarity, be passed over for the present. But the following pairs, κμ : χμ, θμ : τν : φν, though not *initial* yet within the same word *permissive*, deserve to be stated here, as they will afterwards be noticed.

3. More than twenty other combinations of consonants, (along with ψ, ξ, ζ,) though qualified to be *initial*, are of course foreign to the purpose, as never being *permissive* also; at least in the practice of those authors to whom these remarks are confined.

The combinations last mentioned it may be allowed in future to call *non-permissive;* and for this reason, that neither within the same word, nor between one word and another, (of verse at least,) do they permit a preceding short vowel to be pronounced distinctly apart: it seems to be coupled with them always by an irresistible attraction.

In turning from the Comic trimeter of Aristophanes to the stately hexameter of Homer, the difference of syllabic quantity must be strikingly felt: and that contrast is here purposely taken, to show more clearly in what the great difference consists betwixt the prosody of heroic and that of dramatic verse.

2 D

4. Homer seldom allows a short vowel to form a short syllable before any of those *permissive* pairs lately detailed, and only before some few of them. The following cases occur betwixt one word and another : such corrcptions within the same word are yet more uncommon.

A. 113. Οἴκοι ἔχειν· καὶ γάρ ῥα Κλυταιμνήστρης προβέβουλα.
— 263. Οἷον Πειρίθοόν τε, Δρύαντά τε, ποιμένα λαῶν.
— 528. ᾽Η, καὶ κυανέῃσιν ἐπ᾽ ὀφρύσι νεῦσε Κρονίων.
— 609. Ζεὺς δὲ πρὸς ὃν λέχος ἤϊ᾽ Ὀλύμπιος ἀστεροπητής.

5. Aristophanes (with very few exceptions in Anapestic verse, pointed out by Porson, pp. ix. lxi. = p. 54) never allows a short vowel *cum ictu* to form a long syllable with any permissive pair, even within the same word.

$$\overset{|}{}\quad\overset{\|}{}$$

Plut. 419. ποιοισιν ὁπ-λοις ἢ δυνάμει πεποιθότες;

Such was, indeed, the vulgar reading, till Dawes (*M. C.* p. 196) anticipating, as usual, the Ravenna MS., gave the true text :

$$\overset{|}{}\quad\overset{\|}{}$$

Ποιοις ὁ-πλοισιν ἢ δυνάμει πεποιθότες;

6. Homer, on the other hand, not only in the same word *cum ictu*, but in the same word *extra ictum*, and even between two words in the same *debilis positio*, makes the syllable long.

A. 13. Λυσόμενός τε θυγατ-ρα, φέρων τ᾽ ἀπερείσι᾽ ἄποινα.

— 77. ᾽Η μέν μοι πρόφ-ρων ἔπεσιν καὶ χερσὶν ἀρήξειν.

— 345. ῾Ως φάτο· Πατ-ροκ-λος δὲ φίλῳ ἐπεπείθεθ᾽ ἑταίρῳ.

Δ. 57. αλλαχ-ρη καὶ ἐμὸν θέμεναι πόνον οὐκ ἀτέλεστον.

H. 189. γνω δεκ-ληρον σῆμα ἰδών, γήθησε δὲ θυμῷ.

7. The only possible case in which Aristophanes might prolong such a syllable would be in the use of verbs like these, ἐκ-λύω, ἐκ-μαίνω, ἐκ-νεύω, ἐκ-ρέω, if compounds of that kind ever occur; because, from the very nature of the compound, ἐκ must always be pronounced distinct from the initial consonant of the verb.

8. In Homer, on the contrary, even the loose vowel of augment (ε) or reduplication, when it precedes πλ, κλ, κρ, τρ, &c., initial of the verb, not only *cum ictu*, but even *extra ictum*, is made to form a long syllable.

Δ. 46. ἐκ-λαγξαν δ' ἄρ' ὀϊστοὶ ἐπ' ὤμων χωομένοιο.

— 309. 'Ες δ' ἐρέτας ἐκ-ρινεν ἐείκοσιν, ἐς δ' ἑκατόμβην.

H. 176. Πεξαμένη, χερσὶ πλοκαμους ἐπ-λεξε φαεινούς.

N. 542. Δαιμόν τύψ', ἐπί οἱ τετ-ραμμένον, ὀξέϊ δουρί.

9. In Homer no dissyllabic word like πατρός, τέκνον, ὄφρα, &c., which can have the first syllable long, is ever found with it otherwise: in Aristophanes those first syllables are constantly shortened.

10. Briefly, then, it may be said, that in Homer, whatever can be long is very seldom (and under very nice circumstances) ever short: in Aristophanes, whatever can be short is never found long.

To complete the purpose of this little sketch, the tragic prosody also (of Euripides, for instance), in a few correspondent points, may as well be presented.

11. Aristophanes, even in the same word, and where the *ictus* might be available (§ 5), never makes a long syllable: Euripides, who excludes the prolongation even *cum ictu* betwixt one word and another,

(*Orest.* 64, παρθένον, ἐμῇ τε μητρὶ παρέδωκεν τρέφειν,

i. e. not παρεδωκετ ρεφειν,)

within the same word, readily allows it:

Med. 4. τμηθεῖσα πεύκη, μήδ' ἐρετ-μῶσαι χέρας.

—— 17. προδοὺς γὰρ αὐτοῦ τεκ-να, δεσπότιν τ' ἐμήν.

—— 25. τὸν πάντα συντήκουσα δακ-ρύοις χρόνον.

12. In Euripides, even those dissyllabic words (alluded to § 9), wherever, from its position, the syllable is decisively long or short, exhibit that syllable *thrice short* to *one* case of *long*. Consequently, in certain positions (unictuated) of Iambic or Trochaic verse, which indifferently admit either quantity, there can be no reasonable ground for supposing that syllable to be lengthened: of course, therefore, the following lines are thus read:

Med. 226. πι-κρὸς πολίταις ἐστὶν ἀμαθίας ὕπο.
Iph. A. 891. ἐπὶ τίνος σπουδαστέον μοι μᾶλλον, ἢ τέ-κνου πέρι;

13. In cases where the augment falls as in *ἐπέκλωσεν* or *κεκλῆσθαι*, or where, as in *πολύχρυσος* and *ἀπότροποι*, the short vowel closes the first part of a composite word, the prolongation of that syllable in Euripides, though not altogether avoided, is yet exceedingly rare. (R. P. *ad Orest.* 64.)

14. One great cause of the many mistakes about syllabic quantity should seem to be involved in that false position of S. Clarke's (*ad Il. B.* 537), that a short vowel preceding *any* two consonants with which a syllable can be commenced may form a short syllable. Nothing was ever more unluckily asserted, or more pregnant with confusion and error.

15. To the perspicacity and acuteness of Dawes (*M. C.* pp. 90, 1, 196, 146, 7) we are indebted for the first clear statement of the principal points in this department of prosody: to the deliberate and masterly judgment of Porson (*ad Orest.* 64, and elsewhere) we owe whatever else is correctly and certainly known.

16. Some little things, however, may serve to show that an English ear, especially on a sudden appeal, is no very competent judge of *Attic corrections*, so called.

For instance, in the following lines:

> *Phœn.* 1414. *ἐν τῷδε μήτηρ ἡ τάλαινα προσπίτνει,*
> *Alc.*   434. *ἐπίσταμαί γε, κοὐκ ἄφνω κακὸν τόδε,*

it is not from any practice of our own, certainly, that we should pronounce the words *προσπί-τνει* and *ἄ-φνω* with precision and facility in that very way.

17. So, too, if *ἀκμή* and *ἔσμεν* were on a sudden proposed as to the shortening of the first syllable in each, it might seem to an English ear just as improbable in the noun as in the verb; although in Athenian utterance we know very well the fact was quite otherwise.

Toup (vid. Emendd. Vol. I. 114, 5; IV. 441) maintained in his day (what is now called) the *permissiveness* of *σμ*: and actually, on that ground, suggested the following as an emendation of a passage in Sophocles, for *ἐμέν* or *ἴμεν*:

> *Elect.* 21, 2................*ὡς ἐνταῦθ᾽ ἐ-σμέν,*
> *ἵν᾽ οὐκέτ᾽ ὀκνεῖν καιρός, ἀλλ᾽ ἔργων ἀκμή,*

(where *ἀκμή*, of course, is right enough, being pronounced *ἀ-κμή*). Since Porson's delicate correction of that error (u. s. p. 441) no argument has been advanced in its defence. And yet, *à priori,* why should not σμ be *permissive*, as well as θμ, for instance? " The consonants σμ can begin a word; why not commence a separate syllable? How can θμ commence a syllable, when notoriously it cannot begin a word?"

18. The plain truth, however, stands thus : that κμ and θμ, (with χμ, φν, τν,) though never used as *initial* to any word, yet within the same words are found *permissive* much too often to admit the shadow of a doubt on that head.

Phœn. 351. Καὶ γὰρ μέτρ' ἀνθρώποισι καὶ μέρη στα-θμῶν

may be taken for one undisputed example; there is no want of more.

19. How far in the different pairs of consonants which have been defined as *non-permissive* (§ 3), a physical necessity was the obstacle, in some at least, if not in others, might be a question for anatomy rather than for criticism.

Special Rules of Quantity.

1. Ἡμῖν and ὑμῖν, when so written for ἡμῖν, ὑμῖν, have the last syllable short in Sophocles. Elmsley has thus stated the case.

Solus e tragicis secundam in ἡμῖν et ὑμῖν corripit Sophocles, monente Porsono *Præfat.* p. xxxvii. Id in integris fabulis bis et quadragies extra melica fecit. Septies autem necessario produxit ante vocalem; *Œd. Tyr.* 631, *Œd. Col.* 826, *Trach.* 1273, *Aj.* 689, *El.* 355, 454, 1381. Quæ omnia emendationis egere suspicari videtur Porsonus. Ego vero casu potius quam consilio factum puto, ut tam raro ancipitem vocalem necessario produceret Noster. Nam simile quid Euripidi accidisse video. Is, ut monuit Porsonus, posteriorem horum pronominum syllabam nusquam corripuit.—Quod ad accentum correptæ formæ attinet, alii ἡμιν et ὑμιν, alii ἡμὶν et ὑμὶν scribendum arbitrantur. Hanc scripturam adhibuit Aldus in *Ajace* et *Electræ* versibus primis 357, dehinc vero ἡμιν et ὑμιν usque ad finem libri. Ἡμὶν et ὑμὶν ubique editiones recentiores, quarum scripturam post Brunckium adoptavi. Elmsley, *Præf. ad Œdip. Tyrann.* p. x.

2. I is common in ἰάομαι, ἰατρός, λίαν, ὄρνις. The quantity of this vowel varies in ἀνία and ἀνιαρός.

Nomen ἀνία, vel ἀνίη, plerumque penultimam producit, aliquando corripit, ut in quatuor exemplis a Ruhnkenio, *Epist. Crit.* ii. p. 276, adductis.—Verbum ἀνιάω vel ἀνιάζω, apud Epicos poëtas secundam plerumque producit, ut et in Soph. *Antig.* 319. Verbum ἀνιῶ apud

Aristophanem penultimam ter corripit, semel producit *Eq.* 348.
(349, Bekk.)—Semper, nisi fallor, secunda in ἀνιαρὸς ab Euripide et
Aristophane corripitur, producitur a Sophocle *Antig.* 316. Sed
ubique tertia syllaba longa est. l'orson. *ad Phœn.* v. 1334.

3. I is long in κόνις, -ιν, ὄφις -ιν, e. g. Æsch. *Pers.* 1085, *Choeph.*
928

EXAMINATION PAPERS

ON THE

GREEK TRAGEDIANS.

EXAMINATION PAPERS

ON THE

GREEK TRAGEDIANS.

ÆSCHYLI PERSÆ.

TRINITY COLLEGE. *June*, 1832.

MR. THIRLWALL.

1. DEFINE your notion of epic, lyric, and dramatic poetry. What species of composition is implied in the term lyrical Tragedy? Mention the various meanings that have been derived from the etymology of the words τραγῳδία and τρυγῳδία. Which of these explanations is most conformable to analogy?

2. On what grounds, according to Aristotle, did the Dorians lay claim to the invention of Tragedy and Comedy? Point out the fallacy of the argument he mentions. In what Greek cities out of Attica were early advances made toward dramatic poetry? Where was any of its branches brought to its perfection earlier than at Athens? Explain the proverb οὐδὲ τὰ Στησιχόρου τρία γιγμώσκεις. Mention the age, country, and inventions of Stesichorus, and the character of his poetry as described by the ancients.

3. Relate the principal Attic legends concerning the introduction of the worship of Bacchus into Athens. How did the oracles contribute to this end? By what means does the worship of Bacchus appear to have become connected with that of Apollo at Delphi, and with that of Ceres at Eleusis?

4. Enumerate the Attic Dionysia, and explain the origin of their particular names. In what Attic month, and at what season of the year, was each celebrated? To what division of the Greek nation did the month Lenæon belong? To what Attic month did it cor-

respond ? What is the origin of the name, and what inference may be drawn from it as to the place of the month in the calendar? Which was the most ancient of the Dionysia at Athens?

5. At which of the Dionysia were dramatic entertainments given? In which were the dithyrambic choruses exhibited? What were the peculiar regulations affecting the performances at each festival? In which were the τραγῳδοὶ καινοί? What authority is there for believing that women were admitted to these spectacles?

6. Translate: εἰσήνεγκε νόμον τὰς τραγῳδίας αὐτῶν ἐν κοινῷ γραψαμένους φυλάττειν καὶ τὸν τῆς πόλεως γραμματέα παραναγιγνώσκειν τοῖς ὑποκρινομένοις. Who was the author of this law, and what were its objects? Translate and explain: οἱ ποιηταὶ τρεῖς ἐλάμβανον ὑποκριτὰς κλήρῳ νεμηθέντας ὑποκρινομένους τὰ δράματα, ὧν ὁ νικήσας εἰς τοὐπιὸν ἄκριτος παραλαμβάνεται. What were the particular denominations of these actors? How were the parts in the Persæ probably distributed among them? What was the general name for the other characters in a play?

7. Give some examples to illustrate the different light in which actors were regarded by the Greeks and by the Romans. How is the fact to be explained? From what causes did the profession of an actor rise in importance in Greece between the age of Æschylus and that of Demosthenes?

8. What part of the expense of the theatrical entertainments was defrayed by the Athenian government, and what by individuals? Mention the various duties and charges to which the χορηγοί were subject. With what powers did the law invest them in the execution of their office? Explain the origin and nature of the Θεωρικόν, the changes that took place in the distribution of it, and its political consequences. Who were the θεατρῶναι and θεατροπῶλαι? Explain the allusion in the characteristic: καὶ ξένοις δὲ αὐτοῦ θέαν ἀγοράσας μὴ δοὺς τὸ μέρος θεωρεῖν. ἄγειν δὲ τοὺς υἱοὺς εἰς τὴν ὑστεραίαν καὶ τὸν παιδαγωγόν.

9. Mention the various ways in which Greek Tragedy was made to answer political purposes, and produce some illustrations from the extant plays. By which Tragedian was the drama most frequently so applied? What arguments beside that of the Persæ were taken from events subsequent to the return of the Heracleids? How do you explain the saying attributed to Æschylus: τὰς αὑτοῦ τραγῳδίας τεμάχη εἶναι τῶν Ὁμήρου μεγάλων δείπνων?

10. State the best attested dates of the birth and death of Æschylus. Enumerate his dramatic predecessors and contemporaries in the order of time. Mention the leading occurrences in

his life, the honours paid to him after his death, the members of his family whose names are known, and the causes of their celebrity. Do his plays contain any intimation as to his political sentiments? What grounds have been assigned for the charge of impiety said to have been brought against him? What reason is there for believing that he made more than one journey to Sicily? When did Hiero become king of Syracuse, and how long did his reign last?

11. What were the plays that made up the Tetralogy to which the *Persæ* belonged? State the principal features of the legends connected with their names. What ground is there for supposing that the Trilogy had a common title? In what manner may the argument of the *Persæ* have been connected with those of the other two pieces? What other poets wrote plays of the same name?

12. Quote the lines of Aristophanes which relate to the chorus of the *Persæ*. What difficulty have they occasioned? How may they be understood, without supposing them to refer to any other edition of the play than the one we have? What other references are made by ancient writers to passages of the *Persæ* not contained in the extant play of that name? How may this be accounted for, without supposing them to have dropped out of the latter? How does Stanley conjecture the chorus of the *Persæ* to have been composed? How may this conjecture be reconciled with the usual number of the tragic chorus? How is it confirmed by the distribution of the dialogue?

13. Make out a list of the Median and Persian kings, down to the fall of the Persian monarchy, noticing the variations between Æschylus, Herodotus, and Ctesias. Who was Ctesias? when did he live, and what were his sources of information? Give the pedigree of Xerxes, and show how he was related to Cyrus. How many kings of the name of Darius are mentioned in history?

14. Mention the divisions of the Persian nation according to Herodotus. How is Xenophon to be understood when he says: λέγονται Πέρσαι ἀμφὶ τὰς δώδεκα μυριάδας εἶναι? Mention the divisions of the Persian empire accordingly to Plato, Herodotus, and the Old Testament. How may the three accounts be reconciled? Trace the frontier of the empire under Darius in the last year of his reign, and mention the modern names of the countries through which it passes. Give the modern names of Susa and Ecbatana, and mention the different opinions on these points. By what name is Susa described in the Old Testament? What is the meaning of the word? Mention the mythical and the historical person to whom the foundation of the city is attributed.

15. What is known of the circumstances and life of Darius before

his accession? How does Æschylus allude to the manner in which he obtained the crown? Give a short account of his wars, and show how far their several issues justify the language of Æschylus: νόστοι ἐκ πολέμων ἀπόνους ἀπαθεῖς εὖ πράσσοντας ἄγον οἴκους.

16. Give an account of the invasion of Greece by the Gauls, mentioning the time, the occasion, and the leaders of the expedition. Describe the line of their march, and compare the principal incidents of the campaign with those of the Persian invasion.

17. Draw a map of Salamis and the adjacent coast, marking the situation of the towns of Salamis, Megara, and Eleusis, and the ἀκταὶ Σιληνίων, the spot from which Xerxes viewed the battle, and the island of Psyttaleia. Translate ἐπειδὴ ἐγίνοντο μέσαι νύκτες, ἀνῆγον μὲν τὸ ἀπ' ἑσπέρης κέρας κυκλούμενοι πρὸς τὴν Σαλαμῖνα· ἀνῆγον δὲ οἱ ἀμφὶ τὴν Κέον τε καὶ τὴν Κυνόσουραν τεταγμένοι, κατέχον τε μέχρι Μουνυχίης πάντα τὸν πορθμὸν τῇσι νηυσί. Describe the position of the three last-mentioned places.

18. Give a short account of the history of Salamis, and of the way in which it fell under the dominion of Athens. On what evidence did the Athenians found their claim to the island? What other ancient name had it? What is its modern one? Mention the meaning of each. Does Homer (as quoted by Stanley) throw any light upon the epithet πελειοθρέμμονα? Explain the epithet in the words ἀκτὰς ἀμφὶ Κυχρείας.

19. Translate:

Ἦρξεν μὲν, ὦ δέσποινα, τοῦ παντὸς κακοῦ
Φανεὶς ἀλάστωρ ἢ κακὸς δαίμων ποθέν.
Ἀνὴρ γὰρ Ἕλλην. κ. τ. λ.

Who is the person here alluded to? Is he accurately described as ἀνὴρ Ἕλλην? How was he rewarded for his services?

20. Translate:

—— Ἕλλησιν μὲν ἦν
Ὁ πᾶς ἀριθμὸς ἐς τριακάδας δέκα
Νεῶν, δεκὰς δ' ἦν τῶνδε χωρὶς ἔκκριτος.

What is the difference between the numbers of the Grecian fleet described in this passage and in Herodotus? What part of this fleet was furnished by Greeks of Ionian extraction? Compare the statements of Æschylus and Herodotus as to the numbers of the Persian fleet. Supply the principal events omitted by Æschylus that intervened between the battle of Salamis and the retreat of Xerxes, and between his arrival at Sardis and his return to Susa.

21. Translate;

"Ἐλθ᾽ ἐπ᾽ ἄκρον κόρυμβον ὄχθου
Κροκόβαπτον ποδὸς εὔμαριν ἀείρων
Βασιλείου τιάρας
Φάλαρον πιφαύσκων.

Explain the allusion in the last part of this passage? Is the evocation of Darius founded on Grecian or on Persian usage? Where was Darius buried?

22. "Ἀργύρου πηγή τις αὐτοῖς ἔστι, θησαυρὸς χθονός.

Describe the district in which this treasure lay, and mention the ancient and modern names of the principal towns in it. Give an account of the manner in which its produce was applied before and at the time of Æschylus. By what peculiar privileges did the government encourage the cultivation of it? Explain Xenophon's project for increasing its productiveness.

23. Explain the allusion in the words ἰὰν Μαριανδυνοῦ θρηνητῆρος πέμψω, and give some other examples of similar national usages. Why is Atossa made to describe Greece as Ἰαόνων γῆν, and afterwards to say, ἡ μὲν πέπλοισι Περσικοῖς ἠσκημένη, ἡ δ᾽ αὖτε Δωρικοῖσιν? Why do the Greek writers speak of the Persian war as τὰ Μηδικά? Why is Xerxes described as Σύριον ἅρμα διώκων? Translate: δίρρυμά τε καὶ τρίρρυμα τέλη? What mention is found in history of the use of chariots in the Persian armies?

24. Translate the following passage, and arrange it in metrical order, naming the verses into which you divide it. δολόμητιν δ᾽ ἀπάταν θεοῦ τίς ἀνὴρ θνατὸς ἀλύξει; τίς ὁ κραιπνῷ ποδὶ πηδήματος εὐπετοῦς ἀνάσσων; φιλόφρων γὰρ σαίνουσα τὸ πρῶτον, παράγει βροτὸν εἰς ἀρκύστατα τόθεν οὐκ ἔστιν ὑπὲρ θνατὸν ἀλύξαντα φυγεῖν.

25. Define and exemplify the metrical terms, arsis, thesis, basis, anacrusis, anaclasis, cœsura, prosodia. What is meant by metres κατ᾽ ἀντιπάθειαν μικτά? What is an asynartetic verse?

Explain the grounds on which Hermann objects to the ancient mode of measuring the Iambic verse.

26. Explain the terms, hyperbaton, zeugma, prolepsis, and give an instance of each. Translate: τίς οὐ τέθνηκε, τίνα δὲ καὶ πενθήσομεν Τῶν ἀρχελείων, ὅς τ᾽, ἐπὶ σκηπτουχίᾳ Ταχθείς, ἄνανδρον τάξιν ἠρήμου θανών. In the lines: ὡς εἰ μελαίνης νυκτὸς ἵξεται κνέφας, Ἕλληνες οὐ μένοιεν, ἀλλὰ σέλμασι Νεῶν ἐπενθορόντες ἄλλος ἄλλοσε Δρασμῷ κρυφαίῳ βίοτον ἐκσωσοίατο—what corrections have been proposed? Translate the lines as they are here written. Explain the construction of the lines: ἐνταῦθα πέμπει τούσδ᾽, ὅπως ὅταν νεῶν

Φθαρέντες ἐχθροὶ νῆσον ἐκσωζοίατο. In what cases are adverbs of time properly followed by the indicative, in what by the subjunctive or the optative mood? When is the subjunctive, and when the optative required after a relative pronoun or adverb? Explain the distinction between the grammatical and the rhetorical ellipsis. To what figure does the construction of the following words belong? τυτθὰ δ᾽ ἐκφυγεῖν ἄνακτ᾽ αὐτὸν ὡς ἀκούομεν Θρῇκης ἀμπεδιήρεις δυσχίμους τε κελεύθους. Distinguish the different meanings of the following words according to the difference of their accentuation: αγη, βιος, βροτος, γαυλος, δημος, θερμος, θολος, καλος, κηρ, ληνος, λις, νειος, νομος, τροπος.

SOPHOCLIS PHILOCTETES.

1. (*a*) Give the dates of the birth and death and first tragic victory of Sophocles.

   (*b*) In what war was he engaged? What was its duration and event?

   (*c*) How long after the death of Sophocles and Euripides did Aristophanes produce his *Ranæ*?

   (*d*) Translate and explain:

   HPA. Εἶτ᾽ οὐχὶ Σοφοκλέα, πρότερον ὄντ᾽ Εὐριπίδου,
   Μέλλεις ἀναγαγεῖν, εἴπερ ἐκεῖθεν δεῖ σ᾽ ἄγειν;
   ΔΙΟ. Οὐ πρίν γ᾽ ἂν Ἰοφῶντ᾽, ἀπολαβὼν αὐτὸν μόνον,
   Ἄνευ Σοφοκλέους ὅ τι ποιεῖ κωδωνίσω. (*Ran.* 76.)

2. (*a*) How far does Phrynichus appear to deserve the title of Father of Tragedy?

   (*b*) Why was a fine imposed upon him for his Μιλήτου ἅλωσις? Where is the story related?

   (*c*) Translate and explain μινυρίζοντες μέλη ἀρχαιομελισιδωνοφρυνιχήρατα. (Arist. *Vesp.*)

3. (*a*) What do you consider to be the object of Epic, and Dramatic poetry?

   (*b*) What the chief characteristic of *Grecian* tragedy?

   (*c*) How was the Drama encouraged at Athens?

(*d*) At what seasons of the year, and at which of the Dionysia, were dramatic entertainments given?

(*e*) What is the controversy respecting the Lenæa?

(*f*) What was the nature of the laws περὶ τῶν θεωρικῶν? When introduced, and with what object? How does Demosthenes allude to them?

4. (*a*) What account does Homer give of Philoctetes? How many ships did he bring to the war?

(*b*) Does he allude to his aid as requisite for the taking of Troy?

(*c*) Is his fate after the fall of Troy alluded to by Homer or Virgil?

5. (*a*) What is the situation of Lemnos with respect to Athens?

(*b*) How came it to be inhabited by the Pelasgi? (Herod. B. VI.)

(*c*) How did it fall under the power of the Athenians? (*ibid.*)

(*d*) Where was the island Chryse situated? What account does Pausanias give of it?

(*e*) How was Hercules connected with it?

6. Explain the terms 'cæsura,' 'quasi-cæsura,' and 'pause' in the Iambic trimeter of the tragedians.

7. Ἑρμῆς δ' ὁ πέμπων δόλιος ἡγήσαιτο νῷν. (v. 133.)

(*a*) In what sense is Mercury called πομπαῖος in the *Ajax?*

(*b*) Illustrate πομπαῖος and δόλιος from Horace.

(*c*) What is the meaning of the Homeric epithet ἐριούνιος?

(*d*) Translate:

> Ἀλλά σ' ὁ Μαίας πομπαῖος ἄναξ
> Πελάσειε δόμοις,
> Ὧν τ' ἐπίνοιαν σπεύδεις κατέχων
> Πράξειας. (Eurip. *Med.* 755.)

8.
> Ὀρεστέρα παμβῶτι Γᾶ, μῆτερ αὐτοῦ Διός,
> Ἰὼ μάκαιρα ταυροκτόνων
> Λεόντων ἔφεδρε. (v. 380.)

(*a*) Illustrate παμβῶτι Γᾶ from Lucretius (B. II.). What reason does he assign for the Greek poets representing Cybele (or Tellus) in a chariot drawn by lions?

(*b*) Why was she called 'Idæa Mater'? What ambiguity has the word 'Idæa' caused?

(*c*) How does Euripides connect Bacchus and Rhea? (*Bacchæ.*)

9. (a) Translate:

Ἰδοὺ δέχου, παῖ· τὸν φθόνον δὲ πρόσκυσον,
Μή σοι γενέσθαι πολύπον' αὐτά. (v. 759.)

(b) Does the expression τὸν φθόνον δὲ πρόσκυσον, or a similar
one, occur elsewhere?

(c) Why was Nemesis called 'Αδραστεία?

10.   —— ἐπεὶ πάρεστι μὲν
Τεῦκρος παρ' ἡμῖν, τήνδ' ἐπιστήμην ἔχων. (v. 1038.)

(a) In what sense, and by whom, is Teucer called ὁ τοξότης
in the *Ajax*? Translate Teucer's reply οὐ γὰρ βάναυσον
τὴν τέχνην ἐκτησάμην. What difference in the sense
would be caused by the omission or different position of
the article τήν?

(b) Which of the Greeks at Troy was the most famous for the
use of the bow? (Hom. *Od.* VIII.)

(c) How do you account for the use of the bow being held in
contempt by the Athenians?

(d) What was their peculiar offensive weapon? (*Æsch. Pers.*)

11.   Ὕπν' ὀδύνας ἀδαής, Ὕπνε δ' ἀλγέων,
Εὐαὴς ἡμῖν ἔλθοις
Εὐαίων, εὐαίων, ὦναξ.
Ὄμμασι δ' ἀντέχοις τάνδ' αἴγλαν,
Ἃ τέταται τανῦν. (v. 810.)

Give Welcker's interpretation of this passage, with the grounds on
which it rests.

12.   Χὠ Κεφαλλήνων ἄναξ. (v. 262.)

(a) What do we find respecting the Κεφαλλῆνες in Homer?

(b) Translate:

ἀλλ' οὐχ ὁ Τυδέως γόνος,
Οὐδ' οὑμπολητὸς Σισύφου Λαερτίου,
Οὐ μὴ θάνωσι. τούσδε γὰρ μὴ ζῆν ἔδει. (v. 411.)

What is the objection to Hermann's interpretation?

(c) To which of the generals in the *Iliad* is Sisyphus said to be
related? (*Il.* VI.) What character is there given of
him?

(d) How may οὐ μὴ θάνωσι be explained by an ellipsis?

(e) What is the chief distinction in the use of οὐ and μή?
Distinguish between ψυχὴν σκοπῶν φιλόσοφον καὶ μή,
and ψυχὴν σκοπῶν φιλόσοφον καὶ οὔ.

13. (a) Distinguish between φυλάξεται στίβος (v. 48) and φυλαχ-θήσεται στίβος.

(b) What is the rule with respect to the use of πρὶν followed by an infinitive, or a subjunctive or optative mood? What is there remarkable in ὁ δὲ ἀδικέει ἀναπειθόμενος πρὶν ἢ ἀτρεκέως ἐκμάθῃ? (Herod. B. VII.)

14. Translate the following passages and explain the construction :

(a) ὅστις νόσου Κάμνοντι συλλάβοιτο. (v. 279.)

(b) τίνος γὰρ ὧδε τὸν μέγαν Χόλον κατ' αὐτῶν ἐγκαλῶν ἐλήλυθας ; (v. 325.)

(c) ὃν δὴ παλαί' ἂν ἐξ ὅτου δέδοικ' ἐγὼ Μή μοι βεβήκῃ. (v. 488.)

(d) πλησθῇς τῆς νόσου συνουσίᾳ. (v. 512.)

What peculiar sense does ἀναπίμπλασθαι admit? Is 'impleri' ever used in the same manner?

(e) πρὸς ποῖον ἂν τόνδ' αὐτὸς οὐδυσσεὺς ἔπλει; (v. 564.)

Explain the force of ἂν here, and in ἐνθένδε ἄνδρες οὔτε ὄντα, οὔτε ἂν γενόμενα, λογοποιοῦσιν. (Thucyd.)

15. Translate the following passages :

(a) Σκοπεῖν θ' ὅπου 'στ' ἐνταῦθα δίστομος πέτρα
Τοιάδ', ἵν' ἐν ψύχει μὲν ἡλίου διπλῆ
Πάρεστιν ἐνθάκησις, ἐν θέρει δ' ὕπνον
Δι' ἀμφιτρῆτος αὐλίου πέμπει πνοή. (v. 16.)

(b) Τί χρή, τί χρή με, δέσποτ', ἐν ξένᾳ ξένον
Στέγειν, ἢ τί λέγειν πρὸς ἄνδρ' ὑπόπταν ;
Φράζε μοι.   τέχνα γὰρ τέχνας ἑτέρας προὔχει,
Καὶ γνώμα, παρ' ὅτῳ
Τὸ θεῖον Διὸς σκῆπτρον ἀνάσσεται. (v. 135.)

(c) Εἰ δὲ πικρούς, ἄναξ, ἔχθεις 'Ατρείδας,
'Εγὼ μὲν τὸ κείνων κακὸν τῷδε κέρδος
Μετατιθέμενος, ἔνθαπερ ἐπιμέμονεν,
'Επ' εὐστόλου ταχείας νεὼς
Πορεύσαιμ' ἂν ἐς δόμους. (v. 504.)

(d) Εἶρπε δ' ἄλλον ἄλλοτε
Τότ' ἂν εἰλυόμενος,
Παῖς ἄτερ ὡς φίλας τιθήνας, ὅθεν εὐμάρει' ὑπάρ-
χοι, πόρον, ἀνίκ' ἐξανείη δακέθυμος ἄτα.
Οὐ φορβὰν ἱερᾶς γᾶς σπόρον, οὐκ ἄλλων
Αἴρων, τῶν νεμόμεσθ' ἀνέρες ἀλφησταί,
Πλὴν ἐξ ὠκυβόλων εἴποτε τόξων πτα-
νοῖς ἰοῖς ἀνύσειε γαστρὶ φορβάν. (v. 690.)

What are the metrical names of the lines (b) and (d)?

16. Give the meaning and derivation of the following words:

ὀγμεύω, σμυγερός, παλιντριβής, ἔμπυος, ἐχθόδοπος, οὐρεσιβώτας. In what other authors does ἐχθόδοπος occur? What different forms of οὐρεσιβώτας occur in Sophocles?

EURIPIDIS ALCESTIS.

TRINITY COLLEGE. *May*, 1837.

MR. DONALDSON.

1. TRACE the epic and lyric poetry of Greece to their respective sources, and show how each of them was related to the Athenian drama. Translate, γενομένη οὖν ἀπ᾽ ἀρχῆς αὐτοσχεδιαστικὴ καὶ ἡ τραγῳδία καὶ ἡ κωμῳδία, ἡ μὲν ἀπὸ τῶν ἐξαρχόντων τὸν διθύραμβον, ἡ δὲ ἀπὸ τῶν τὰ φαλλικά, κατὰ μικρὸν ηὐξήθη. Explain and justify this statement, particularly the former part of it. What other name was given to the διθύραμβος, and why? Of how many persons did the dithyrambic chorus consist? How did it differ from or agree with the chorus in a tragedy?

2. When did Arion flourish? How could he be said τραγικοῦ τρόπου εὑρετὴς γενέσθαι? Explain the word τραγῳδία consistently with your interpretation of this statement. What do you understand by a *lyrical tragedy?* What is known of Stesichorus, and what was his real name? Mention some of the principles which regulated the formation of proper names among the Greeks. Why was the name Aletes given to the founder of the Dorian dynasty at Corinth, and what name was for a similar reason borne by the son of Cimon? To what circumstance did the poet Euripides probably owe his name? Thucydides mentions Xenophon, the son of Euripides, as an Athenian general in the year 422 B.C.; could this Euripides have derived his name from the same cause?

3. By whom was the custom of performing tragic Trilogies introduced, and by whom was it first abandoned? What was the nature and origin of the fourth play in a Tetralogy? What place did the *Alcestis* occupy in the Tetralogy to which it belonged, and what were the other three plays? Is the inference which you might draw from the place of the *Alcestis* confirmed by any peculiarities in the play itself?

Translate:

> Nunc, quam rem oratum huc veni, primum proloquar,
> Post argumentum hujus eloquar tragœdiæ.
> Quid contraxistis frontem, quia tragœdiam
> Dixi futuram hanc? Deus sum! Conmutavero
> Eadem, si voltis. Faciam hanc ex tragœdia
> Comœdia ut sit omnibus isdem versibus.
> Utrum sit an ne voltis? Sed ego stultior :
> Quasi nesciam vos velle, qui divos siem!
> Teneo quid animi vostri super hac re siet.
> Faciam ut conmista sit Tragicocomœdia :
> Nam me perpetuo facere ut sit comœdia,
> Reges quo veniant et Di, non par arbitror.

Of what play is this said? Mention other instances of an extravagance, similar to that on which the plot of it depends, in the dramatic literature of ancient or modern times.

4. How was the iambic trimeter derived from the dactylic hexameter? Give a scheme of the iambic trimeter acatalectic both tragic and comic. What is Porson's rule about the pause in the tragic trimeter? Can you mention any exceptions to it? We learn from Joannes Laurentius Lydus that Rhinthon wrote comedies in hexameter verse; what remarkable fact in the literature of Rome is explained by this? To what classes of Greek plays did the *prætextata, togata, Atellana* and *planipes*, respectively correspond? Explain the last word, and show from Horace that the *prætextata* and *togata* were different. What is Niebuhr's opinion about the *prætextata*?

5. Translate :

> Ἐγὼ καὶ διὰ μούσας
> Καὶ μετάρσιος ἦξα, καὶ
> Πλείστων ἀψάμενος λόγων
> Κρεῖσσον οὐδὲν ἀνάγκας
> Εὗρον, οὐδέ τι φάρμακον
> Θρῄσσαις ἐν σανίσιν τὰς
> Ὀρφείᾳ κατέγραψεν
> Γῆρυς, οὐδ' ὅσα Φοῖβος Ἀσκληπιάδαις ἔδωκε,
> Φάρμακα πολυπόνοις ἀντιτέμων βροτοῖσι.

(a) Explain and illustrate by examples διὰ μούσας—ἦξα, and φάρμακα—ἀντιτέμων.

(b) To what branch of his studies does Euripides allude when he says, μετάρσιος ἦξα?

2 E 2

Translate:

Οὐ γὰρ, μὰ Δί̓, οἶσθ᾽ ὅτι ἡ πλείστους αὗται βόσκουσι σοφιστὰς,
Θουριομάντεις, ἰατροτέχνας, σφραγιδονυχαργοκομήτας,
Κυκλίων τε χορῶν ᾀσματοκάμπτας, ἄνδρας μετεωροφένακας.

Also:

Σύ τε λεπτοτάτων λήρων ἱερεῦ, φράζε πρὸς ἡμᾶς ὅ, τι χρῄζεις.
Οὐ γὰρ ἂν ἄλλῳ γ᾽ ὑπακούσαιμεν τῶν νῦν μετεωροσοφιστῶν,
Πλὴν ἢ Προδίκῳ· τῷ μὲν σοφίας καὶ γνώμης εἵνεκα, σοὶ δὲ
"Οτι βρενθύει τ᾽ ἐν ταῖσιν ὁδοῖς καὶ τὠφθαλμὼ παραβάλλεις,
Κἀνυπόδητος κακὰ πόλλ᾽ ἀνέχει, κἀφ᾽ ἡμῖν σεμνοπροσωπεῖς.

And explain all the allusions in both passages. Who were the Sophists? What is known of the Prodicus mentioned in the second passage?

(c) Give some account of Anaxagoras and his peculiar doctrines.

Translate:

᾿Αναξαγόρας ἀπείθους εἶναί φησι τὰς ἀρχάς· σχέδον γὰρ ἅπαντα τὰ ὁμοιομερῆ, καθάπερ ὕδωρ ἢ πῦρ, οὕτω γίγνεσθαι καὶ ἀπόλλυσθαί φησι συγκρίσει καὶ διακρίσει μόνον, ἄλλως δ᾽ οὔτε γίγνεσθαι οὔτ᾽ ἀπόλλυσθαι, ἀλλὰ διαμένειν ἀΐδια.

And,

Τουτέων δὲ οὕτω διακεκριμένων γινώσκειν χρὴ ὅτι πάντα οὐδὲν ἐλάσσω ἐστὶν οὐδὲ πλέω. οὐ γὰρ ἀνυστὸν πάντων πλέω εἶναι, ἀλλὰ πάντα ἴσα αἰεί.

What was the connexion between Euripides and Anaxagoras? Mention any instances in which Euripides has expressed the opinions of this philosopher.

(d) What are the σανίδες Θρῆσσαι here alluded to?

(e) In what metre are these lines written?

6. Describe the general features of a Greek dramatic representation. Where was the Theatre of Athens situated? Quote instances of allusions made by the dramatists to the locality of the Theatre and the surrounding scenery.

7. What was χορὸν διδόναι? When did the tragic contests take place? In what year did Euripides bring out the Tetralogy to which the *Alcestis* belonged, and what was his fortune on this occasion? What play in this Tetralogy was continually ridiculed by Aristophanes, and why? How is it parodied in the *Acharnians*?

Translate:

Σὺ δή με ταῦτ᾽, ὦ στωμυλιοσυλλεκτάδη
Καὶ πτωχόποιε καὶ ῥακιοσυρραπτάδη;

What was probably the object of Aristophanes in composing the *Frogs?*

Translate and explain :

ΞΑ.   κἄπειτα πῶς
     Οὐ καὶ Σοφοκλέης ἀντελάβετα τοῦ θρόνου ;
AI. Μὰ Δί᾽ οὐκ ἐκείνος, ἀλλ᾽ ἔκυσε μὲν Αἰσχύλον,
     Ὅτε δὴ κατῆλθε, κἀνέβαλε τὴν δεξιάν,
     Κἀκεῖνος ὑπεχώρησεν αὐτῷ τοῦ θρόνου.

8. Give the general rule for the construction of verbs with the particle ἄν. What do you conceive to be the origin of this word? Show that there is no need of alteration in οὐ γὰρ αἰδ᾽ ἂν εἰ πείσαιμί νιν, and confirm this reading by adducing a similar construction in Latin.

9.   Τί σεσίγηται δόμος ᾿Αδμήτου ;
     Οὔ τ᾽ἂν φθιμένας γ᾽ ἐσιώπων.

Distinguish between σιγᾶν and σιωπᾶν. Which of these words corresponds to *tacere* and which to *silere?*

10. Translate :

     Κλύει τις ἢ στεναγμὸν, ἢ
     Χερῶν κτύπον κατὰ στέγας,
     ῾Η γόον ὡς πεπραγμένων ;
     Οὐ μὰν οὐδέ τις ἀμφιπόλων
     Στατίζεται ἀμφὶ πύλας.
     Εἰ γὰρ μετακύμιος ἄτας,
     ῏Ω Παιάν, φανείης·

     Πυλᾶν πάροιθε δ᾽ οὐχ ὁρῶ
     Πηγαῖον, ὡς νομίζεται,
     Χέρνιβ᾽, ἐπὶ φθιτῶν πύλαις·
     Χαίτα τ᾽ οὔτις ἐπὶ προθύροις
     Τομαῖος ἃ δὴ νεκύων
     Πένθει πίτνει, οὐδὲ νεολαία
     Δουπεῖ χεὶρ γυναικῶν.

Explain the words στατίζεται, μετακύμιος, and χέρνιβα. Why does Elmsley object to πιτνεῖν and ῥιπτεῖν, and how are these forms supported by Hermann and Lobeck? What is, according to Hermann, the difference between ῥίπτειν and ῥιπτεῖν? Is it borne out by usage? What is generally the difference in signification between contracted and uncontracted verbs from the same root in Latin? Explain the formation of δυστυχεῖν from τυγχάνειν and of *belligerare* from *gerere*. The MSS. give νεολαία, Dindorf reads νολαία, Monk νεολαίᾳ. Which is right, and why?

11. Translate:

> Τί χρὴ γενέσθαι τὴν ὑπερβεβλημένην
> Γυναῖκα; πῶς δ᾽ ἂν μᾶλλον ἐνδείξαιτό τις
> Πόσιν προτιμῶσ᾽ ἢ θέλουσ᾽ ὑπερθανεῖν;

What is the difference in Plato between ἐνδείκνυσθαι and ἐπιδείκνυσθαι? What was the ἐπίδειξις of a Sophist? In what cases could an ἔνδειξις be brought according to the Athenian law, and how was it connected with an ἀπαγωγή?

12.   Λέξαι θέλω σοι πρὶν θανεῖν ἃ βούλομαι.

Distinguish accurately between θέλειν and βούλεσθαι. Translate: ἂν οἵ τε θεοὶ θέλωσι καὶ ὑμεῖς βούλησθε. Which is the older form, θέλειν or ἐθέλειν? What is the oldest form of βούλεσθαι?

13. Translate:

> Καὶ πῶς ἐπεσφρῶ τήνδε τῷ κείνης λέχει;——
> Καὶ μὴ 'πιγήμῃς τοῖσδε μητρυιὰν τέκνοις.——

And,

> ὃς ἐπὶ θυγατρὶ ἀμήτορι, τῇ οὔνομα ἦν Φρονίμη, ἐπὶ ταύτῃ ἔγημε ἄλλην γυναῖκα, ἡ δὲ ἐπεσελθοῦσα ἐδικαίευ εἶναι καὶ τῷ ἔργῳ μητρυιὴ τῇ Φρονίμῃ.

What is the force of ἐπὶ in these passages? What different signification does it bear in the word ἐπιγαμία? Give some account of the marriage law at Athens. How does Æschylus use the word μητρυιὰ metaphorically?

14.   Translate, explain, and compare the following passages:

> Σοφῇ δὲ χειρὶ τεκτόνων δέμας τὸ σὸν
> Εἰκασθὲν ἐν λέκτροισιν ἐκταθήσεται,
> Ὧι προσπεσοῦμαι καὶ περιπτύσσων χέρας
> Ὄνομα καλῶν σὸν τὴν καλὴν ἐν ἀγκάλαις
> Δόξω γυναῖκα καίπερ οὐκ ἔχων ἔχειν,
> Ψυχρὰν μέν, οἶμαι, τέρψιν, ἀλλ᾽ ὅμως βάρος
> Ψυχῆς ἀπαντλοίην ἄν· ἐν δ᾽ ὀνείρασι
> Φοιτῶσά μ᾽ εὐφραίνοις ἄν· ἡδὺ γὰρ φίλους
> Κἂν νυκτὶ λεύσσειν ὅντιν᾽ ἂν παρῇ χρόνον.

> Πόθῳ δ᾽ ὑπερποντίας
> Φάσμα δόξει δόμων ἀνάσσειν.
> Εὐμόρφων δὲ κολοσσῶν
> Ἔχθεται χάρις ἀνδρί,
> Ὀμμάτων δ᾽ ἐν ἀχηνίαις
> Ἔρρει πᾶσ᾽ Ἀφροδίτα.

Ὀνειρόφαντοι δὲ πενθήμονες
Πάρεισι δόξαι φέρουσαι χάριν ματαίαν.
Μάταν γὰρ εὖτ' ἂν ἐσθλά τις δοκῶν ὁρᾶν
Παραλλάξασά διὰ χερῶν
Βέβακεν ὄψις οὐ μεθύστερον
Πτεροῖς ὀπαδοῖς ὕπνου κελεύθοις.

15. Translate:

Πολλά σε μουσόπολοι
Μέλψουσι καθ' ἑπτάτονόν τ' ὀρείαν
Χέλυν ἔν τ' ἀλύροις κλέοντες ὕμνοις,
Σπάρτᾳ κυκλὰς ἁνίκα Καρνείου περινίσσεται ὥρα
Μηνὸς ἀειρομένας
Παννύχου σελάνας
Λιπαραῖσί τ' ἐν ὀλβίαις Ἀθάναις.

What was the origin and nature of the Carnea, and in what month were they celebrated? Why is the epithet λιπαρὸς applied to Athens?

16. How is the legend about the death of Alcestis and the servitude of Apollo to be explained?

Translate:

Οὑμὸς δ' ἀλέκτωρ αὐτὸν ἦγε πρὸς μύλην. (Soph. *Adm.*)

What is probably the meaning of the name Ἄδμητος as applied to this mythical King? How do you account for the introduction of Hercules? Was he a Dorian divinity? How does it appear from this play that Apollo and death were dressed? How are they represented in ancient works of art?

17. Translate:

καὶ σάφ' οἶδ' ὁθούνεκα
Τοῦ νῦν σκυθρωποῦ καὶ ξυνεστῶτος φρενῶν
Μεθορμιεῖ σε πίτυλος ἐμπεσὼν σκύφου.

And,

ὅ τε ἐκ γῆς πεζὸς ἀμφοτέρων, ἰσορρόπου τῆς ναυμαχίας καθεστηκυίας, πολὺν τὸν ἀγῶνα καὶ ξύστασιν τῆς γνώμης εἶχε.

Explain the word πίτυλος. Does μεθορμίσασθαι usually govern the genitive? If so, mention some instances.

18. Translate:

Ἀλλ' εὐτυχοίης, νόστιμον δ' ἔλθοις πόδα.
Ἀστοῖς δὲ πάσῃ τ' ἐννέπω τετραρχίᾳ
Χοροὺς ἐπ' ἐσθλαῖς συμφοραῖσιν ἱστάναι
Βωμούς τε κνισᾶν βουθύτοισι προστροπαῖς.

And the following oracle:

Αὐδῶ Ἐρεχθείδαισιν, ὅσοι Πανδίονος ἄστυ
Ναίετε, καὶ πατρίοισι νόμοις ἰθύνεθ' ἑορτὰς,
Μεμνῆσθαι Βάκχοιο, καὶ εὐρυχόρους κατ' ἀγυιὰς
Ἱστάναι ὡραίων Βρομίῳ χάριν ἄμμιγα πάντας
Καὶ κνισᾶν βωμοῖσι, κάρη στεφάνοις πυκάσαντας.

(a) What was the Tetrarchy here alluded to? Give some account of the ethnography and old constitution of Thessaly. Who were the Aleuadæ, and where did they reign? Where was the kingdom of Admetus? .

(b) Why does κνισᾶν govern an accusative in one of these passages and a dative in the other?

(c) What relation subsisted between Bacchus and Demeter? When was the worship of the former introduced into Attica, and when and by what means established at Athens?

19. Are μάρπτω and εὐμαρής connected? What is the root, and where does it appear in its simplest form? Derive ἀρταμεῖν, πλημμυρίς, (what is the quantity of the penultima in Homer?) μονάμυξ, ὀκνῶ, ὀρφανεύειν, κεδνός, σεμνός, and ἀνάγκη. Which is right, οἶδας or οἶσθα? What is the syntax of πρίν? Distinguish between ὁ ἄνθρωπος αὐτός, and ὁ αὐτὸς ἄνθρωπος. Is οὔ σοι μὴ μεθέψομαί ποτε an allowable construction? If so, what do these words mean? Are there any other instances of a similar construction? If so, adduce and explain them. Accentuate the following words according to their different significations: μητρο-κτονος, αθωος, σιγα, ποιησαι, νυμφιος, μυριοι, πειθω, and λιγυς. What are the futures of ἐσθίω and πίνω?

20. Translate the following passages, and point out any peculiarities which you may think deserving of notice:

(a)   συμμέτρως δ' ἀφίκετο
Φρουρῶν τόδ' ἦμαρ ᾧ θανεῖν αὐτὴν χρεών.

(b)   Πρὸς τῶν ἐχόντων, Φοῖβε, τὸν νόμον τίθης.

(c)   Πόλλ' ἂν σὺ λέξας οὐδὲν ἂν πλέον λάβοις·
Ἡ δ' οὖν γυνὴ κάτεισιν εἰς Ἅιδου δόμους.

(d) ΗΡΑ. Τίνος δ' ὁ θρέψας παῖς πατρὸς κομπάζεται;
ΧΟΡ. Ἄρεος, ζαχρύσου Θρηκίας πέλτης ἄναξ.

(e)   Τί χρῆμα κουρᾷ τῇδε πενθίμῳ πρέπεις;

(f)   Ἆ, μὴ πρόκλαι' ἄκοιτιν, ἐς τόδ' ἀναβαλοῦ.

(g)   Τοί γὰρ φυτεύων παῖδας οὐκέτ' ἂν φθάνοις.

(*h*) 'ΑΔΜ. Ὡς μήποτ' ἄνδρα τόνδε νυμφίον καλῶν.
'ΗΡΑ. Ἐπήνεσ' ἀλόχῳ πιστὸς οὕνεκ' εἶ φίλος.
(*i*) 'ΗΡΑ. Τόλμα προτεῖναι χεῖρα καὶ θιγεῖν ξένης.
'ΑΔΜ. Καὶ δὴ προτείνω, Γοργόν' ὡς καρατόμῳ.

SOPHOCLIS ANTIGONE.

Trinity College. *June*, 1860.

Mr. Hammond.

1. Quote Horace's account of the origin of the Greek Tragic Drama. Point out its errors. What writers composed tragedies at Athens ·before the time of Sophocles? What improvements in tragic art were successively introduced by them? What changes are attributed to Sophocles? Quote passages from Aristophanes in which allusion is made to Sophocles and his predecessors.

2. Give the dates of Sophocles' birth and death and of his first tragic victory. What was the title of his first Tragedy, and what the circumstances attending its representation? Discuss the date of the *Antigone*. Point out any passages which seem to you to refer to the political state of Athens. How does this play serve to connect Sophocles with Herodotus? What further evidence have we in support of this connection?

3. Give a general description of a Greek theatre, and show how it differed from a Roman theatre. Explain the terms:

θυμέλη—λογεῖον—προσκήνιον—περίακτος—βουλευτικόν.

Describe the locality of the theatre of Dionysus at Athens, and quote passages from the dramatists in which special allusion is made to its situation and construction.

4. Discuss the following questions, (1) The number of Dionysia at Athens: (2) The time of year at which each festival was held: (3) The peculiar circumstances and regulations affecting the audience and the performances at each festival.

5. How were the general expenses of the Dionysiac performances defrayed? What portion fell upon the choragus? What were the duties, privileges and powers attached to this office? To whom were the actors allotted? Mention the names of any who performed

2 E 3

in Sophocles' dramas. Assign the several parts of the *Antigone* to their respective actors. Is there any change of scene in this play? Is the Eccyclema employed?

6. (a) Ἔτι δὲ τρίτον παρὰ ταῦτα τὸν μέλλοντα ποιεῖν τι τῶν ἀνηκέστων δι' ἄγνοιαν ἀναγνωρίσαι πρὶν ποιῆσαι. καὶ παρὰ ταῦτα οὐκ ἔστιν ἄλλως. ἢ γὰρ πρᾶξαι ἀνάγκη ἢ μή· καὶ εἰδότας ἢ μὴ εἰδότας. τούτων δὲ τὸ μὲν γινώσκοντα μελλῆσαι καὶ μὴ πρᾶξαι χείριστον. τό τε γὰρ μιαρὸν ἔχει καὶ οὐ τραγικόν· ἀπαθὲς γάρ. διόπερ οὐδεὶς ποιεῖ ὁμοίως εἰ μὴ ὀλιγάκις· οἷον ἐν 'Αντιγόνῃ τὸν Κρέοντα ὁ Αἵμων.

Translate this passage and explain the allusion. How does the Scholiast excuse the incident? What is your own opinion on the subject?

(β) ΧΟΡ. Ἄμφω γὰρ αὐτὰ καὶ κατακτεῖναι νοεῖς;
ΚΡ. οὐ τήν γε μὴ θιγοῦσαν· εὖ γὰρ οὖν λέγεις.

Give the substance of Hermann's comment on these lines. How would you explain their introduction by Sophocles?

Assuming the coexistence of an *ethical* and an *artistic* element in this play, show how Sophocles attempts to satisfy the requirements of both in the development of the plot and of the two leading characters.

7. Quote Horace's lines on the duties of the Chorus, and apply them to the particular case of the Antigone. Distinguish between the terms πάροδος, στάσιμον, and ἐμμέλεια, and explain the connexion existing between the odes in this play and the dramatic action of the piece.

8. Τοῦ πρὶν θανόντος Μεγαρέως κλεινὸν λάχος.

By what name is Megareus known in the *Phœnissœ?* How is his story introduced into that play? Does his death precede or follow that of Eteocles? Do you suppose that Sophocles intended to follow the ancient legend in all the subordinate incidents of this play? Mention an instance from the *Œdipus Coloneus* in which he has departed from the account of the Cyclic Thebais. In which of his plays has Sophocles violated the so-called Unities of Time and Place?

9. Draw a map which shall contain Bœotia, the islands of Eubœa and Naxos, and the Saronic Gulf.

10. Translate the following passages, and, wherever the meaning or the text is a matter of dispute, give your own opinion on the subject and your reasons for it:

(1) Ὦ κοινὸν αὐτάδελφον Ἰσμήνης κάρα,
ἆρ' οἶσθ' ὅτι Ζεὺς τῶν ἀπ' Οἰδίπου κακῶν

ὁποῖον οὐχὶ νῷν ἔτι ζώσαιν τελεῖ ;
οὐδὲν γὰρ οὔτ᾽ ἀλγεινὸν οὔτ᾽ ἄτης ἄτερ
οὔτ᾽ αἰσχρὸν οὔτ᾽ ἄτιμόν ἐσθ᾽ ὁποῖον οὐ
τῶν σῶν τε κἀμῶν οὐκ ὄπωπ᾽ ἐγὼ κακῶν.

(2) Τοῖος ἀμφὶ νῶτ᾽ ἐτάθη
πάταγος Ἄρεος ἀντιπάλῳ
δυσχείρωμα δράκοντι.

(3) Καθήμεθ᾽ ἄκρων ἐκ πάγων ὑπήνεμοι,
ὀσμὴν ἀπ᾽ αὐτοῦ μὴ βάλῃ πεφευγότες,
ἐγερτὶ κινῶν ἄνδρ᾽ ἀνὴρ ἐπιρρόθοις
κακοῖσιν, εἴτις τοῦδ᾽ ἀφειδήσοι πόνου.

(4) Ἀλλ᾽ εἴτ᾽ ἀδελφῆς εἴθ᾽ ὁμαιμονεστέρα
τοῦ παντὸς ἡμῖν Ζηνὸς ἑρκείου κυρεῖ
αὐτή τε χὴ ξύναιμος οὐκ ἀλύξετον
μόρου κακίστου.

(5) Ἀλλ᾽ εἶκε θυμῷ καὶ μετάστασιν δίδου.

(6) Ἔρως, ὃς ἐν κτήμασι πίπτεις.

(7) Ἔψαυσας ἀλγεινοτάτας ἐμοὶ μερίμνας,
πατρὸς τριπόλιστον οἶκτον,
τοῦ τε πρόπαντος ἀμετέρου πότμου
κλεινοῖς Λαβδακίδαισιν.

(8) Ἀλλ᾽ εἰ μὲν οὖν τάδ᾽ ἐστὶν ἐν θεοῖς καλά,
παθόντες ἂν ξυγγροῖμεν ἡμαρτηκότες·
εἰ δ᾽ οἵδ᾽ ἁμαρτάνουσι, μὴ πλείω κακὰ
πάθοιεν ἢ καὶ δρῶσιν ἐκδίκως ἐμέ.

(9) Βωμοὶ γὰρ ἡμῖν ἐσχάραι τε παντελεῖς
πλήρεις ὑπ᾽ οἰωνῶν τε καὶ κυνῶν βορᾶς
τοῦ δυσμόρου πεπτῶτος Οἰδίπου γόνου.

(10) Ὦ πρέσβυ, πάντες, ὥστε τοξόται σκοποῦ,
τοξεύετ᾽ ἀνδρὸς τοῦδε, κοὐδὲ μαντικῆς
ἄπρακτος ὑμῖν εἰμί, τῶν ὑπαὶ γένους
ἐξημπόλημαι κἀκπεφόρτισμαι πάλαι.

(11) Ὦ πάντες ἀστοί, τῶν λόγων ἐπῃσθόμην
πρὸς ἔξοδον στείχουσα, Παλλάδος θεᾶς
ὅπως ἱκοίμην εὐγμάτων προσήγορος·
καὶ τυγχάνω τε κλῆθρ᾽ ἀνασπαστοῦ πύλης
χαλῶσα καί με φθόγγος οἰκείου κακοῦ
βάλλει δι᾽ ὤτων.

(12)   Παραστάντες τάφῳ
ἀθρήσαθ᾽ ἁρμὸν χώματος λιθοσπαδῆ
δύντες πρὸς αὐτὸ στόμιον, εἰ τὸν Αἵμονος
φθόγγον συνίημ᾽ ἢ θεοῖσι κλέπτομαι.

11. Discuss the grammatical peculiarities of the following passages :

(1) 'Αμήχανον δὲ παντὸς ἀνδρὸς ἐκμαθεῖν
ψυχήν τε καὶ φρόνημα καὶ γνώμην, πρὶν ἂν
ἀρχαῖς τε καὶ νόμοισιν ἐντριβὴς φανῇ.

(2) 'Ως ἂν σκοποὶ νῦν ἦτε τῶν εἰρημένων.

(3) Τεὰν, Ζεῦ, δύνασιν τίς ἀνδρῶν
ὑπερβασία κατάσχοι ;

(4) 'Αλλ' ἄνδρα, κεῖ τις ᾖ σοφός, κ.τ.λ.

Explain the use of the negatives in the following :

(a) 'Εγὼ δ' ὅπως σὺ μὴ λέγεις ὀρθῶς τάδε,
οὔτ' ἂν δυναίμην μήτ' ἐπισταίμην λέγειν.

(β) Ἥτις τὸν αὑτῆς αὐτάδελφον ἐν φοναῖς
πεπτῶτ' ἄθαπτον μήθ' ὑπ' ὠμηστῶν κυνῶν
εἴασ' ὀλέσθαι, μήθ' ὑπ' οἰωνῶν τινός.

Accentuate the word οποια in the line

ἀλλ' ἴσθ' ὁποια σοι δοκεῖ.

12. Derive, illustrate, or otherwise explain the following words :

τανταλωθείς—δεξιόσειρος—πάσασθαι—περιβρύχιος—ὑπίλλουσι—
περισκελής — καταρτύειν — ἐπήβολος—ἐρεμνός — θυστάς — ὄργια —
παστάς—κνώδοντες.

INDEX.

www.ingramcontent.com/pod-product-compliance
Lightning Source LLC
Chambersburg PA
CBHW030949110726
47900CB00004B/1188